I0615442

Published by BookPop Media LLC

Edition 1

ISBN 978-1-956918-11-3

25.11.25.4R

1st Edition date of publication: November 25, 2025

1st Edition eBook ISBN: 978-1-956918-10-6

1st Edition Print ISBN: 978-1-956918-11-3

Cover design by Fay Lane (https://faylane.com/)

Symphony of Crowns and Gods Official Website:

https://www.theauthorbrian.com

A NOTE ON SERIES THEMES:

Symphony of Crowns and Gods is a fantasy series filled with unexpected twists and turns. This narrative explores a rich and complex world, including sudden transitions to themes and motifs that may provoke strong emotions or discomfort for some readers. These elements include, but are not limited to, dark magic, violence, moral complexities, psychological manipulation, trauma, and crises of identity. Characters in this series must overcome the darkness within themselves and confront the harsh realities of their world to ultimately discover their inner strength and resilience. Their journeys will not be without their scars.

JOIN BRIAN A. MENDONÇA'S EMAIL NEWSLETTER

WHY SIGN UP?

It's simple: fans on this email list get my official updates before anyone else, including any other blogs and social media websites. Here's the news you can expect:

- Upcoming releases and previews of upcoming books
- An open dialog about my author journey
- Deals and sales
- Opportunities for ARCs (Advance Reader Copies)
- Info about fantasy books from other indie authors

Sign up link:
https://theauthorbrian.com/join-brians-newsletter

Greater Events of the World

as verified by Iris Thorne, Councilwoman
of Internal Affairs of the Second Darian Kingdom

The Human Uprising
(Years 1 -171)

Scourge of the Dragon Slavers
(Years 171-401)

The First Great War
(Years 441-449)

Downfall of the First Darian Kingdom
(Years 441-446)

Lucidian Civil War
(Years 445-449)

Founding of the Second Darian Kingdom
(Year 450)

The Blooming of All Nations
(Years 450 -)

Wedding of the Torn Rose
(Year 474)

Leonia
Temple of Dragons
Twilight Haven
Bricktown
The Twins
Umbral Rot Wastelands
Northern Yaenia
Shield Haven
Haventown
Sky Tower Coast
The Lowland Graves
Hillside

Haventown
Sky Tower Coast
Wargonne
The Lowland Graves
Hillside Reach
Gale Village
New Ginstown
Last Hope
Emil
The Leila Kingdom
Lucidian Enclave
Southeast Yaenia
Starlight Beach

Throatian Island

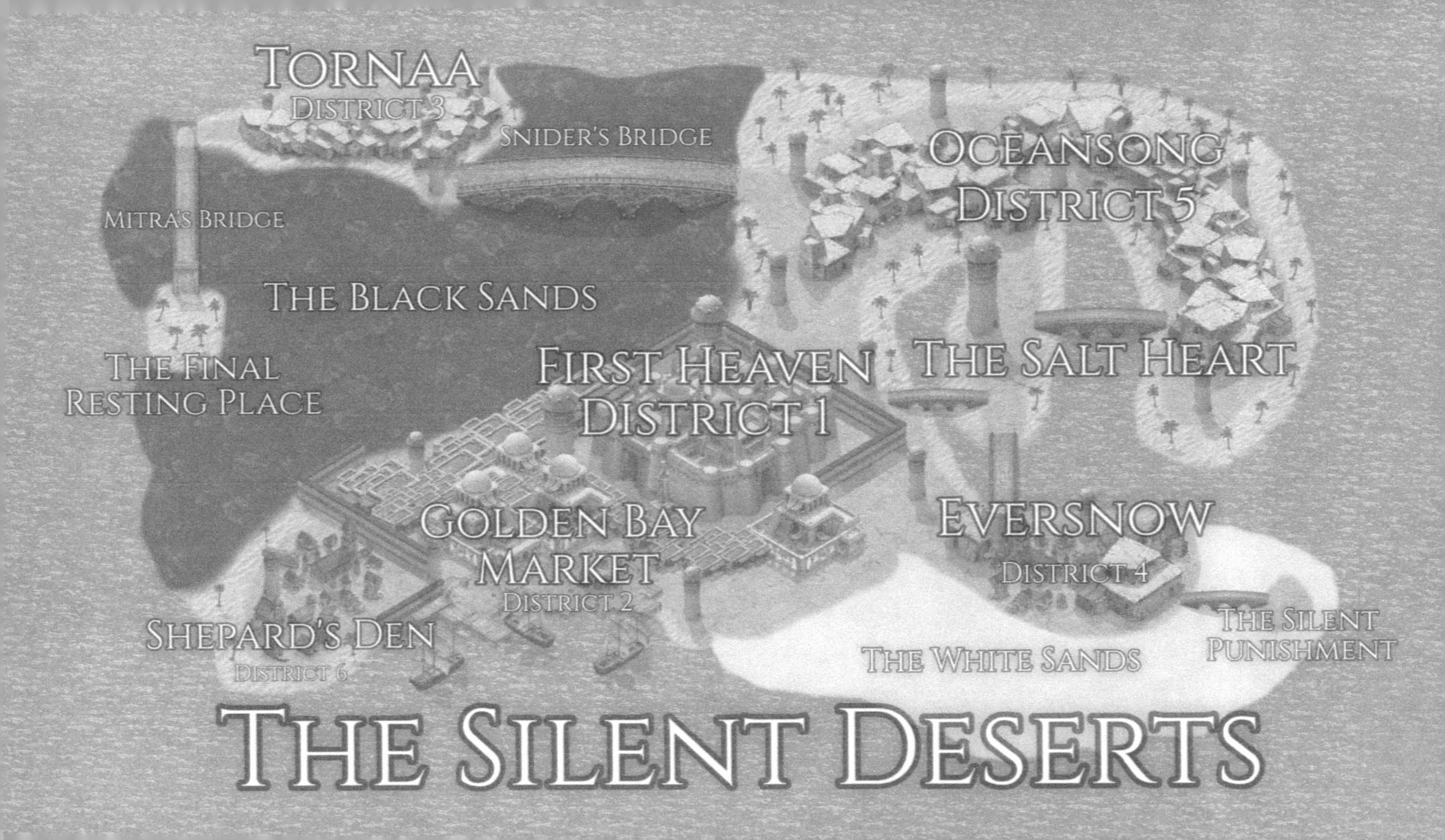
Tornaa
District 3
Snider's Bridge
Oceansong
District 5
Mitra's Bridge
The Black Sands
The Final
Resting Place
First Heaven
District 1
The Salt Heart
Golden Bay
Market
District 2
Eversnow
District 4
Shepard's Den
District 6
The White Sands
The Silent
Punishment
The Silent Deserts

PROPHECY
OF
TEARS
AND
SACRIFICE

SYMPHONY OF
CROWNS AND GODS
BOOK THREE

BRIAN A. MENDONÇA

1

KIRA - THE MIRROR OF PRINCESS LYDIA

Kira stood outside Lydia's old room, her hand hovering near the cold, white doorknob. The door, painted by Lydia with patterns of ivy, stones, and roses, loomed over her, an intimidating yet beautiful barrier to memories Kira wasn't sure she was ready to confront. Since the tragedy, she'd walked past it every day, several times, but she'd never opened the door. Everything past it was filled with reminders of the sister who'd once graced their castle with smiles and light, but Kira was darkness.

She took a deep breath, preparing to face what she'd been avoiding. Today, she couldn't avoid it anymore. Lydia wouldn't have wanted her to stay away forever. They'd shared more happy memories inside of that room than not, but now everything would be different. With a shaky hand, she grasped the doorknob and turned it. The door creaked open, its sound echoing through the empty hallway like a nervous sigh.

Stepping into her late sister's bedroom, the comforting scent of lavender and flowers—Lydia's cherished fragrances—welcomed Kira. The room remained untouched since her death except for the vase on the windowsill, which servants refilled with fresh roses twice a week. Everything else stayed frozen in time, just as it had been on Lydia's wedding day. The embroidered quilt that Lydia had thoughtfully crafted covered the neatly made bed. On the bedside table sat a stack of well-loved books, their pages worn from so many readings.

Kira's eyes wandered to the balcony where Lydia used to spend hours gazing out at the gardens. On the window seat beside her reading chair rested Lydia's unfinished needlework, as if she'd only stepped away for breakfast and would return soon. She pictured Lydia working on dress sleeves or maybe useful things like tablecloths or scarves.

A portrait painted two summers ago hung above the fireplace, depicting them arm-in-arm, holding baskets of strawberries, Kira's favorite fruit. They had spent the day picking them in the field. When they returned, their father, moved by their warmth and closeness, commissioned the painting that same evening. Neither sister had wanted to sit still for the artist on that occasion, but Kira was grateful they had.

Her eyes fell upon the vanity, where a strand of Lydia's auburn hair remained on the silver-backed brush.

"Oh, Lydia," Kira whimpered. "Why did you leave me alone?"

A single tear rolled down her cheek and struck the polished wooden floor by her feet. She quickly wiped it away with her shoe, embarrassed by her vulnerability, even though no one was there to witness what was running down her face. The princess collapsed, her knees bending as she sobbed, her hands gripping Lydia's vanity stool for support. Yet even her tears couldn't ease the loss—nothing would bring her back.

For what seemed like an eternity, Kira sat on the ground, weeping uncontrollably, unable to let go of her grief. Eventually, she forced herself to rise and carry on with her visit.

She caught her breath between sobs and took a gulp of air before venturing deeper into the room. The bed, once her sister's, appeared both inviting and empty. Would Lydia have minded if Kira rested there now? Kira brushed her hand over the cool quilt fabric, recalling how Lydia had always chosen the softest materials for her crafts. Everything still belonged to her, even though Lydia was gone.

Her eyes drifted to the brush on the vanity. As she picked it up, memories of the wedding morning resurfaced. Lydia and Kira had spent hours preparing, Lydia's nervous laughter sounding through the room as Kira combed her hair.

"Are you really going to get married?" Kira had asked anxiously, though for the wrong reasons at the time.

Lydia had simply smiled without looking away from her mirror. "I have to, Kira—it's what's best for our kingdom."

"But are you truly sure? You don't love him. Prince Thane may be handsome and speak the Common Tongue well enough, but you've only had a few brief conversations with him. How can you marry him after such a short time together?"

Lydia had looked into the mirror, her green eyes shining with determination rather than anger at Kira's words. "Sometimes, what's better for our people comes before personal desires. I understand that now."

That day, Kira's stomach twisted knowing her sister was sacrificing her dream wedding for an alliance with the Throatians. Lydia, though strong-willed, had fled the castle a few days earlier, only to return after a monster attacked her. It was the new retainer, Kaine, who had saved her from death.

Kira wiped away a tear and combed, gripping the brush so tightly that her hands trembled. She could almost feel Lydia's soft hair between the bristles and hear her sister's voice again. Looking into the hand mirror, Kira's face reflected back, this time alone.

Sadness, nostalgia, anger, and even a touch of guilt flooded her as she continued brushing. Their future had been stolen. Kira's thoughts only grew more bitter as she recalled the day she learned of Lydia's death. After the wedding, she had just finished bathing when she heard servants whispering outside her door about knights pursuing the Throatians. At first, she misunderstood—why would anyone attack them? Could it have been bandits?

"What's going on?" Kira inquired as she stepped into the hallway after getting dressed.

One attendant replied, "Nothing is certain yet, my princess. Please return to your room for now. The guards are on their way to stand watch outside your door, just in case."

It was as if the servant had punched her in the stomach. Lydia had left with the Throatians without a word. Was everyone safe? The uncertainty was unbearable.

"Tell me what's happened."

"I'm sorry you overheard us," the servant replied, "but we don't know what's true, and we don't want to worry you with what may be false rumors."

But Kira needed to know, and she did something she'd never done before: issued a royal command, just like her brother Xander did when he wanted servants to obey his wishes against their father's orders.

"As Princess Kira of the Darian Kingdom, I order you to tell me what you have learned."

And then it came—rumors surfaced that a spy was traveling with the carriage carrying Lydia, her father, and the Throatians. Because someone was concerned about a planned attack, extra guards went toward Starlight Beach to guard against potential threats.

Kira had worried, though perhaps not as much as she should have. She hadn't questioned whether the servant spoke the truth or if their words had been toned down to soften the reality of what truly occurred.

As news spread, long before the king returned, many of the rumors turned out to be true. Lydia had died that same day, and her father disappeared for many weeks afterward. Kira feared she would never see either of them again.

Prince Thane and the Throatians had murdered Lydia for her magic, prompting their father to pursue them to the sea. From there, a war began, and the king's return to Last Hope was uncertain. The Throatians proved as treacherous as they were dangerous, leaving Kira's world in disarray. They had pledged an alliance through a loveless marriage but taken Lydia's life instead.

When her father returned from the ocean, he had become a broken man, transformed from a joyful and thoughtful king into one reserved and isolated. Now, he often stayed in his room, claiming to work on war plans, but Kira suspected he was still in shock, hiding his grief and vulnerability from everyone he knew.

Like their father, Kira's brother Xander became cold and silent, retreating into his thoughts and spending much of his time hiking in the woods with twice as many guards as usual. He rarely spoke at dinner unless Kira started the conversation, his voice reduced to a monotone. Would any of them ever return to their former selves?

Kira recognized she had changed too—as though someone was squeezing her lungs and all she could feel was an overwhelming curse of loss and rage.

She continued sitting at Lydia's vanity, brushing her hair, until she noticed a small bottle—a familiar shape and color she had seen countless times. It was Lydia's favorite perfume. She removed the cap and inhaled the crisp, woody apple scent. Lydia had worn it on the day of her wedding.

In a sudden fit of anger, Kira lost control, letting out a desperate cry as she hurled the glass against the wall. It shattered instantly, perfume spilling amid the shards of glass. She stared in shock, regretting her actions even as she burned with frustration, with herself and the Throatians.

"Burn in the Black Sands!" she yelled, nearly slamming Lydia's

"Okay. I'll meet you downstairs in a minute."

Ursula rushed out into the hallway on her way to her room, leaving Kira to look over Lydia's things once more.

Alone again, she neared the vanity and picked up Lydia's mirror. As Kira gazed at her own reflection, she imagined her sister's face next to it.

"The world is so dark," Kira whispered to the empty room, hoping her sister might somehow hear her. "But I will try to bring it some light. I'll do my best to make you proud."

2
THANE - THE DRAGON HORN

"I still don't understand how a god can die," Prince Thane muttered as he sipped what he swore was the worst beer he'd ever tasted. He hoped Somnius had been right about leading him here—the entire kingdom had a price on his head.

He and Somnius were stopping for the evening at Hillside Reach, a small town known for its tavern, which looked more run-down than any he'd seen in Yaenia. The goddess had insisted they stay there, claiming an important figure would arrive later that night.

"A god is capable of unexpected acts, even death under certain circumstances," Somnius replied solemnly. "It's difficult to explain, but I assure you, it's possible—even I am not invulnerable. Such is the foundation of the Prophecy of Tears and Sacrifice."

Thane remembered it well from what she'd told him:

> *A god will fall, and a corrupt pretender will rise in his place.*
> *A great sacrifice will yield an unyielding savior, one destined for using the Tears of Asura to cast the darkness from this world forever.*

Thane's eyes briefly glanced at the rounded swell of her abdomen beneath the table, the fabric of her dress slightly tighter than the night before. "Your child has a great responsibility ahead."

They had a destiny to defeat both Bios Auras and Zann-Xia-Czul, becoming a god and the savior of their world. The child's father, if still alive, was someone Somnius must have left behind in her former homeland. That she avoided mentioning him revealed her reluctance to discuss the matter further.

Thane had walked with Somnius for days without knowing his purpose. Each time he asked, she promised to explain his role once they reached Hillside Reach. Soon she would reveal the tasks and the people they would encounter. Sometimes, it was hard not to doubt whether Somnius truly knew what she was doing.

"It will take years before everything else happens," Somnius said, taking a sip of water and resting her hand on her growing stomach. "Until then, we must avoid Bios Auras and prepare for the coming conflict with Zann-Xia-Czul. The one who meets us tonight will grant me safe passage to the Black Moon Tribe and show you where those who speak like dragons dwell."

"Are you still certain this was the best place to meet your acquaintance?" Thane asked. The chipped, worn tankard only added to his poor opinion of the bar.

Suspicious characters filled the venue—gamblers huddled over card tables, their faces shadowed and untrustworthy. Thane felt a growing unease despite his sword, magical armor, and Somnius's abilities. He prayed no one would recognize him as the former groom of Princess Lydia.

"This situation is new to me as well," Somnius admitted. "Still, the woman coming to help me is a trusted ally—I've met her before."

As the evening wore on and the customers grew rowdier, Thane began to doubt that anyone would show up. Only when the patrons had grown wilder and empty tankards littered the tables did someone finally approach their table.

"Herja," Somnius greeted. "Welcome. Please sit."

The woman stared in disbelief. "How did you already know my name?" she asked, surprised. She was a knight in ill-fitting armor, her flowing dark red hair contrasting with her pale skin.

She clearly did not know who Somnius was, despite the goddess's claim of having met her already. Thane suspected she'd spoken the truth indirectly. The first time Thane had encountered Somnius, she had been hiding in plain sight and he had assumed she was a commoner. It wasn't until after the Wedding of the Torn Rose that Somnius had revealed her true identity to him—she was a goddess.

"I sought your tribe's aid and paid upfront," the deity said. "Given their current situation, I expected their leader to investigate the matter."

Herja sat across from them, wincing as her armor pressed against her body. "You should never have sent so much gold without checking if we'd accept your offer first."

"I knew beforehand that you would agree to my terms," Somnius said with confidence. "The Black Moon Tribe has always led the hunt against its legendary enemies. You've long awaited this chance to prove yourself since your father's death. Your only doubt was whether the dragon was real, but why else would I have paid you if I weren't certain?"

Herja raised an eyebrow, as if considering whether Somnius had been watching her all this time. Still, she remained focused on their business matters. "So there's little left to discuss," she said. "All you ask is that we follow the instructions in your letter. Nothing else?"

"What I've written is all I need from you," Somnius confirmed. "But I expected you'd bring allies tonight."

"I would have them here if they hadn't abandoned the cause," Herja growled in response. "I'd rather they prove their cowardice now than reveal it on the battlefield later."

The goddess nodded slowly. "So, it came earlier than I anticipated."

"Pardon?"

"Never mind," Somnius said. "Moving on, my companion here can retrieve the dragon horn alone."

Herja gazed intently at Thane, studying his frame. "What's his name?" she asked.

Thane looked to Somnius for guidance, unsure if revealing his true identity was wise. Luckily, the goddess had a response prepared.

"My knight's name does not bear relevance at this time," Somnius said. "He will retrieve the horn from the Whisperers and bring it to us in Twilight Haven."

"A dragon horn?" Thane asked in disbelief. He hadn't heard of it before.

"It is an important item," Somnius explained, "that can summon Zann-Xia-Czul when the time comes."

"Only two were ever made," Herja explained. "A dragon destroyed the first, along with its creator, and the knowledge of how to make the horns died with him." She turned to Somnius, her voice filled with disbelief. "I can't believe you've found the second one!"

Somnius smiled lightly. "My experiences led me to uncover its location. I have full confidence in my knight to retrieve it."

"Then it's settled," Herja declared, brushing her hair from her eyes. "Your carriage to Twilight Haven awaits outside, my lady. Your mysterious knight will have to find his own way to where the dragon horn resides."

The Black Moon Tribe's leader appeared eager despite her long journey. Thane had other concerns, suspecting his upcoming quest held more complexities than he could foresee. Somnius's insight could provide clarity before they parted ways.

"Wait, I don't even know where to look for the dragon horn," he said, as Herja shot him a disapproving glare.

"Fear not—I wouldn't send you on such an important mission without the details," Somnius said, glancing at Herja. "Though I'd imagined explaining it to you alongside two others."

Herja seemed surprised, as if Somnius was accusing her of driving her allies away. Neither had said enough to explain why Herja's companions might have abandoned her, but it seemed more like an annoyance to Somnius than a direct attack on Herja as the leader of the Black Moon Tribe.

"I will find the dragon horn, even if alone," Thane promised.

"Buy enough Red Cloud material from Sky Tower Coast's markets to protect your mouth and nose," Somnius instructed, her gaze caring as it locked onto Thane. "The air in the swamp west of there is filled with poisonous gases."

Thane blinked in surprise. "There's a swampland in Yaenia?" he asked.

The goddess produced a map from her small white leather satchel and laid it out on the table so they could look over it.

Somnius confirmed, pointing to an area on her map nearly twice the size of Last Hope. "Once you arrive there, wrap your face using the cloth. Upon reaching the other end of the swamp, head southwest until you see the walls of the Lucidian Enclave. Stay close to the northern mountains until you find a path through them. Enter the white trees and search for the Whisperers in the valley at the summit."

Herja shifted uneasily. "The Lucidian Enclave is dangerous," she warned. "They're known for their secrecy and ruthless methods. If they catch him—"

Somnius raised a hand, silencing Herja. "He'll be careful," she said. "The Lucidians won't go near the swamps because of their history."

Herja's lips tightened and she said nothing more. She apparently had doubts, but as for Thane, he had no way of knowing how absurd or logical Somnius's statement might have been. Like with everything else, he would have to trust her and assume she knew more than they did.

"The Whisperers have the dragon horn," Somnius continued. "They believe it holds clues to unlocking more of their powers. However, they are wary of outsiders and misguided in their beliefs. Approach them with caution."

"I will be careful the entire way," Thane said.

"The Whisperers are a most corrupt people," Somnius added. "Befriend them if possible, but do not take part in their rituals, no matter what dragon magic they promise to give you in return. Among their hidden relics, you will find what you seek. Retrieve it by any means necessary and bring it to me at the Black Moon Tribe's home in Twilight Haven. Do you understand?"

Thane studied the Yaenian map once more. The route seemed simple, but he knew maps often omitted dangerous obstacles. Thankfully, Somnius had given him magical armor when he'd pledged himself to serving her. She had saved his life rather than kill him, after all. Fetching an item was the least he could do to repay her.

"I'll bring the horn to you at the home of the Black Moon Tribe," Thane said, "though the journey will be long."

Somnius smiled warmly. "I am confident you will succeed, my knight. Take your time. The horn won't be needed for many years, but ensuring its safety until then matters most."

Herja stood, her armor creaking. "If that's all, I'll take my leave," she said with a bow. "The carriage waits outside. We can depart for Twilight Haven whenever you're ready, my lady."

Somnius nodded. "Thank you, Herja. You have my gratitude. Leaving in the middle of the night isn't unwise given our circumstances. I'd like to reach Twilight Haven as soon as possible."

Herja gave a curt nod and left the bar with a proud stride.

Thane watched her go, his mind already thinking ahead: Sky Tower Coast, the swampland, the path to the mountain ranges, and finally, the Whisperers. Determined to ensure the goddess received the dragon horn, he would face each challenging segment of his journey. Somnius had saved Thane's life, even though he'd been about to try to take hers. One day, both Zann-Xia-Czul and Bios Auras would suffer judgment for their lies.

More importantly, he needed to find a way of getting home to

Cereene. They had been separated for too long, and there were many words left unsaid between them. His love for her remained strong, but the pain of his actions burned his heart, making safely returning to her his greatest goal. Yet as long as Zann-Xia-Czul and Bios Auras held control over his homeland, rescuing her—and freeing his people from the barbaric traditions that had taken root—would remain a challenge. Still, he was determined to act, no matter the risks. Helping Somnius, in a way, was helping himself.

"Are you ready to begin your journey?" Somnius asked, her voice soft yet firm.

Thane met her gaze. "I am," he said, standing up and sliding the cracked tankard to the center of the table.

She smiled but her expression seemed forced, as if she were quietly trying to tell him not to worry despite their situation being more dire than she was revealing.

"Never forget, you are the right person for this mission," the goddess said. "It will be some time before we meet again, and though our time together was brief, I appreciate you having journeyed with me this far."

3
KAINE - THE RETAINER

Cherry blossoms fluttered towards the pink-covered ground as a gust of wind blew past Kaine and Xander's training weapons. Their wooden swords clashed as Kaine pretended to retreat, hoping to lure the young Darian prince into a trap.

Xander exclaimed, "It's not fair!" His voice faltered under the strain of his growing muscles and new responsibilities. His face flushed with frustration and exhaustion. Kaine, a towering figure despite his injured arm, stood before him, guiding him through complex steps while watching the prince's boots.

"Battles are matters of life and death, not fairness," Kaine replied, his voice stern. He tightened his grip on the wooden sword, feeling its unfamiliar weight. "Let's try again. This time don't chase me. Either let me return to you or be ready for me to slip away to the other side. Watch my feet—they'll reveal my next move."

With a hint of mischief, Kira shouted from the sidelines, "Look down while he's trying to maintain eye contact." She sat on a small bench, her fingers stained with peach juice. Kira resembled her late sister Lydia, with soft white skin and green eyes, curious yet insightful.

"You're making that up!" Xander scoffed, disbelief clear in his voice. He tensed his shoulders, preparing his sword for the next round.

Kira stuck her tongue out playfully and resumed eating her

peach. Beside her on the bench sat Ursula Frost, Councilwoman Frey's niece.

Kaine raised his sword once more. "Let's try again and test your theory, my young prince."

Unfortunately, the second round of sparring went worse than the first. Kaine stole away Xander's opening before he could side-step again, delivering a decisive blow to Xander's shoulder with his wooden sword and securing a clear victory in their practice session.

"Why didn't you jump back like before?" Xander snapped. He rubbed his shoulder where Kaine had struck him.

"Even if I had planned to, you left yourself exposed," he said, disappointed. "I couldn't ignore it."

They clashed their wooden swords for another few minutes, the morning air rising in temperature as they continued to spar. Yet it was clear Xander's mind wandered, his focus lost in the swirling circles of his thoughts. Finally, Kaine tapped the prince on the shoulder once more, signaling the end of their session.

Xander hurled his training sword to the ground with a force that would have been impressive, if not for the immaturity behind it. Rolling up the sleeves of his tunic, he stormed toward the castle's entrance, his footsteps raising dust in the courtyard.

"Xander," Kaine warned, resting his wooden weapon. "We've been over this—it goes against proper etiquette to leave during a duel, even for training."

The prince paused at the bench where Kira and Ursula were seated, turned toward Kaine, and gave a brief, obligatory bow. "Thank you, Lord Khalia," he muttered. Just as Kaine thought the prince had calmed down, Xander slapped Ursula's book from her hands. It fell to the ground as the silver-haired girl shrieked.

"Xander von Stonewall!" Kaine's voice bellowed, loud and deep from his many years spent communicating with sailors at sea. He'd never imagined he would one day use it to discipline the Darian royal children.

"I'm going to have breakfast!"

"Apologize to Ursula!"

He suspected Xander would continue his tantrum. As he prepared to yell again, Prince Xander swooped the book from the ground and returned it to Councilwoman Bridgette's niece. With a muttered apology, he disappeared into the castle.

Once her brother was out of earshot, Kira asked, "So, is it my turn now?"

"Of course," Kaine said warmly, offering her a faint smile. "You were next in line."

Kira hopped up from the bench with a lightness in her step, leaving Ursula to resume reading her book. She picked up the training sword her brother had left on the ground and approached Kaine.

"Ready!" she eagerly confirmed, pointing her weapon's tip at his chest. A cherry blossom petal touched her face, and she brushed it away without breaking eye contact.

Kaine stepped forward, standing tall to maintain his height advantage over the young girl. Kira made the first move, but her attack lacked commitment. She pivoted to his right, targeting his injured arm still in a sling, and swept her sword horizontally. He easily parried the move, as she often tried to distract him that way. Instead of countering as he typically did, he retreated, repositioned his weapon, and lunged in her direction.

The princess gasped, retreating and throwing another horizontal arc as a barrier. The wind aided her swing, sending fiery pink leaves swirling in her path. As Kaine extended his reach, Kira retaliated by closing the distance and counterattacking with a precise stab of her own.

Kaine's instincts took over as his right arm, confined to the sling, slipped free, tightening the strap at his shoulder. Kira's wooden sword caught him in the gut before his left side could react.

A surge of pride and guilt rose within Kaine as he acknowledged Kira had bested him in their practice session. Though she was a child with only a month's training, her skill with the sword was remarkable. While he took pride in her progress, his worry remained. As a sailing merchant, he had fought pirates and slavers, but his greatest triumph was the defeat of the Throatian Queen Urith Asche during the previous battle. However, in their final clash, her war hammer shattered his forearm, leaving him with a lasting injury. Now, he could only train the children with his non-dominant arm.

Upon returning to Last Hope for treatment, the healer promised full recovery within eight weeks, yet four months had already elapsed. He kept his arm in a sling, hoping it would heal and return to its original state, but each passing day ate away at his hope of his life returning to normal.

"I'm a fast learner, aren't I?" Kira said gleefully, her eyes sparkling with excitement. Though she was more skilled in combat than her brother, Kaine couldn't help but wonder if his limitations were giving her an unearned confidence. Kaine wasn't a sword master or a teacher, even though he had been capable with a blade before his injury. He felt a deep sense of failure, realizing he couldn't provide the children with the instruction they needed to protect themselves and their kingdom.

He'd already offered to resign as their retainer if his arm didn't fully heal; training them was one of his essential duties. Their father dismissed his resignation, saying, "You swore an oath for life, Kaine Khalia. Whether you have two arms, one, or none, you are bound to it. You are part of my house, and we will do everything to restore your arm." Over the months, Kaine grew to understand Ether von Stonewall well enough to know his sincerity wasn't driven by pity or obligation. Still, he couldn't help but wonder whether he might become a burden if his wound never healed.

"You're the fastest girl with a sword I've ever seen," Kaine praised, hoping to encourage her.

"Do you think I'll be slaying lots of monsters someday?"

Kira was referring to the time Kaine had saved Princess Lydia from a beast in the forest. At the time, Lydia had stolen a God Stone from her father and unleashed its magic, accidentally transforming one of her handmaidens into a winged abomination. Kaine happened to be there, saving the princess and inadvertently setting off the chain of events that led to the Wedding of the Torn Rose. He couldn't help but recall the memory, knowing he had helped shape history. However, he also understood that the future was uncertain, and he would need to remain adaptable and rise to whatever new challenges came his way.

"We'll hopefully never see a monster again, but if we do, you'll be ready for it," Kaine said, his voice filled with confidence. As long as no one used the God Stones, there was nothing to worry about. Kira likely didn't know about them, and he was uncertain whether her father would reveal their existence once she matured. Before she died, Lydia expressed regret about misusing them, admitting she hadn't been responsible enough despite nearly mastering their magic. Given everything that had happened, Ether von Stonewall would likely forbid Kira from using them, fearing enemies like the Throatians who sought such power.

Kaine and Kira continued their sparring. Kaine's muscles flexed and relaxed with each precise swing of his sword, while Kira's graceful movements matched his precision. The breeze picked up and Kaine felt the warmth of the sun seeping through his tunic, making him uncomfortable. Then unexpected raindrops fell, first grazing the upper part of his face, then his cheekbone. Ursula sat absorbed in her book in the courtyard, oblivious to the world around her.

"That's enough for today," Kaine said, wiping his forehead. "We should head to the council chamber for breakfast before the rain pours down."

Because of the war against the Throatians, King Ether required his council members to hold daily meetings over breakfast to discuss new plans, overnight developments, and other relevant matters before their official duties began. Despite the sensitive nature of the information, the king insisted the prince and princess observe the discussions quietly. King Ether also expected Ursula, Councilwoman Bridgette Frey's niece and heir to her role, to attend.

With a training sword clutched under each arm, he escorted Kira and Ursula into the castle through the doorway Xander had stormed into earlier. He handed the weapons to another servant, who would store them in a nearby closet, then led the girls up a narrow spiral staircase. Sunlight filtered through the cracks of the castle's neglected bricks, casting shards of light on their faces. Though the stronghold had been tidied for the wedding, thorough cleaning and repairs required the king's approval. Ether von Stonewall, a practical leader, put safety above aesthetics, delaying restorations until the structure's integrity became compromised.

As they headed up the stairs, Kira asked, "Between me and Xander, who would win in a duel?"

"You have the advantage for now," Kaine said. "But all it would take is a few good days of training, and he could rival you. Keep up your efforts if you want to stay ahead."

The guards blocking the doorway stepped away as the trio approached. Candles hanging from the walls illuminated the spiral steps, their flickering flames dim. It exuded an ancient, dark aura, as if someone had taken the passage from the dungeons and repurposed it for the council chambers. Despite climbing this flight of stairs every week, Kaine hadn't grown accustomed to the eerie thought that the candlelight might suddenly flicker out, plunging them into darkness within the narrow corridor. The idea made him uneasy, but he pushed it aside.

"Ursula," the princess said. "Would you mind going ahead?"

"Of course," the young girl replied with a nod.

As Ursula continued up on her own, carrying her book, Kira and Kaine stalled halfway up the stairs. Kira turned to him, her fingers nervously twisting a strand of hair. "Ummm... Kaine, can I ask you something else?"

He placed one foot a few steps higher to stretch his leg. "Of course. What is it?"

Kira took a deep breath, her eyes filling with tears as she tried to blink them back. "Do you know how to stop bad dreams?"

The question seemed straightforward, but the answer wasn't so simple. Helping her understand it might at least make her feel better. "I wish I knew, but I don't. Whether they are pleasant or nightmares, we can't control our dreams or when they happen, but we can choose how we react to them."

"But how do you approach it?" Kira asked.

Kaine took a quiet breath of the cramped stairway's air, searching for the right words. "Try to have heart, and remember courage will come if you let it," he said finally. "It's easier said than done, but face whatever is troubling you. Start by pretending to be brave, and the rest will follow."

Kira absorbed his words; her eyes filled with both openness and unease. "I don't know what to do," she admitted softly. "I just don't want to keep dreaming about Lydia in pain. I keep trying to hide it and pretend like it's not affecting me, but it does."

He nodded, feeling sympathetic toward the young princess. "I understand how you feel," he whispered. "Years ago, I used to fear drowning in the ocean before I learned to swim. But remember, Kira, you have the strength to overcome this. Even if I don't know how, I believe you can rise above this shadow."

Kaine hoped his words had brought Kira some comfort, but he knew Lydia would remain at the center of her nightmares for a long time, if not forever. The memory of that fateful day still haunted him, a reminder of the loss they all endured. He and Eisenbern had pursued the Throatians, only to discover they were too late. The sight of King Ether, paralyzed and shattered, in shock at witnessing Prince Thane sacrifice his daughter before him, was an unforgettable one.

That day, a part of Ether died, and his hollow gray face never returned to its former self from before his daughter's wedding. It was Lydia's day, and he had been so proud of her just moments before everything changed. The Throatians' plot to marry Lydia only to kill her had succeeded, and Kaine still couldn't help wondering if he could have prevented her fate.

Ultimately, he realized that saving the princess would have been impossible, no matter how much he retraced the moments leading up to the wedding. Lydia had drugged his wine, ensuring he could not stop her. Only he understood Lydia intended to die, and the nightmares of that night haunted both him and Kira. The memories tormented him with such frequency and intensity that he struggled to recognize a way forward.

Sometimes, he dreamed of carrying Lydia's cold body back to the Darian ship, only to find the shroud empty when he unwrapped her. Other times, the Throatian Queen shattered his arm with her war hammer and continued crushing him beyond recognition. Still other bad dreams were about the corpses of innocent horses, slain for their blood and left abandoned in the forest, haunting him most vividly. But the worst nightmares involved child hostages hung from ships and set ablaze—torches meant to taunt the few Darians who had pursued the Asche family overseas from Starlight Beach.

"I know she is proud of you," Kaine added. It was all he could do for now, besides train her. "I promised Lydia and your father I'd protect the two of you, and I intend on doing my best."

Candlelight caught the reflection of a tear on Kira's cheek—unnoticed by her. "Xander has the same dreams as I do, I think," she continued. "I've heard him calling her name at night from his room."

"What happened to your sister cannot be easy for anyone who knew her to contemplate," Kaine said. "I'll talk to him about this when I get the chance."

"Thank you, Kaine. He doesn't say it often, but he's thankful for how much you take care of us."

"Such is my will and duty, my young princess."

A dry warmth welcomed Kaine, Kira, and Ursula into the tower's highest chamber as they entered, escaping the torrential rain pounding against the castle walls. The fireplace dominating the southern wall roared with a great intensity, its flames flickering dangerously close to the grand table that spread before them. The table, so large it seemed impossible that it had been brought up the stairs as a singular piece of furniture, was now filled with the council members who had gathered for the morning's meeting.

At the head of the table sat King Ether von Stonewall, his gray hair and broad features betraying the toll of his years. Though his gold-embroidered burgundy tunic and matching surcoat were impressive, they couldn't hide the dark circles under his eyes or the sagging skin. Unaware of his exhausted appearance, the king obsessively scribbled on a piece of parchment.

Sitting to the king's right was Xander, wearing a tunic like his father's, though he wore a black cloak over his shoulders. He glanced at Kaine and Kira as he ate a roll of bread but seemed to actively ignore them. His blond hair fell over his eyes, hiding any persistent anger from the sword training earlier in the courtyard.

Next to Xander, past an empty seat, sat Councilman Ofred, the Darian Master of Agriculture. A stout, middle-aged man with a receding hairline fading from brown to gray, Ofred bore the weathered tan of years spent working under the sun. Once a simple farmer, he had risen to manage the kingdom's food supply. His round face jiggled as he boisterously greeted them with a wide smile, though bits of chicken remained between his teeth.

Across the table from Ofred sat Iris Thorne, the Master of Internal Affairs. Like King Ether, she was engrossed in jotting something down in the journal she always carried. Rumor had it she started a new notebook every other week, but the worn surface of the cover hinted that she replaced its inner pages.

Kaine found himself lost in thought as he took his seat next to her. The king had insisted he attend their meetings as an advisor, but Kaine suspected there was an unspoken motive. Perhaps Ether wanted another perspective or was considering assigning him less physically demanding tasks if his arm failed to heal. Nonetheless, Kaine had earned the king's trust through his actions during the Wedding of the Torn Rose, and he sensed that still greater challenges lay ahead.

King Ether flipped through his notes and cleared his throat before beginning the meeting. "We've received a letter from Councilman Conan, who regrets to inform us he has made no progress in piercing the Throatians' defensive veil. He will be returning the fleet to Wargonne to resupply and then setting sail once more. I'll proceed around the table from here. Councilman Ofred?"

The portly man squinted as he spoke. "The thieves have been

raiding our storehouses once more. Last night alone, they stole a hundred crates of wheat, fifty sacks of rice, and assorted goods."

"Again?" The king's thin face grew a little thinner as he asked, "Iris, I thought you'd resolved this?"

"I handled it," stated the Master of Internal Affairs. "In my report to Councilman Ofred, I determined that the missing supplies were because of mistakes in inventory keeping."

"Impossible!" Ofred exclaimed, trading his typical buoyancy for petulance. "The stock records are triple-checked by my staff every week. Not a single grain goes unaccounted for!"

King Ether interjected, "Then why does this keep happening, and how?"

Before Ofred could speak, Iris seized the chance. "Ofred's team took inventory at sunset and locked the doors," she said. "I randomly assigned guards each night. By morning, they reported nothing unusual, but when Ofred's men unlocked the doors, inventory was missing. A significant number of crates and barrels vanish every few weeks—on random nights. The discrepancy must lie in the counting process."

"Someone in the city guard is being bribed!" Ofred declared vehemently. "Such a massive theft couldn't happen without inside help. It's not my people who are responsible—it's your city guard who were supposed to be securing those doors!"

"But since Iris randomly selected the watchers," Bridgette added, "it would be difficult for thieves to coordinate the removal of so much cargo. Even if the guards themselves were moving it, they would have needed considerable help."

"Finally, some levelheadedness," Iris said. "The guards didn't have the key to the stores either—only Ofred's workers did. This means nobody has stolen the food. The person tallying everything must be making a mistake. Councilman, can you confirm that no one has ever made inventory errors before?"

Ofred's face was red, and Kaine couldn't tell whether it stemmed from anger or embarrassment. "Yes, mistakes have occurred in the counting process before, but only minor ones—such as a crate or two missing from a shipment, or one being spoiled and discarded without being recorded," Ofred said. "Hundreds of crates disappearing overnight, however, is no mere mistake. Someone has certainly stolen them!"

Ether adjusted his crown. "I trust in your hands' competence that there was no error in record-keeping. Iris has shown this isn't just a simple theft. Let's keep randomly selecting the guards each night, and the truth will come out sooner or later. And Bridgette..."

"Yes, your highness?"

"The kingdom is well-fed for now, but if our stock continues to go missing, we'll need to make up the difference. Can you find the gold necessary to import more supplies from the Silent Deserts?"

"Of course. I'll ensure that Councilman Ofred receives additional coin."

Merdel, the Master of Foreign Relations, burst through the door, brushing past the table with his narrow frame as he hurried to the nearest chair. Like Kaine, he was born in the Leila Kingdom but now served the Darian Kingdom. His tendency to over-commit to tasks often left him tardy, and arriving so late to even a breakfast meeting suggested he hadn't slept at all the previous night.

"Apologies, everyone," the Councilman huffed, struggling to compose himself. Sweat trickled down his dark forehead, soaking into his forest-green robe. "I've just returned from the Leila Kingdom with—"

"No need to explain," Ether interrupted. He sipped the red juice from his goblet then wiped his lips. "There's no harm done. Besides the previous task I assigned you, do you have any other news?"

"Sir Eisenbern has been facing increased trouble from the People's Army within their city," Merdel said.

Jarret Eisenbern, leader of Queen Blanche's Purple Guard, held a powerful position in the Leila Kingdom, but to Kaine, he was an old friend. Long before Kaine rejected his parents' expectations to become a knight, Eisenbern had been a constant presence in his life, always ready for serious conversations, intense training, and lively nights of drinking. If Kaine had followed the path his mother and father set out for him, he likely would have served alongside Eisenbern as one of Queen Blanche's knights. Instead, Kaine abandoned his upper-class lifestyle and took to the ocean as a merchant, disappointing his family, severing ties, and beginning a new life.

Despite the long period away from his birthplace, he had returned full circle. He unexpectedly reunited with Eisenbern during Princess Lydia's wedding rehearsal dinner, their first meeting in years. Eisenbern teased him about not staying in touch during his time at sea yet remained as charismatic and jovial as ever. His charisma, along with his skill with a sword and cleverness, was likely what had made the queen trust Eisenbern enough to put him in charge of her special knights. Though Kaine deeply admired his friend, he felt he had let Eisenbern down twice: once by leaving the Leila Kingdom and again when his arm failed to heal.

"The People's Army is also protesting over in the Leila Kingdom?" Ofred exclaimed. "They're at our market right now. I just passed by their unruly mobs as I came in."

Kaine avoided taking Xander and Kira to Last Hope's crowded public areas, fearing potential danger. These districts, usually peaceful, had become hotbeds of crime, with weekly outbreaks of shouting, fights, and looting of merchant carts. Some Darians opposed the war against the Throatians, despite the princess's demise. If people recognized the prince and princess in the streets, the situation could turn violent. For weeks, Kaine had kept them confined within Serenity Keep, where they occupied themselves with their training and studies while the guards protected them.

"I haven't determined who leads the group," Iris said. "My patrols questioned the arrested violent individuals, but we gained no insight into how they organize."

"An idea doesn't need a leader to ignite a movement," Ether von Stonewall declared. "Yet it shames our kingdom how apathetic and cruel they've become. Even their own princess, Lydia, was murdered. How can they remain so indifferent to that?"

"They may feel outrage but remain unwilling to engage in warfare," Bridgette said.

"It wasn't just Lydia," Ether said harshly. "Never forget that the Throatians burned the men, women, and children of Starlight Beach alive."

"The betrayal we suffered justifies invading their island," Merdel said as Xander gave him a quiet smirk of approval. "Any other kingdom would have done the same."

Ether maintained a neutral expression but remarked, "I cannot understand why those protesting don't see it. They've chosen the opposite side of justice."

Merdel rubbed his fingers across his chin. "We need to communicate what's at stake. Perhaps we can organize a memorial for those abducted from Starlight Beach. We must remind everyone that the crown hasn't forgotten those murdered by the Throatians. This might inspire some protesters to shift their perspective and even consider joining Councilman Conan at sea."

"A fine idea!" Ether exclaimed.

"I trust you can handle the arrangements?" Bridgette asked.

"Of course," Merdel replied with a confident grin. Kaine could see the wheels turning in his mind as Merdel added, "The remembrance will take place within the fortnight."

"No, Rufus," the king said. "This time, Councilman Ofred will oversee the event instead."

Ofred's face went white. "Me?"

"May I ask why, Your Majesty?" Merdel said curtly. "I'm usually the one in charge of organizing these sorts of—"

"While the memorial gathering is important to me, I will soon need your help even more," King Ether said, his tone reassuring. Turning to Ofred, he continued, "Your efforts will lead our streets toward peace—I am confident of it. The People's Army is a constant challenge, and my priority is to remove them without resorting to violence. Instead, we must focus on changing their hearts."

Xander leaned forward, his eyes widening with determination. "What if they continue to spread chaos and destruction in the city—or even want to overthrow us?"

Ether looked at his son with surprise and concern. "Xander, I understand your anger, but we cannot resort to violence without careful thought. We must remember the innocent lives at stake. Darians are still Darians, even if their beliefs differ from ours. The People's Army is not a rebellion; it's a movement."

Ofred coughed. "Your father speaks wisely, young prince. If you confront the People's Army with a sword, they will unsheathe their own. But if you choose to speak, they might lower theirs."

Xander looked down at the table, his shoulders drooping in defeat as he muttered, "They haven't earned my trust yet."

Ether smiled. "I know, Xander. We all feel that way... and now we know that trust must be earned, not given freely."

4
BIOS AURAS - THE ARRANGEMENT

The backroom of the butchery was a narrow, secretive nook within the vastness of Last Hope's market, filled with smells of fresh blood. His crimson armor rested against the rough edge of his chair as Bios Auras smiled. Across from him, Darian Councilman Ofred's massive frame sat in a seat that creaked under his weight. His sausage-shaped fingers tapped on the table and greed shone in his eyes as he estimated the heap of gold before him.

"You understand the price has gone up, my charitable knight?" Ofred said, his voice carrying an obvious note of satisfaction.

Bios Auras curled his lips into a wider smile. Human nature was as predictable as the sunrise. Profit, ambition, and risk were Ofred's strengths, but to Bios Auras, they were tools to exploit.

"Your guards finally noticed the missing grains," he acknowledged, sliding another pile of coins across the table. "Your information becomes more valuable. I understand your predicament, of course. Whatever amount of gold you need to make this worthwhile, you'll receive from me—but don't forget, I've been a consistent business partner."

Ofred grabbed the second bag. "They're planning to tighten security around the silos and granaries starting next week," he revealed after a brief pause. The only sound was the distant chatter of market vendors outside and above the basement.

"What about the guards' patterns and rotations?" Bios pressed further, assessing Ofred's willingness to say more.

The councilman shifted uncomfortably. "It's unpredictable now. Iris Thorne will monitor this more closely than ever before."

Bios considered the recent development with an expressionless face. His plans demanded precision; unpredictability was a liability unless he created it. Still, as long as the granaries remained locked and unguarded at certain times, opportunities would arise. "Your assistance ensures that those who are hungry will be fed," he said.

Ofred grunted noncommittally, eyes fixed on the two piles of coins.

"And in return for taking more risk," Bios said, counting out coins from his satchel with deliberate slowness, "you'll receive proper compensation."

"This should suffice for now," the councilman muttered. "But be cautious, my charitable, red-armored knight. Your opportunities for heists are dwindling."

Bios Auras stood from his chair. "I've faced worse than guardsmen," he assured Ofred with a cold confidence.

The councilman slid a note across the table to Bios, who unfolded it without saying a word. Inside was the information he had paid so much gold to receive:

Don't wait too long—tonight might be your last chance for a while.

"You're a peculiar person, my deep-pocketed stranger," Ofred murmured, leaning closer to ensure his words stayed hidden from the outside world. "One might wonder if your philanthropy has a cause or purpose. The amount of missing food tied to our arrangement is substantial. Who could need such a large quantity?"

Bios's eyes narrowed just a fraction, sharpening his focus without revealing his ignorance. He stayed silent, allowing the councilman to reveal more of his thoughts.

"Could it be that you are affiliated with the People's Army?" His choice of words was deliberate, drenched in implications. "They have significant resources and influence—and certainly would have use for the food you've been taking."

The accusation persisted like the musty odor of raw meat around them. Bios Auras released a quiet chuckle, not loud enough to draw attention from outside the butchery but sufficient to show he found it amusing. It wasn't clear how Ofred would proceed.

"The People's Army?" Bios let a smirk escape. "Friend, your mind wanders into fascinating fantasies." He paused, gauging the councilman's reaction.

"But who else would need so much stolen food from Serenity Keep?" Ofred pressed. "The poorest of Last Hope have always been hungry, but I've learned of no unusual increase in the number of mouths being fed."

Bios sat back in his chair, his armor clinking softly as he pondered his next response. His actions could easily be mistaken for supporting the People's Army, a notorious group of protesters known for their conspiracies, swindling, and opposition to King Ether von Stonewall's rule.

"I assure you," Bios began slowly, letting each word drip with sincerity and hidden meanings, "my interests are... my own. As I told you, the food is for those who are hungry."

"Is that so?" Ofred said, seemingly unsatisfied with the cryptic answer. His eyes remained observant, as if calculating how much he might extract from the arrangement if it could endure indefinitely. Despite his oafish appearance, the man had a cunning intellect lurking beneath the rolls of his skin.

"It is," Bios affirmed.

Ofred's triple chin paused in contemplation before he nodded. "Well then," he said with resignation while gathering his gold coins. "Frankly, it matters little who you serve—or even if you are dumping food into rivers—so long as you pay me."

Bios Auras watched the councilman hesitate. Though Ofred had a reputation for corruption, his loyalty to King Ether remained uncertain. Bios noticed the tension in Ofred's shoulders—a sign of someone hiding something but also seeking an ally. If Ofred were to be involved with the People's Army, it would explain his behavior. It would also give Bios more reason to win Ofred's trust. There was more Ofred could offer than just his food stores, after all.

After the Throatian Royal Family and their subjects failed in their attempt to steal the Tears of Asura from King Ether, the Darian council members emerged as the next potential way of finding them. Bios's primary goal was to acquire the God Stones, and bribing the councilman with exorbitant amounts of gold was a means toward building trust and achieving this. While access to Last Hope's food stores was a consideration, it was not Bios's greater interest.

If Councilman Ofred was a member of the People's Army, that

suggested he would betray the king for the right price. But Bios Auras knew better than simply offering more gold. Turning Ofred from a business partner into a loyal servant would require something more than money. Bios would need to create a series of unfortunate circumstances, surrounding Ofred with four walls of pressing and dangerous situations, each more dire than the last. This would force Ofred to a breaking point, where he would have no choice but to seek Bios's protection. But to gain Ofred's loyalty born from desperation, Bios first needed to earn his trust.

"Councilman," he called out, keeping his voice hushed. "Before you go, indulge my curiosity for a moment."

Ofred raised a questioning eyebrow and asked, "What more is there to discuss?"

"The People's Army," Bios began slowly, each word chosen to deceive. "Your insight into their affairs strikes me as unusually sharp. You're a powerful man, someone with the capacity to wield influence over lesser powers if he chose."

"I serve King Ether and the Darian Kingdom," he sneered, his eyes betraying his words as he hesitated while half-risen from his chair.

"And yet," Bios continued, allowing his declaration to unravel the truth, "one might wonder if you serve more than one master."

As Ofred stood, his round face tightened into an unconvincing mask of outrage. "I am loyal to my king!" he declared, cringing when he realized he had spoken too loudly.

"Of course you're loyal to the king, like anyone else," Bios said kindly. "I didn't mean to suggest otherwise. It's just that you speak of the People's Army as someone familiar with its inner workings. Are you acquainted with them? I'm quite curious about their group. Whether you're a member or doing business with them is none of my concern."

The silence overtook the basement as he waited impatiently for the councilman to yield.

"I've... heard some things," Ofred finally muttered. "You know how rumors and whispers spread through the council's halls. They're a problem for King Ether, so Councilwoman Iris has been investigating the group."

Bios pressed, sensing Ofred's rapid heartbeat and the sweat on his face. "But you're not one of them?"

"No!" The denial was quick and shallow, and the man was halfway across the room at the doorway.

Bios stood, palms open and hands raised above his waist, keeping them well away from his sword.

"It seems odd to me," he said as he approached the councilman, "that you would risk so much for mere coins with people like me when nobler causes are at stake. We both know King Ether isn't perfect—given the issues we've seen, for example, the recent troubles with the Throatians. What if I told you that my interests align more closely with those who seek change in the Darian Kingdom? What if I sought... a partnership with such an organization?"

His bait now lay enticingly before him, shiny and tempting.

Ofred shifted from foot to foot, his eyes darting like a trapped rabbit.

"I'm not—" he said, and swallowed hard, before continuing. "If I were involved with such people, it would be dangerous for either of us to talk about it."

Bios smiled. "These walls have always been secure for our previous dealings," he replied. "A few more moments shouldn't matter, if anyone is listening. If you're concerned, check outside the exit for eavesdroppers."

Ofred nervously glanced up the stairway, his senses likely overwhelmed by the aroma of fresh hanging meat.

"If someone like me had connections..." he whispered, leaning in so close that Bios could smell the sweat beading down his nose.

"Yes?"

"Then it would be with those who hold great influence within their group," Ofred confessed, his own pride poisoning him.

Bios offered a small, calculated smile, revealing only interest and approval. "What if your hypothetical friends could use someone like me—a swordsman who is also stealthy and adept at entering and exiting places undetected?"

Ofred's eyes widened slightly. "Hypothetically," he said with caution, "someone like you could be invaluable. The People's Army would offer you work—and coin, of course."

"Perhaps it's time to align myself with those powerful enough to recognize my value." Bios paused to let the words settle before extending his hand.

Ofred wiped sweat from his pudgy face and took it. The councilman's grip revealed eagerness and fear.

"Let's stop talking in hypotheticals," Bios murmured, "and tell me more about these friends of yours."

Ofred's breath fogged the cold, musty air as he spoke. "There was an ambush at Wargonne," he said. "A group of assassins sent by the People's Army all died. Rumors suggest King Ether's forces knew they were coming. I believe Councilman Conan remains unsusceptible to surprises as long as he's within the walls of the fortress."

Bios Auras nodded. Every disaster stemmed from others' missteps, whether because of inadequate planning or a lack of caution. The news Ofred shared wasn't just of a failed assassination —it opened the door to new possibilities. As the heart of the Darian military, Wargonne would be the safest place for King Ether to hide the God Stones from the Throatians and Lucidians.

"The People's Army won't let this setback stop them," Ofred continued, his eyes darting around the dimly lit backroom as if King Ether might appear at any moment. "They're assembling a new team —warriors for sensitive missions across the kingdom."

Could the word "sensitive" be a clue pointing to the God Stones? Bios leaned back against the cold stone wall, crossing his arms and shifting uncomfortably. "And you believe I could be part of this new team?" he inquired, letting a touch of eagerness grow in his voice.

Ofred's confirmation came slowly and thoughtfully. "I might recommend you," he said, "but you must understand the stakes are high. These missions are not for the faint-hearted or those unwilling to get blood on their armor."

A thin smile stretched across Bios's lips. "My armor is the color of blood for a reason," he said coldly. "I have more experience with such matters than most men have in their lifetimes."

The councilman studied him before speaking again. "If I put your name forward, they'll test you," he remarked. "They will want proof of your loyalty and competence."

Bios declared, "I welcome their tests—but only if the work is truly as interesting as you claim."

Ofred accepted the response and extended his hand for a final handshake. "I'll make the arrangements," he said, "but remember— they are not tolerant of failure. Those who perished in Wargonne were better off dead than returning without fulfilling their mission."

"Then it is fortunate that I cannot fail."

He advanced toward the front of the butcher's shop. By becoming an assassin for the protestors, he could use their political goals against them until all their secrets spilled out, including Ofred's knowledge of the God Stones. The councilman was a means to that end, and his weaknesses made him the easiest path.

"Wait," Ofred called. "To submit your name, I'll actually need it."

"Call me Hellvar." It was a lie.

"Very well, Sir Hellvar. Go to the Golden Mare at Hillside Reach. In five days, inquire with the bartender about a drink called the Strega Generatrice. He will provide you with the information you need. I will ensure he is prepared for your arrival. Is that clear?"

"I'm to order a Strega Generatrice at the Golden Mare," Bios confirmed. "Understood. Farewell until next time."

He left the butcher's shop and walked through Last Hope's markets, checking every few moments to ensure nobody was following him. Though King Ether's knights patrolled from dawn until dusk, the public commonly knew where and when the knights patrolled. They followed regular paths unless a common pickpocket or a brawl caused a scene that might delay them.

Two markets thrived within Last Hope—the stalls selling produce, essentials, and trinkets, and the shadowy dealings between them. Bios Auras was adept at reading the second market, the more interesting one. Moving through the crowd, his crimson armor hidden beneath a black cloak, he observed the covert exchanges.

In a dim corner beyond a potato stall, where sunlight seldom penetrated, a woman with a snake tattoo winding up her arm traded vials of green ooze for a glass-bladed knife. Her buyer, a young boy with nervous, darting eyes, pocketed the containers and vanished into the crowd.

A few stalls down, an old man with weathered skin sold necklaces with counterfeit jewels. Though everyone knew they were fake, his low prices and sparse sales kept the guards from bothering him. Every day, he sat at his stall, and rarely would anyone care to look at his wares. But Bios noticed something unusual when a woman with golden hair approached him. She handed him a simple pouch of carrots, and in return, he gave her a large bag of coins—far more than the vegetables were worth.

A group of children ran through the crowd, crashing into people while pretending to play a game of chase. In truth, they were distracting the onlookers while their quieter friends sifted through the pockets of those who'd fallen victim to their own curiosity.

He took advantage of the situation and darted straight into an empty alley where nobody waited. He centered his focus within himself, sensing the Tear of Asura dormant within his body.

To fully utilize his gift, he'd sewn the God Stone underneath the skin of his right forearm, between the surface and bone, and allowed his body to heal over the wound. Now, it would be impossible for him to become separated from his God Stone unless he somehow lost his arm. After all, to use the Teleportation Stone, he only had to be touching it. Keeping it inside his body was both the safest and most convenient option. Though Bios Auras had secured only one God Stone so far, the Teleportation Stone was undoubtedly the most powerful among them.

To activate the Teleportation Stone, he needed only to visualize the destination. If he imagined the location vividly enough, an invisible portal would open and lead him there. The power had two limitations: he could only maintain one gateway at a time, and it would stay open until he mentally instructed it to close. Years of practice had refined the process to the point where opening and closing gateways felt as natural as recalling a memory.

And now, he wished to visit the Temple of White on the Throatian island, where the Elders gathered to oversee all blood sacrifices and related religious activities for the island.

His mind's eye focused on its inner chamber, a place he'd recently visited more frequently than in the past. He visualized every detail—the way sunlight passed through the glassless windows, the shiny polished stone walls and floors, the musty smell of the incense that perpetually infested in the air. The three obelisks stood at the center of his memory, their ancient history shrouded.

With a gentle shift in his awareness, a tingling sensation traveled up his arm. The world around him blurred at the edges as reality folded upon itself, revealing a faint shimmering physical outline—an invisible portal, unseen by everyone else. Though he couldn't see it either, he sensed its magic, knowing he had summoned it.

5
KAINE - THE CRYPT

After the council meeting ended, Kaine found himself alone with Xander. The others had dispersed, leaving an uncertain atmosphere throughout the chamber. Xander sat at the table, his chin resting on his hand. Kaine hesitated before nearing, unsure if he should interrupt the prince's thoughts.

"Xander," Kaine murmured, approaching without startling him, "may I speak with you for a moment?"

The prince looked up from the table, his weary eyes revealing exhaustion. "Of course," he responded.

It must have been the nightmares Kira mentioned. Kaine moved to sit next to the prince and examined his face for any signs of emotion. Xander appeared neutral, yet there was something about him that seemed more tired than just a lack of sleep would explain. "You seem troubled," he noted gently.

"I'm fine," he replied. "I have my new duties as prince to fulfill. It's a lot, but I'll learn how to bear them."

Kaine nodded, sensing that Xander wasn't being entirely truthful. "I understand," he said, "but I can't help noticing that something's bothering you. Is there anything you'd like to talk about?"

"There's nothing going on," he said. Yet Xander avoided eye contact, and his face told a different story.

"I know losing Lydia has been hard on all of us, and it's been especially difficult for you. Please don't feel as though you need to hide your feelings from me. I'm here for you."

"I wasn't hiding anything!" Xander exclaimed. Yet, to Kaine's surprise, Xander pressed on. "But how can so many people doubt Lydia is gone? Could they be right? I never saw her after the wedding. Maybe the People's Army is correct—perhaps she's not dead, just missing."

That dark day marked Kaine's first meeting with Xander and Kira. The somber encounter left a lasting impression, and from that moment, Kaine vowed to protect them as if they were his own siblings—a promise he'd made to Lydia herself.

Lydia's coffin had been closed during the funeral. Her lifeless form was unpresentable, and King Ether had insisted that the kingdom's last memory of her be of her wedding day, dressed in beauty. The king had seen his daughter's body only once and could not bear to view it again. Closing the casket spared Xander and Kira from carrying that image in their hearts and minds as well.

Kaine looked at Xander with empathy. "I understand your doubts, my prince," he said, "but I saw her body. Moreover, I carried it from the Throatian ship back to your father to confirm it was indeed Lydia and not a deception the Throatians were attempting against us."

Xander stared at Kaine in disbelief. "You did that?"

Kaine nodded solemnly. "I was there when we exchanged Lydia for Throatian hostages. It was... a horrifying sight."

Tears streamed down the prince's face. "Why would they kill her? I know the reason—they killed her for her magic. But why target her specifically?"

"Not all religions are honorable or good, especially that of the Throatians. It's hard to accept, but believe me, she's gone," he said gently. "It is important that we move forward and honor Lydia's memory."

"I'll… I'll try."

"You're not alone, Xander. We're all here with you."

"I don't care what anyone says," the prince declared. "The Throatians must pay for their betrayal. Teach me, Kaine—make me the greatest swordsman in the world so I may join Councilman Conan at sea."

Kaine nodded, though only to please his prince. "I'll do everything in my power to train you," he promised, jovially pointing to his arm in a sling. "If fortune favors us, Councilman Conan will breach their island and end the war long before you ever have to set foot on a ship."

"Xander, shouldn't you be studying with Kira and Ursula?" Ether boomed, his voice echoing through the chamber as he returned from wherever he had just gone.

Kaine rose from his chair, bowed respectfully to the king, and said, "He should be, but it was my fault for keeping him here."

Xander, with an equally respectful tone, responded, "I'll go now, Father."

The prince exited the room, and as Kaine prepared to leave, the king raised his hand to stop him. Kaine noticed a new sword at his side, its emerald-green sheath gleaming. The king explained, "I came back here to find you, Sir Khalia. Come—we need to move somewhere private to talk."

Kaine noted the closed door at the end of the room and asked, "Is it not secluded enough here?"

The king replied, "It's not necessarily free from all who might hear us."

He led Kaine down the stairwell to the castle's lowest floor and then through the open area where Kaine had trained Xander and Kira that morning. The downpour had ended as suddenly as it had begun, leaving behind a muddy landscape. Each step squished beneath their boots as they walked. The courtyard, now peaceful, seemed frozen in time, except for the occasional pink cherry blossom drifting down. For a moment, Kaine thought the king was heading toward his chambers, but Ether guided him through the main gate, down a short hill, and in the direction of Serenity Keep's graveyard.

As they walked through the cemetery, Kaine's mind drifted back to the night Lydia had invited him there—the night before the Throatians killed her. Worse still, he'd heard rumors that the church had declined to annul their marriage even after her death. As far as the records went, Thane was now a widower.

They approached the princess's tombstone and headed toward a large stone archway leading to the royal crypt. Every von Stonewall family member had two graves—one for public display and another in the private rooms buried deep underground. Kaine speculated that the reason behind multiple burial sites was to let the departed rest undisturbed by onlookers. Though he had never entered the crypt and hadn't heard of others gaining access, it seemed the king intended for them to enter.

Upon reaching a large gate bolstered by three locks, King Ether produced the keys and opened the entrance more quickly than Kaine could believe.

Kaine said, "I'm surprised you allowed me to come here. It's an honor."

The king gave him a rare smile as they reached the bottom of the steps. He lit a torch and mounted it on the wall. "Do you remember the first time we met, Kaine?"

It was unforgettable. Before meeting King Ether, almost thirty years had passed since he'd last stepped into a throne room. After rescuing Lydia from the monster, Kaine returned her to the castle, more concerned about his muddy clothes than anything else. Councilman Merdel provided him with clean attire, but the thought of being formally presented to royalty after so long was overwhelming.

"I remember it well, Your Highness, but it feels as though years have passed."

"The busiest of years are the fastest stolen by time," Ether replied cryptically. "Lydia insisted I give you a role in my household, although we had never met. I didn't know whether you were a pirate or a merchant. But our meeting, and our friendship, were meant to be."

He led Kaine deeper into the cavern-like tomb, lighting additional torches as they moved. The damp walls mournfully reflected the orange glow of the flames, while the narrow hallways carried the subtle scent of lavender from an unseen source. Their footsteps sank into the wet soil as they entered a spacious chamber filled with more graves, tombstones, and shrines than Kaine could have imagined fitting beneath the ground.

"Only Lydia is down here," Ether said. "My kin passed away before I established the kingdom, so they are buried elsewhere in Yaenia. Despite their absence, their statues occupy places in this room. Other graves are for the future—I just never expected to use my daughter's."

It was evident the king's purpose for the underground building went beyond mere stone; it immortalized his family's lineage and created a resting place where his descendants could be laid to rest. Perhaps Ether most wanted the crypt to remind him of where he'd come from and the family he had lost to forge his crown. Still, there was one other person who should have been buried down here next to Lydia—her mother, Lily von Stonewall.

Kaine eyed the enormous statue of a woman next to Ether's future grave. The craftsmanship was exceptional—despite never having met Queen Lily, the statue's detailed features bore striking resemblances to both Lydia and Kira. Her long, bushy hair cascaded down her smooth face and over her dress. Though her expression was neutral, like most statues Kaine had seen, her eyes held a quiet passion that hinted at deep power and determination.

"You said only Lydia is here, but isn't this the queen's grave?"

Ether nodded, leaving his hand on the statue's base beside an empty spot that would one day mark his future burial site. "I wanted Lily to be laid to rest here, but she chose the mountains of Gale Village. It was where she had spent much of her life before we met. Knowing we'll be buried apart fills me with great sorrow, but as king, I must ensure that this tomb remains my resting place."

In his position, Ether could have changed the law if one existed. However, Kaine understood his reasoning—what king wouldn't want his grave near his castle? The more intriguing question was why the queen had chosen to be buried so far from her kingdom and family. They had likely argued about her decision years ago.

"As grim as a crypt should be, there is a certain peacefulness among the shadows of this place," Kaine commented, trying to lighten the mood.

Ether nodded approvingly. "I see it that way too," he said. "In fact, I wanted to discuss Lily's grave with you today. But first, I'd like to hear your thoughts on the council meeting we just had."

It was an odd topic. Ofred and Iris had been shifting blame for the missing food supplies between themselves, and Xander had erupted in anger. Which of these two incidents had most disturbed the king?

"I suspect everyone is more on edge than usual," Kaine said. "More than one attendee was snappier than the coldest of ocean winds."

"Have you noticed the lack of progress between Ofred and Iris lately?" The king appeared to have a fixed opinion and was weighing his intuition.

Kaine accepted the invitation and responded, "If the missing food comes from criminal activity rather than an accounting error, then it appears to involve well-planned heists. Solving this mystery won't be simple, but the cause will probably boil down to either thievery or incompetence."

Dark circles shadowed the king's eyes as he stared at his wife's statue and shrine. "Iris and Ofred are both capable in their duties. Neither is so incompetent that they would misplace or make errors at the scale of the missing food. They're skilled enough to identify any mistakes if they exist. If both were fulfilling their obligations as they claim, the problem would have been resolved by now. Since the issue persists, thievery must be the cause."

It then became clear why Ether had brought him underground to avoid discussing the matter publicly in the council chamber—the king was suspicious of his council members' loyalty and did not want them to discover his doubts.

"Between Iris and Ofred, who has the greater incentive or advantage for stealing the supplies?"

"That's what I don't understand," Ether said. "If Ofred is corrupt, he could have made the food unrecorded, forged the records with incorrect numbers or false sales, or manipulated them in countless other ways. Only a few people would need to be involved for him to succeed. I wouldn't even know the supplies were missing. None of us would realize the truth unless the kingdom faced starvation."

"But he is the one drawing the most attention to the issue," Kaine said. "If he had a hand in the heists, he wouldn't want to draw attention to himself. What, then, could Iris be doing? She would need more than a handful of corrupt guards at her disposal. Alternatively, the watchmen themselves might be untrustworthy and lying to her. Someone could be deceiving both of them."

"Her randomized selection of guards would thwart any such efforts, if that were the case," Ether said, "but there's another explanation for what's happening here."

"And that possibility would be what?"

"Perhaps the food isn't disappearing at all," King Ether surmised, "and someone intends for this situation to distract us from more pressing issues."

"A distraction? From what kinds of problems?"

"From the war," Ether said. "You've seen the protests, and the pamphlets posted on every street corner. The People's Army is urging us to bring our ships home and ignore the fact that our conflict with the Throatians is far from over. If famine strikes, our military efforts will starve as well. Either someone is truly stealing the food, or they want us to believe they are."

"You really think the protesters have the resources and influence to sway one of your council members?" Kaine asked. The People's Army was merely an informal name adopted by some citizens. Nobody had even claimed leadership or to represent them.

"In all my years as king, I've never witnessed a resistance movement of commoners emerge so suddenly or grow so large so quickly. Someone sympathetic to their cause must be funding them with gold—it's the only plausible explanation. Also, the fake letter you received from Prince Thane shows they may have significant influence within Serenity Keep."

"I fail to see the relationship between the letter and the missing food."

After battling the Throatians at sea and returning to Serenity Keep, Kaine had discovered an envelope beneath his door. The letter revealed that he and the Throatian prince were being manipulated for a greater purpose and that a knight in crimson armor was the true threat behind the Wedding of the Torn Rose. It warned him to protect the God Stones at all costs and hinted at a more significant war yet to come.

The most peculiar aspect was that the message supposedly came from Thane, or at least his initials were scribbled at the bottom. However, Kaine immediately recognized it as Lydia's handwriting, recalling the previous letter she had given him before her death. He spent three days trying to determine whether Lydia had written both letters beforehand and, if so, why. If she hadn't, then the second letter, signed as Thane, was likely a forgery. Kaine couldn't understand why someone would mimic Lydia's writing style only to sign Prince Thane's initials at the end.

Puzzled by the mystery, Kaine revealed the letter to King Ether and the council, expecting them to recognize Lydia's handwriting. They scrutinized the letter's penmanship, paper, and wording, but ended up as confused as Kaine. They claimed it wasn't the handwriting of Lydia, and everyone doubted Prince Thane's involvement.

Someone else likely wrote the letter, but what was alarming was their knowledge of the God Stones. According to Ether, only he, his council, and Kaine were supposed to know of them. If the king's suspicion was correct and the People's Army had somehow discovered the God Stones, they might attempt to steal them. However, the letter requesting their protection contradicted this possibility, leaving everything confusing and unclear.

"If we assume the People's Army is trying to undermine our war efforts, it explains the strange occurrences we're witnessing," King Ether said. "At present, the only council member I fully trust is Merdel. Everyone else seems suspicious to me. I must assume that at least one of them could manipulate what we observe. It's the only way to explain the letter sent to you and the missing food."

In Kaine's view, the relationship between the topics they had discussed was fragmented. While all the events Ether mentioned were genuine, they seemed parts of unrelated plans. The problem lay in Ether's approach: instead of recognizing that each event served its own distinct purpose, he was attempting to merge them into a single, overly complex mosaic. Whether the missing food and Thane's letter were related or separate, the meaning behind them was unclear and lacked coherence.

"I still don't think the People's Army and the letter are related," Kaine said openly, "but this situation involving the letter keeps me awake at night, trying to figure out who wrote it and why."

Ether said, "I suspect our corrupt council member is behind this." He paused, his eyes narrowing. "These distractions are pulling us away from the war against the Throatians—exactly what the People's Army wants. That's why I've called you here. I have a task for you, something I can't discuss with the entire council."

Although Kaine still doubted the connection, debating the details was pointless since neither of them could prove anything yet.

"But how do you know I didn't write the letter?" Kaine asked. "I could be the one trying to sabotage the war effort."

"As you know, I've been suspicious lately, Kaine, but questioning your loyalty is pointless. When you were a merchant and first entered my throne room, you were not swayed by my gold, and that's why I know no one can bribe you against me. You helped me with Lydia, supported me through everything that followed, and have proven your loyalty countless times. Plus, I've seen how you watch over Xander and Kira, guiding them with such care and devotion. Although they lost their older sister, they've gained you as a brother, in a way."

The king overestimated his worth, though his reasoning seemed sound, assuming that was his genuine belief. "I appreciate your continued faith in me," Kaine replied, "and I pledge my loyalty to your family."

Ether warned, "Just don't lose faith in yourself," as Kaine felt the hairs on his neck prickle. "Especially since I'll be sending you and Merdel to do this task."

As the Master of Foreign Relations, Merdel was well-versed in speech and suggestion and had served as the royal family's primary host before the wedding. If Ether intended to send them to negotiate across the sea, it would be a lengthy and challenging journey, especially if granted the opportunity to meet Prince Thane in his homeland.

"Sending our best diplomat into hostile territory might not be wise," Kaine warned. "Given the Throatians' reputation, I wouldn't be surprised if they murder anyone we send, especially since none of our birds came back from their island."

Ether scrunched his face, confused. "I'm not sending you to the Throatian island—though you're right, that would end badly. Instead, you, Merdel, Xander, and Kira, will travel to Gale Village."

It was no accident that Ether guided him to his family's crypt and revealed the secret about Lily von Stonewall's grave. If the king felt his children's safety was at risk, sending them to a remote location made the most sense—especially if he couldn't reveal the plan to most of his council members.

"You want us to hide the children there," Kaine concluded. "But what's the point of bringing Merdel with us?"

"You've almost got it," Ether replied. "Officially, I'll inform everyone that you'll take Xander and Kira to Wargonne for military training. In reality, you'll go to Gale Village instead. There, you can tell the locals that you've brought the prince and princess to visit their mother's grave. However, your true mission is to bury the God Stones alongside her. Merdel will accompany you to meet with the village head, an old friend of mine."

"A clever plan," Kaine said. "I agree that moving the God Stones to a safer location is necessary. If the Throatians attempted to steal them again, they'd be unlikely to search such a remote spot."

"Honestly," Ether admitted, "I'm not sure who I can trust right now. That's why I have to lie to my council members until I discover who is working against me. I've also hired body doubles for Xander and Kira—Merdel found two children who are the exact likeness of them in the Leila Kingdom. This is why he was late for the meeting earlier."

Using children as decoys was likely one of the king's coping mechanisms after losing his daughter. Merdel must have traveled to the Leila Kingdom with a cartload of gold and a silver tongue, securing not one but two children to serve as potential sacrifices if an attack happened while they were gone. The thought of how much he had paid their parents was unsettling, a darkness Kaine preferred not to dwell on. Still, as long as the Throatians never returned to Last Hope, Xander and Kira, and their doubles, would remain safe.

"You're certain the problem is so deep-rooted?" Kaine asked.

"The letter you received suggests that much. I plan for you to spend at least a few weeks in Gale Village while I sort this out."

Ether's caution was justified, given the many unexplained events. With such high stakes, protecting both his children and the powerful magical stones demanded careful planning. "We will move discreetly," Kaine promised, "so that nobody along the road recognizes us."

"Thank you again, Kaine Khalia," the king said, unlatching his sheathed sword and, with both hands, offering it to him. "You're the only one who can set things right in uncertain times."

"You're giving this to me, Your Majesty?"

"It's a blade from my personal stores," the king said. "I used it in the first war, though it wasn't my main weapon. Nevertheless, it played a significant role in the previous conflicts. Its name is White Oath."

"White Oath—it's a fine name," Kaine replied, examining the emerald-green sheath. The handle was the color of bone, and the blade beneath, forged from steel unblemished and shining, seemed to bear both honor and serenity.

"I need you to protect my children above all," the king continued. "If anything happens to Xander or Kira, I'll be as good as dead."

"My life will be their shield, Your Majesty," Kaine promised.

"I know it will, Sir Khalia," King Ether said solemnly. "It is your destiny to be this, and that is why I am certain you are the right one to choose."

But what good would a new sword do him if his arm failed to heal?

6

THANE - THE NULL MAGE

Sea breezes brushed Thane's cheeks as he wandered through Sky Tower Coast's crowded streets, his magical armor hidden by his brown cloak. Just a short walk from the docks, a vibrant market lined the northern edge of the city and shoreline, offering a variety and quality of goods unmatched by White Boar's Landing from his motherland.

Most merchants sold fish, crabs, oysters, and other seafood, while others offered decorations and jewelry crafted from seashells. These crafts likely appealed to tourists, as there were more vendors selling trinkets than essential items. The abundance of shells reminded Thane of his mother's childhood punishments, recalling how she'd forced him to kneel on broken ones as a boy.

Urith Asche was strict, cold, and almost cruel. Yet she raised him to be stronger than the other children on his home island. When the Darians defeated her and his father at sea, a peculiar numbness enveloped him, similar to that in his kneecaps during his mother's punishments. He knew his reaction was not normal—even the weeks spent in jail with Hrodspire had stirred no grief or tears for him. Perhaps growing up around the Loyalty Circles had numbed him to the sorrow he should have felt at their loss.

Tension had run high during his family's last days together. The brutal Loyalty Circles seemed tame compared to what his father had commanded them to do to the Darian captives aboard their ships. Although Thane pleaded, King Harkbin and Queen Urith ordered the men, women, and children to be burned alive in the name of

Zann-Xia-Czul. At that moment, Thane's family had met their true end, even though they were still living.

Despite his parents' last chain of decisions being driven by desperation, Thane couldn't shake off his suspicions. Had the disasters following Thane's wedding revealed their genuine natures, or had it changed them? Ultimately, Harkbin and Urith showed that worshipping Zann-Xia-Czul led only to gratuitous violence, suffering, and death.

There was no point in letting his thoughts linger on the darker memories, so he searched the market for what Somnius had advised him to purchase. Finding the specific medicinal roots and mushrooms he needed was effortless, and within twenty minutes, he'd already located an herbalist who had exactly what he required.

The shop owner's question about searching for diamonds in the volcanoes near Gale Village led Thane to conclude Red Cloud was commonly used for safer mining. He paid the elderly woman a few coins from the small purse Somnius had given him and moved on to find his lodgings. The next morning, he would head west in search of the Whisperers as Somnius had instructed.

With a rumbling stomach, he entered the nearest inn, named The Lucky Fish Hook. He headed straight for the bar, taking one of the vacant stools. A middle-aged man with graying hair managed the pub, assisted by a young boy carrying drinks who Thane took to be his grandson.

"What'll it be?" the bartender asked, his curious eyes studying Thane.

The Throatian prince, wary of revealing too much about himself, enunciated slowly in the Common Tongue: "I'd like a meal for dinner."

"Say what?"

Thane repeated himself, speaking as naturally as he could.

Setting aside the drink he was mixing, the bartender stepped to face him across the bar. "Your accent—I can't quite place it. Where are you from?"

"I am from the Silent Deserts," Thane lied. "I'd like any kind of dinner dish you have."

The bartender looked him over, then offered swordfish—their priciest meal. Seeing a tourist trap, Thane retreated.

"A simple fish will suffice," he said. "I'm not as wealthy as you imagine."

A figure cloaked in a charcoal robe with their head concealed beneath a hood approached the bar and sat a few seats away. He glanced their way, but the baggy cloak hid their gender. Only a pair of eyes were visible, the rest of their face shrouded in darkness and bandages. Thane knew the bartender wouldn't succeed in exploiting this person either.

"Fair enough," the bartender said to Thane, his grin wide. "Four bronze will get you half a fish and vegetables. Add two more, and I'll give you a beer as well."

"Deal. Six bronze it is." The bartender took the coins and examined each one. His scrutiny suggested he was verifying their authenticity, leading Thane to suspect he wasn't in one of the city's more affluent areas. For someone to scrutinize even low-value coins hinted that scammers, thieves, and cheats were prevalent here.

After pocketing the money, the bartender forced a strained smile. "So, traveler, which district of the Silent Deserts are you from? You must be from District One to have reached my place. Are you working for someone?"

Thane was unaware of the districts but deduced from the man's tone that District One was the wealthiest. Since he had claimed not to be a wealthy visitor to Yaenia, Districts Two or Three were likely safer choices to use for his imaginary backstory.

"I'm a farmer from District Three," Thane lied as he spoke clearly and puffed out his chest, "and visiting the city for a few days to trade."

"Ah, you must be the fifth person this week from there," the bartender remarked. "Isn't that something?"

The bartender's attempts at small talk were growing annoying. It would be better to sit in silence until his food arrived. Thane nodded and glanced at the hooded stranger next to him, who hadn't spoken since arriving.

"The world grows smaller every day," the man commented as he scribbled Thane's order and handed it to the young boy. The child quickly scanned the note before rushing with it to the kitchen. Then, the bartender called out, "What can I get you?" to the stranger concealed under a gray hooded robe.

"Something sour," he muttered, his voice deep and tired, as if he'd just completed heavy labor.

"Two bronze."

A thin, clenched hand emerged from the stranger's sleeve, wrapped entirely in bandages. A pair of coins dropped onto the bar countertop, then the man's fist retreated into the cloak. Meanwhile, the bartender pocketed the coins without inspecting them. Perhaps the hooded man was a regular who had already proven he didn't carry counterfeit money.

The bartender poured him a golden beer in a chipped tankard, then moved on to serve other customers. Thane folded his arms on the table, glancing toward the other end of the room where a woman, presumably the barkeep's wife, sat near the southern wall knitting a blanket. The establishment's empty atmosphere and lack of crowds reassured Thane he could rent his accommodations for the night after he finished eating.

The kitchen, however, seemed unusually busy, as nearly half an hour had passed without Thane's meal arriving. As a former prince, he had never once waited for his food, and now he was uncertain whether it was culturally appropriate to inquire about the delay. Minutes dragged on, stretching into what felt like hours. He tried to imagine how a farmer might bring up the topic and guessed they wouldn't be so timid.

Earlier, Thane had considered eating in one of the cookery lanes, though those seating locations were outside and left him vulnerable to being seen by more people walking by. While indoor options provided better privacy, the kitchen wouldn't have prepared his meal in advance. Now he regretted his choice: if his plate didn't arrive soon, he'd be better off leaving and finding another place to eat.

"Hello, bartender!" Thane called out.

"What?"

"Could you tell me how much longer until my food arrives?"

"What in Asura's ass do you think I am? A fortune teller?" Then, Thane realized his question was inappropriate.

"Sorry."

"I'm just toying with you," the man replied. "Give it a few more minutes."

He summoned his grandson over, muttered something into his ear, and the boy hurried back into the kitchen. Thane suspected they had forgotten about his food and were now going to ask the cooks to prepare it. Still, to save time, Thane could eat sooner—and that meant he could find a quiet spot out of sight sooner, too.

Though the kitchen had made a mistake, it hardly mattered. A late meal was a minor inconvenience compared to what Thane had endured in recent weeks. He had lost his royal status to his uncle, Grimm Kathaar, and watched his closest friends and family die, some even at his own hand. Now, defeating Zann-Xia-Czul and Bios Auras remained his and Somnius's shared goal.

Before he could think further, the bartender placed a plate of tilapia, carrots, and sprouts in front of him. "It shouldn't have taken this long," he grumbled. "Almost seems as if the cooks had to venture to the ocean to catch it."

Thane's mouth watered as the dish slid towards him. "Even so, it would be fresh. Thanks!"

The man poured him two drinks—one as a silent apology for the delay—then left to tend to other customers. Thane sliced a thin piece of fish and took his first bite, only to discover it was rotten to the core. He spat the mouthful back onto his plate and turned to the vegetables, which, though not outstanding, were at least edible. He devoured them quickly before picking up a beverage. Just as he sipped, the inn's door creaked open, and five armored city guards strode in, their armor clanking.

The bartender's grandson approached them to guide them to a table, but Thane's gut churned as the boy pointed at him from across the room. Thane dropped his gaze back to his plate, while his right hand edged towards his hip where his weapon lay sheathed. Unlike the armor that Somnius had provided, his sword was ordinary.

"You there!" the largest guard roared. "Put your hands flat on the table. Stay still! You're under arrest!"

The bartender snatched a dagger from the shelf and pointed it at Thane. "Go quietly and don't mess up my inn," he said.

"I've done nothing wrong!" Thane exclaimed.

"Being a Throatian is terrible enough," the bartender declared.

Thane's heart stopped. How could they have known?

"I-I'm not Throatian," he stuttered. "I'm from the Silent Deserts."

"And I might as well be called Red Eyed Martin," the bartender retorted. "You said you're from District Three, the Black Sands of Tornaa—unfit for farming and uninhabitable. I doubt you've ever set foot anywhere near there."

"Your accent gives it away," the lead guard added. "It's not one I've heard before. It's obvious you are trying to hide from someone —and you're not from around here, nor from the Silent Deserts. Come with us, and everything will be fine. You'll get a fair trial, we guarantee."

Fortunately, it seemed they only suspected him of being Throatian and were uncertain of his true identity. Though they hadn't recognized him as Thane Asche, prince of his kingdom, an arrest could lead to someone more powerful recognizing him. Since many Darian guests had attended his wedding to Princess Lydia, he realized his best chance of survival was to fight his way out of the bar rather than risk capture.

"We both know such a trial would be a sham," Thane said. "I'm not a Throatian, and you have no claim on me." Standing, he placed a hand on his sword. "Now, will you let me pass?"

Most patrons rose from their seats and headed toward the lobby to exit. A few stayed, including the one in the gray cloak. Thane thought they either wanted to watch or believed the fight would end soon.

The leader of the guards stepped ahead, grinning. "What are you going to do? Conjure up a storm?"

Thane wasn't sure what he was referring to, but he drew his sword in response. "This will do just as well, if it has to be this way."

Without another word, the guard leaped forward, thrusting his steel. Thane let it pierce his cloak and strike his armor. The magical protection deflected the blade, sending it flying to the floor with a clang of defeat. As the knight stammered in surprise, Thane struck, swinging his weapon in a sharp arc that nicked the leader's arm. The first foe yelped and stumbled back, making way for two allies to rush into the fray.

As he engaged the multiple fighters simultaneously, his heart pounded. His armor assured his protection from any misstep, but he was determined not to waste his years of training in the Loyalty Circles. With precise swings and stabs at the guards' weak points, they fell. The bartender fled to the kitchens, retreating from behind the bar.

"Get him now, dead or alive," the lead guard snarled to his last two allies.

Unlike his previous foes, who wielded swords, Thane's final adversaries brought out morning stars equipped with long spikes. Any blow from the spiked iron balls could compromise his armor's integrity, and a direct hit to his head would be fatal.

He aligned his blade with his shoulder, poised to strike first. Before anyone could move, a sharp hiss pierced the air. The ground before him erupted in a puff of white smoke, overtaking the entire bar. Thane and the guards coughed uncontrollably as the thick clouds filled the room. A hand grabbed Thane's upper arm, startling him.

"Come with me if you value your freedom," a deep, solemn voice whispered into his ear.

He realized why the person previously sitting next to him had worn a gray cloak—it made him disappear into the fog. Even at less than two feet away, Thane reached out to confirm he was real, unsure if his eyes deceived him. If the man were any more distant, the haze would have rendered him invisible, blending him seamlessly into the surroundings.

"Very well," Thane muttered between his coughs. If the cloaked person had wanted him dead, he could have already killed him outright.

The duo navigated around the counter, guided by the edges of the bar stools. The hooded man pushed the kitchen door open and dashed through.

"Come, Throatian," the stranger called out, and another thud echoed from beyond the doorway. "Walk straight ahead."

He moved forward, bracing himself for the sight of the bartender or his grandson's body on the floor. The man was skilled and well-prepared, but Thane couldn't understand why he was helping him.

Reaching the back alley bordering the inn, Thane stepped outside and closed the door behind him. The cloaked man surveyed his surroundings for a moment before speaking. "Keep following me."

Still hooded in gray, his new acquaintance broke into a run. Thane hadn't seen his face yet, but with guards likely still close, he chose to trust his mysterious ally. However, he knew nothing comes without a price.

"Why are you helping me?" Thane asked as they ran. The wind—or perhaps his running style—caused the man's head covering to fly back. Even with the hood down, gray cloth strips wrapped around every part of him above the neck, suggesting he intended to hide his identity regardless of whether he wore the cloak. Only his eyes, a narrow slit for his nostrils, and another small opening for his mouth remained visible.

"We're the same, you and I," he replied. "Enemies of the common narrative."

"What does that mean? Who are you?"

"A friend, perhaps, if you are what they claim."

The man spoke the Common Tongue perfectly, which made him unlikely to be a Throatian. No one would offer protection to an enemy of the Darian Kingdom unless they were their foe.

"So, you're some sort of rebel, then?"

The cloth face coverings masked the nuance of the man's response. "I've been called worse."

As they approached the townspeople, they slowed from a run to a brisk walk. Thane sighed in relief, checking behind them to confirm they weren't being pursued. The remaining guards, the ones with the morning stars, were probably gathering reinforcements and starting a citywide search. Since the commotion at the bar wasn't minor, the knights needed to find and capture the perpetrators to maintain their credibility.

They went past the marketplace where Thane had bought some Red Cloud earlier that day. Though the sun had long since set, the plaza was still active with large numbers of people. The shifting crowd, divided into two streams—one flowing up the alley and the other down—offered Thane and his new ally the perfect cover. However, he knew the guards were likely aware of this and had already sent a search party to patrol the area.

"How much further?" Thane asked.

"Here," the man in the cloak said as they approached a doorway in a row of connected homes. "We should be alright inside—I hope."

THE MYSTERIOUS CLOAKED MAN DREW A KEY FROM A HIDDEN POCKET and fumbled with the rusty lock until the entryway creaked open with a grinding sound. He gestured for Thane to enter first, then scanned the alley to ensure no one was watching before following him inside and closing the door behind them.

The man's dwelling was sparse, containing only necessities. An old wooden table stood in a corner, alongside two worn crates used as chairs. A small kettle without its lid sat near a sooty fireplace blanketed in gray ash. Balanced against the wall were a thin saber and a shield just larger than a dinner plate. Beyond these few items, the man's one-room home held little else—no bed and no belongings. Instead, a single mat lay on the floor.

"It's not much," he remarked, "though I always meant it to be a temporary home."

"I don't need a room in a castle," Thane replied. "Are we safe here?"

"There's no place truly safe for people like us," he said.

"Who exactly are you?"

"Zeere. Zeere Malaak."

The man, wrapped in cloth from head to toe, made his way to the fireplace and gently tossed some logs into it. He reached into a small, hidden shelf inside the chimney's base and pulled out a flint. With three quick scrapes, a warm, orange glow bathed the room.

Despite them seeing each other distinctly now, Thane still could not figure out much regarding the fellow other than that his whole figure stayed shrouded under the wraps.

"I haven't heard that kind of name before," Thane commented. "Are you from the Silent Deserts?"

"The Silent Deserts is where I plan to spend the rest of my life," Zeere replied. "Once I've finished my business in Yaenia."

"So you're a Darian after all."

"It's not that simple," he said with a shrug. "If living here makes me a Darian, perhaps I am one. However, I don't pledge allegiance to Asura or the von Stonewall throne."

"What else aren't you saying?" Thane asked, sensing his evasiveness.

"Is that how you speak to the person who just saved your life?" Zeere grunted. "If you're really a Throatian, they would have hanged you."

"Sorry," Thane said. "I'm grateful for your help, but still unsure if I should trust you."

"And the same to you," Zeere said. "Trusting a stranger can lead to betrayal. Like sharks in the ocean, people can sense vulnerability from afar, and if you don't flee or fight, they'll seize the first chance to tear you apart. However, if you're truly a Throatian, I might trust you."

Regardless of Zeere Malaak's identity, he evidently harbored animosity toward Darians, potentially turning even a Throatian into an ally.

"Yes, I'm a Throatian," Thane admitted, "and my name is Feiir."

Thane's twin sister, Feiir, had passed away shortly after their birth. Throughout his life, Harkbin and Urith had concealed her existence from him. It wasn't until Hrodspire revealed the truth that Thane discovered his parents had suffered multiple miscarriages, making him the lone survivor of four pregnancies. By adopting Feiir's name, he could ensure her memory lived on for a while longer.

Zeere hesitated, seeking to confirm the pronunciation. "Fay… air?"

"Correct, and you pronounce it well," Thane said. "I came here for Prince Thane Asche's wedding, but after the ceremony, my people abandoned me, leaving me to die. I seem of little worth to them, seeing as I played no part in the scheme to kill the Darian princess."

Zeere plopped onto a crate and scooted it closer to the table. "You're telling me you knew nothing about the Wedding of the Torn Rose?"

Thane deliberately lied when he said, "My invitation to attend the event happened as a courtesy. I am connected to the Asche family through marriage, not blood."

"Understood," Zeere said. "If you were their direct family, they wouldn't have abandoned you. They would have involved you in their treasonous plot as well."

Thane said, "My people are deeply tribal—secrets rarely go beyond their bloodlines."

So far, his new companion believed his story, which was the best for now. While the man might be trustworthy, it was impossible to predict how he would react if he uncovered Thane's true identity. Even if Zeere favored Throatians for some reason, the less he knew, the safer Thane would be.

Zeere leaned forward, his eyes narrowing between the slits of bandages surrounding them. "And what of your magic?"

"Pardon?"

"Throatian magic—is it also connected to bloodlines?"

"There is no Throatian magic."

Zeere shifted in his chair. "You cannot hide it," he said. "Your kingdom's discovery of such power was the sole reason King Ether von Stonewall arranged the marriage between his daughter and your prince."

"The Asche family lied," Thane declared. It was now clear that Zeere had rescued Thane from the bar to observe his abilities.

"Did they now, Feiir?" Zeere pressed too hard. Why was he so insistent on believing Throatians had powers?

Resisting the urge to shout, Thane maintained his composure and spoke calmly. "The Asche family's deception was too convincing. The magic they promised to King Ether was a mere trick to abduct Princess Lydia. Our culture's tradition of blood sacrifices, despite the countless innocent lives it claimed, achieved nothing in the end."

Zeere pounded his fist on the table. "Black sand..."

Thane sat on the crate, looking over the surface at him. "You saved me from the guards so that you could learn, didn't you?"

"Obviously." Zeere's arms folded over his chest. Thane couldn't see his face, but he sensed his high level of disappointment.

"If I could teach you magic, I would, but I have nothing to offer you."

"Fair enough. You're free to go, then," Zeere replied. "Just be careful from now on. The Darian Kingdom isn't safe for your kind. In a war, villains are worth their weight in gold—even if they're innocent."

Thane headed toward the door but stopped halfway and gave a last glance at Zeere. "Before I leave, I have to ask," he said, "why do you always cover yourself in those bandages? You don't appear to be injured since you handled the guards earlier with ease."

"Flames of a civil war are both a blessing and a curse," Zeere replied.

"I don't understand what you mean by that," Thane said. "The Darians never had an internal conflict."

"I'm not a Darian," Zeere said, "and as one outcast to another, the truth is I'm a Lucidian."

Thane took a step back towards him, unsure whether to stay or go. Lucidians were the only people capable of using magic, and Zeere would possess abilities of his own. That explained his curiosity about Throatian magic—understanding how it compared to the power of the Lucidian Enclave's would be crucial knowledge for their citizens.

"And here I thought you wanted to learn magic since you are a human," Thane said.

Zeere's crimson eyes revealed his crisis. "I don't have any powers because I'm a Null Mage."

"A...Null Mage?"

"A Lucidian born without powers," Zeere explained, "not to be confused with a Dead Mage or a Fallen Mage."

Thane observed the man standing before him. Nothing in his words made sense. Perhaps Zeere was mentioning titles or statuses, but Thane couldn't piece together what they meant.

"A Lucidian who can't use magic? I've never heard of such a thing."

Zeere gestured to the empty crate next to him. "I suspected as much from your blank stare. Sit down, and I'll explain, if you're interested. But you'll have to tell me about the Throatian way of life in exchange. Do we have a deal?"

NATURALLY, THANE WAS EAGER TO UNDERSTAND MORE.

"The night grows darker, and this is the safest place until morning," he replied to the Lucidian. "You've taught me a valuable lesson about your people, but what would you care to know about mine?"

"I have one question for you, Feiir the Throatian... What is life really like on your island?"

Zeere had asked a broad strategic inquiry, not revealing what he already knew. Perhaps it was a test of Thane's legitimacy or an attempt to determine if "Feiir" was close to the Asche royal family. Regardless, Thane found it important that as many people as possible learned of the cruelty Zann-Xia-Czul had inflicted upon his homeland. That part was safe to share.

"A false god has ruled our island for generations," he said, his voice low. "Worship is the foundation of our culture. Every day, the Son See'ers kill each other in Loyalty Circles. Others must create new children in the Breeding Farms. They offer the blood of our people as a sacrifice to Zann-Xia-Czul, but this is all a lie. The truth is dark: our god is evil and cruel, manipulating us all for no reason. Living in my homeland is a suffocating cage of worship and obedience—nothing more."

Zeere peered back at him. "If your deity is false, then why hasn't there been a rebellion? It seems your kingdom starves for revolution."

"It's not that simple," Thane said. "Zann-Xia-Czul has magic—he can read our minds and communicate directly within them. No one has seen his physical form."

Zeere, who had been pacing, paused. "Some Mind Mages can influence thoughts and emotions, but not in such a direct way. If that were the case, the Enclave would have already tracked them down. Something doesn't add up here." He looked back at Thane with curiosity. "Are you familiar with dragons?"

"I assume you know more about them than I do," Thane said.

Zeere's fiery eyes lit up. "A dragon would possess those powers—if any still existed," he said. "But dragons are long gone. Unless..."

"Zann-Xia-Czul is the last dragon," Thane admitted. "And as evil as you'd expect. That's why I have to defeat him and free my homeland."

"It's twisted—highly twisted," Zeere replied. "If I had to guess, your god designed your entire religion as a means of revenge. After all, in Yaenia, humans defeated all his kind, and now he's making up for it by murdering as many of you as possible. A single island-wide culling, even if it claimed thousands of lives, wouldn't satisfy him. Generations of sacrifice, an endless cycle of life and death within your Breeding Farms and Loyalty Circles—that is a slow, agonizing, and infinitely more satisfying vengeance. Am I correct?"

Thane had never realized it, but the Lucidian was right—the blood sacrifices had been meaningless all along. Blindly devoted, the Throatians had been murdering themselves for centuries while Zann-Xia-Czul watched from Mount Sephorr. Their deity not only desired to annihilate his followers but reveled in endless generations of suffering and death.

He couldn't believe he hadn't seen it sooner. The truth was now painfully clear, yet it still felt like an aching wound in his heart. What else would an outsider notice about his homeland? Nearby, the fireplace crackled as a slab of wood fell deeper into the flames, sending up orange sparks.

"Everything about Zann-Xia-Czul is evil," Thane said. "I have to move past what he's done and fight back, somehow."

"I understand your anger, but waiting for the dragon to die naturally is better than creating more wounds," Zeere said. "Those creatures have destroyed entire armies, even when there were Azure Mages. Fighting something that can read minds, breathe fire, summon lightning, or crush you with its tail is too difficult."

In that moment, Thane realized Zeere could assist in Somnius's quest. He would know the way to the Lucidian Enclave, which was the main part of Thane's journey west.

"I am aware of the odds," Thane said, "and understand I cannot fight him directly. That's why I need your help to reach your Enclave."

"My people won't aid you, I'm sorry," Zeere said. "The Enclave only looks after its own. A single dragon on a faraway island isn't a threat. Only if two dragons were breeding and multiplying would it pose a concern to them."

"I'm not searching for their help," Thane said. "There's somewhere else nearby I must reach. If I can locate the Enclave, I'll be able to get to my destination."

"And what do you hope to find?" Zeere asked. "My government would have already seized anything, or anyone, powerful enough to defeat a dragon."

"A group of people capable of speaking directly into others' minds, just as the dragons," Thane said. "Have you ever heard of the Whisperers?"

"It seems to be a false rumor," Zeere said. "Lucidians don't have that kind of power."

"They may not be Lucidians, but my information is reliable," Thane replied. "Those in the mountains can speak without moving their lips and know a great deal about dragons. They might also know a weakness."

"Do you believe in this power without a doubt?" Zeere asked. "Is it an innate ability, earned through merit, or a birthright like my people?"

Thane didn't grasp the second part of the question, but the first part was easy to understand.

"Though I haven't witnessed their powers firsthand, my source is reliable. I believe they've mastered the art of mental speech. While their origins remain unclear, their power is real," he said.

"Then I'm coming with you," Zeere said. "Trying to find a ship to Leonia by working as a fish gutter was proving to be a dead end. Perhaps these Whisperers hold secrets the Enclave has missed or forgotten. They might help both of us."

Somnius's warning echoed in his mind—avoid the Whisperers' rituals at all costs, no matter how tempting their dragon-like magic might be.

Hesitantly, he countered, "They might be dangerous, and we must be realistic—we have no guarantee they'll freely share their knowledge."

"I'd rather know the price of what's real than wonder whether any of it was real all along," Zeere replied with a grin. "We'll leave tomorrow morning to find these Whisperers and learn the answer."

7
EISENBERN - THE PURPLE KNIGHT'S PRAYER

Rain beat against Jarret Eisenbern's violet armor as he growled at the young man darting down the alleyway. The towering buildings loomed overhead, their silhouettes dark against the foggy, gray sky. The boy's baggy brown tunic suggested he was a beggar from Last Hope or another distant town, not a Shadow Walker of their kingdom. Only Leilans knew the city's maze-like streets well enough to navigate them quickly. A single wrong turn or stroke of bad luck could lead to a dead end. As Eisenbern had suspected, the criminal was unfamiliar with the hidden pathways. Now, the boy was trapped.

"Oi, scum! Give it up already! You're caught!" Eisenbern called out, his voice echoing through the narrow alley. The skinny boy realized his mistake and frantically searched for another escape route. The chase had lasted ten minutes, and his simple error in making a wrong turn had become critical.

The road was so tight that neither of them could fully extend their arms. Escaping was impossible unless he could scale the towering walls above them.

"I've done nothing illegal," the young boy protested.

Eisenbern sheathed his sword and extended his hand in a warm offering. There was no need for bloodshed. "I've been watching your every move in the market square for two weeks. The letters you've been handing out to random people look highly suspicious. Let me check your bag, and then you can go."

"I don't know what you're talking about!" The young man

clutched tightly at his pouch, his trembling voice betraying his denial of the accusation.

"Yeah, you do."

"I really don't know!"

Eisenbern stepped closer, and the boy's eyes darted up to the walls. The idea of pressing his hands against the buildings and climbing up, spider-like, might have crossed his mind, but the fifty-foot drop was too risky.

"Even though you're scrawny, falling will still hurt you," Eisenbern warned. "You're a member of the People's Army, and I've seen you running around delivering messages to your comrades. But it's not worth it to keep running. You're an informant, and I want the information you've gathered. I won't punish you like a common thief. You can keep your things, provided none of them were stolen."

The young man hesitated, glancing between his bag and Eisenbern, then asked, "You sure you won't take anything from me?"

Eisenbern was uncertain what he would find in the letters, but they likely contained orders for other members or requests for funds. The People's Army had gained considerable influence among the youth of the Leila Kingdom before the outbreak of the War of the Torn Rose. What began as a group notorious for scamming naïve individuals out of their money had strengthened into a political force. Now, with the resources it had amassed, the People's Army spread misinformation, funded protests, and circulated conspiracy theories throughout the populace. Eisenbern had heard reports of large rallies at the University of Starlight Beach, where students claimed that Princess Lydia hadn't been murdered, but was in hiding. Other rumors suggested that King Ether had faked his daughter's death and was using the war as an excuse to steal the magical secrets of the Throatians. Every word of it was a lie.

"You will have your things back after I check them over," Eisenbern promised.

"Okay, I guess. You can look," the suspect said, undoing the straps on his satchel and tossing it to the ground.

The leader of the Purple Guard smiled. "I appreciate your cooperation."

He opened the battered pack and sifted through its contents: a roll of stale bread, an empty canteen, a coin purse with a few bronze pieces, and an unmarked sealed envelope. Renato, the most scientific-minded member of the Purple Guard, would likely want a copy of the instructions inside. Unable to resist his curiosity, Eisenbern unfolded the letter.

"For the kingdom's security, I'm going to read this," he announced. He slid his finger under the seal and let the envelope fall to the ground. As he scanned the contents, his satisfaction faded into a scowl:

This week's special at the Drunken Hornet: Strega Generatrice

1.5 ounces whiskey

0.5 ounces white vermouth

0.25 ounce saffron liqueur

1 ounce fresh-squeezed lemon juice

Mix well and serve with raspberries, if available.

The Drunken Hornet was a famous local tavern, known more for its overpriced menu than anything else. Eisenbern had visited once with his fellow knights, but they discovered the bar overcharged on every item. It was a complete waste of money, and better places existed to stretch one's coin purse thin and fill one's belly with drink.

"Asura's ass. It's just a recipe." Eisenbern let the letter drop to where its envelope had fallen. "You made me chase you all this way for some bartender's instructions?"

"You were chasing me with a sword! What was I supposed to do?" the young man protested. "Can I please go now?"

"Black sand… Yeah, get out of here." Eisenbern said, wiping rain from his forehead. He let the boy pick up his things, including the letter. How could he have been so wrong?

This chase for nothing was a major setback. Eisenbern's appointment as leader of Queen Blanche's Purple Guard happened shortly before the war began, and so far, he'd not proven himself worthy of the role. He had promised to uncover the inner workings of the People's Army but had nothing to show for it yet except what Renato's informants learned. Eisenbern had contributed nothing to their shared knowledge.

Though he'd come to his upcoming meeting bearing no news, it was better to have less proof of the People's Army's growth and influence than confirmation their power had spread. As he strolled back toward Aeon Eve, where the queen awaited his return, the rain drifted away, the same as his luck.

A SOFT BREEZE BLEW THROUGH THE AIR AS THE CLOUDS FADED, revealing the elegant, iris-tinted castle of Aeon Eve. Dusk's fiery light reflected off the polished surfaces, highlighting the superb craftsmanship and the mimicry of the Shadowstones in the nearby mountains. Like every other project the queen had started, this one demanded the greatest aesthetics and showmanship possible. The palace's exterior resembled Shadowstone, but in reality, stained glass panels covered rock to achieve the appearance Queen Blanche envisioned.

As Eisenbern neared the front gate, the archers in the nearby towers greeted him. He strode through the vast garden, the night air brushing his face. After passing through two rows of massive stone pillars, each as carefully carved as the rest of the castle, he entered the throne room.

Queen Blanche sat on her silvery-purple throne, surrounded by Ilya, Gustav, and Renato of the Purple Guard. Sumani's chair was empty, as she was out at sea supporting the Darian fleet near the Throatian island.

"Jarret, you're late," she noted. "Was your mission a success?"

He bowed on one knee, his eyes fixed on the floor. "I caught the boy we'd been following, but there was no evidence he was with the People's Army. The trail may have been leading to a dead end all along."

"Hmm..." She often relied on awkward silence to convey her thoughts, and as she waited, the room grew tense. The Purple Guard members knew that a pause longer than five seconds meant she wanted more information.

"Regardless, we still could have underestimated how widespread they are," Eisenbern said, sitting next to the queen. "From the crime reports, their numbers have likely grown, or they've gotten bolder at swindling our citizens." He glanced at Gustav. "Do you agree, Sir Reed?"

Gustav, the bulkiest member of the Purple Guard, towering over the queen's high chair, shrugged his broad shoulders and released a quiet breath. A massive broadsword leaned against his leg, far heavier than Eisenbern cared to use. "There's so much we are unaware of," he replied.

Ilya, who had been fiddling with her knife, sheathing and unsheathing it, let her blade rest at her side. "Nobody here doubts they are a threat," she said. "The People's Army may already be hiding within our city walls. We don't know whether they're only a few or a large force, but their influence is growing."

The queen shifted her gaze from one person to another, like a cat watching them from behind a window. She often held her tongue to let her advisors and guardians discuss details before weighing in. Eisenbern studied Blanche's wrinkled face but couldn't read past her pursed lips.

"You can't verify what isn't there," Eisenbern said. "The boy we'd tracked for weeks in the market—what did I find on him? A recipe for a drink, some bronze pieces, and old bread—nothing else. This was supposed to be our big breakthrough. I'm sorry it led to nothing."

Renato, the most analytical member of the Purple Guard, chimed in next. "Finding no evidence on the boy doesn't mean we can let our eyes rest. His behavior in the market was too predictable to be coincidental. He may have gotten lucky today, but perhaps not tomorrow."

Ilya began playing with her knife again, now removing the blade before shoving it back in. "We don't have the time to monitor every questionable person. Anyone can seem suspicious if stared at long enough. The regular guards are growing impatient with these endless investigations. We've received only complaints and rumors about the People's Army, not concrete evidence. It's better to focus on the fact that the actual war is far out at sea, not here at home."

"Lady Ilya," Queen Blanche said, raising her hand. "You're correct. However, the People's Army is like a weed—small and harmless at first, but if left unchecked, it will spread until it dominates everything around it. You've heard of what's happened in Last Hope, yes?"

"Everyone knows about the protests, but—"

"And the damages that came with them," Blanche finished. "It doesn't matter if it's bricks or arrows flying through the windows—their activities endanger ordinary people's lives. Crime is crime and war is war, regardless of the underlying ideologies or the aggressors' backgrounds. We must burn the seedlings within our borders before they grow into the same blight infesting Last Hope. Unfortunately, King Ether is more focused on getting to the Throatians."

Eisenbern took a deep breath and stopped himself from debating further. The Darian Kingdom's population far exceeded the Leila Kingdom's—of course there would be more rotten apples in their barrel overall. The People's Army's goals remained unclear, beyond cheating people out of their money and demanding a stop to the war against the Throatians.

"Both situations need to end soon," Eisenbern commented. "King Ether's campaign for retribution is justified, but it has gone on long enough. We have sent our ships out to sea several times to join him, only to have them wait for weeks in the ocean for a storm that never subsided. This has become a waste of resources."

The Throatians had posed a formidable challenge: a magical water barrier that emerged after the Wedding of the Torn Rose. A sudden storm had swept in as the battle ended and Eisenbern pursued the Asche family at sea alongside King Ether von Stonewall and Kaine Khalia. Initially seen as a coincidence, the abnormal weather returned when the Darian King declared war and his fleet set sail from Wargonne to the Throatian island. It hadn't stopped since then.

Every part of the enemy's land, including White Boar's Landing, remained encircled by the magical water. The Darian ships urged patience as they waited for the storm to fade, but this strategy caused only failed missions and vessels returned home, depleted of supplies. Any ship attempting to breach it would be destroyed, and one had already proven this.

"We should call it a stalemate," Gustav said. "This is the longest war without a fight I've heard of."

Queen Blanche snorted. "Ha! As if Ether would ever agree to a draw. He's the type to win or die trying—that's how he was when I fought alongside him. We never faced a magical wall in our battles against the Lucidians—they were always on the offensive, never a reclusive defense. Something is different this time, something big."

Ilya fidgeted restlessly in her chair; she rarely stayed still for long. The only occasion Eisenbern had seen her focused was during their sword training.

"The Lucidian Enclave's declaration of neutrality worries me most," Renato said. "If there was magic they couldn't control, they'd seek to obtain or destroy it. Distancing themselves from the situation suggests they're either protecting the Throatians or allowing others to test the magic's limits before risking their own people."

The queen looked down at her dyed ivory woven cloth boots. Despite their elegance, rumors had spread around the castle that they were the same footwear she'd worn in her younger years as a warrior. Eisenbern doubted the gossip was true—the shoes were too pristine to have survived a war and daily use. Nevertheless, the queen had a habit of keeping mementos to remind her people of where they'd come from and the cost of forming the Leila Kingdom. Much of the artwork hung throughout Aeon Eve's walls referenced those earlier times.

"Regardless of whether the Throatians have a mage on their island, I agree the Lucidians are acting suspiciously," Queen Blanche said. "But I believe I know the actual source of their magic."

She rose from her chair and moved toward the eastern wall of the throne room, where a stained window depicted the history of the Yaenian continent. Though it was late, the vibrant colors and elegant craftsmanship of the glass shards were as impressive as always. Everyone present was familiar with its imagery: a hammer symbolizing the Human Uprising and, to its right, a dragon representing the Scourge of the Dragon Slavers.

"Apart from Lucidians, those beasts are the only other magical beings," she said, resting her hand just below the dragon's mouth. "This explains the storm wall surrounding their island. The Throatians certainly made a deal with a dragon or hatched or captured one to protect them."

"But your highness, the dragons are long dead," Gustav replied. "Besides, none of them sympathized with humans during the Scourge, nor did any cooperate by surrendering. They were monsters, after all."

Though Renato nodded, Eisenbern sensed his reluctance. "I'm open to the idea that their magic comes from a dragon," he said, "but I doubt any remain alive. The Black Moon Tribe documented every dragon during their war and recorded each one when they fell."

"They could conjure storms, breathe fire, and read the minds of both humans and other dragons," Eisenbern warned. "One must have survived somehow. But how could it protect an entire country?"

"Maybe the Throatians have several of them?" Ilya suggested.

"Impossible," Eisenbern said. "Kaine Khalia left us years ago to become a merchant and sail the seas. He's been to the Throatian island many times. If there were dragons in the sky, he'd have noticed. Of all the traders, nobody thought to mention anything about seeing one of them?"

Ilya's face went blank during his anecdote about White Boar's Landing. Perhaps she had also been there before? Eisenbern raised an eyebrow until she regained her composure and said, "Maybe they have a baby dragon, then?"

"It's unlikely for one to be living in the Throatian homeland," Queen Blanche stated, choosing to ignore Ilya's peculiar behavior. "As I said, two forms of magic exist: dragons' abilities and Lucidians'. No human has ever learned either. The storm protecting their island seems more dragon-like, so we should assume it comes from them. Maybe the Throatians studied a corpse and unraveled the principles of dragon magic. If so, this is very dangerous."

Renato nodded again. "The queen is correct—the source of their magic isn't conventional. I just don't understand how Throatian blood sacrifices fit into everything. We'll need to figure out the relationship between what the Throatians did and the storm wall before we can breach their defenses."

"We should talk to the Black Moon Tribe," Gustav suggested.

Eisenbern had heard of them before; they were the people who'd killed off the dragons over many years. They'd lived underground to avoid detection by their enemies. How they managed the feat without magic puzzled Eisenbern, but every human alive today owed their existence to their achievements.

"The dragons have been dead for so long. I thought the Black Moon Tribe was only a part of history—would they still be hiding in their caves? Do you really think they'll remember at this point?" Eisenbern asked.

"That they'll remember what?" Ilya asked.

"He means the specifics of dragon magic," Gustav said. "How does it work? Lucidians can use their powers only until they lose too much blood. The Throatian royal family murdered Princess Lydia for her blood, and Eisenbern told us about the Throatians harvesting it from horses in a forest. Why does that help a dragon's powers, assuming that was the goal? The Black Moon Tribe might understand what they were trying to accomplish."

Queen Blanche sprang from her purple throne, clapping her hands and beaming at her subjects.

"Eisenbern, you must go north and find the Black Moon Tribe. They fought dragons for over two hundred years, and their legends and creed would have kept them ready to fight them again if they ever returned. They'll know better than we do. Any other discussions on our end are only baseless speculation. I hate to admit it, but we should assume they have a dragon until we learn otherwise."

The queen's command was fair, but Eisenbern's stomach lurched at the idea. While he was content to serve and protect his queen, he hadn't expected to be sent so far from their kingdom. The journey didn't bother him, but the time he would be away from Ophelia did. Would he return before it was too late? What if she needed him while he was gone? Before his worries overwhelmed him, Eisenbern admitted he'd made his oath and sworn his life to the queen. Even if he wanted to, there was no turning back—he'd pledged himself to his kingdom, and Ophelia would have to wait.

"Then I will head north," Eisenbern said. "I'll find the Black Moon Tribe and confirm whether the Throatians have allied themselves with a dragon or learned its magic. More importantly, I'll learn how to defeat it."

"I'll join you," Ilya offered. "The distance between here and North Yaenia is too great for you to go alone."

"I want both you and Gustav to come," Eisenbern replied. "Sumani is patrolling the seas by the Throatian island with Captain Ellebar and won't return for another month. Renato will be the last Purple Guard at Aeon Eve and should remain near the queen. Does everyone agree?"

"Asura's ass," Blanche replied. "Though I'm old, I'm not that fragile. Take the three of them with you." Known for her tongue and leather-like toughness, the queen's body was aging faster than her ego would admit.

"Pardon me, my Queen," Gustav interrupted, "but what is our relationship with the Black Moon Tribe? To my knowledge, we don't have one. Shall we send them a bird to introduce ourselves?"

She nodded, scratching her wrinkled cheek. "You're right—we have no ties to them. Diplomacy is challenging because they're an underground society that avoids using birds to stay hidden. In fact, they might not even be aware of our kingdom's existence. That's why I want more of you to go—to show our commitment to trade. If Renato isn't joining you, bring a Shadowstone spear as a gesture of goodwill."

Eisenbern stared at the queen in disbelief as his stomach growled so loud he swore he heard it echo throughout the throne room. "A Shadowstone Spear? You'd truly give one of those away?"

The spears were exceptionally time-consuming to forge, but timeless when finished. Made of the seemingly unbreakable material found in the nearby mountains, each spear required over a year to create. Though Eisenbern didn't know the exact process, he'd heard rumors that a single weapon involved more than a hundred thousand rounds of sanding and polishing. The Purple Guard had only two completed weapons in its armory. The spears were perfectly balanced and as light as they were deadly.

"We'll give a spear to them to start and hint that more are available," the queen explained. "Their knowledge about killing dragons is invaluable. A lone dragon could destroy a nation overnight, if it chose. Even an army of Shadowstone spears couldn't stop it."

"Understood. I'll bring them a spear," Eisenbern said, "but one knight should remain to protect you alongside the city guard, my Queen."

"Very well," Blanche replied. "Renato will stay in Aeon Eve with me to continue investigating the People's Army, while Ilya and Gustav can accompany you. Remember, this is a diplomatic mission —keep your wits and words about you!"

"Merdel is the best diplomat," Renato chimed in. "Perhaps we might borrow him from the Darian Kingdom for a while and send him along, too."

The queen waved her hand. "I considered asking for the favor, but I'm not sure I want to reveal the details of our suspicions to our allies so soon."

She was right. Though born a Leilan, Merdel, as Darian councilman of foreign affairs, was obligated to the von Stonewall family now. Whatever information he learned from the Leilans, he had to disclose. If their conjectures about the dragon were mistaken, it would cause issues. Leilan culture frowned upon presenting a problem without a definitive solution. It was better to know how to defeat a dragon and whether the Throatians actually had one before spreading wrong or fear-inducing reports.

Eisenbern rose from his chair, grabbing the fine leather hilt of his sword as he stood. "This will be an opportunity to expand our kingdom's influence and reputation."

Queen Blanche smiled warmly, a rarity in the past months. "I know you'll make allies of the Black Moon Tribe. When I appointed you to the Purple Guard, Sir Eisenbern, as well as your companions, I wanted those most skilled not only with their blades but likewise in mind and honor. You are both the first and last protectors of our growing kingdom. Do everything you can to succeed."

THE WOMAN'S FLUTE PLAYED GRACEFULLY AGAINST THE BACKGROUND hum of gossip and laughter. Eisenbern didn't know her name, but he knew she performed at Miner's Kitchen at least four nights a week. The melodic songs she played were familiar; he and the knights of the Purple Guard frequently visited the establishment to unwind and socialize. Her style blended old Yaenian and modern influences, yet she maintained a brisk tempo. Her cheerful melodies often replayed in Eisenbern's mind during his sword training.

Nearby, three leather-armored women—likely mercenaries given their mismatched clothing and lack of the gray capes worn by the city guard—urged each other to drink shots of golden rum. Underneath their table was a small cage holding a sleeping brown dog. Eisenbern suspected they were returning the animal to its rightful owner or selling it to someone wealthy who could claim it as a pet.

Miner's Kitchen wasn't the Leila Kingdom's most popular tavern, but it served as a reminder of the citizens' primary trade: mining Shadowstone. Meals were hearty and fulfilling, perfect for anyone after a hard day's work. Every dish featured a generous portion of beef, pork, or chicken, accompanied by bread, potatoes, or both. Despite its name and theme, the bar's patrons were rarely miners. Eisenbern suspected workers didn't want to spend their free time at a place that reminded them of their job. Most visitors were guards, travelers, or the hungriest in the kingdom, regardless of their reasons.

After meeting with the queen, Eisenbern, Ilya, and Gustav gathered at their usual edge of the tavern. Though the round table was nearly too small for their tankards of drink, plates of steak, and baked potatoes, they preferred this corner because it was the perfect spot to soak in the tavern's ambience. The table's surface was sticky from Gustav's spilled drink—an accident that had occurred an hour earlier. While trying to clean it up, he'd knocked over Ilya's drink as well. In a fit of laughter, Eisenbern ordered them replacement drinks and added a punishment shot of rum for Gustav.

"I still can't believe the queen wants to give away a spear," the largest member of the Purple Guard said, taking his glass after.

"Me either," Eisenbern replied, grabbing his fork and stabbing into his potato. The butter and chives inside filled the air with their aroma, complementing the steak he had just eaten. "She must think the Black Moon Tribe is a tough crowd to negotiate with; otherwise, why send all three of us?"

"She has her reasons, even if they aren't clear yet," Gustav said.

Ilya, struggling to cut her meat with the provided knife, placed it back on the table and reached for her personal blade, strapped to her waist in a scabbard. Equipped with her preferred weapon, she carved through the slab effortlessly. "If a dragon exists on the Throatian island," she mused, "a spear would be of little use against it. Understanding how to defeat it or its magic would be far more valuable. She said so."

"I'll retrieve the weapon from the armory tomorrow morning before we depart," Eisenbern replied, "though it pains me to offer something so rare. But you're right—it must serve a higher purpose."

Ilya wiped her mouth, then spoke again. "Do you think Renato would have wanted to join our quest?"

Gustav shook his head. "Probably not. He always preferred a simpler daily routine. Castle life is predictable, provided there are no unexpected events. As for me, I'm grateful to have the chance to explore more. Sumani is the one who's missing out."

"She won't be back from the sea for a while," Eisenbern said. "If she were available, she would have loved to join us." He raised his tankard in a toast to her.

"Hm..." Ilya let out a sigh.

"What's wrong?" Eisenbern asked.

"Nothing."

"Come on," urged Gustav. "Spit it out—there's no point in holding onto those troubles. We're about to travel halfway across Yaenia together."

She stared at the half-eaten steak on her plate before taking a large swig of beer. Despite Ilya's slender frame, she could drink double her weight without feeling tipsy or sick. "I-I just wondered..." She hesitated. "No, wait. It's stupid."

"Are you nervous about heading toward central Yaenia?" Eisenbern asked, crunching fried potato slices. "The journey ahead may be long, but we'll watch each other's backs."

At first, her chin dipped, as if she were about to nod, but then she shook her head. "No, it's not about the trip. I was just thinking… when you mentioned Sumani at sea, it reminded me of Kaine. I wonder how he's doing. We haven't talked since he left to become a merchant. But you met him in the Darian Kingdom recently, right? How was he?"

Eisenbern sensed she sought more information than what he'd provided in his official account upon returning home months ago. Ilya already knew everything he had seen in Last Hope throughout the Wedding of the Torn Rose. What else could she possibly want to know?

"Yeah, we caught up at the rehearsal dinner," Eisenbern said. "He's supposed to visit once his arm heals. I've sent several letters but haven't heard back. I guess his new role serving Prince Xander and Princess Kira keeps him busy."

Ilya studied his face. "But did he ask about us?"

Truthfully, Kaine hadn't asked about the other Purple Guard members, but Eisenbern and Kaine had little time to talk. They shared a meal, but chaos erupted the next morning, leaving them no chance for idle chatter after learning of the Throatians' betrayal.

"Yeah, he asked," Eisenbern lied. "I told him you were all doing well."

Ilya stared down at her almost empty drink in apparent disappointment. "I see… So, he plans on remaining in the Darian Kingdom."

Gustav clanged his tankard onto the table. "If you miss him, you can travel to Last Hope after our mission. If that's what you want."

She shivered, squirming in her chair. "I feel so… so childish," she whispered. "The truth is, I rejected Kaine years ago."

"Say what?" Eisenbern blurted. "I always suspected you were interested in him—at least back then. Were you two actually together?"

"We were, but…" Ilya paused, taking a deep breath. "What was I supposed to do? Marry him and abandon everything we'd worked for?"

Eisenbern spat out his beer. "Wait! Kaine proposed to you?"

Ilya fidgeted in her seat, uncomfortable at revealing a secret she'd likely kept for years. "Well, no, he didn't propose to me, but he came close to it. Something happened just before he left the Leila Kingdom to become a merchant. I don't know what it was, but it changed everything. If it hadn't gone that way, I think he would have proposed. Whatever happened bothered him so much that he wouldn't even tell me, and he left the Leila Kingdom because of it."

Eisenbern wondered where to begin. Kaine had never explained why he resigned from his position with the Leilan City Guard, but now it seemed his reasons went beyond a mere shift in interests. As for whether Kaine and Ilya would have eventually married, Eisenbern couldn't say. From what he knew of Ilya, she wasn't the type to rashly assume he would propose unless he showed clear signs of intent. Even if Kaine intended to follow through, Ilya was right that such a relationship would have jeopardized both of their chances of advancing from the Leilan City Guard into the Purple Guard. While there was no official rule against romantic involvements among Purple Guard members, it was likely that Queen Blanche would disapprove if the situation arose.

Nothing—not even Kaine—could have tempted Ilya to abandon her ambitions. Relationships between knights carried their own complications, and the cost would be high. Perhaps Kaine expected that proposing to Ilya would be too much trouble to cause, regardless of if they were both in love. Still, there must have been more to it than that. Was that the real reason Kaine left the City Guard to become a merchant?

"Would you consider reigniting that fire if the chance came up?" Gustav asked.

"I do not know. He hasn't returned to our kingdom since he left."

Eisenbern nodded, recalling Ophelia, and said, "He might feel ashamed returning or guilty for leaving, as I've learned from experience."

"How would you know?" Ilya exclaimed. "I've never seen you back down from anything!"

"Our newly assigned mission isn't without its complications," Eisenbern admitted. "Ophelia hasn't been well lately, worse than usual in fact. I'm not sure that leaving her right now is the best choice for her. She might need me."

He sipped his beer before the others could respond. Across the table, Ilya nodded slowly, choosing her words carefully as Gustav continued the conversation.

"Are you certain that it's that dire?"

"It is. Time is running out for Ophelia. I don't want to delay our mission to the Black Moon Tribe either; this is my first chance to prove my worth as your lead knight."

"You already proved yourself during the Wedding of the Torn

Rose," Ilya said. "You commanded a ship that chased the Throatians and fought their king. You made an impact that most knights can only dream of. There's nothing left to prove—you're completely worthy of leading us."

Eisenbern could only smile at her words as he paused. What she said was true; he was grateful it was enough for now. Still, what he'd done before didn't change what his queen and kingdom expected of him presently and in the future. If their enemies had a dragon or dragon magic at their command, Eisenbern's work was far from over. There was no time to divert his attention from the greater needs of the world.

"Thank you," he mustered, "but I'm still not sure what to do about Ophelia."

"It might be the day to say goodbye," Ilya began. "Sorry for being blunt, but you must be prepared for anything."

"No, she'll be fine," Gustav said. "Finish your drink, then talk to her about your fears—I'm sure she'll understand and support you. Pray to Asura that she holds on until you return. Encourage her; she'll cling to her will to live."

"We have to be realistic," Ilya said. "It's important to consider how long we'll be away from home."

"Fair enough—I'll have a heart-to-heart with her," Eisenbern said, bringing the tankard to his lips. He downed his drink and added, "Let's order another round, on me. Might as well try the thing that young man I stopped had the recipe for."

He called over a middle-aged woman wearing a dark cloak and carrying a tray of maroon-colored drinks. "Pardon, miss, but would you bring us three Strega drinks?"

"Strega what?"

"A Strega Generatrice," Eisenbern said, quietly congratulating himself on remembering the name. "I think it has whisky, raspberries, and some other things."

The woman gave him a confused look. "I've never heard of that drink, but I'll check with the bartender to see if he can make it for you. If not, would whisky alone work?"

"It's an interesting choice to end the night on, but sure!" Eisenbern said. Once the woman moved on to the crowded bar, he turned again to his companions. "So, back to Ilya—if Kaine doesn't reply to my letters by the time our mission ends, we'll drop in on him in the Darian Kingdom. He owes us a visit, and if he doesn't settle the debt, we'll have to remind him in person."

Ilya finished her beer and placed the empty tankard in the collection bucket under their table. “I hope it’s not my fault he doesn’t want to come home. Still, let me think about it. I don’t know if I’m ready to see him yet.”

“Just how many years has it been?” Gustav asked.

“Too many,” Ilya said, “and no matter how many more pass, it never becomes easier.” She gave a smile but remained reluctant to say more. Their conversation paused until she inquired, “Now, Eisenbern, where are those other drinks you ordered?”

Just then, the woman who had taken their order returned, carrying a tray of straight whiskies. “Nobody’s heard of the drink that you asked for,” she apologized.

Eisenbern handed a glass to each member of his team. “No problem,” he said. “Better to end the night with a liquor we know than risk a hangover from a mystery one.”

They raised their drinks and made them disappear as quickly as they had appeared. Though they hadn’t gotten to taste a Strega Generatrice, Eisenbern found himself losing interest in it. What Ilya had said earlier about Kaine made him consider his own situation. If the three of them truly were going to leave so soon, then he needed to stop by the church and speak to Ophelia. Regret, as likely as it might come, needed to be put at bay.

“I’m heading out to go have that heart-to-heart now,” Eisenbern said to Ilya and Gustav. “We’ll depart in the mid-morning.”

Ophelia’s frail hands motioned for Eisenbern to approach as he descended the stone stairs into the pool meant to cleanse him. If the water could cure Scarlet Cough, Eisenbern would have urged Ophelia to enter instead. But the water, though blessed by Asura, held no remedy for her illness. For him, however, it at least gave some solace, even if only for a moment.

The night was old, but the candles were young as Eisenbern settled to his knees. He clasped his hands, interlocking them in front of his breastbone, as he prayed in silence. His wishes to Asura, as in the past four nights, included Ophelia’s health improving, success on his approaching journey with Ilya and Gustav, wisdom for his new tasks from Queen Blanche, and the downfall of the People’s

Army. If grace would have it, all would come true in the upcoming days.

"You'll head north?" Ophelia, the priestess of the church, asked, then broke into a storm of coughing.

"To the north," Eisenbern grunted as cold water rose to his chest. "Though I'm not sure how far I'll need to go."

Eisenbern regularly visited the pool, but that night was different. It would be the last chance for Ophelia to cleanse Eisenbern. She had guided his heart to Asura and to herself. The ceremony, symbolizing the disappearance of sins, felt instead like the washing away of hope. Eisenbern usually visited every few nights, but without Ophelia, it would never feel the same. She was dying, and time was running out.

The priestess scooped her ladle into the water and poured it over Eisenbern's head. "You'll go as far as Asura needs you, and he'll protect you all the way, whether or not you're sober. Though I pray your mind will remain clearer in the future."

She always knew when he'd been drinking, even if he concealed it behind his composed demeanor. Perhaps that's why she stayed by his side. He opened one eye, taking in Ophelia's tired yet captivating appearance. Her golden hair cascaded past her fair skin, framing the shoulders of her robe. He couldn't help staring.

Eisenbern wiped some water from his eyes as he replied, "Spare me the illusions of security, my dear. Nobody can guarantee protection because destiny will return everyone to the ground. Asura calls on our lives to end when they are meant to conclude, and not a moment sooner or longer. One can only wonder if we will be ready when the time comes."

He believed his own words, yet the uncertainty of when it was he would die was more terrifying than death itself. Eisenbern wished he could choose his own ending and that he would be ready when it came. He hoped Ophelia had found peace in her destiny. Her fate was sealed, and he could do nothing to stop it.

"I'm sorry," Eisenbern added. "I let my wandering thoughts get the better of me again."

"Don't worry about it on my behalf," she said, guiding him from the pool and handing him an embroidered towel the color of sanded wood. "As we grow older, life's answers become clearer. We can't deny my time is nearly over. This is likely our last meeting, but at least you're prepared for what waits ahead."

Eisenbern dried himself, ending with his graying hair. "Don't say such things! I'll be back sooner than you can restock your throat ointment. Or perhaps I can petition the queen to delay my journey a bit longer. There's still so much that remains to be done before you—"

He stopped. If he continued, he'd admit Ophelia was right, and she was. There was nothing they could do. This would be their last meeting unless a miracle cured the Scarlet Cough and all the damage it had caused to Ophelia's body. The most common symptom was coughing up blood from the internal wounds, and the illness hadn't spared her. Soon, her tired lungs and throat would no longer endure the pain. Eisenbern's mother and father had shown it all those years ago, before Ophelia recruited him into the church and they grew close. To have the sickness was a death sentence.

"We can only hope time might be kind to both of us," she said, her voice rough as she reclaimed the damp towel. "Yet I see the days ahead passing faster than before. Your new role keeps you busy, and I expect it will grow even more demanding from now on."

"But are you okay with that?" he asked.

"I must be," she said, "because it's my destiny. Asura willed me to serve my church in my recent years. As long as my hands have done what is right by him, I am fine. My body might suffer in this trial, but my soul remains strong. That is enough for me."

They left the cleansing pool and sat on a nearby bench, where they could see the statue of Asura. The sculpture depicted him as a mature warrior holding a spear made of light. Unlike most statues of Asura, which were carved from gray or white stone, this one's spear was crafted from stained glass. Legends said that the weapon existed purely as light, taking physical form only when striking those who incurred Asura's anger.

"Speaking of moving forward, I wanted to ask you something," Eisenbern started, but she interrupted him.

"Getting married in my last days isn't what I'm meant to do," Ophelia reminded him. "As much as I would treasure it, our destiny will soon become unbound. Save yourself for another, Jarret. You deserve a better fate than what I might offer as your wife."

"Even if it's true, that isn't what I want," Eisenbern said. "We need more time or a cure for your sickness, but wouldn't it be better to be happy, despite it only being for a short while?"

Ophelia drifted to the chapel's table and retrieved a kettle sitting above a flickering flame that was the light color of her hair. Remaining silent, she poured the tea into two chipped cups, as black as Shadowstone, though not unbreakable. She added honey from the church's bee garden, handed a cup to him, and then sipped her own.

"Asura might still save me from this before the end comes," Ophelia ventured. "Certainly, my condition is a test of faith. If I'm in better health when you return, nothing would please me more than to become one with you."

"Just in case I'm delayed on my way back," Eisenbern said as he sank lower into the bench, "do you have any last advice for me?"

The priestess smiled, keeping her eyes on the statue. She wiped the blood from her lips with a handkerchief. "Of course, I always have a lesson ready. Never forget that Asura still lives among us, even though he no longer walks in divine form."

"That's your guidance?" Eisenbern scoffed half-jokingly. "A concept so trivial that it might as well be the teaching a child learns upon entering the church?"

"What I say is not trivial," Ophelia insisted. "Asura is alive, and that is the ultimate truth."

"I don't doubt it," he said, "but I expected your final lesson to be more complex. Or less basic. I'm unsure, to be honest, what I should have thought."

"Well, I'll leave you with one more piece of wisdom. Your loyalty to Queen Blanche surpassed your vows to the church—that's forgivable. Without a stable kingdom, a religion fades. Even though you're bound to live as a Purple Knight for her, you can still be a Holy Knight for Asura beneath your armor. Your heart determines your future, not your title or allegiances."

"Asura blessed my heart all along," Eisenbern declared, "and I am sure I could not have garnered the favor of Queen Blanche without Asura's will behind it. Fear not—I vow to be both a Holy Knight and a Purple Knight of the Leila Kingdom."

"You recognize good from evil," Ophelia added. "And so there's little else I can teach you that you could not have otherwise discovered for yourself. Most who come to me for advice already know the solutions to their problems but merely need reassurance. From today forward, Sir Eisenbern, you must find that reassurance in yourself."

"Even if it comes to me someday seeking it," he said, "I'll try to imagine what you might say. I can't thank you enough, Ophelia, for everything you've taught me and for who you are."

And finally, his lips met hers, for both the first and the last time.

8
BIOS AURAS - THE THROATIAN PRIESTESS

With quiet confidence, Bios stepped through the portal of the Teleportation Stone and emerged into the sacred silence. The seamless transition transported him from the shadowed alley in Last Hope to the distant Temple of White, a place reserved only for the Son See'er Vrai and the Throatian Elders.

The obelisks towered over him, their imposing yet lifeless presence resembling three dead trees. It was likely that Somnius knew of the unique writings carved into each one, and perhaps one day he would force her into revealing her knowledge. They held ancient secrets, secrets that could unlock greater power if he could decipher their code—but that was a task for another day.

His arrival had gone unnoticed by Grimm Kathaar, who meditated nearby with a serene focus that belied his formidable nature. Scarred and sharp-eyed, he was a balanced and refined warrior, yet trapped within his own armor. His body bore the wounds of countless battles and grueling rituals within the Loyalty Circles. Now, he knelt before the obelisks, seeking strength and guidance from their ancient power. As the latest Throatian king, Grimm had been next in line after the Asche family had perished. Bios had played a crucial role in overcoming the last obstacle blocking Grimm's path—Thane Asche.

Thane had questioned too much about Zann-Xia-Czul—a dragon, not a deity—and while he had been useful in life, his weak-mindedness made him a liability. If he had only become a puppet king, Bios could have easily manipulated him to serve his interests.

His wavering loyalty to the dragon and persistent inquiries carried significant risks. Thane needed removal.

Grimm Kathaar, Thane's uncle, emerged as the most suitable candidate to rule the Throatians. His goals aligned perfectly with Bios's vision of an army bound and blinded by religious faith. At first, Bios had nearly ordered Grimm's assassination—much like he had done with Thane—when he discovered Zann-Xia-Czul's true nature. Grimm's reaction, however, surprised Bios. Rather than growing angry, distraught, or rebellious upon learning the truth about the Throatian god, Grimm doubled down on his commitment.

"Our religion is essential for power, even though its foundations are untrue," Grimm had told Bios that day after they had sent Thane to his death. "The Son See'ers don't need to know that Zann-Xia-Czul is a dragon—they only require a symbol to fear and center their lives. You should pose to them as the symbol they fear. Your powers will make you more godlike in the end."

"I'm not a god," Bios Auras replied, "but one day, I will become one. Zann-Xia-Czul and I have a binding agreement, and it's a long-term arrangement."

Everything was connected. Zann-Xia-Czul wished to revive his fallen dragon kin, while Bios Auras desired the God Stones. If Bios obtained all the stones, he could presumably grant Zann-Xia-Czul's wish. The Throatians belonging to the dragon would help Bios achieve his goal. The vastness of the world made it difficult for him to locate all the God Stones on his own, as their hiding spots were too numerous and scattered. However, with an army of religious fanatics, he could gather more resources and eyes to assist him in his search. For Bios, the stones were not an end in themselves but a means to fulfill his destiny of purging the world of evil, as foretold by Asura.

His goal aligned with the prophecy Somnius had once told him long ago. At the time, he hadn't understood its meaning, but in recent months, clarity arrived: the dragon and the Throatians were meant to help him collect the Tears of Asura.

Bios Auras had no intention of using the God Stones to revive the dragons, even if it were possible. Zann-Xia-Czul and his Throatian people were only his tools. Unaware of their fate, they would eventually be sacrificed, a grim reflection of their culture's brutality. The Throatians—and their dragon god—all deserved death, and he would bring it to them one day.

Bios smiled at the group of Throatian soldiers kneeling in rows behind Grimm, their heads bowed. Each wore white robes with golden trim and decorative embellishments across their chests from their necks to their legs, along with masks of the same color that hid their true identities. Grimm's armor was dark gray, resembling a stormy sky, but with similar gold patterns painted over its surfaces.

Closer to the obelisks stood Cereene Cirixaa, the newest of the Throatian Elders. The white robe clung to her figure, symbols of her faith woven into the fabric. Each symbol represented her dedication to and knowledge of her people's religion and lore. Her delicate yet firm hands clasped a book above her waist. She held her head high, projecting the image of the priestess she had become, but Bios knew better than to trust appearances alone.

Cereene's eyes met his from across the room, and he could see the anger and fear brewing within them. It was Bios who had ordered Thane's death, who had manipulated everything leading to that event. And it was he who had used Cereene as a prize and dangled her life before Thane as both a reward and a punishment.

He clearly remembered how her pleas had sounded when Bios forced Thane to choose between his own life and hers. That moment had been a stroke of genius—a test of loyalty for Thane and a cruel twist of fate for Cereene. Now she stood here, taking the place of Elder Hrodspire, who'd met his tragic end at Thane's hand —another act orchestrated by Bios.

Cereene's convictions were shattered that day when Bios had grown tired of Thane's lapses in faith. Unlike the other Elders, Cereene was vulnerable—she had neither won a battle in a Loyalty Circle nor served on the island's Breeding Farms. She had been a privileged, well-studied lover to Prince Thane, but now that the Asche family was gone, she was demoted to just another pet of the island's religion.

"Grant us your protection and blessings as we gather food for our growing people," Cereene's voice echoed through the temple as her prayer continued.

Bios stepped forward, closing the distance between them. His smile rested on her face a moment longer than necessary before he gave her a menacing nod—a wordless reminder of the power he still held over her fate. The priestess stuttered in her next sentence, then carried on.

"As you slumber, we will serve you and give thanks daily for your protection," Cereene recited. Her voice rose as she said, "Protect us against those who would harm or deceive us, and shield our souls from the darkest evils of this world!"

"Protect them from me," Bios wanted to say, but he dared not risk any unnecessary complications.

Nevertheless, he found pleasure in their subtle exchange. To provoke such reactions with his mere presence alone strengthened his confidence. Those who knelt before the stone pillars were truly bowing to him, unknowingly acknowledging his power and mercy.

Cereene took her place beside Grimm, settling her knees on the floor as she bowed to the obelisks with reverence. Her role as a priestess demanded daily ceremonies, even though she too now knew the truth about Zann-Xia-Czul. Trapped by the beliefs expected of her, she was a prisoner on an island of religious fools.

As he watched them bow and straighten in unison, Bios recalled how he'd leveraged Cereene's new status to his benefit. Since Thane was gone, her influence as an Elder and Son See'er Vrai was too significant to overlook, and she had proven invaluable in maintaining control over Grimm and the kingdom. Bios Auras had already pressured Cereene to denounce Thane as a traitor to their island. She could serve him through her words, even if they were coerced.

Meanwhile, Grimm turned his head, acknowledging Bios's presence without drawing attention from others. While Grimm appeared to rule the kingdom, it was Bios who held the power—the strings that could unravel everything. Before Zann-Xia-Czul had entered his hibernation, he had directed the Elders and Grimm to follow Bios Auras's orders. Because Zann-Xia-Czul's voice had resonated inside their minds, they had no choice but to accept his divine word as truth.

"Zann-Xia-Czul, we are your Son See'ers, and all that we do serves you as you slumber," Cereene continued. "Upon your awakening, we shall present an army prepared to carry out your will across the world."

She rose from the ground, and Grimm followed after. Together, they faced the masked warriors, lifting their arms. The Throatians' eyes gazed through their golden masks, their attention fixed on Bios Auras.

"Shivanna Adul," Grimm greeted him. "Do you bring us good news?"

He was referring to their food supply. The Throatians had been striving to boost their population, but they lacked the farmland necessary for their future needs. Before the conflict with the Asche and von Stonewall families, White Boar's Landing served as an essential trade hub, allowing them to secure any provisions they needed. The closure of the port for nearly a year worsened the scarcity of food.

"We are going to have another chance for a raid on Last Hope's silos next evening," Bios said. "We'll have two or three minutes. The guards are getting suspicious, but my contact assures me that they will only station the guards outside and not inside the building."

Bios was fluent in Throatian, a language he had mastered over ten years of wandering White Boar's Landing. Though he despised its harsh, argumentative tone—each syllable seemed to clash like a brief, sharp song—he couldn't deny its one redeeming quality: every sentence carried an implicit threat.

"How many more raids can we expect you to arrange for us?" Grimm asked. "I love the idea of stealing so much from our enemies, but eventually, they will place guards inside the storage rooms. Our constant thefts can't go on forever."

"Of course not," Bios agreed, "but like you, I derive pleasure from taking from the Darians first. Once they become wise enough, we'll stop our raids in Last Hope and move on to the food belonging to Wargonne."

"Wargonne," Grimm said. "Were it anyone but you, I'd deem them mad to even dream of breaching that fortress."

Wargonne was an isolated stronghold accessible only by ship. To prepare for sieges or emergencies, it maintained ample supplies in reserve. Normally, entering and exiting the secured castle posed challenges, but the Teleportation Stone allowed him to circumvent these obstacles. The most effective solution to secure the food provisions for the Throatians was to execute a single, bold heist.

"With me at your side, we'll conquer the world when the time comes. For now, let's focus on thievery," Bios said. With his Teleportation Stone, they could launch simultaneous attacks in many places, but they needed more people.

Cereene stood by, frozen and unable to speak.

"A fine prayer performance, Cereene," Bios praised, "and what a loyal Son See'er Vrai you've been. Prince Thane would have been proud."

Cereene's jaw dropped open in shock before she muttered an insincere "Thank you" and scurried toward the temple exit like a scared mouse.

The soldiers, their faces hidden behind masks, filed from the room in single file. After each worship session, they proceeded to their respective Loyalty Circles. There, they performed the Reminder of Suffering, a ritual battle to the death between two warriors. The winner of the one-on-one combat was considered the most loyal to Zann-Xia-Czul. The dragon had devised this religion for his followers, though it wastefully culled many humans. Despite this, the cycle unintentionally produced a bloodline of soldiers. However, sustaining an entire population required food, which he supplied.

"Now, Grimm," Bios said, "the food supply issue is already resolved. What we need to move forward we almost have, but your people must continue following my lead to secure it. Are they ready?"

"You'll have the warriors, as always," the latest Throatian king promised. "But if I can pose you an unrelated question?"

"Ask."

"You seem to find terrifying Elder Cirixaa amusing," Grimm commented. "You're free to do as you wish, but I'm genuinely curious why."

Bios smiled. "It's simple. Cereene's fear brings me pleasure."

"Is that the only reason?"

"It doesn't need to be more complicated than it already is," Bios replied with a knowing smirk. "Everyone reacts when somebody pushes them. Finding what it takes to break someone with words alone is what I find more fascinating."

Grimm grinned cruelly. "Blades and whips are a quicker way of breaking others down."

After Urith Asche, Thane Asche's mother, murdered Grimm's brother Desaii, the latest Throatian king had shown plenty of insight and potential. A thirst for vengeance, a mind for cold-blooded calculation, and a steadiness that kept him calm guided Grimm toward stealing the crown from the Asche family while they'd been away on their mission. Bios had arranged everything beforehand, but Grimm didn't need to know that.

Grimm's reach for power had been a test all along—could he lead the Throatians with his eyes fully open to the truth about their religion, yet still yield total loyalty to Bios Auras and Zann-Xia-Czul despite it? Could he do what Thane Asche would not, or would he waver?

"What you say is true—physical harm breaks people's wills the fastest," Bios explained. "But what do they feel before they reach that point? Fear, anger, and desperation, perhaps, before it's over. So, wouldn't it be more intriguing to give them a sense of something far greater? Hope or confidence, for instance. Let them devise plans to escape your control, only to fail. Let them believe they might defeat you but ensure they never can. Then, as you reveal the truth, crush them with the weight of losing everything and watch them squirm until they can't anymore. You cannot achieve this state with weapons alone. The human soul is resilient, but never immortal."

"You're an interesting one, Bios Auras," Grimm remarked, "and I thought Zann-Xia-Czul held the darkest soul on this island."

He turned away from the Throatian king, his mind weaving through the king's words. Indeed, Zann-Xia-Czul had spread despair and torment, but Bios's own secretive, complex actions—planned over time—might one day rival the dragon's cruelty. He let the thought linger as he considered Grimm's potential for the future.

During Grimm's ascent to power, Bios observed a ruthless determination in him, initially masked by hesitation, that led to him casting aside his own family for the crown. Grimm had known Desaii wasn't fit to rule and that the Asche family would lose their positions, yet he did nothing—no protest, no resistance. In fact, Zann-Xia-Czul noted that Grimm showed little concern for his extended family's fates. Could he, like Bios, master the art of manipulating fear and hope to tighten his grip on power? Soon, they would discover the truth—and if Grimm proved unprepared, they would replace him, just as they had replaced Harkbin, Urith, Thane, and Desaii before him.

The temple's atmosphere clung to him as he pondered. The walls and floor of the temple were ivory and as pure as could be, but the blood spilled both outside and in remained invisible.

To Bios, the darkness Grimm spoke of was merely a tool, something to be wielded until he obtained all the Tears of Asura. Once he wielded the full blessings of Asura's gifts, the shadows—and the trail of sins Bios had left behind—would vanish.

"I do only what is necessary," he replied. "Lesser people are assets to me, and I must break their shells to determine if they will be obedient and useful—or shattered and useless."

"Finally, I understand you better," the Throatian king said. "You tested Thane and found he had little to offer. I will provide you with far more. I seek only one thing: power. You may have the rest of the world but give me control of this island. Naturally, I can assist you in your conquest."

He extended his hand to shake Bios's, but Bios didn't extend his own. "I have a question," he said. "Remind me why you are so willing to serve me?"

"It's as simple as your answer about Elder Cirixaa," Grimm replied. "I have no interest in ruling the entire world—I can only be in one place at a time and can't move as freely as you. There's no point in owning land I'll never see in my lifetime. This island is large enough to be a home for me, with plenty of people to fulfill my every trivial desire. Like you, I'm curious about humanity's limits. Can my servants rise to conquer Yaenia, the Silent Deserts, and the rest of the countries I haven't seen? The question interests me, but I have no yearning to rule over it once I find my answer. Conquering everything else is one goal, but holding power afterward is a far more complicated and grueling ordeal. If my kingdom will survive on its own after helping you, then that's all I need."

Bios grinned. "You're a practical-minded man, Throatian King Kathaar. But what of Zann-Xia-Czul? He remains your god—or at least the one to whom you must still answer."

"When he's asleep, he can't read our thoughts," Grimm said. "That's why I can speak plainly to you. Do you understand?"

"I'm surprised you've noticed," Bios remarked. "Could the same be said for the other Son See'ers?"

"They'll discover it too eventually, I suspect," the Throatian King replied. "But it doesn't matter. I think I know what you plan to do later, maybe even before he wakes up."

"And what is that?"

"You need Zann-Xia-Czul only to protect our island from the Darians as we build our army," Grimm said. "Once that's done, what purpose would he serve beyond continuing to pose as a god?"

Grimm proved smarter than Bios had expected but revealing the entire truth to him wasn't worth the risk—not yet.

"Zann-Xia-Czul will remain useful in times to come," Bios deflected. "A dragon on the battlefield is a formidable adversary. Your god despises humans and delights in killing them. Retribution shall guide Zann-Xia-Czul's later actions more than conquest."

"If I can fight alongside Zann-Xia-Czul, our future will be most promising," Grimm said. "Our warriors are sure to be inspired. Speaking of that, Elder Valenti wanted to speak with you about the latest newborns."

Elder Valenti managed the island's Breeding Farms, sustaining the Throatian population despite the losses from the Loyalty Circles. These farms were the sole safeguard against the Throatians' self-destructive religious rituals, requiring careful planning and foresight, unlike brothels in other lands. While she arranged the procreations for her people's future, Bios Auras could still offer help. Time was the primary constraint on growing their numbers, and Bios had methods to overcome this limitation.

"Very well, I'll go see her," Bios said. "This has been a fine conversation with you." If Valenti had already requested his aid, she must have prepared the cart he needed to move.

"Likewise, it's been an interesting exchange, my new friend," Grimm replied with a solemn bow. "We'll reunite when the time comes for the raid in Last Hope."

Valenti was waiting at Breeding Farm One, so Bios pictured the main hallway of the inner chamber. The memory came easily, though it was a place he'd visited more out of necessity than desire. He had no interest in participating in the activities there. The dim candlelight along the stone walls reminded him of a dungeon, and to some, that's what it was.

The Teleportation Stone obeyed, opening a portal to where he wanted to go next.

"I'll return in a few hours," Bios Auras promised. "Prepare your men for the raid."

The Temple of White was a twenty-minute walk from Breeding Farm One, but he arrived instantly as the portal closed behind him. The sudden smell of perfume overwhelmed his nose, struggling against cheap incense, alcohol, and sweat. He'd never ventured beyond the doors on either side of the main hallway, where the activities took place.

He marched toward the end of the rows, where a short staircase led to where Valenti would be. Along the way, he noticed the paintings hanging crooked on the walls—simple scenes of forests, oceans, and grassy plains. All were likely imported from White Boar's Landing, for the Throatian island had no such peaceful places.

The soft strum of a lyre filled the background, echoing a melody that was both calming and ominous. It welcomed first-time visitors to the Breeding Farm but tormented those who had fulfilled their religious duty to procreate and were required to return.

Valenti's door was ajar, so he stepped inside. Bookshelves crammed with old volumes lined the walls; their spines showcased generations of records detailing bloodlines, physical traits, and the circumstances of each child conceived in the Breeding Farms. Between the shelves, rolled parchments were stacked in cylindrical holders, each labeled with fine handwriting that revealed the inner references Valenti regularly used. Based on the titles, Bios surmised they were schedules showing who would enter the Breeding Farms and with whom they would go.

The Elder sat at her desk, poring over a large ledger. To neatly contain her gray hair and avoid distraction, she pulled it back into a tight bun. Her formal yet functional charcoal robe was plain except for a silver chain around her waist, from which several keys dangled.

She didn't look up as he entered, her quill continuing to scratch across the page in quick, confident strokes. Her focused demeanor showed she wasn't easily disturbed.

"Shivanna Adul," she greeted, finishing her final record and looking up. "The cart is being loaded now."

He nodded firmly, appreciating her directness. "Are all of them healthy?" he asked.

"All fifty."

"And the bloodlines?"

"Beyond the twentieth tier," Valenti answered. "Problems from inbreeding will likely take several years to appear, if they do at all. Your business partner won't notice any symptoms yet."

"Agreed," Bios said. "I will turn your fifty into at least twenty-five."

She smiled approvingly. "Your ability to make these trades is astounding. How do you manage to do it?"

"I'm good at making deals, that's all," he replied. "Now where are they?"

"Come, my friend," the Throatian Elder of the Breeding Farms said, "and I'll show you."

She led Bios Auras through the shadowy passage, where their footsteps echoed off the ceiling. A musky scent of wet soil dominated the air, and faint wails seeped from the numerous chambers on the other side of the walls. Suddenly, as if in response to their approach, the main door burst open with a force that hinted at urgency from the other side.

Cereene Cirixaa filled the doorway, an unexpected yet commanding presence silhouetted against the dying sun. The light carved her into something more than a priestess—one of solemn intentions.

"I must accompany you," she said, her voice a soft rasp cutting through the hallway's dreadful scents.

Bios Auras scoffed. "Why would you join me?" he challenged. "The place I'm taking them isn't one for worship."

Cereene lowered her chin, eyes steady. "Grimm spoke of where you'll bring them. It's because of where you're taking these children that they need Zann-Xia-Czul's blessing—a prayer from me to protect them from what's ahead."

Valenti interjected with diplomacy, "It would be an honor for this set of children to be blessed by Elder Cirixaa, and it might even ease the minds of those who have given them over."

Bios studied Cereene for a moment, trying to discern whether her sudden insistence held a hidden motive. His instincts suggested there was more to Cereene's request than solely religious devotion. While she may have felt empathy for the newborns, it was unlikely she still believed in the authenticity of her own prayers now that she knew the truth about Zann-Xia-Czul. What was she after?

"You don't need to attend," he said curtly. "Your prayers can be offered from here. My journey doesn't require your blessings—nor a divine intervention."

Cereene nodded, seizing the moment, yet still stepping aside to let them pass. "I insist you let me come," she said. "You aren't a Throatian, after all."

"What you say is true," Bios snapped, "but I'm destined for more than just being a Throatian."

"But a Throatian must escort their kind into exile," Cereene said. "These infants will never return to this island. You know this."

What was she really asking? Bios suspected she wanted to escape the island. Regardless of her reasons, he distrusted appearances, especially when it came to someone who had been so close to the prince he had recently killed.

"Very well, you may join me in delivering Valenti's newborns to the Silent Deserts," Bios said. "But if you should flee, I will send you straight into the Black Sands of Tornaa."

For the next part of his journey through the Teleportation Stone's portals, Bios arrived in the Golden Bay Market of District Two in the Silent Deserts. He, Cereene, and the infants were as far as possible from Yaenia and the Throatian island. Guiding the horse and cart through the crowded marketplace, the endless wailing of the newborns and Cereene's disapproving glares seemed to drag time to a halt.

He routinely came to the land of slave traders for business, building relations with the masters alike the Throatians. Yet, the cart of newborns, each in its own basket, bore a unique sound he'd never forget. Soon, they would trade them to the world across the ocean. Cereene hadn't been wrong in claiming they'd never return to their homeland.

A rigid caste system controlled every aspect of a slave's existence. The Salt Heart in District Five relied on massive labor for their operations, so there was no mobility. However, those born in District One's First Heaven or District Two's Golden Bay had a far greater likelihood of being assigned to a higher caste.

The people of the Silent Deserts had mastered the art of oppression, trading lives as casually as salt or spices in other countries. District Two's Golden Bay market was notorious for its daily dark yet open transactions. Long ago, the native people there began enslaving their own kin and selling them, a practice that grew so embedded in their culture that the Golden Bay trading port eventually opened to foreigners seeking slaves.

To Bios, slavery was the most primitive form of life, a bleeding wound of humanity's progress. No other creature behaved like humans. For today, however, he needed to exploit their lack of morality for his own ends.

Beneath his disgust, Bios concealed a complex conflict. Currently, he depended on these systems to fulfill his objectives. Unlike the corrupt, misguided slavers he despised, Bios believed his own cause was grander and nobler. His actions, he told himself, were temporary—a necessary harm on the path to a greater good. Once he could gather the remaining Tears of Asura, he could undo everything he had done and was about to do. He would eradicate all evil, not just slavery.

The market buzzed with a symphony of haggling voices, the clang of coins, and the scents of dried fish mingling with the sea's air. The sun beat down upon the Golden Bay, casting a similarly tinted hue over the rows of tents and stalls where the vendors peddled their wares. Amid the energy of the traders, Bios Auras steered his horse-drawn cart through the crowd, unnoticed.

Cereene walked alongside him, her arms crossed and face filled with disapproval. "These children deserve better than being sold to slavers in your twisted schemes," she said, her voice cutting through the disturbing newborns at their rear.

Bios shot her a sideways glance. "Evil? Is that your word for me? Look around you. This place trades men, women, and children like sacks of grain, and it's ordinary here, not a scheme. What I'm doing—"

"What you're doing isn't any different!" she snapped angrily. "You hide behind the excuse that it's normal or for the greater good, but we both know it's not right." She gestured back to where infants lay in their small baskets lined with thin blankets. "They're innocent! Don't pretend you aren't aware of what's going to happen to them."

"And what of your Throatian rituals?" Bios challenged, his voice low but sharp enough to cut through the noise of the market. "You already know the truth about the blood sacrifices to Zann-Xia-Czul. How many people suffered and died because of your false religion? Is a life of slavery here truly worse than suffering and dying in a Loyalty Circle? At least here they'll live and not suffer in the name of a fictional deity."

"That's different," Cereene argued back, her eyes never leaving his face. "We don't trade our children to strangers."

"No?" Bios quirked an eyebrow. "Then what are we doing here? This is happening, and the Elders supported it. Even before I came along, your people traded slaves to diversify the Breeding Farms. You might not have been aware, but it's how—"

Cereene flinched at his words. "Our faith—"

"Is just as flawed as this market's morality," Bios concluded for her smoothly. "Don't pretend your hands are clean while accusing me of being beneath you. Did you come here solely to lecture me on how you view me as evil? Have you ever considered there's a greater purpose behind what I'm doing?"

She was a fragile soul born into a harsh reality and owed her survival to Prince Thane's royal influence. Had he not intervened, she would have perished in the Loyalty Circles long ago. Cereene's reputation betrayed that she had never faced another Son See'er in combat.

"You killed him," she finally said, trembling. Now the truth was out.

"Don't be sad, Elder Cirixaa—your prince was useful to me until he was no longer needed."

Her lips shivered. "But why? Why would you send him to fight the sorceress when you knew he couldn't survive?"

So that's why Cereene had insisted on coming along to the Silent Deserts. She wanted answers, not to run away. Perhaps she'd imagined he'd more freely reveal the truth if none of the other Elders or Grimm were present. Aside from the cartload of newborns they were hauling through the market, there were no other Throatians nearby to hear what they'd speak of.

He wasn't obligated to tell her anything, but it was unlikely that anyone else knew the reason he had sent Thane back to Last Hope—except possibly Somnius.

"She's not a sorceress," Bios said. "She's a goddess, and we are still at war with her."

"A goddess?"

"A goddess," he revealed. "It was better for your people to believe Zann-Xia-Czul is the only god. Long ago, she betrayed me, and now I must destroy her."

She paused, digesting the new information. "But why did Thane have to get involved?"

"The goddess has many eyes," Bios said. "She's trying to kill me, and I her. Sending Thane to Somnius alerted her that I knew where she was hiding. I aim to keep her cautious while I prepare."

The problem was with the Tears of Asura—if Somnius had even one of them, she might overpower him. He needed to locate the remaining stones and avoid confronting her until he understood her full capabilities. Whether he possessed more—and more useful—stones than her, he would have to face her to fulfill his destiny from Asura.

Finding them was no simple task—the world was vast, and they were as small and indistinguishable as any ring or necklace's centerpiece. However, whenever humans activated their magic, Bios could feel the God Stone's call, like a fire's smoke beckoning him.

"That's the reason Thane died?" Cereene cried. "For sending a message? Don't you feel guilty for ending his life for that?"

Bios smiled. "There are many things I've done that I should feel ashamed about, but guilt slows down progress. We are nearly there. Keep silent."

She continued weeping while he guided the horse into another main aisle of the Golden Bay marketplace. The infants, too, wailed without pause, and time dragged on as he steered them through the dense crowd. His eyes narrowed, ignoring their cries as he gave the reins a swift tug. He needed to do this, even if it was wrong.

As he led the horse through the Golden Bay Market, each visitor wore a large silver or gold chain around their neck, symbolizing their mastery over something or someone. Bios Auras, however, had no need for such vanity—he neither flaunted his wealth nor sought extra attention. His destination was the stall just ahead, and that was all he needed for the moment.

The cart whined as he guided it to where Klein Pene, a slave trader, waited. Born in District One to a wealthy family, Klein had more wealth than most people could earn in a lifetime, though now he lived in District Four where his workers toiled. He wore purple robes and a maroon hat covered with red jewels worth ten times their weight in gold. Two thick metallic snakes hung from his neck —one made of gold, the other of silver. Bowed under their weight, he bent over his table, scribbling the day's transactions.

"Hellvar," the slaver greeted in Harsani, the language of the Silent Deserts. Hellvar was the alias Bios adopted while conducting business in the region to preserve his true identity.

"I hope you have a good stock for me today," Bios replied in Klein's native tongue. "I trust the Golden Bay has been treating you well since my last journey from District One?"

As ordered, Cereene idled nearby in silence, unable to understand the Harsani language. She stood by the cart, comforting some infants with her delicate hand.

"Business is always good for me when you come to visit," Klein replied with a smile. He gave Cereene a curious stare. "What do you have for me today?"

"Fifty healthy, unmarked infants," Bios replied. "And there's gold too, of course."

"And gold?" Klein exclaimed. "You must have urgent needs to be offering so much upfront."

"I want twenty-five of your best," Bios said.

Klein grinned, revealing his golden tooth. "My people are always the best, but what skills do you need?"

"Adults. It doesn't matter what their current roles are."

"Fifty infants for twenty-five adults... the amount of gold you'd need to put forward would be significant. I trust you have not forgotten the cost."

Bios recognized the customs of the Silent Desert, where people treated infants and children as having little value until they could work. Unlike adults who could generate income, people considered children investments for the future. To offer a child, Bios would need to provide enough gold to cover their living expenses until they could become profitable. The locals frequently sold their people into various forms of servitude, making this practice as commonplace and traditional as it was grotesque.

"You speak as though I haven't made this kind of transaction with you before," Bios told him with a playful wink.

"It's hard to forget someone who so often trades for losses, Hellvar," Klein replied. "I can't understand why you keep doing business with me. It's not worth it for you. You're offering me more than what full-grown workers would cost if you had bought them outright. A wiser man would keep his infants and save the gold. You know this, don't you?"

It was true—exchanging infants and coin for half as many adults proved costlier than simply purchasing them outright. However, there was far more to the trade than mere economics; the true benefit lay in the illusion he created—one that deceived the Throatians and the slavers alike. His influence grew on both sides, and Klein hadn't yet witnessed all that Bios had planned for him. Later, there would be a silent justice.

"I understand the concept of losses," Bios Auras replied with gritted teeth. "But you're saving me from my impatience. What I'm offering you now is useless to me in the immediate future. Fifty crying children are quite noisy. Your fully grown Whitesands can serve me today."

"My patience will be your loss." Klein snickered. "Well, if that's what you insist, I'll make the exchange. Given your status as a prominent member of District One, Hellvar, I suppose you must know what you're doing."

"I do."

"Very well, then. Now, if you don't mind..."

"Go right ahead. Look them over."

Bios gestured for Klein to continue, and a thin woman in a yellow dress emerged from behind the stall and approached. She carefully lifted one of the wailing infants, looked it over closely, and then set it back down. She continued by examining three more children, inspecting their wrists, necks, and bodies. Meanwhile, Cereene glared at the woman, then Klein, and back again in pure disgust.

"They are unclaimed and healthy," the woman announced, glaring back at the priestess.

"Take them to the inker," Klein motioned with a wave of his hand. The babies might never receive individual names, but their culture would likely curse them with the surname Whitesand.

"Here is your payment," Bios announced, revealing a large bag of gold. He placed the sum on Klein's table, letting the slaver count the coins.

"I see you already knew the fair going rate," he commented.

"This isn't our first transaction, and it won't be our last," Bios replied.

"Speaking of transactions," Klein said in a hushed tone, "the foreigner you're with today—is she…?"

"She's not for sale," Bios warned, though Cereene didn't comprehend their conversation. She was useful as a suitable replacement for Elder Hrodspire, at least for now. As long as she remained under his control, there was no need to remove her. Besides, Bios already knew what Klein would do to her, and there was no greater purpose in letting him have that.

Klein smiled warmly. "I understand your desire to keep her, my friend," he said. He called out to one of his servants, then turned back to Bios. "Your new companions, all adults, will arrive shortly. Honestly, I didn't expect to exchange so many people today. Their seals are being crossed off and invalidated by the inker as we speak."

"Time waits for no one but me," Bios said. The minutes trickled by as Klein's worker unloaded the last of the Throatian infants and took them behind Klein's stall.

Another servant emerged, leading a line of twenty-five men and women. Their movements were subdued by the shackles around their wrists. With each step, their chains clanged in unison. They stepped past Cereene, as if she were invisible, and approached their new master.

Bios Auras studied the row of adults, observing their faces. Most had naturally fair skin, tanned from working in the sun, with no signs of wrinkles. He observed their strong builds and evaluated their potential usefulness for future plans. As usual, Klein's people were well-cared for, and he seemed proud of their nourishment.

The same couldn't be stated for other slavers, which was why maintaining Klein's favor remained beneficial for Bios.

He nodded in approval. "They will suffice," he said to Klein's servant. "Remove their chains."

"Truly sir?" the servant replied in Harsani.

"I rule without chains," Bios replied. "Remove them. Though they will be freed physically, they cannot escape their destiny."

"As you wish, sir." Klein's servant unshackled them, and each slave glanced at Bios. When his gaze met theirs, he smiled mysteriously. The people he'd just bought would have their freedom, but only so they could face a choice: whether to worship Zann-Xia-Czul and assimilate into Throatian society, or refuse. If they chose poorly and were sent to the Loyalty Circles for not pledging loyalty, at least the choice would have been theirs.

With the exchange concluded, Bios waved goodbye to the slaver. "May your bags remain full," he said to Klein as he turned the cart around. He then switched back to speaking Throatian. "Come, Cereene."

Leading his horse, he retraced his steps by the marketplace's light. The trudging of his followers' bare feet echoed behind him as he led his new servants. The lonely alley from where he'd come waited ahead. Long ago, he carved a snake into the wall to remember it.

At the dead end, Bios halted and faced the group. His attention swept over them once more, this time with a sense of finality. "Step forward," he commanded in Harsani, his voice carrying an authoritative tone. "Do not stop."

The twenty-five servants obeyed without hesitation, approaching him in silence. He closed the invisible magic gateway as the last of Klein's people disappeared from the alleyway's heart. Bios Auras would never see them again.

"So that is how the Breeding Farms worked," Cereene commented. "You must have been doing this for—"

"I have been involved for a long time now, though only Zann-Xia-Czul and Valenti were aware of my influence. The other Elders, as well as the Asche family, were oblivious to my presence and influence within your society until recently."

"But I always thought the obelisks at the Temple of White were how new people arrived on our island," Cereene said. "Elder Kaelgeth suspected there was a World Vein there, but Zann-Xia-Czul commanded us not to touch them. Was he right, or was it really you all along?"

"Both were true," he said, "and Kaelgeth had moved the obelisks in the main chamber up from the basement and switched them with the replicas. It's more important that they stay accessible to me. Somehow, a World Vein is bound to the real ones."

World Veins were naturally occurring phenomena similar to the portals Bios created. Before acquiring the Teleportation Stone, Bios had studied these mysterious rifts, which he sensed as cracks in reality's fabric as he approached. Yet he discovered no further information about them. Except for the one in the Temple of White, World Veins moved unpredictably, lasted for random durations, and connected only through their paired endpoints. Entering a portal was risky, offering no way to know where it led or if it would stay open long enough to return. Thankfully, the Teleportation Stone gave Bios greater control and precision, making World Veins obsolete for practical use.

"But why such secrecy?" Cereene asked. "Our lore suggests the original Throatians emerged on the island through those obelisks, and sometimes even more people come through. Every one of them is strange, cannot speak our language, and seems malnourished. Nobody can read the inscriptions carved on the obelisks either. Do you know the reason? Are those slaves from the Silent Deserts as well?"

"It's true that I've brought many newcomers to your island, but I doubt anyone ever came through the World Vein," Bios replied, leaning against the alleyway's wall. "The portal nested between the three obelisks leads to a place unlike any other—an empty wasteland. The first time I stepped through it, I found something unsettling and a man who claimed to know me."

As the words left his lips, the memory surged back to him—the snow, the ruins, and the stranger who had warned him of a fate yet to come…

9
KAINE - THE SECRET OF GALE VILLAGE

To Kaine's surprise, neither the prince nor the princess had any interest in visiting Gale Village. The night before, in the throne room, King Ether had announced to Xander, Kira, Kaine, and Merdel that they would embark on a journey. The following drama only highlighted the significant stress and turmoil the von Stonewall family had recently endured.

Ten-year-old Kira's tears flowed endlessly as she argued against leaving the safety of Last Hope. She feared the unknown dangers outside Serenity Keep's walls, away from her father and his guards for the first time. Xander, two years older than her, agreed, displeased that their father had planned the trip without consulting them. The prince had already arranged a hunting expedition with friends in the king's guard, scheduled for the same period.

The idea of visiting their mother's burial site to find peace after the recent events deeply troubled Kira and Xander, despite Ether's insistence. They argued that if it was so crucial for them to go to her grave immediately and with no flexibility on the timing, why shouldn't the king accompany them? Ether's vague and unconvincing explanation about his duties in Serenity Keep left both children unsatisfied.

Kaine concurred with Ether and Merdel that Xander and Kira should remain unaware of the true purpose behind their journey, given the sensitive nature of the information about the God Stones. Keeping them in the dark would ensure their safety in the days to come. The children were not yet mature enough to grasp that their father suspected a traitor within his council. While Ether aimed to uncover the disloyal member, he had not disclosed his methods. Remaining in Last Hope while their father addressed the issue could endanger Xander and Kira. Ether would concentrate on the urgent matters, while Kaine and Merdel would handle any grievances from the children as they departed.

"I can't believe Father planned this trip without telling us first. Why couldn't we bring a carriage?" Xander complained just twenty minutes outside the city gates. He pulled a purple hood over his head to block the sun, reluctantly settling for their form of transportation. Kira couldn't resist snickering at her brother's discomfort, while Kaine brushed his hand against the hidden satchel at his chest, hoping she wouldn't notice it.

"The terrain has changed since your last visit," Merdel explained. "The usual path is now blocked by rockslides, forcing us to take a more treacherous route. Carriages can no longer pass through the Shadowstone Mountains, and the roads are now mere narrow paths, only a few feet wide, blocked by towering walls of the thick, black glass. Even our horses won't be able to navigate these roads, so at some point, we'll have to leave them behind and continue on foot."

Xander swore loudly; Kaine felt Kira restraining another giggle. When Kira's back pressed against his satchel, he shifted it aside, hoping she wouldn't grow curious about its purpose.

Kaine felt unease regarding the God Stones hidden beneath his shirt. Though they traveled at a relaxed pace, he couldn't help but want to reach Gale Village as soon as possible. Only after he buried the stones with the queen would he feel a sense of relief. When Kaine requested escorts, the king refused, citing the mission's secrecy as more important than the risk of involving loose-lipped guards. Instead, he provided them with plenty of gold to bribe any ill-intentioned bandits they might meet along the way.

"The journey to the base of the mountains will require nearly a week," Merdel said. "From there, we'll hike to the summit, which might take another three or four days. I thought you'd both already visited Gale Village many times."

"Even though we've been there before, I still don't want to go," Xander said. "It's hardly a fun place to visit. Why would anyone in their right mind build their homes near a bunch of volcanoes?"

"Perhaps the people living there do so to avoid listening to complainers," Kira retorted, her wit as sharp as her tongue. Noticing

Xander's impatience, Kaine planned to help him develop better emotional control during their next sparring session.

They traveled the rest of the day without incident and set up camp a short walk from the main road. Their group brought two tents—one for the children and another for Kaine and Merdel. For dinner, they ate boiled potatoes, which Xander commented were boring compared to what they normally had at the castle. Though she didn't say so aloud, Kira's scrunched-up face revealed she agreed. To add more flavor, Kaine fried a small piece of lard, sliced the potatoes into wedges, and reheated them.

After the children were full and satisfied, they retired to their tent for the night, leaving Kaine and Merdel by the dying campfire to keep watch. The evening was alive with chirping crickets, creating a gentle sound barrier.

"About that package you're carrying," Merdel said with an inviting wink, "I couldn't help wondering—do you think hiding it at our destination is the best plan?"

"The king gave us the instructions," Kaine said, unsure of what to make of Merdel's suggestion. "I suppose he already put a great deal of thought into whether it made the most sense."

While the councilman was fully aware of their mission, Xander and Kira were not. They discussed the matter vaguely and out of earshot to avoid arousing the children's curiosity. After all, it was Lydia's sense of wonderment that led her to steal the God Stones from her father.

"Hiding them or using them are the most reasonable options," Merdel said. "But each has its own drawbacks."

"Agreed," Kaine said. "The power is not something to be taken lightly. The responsibility it entails would be a far greater burden than a gift, I suspect. Better to keep them hidden so nobody can abuse them."

"It's comforting to know you believe tucking them away is the best option for now," the Master of Foreign Relations remarked. "Many would disagree."

A sudden chilly breeze brushed Kaine's cheek as he recalled how Lydia's demeanor had shifted once she'd read the Throatian royal family's memories and seen what they'd planned to do to her. "I fear such power could corrupt someone or leave lasting scars," he said. "Under what conditions would the risk be worth it? Perhaps when the children are old enough to decide?"

Merdel let out a quiet chuckle. "Who knows what this war may bring us, or how long it might last? The prince and princess have much to learn, no matter how their circumstances change. Kira, like her elder sister, is enthusiastic and curious but unaware of the harsh and manipulative nature of the world. Xander has a good sense of predicting an enemy but lacks nuance in his words and decisions. I hope you teach them well, Sir Khalia. Ready or not, they are eventually going to inherit the burden of what we've set out to do."

Kaine glanced back at the large tent where the children slept, listening for any signs they might be awake. So far, he had heard no rustling or arguing. Merdel was right—they were the future. "Perhaps one day, Kira might steward over Last Hope while Xander defends the border. Each can use their strengths to protect the other's weaknesses."

"I appreciate your candor, Sir Khalia," Merdel replied. "You are considerably more straightforward than many of the upper-class members I've encountered."

Kaine forced a weak smile, wondering if the campfire light would expose his unease to Merdel. The renowned diplomat, known for his strict personality, seemed unusually relaxed, as though he had shed his usual guarded composure. Was he truly this at ease drinking no alcohol, or was his behavior an attempt to extract information from Kaine?

Merdel was likely seeking insight. If so, sharing the truth posed no harm—and might even reveal more about Merdel himself.

"The vanity of the privileged is why I abandoned the Leila Kingdom and became a merchant," Kaine said. "You have more tolerance than I for those who party, gossip, and live vicariously through their hollow lifestyles. But why did you leave? Like me, you could have only served Queen Blanche. Yet here you are, serving King Ether while still reporting to her."

The Master of Foreign Relations chuckled as he rose and began pacing around the campfire. "You see through my facade, don't you?" Merdel admitted. "Honestly, it was the influence that drew me to swear allegiance to the von Stonewall family rather than Queen Blanche. Our home kingdom is small and often mistaken for a mere city within the Darian Kingdom. Long ago, with more hair and less gray, I believed serving the Darians would grant enough power to keep tensions low. The Leila Kingdom needs to remain independent of them. That said, so long as the two kingdoms remain allies, I'm able to serve both of them, despite being obliged to one and not the other."

"How noble of you." Kaine snorted. "There must be more to it than that. The Leila Kingdom will always be self-governing."

"That's the truth, I swear to it by Asura," Merdel said. "The Leila Kingdom's founding was an afterthought, made possible only by those who died aiding King Ether in his war against the Lucidians. Alliances shift over time, and who knows what challenges the future may bring."

Blanche Voussoir, once a formidable warrior, had pledged her people to Ether von Stonewall's cause for land. However, the battle resulted in unforeseen casualties, prompting Blanche to ask for an independent realm as compensation to preserve her people's identity. This demand sparked a fierce debate, but Blanche ultimately succeeded, becoming queen and establishing the Leila Kingdom, which remained separate despite being geographically within the Darian Kingdom's territory.

"My apologies, Councilman," Kaine said. "I tend to distrust politicians. Perhaps I misjudged you."

"No offense is taken, my new friend," Merdel replied, seating himself on the ground. "It's wiser to distrust them all than to believe even one has the world's best interests at heart."

"Then it looks like we'll get along fine on this trip," Kaine said, his shoulders relaxing.

Merdel leaned closer to the fire's warmth. "Given the history between Queen Blanche and King Ether, are you familiar with the leader of Gale Village, Orin Axemonger? He was their companion during the war. You'll likely meet him soon."

He couldn't recall where he'd heard the name before. It might have been from a bard or someone with whom he traded who shared a similar name. Kaine had never been to Gale Village, a remote place so far from other towns.

"Is he a hermit?" Kaine asked. "The prince pointed out how unusual it is to choose to live so close to volcanoes. It's an intriguing question, and I'm sure the answer is equally interesting."

"You're not the first to think that," Merdel said. "Orin lost many of his people, along with his right eye, in his chaotic last battle against the Lucidians. That event transformed him."

"I've heard the stories from before, but none of them mentioned Orin Axemonger," Kaine replied. Ether von Stonewall had led the migrating humans to southeast Yaenia to escape the Lucidian Civil War, uniting the native people of Starlight Beach, Sky Tower Coast, and smaller villages under his rule. He carved out his kingdom from the shared territory. "I'm guessing that Orin founded Gale Village after it all settled down?"

"Correct," Merdel said. "Orin wanted isolation from anything that reminded him of the past. That's why he's moved so far away from everything else. Most of us who remember that conflict assumed the Lucidians would counterattack within the year, and Orin likely shared this belief. If the fighting resumed, they would have overlooked Gale Village because it lacks valuable resources, and its population is too small to matter compared to other settlements."

Kaine then realized why it was the ideal hiding place for the God Stones. "If Orin was close to King Ether," Kaine said, "he would already know about what I'm carrying."

"He's aware of the stakes," Merdel confirmed. "But I must warn you: there are unresolved conflicts between Ether, Blanche, and Orin. I came along in case tensions arose. Avoid mentioning the war or expressing your fondness for working for the von Stonewall family. If Orin asks about your opinion of the king, it would be best if you called him selfish."

Had the years of peace somehow changed him into the kinder man that Kaine knew now? Ether von Stonewall seemed to be anything but selfish.

"What kind of disagreement caused so much tension?"

"I'm not at liberty to say, unfortunately," Merdel replied. "The king wouldn't want me to share his personal affairs; neither historic records nor even the tavern songs record such details."

Ether's reluctance to join them on their journey likely stemmed from those longstanding disagreements. Perhaps Orin had contested Ether's right to the throne, or the issue may have been trivial compared to the broader events unfolding since their war. Whatever the root of their tension, Merdel would need to mediate and resolve it.

"Your task sounds much more delicate and complicated than mine," Kaine commented.

"Perhaps, but if I fail in my mission, it will only hurt two men's feelings," Merdel said. "If you fail, it will destroy the entire world—or something equally catastrophic. If you're offering to trade places with me, I must respectfully decline."

The two of them burst into laughter as the campfire smoke rose into the night air. Chatting about life and the world, the evening turned into the late hours before they fell asleep. Their conversation had kept them up later than planned, but being away from Last Hope and his daily duties reminded Kaine of simpler times aboard the Lion's Paw, when he only concerned himself with profits.

Now, serving King Ether, he faced additional responsibilities and people, each with their own demands and rewards. His oath to the von Stonewall family had led him to a life of service filled with purpose. Though now tethered to land instead of the sea, Kaine eagerly awaited what the next day might bring. His world had changed, and he had changed too.

DURING THE FOLLOWING DAYS, TRAVELING THROUGH THE MOUNTAINS of southeast Yaenia seemed darker than black and as lifeless as diamonds. To the north awaited Gale Village, accessible only by a steep, winding path through the mountains. But the ridges' walls had collapsed as Merdel had said, making it impossible for them to proceed on horseback. They set the horses free, and the group had no choice but to continue their journey on foot.

"Are you certain Cocoa and Strawberry can find their way home alone?" Kira asked.

"The finest stable keepers in Last Hope trained those horses," Merdel replied with confidence. "They'll navigate back to Serenity Keep more easily than us."

The day stretched on as Kaine and his companions trudged up the mountain path. In the distance, rivers of orange lava flowed down the slopes, heading eastward toward the sea. The landscape was a strange mix of black and green mountains, as if the black ones had formed a scab over the more vibrant peaks. The lower regions were filled with toxic fumes, too hot and dangerous to support life, yet the summits somehow remained explorable. It was remarkable that any village could survive in such an inhospitable environment.

"How long must we stay in Gale Village?" Xander asked impatiently.

"A day or two," Kaine replied, turning his attention to Merdel. "That should give you enough time to finish your tasks, correct?"

"Sometimes, it can take months to persuade someone who disagrees with my king's political ideologies," Merdel said. "But a single deep conversation might prove sufficient."

The group spread out and walked freely again, abandoning the single-file line. The burning heat forced them to drink water multiple times every hour to stay hydrated. Fortunately, the mountainous environment provided them with abundant sources of fluid. Boiling water flowed down the sides of the surrounding rocks, and Merdel, the expert on the land, assured them they could safely consume it after cooling and filtering it through the special cloths they carried. Climbing the mountain pushed Kaine to his physical limits, but his earlier worries about dehydration had lessened.

"I still don't understand why you're with us, Councilman Merdel. Why would someone disagree with my father?" Xander said. He had been silent most of the day, unlike Kira, who had been humming loudly and asking unimportant questions since dawn.

"People often have the same desired outcomes for their society," Merdel said. "However, they can have vastly different approaches to achieving them."

Xander took a moment to contemplate his words as their group approached a fork in the road. The neighboring cliffs branched into two equally similar paths, but one wall had a streak of red paint along it. These markers left by travelers aimed to help prevent others from getting lost in the endless, maze-like switchbacks.

"But the king decides what's best in the end," Xander said firmly, not noticing the mark.

"Indeed, the king always gets the final say," Merdel admitted as he slowed his pace and led the group on the path not painted.

"A noble king must ensure his people understand the reasons for his decisions," Kaine added, wiping the sweat from his forehead. "Even if they disagree."

"And what if they refuse to understand?" the prince asked.

The two adults exchanged a knowing glance, reflecting on the years to come. King Ether still had many years remaining before Prince Xander would inherit the crown, but the young prince had much to learn in the meantime. Both Kaine and Merdel knew their futures would involve serving Prince Xander, just as they now served King Ether.

"That's why a king's counselors are so important," Kaine replied, "and why selecting them is the most crucial decision you'll ever make. You need people who not only master their roles but also have a genuine character."

"People like Kaine and I assist your father in whatever he needs," Merdel said. "If he ever makes a mistake, he can count on us to tell him. A king left unchallenged risks becoming drunk on his own power."

Xander kept his pace, staring at the ground. "I disagree."

"You disagree someone ought to challenge a king when he's wrong?" Kaine asked.

The prince spoke sternly. "I don't think you would understand."

Before Kaine or Merdel could react, Kira dashed ahead of the group and spun around dramatically. "Shut up, Xander!" she teased, her arms held behind her back as she leaned toward them. "When you're the king, keep people happy. Otherwise, they'll steal your crown… and your head!"

"Kira!" Kaine warned.

"She's not wrong, you know," Merdel whispered.

Before anyone could say anything else, the princess screamed with excitement, pointing out Gale Village in the distance, and hurried ahead. Kaine climbed the dark hill, spotting a plain wooden barricade that seemed meant to contain animals instead of keeping people out. Beyond the fence stood three old shacks, all clearly neglected for years. One had a collapsed roof, while the other two remained standing but in disrepair.

"This can't be it, right?" Kaine blurted. "The village is abandoned."

"Now you know why I'd have rather gone hunting," Xander remarked.

It had slipped Kaine's mind that the prince and princess had already been to Gale Village several times before. Perhaps one of them could explain what had happened between King Ether and Orin Axemonger.

As they quickened their pace to catch up with Kira, Kaine asked, "Do you have many friends here?"

"There weren't any other children here the last time we visited."

"Perhaps you have some aunts or uncles?" he inquired, believing it was worth a try. After all, their mother might have family there.

"We only know Finnegan," the prince replied as they walked along a fence. "Everyone else stays in their homes whenever we visit. They give us privacy."

Giving them privacy seemed like a strange decision. Was the entire village, along with Orin, also displeased with King Ether? It was perplexing why they all stayed inside every time the royal family arrived. What had happened between the Darian king and the people living there?

"Who is Finnegan?"

"The chicken breeder."

"A chicken farmer?" Kaine looked over at Merdel. "Have you met him?"

"I met him on a previous occasion, but I did not have the chance to get to know him well."

They caught up with Kira, who waited near a towering gray boulder. "A lady saw me, but she ran away," she said.

The intense heat of the charcoal-like ground must have dulled his senses, but something about Gale Village felt off. Beyond Kira, fifteen more wooden shacks stood, all worn down and out of place in the harsh volcanic environment. Its isolation from neighboring villages and kingdoms, combined with the lack of horse access, made trade and supply acquisition challenging. To the east, across the volcanoes, was Wargonne, a Darian military stronghold accessible only by sea. Merchants might have found alternative routes through the mountains to get supplies; otherwise, the Leila Kingdom was the closest source of a market.

He wondered about the secluded town and whether anyone would offer information. The village seemed empty, and not a single person was to be found. Everyone had retreated into their homes, as Xander had suggested, or perhaps nobody but Orin actually lived in the village at all.

Merdel tried repeatedly to announce their arrival and declare they were there on behalf of King Ether, but his attempts went unanswered. Meanwhile, Kaine noticed a curtain closing suddenly in a second-floor window of one of the shacks. The villagers seemed to fear outsiders, the king, or both.

"Perhaps we should find Orin Axemonger first," Kaine said. "If we assure him we mean no harm, he might help us communicate with the rest of the villagers."

Xander pointed to the shack on the far left side of the street and said, "He lives there—the smallest of the lot."

The house, barely larger than a single room, seemed more like a modest shelter than a proper residence. Its weathered wood showed signs of insect damage and humidity, and its surface was dark gray, covered in soot and ash that had accumulated over the years. Even if the structure were brand new, it would still be a humble home, ideal for someone who preferred solitude.

The four of them approached the shack, and Kaine almost

expected it to be abandoned. Merdel stepped forward and rapped on the door with his knuckles.

"Orin Axemonger, are you inside?" the councilman called. "We mean you no harm and come in peace."

A light breeze fluttered the dry patches of grass at their feet. As they waited, campfire scent and ash filled Kaine's nostrils. He patted his chest again to check that the God Stones were still there. If the villagers planned an ambush, White Oath hung at his waist. His injured left arm made wielding it difficult, but it was better than being unarmed.

A brilliant rainbow of light suddenly glowed from beneath Kaine's shirt—the God Stones were activating! He whipped the satchel containing them behind his back, desperate to hide it from the others. Though he'd carried the stones undetected this whole time, they'd lain dormant. Why now? he wondered, baffled by the sudden glow. He had never seen them activate before, not even when he'd handled them barehanded!

His heart pounded in his chest. Fortunately, Merdel, Xander, and Kira remained occupied with the doorway ahead, oblivious to the strange occurrence happening beside them. The stones went dormant again, and the radiance disappeared as rapidly as it had come. Kaine hoped they wouldn't reactivate and waited before checking the satchel. The stones looked ordinary now—like any other jewels—but something between him and them had changed in that moment, leaving him without an explanation.

A faint creak echoed from within the shack, but no one answered. Kira moved forward and pounded her fist against the splintering wood.

"ELDER ORIN! THIS IS KIRA! STOP IGNORING US AND ANSWER YOUR DOOR!"

The shack creaked open to reveal an elderly man far older than King Ether and Queen Blanche. He wore a simple black robe that clung to his frail frame, with shiny green linings that matched his single remaining eye. A dark leather patch that complemented his attire covered his other eye. Though he was bald, his smooth head shone as if he oiled it every morning. The only hair left on his body was a lengthy white beard that reached his chest, yet it failed to hide his embarrassment.

"Princess Kira and Prince Xander, I didn't know it was you!" he exclaimed. He hobbled over, embracing her with one arm while gripping his dark wooden cane with the other. "How are you both?"

Though he acted like a long-lost grandfather, Kaine remained suspicious of his motives. Kira and Xander exchanged brief, vague answers with him, and they shared a few pleasantries until Orin revealed how isolated Gale Village truly was.

"Why didn't you bring your sister along?" he inquired. "And where are your crowns?"

"Much has changed since our last visit," Merdel said.

"Rufus, it has been a while," Orin said. "Tell me, what news do you bring from Last Hope?"

Kaine wondered if perhaps the village didn't have birds or if Ether had purposefully left him off the list of those whom he'd invited to Lydia's wedding and funeral. Orin was clearly unaware of the events of recent months, including the new war. Now, it would fall upon the four of them to inform him.

"Too much news," Merdel said. "Far too much."

THE FIVE OF THEM HUDDLED AROUND A TABLE INSIDE ORIN'S ONE-room shack. His accommodations could barely fit two people, so the elder fetched additional chairs from another villager's house. In the back of his home, near his small single-person bed, stood a weathered old armoire that looked like it had rolled down a nearby mountain.

Merdel dominated the conversation for the next hour, providing the latest updates. As he spoke, the air in the shack grew mustier with tension, while the smell of damp earth and old wood mingled with the faint scent of burning embers outside. The flickering candlelight made Orin's single eye seem to glow. Lydia's arranged marriage and the subsequent events caught Orin off guard, revealing he had known nothing of what happened in the Darian Kingdom.

"I apologize for my ignorance regarding the Wedding of the Torn Rose," Elder Orin said. "We've always lived in isolation, removed from the world's affairs. Yet this pain burns more than lava on bare skin. May Lydia rest in peace while her father seeks vengeance."

"The entire kingdom mourns her," Merdel said. "The princess's life ended too soon. Kaine Khalia's intuition uncovered the Throatians' true motives for the wedding. Without him, the Asche family would have fled back to their island, and we wouldn't have discovered their betrayal for months."

Orin's cane tapped against the wooden floor as he pointed accusingly at Kaine. "This is Kaine? Kaine Khalia?" as if to confirm.

Kaine sank into his chair under Orin's single eye, which seemed to pierce his soul. "How did you guess?" Kaine asked, his voice remaining steady yet trembling. Though he hadn't introduced himself, he sensed the elder was sizing him up.

Orin glared at him as if they had crossed paths before and once been enemies. But Kaine was certain they had never met.

"Years ago, when I visited her Majesty, she spoke of you." He tapped his index finger on the side of his head, as if recalling a distant memory. "A wise man never forgets even the most inconsequential conversation."

Kaine kept his face neutral. Orin's words puzzled him. At no point had Queen Lily von Stonewall met Kaine, and it was likely she had never even heard of him. Orin had mistaken him for someone else.

"Indeed, it is you," Orin said, nodding. He turned to Merdel and directed his single eye toward him. "And I suppose Ether sent you to fetch me for another one of his wars? Doesn't he realize I no longer carry an axe?"

Orin's words didn't faze Merdel, who seemed to have expected resistance. "Far from it," the councilman said with a confident smile. "He instructed you to stay hidden among your volcanoes."

Orin chuckled, nudging Xander and winking at Kira. "Your father points out the obvious, doesn't he? Well, he's not welcome here in my lands. Not that he'd bother making the trip here. But the two of you can visit anytime you'd like. I shall not punish children for the inadequacies of their father."

"Go on now, the three of you," Merdel urged suddenly. "I have more to discuss with Orin."

Smoke and black haze seared Kaine's nostrils as he led Xander and Kira outside. The other shacks were eerie, their windows covered with sheets or cloth to block anyone from looking inside. Those who lived there either did not wish to be seen—or had abandoned the place entirely.

"Do you know where your chicken farmer friend lives?" Kaine asked the children, hoping to discover more about the oddities of Gale Village.

Kira's eyes lit up with excitement. "Finnegan was the one who lent us the chairs."

"Would you like to talk with him?" Kaine suggested, his voice filled with curiosity. "We have nothing else to do until Merdel and Elder Orin finish their business."

"It's fine," Xander said hesitantly. "We aren't close, but he'll help if needed. We don't need to visit him."

"That's fine," Kaine said. "What would you like to do? We could practice sparring again if you'd like."

Kira gestured toward the east. "Let's check out the volcanoes!" she exclaimed.

She led them to the peak of a hill, where the sight of the volcanoes left Kaine in awe. Their bright lights cast an ethereal glow over the grassy field, yet there was something magical about them.

He murmured, "I've never seen such a dark and solemn but beautiful scene."

"You can't admire them from Last Hope," Kira informed him. "Only from Gale Village can you get a good view of everything."

For about half an hour, the three of them sat on the ground, taking in the lonesome surrounding scenery. Then Merdel arrived, looking flustered, as if he'd been hurrying to find them.

"I thought I would have found you here," he said, out of breath. "Come with me, Kaine—we have more to discuss."

Looking at the prince and princess, Kaine asked, "What about these two?"

"They'll be safe as long as they stay here and don't leave the village," Merdel replied, though his voice was still concerned. "Gale Village's people are reclusive, yet I feel they'll protect them. After all, their mother once lived here too."

Though reluctant about leaving the children alone, Kaine followed Merdel back to the shacks. "What's happening?" he asked when they were out of earshot.

"I rarely want to ask favors," Merdel said, "but I need to ask one of you, Kaine. Orin has a letter King Ether received from Queen Lily von Stonewall before her death. My mission involved retrieving the letter and returning it unread, but it's clear I can't persuade Orin to give it to me, no matter how hard I try to negotiate. Convincing him is like talking to a rock. Can you steal it for me tomorrow? It's somewhere in his shack."

Kaine's pulse quickened at the request. "That seems extreme," he responded. "Is their feud so intense that Orin would cling to a personal letter out of spite?"

"You've seen how the elder speaks," Merdel said. "His exact words were to tell the king to grow some balls and retrieve it himself if he cares so much."

"I was correct about him being a petty man," Kaine replied. "The letter belongs to Ether by right. Orin has no claim to the late queen's belongings because of a dispute."

"So will you do it?"

"I'll try," Kaine promised after a moment's hesitation. "There's something unrelated I wanted to ask you. The God Stones glowed when we first approached Orin's shack. Could it have been a warning of danger?"

"They lit up?" Merdel asked, clearly surprised.

"Yes, I'm sure of it."

"Only if Kira touches the stones could it trigger that outcome, but they've been around your neck all along, right?"

"Yes, I've never seen it happen before."

"Let me see them," Merdel said.

Cautiously, Kaine pulled the pouch from his shirt and poured the four God Stones into the councilman's open palm. Merdel examined them, searching for signs of anything unordinary. Finally, he returned them to Kaine's hand, but they remained dormant.

"It must have been a trick of the light," Merdel suggested. "Perhaps it was a reflection from the volcano's lava or another natural phenomenon. They can glow if activated, but not randomly. Their behavior is consistent; the king used this fact to test Lydia, Xander, and Kira when they were younger. Only Kira and Lydia could make them glow."

"That makes sense," Kaine said. "Perhaps the journey made me more tired than I realized."

Merdel smiled reassuringly, saying, "It's okay to feel nervous holding them. They are quite powerful, after all—for those who can wield their strength, at least. For ordinary men like us, they are only jewels."

"Are we sure we should trust Orin not to dig them up again after we leave?"

"He doesn't know we're keeping them and has no idea what we're planning to do," Merdel said. "As far as he is aware, the stones are still hidden in Last Hope."

"Okay, fine. It's just that I'm not sure I trust him."

Merdel let out an unrestrained laugh. "Likewise, the distrust runs both ways. I noticed him staring at you earlier, studying your face as though he'd seen it on a wanted poster somewhere."

"Perhaps he wonders why the king chose a man with just one good arm to guard his children," Kaine muttered, as he pointed to his sling.

"Let him distrust you all he likes," Merdel smirked. "But if he underestimates you as well, that works even better in our favor. It means he won't suspect our plan to steal the letter."

FINNEGAN'S SHACK OFFERED REFUGE, ITS MILDEW AND BURNT GRASS scent a minor nuisance for the roof they needed. The humid night clung to their bedsheets, leaving Kaine to wonder how long the lingering residue would remain on his skin. While the others slept, Kira's sudden shriek jolted him awake.

He fumbled White Oath from between the bed and wall, flinging the sheath across the room as he glided into an offensive stance. His eyes already adjusted to the darkness, he saw Kira standing by the window, her hand over her mouth, staring at the village beyond. Merdel sat up in his bed, defenseless.

"Stand back!" Kaine snapped, positioning himself between Kira and the unknown threat lurking outside.

"Look!" Kira exclaimed, her voice radiating excitement instead of fear. She pointed toward the village, where glowing orbs rose into the night sky.

The tension on his face softened as he watched the display unfold. Fireflies floated upward, their gentle luminescence illuminating the evening. The sight was breathtaking, yet it did little to ease the shock that had overwhelmed him.

"You shouldn't scream like that unless it's an emergency," Kaine scolded Kira, lowering his sword as the last fireflies disappeared into the night.

"Sorry, Kaine—I just forgot about the tribute," said Kira.

"The what?"

Merdel sat up in his bed and explained, "It's a local tradition. Instead of releasing paper lanterns similar to how most Asuras do, the people of Gale Village capture and release fireflies. This symbolizes the fragile boundary between life and death, urging everyone to seek Asura's light."

Kaine scoffed, "As beautiful as it is, the middle of the night should be for rest. If no one sees anyone outside, even though every household supposedly takes part in the event, then we should sleep through it."

Yet, as Kaine spoke, his anxiety remained. The villagers' secrecy and isolation were unlike anything he'd ever encountered. He wondered about their motivations and culture, pondering whether their reclusiveness stemmed from fear of diseases or a cult-like devotion to Elder Orin himself.

The next morning, Kaine and the others followed the elder for almost an hour as they hiked toward the graveyard as planned. Adding to the oddities, Orin had left his cane at home and was walking energetically, as if to prove his strength and impress them, despite having no logical reason except to heighten his ego.

When Kaine asked him for hints about the Gale villagers' identities, Orin responded with a practiced answer: "The people here have a closely knit culture that needs to be guarded."

As they neared their destination on the other side of the mountains, Kaine noticed Orin staring at him constantly, which made him uncomfortable. Kaine assumed it was because he was the only one who'd never been to those elevated lands before. Deciding it was best to ignore Orin's awkward glances, Kaine instead focused on keeping pace with Kira.

As they walked, Kaine's thoughts drifted back to the God Stones. During Princess Lydia's time, she had frequently used the Memories Stone in public, including in front of Kaine and others, yet it never glowed. Perhaps the God Stones did not emit light even when activated, or Lydia might have turned her rings inward toward her palm whenever she used them. Kaine realized Merdel was right; the issue lay with his own eyes all along.

The group arrived at a small plateau scattered with several graves overlooking a valley of magma. Carved with rudimentary techniques and varying skill levels, each tombstone differed from the others. They all seemed to be made of a natural glass rock, suggesting the villagers had hauled them to the graveyard. Each stone bore the name of a deceased individual, laboriously inscribed without proper tools.

Orin led them to a semi-oval grave with a broken corner, where he bowed in reverence. He appeared to grow tired as he stepped back and leaned against another tombstone.

"He should have brought his cane—or at least a walking stick," Merdel muttered.

Orin gestured toward the burial site of their late queen, and said, "We're here. Xander, Kira—give yourselves some time to say hello and pay your respects."

The prince and princess knelt at their mother's grave, praying as Kaine and everyone waited nearby. Kira pulled a small paper lantern from her pocket, her trembling fingers unfolding it. From a distance, Kaine couldn't read the details but noticed her penmanship covered most of the lantern. She shaped the wire base into a rectangle and threaded it through the lantern's edge slit. Once stable, she placed it on the ground and lit the flame with a flint and dry grass.

"I'm doing my best for you, Mother," Kira whispered as tears streamed down her face. "The world is so dark, but I'm trying to bring it some light."

She lit the lantern's inner chamber, and it burst into a small ball of flame. She held it close to warm the air inside, hesitating before releasing it. Kaine sensed her fear that the fragile object might crash to the ground, but it rose silently above the princess's face and drifted into the sky.

With a thin smile, Kira stepped away from her mother's grave, content that the lantern would reach its destination high above them. Xander stayed behind, tilting his head toward the tombstone at his feet, frozen in a silent thought or prayer. He pulled a letter from his pocket and used Kira's flint to ignite it. As the paper turned to ash, he stamped out the flames, leaving a smoldering pile on the ground. Gazing up at the sky, his expression remained unreadable.

"Let's go back," Xander finally said, breaking the silence.

Merdel, watching them closely, suggested, "Kaine, you might appreciate a moment with the queen."

"Sure," Kaine said. "If you all want to head down, I can catch up in a few minutes."

Orin, sensing the tension, stepped forward. "I'm certain you appreciate the offer to start early," he said, his voice dripping with sarcasm.

Orin took the lead, guiding Xander, Kira, and Merdel back

towards Gale Village. As they walked, Kaine found himself alone in the graveyard. He counted to sixty to ensure none of the children returned, then removed the small coin purse he wore around his neck. He carefully poured the four God Stones into his hand and examined each one for the last time. He pinched each of the four stones of different colors, searching for any sign of magic. But no matter how hard he squeezed, they remained unresponsive.

He approached Lily von Stonewall's grave and knelt, his heart uncertain of whether what he was doing truly fulfilled his responsibility. He dug a small hole in the ground, deep enough to prevent nature from erasing his work. Solemnly, he placed the God Stones into the hole, one by one. His voice murmured, "This was King Ether's wish. And I'm sorry I couldn't save Lydia... But I swear on your daughter's grave, I won't let anything happen to Xander or Kira."

He prayed that leaving their father's magic with their mother would help him accomplish that. The God Stones were unknown to him, but hiding them in a place where no one would think to look seemed like the best course of action. As Ether had warned and Lydia showed, their power was dangerous if it were to fall into the wrong hands.

He filled the hole with dirt, scattering ashes from Xander's letter as he covered it to conceal his actions. Confident that no trace of his intrusion remained, he stood up and headed back toward the village.

As he caught up to the group, Merdel faltered to the side and crashed sideways into the ground, crying out, "OW! MY LEG! IT'S BROKEN!"

"Merdel!" Kaine shouted, trying to keep his voice realistic. "Are you okay?" He wasn't sure how he would have reacted if Merdel's fall hadn't been a ruse, but what mattered was whether Orin believed the fall to be real.

Orin approached Merdel and examined his lower limb. "It's not broken," he said, pulling up Merdel's pant leg to reveal the injury. "Just a sprain, perhaps?"

"It's badly twisted," Merdel protested, his voice strained with false pain. "I heard a pop and now it hurts. I think I've injured my leg. Asura's ass!"

Kaine smirked at Merdel's sudden outburst, his formal demeanor replaced by a crude exclamation. Kira offered him water from her canteen while Orin continued to examine Merdel's leg.

"We're close to the village," Orin said. "You can hobble the rest of the way on one leg. We'll move slower to make it manageable."

"Easy for you to say!" Merdel snapped back, his eyes wide with a forced fear. "I feel... dizzy. Did I hit my head? Someone carry me—"

Xander let out a chuckle at Merdel's dramatic display, his laughter ringing through the graveyard. "How fragile are you?"

"I'm serious," Merdel groaned, his face squinting with pain.

"I'm too small to lift you," Kira said, her voice filled with genuine concern that made Kaine feel guilty. "But I wish I could."

Kaine pointed to his sling. "And I've only got one good arm," he added.

Merdel looked at Orin with a smile. "Can we really ask the prince to carry me?"

Xander shook his head. "Even if you did," he said, turning to Elder Orin, "I would decline."

Orin sighed. "I carried many wounded warriors in my youth, but the years have taken that ability away."

"So, what should we do about me?" Merdel whimpered, his performance growing more convincing.

Kaine stepped forward and said, "I'll head back to the village to find Finnegan and see if he and others can help. You should rest there while I'm gone."

Orin scoffed. "It's a waste of time," he said dismissively. "Merdel could make it home on one leg, especially since he could lean on someone. But if he insists on acting like a child and being a burden, may he suffer in useless agony until you return."

"I'll be back soon," Kaine said with a playful smile. "Don't die on us while I'm gone."

TWENTY MINUTES AFTER LEAVING THE GROUP BEHIND, KAINE SLIPPED through the open wooden gate into the silent Gale Village. Having no witnesses meant fewer complications. With this advantage, he moved to sneak into Orin's shack and retrieve King Ether's letter.

The elder's home stood isolated at the edge of the village, its solitude hinting at Orin's true nature. Kaine approached stealthily in case anyone was nearby. Pausing at the entrance, he peered through a small, decayed hole in the wood. Seeing no one, he let himself inside and closed the door behind him.

Orin's single-room shack had few places to hide anything, which was to Kaine's benefit. A bed, an armoire, and a few simple furnishings filled the home, nothing out of place. Yet, Kaine knew better than to underestimate the elder. He began his search with the bed, which yielded only a small hand-axe hidden underneath the mattress. The armoire, however, had its own secrets.

Kaine's scrutinizing brown eyes spotted the slightest irregularity on the bottom shelf—an unnatural scratch along its edge. Pressing his fingers into the crevice, he felt the board give way, revealing a secret compartment beneath. Inside, he discovered a small leather bag and a letter beside it. The wax seal was missing, and the envelope's lip hung loose. Kaine hesitated, recalling Ether's instructions to return the note unread. However, the missing emblem bothered him. What secrets that he should not see did the letter contain?

He promised himself that no matter what he read, he would not destroy the letter this time. Clutching it, his eyes devoured the words:

Ether,

I wish I could tell you this in person, but we both know that's not possible for me to be at Serenity Keep. I miss you deeply and regret having to train so far away. There was no other choice, and the woman you met last time is doing her best to care for me.

The Prophecy of Tears and Sacrifice was not as we thought. I am not the savior who will restore balance; instead, my role is far different. I must die. It pains me to admit this, but I'm fading. You know I'm not a goddess, but I've been pretending to be one by using these stones.

Everything comes with a price, and I'm uncertain if I can pay the cost. Using multiple stones is causing irreparable harm to my body and soul. Unless I find a solution, my time is running out—nothing else we've tried might save me.

Despite my wishes, you must take care of Lily Ashthorne if you haven't already married her. This news may not please you, but using the Time Stone revealed she shares my bloodline. If I fall, it might be up to her to fulfill the prophecy. This was a shock to me as well, but history cannot be disputed. You know what this means, though it's for the greater good of all.

Please take five God Stones in this envelope and test if Lily can activate them. If she succeeds, the person who trained me will attempt to train her instead. Perhaps I was never meant to use the God Stones—and perhaps our roles were mistaken all along.

There are too many things I wish I could say but cannot fit on parchment. You showed me strength when you took me in your arms, and for that, I am grateful. It pains me deeply that our circumstances prevented our dreams from coming true.

Zelia

The confusion grew in Kaine's mind. Who was Zelia, and how was she connected to the von Stonewalls? Where was the fifth God Stone?

Before he could think more, a knock interrupted his concentration. "Orin? I thought you went to the graveyard," someone called out.

Kaine froze in place because he realized he had nowhere left to hide.

The door swung open, and the woman who entered revealed why the people of Gale Village had been hiding in their homes. Her weathered face bore a wrinkle for each year she'd lived, but it wasn't her age that caused Kaine to drop the letter and reflexively draw his sword—it was her skin, a fading grayish-purple.

To have such a skin tone meant only one terrible fact—Queen Blanche had often warned him that if such beings should ever capture him, it would be easier to take his own life than subject himself to their cruel whims.

"They'll cut your chest open for fun, just to see what you ate for breakfast," she once said as they drank wine together. "Most of the time, they don't even need a knife—their minds can slice sharper than a blade, and they don't care how loud you scream."

Lucidians were perhaps the most dangerous beings in existence, and now Kaine was alone in a room with one.

10
BIOS AURAS - THE TEMPLE OF WHITE'S WORLD VEIN

Long before Bios traveled with Cereene in the Silent Deserts, the obelisk's World Vein always opened to the same place: a collapsed castle buried in white. When he had first stepped through, he'd found himself in an unknown landscape of frozen wasteland—a bleak, scarred plain where the snow clung to the ruins like ash. The castle itself hovered on a levitating platform, suspended two miles above the flatlands, its remains defying gravity. Despite its magic, the location was desolate, and there was no way to return except by the Teleportation Stone. The obelisk's World Vein and its destination were unlike any others, and Bios couldn't comprehend why.

During his first journey there, after he spent hours exploring every accessible corner of the floating base and assuming the area was deserted, a strange, yet still living, man suddenly startled Bios.

"You're not supposed to be here," the scholarly-appearing man had announced in the Common Tongue, his voice strained with weariness. His long white beard rested on his black and maroon hooded robe, which was embroidered with symbols of the sun and moon. "There is no purpose for you in this place. The time is almost upon us. Turn back before you're destroyed."

The man's tone trembled with fear, suggesting he was either paranoid or telling the truth.

"I have nothing to be afraid of," Bios Auras said. Whatever calamity or destruction that had happened to the castle and its people had occurred centuries ago.

He replied solemnly, "You ought to be frightened in this place, chosen one, even if you can't recall why."

"Chosen one?" Bios replied, tightening his grip on the sword at his side. Why had he referred to him like that? Was his remark meant to be a subtle threat?

"Who are you and where are we?" Bios added.

The man in the maroon robe froze, unnervingly calm, as if the snow had wrapped him in ice. His wrinkled face momentarily bore a puzzled expression before regaining its original solemnity.

"I'm a friend and a guide," he said as he removed his hood, "and now I understand a significant event must have happened if destiny brought you here. Where is Somnius? Did something happen to her? How many God Stones have you gathered?"

The stranger before him appeared oblivious. Who was this mysterious figure cloaked in the robes of the sun and moon? Didn't he know the goddess had betrayed him? Was he another of her allies?

"You didn't answer my question," Bios said accusingly.

The enigmatic elderly one smiled. "When time runs out, everything returns to how it was. You weren't here in the beginning. That's why you must leave now if you intend to complete your mission."

"My mission?"

"The Prophecy of Tears and Sacrifice. You are aware of it, yes?"

"I am. But what are you going on about?" Bios had urged, hoping for more context. "Who are you, and how do you know about any of this?"

"I see. Something must have happened to you, but I shouldn't inquire further, especially if the prophecy brought you here. You left me as steward of this place, and your instructions were clear," the elderly man said. "Return to your world and continue collecting the Tears of Asura. Everything else will fall into order once you've gathered them. If you stay here much longer, you'll fade away, like a flame without a wick."

Despite the confusion surrounding him, Bios sensed the man's truthfulness. His demeanor was unsettling and almost artificial, yet he appeared genuinely concerned, though the source of his restlessness remained obscure.

"What else do you know?"

"I understand only what you revealed to me," the stranger

insisted, "and I can say only what is relevant now. These were your instructions."

"Stop playing games and speak the truth!"

"Enough. I've said no lies. Leave this place now, or it will erase you as well. You're not supposed to be here. You told me."

The elderly man pulled a small vial from his robe pocket and chugged it down. Before Bios could react, the man collapsed, and white foam leaked from his mouth. Now, he was dead, having taken his own life to avoid whatever fate "it" held. His willingness and preparations suggested there was no room or time to argue. The area must truly have been dangerous.

Bios had sighed at losing his one avenue of truth but heeded the warning and used the Teleportation Stone to retreat to the Temple of White. Over the next few weeks, he pondered the strange, shocking encounter. Why had the old man been aware of his goals?

More importantly, he had referred to Bios as "the chosen one". Maybe he would become the new Asura and fulfill the prophecy. However, perhaps Bios Auras acted prematurely and should not have used the Temple of White's World Vein until the prophecy's completion. If this theory were correct, gathering all the God Stones would grant him the power so that he could become a god.

So many questions remained in his mind. Was his new interpretation of the prophecy valid? Where were the castle ruins located?

He speculated about the set of obelisks. From this recent phenomenon, he reasoned they must be some kind of magical artifact or device capable of altering the World Vein's usual behavior.

After days of pondering, he summoned the courage to revisit the ruins, determined to uncover more clues about the challenges he might face in the future. As he approached the site, he envisioned the slippery stones of the ruined Temple of White and the snow drifting from the sky.

Yet, for the first time, his Teleportation Stone failed to create a portal. Bewildered, he tried again to return to the platform, wondering if he had misremembered the ruins' details. Despite his confidence in his recollection, the portal to the snowy ruins wouldn't appear. Why was the God Stone preventing him from coming back? Had the strange man been right about everything being destroyed? Was it all now gone, making it impossible to manifest a passage based on his memory alone?

Testing the Teleportation Stone by creating portals to other locations confirmed his suspicion—he could travel around the world but only in the present moment. Without the Time Stone, he realized, he couldn't access pathways to the future. For now, the obelisks' World Vein seemed to be the only way of traveling forward in time.

He ventured once more into the gap between the obelisks, where the teleportation magic accepted him. As he stepped around the ruins for the second time, he tried to understand what had occurred since his previous visit, but everything appeared unchanged. The only notable fact was that the elderly man's body was gone. Bios searched the area where the man had drunk his poisonous potion and died but found no trace of him. Someone else must have removed his body, yet there were no footprints in the snow. It was as if nobody had been there.

The unexplained event made Bios's neck hairs curl, and his instincts confirmed the urgency of the warning to flee. He returned to the Temple of White. No matter what, the Prophecy of Tears and Sacrifice revealed his purpose—he would use the Tears of Asura to purge the darkness from the world, across all time, now and forever.

Back in the Silent Deserts' Golden Bay, Bios finished telling his story about the World Vein to Cereene. If she could only understand his motives as deeply as she feared his power, the inconvenient moral quarrels between them would fade. Yet he'd revealed what he'd seen only to manipulate her—just as he had done to Prince Thane.

He reminded her, "When I fulfill my destiny, I will erase all sins and darkness. Once I collect the Tears of Asura, I can wash the blood from my hands. No cost is too high if it means ridding the world of all that is wrong."

"Even if you yourself are part of the problem?" Cereene whispered, her scowl showing she was serious. "And I don't believe your story."

"There's no need for you to trust a single word I say," Bios said. "But you were there, too."

"I was?"

"In the future," Bios said. "I once took you there myself."

"I... I don't remember any of that."

"You were unconscious," he explained, "but you were there."

"But why? How?"

He gave her a smug look. "I used you to test your beloved prince, of course. He saved you over his newlywed wife, if that offers you any consolation."

Bios recognized Lydia, King Ether's eldest daughter, as an immediate threat the moment she showed her use of the God Stones. Though he struggled to comprehend why she had wielded their power, he knew one truth: anyone capable of channeling such magic had to be eliminated. The desolate future he envisioned—one of ruin and despair—was likely tied to Lydia or Somnius, the only other living beings besides himself who could activate the stones' abilities.

"You're a coward," Cereene shouted. "You made Thane kill so many people, even those who weren't involved in your plans!"

There was a reason for his orders, but he chose not to reveal it. Bios Auras couldn't kill anyone directly. If he did, the God Stone's magic would temporarily stop working for him. He had experienced losing his powers before, and every time he took a life, his abilities vanished for an unpredictable period—sometimes for minutes, other times for days. To keep his abilities active, it was easier to have another person carry out the killings, though this was inconvenient and less satisfying.

Whenever he wanted to kill someone, the easiest way was to use the Teleportation Stone to create a portal beneath his victim, sending them through to a Loyalty Circle. There, the Throatians would subject them to the Reminder of Suffering rites. Although this method was efficient, it bored him. Using trickery, manipulation, and force was far more engaging to him. Occasionally, he found it even more entertaining than if he'd performed the task himself. As long as the God Stones continued to provide him with magic, then it followed he had done nothing wrong to warrant losing their powers.

"It doesn't matter what you or anyone else believes," Bios Auras said. "They wouldn't have died if fate hadn't meant for them to die."

"You're a monster!" Cereene stepped back, edging toward where the alley opened onto the street. She poised herself to flee, but he sensed her hesitation. "You trade children for slaves, make people kill each other without purpose and—"

"I will become a god," he declared. "Who I am now doesn't matter, as long as I control the future. I can undo all the evil later."

Cereene hesitated, her voice trembling frantically as she turned away. "I can't do this," she said, her words trailing off. "Let me go—"

"Let you go where?" he interrupted. "You can't speak Harsani, and the slavers here would claim you as their own without a second thought. Klein, who bought the infants, showed interest in purchasing you. There are far more dangerous individuals out there than him. Is that really what you want, priestess? Freedom in a land of slavery? You wouldn't survive."

She was shaking, now that her plan had failed. "Then what am I supposed to do?"

He recalled what he had told Grimm about the human soul's lack of immortality. Anger, fear, desperation—all of them, Cereene had felt. He'd let her devise her plans to do what she'd wanted, only to let her fail once the truth became evident. He'd done what physical weapons alone could not, and now, she had no choice but to obey him.

Bios extended his hand. "Stay by my side, Cereene, and you'll have the safety you need. No one, not even I, will harm you."

"I can't trust you," she muttered. "Not even for a moment."

"You understand the truth about Zann-Xia-Czul," Bios said. "Serve me instead, and he can't harm you."

Manipulating her—pushing her away and pulling her back—filled him with satisfaction. She reminded him of Thane, and perhaps that's why she fell into his trap. Cereene and Thane were equally easy to control.

"Okay."

He smiled, moving his outstretched hand closer to hers. "I keep my promises, Elder Cirixaa, no matter how terrifying they may be. Do as I say, and you'll be under my protection."

Her small hand clasped his, and a delicate warmth came with her trembling touch. "Please."

Her wishes were irrelevant—maintaining control over the Throatians was his priority. If Grimm's ambition ever grew too great, Cereene could replace him as a queen. The Throatian army would continue expanding, and by controlling its leadership, Bios would rule everything, no matter who sat at the top.

He brushed back his blond hair. "Though I'm the monster you claim, it's a relief knowing you've agreed to stay with me," he said. "I feared you'd try to escape. The world is a dangerous place."

"I won't run."

He still sensed her fear, even after releasing her hand. His promise offered safety, a better alternative to surviving alone in the Silent Deserts as she'd first intended. Everything had benefited him.

"Now, join me in the next order of business," he said.

"Are we going back to the Temple of White so Grimm can begin his raid?"

"No, somewhere else," Bios said, gathering his thoughts as the magic in his arm pulsed with invisible energy. "Come with me, and you'll understand why Klein the slaver's bedroom is our next destination."

He could recall Klein's bedroom as vividly as he remembered the crimson armor he wore. The memory was sharp, detailed from his frequent visits. Lavish silk curtains hung across tall windows that framed the bed's pillows, while scents from perfumes and oils lingered on the sheets. Several jewels and trinkets lay on a massive mahogany armoire—where, he suspected, the slaver placed his heavy gold and silver snake necklaces every evening.

Bios noted the bulky wooden door's location, the patterns of the stone floor tiles, and even the crack in the wall—evidence of the slaver's hidden rage when he might have hurled something in a sudden outburst. These details had become Bios's invisible map, allowing him to return to Klein's bedroom as often as he wished.

Now, he and Cereene stood still, taking in the rich atmosphere. His gaze shifted to the dresser, where rows of precious jewels captured his attention. If only they were God Stones, he thought, yearning for their divine power.

He ensured there were no servants wandering nearby before opening the bottom drawer. Inside rested the ledger containing his records of decades of transactions. He placed the book on the desk and opened it to a random page from years past. Scanning the numbers, he searched for exchanges with nines and carefully altered them to eights using Klein's quill. He even dared to cross out larger figures, reducing 800s to 600s and authenticating them with Klein's signature—a forgery he had perfected. Bios spent the next several minutes editing the ledger, tallying the total of missing gold until he found the amount satisfactory.

"What are you doing?" Cereene asked.

"I'm raising the price of the infants we sold him," he replied.

"So you're stealing from him?"

"Yes." And it was very unlikely that Klein would discover what he'd done.

Once Bios finished with the ledger, he replaced it inside the drawer and reached underneath the desk, where a loose tile covered a vulnerable hiding spot. Klein, greedy and paranoid, trusted nobody but himself, and kept much of his wealth hidden beneath the floor. Bios took the gold he had deducted from the records, tucking it in a small cloth satchel he had sewn into the pocket beneath his armor.

Klein would never find the missing coins, and even if he did, it would be too difficult, or perhaps impossible, to figure out how much was taken and which transactions were fraudulent. While Klein might possess a second, hidden copy of the ledger that Bios didn't know about, given they were acquaintances at best, it was more plausible that he would suspect disloyalty among his servants. As for Bios—or rather, the wealthy Hellvar—he was so wealthy that he wouldn't even be considered a suspect in the recent thievery.

As Cereene hovered behind him, he squatted to replace the loose tile, having taken everything he wished for the day. He had ample coin to bribe Councilman Ofred at their next meeting and some to keep for himself.

Suddenly, a sharp pain pierced his head as he crashed forward into Klein's desk, followed by a sudden warmth trickling down the back of his neck. His vision blurred, and his consciousness waned.

She'd stabbed him!

"You fool," he muttered as Cereene screamed from behind. Pushing himself up, he faced her as warm red liquid flowed down his nape and onto his shoulders.

Sweat cascaded down Cereene's face as her eyes widened in disbelief, wider than he'd thought possible. Her mouth hung open in a silent, desperate "no," as if something had torn the words away from her. She'd expected to kill him with her cowardly stab, but failed.

He reached behind his head and pulled the blade from where it had penetrated him. Although the weapon was small and perhaps intended only for opening letters, blood covered four inches of its length. Only after licking away the red did Bios recognize the familiar gold and the jewel on the hilt. The dagger had once belonged to Harkbin Asche, Thane's father, before being passed down to the prince. How Cereene had obtained it was irrelevant. He realized why she had joined him on his journey to the Silent Deserts: Cereene hadn't intended to flee from the Throatians; she'd planned to murder him!

"I told you I am Asura's chosen one," he declared as the wound in the back of his head sealed itself. "My destiny protects me even from mortal wounds."

Cereene needed to be taught a lesson. He took a step forward as she ran toward Klein's door. His armor jostled as he intercepted her and shoved her onto Klein's bed in a single swift motion. Cereene screamed as she fell backward onto the sheets. He moved closer and stood over her. His hand rested on his sword, though she didn't realize he could not use it.

"I promised not to harm you," he reminded her. "Don't betray me again."

Bios dropped the knife harmlessly onto her stomach, his blood staining her white robe. Cereene met his eyes, filled with remorse, and he waited for her to breathe three times before taking his first step away from the mattress. From a distance, he extended his hand once more. "This is your last chance to do right by me. Serve me, and you will be safe."

"I'm… I'm sorry," the priestess whispered. "I won't do it again."

"Then there is no harm done," Bios said with a friendly smile. He helped Cereene rise from the bed. "Nobody can kill me. Not you. Not even me. Now we shall return to—"

Suddenly, Klein's bedroom door swung open and thudded against the wall. In the doorway stood a man dressed in tan leather armor, wielding a fire iron. Cereene's screams earlier must have drawn his attention.

"Black sand," Bios muttered.

"Thieves!" Klein's servant hissed, pointing the fire iron at them.

Bios knew being seen in Klein's room was unacceptable. Though the servants had never noticed him before, he'd prepared for this moment. He focused on the far side of the chamber—away from the doorway and the bed—and activated the Teleportation Stone. Cereene gasped as the servant vanished. He reappeared headfirst on cold tiles in another room, the fire iron clattering uselessly out of reach beside him.

The servant cried out in pain as he crashed, and Bios Auras suspected he'd broken his collarbone or shoulder from the impact. However, the injury wasn't severe enough to stop him.

"You've made a fatal mistake," he told Klein's worker. Raising his hand, he focused his mind's eye. A tingling sensation coursed through his body as the servant vanished again, dropping through the floor and landing hard on the other side of the room, back near where he'd entered. On the second drop, the man lost consciousness.

"Is he dead?" Cereene stammered.

"Not yet," Bios said. "Do you still have that knife?"

"I do."

"Then use it. Prove your loyalty to me."

Cereene's rose-colored lips trembled as she hesitated. "I—I can't."

"You've already proven you're willing to kill someone when you stabbed my head," he said. "Now do it for me. We must return to the Temple of White so Grimm may begin his next raid."

"I can't."

"You can," Bios insisted, "and you will."

11
EISENBERN - THE GOLDEN MARE

Eisenbern, Ilya, and Gustav departed the Leila Kingdom the next morning after receiving their mission assignment. The Black Moon Tribe was in Yaenia's central region, a lengthy journey from the southeastern Leila Kingdom. Their first stop, Hillside Reach, was a week's ride away. From there, two and a half days of traveling brought them to Sky Tower Coast, the northern counterpart to Starlight Beach. This would be their last chance to restock before a long trek through the wilderness.

Riding their three horses—Gustav on a large stallion, Ilya on a small pony, and Eisenbern on an average-sized horse—they made an unusual sight to any passerby.

"You're sure we can find the tribe based on rumors?" Ilya asked, riding at Eisenbern's right. The Shadowstone spear rested strapped to her back. Of the three of them, Ilya was the only one skilled enough to wield it. If they encountered brigands, she would be their first line of defense, guarding both her companions and the precious treasure destined for the Black Moon Tribe.

"It should be straightforward," Eisenbern replied. "They live in black mountains similar to the Shadowstone ones we have at home. Their homes are underground, with entryways hidden in small crevices."

"But wouldn't the dragons have found a way to blow fire down there?" Gustav asked.

"The dragons of old couldn't easily melt the stone with their fires," Eisenbern explained. "That's why the Black Moon Tribe made the mountains their shelter. Why they still live there, now that the dragons are gone, remains a mystery. None of the lore Renato summarized to me before we left went over that."

"I can't imagine life without sunlight," Ilya said. "Maybe they've grown so accustomed to living underground that the surface feels uncomfortable to them?"

"That's possible," Eisenbern agreed. "Centuries of hiding in the mountains and hunting dragons must've shaped their culture in unimaginable ways."

"How did they kill all the dragons, anyway?" Ilya asked.

"Renato spoke of a special crossbow," Eisenbern said. "Dragon skin is impenetrable. However, if you can trick a dragon into breathing fire while armed, a quick shot into its mouth may pierce its throat. With luck, you might strike its stomach or a lung."

Gustav clapped his hands and said, "You sound confident enough to take on a dragon by yourself! Why are we on this quest when we could have sent you to deal with the Throatians?"

"Don't flatter me!" Eisenbern chuckled. "I have no skill with such a weapon. I'd probably shoot myself in the foot before the dragon even had a chance to cook me."

Ilya reached behind her and gently touched the spear. "Do you think this could pierce their skin?"

It was a valid question. Shadowstone was invulnerable to anything but itself, and no one had thought to mine it back then. The tip of the weapon would need to be sharp, and the wielder must provide sufficient force.

Eisenbern replied, "It's never been tested, but I'd like to see. Perhaps our hosts will have dragon scales we can use."

"Even if Shadowstone works, these weapons are difficult to forge in large numbers," Gustav said. "We can hardly produce enough for the Purple Guard, let alone an entire army."

"True, but if it proves effective, we could bring in specialized blacksmiths or train new ones," Eisenbern said. "There's enough dark rock north of the kingdom to build an entire city from Shadowstone, but we lack the skill and numbers to handle it."

As they rode on, the western mountains, golden with dried grasses, stretched before them. At their base lay the small township of Hillside Reach, known as a resting place for travelers and a haven for hikers who sought the area's challenging trails. Ilya once described Hillside Reach as "a worn-out old inn surrounded by a bunch of old, worn-out hermit shacks."

Eisenbern agreed. He had visited Hillside Reach a few times en route to Sky Tower Coast to sail to Wargonne. The town had little to offer beyond hiking up lifeless hills. The beer at the pub tasted like horse sweat, and the only menu item, steak, was like wet leather. But it would be nightfall soon, and it was better that they take the opportunity to rest in beds now, while they still could.

"We'll relax here for the night, then press forward toward Sky Tower Coast in the morning," he said to Ilya and Gustav.

"Is the food here as bad as you claim?" Gustav asked, dismounting his horse and walking alongside it toward the Golden Mare.

"You'll be telling me about it when you're done chewing for the hundredth time and it's still too thick to swallow," Eisenbern said.

"Do they seriously serve only meat and alcohol at the inn, or is there something else?" Ilya wondered.

He shrugged as his horse pulled ahead of the others. "Unless you prefer moldy bread with a crunch?"

"Come on," Gustav replied. "It can't be that horrible."

"You don't believe me now, but you'll see later; I'll get a drink, but I won't be eating."

Eisenbern and Ilya dismounted and moved past various shacks weathered by rain, wind, heat, and rot. Some seemed abandoned. Further down the dirt path winding through the town's center stood the Golden Mare, the largest building. Like most others, it was nearing total collapse. The eastern side was lopsided, sinking into the dirt, with a large crack running from roof to ground. Someone had nailed wooden planks haphazardly onto the main wall, covering missing and broken sections. Though the sun shone across the top, Eisenbern spotted rats darting across it and into uncovered holes.

"I'm still not going to eat there. You shouldn't either," he warned Gustav.

Gustav reached down to a large satchel near his left leg and lifted it. "We've got one loaf of bread and likely six or seven potatoes. Take your pick for dinner. You really don't want to dine here, do you?"

"The restaurant only serves steaks, yet there are no cows

around," Eisenbern proclaimed. "I only see rats. Make of it what you will."

Ilya giggled. "There's no way. People would know if they were eating rats."

"Show me a single cow," Eisenbern demanded. "Just one."

They approached the inn, and Eisenbern handed the stable boy a few coins to board their horses at a small building on the other side of the street. Carrying their bags, he, Ilya, and Gustav entered the lobby of the Golden Mare. Several cracked wooden tables were scattered throughout the open space, though ropes and wood blocks patched some chairs with uneven or broken legs. Candlelight struggled to illuminate the foggy glass cups spread about, giving the room a musty, dark feel. To Eisenbern, the venue seemed like a tavern that had already closed for the night.

An elderly man stood behind the bar, idly cleaning the glasses.

"It must be their beef comes from Sky Tower Coast," Gustav ventured.

"They don't have cows there either," Eisenbern said. "Why bother raising cattle when they've got the sea and all the fish they could ever need?"

"Stop panicking with excuses, Eisenbern," Ilya replied. "I'll tell you if the steaks are made of rat meat."

"How?" Gustav said, lowering the heaviest supply bag to the ground.

"My sister and I often munched on them while we were growing up," she explained. "They weren't our first choice, but we had nothing better."

Gustav's brown eyes widened in bewilderment. He'd either forgotten or was unaware of the details of Ilya's origin. "Surely, you're jesting! There's no way you ate rats!"

"It's true," Eisenbern said. "Before Ilya joined the City Guard, she was a Shadow Walker."

Gustav's face stiffened as quickly as it turned red. "You were one of them? Apologies, Lady Ilya. I didn't know."

Shadow Walkers were the orphans of the newly founded Leila Kingdom. They survived by living in the darkest corners of the streets and markets. The war against the Lucidians had claimed many lives, including those of Ilya and her sister's parents. The kingdom, still recovering from the conflict, struggled to support its people, leaving groups of children without homes. Eisenbern knew Ilya would have eaten rats, scraps, or any edible morsel she could find. Growing up in better circumstances, he couldn't fathom the hardships she had endured to survive.

Once Queen Blanche recognized the Shadow Walkers—poor children and young adults on the verge of turning to crime—she used her leadership to give them a chance at changing their fate: integration into the City Guard. Those who thrived adapted well to the structure, found motivation, and dedicated themselves to the kingdom. Ilya was one of them, and she had told Eisenbern how she'd escaped the life of a Shadow Walker. Besides Ophelia, she was perhaps the strongest-willed woman Eisenbern knew. Her rise from the lowest status in their society to become a Purple Guard was an accomplishment unmatched by anyone else.

"We skinned them first and cooked the meat thoroughly," Ilya explained. "It wasn't enjoyable, but it minimized the risk of getting sick. When you're desperate enough, it will do."

"Enough about the rats," Eisenbern said. "Let's get our accommodations."

As they moved deeper into the inn, the old man behind the bar eyed the spear strapped to Ilya's back and their purple armor.

"You all look tired. Care for a drink?" the innkeeper asked as Gustav placed the largest of their luggage on the floor.

"We're looking for lodging," Eisenbern said. "Three beds. We can pay for two rooms if needed. Just for one night."

The innkeeper set down the cloudy glass and leaned closer, murmuring, "Are you all certain you want nothing to drink or eat?"

Something about the Golden Mare's owner felt unsettling, and Eisenbern suspected he was trying to push off spoiled food on them before the end of the day.

"We'll be fine with just the room for now," he replied. "We've had a long journey, and a night of not sleeping on the ground would be good for us."

The innkeeper gave a sigh. "I apologize, sir, but we have no vacancies. We have no available rooms at all, not even a single one, unless you have made reservations."

"This lobby's empty though," Ilya said. "Shouldn't there be more people here?"

"An extensive tour of the mountains is happening soon," he explained. "We're expecting many travelers who'll be staying for several days. They've already reserved their rooms and paid in advance, so I can't have you stay here tonight. Still, let me make up for the trouble." He reached under the countertop, fumbled for a moment, then produced beers for the three of them.

Eisenbern accepted the tarnished tankard, noticing he could see through the drink to the bottom. "This is kind," he said weakly.

"It's on the house," the innkeeper confirmed. "Rest your legs here for a while. My kitchen will open for dinner in an hour."

"Thanks," Gustav grunted as he heaved up the largest bag again. "I'd like a meal once your cook is ready. Say, what kind of food do you have?"

"Steaks," the innkeeper replied, "and lots of them. It's the only meal an adventurer needs besides alcohol and water."

"Just no rooms," Eisenbern muttered, claiming a sturdier set of tables and chairs. "I guess we'll camp outside later tonight."

Ilya took her first sip of the free drink and cringed in disgust. "This beer tastes like two-thirds water," she whispered so the barman wouldn't hear. "You're right; they're taking shortcuts everywhere. Are there any other inns nearby we could try?"

"This is the only place in town, of course," Eisenbern said, shifting in his chair until he was close enough to his friends to avoid being overheard. "It would have been nice to have a bed, but the quality here has declined since my last visit. Who knows what critters would have infested the beds by now? Getting denied a room may have been a blessing in disguise."

Gustav reached into a small bag at his side and pulled out slices of bread. He then took out a little wedge of butter and used his pocket knife to spread it across each slice. "I don't understand why they would need a tour to go over the hills. It's not like one needs to read a book to make the climb."

"You can probably see all of Yaenia from up there," Ilya replied. "I'd love to join the outing sometime too. There's so much more of the world I haven't explored yet."

"You're exploring now," Gustav reminded her.

"On our way home from the mission, maybe we could stay here for a few days," he suggested. "Still, I won't eat the food."

Eisenbern wondered whether Ilya would have become a merchant with Kaine if he'd asked. It tempted him to pry, but he resisted his curiosity. He would wait until they were well under the influence of some quality beers before asking more about her relationship with Sir Khalia. Though the Golden Mare's lobby was empty, its run-down state made the atmosphere feel uncomfortable.

"It's a deal." She raised her beverage to toast but set it down without taking a sip. "I-I think I'm done with this. Gustav?"

The knight bellowed and slapped his knee. "Nice try," he said, "but I'm not finishing your drink tonight."

"Even if you did, you wouldn't need to worry about getting drunk off it." Eisenbern winked at his comrades.

The inn door creaked open, and a lone man stepped inside, cloaked in shadowy fabric with a sword at his side. Surveying the room, he nodded to the three of them before heading toward the bar. Approaching the innkeeper, he removed his hood, revealing dark blond hair and a sun-tanned face. From his bulky, oddly shaped figure, Eisenbern knew the visitor wore armor beneath his cloak.

The innkeeper busied himself wiping down the glasses, as if ignoring the new guest.

"I'm here for a Strega Generatrice," the man declared, bypassing any greeting. He reached into his cloak, revealing a small leather coin purse. His fingers dug through the bag, extracting a handful of bronze pieces. As he held them out, Eisenbern spotted the man's gauntlet, painted crimson.

"A what?" the innkeeper asked.

"A Strega Generatrice," the newest visitor repeated. "You have it, do you not?"

The innkeeper set down the tankard he had been working on. "Apologies, sir," he said. "My hearing isn't what it used to be. I just wanted to make sure I heard you correctly." He gestured for him to sit. "I'll bring it to you shortly." He ignored the coins the man offered.

"Very well." The knight left some coins at the edge of the bar anyway and made his way to where Eisenbern, Ilya, and Gustav were sitting. Choosing a table in the corner, he undid his cloak, revealing his beat-up crimson armor. Every piece had a red shade, like his gauntlets. Without removing his chest plate, he sat on one of the wobbly chairs and surveyed the surrounding room.

Ilya touched Eisenbern's shoulder. "Isn't that the drink you ordered for us at Miner's Kitchen?"

It was the same drink. Strangely, their favorite bar back home had never heard of it, yet here, in the middle of nowhere, the bartender at the Golden Mare knew exactly how to prepare it. The bar's selection of bottles and drinks was sparse, mirroring the restaurant's limited "menu," so the fact that the host could make the drink only deepened Eisenbern's curiosity. Instead of asking the bartender directly, Eisenbern investigated, hoping the customer might reveal more about the odd coincidence.

"I'll find out what I can," Eisenbern replied.

He stood and approached the knight sitting two tables away.

"Hey there," he said to the stranger who'd ordered the Strega Generatrice. "People say good things about that drink. Mind if I join you for a moment?"

The stranger in crimson armor nodded. "I've never ordered this before, but I hear this is the place to get it."

"It's a rare beverage, isn't it? I've tried ordering it elsewhere, but no one seems familiar with it. Where did you first learn of it? I theorize it comes from the University of Starlight Beach because of how complicated the name is to remember. Someone well-educated must have made it up."

The knight in crimson armor eyed him with a puzzled expression, then smiled. "I learned of it in the Leila Kingdom. Have you heard about the rats infesting the alley here?"

"Oh, you're from the Leila Kingdom too?" Eisenbern asked, squinting at the man's odd question. "There are a lot of rats around here, but at least back home, they stay hidden in the sewers, out of sight, as they should be."

The man sat quietly in his chair. Just when Eisenbern thought he wouldn't respond, he said, "So what's next?"

"Next?" Eisenbern replied. Something about the stranger hinted that he was lying, and that he wasn't from the Leila Kingdom; otherwise, he would have been more forthcoming. To test him, Eisenbern chuckled. "Let's share a refreshment. A Strega Generatrice, as befits us Leilans."

"Fine, then," the knight said, rolling his eyes. "Whatever you want."

Eisenbern called out to the innkeeper for another drink. While they waited, Eisenbern glanced around the lobby to ensure no one unexpected was nearby. "So, at the market, do you prefer Frank's or Edna's famous berry pies? My friends over there like Edna's, but I find hers too tart. Frank's are pricier, but the buttery crusts make them worth the extra cost."

"Edna's," the knight said. His answer was incorrect, for neither Edna nor Frank were real—they were names Eisenbern had just invented himself.

Whoever this person was, he was trying to hide his identity.

Could there be a connection between the boy Eisenbern apprehended back home, the Strega Generatrice drink, and the mysterious knight sitting before him? Was the stranger perhaps a member of the People's Army?

"You're not a fan of berries, eh?" Eisenbern asked, leaning in closer to push his bluff further. "Truth be told, your pie preference doesn't matter at all. We've been waiting for you, sir. I'm in the People's Army, just like you."

The knight studied his face, then glanced toward the other end of the bar. The innkeeper was nowhere in sight. "What do you mean by that?"

"The People's Army," Eisenbern repeated in a whisper. "The Strega drink—it's a secret set of instructions, correct?"

"You must be drunk out of your mind," the crimson knight said, shifting in his seat. "I don't have the faintest idea what you're talking about. Go away."

Eisenbern looked over his plain, scowling face. He now appeared genuinely annoyed, though Eisenbern couldn't tell if he was a masterful liar hiding his true feelings or being truthful. Either way, the man's guard was now up. After all, people often concealed their identities while traveling for various reasons. Perhaps the man was fleeing from debt or a crime. Interviewing him further seemed futile. Perhaps Gustav and Ilya had noticed something unusual.

"Sorry to bother you," Eisenbern said, pushing back his chair. "Let's share that glass another time."

The crimson knight remained silent as Eisenbern returned to his companions' table. Approaching Ilya and Gustav, he chose a chair facing away from the knight's table.

"What were you doing?" Ilya asked.

"Did you find something out?" Gustav added.

Eisenbern kept his voice low. "Tell me if you noticed anything first, then I'll say my piece."

Ilya gave a not-so-subtle glance back to the other table before taking the first guess. "The man seems to be a mercenary. He carries only a sword at his hip and whatever fits in his pockets."

"A mercenary traveling southward to join the Darian military, perhaps," Gustav concluded. "There's good money for strong warriors, especially if he can fight."

Eisenbern nodded approvingly. "Did you notice anything else?"

"What more is there?" Ilya asked. "Something about the Strega Generatrice he ordered?"

"You pointed out that he looks capable of fighting; look at that worn armor, full of dents and scratches. If he was wearing it when his metal took the hits, we can assume he's a seasoned warrior. He's traveling alone, but wouldn't a battle-hardened soldier have already volunteered, or been recruited by King von Stonewall for his cause? That part stands out as strange. Mercenaries of his status rarely perform by themselves. It's safer for them to cooperate in small groups, even if they must split the payments. This guy isn't a soldier or a mercenary, yet he ordered a drink nobody had heard of before, except for a suspicious boy whom we long suspected was a People's Army member."

From habit, Gustav almost sipped his beer but caught himself and set down his tankard before it touched his lips. "You might have a valid theory, but you're taking excessive liberties with your assumptions. While we spend hours at the taverns, it's unreasonable to expect us to know every new drink recipe. We're getting older—and out of touch."

"Maybe you two are behind the times!" Ilya protested. "But not me. I haven't aged a single day in years!"

Eisenbern and Gustav chuckled. "Whatever you say," the leader of the Purple Guard replied with a wink. "We know better than to disagree with you, after all." He jabbed Gustav's shoulder.

"So, should we follow this guy when he leaves?" Gustav whispered.

"No," Ilya said. "We have our own mission to focus on for now. Isn't that right, Eisenbern?"

He sighed lightly. "I was too bold, and now the knight is suspicious of me. Though I may regret this, our top priority must remain reaching central Yaenia. We can't let him distract us from our goal. We'll keep watch while we're here, set up camp outside town before nightfall, and continue north in the morning. Sound good?"

"Yes, sir," Gustav replied. "That's the best decision for the long term. The sooner we reach the Black Moon Tribe, the sooner we'll be back where we belong."

"Renato is responsible for managing the People's Army investigation while we're away," Ilya said. "We can tell him what happened later or send a letter once we arrive at Sky Tower Coast."

The innkeeper reappeared, having been downstairs in the basement preparing the drink the knight had ordered. Timidly, the owner of the Golden Mare approached the lone patron, apologized for the delay, and requested that he wait a bit longer, offering a meal at no charge.

Before the free dinner arrived, a massive crowd of young adults entered the establishment and swarmed the remaining empty tables. The inn and its bar were oddly livelier than Eisenbern had expected for such a run-down old building. Luckily for the inn's owner, a handful of servers had shown up amongst the new guests and began delivering everyone plates of steak and the semi-tasteless beer that Eisenbern and his friends had tried earlier.

"No wonder they were out of rooms," Eisenbern said loudly to Ilya and Gustav.

"The problem is, I don't think there are enough of them," Gustav replied.

"What?" Eisenbern could barely hear her above the noise of the crowd.

Gustav continued, "There aren't ample rooms here. Given the inn's size, there are probably no more than fifteen of them. Look around—there are too many people in this place. They won't fit."

He was right—unless more than half the people intended to sleep on the floor, everyone couldn't stay in the beds. They'd likely have to split into groups of ten or twelve people per room. The innkeeper surely wouldn't approve—such overcrowding would overwhelm his accommodations. But perhaps with an extra payment, the owner would have looked past it.

"Perhaps some of them are sleeping outdoors," Ilya suggested. "After all, they're visiting to hike. Maybe this is just dinner?"

"Possibly," Eisenbern said. "If that's the case, we should head out and stake our spot for the tent. Who'd have thought there would be so many people here for a hiking tour?"

Eisenbern glanced back at where the knight in crimson armor had been sitting, but the stranger was gone—either already left or vanished into the crowd. Likely, the sudden influx of travelers had spooked him, prompting him to flee outside. For a moment, Eisenbern acknowledged that he might have overanalyzed the situation. After all, a lone knight resting at a remote bar wasn't unusual or suspicious. Still, he decided to mention what he'd seen to Renato later.

Meanwhile, Gustav stood, heaving the large bag of supplies onto his shoulder. "After we set up camp, could I come back here?"

"Why?" Eisenbern asked. "Did you see something?"

"I'm still curious about the steaks," he admitted. "I didn't get to order yet."

"If you want to waste your coins and get a plate, I am not going to stop you," Eisenbern said. "But first, you'll need to help set up camp."

THEY STEPPED OUTSIDE AND CARRIED THEIR BAGGAGE DOWN THE street toward the edge of town. Carriages lined the road, with more arriving and unloading travelers. The sudden activity startled Eisenbern, but he was relieved that he and his friends would not stay at the Golden Mare. The thought of too much commotion downstairs making sleep difficult was unappealing. Camping outdoors without a bed wouldn't be as comfortable, but it would be quieter and more restful.

They found a small clearing beyond the last shack in the town and set up their tents. After gathering firewood and preparing for the night, Gustav and Ilya returned to the Golden Mare, leaving Eisenbern to tend the campfire. He sat on a rock, watching the flames dance under the pot boiling his single potato. Eisenbern knew his simple potato, especially when smothered in butter, would taste better than the inn's "steak," and need no additional spices.

"Eh, whatever keeps them happy," Eisenbern muttered. The crackling fire and distant chirping of crickets filled the air, and no one else could hear him.

The night's silence invited him to reflect. Months had passed following his last rest. He'd lost count of how many moons had gone by since Queen Blanche had appointed him leader of the Purple Guard. Though Eisenbern had taken his oath sincerely, he'd spoken those words in a time of peace, before the Wedding of the Torn Rose. The evening before the tragedy, Eisenbern had been drinking and enjoying himself with Kaine, declaring his new role easier than expected. Little did he know everything would change. No one could have predicted the Throatians would kill the princess they had just wed. How could someone pledge themselves in marriage and then murder their wife on the same day? Eisenbern still couldn't forget Prince Thane's emotionless face as King Ether von Stonewall slashed the Throatian king's throat in a fit of revenge. The foreigners were evil at their core.

He pondered Ophelia's current condition and wondered if she had enough warm fluids to ease her pain, whether she was resting or at the market, and if the others in the church were taking care of her as they'd promised before Eisenbern left.

Then, a harsh chill ran down Eisenbern's arm as he lowered his head. He wrapped his hand in a shirt to remove the boiling pot from the flames and retrieve his potato. As crickets chirped in the background, he cut it in half and placed a small chunk of butter inside. It wouldn't be the most flavorful meal, but it would suffice. Those who fought in previous wars likely faced worse food and greater worries.

The larger question ate at him: would his actions on this journey matter? This war against the Throatians was unlike wars before, unpredictable and indefinite. He yearned for the next piece of information that could shift the balance of power in favor of the Leila Kingdom. Such knowledge could also restore his sense of purpose. Joining the Purple Guard had brought him prestige, but at what cost? The time and effort required to earn his place had demanded significant dedication, yet that hardly cured his deeper concerns.

Someday, someone would inscribe his name on his tombstone, but what else would remain of him? His comrades and the queen might remember his deeds, but how long would he linger in the minds of others? What legacy would a knight on a diplomatic mission leave behind? His sword may never need to be drawn.

No, Eisenbern wouldn't achieve immortal glory unless he wielded a weapon and accomplished something extraordinary. While Ilya had reminded him of past feats, he sought a greater achievement to be remembered for. The Throatians remained out of reach, and the People's Army had become secondary in the queen's eyes.

He bit into his potato, but the center was still hard. "Asura's ass," he grunted, gnawing around the uncooked parts. After eating everything but the core, he tossed the remains into the fire. Just before dumping the water into the bushes, he reconsidered and added two more potatoes to the pot.

They cooked as Eisenbern sat back down, running his hands along his cheeks contemplatively. He might have been better off patrolling the city streets, catching criminals, and delivering justice, rather than journeying across the country to the town his parents had fled from during the previous war. His mother and father had passed away long ago—he'd been born late in their lives. If they had still been alive, they would have urged him to turn back and stay out of the north. During their time, Lucidians and humans had coexisted in that part of Yaenia, though racial tensions simmered beneath the surface. But as conflicts escalated, his parents left for the newer lands in the southeast, seeking safety. Their desire to avoid becoming collateral damage in the Lucidian Civil War motivated their decision or, worse, facing persecution from the Enclave's troops. Everything had changed; most of what waited ahead was now abandoned. Was it wise of him to go further?

As Gustav and Ilya's chatter grew louder, signaling their approach to camp, Eisenbern estimated they'd been gone only half an hour. He rose from his rock and greeted them.

"You're back already?" he said with his arms outstretched.

"Throw the whole inn into the Black Sands of Tornaa!" Gustav yelled. "Burn down the entire building, the innkeeper, the rickety chairs, and the rats! Burn them down, and don't leave even their ashes behind!"

Behind him, Ilya giggled uncontrollably. "I gave it a taste after him, and it was rat meat all along," she said.

"I told you your bowels would thank you if you didn't eat there!" Eisenbern said.

"If they were in our kingdom, I would arrest everyone—even the rats," Gustav declared.

"Come here, both of you," Eisenbern said with a smile, pointing toward the boiling pot. "I have dinner ready for you. Tell me you didn't finish your so-called steaks."

"Not a chance," Ilya said, shaking his head. "Only Gustav ordered it, and I wasn't about to take more than a bite. Believe me, I've had more rats in my younger days than anyone should ever eat."

Gustav stripped off his armor and sat on a rock close by that matched the size of Eisenbern's. "You're far more resilient than I, Lady Ilya," he said. "I owe you a beer at the next bar we find."

"I don't need your pity," Ilya replied with a forgiving smile. "My sister and I did what we needed to survive back then. No matter what sauces you add or what you cook it with, at the end of the day, it's still just a rat—not an emblem of honor. But I accept your offer for a drink."

"And so, what's everyone's lesson for today?" Eisenbern bellowed, his grin further illuminated by the campfire's glow.

"Don't eat cheap steaks at a run-down old inn that should have collapsed years ago," Gustav guessed.

"The answer is to listen to Eisenbern," Ilya snickered. "He warned you several times not to eat here. Speaking of which, remember the crowds of people we saw earlier? They're all gone now."

"Gone?" Eisenbern exclaimed. "Gone up the hill this late in the day?"

"Well, yes," Ilya said. "When Gustav and I returned to the Golden Mare, it was empty—just as it had been earlier when we first arrived. The people had also deserted the town. The hikers hadn't set up tents, and the carriages they came in were still there."

"That's strange," he commented. "Is there another restaurant here we don't know about?"

"When I asked the innkeeper where everyone had gone, he seemed suspicious," Gustav added. "I ordered my steak, and he appeared fine, but when I inquired about the hikers, he got all quiet and claimed they had already left for their tour."

"Who starts a hike at dusk?" Eisenbern said. "That doesn't seem wise."

"Nor is it plausible," Gustav continued. "Organizing hundreds of people to finish their meals and then go up the hills in less than an hour seems too efficient to be true. I don't think they went up the mountain; they must have gone somewhere else."

"They didn't come this way," Eisenbern said. "So, if they left town, they probably headed off south."

"But why south?" Ilya asked. "Are we even sure they came from the north? I can't imagine many people from the Sky Tower Coast who hike."

"Unless they aren't here for that," Eisenbern suggested. "Maybe the innkeeper lied, or someone gave him the wrong information. But if the knight we saw was from the People's Army, then—"

"Jarret," Gustav said. "You're overthinking it. They were likely hikers; most were no older than twenty-five. The thrill of hiking at night could be a popular activity we don't know about. Rat meat aside, there has been nothing out of the ordinary since we arrived. You want to catch the People's Army and won't stop until you make progress, but I doubt the people at the inn are involved in any protests. It's more logical to assume they're in the cities, not this run-down small town."

"I agree with Eisenbern's thoughts," Ilya said. "It might be worth checking if they're truly hikers. If they are, then they aren't members of the People's Army. If they aren't, they could be protesters heading to or from Last Hope."

"You're paranoid about them too?" Gustav questioned, face palming. "You've got to be kidding me."

"What caught my attention is where the crowd has gone," Ilya said. "We know they aren't at the inn and didn't pass our camp at the northern edge of town. So, the people either abandoned their carriages to continue south or headed up the hill."

"And which one of those is more likely?" Gustav pressed.

"Ilya, will you run up there and check?" Eisenbern said. "If they're up there, we can rest easier tonight."

With the Shadowstone spear strapped across her back, Ilya broke into a jog toward the main street. There, they'd spotted a dirt trail leading to the base of the nearest mountain. Eisenbern and Gustav stayed behind, watching for stragglers or signs of the departing crowd. The town seemed abandoned as dusk approached.

Gustav passed the time away singing an ominous song about a girl locked in a high castle who broke down the walls with a hammer only to be crushed by the weight of her own destruction. Eisenbern found the lyrics depressing, but Gustav had an oddly charming voice as he sang.

Just as the sky grew dark, Ilya returned, reporting she'd seen no one on the mountain or at the inn. The search trail had grown cold.

"This is so strange," Ilya commented, "and frustrating. Why did the crowd come here, and where did they go after?"

"We should send a letter to Renato as soon as we arrive at Sky Tower Coast," Eisenbern declared. "He may have deeper insight into who they were or what they were doing. Even if those we encountered weren't part of the People's Army, what happened there was too unusual to ignore."

"This whole town rubs me the wrong way," Gustav said, "and I'm not sure I can eat a steak again."

12
BIOS AURAS - THE PEOPLE'S ARMY

Bios sat alone at the Golden Mare, as Councilman Ofred had instructed, sipping his Strega Generatrice—a drink unfamiliar to him. His eyes darted around the dim bar, scanning every detail. Nearby, the only other patrons were a group of knights whose armor reflected purple under the flickering candlelight. Though engrossed in their own conversation, their eyes wandered, lingering on Bios as if they sensed his greater power.

The knights were likely members of the Leila Kingdom's Purple Guard, and Bios suspected their presence here was no coincidence —they were searching for or waiting for something, or perhaps someone. Earlier, the man who'd approached him had suggested they might be looking for the People's Army, and the possibility troubled Bios. Were the Leilans about to uncover the secret meeting arranged by Ofred?

The bartender, likely Ofred's point of contact with the People's Army, was the key. The councilman had emphasized ordering a Strega Generatrice, which suggested the drink held significance. However, neither Bios nor the Purple Knights knew where to search next or how to use that information.

The taller of the knights turned, and his eyes met Bios's. Time seemed to freeze between them. Suspicion flickered in the knight's eyes before he masked it with a look of indifference and refocused on his companions.

Bios scowled into his drink. The Purple Knights needed to leave before he could make his next move or the bartender could act. Teleporting the Leilans away might make them disappear, but the risks were too high, especially if their presence was a test of his intentions. He aspired to join the People's Army but wasn't one of them yet. The Leilan Knights' arrival seemed too convenient to be a coincidence.

He was prepared to out-wait them. So he waited, keeping one eye on the knights and the other on the bar's entrance. He ordered a second beverage and then a third, shifting his gaze between his observers and the doorway. Everything about the Golden Mare so far seemed odd, and he also sensed a World Vein, but no one else around him appeared to notice it.

After finishing his third drink, the door of the Golden Mare swung open more frequently, letting in more patrons whose laughter and voices filled the room with a low, buzzing energy. The formerly quiet bar was now alive with noise, providing unexpected but welcome cover. For Bios, the sudden influx of newcomers obscured the Purple Knights, allowing him to approach the bartender and wait for his turn to order.

"Another Strega Generatrice," he said smoothly.

The bartender leaned in closer, his voice hidden underneath the crowd's laughter and banter. "The Purple Knights have finally left," he murmured. "Wait ten minutes, then follow the others downstairs."

Bios nodded and returned to his table, drink in hand. His mind counted the time as he watched a mix of young and middle-aged patrons shuffle one by one toward the stairway at the back of the bar, which led down into the basement.

After more waiting, Bios rose from his seat, noticing that those who had entered the cellar hadn't returned. He approached the door and stepped down into a cooler air that smelled slightly of wet dirt and old rags. At the bottom of the stairs, he found himself in a dim corridor surrounded by shelves overcrowded with barrels and crates. The space was eerily quiet; most of those who had gone down seemed to have disappeared into a hidden passage. The World Vein that he'd sensed earlier might indeed be buried beneath the Golden Mare.

A scratchy voice called out from behind the shelves, "Your belongings, please."

"And who are you to request them?" Bios snorted in reply.

The bartender appeared, looking haggard, as if he'd been trampled by horses and left without sleep.

"I am the gatekeeper," the man replied with a pride that matched his stature. "If you are to serve the Common People, you must become one of them—unless you already are."

Bios struggled to grasp the man's words. Was a "common person" another word for a peasant in their view?

"Suppose I am already a Common Person," Bios replied. "What items would my brethren ask me for?"

"You can keep small belongings," the bartender explained, "but valuable things like jewelry or coins should go toward our cause. We've all sacrificed for the greater good."

"And my armor and sword?" Bios said. "If I hand them over to you, I won't be able to serve as well as I'd hoped to."

He said, "Keep those if you like, unless your equipment is gold or silver, like Prince Xander's. Everything contributes to the overall benefit."

Bios reached into his pocket and pulled out his coin purse. Unless he had a specific reason, he rarely carried much coin and had almost entirely spent the amount he brought with him today on Strega Generatrice drinks. He could easily teleport to one of his houses in the Silent Deserts where he stashed his reserves, but he wasn't yet convinced to be charitable.

"This is all I have to my name," he lied, handing over the last of his coins. If that was the price to enter, it was well worth the cost. "Now, what lies on the other side of the World Vein you've kept hidden beneath your inn and tavern?"

With twig-like fingers, the bartender accepted the donation. His eyes seemed to age another decade as he spoke. "A recruitment rally, where others similar to you are preparing to find their place within our cause. Over the years, I've seen many come and go—some driven by ambition, the rest simply searching for a sense of belonging. But all of them, in their own way, contribute to the greater good."

THE DAMP BASEMENT OF THE GOLDEN MARE FADED INTO THE blinding light of day, replaced by a massive crowd in an open field of grass. Bios's boots sank into the soft, muddy ground as he steadied himself, his attention falling onto a tall wooden stage at the center of the gathering. The audience had arrived from the World Vein, and more people continued to pour in from various carriages still arriving.

He navigated through the crowd toward the raised platform where three imposing figures stood motionless, cloaked in black robes. They appeared out of place. Each figure wore an owl mask, symbolizing wisdom and focus, but the central person remained apart, wearing a crimson face covering that mirrored Bios's own armor. Its sharp, menacing, dark eyes seemed to scan the onlookers.

Were these three the leaders of the People's Army? He suspected the truth would soon be clear. The one in the center, cloaked in shadows, raised his hands, and the crowd fell silent.

"I am the Hanged Man," he proclaimed, his voice booming over the murmurs. "We gather here today to open our eyes and break the invisible chains that bind us. We welcome anyone who seeks change —those who yearn for a world illuminated by knowledge, not shackled by lies. You have come here of your own free will, and we embrace you, for we sympathize with your struggles and are here to help. King Ether von Stonewall has ruled too long and abused his power! A ruler stained by corruption becomes a tyrant who enslaves the masses. He has betrayed not just the Common People but you as well!"

Bios crossed his arms over his chest, intrigued by the Hanged Man's words. This meeting was a doorway to emotional manipulation. The surrounding murmurs grew into a unified affirmation, as if the speech had ignited a fire within each onlooker.

"The fruits of our labor line the pockets of the elite, while our families toil in obscurity!" The Hanged Man's fist rose, clenched tight. "We are the backbone of this realm—farmers, blacksmiths, maids, servants, and soldiers. We build roads, harvest grain, till the land, and forge steel. We bleed for this kingdom, and our kin have sacrificed much to give us life. Yet, what do we receive? Scraps from the king's table and hollow thanks."

There had always been a dividing line between the poor and the rich. Jealousy, greed, and the desire for equality typically came from those who had less gold than their wealthier neighbors. The man's words were meant to challenge people who avoided confronting uncomfortable truths, yet most would dismiss his message and seek solace in the deceptive promises of the masked figures instead. Nothing the leaders might promise could change the very nature of the world.

Bios felt a small pull of resentment—the surrounding peasants were not just disgruntled workers but pawns in the People's Army's grand design. They were fools and victims of a tongue that could only spew idealistic words.

The onlookers failed to see the truth: not everyone deserved or earned riches or was entitled to anything other than what the world naturally brought them. Few people were born next to a bag of gold —opportunities to create it required wisdom, foresight, passion, and obsession. Without those, inequality was the natural order and a breeding ground for chaos.

Before he could dwell further, a second figure stepped forward, her cloak flowing. She exuded an aura of mystery that silenced the ongoing whispers of the crowd. She revealed her arms, covered with several golden bracelets that sparkled in the light.

"I am known as the Hierophant," she announced, her voice carrying both authority and charisma. The gold paint on her mask matched her jewelry, and the blue eyes behind it seemed to reach out and beckon those who gazed upon her to listen.

"In this world, it is easy to lose oneself in falsehoods," she began, extending her arms toward the crowd. "I know this from my life. My father worked tirelessly for the king, only to have his name erased once he could no longer labor. Too many voices have bombarded you, offering you convenient lies dressed as truths. It is easier to believe those lies and keep your head down, but you are wiser than those who choose the easiest path."

The men and women in the crowd nodded in agreement, and Bios could feel the Hierophant weaving her spell of unity over their hearts and minds.

"Among us, your greater destiny awaits," she pledged, her arms sweeping across the audience as if gathering them into her embrace. "Here, you will join a fraternity where your voice joins others in unity against the world's injustices. As your Hierophant, I shall guide you on this journey to become genuine members of the Common People. Together we must stand united against all forms of inequity."

Her speech bored him, but he would endure it for now. If the People's Army knew about the God Stones, one of these masked figures might hold that knowledge. Bios Auras wondered how long it would take to speak to them and whether they would prove helpful or a hindrance.

"There can be no equality when a corrupt leader and his castle overlook us from behind their walls," she concluded. "The Darian Kingdom belongs to its workers who nurture and sustain it, not the royal family who sow nothing but chaos and unrest."

She retreated into line with the Hanged Man and the third cloaked figure, her message delivered successfully, as the crowd's cheers confirmed. The third person advanced to the platform's center and another silence descended. This owl mask-wearing leader stood taller than the others, a shadow among shadows, likely the leader of the three.

"I am the Cycle of Death," the next speaker announced, their voice a deep rumble that resonated with finality. The mask they wore was stark white, carved to resemble a skull, perhaps a reminder of mortality.

"Change is the only constant in this world," the Cycle of Death began, arms spreading wide. "We cling to the familiar, afraid to let go of what we know. Endings, like the dawn following night, are natural. They make way for new beginnings and opportunities beyond the horizon. Today is your conclusion as much as your beginning."

"Death to the von Stonewalls!" someone in the crowd cried.

"Discard your beliefs from yesterday," the Cycle of Death commanded. "Question and challenge your previous teachings. Reject the corrupt leadership that stifles our kingdom's potential."

Bios remained motionless as the fading sun warmed his armor from overhead. He doubted the people were willing to overthrow their king. Among them, there must have been a royal spy, loyal to Serenity Keep. The meeting felt staged, too orchestrated to be genuine.

"And so," the Hanged Man concluded, his voice cutting through the field like a sickle through wheat, "defy the injustice and oppression of the Darian Kingdom! Embrace the power of endings and new beginnings to forge a future where you stand tall amidst the graveyards of tyranny!"

"For the Common People!" a call rang out from the crowd. The chant spread, echoing across the field. Bios said nothing, watching with growing curiosity. Not everyone was there for the first time;

some were there to make the group of recruits appear larger than it was.

The chants grew louder, proving the persuasive power wielded by the Hanged Man, the Hierophant, and the Cycle of Death. It was fascinating how readily the peasants latched onto vague promises and ideologies. Here rested an opportunity ripe for exploitation—an army of followers seeking guidance and a perfect world. With carefully chosen words and gestures, Bios might someday sway them to his will if he wished. For now, he let them chant and shout, believing they were on the verge of revolution led by a trio of leaders who concealed their faces.

The Hierophant's voice called for order, interrupting his thoughts. "Form a line," she instructed, her tone firm yet nurturing. "Today, you join your brothers and sisters and find your place among our ranks."

The crowd shifted as the Hierophant and her aides moved through them, gently touching each person on the shoulder to divide them into groups. Various banners flapping in the wind marked each group, representing the different sects of the People's Army. The symbols on the banners included a hammer and anvil, an open book, a flower, a sun, a moon, and a cross surrounded by four stars.

After what felt like hours, the Hierophant's gaze finally met his, and her eyes studied him through her mask.

"And your name?"

"I am Hellvar."

"Sir Hellvar, I've been expecting you," she said with a nod. "A mutual friend in Last Hope has spoken highly of your abilities. We have a place within the Equity Guard that is worthy of your skills. Please walk with me to discuss your role."

The assignment and the group's name intrigued Bios, raising his eyebrow in curiosity. He suspected it was a special faction inside the People's Army, one that handled delicate operations requiring moral flexibility. Following her lead, he moved away from the other recruits, ensuring their conversation remained private.

The Hierophant pointed toward the field where the World Vein had teleported him to the rally. "The bartender at the Golden Mare will serve as your assignment provider and contact for the People's Army," she explained. "Your mission is to infiltrate Wargonne and assassinate Councilman Conan. While this undertaking is challenging, preparations to aid you are already underway. We cannot fail this time."

Bios tilted his head, a gesture of pretended curiosity. Assassinating King Ether's Master of Defense and War would have significant consequences for both the Darians and the Throatians. If Bios succeeded, the Throatians would take the blame, not the People's Army. Was their aim to spread chaos and convince the Darians that the Throatians were still hiding in Yaenia?

"Our mutual friend told me about the events in Wargonne the previous time you sent assassins there," Bios reminded her. "They are all dead. I wonder why you're asking for Conan's removal, since most of the People's Army's protests occur in Last Hope. Is Wargonne a threat, or are you sending a message to the king?"

"Though you are part of the Equity Guard, you are not privy to our inner workings," the Cycle of Death said as he approached. "The People's Army operates by compartmentalizing information among its members to minimize risks of betrayal or accidental disclosure. Remember, other Common People may collaborate with you in secret, supporting your efforts as you assist theirs."

For now, he would comply, but he still wondered why Conan needed to be assassinated. Perhaps the Hanged Man intended to eliminate King Ether's council members one by one until only those under the People's Army's influence remained. Without his advisors, King Ether would lose organization and control of his kingdom.

"We must destroy the crown's corruption," Bios declared, confident they would approve. "I understand it now."

"And yet," the Hierophant pressed on, "there's more you desire for yourself. Speak freely, for you are among allies here."

His eyes met hers as he presented himself as someone prone to imagining conspiracies. "Information," Bios said. "I want to know the truth about what happened during the Wedding of the Torn Rose—and every detail about a particular item involved."

He needed to be direct about what he wanted, yet still vague. If the People's Army didn't have knowledge of the God Stones, then there was no point in his staying and listening to their overly long political speeches.

The Hierophant said, "We are already familiar with everything that can be known about it, but I am unaware of your interests or intentions."

"Princess Lydia's engagement to the Throatian Prince was no secret

—it was a union arranged by King Ether in trade for magic," Bios explained. "That the king bartered his eldest daughter for it suggests the power was genuine. I want to learn what magic he gained and, if there's an artifact, potion, or magical item behind it, claim it for myself."

"It is a fair request, considering what we will ask of you," the Hanged Man said with a nod. "But truths—and such artifacts, if they exist—are earned, not given."

This was the challenge he had expected—the opportunity to assess the depth of knowledge among these passionate individuals. Their reluctance to share what they knew suggested they possessed something significant. The Hanged Man and the Hierophant were equally cautious, and they saw no benefit in revealing their cards until he had proven himself worthy.

"Then consider Councilman Conan dead," Bios promised. "When I complete my mission for you, I expect payment. I want the magical artifact."

The Hierophant exchanged a glance with the Hanged Man. "So, the relic is your goal," she said, her tone leaving no doubt she was the leader of the three masked figures. "We do not possess King Ether's sorcerous items, but know where they are."

"I wouldn't expect you to hand me whatever magic King Ether received," Bios confirmed, carefully avoiding mentioning the God Stones by name, "but if you possess the information, then that will be enough."

"We are familiar with where he keeps them, but to receive that knowledge, you must complete several tasks for us," the Hierophant said.

"Several missions?" Bios replied as he patted the hilt of his sword. "And let me guess—in the end, you'll order me to kill the remaining von Stonewalls."

"The People's Army would not murder the king when it would destabilize the kingdom," the Hanged Man explained.

Bios nodded slowly, understanding his meaning: they had no intention of killing him yet. Instead, they intended to weaken his rule first, through a series of orchestrated events. Like Bios, the People's Army wished to rule from the shadows, and they appeared far more organized and resourceful than he had thought.

"That's enough questions," the Hierophant warned. "Sir Hellvar, you must complete four missions for us. As you succeed in each, you'll receive gold. Upon completing your fourth mission, we'll reveal where King Ether's magical artifact is—the one you mentioned. Do you agree?"

The tasks would involve murdering key figures in the Darian Kingdom. It was a simple job worth the trouble, so long as he gained a lead on where the God Stones waited in the end. "I won't disappoint you."

The Hierophant's eyes narrowed. "Tread quickly, our newest member of the Equity Guard," she said. "We await news of your success—and we will be watching."

13
THANE - THE LOWLAND GRAVES

Thane and his new Lucidian companion, Zeere, journeyed westward from Sky Tower Coast toward the opposite end of the Yaenian continent for several days. The path was empty of other travelers, which put Thane's mind at ease—fewer people meant a lower chance of him being identified as a Throatian. With Zeere's bandaged body and Thane's glowing armor, they were an unforgettable sight to anyone who might pass by. Before reaching a set of dark, hilly mountains, Zeere led them off the path into an expansive marigold swampland shrouded in greenish-yellow fog as far as the eye could see. As they moved through the thickest parts of the dangerous air, they placed the Red Cloud coverings over their faces as Somnius had instructed.

His stomach rumbled as he recalled the memories of sitting with Cereene in her hut, sharing meals together, and he doubted he'd get that chance again. He missed her—her gentle yet resilient nature, her obsession with transcribing ancient texts and books. His greatest wish was for her to be out of harm's way.

"It's been a long time since I've passed through here," Zeere muttered. "The miasma still feels as cursed as before."

The land and trees were rotting, covered by melon-sized mushrooms, while the air reeked of sulfur and ash. Even without Zeere's explanation, Thane sensed something wrong in the environment. Behind them, the occasional slosh of water hinted at bubbles rising from deep below the surface.

"The Enclave will never reveal the truth about what happened here that day," Zeere continued. "The official story of the ground collapsing is a lie. Did you know one of their drugged-up mages destroyed everything you see here? It was an experimental accident that cost them their entire army."

"Regardless of the version of events somebody believes, it doesn't change the fact that this place is deteriorating," Thane concluded. The explosion must have engulfed miles of the surrounding area.

"There were too many bodies to recover," Zeere continued. "Only a handful of soldiers made it back to the Enclave, and only because they arrived late to the battlefield. By the time they reached this place, everyone—two entire armies—were already dead. There was no more war to fight."

"I can't even contemplate what that must have been like," Thane said. In Loyalty Circles, death came one at a time. The idea of whole battalions dying in an instant was unimaginable to him.

"The Lowland Graves is the proper name for this place," Zeere went on. "Thousands of Lucidians died here, including many of my friends. The land changed forever that day. It even smells like death."

"I can't believe I never knew about this history," Thane said. "Zann-Xia-Czul restricted our knowledge of the world beyond our island."

The squishy, unstable ground made building roads or pathways impossible. Setting up a campsite might be impossible unless Zeere already had ideas. The damp foliage and moisture engulfing the trees would make starting a fire difficult. Standing still for too long made Thane's boots sink into the soft ground.

"It's understandable you wouldn't know," Zeere replied. "The Enclave forbids those who know the truth from speaking of it. The Enclave approves only one explanation. That's the reason I never returned home after the war ended."

Thane sensed there was more to Zeere's story than he revealed. Why had the Enclave allowed him to leave?

Thane said, "Sky Tower Coast has beautiful scenery, but that can't be the only reason you decided to live there."

As the Lucidian trudged forward, letting his head sink downward, the croaking of frogs echoed from a nearby pool of yellow water.

"I worked as a mortician during the war and faked my death to escape," Zeere said, avoiding directly answering the question. "The Enclave executes Lucidians who flee our homeland, as leaving is illegal. Sky Tower Coast is the farthest east I could venture on my own."

"I appreciate you bringing me so close to your old home," Thane replied, turning his head toward the south. "Traveling there must be risky. Is the Enclave still looking for you?"

"They've likely kept the belief that I'm dead," Zeere replied. "As for why I'm helping you, it's simple: as I told you, I am a Null Mage. Nothing would please me more than to learn magic and fight back against my corrupt state."

Now it was clear what Zeere had meant back when he referred to them as "enemies of the common narrative." A mage without magic had no more chance of overthrowing his wicked empire than Thane had of defeating the evil dragon that ruled his island. They both needed more power than they currently had.

"Even if you could learn something from the Whisperers, would it be enough?" Thane asked. "I suspect the Enclave has thousands of people with abilities far more powerful than mind speech."

"What I wish for is nearly futile," Zeere grunted. "But it would make me a more valuable person. I've been a coward for too long, Feiir. Too many of us were afraid to stand up against our own government, choosing to maintain internal peace within the Enclave instead. But that was a mistake. At the end of the war, several Lucidians like me fled rather than returning home, and they're hiding somewhere in Yaenia—I'm certain of it. One day, I hope we'll be able to strike back against the Enclave and rid it of corruption."

"Your words have been my thoughts all along," Thane said. "Freeing my island from Zann-Xia-Czul's rule will also require an army."

"Killing the dragon is undoubtedly a noble goal, but what about afterward?" Zeere replied thoughtfully as they continued slogging through the swamp. "Will your people understand why you did it? In my world, everyone leans politically to one side or another—it's a struggle for power and nobody wants to change their beliefs. They refuse to see nuance."

"Some who fought against the Darians were willing to abandon our old ways," Thane said, stepping carefully around a patch of mud. "They cheered me on, vowing to declare me their new king once we returned to my homeland. But upon returning to White Boar's Landing, Grimm Kathaar killed them all."

"How many will support you later?" Zeere asked skeptically. "How many will turn against you? You must have an idea."

"I hope that once Zann-Xia-Czul falls," Thane said, "people will realize humans can slay false gods. Only then might they listen to me."

"We might wish for it," Zeere shrugged, "but individuals dislike change. They'll deny what happens right in front of their eyes if it makes them feel safer."

"Then what's your point?" Thane snapped.

"How can you prove it was their god all along?" The Lucidian turned toward the east, where Sky Tower Coast waited in the distance. "I don't trust in any gods, but for those who do, this contradicts everything people believe a god should be—a giant winged lizard roosting atop a mountain? They wouldn't accept the truth about what they'd been worshipping. They'd call it a test of faith."

The Lucidian was striving to be realistic, but he didn't comprehend losing one's faith. Thane, who had spent his life praying at the Temple of White, knew reality more clearly—what it meant to discover an alternative truth at the cost of unraveling a lie.

"I came to understand my god," Thane said firmly, "despite not seeing it at first. It took time and reflection, but I eventually realized my beliefs were completely wrong. It involved more than a single event and a moment."

He didn't tell Zeere about the significance of the necklace Cereene had made for him as a gift. Even though Thane no longer believed Zann-Xia-Czul was a god, he still wore the silver amulet. Engraved on its cerulean jewel was the Throatian character for his former god's name. If it weren't his only connection to Cereene, he would have thrown it away long ago.

"Perhaps one day, we'll witness if others see the truth alongside you," Zeere said. "In my experience, people would rather believe lies than seek harsher truths."

Their boots squished in the mud as they moved through the marsh, navigating the golden sludge piles scattered among the trees. The sunlight reflecting off the water occasionally forced Thane to shield his eyes by raising his arm.

For a place so desolate and filled with death, there was an overwhelming amount of light. Thane might have found it beautiful if he didn't know of the thousands of bodies buried beneath the soil. The grim truth of what had occurred here brought back memories of his childhood—collecting buckets of blood from the basements of Loyalty Circles.

A splash moved through the tall grass and reeds ahead, though the dense vegetation obscured his view. His fingers instinctively reached for his sword at his waist.

"Do you hear that?" Thane whispered to Zeere, who paused mid-step, shield in one hand and saber drawn in the other.

"If any animals are here, they could serve as food. Cooking them thoroughly would eliminate much of the risk."

Thane wrinkled his nose at the idea—the game would taste no better than the rotting trees around them. Still, it was worth a try. Without protest, he agreed to Zeere's plan to split up and flank the creature hiding in the grass.

By the sound of it, they might have come across a rabbit or a small fawn bathing nearby. If they moved quickly and quietly, they could catch up to it. With a long journey ahead, securing an easy meal now would eliminate the need to search for food later during their trek through the desolate swamp.

The sloshing continued, but Thane couldn't see clearly through the tall nearby brush. Squinting, he crept forward, gripping his sword. Before they could reach the source of the noise, a young man suddenly charged out from behind the brush and reeds. His pale skin looked like salmon flesh covered in bloody cuts, scabs, and scars.

"FEIIR! RUN!"

But Thane couldn't react—an invisible force lifted him off his feet and into the air, leaving him helpless. His legs dangled uselessly as he floated above the ground. He tried to wriggle free, but it was pointless. Whatever held onto him refused to let go, and he couldn't resist something that wasn't physically there.

Although the man carried no weapons, his thrusting of his raw, peeling wrists sent Thane backward as though bucked off a galloping horse. The man was certainly a Lucidian, but he looked more like a reanimated corpse.

Thane plunged toward the ground, splashing into the mud, only to jerk back into the air. Meanwhile, the Lucidian eyed him with desperation, glancing to the trees. Something hurled Thane toward the thickest trunk and he slammed into it with enough force to crack the bark against his armor. He was then pulled away again.

From the ground and out of breath, Thane watched as Zeere sprinted toward the other Lucidian, his saber ready to strike. The telekinetic mage shifted focus from Thane and raised his hand, palm outstretched, in Zeere's direction.

Thane's head throbbed from the collision with the tree. While the rest of his body might have been unharmed, the world around him was spinning. If only he had been wearing his helmet…

"Zeere…" Thane muttered, his voice muffled by blood. The force of the impact—or perhaps the grip—had left him too weak to stand.

As his new ally floated in stasis above, the scarred Lucidian stepped closer to him, examining the bandages.

"Get out of here, Feiir," Zeere pleaded. "He's a Savager Mage."

Whatever a Savager Mage was, it hissed at him, interpreting his words as an insult. He pummeled Zeere to the ground, pinning him on his rear. The saber wrenched itself from his grip, hovered in the air, spun, and drove itself into Zeere's chest.

Zeere's back arched as the blade pulled free and blood spewed. After releasing Zeere's saber, the Savager Mage knelt beside him, bowing his head as if in prayer.

Thane pushed his hands against the sludge, struggling to regain his bearings. Though still dizzy, the Savage Mage had released him, now focused on Zeere. Thane attempted to stand, his legs trembling, but he grabbed his sword from a patch of grass and pressed on. Meanwhile, the strange being leaned closer, pressing its dry lips to Zeere's neck… and moaned.

As the man bit into and drank blood from Zeere's wound, Thane ran in their direction. Before he reached them, the Savager raised his arm toward the sky and flames erupted from his palm. The fire shot twenty feet into the air, leaving Thane confused about the Lucidian's target. The Savager Mage continued moaning almost erotically, only looking up as Thane charged.

With blood trickling from his lips, the enemy harnessed his magic and shoved the prince back toward the tree again. Thane slammed into the trunk, dropping his sword as he struggled to recover his footing.

A sudden hiss broke out, and white haze engulfed the Lucidians ahead. Coughing ensued, forcing Thane to stumble back into the mud. Before the Savager Mage could react, the prince snatched his sword, sprinted forward again, and blindly thrust it into the thick white cloud. The blade connected and a scream rang through the trees as fire erupted in all directions, merging with the smoke to form an explosive orange blaze. Thane shielded his face as the Savager Mage tumbled backward, splashing into the golden waters nearby.

Despite his legs' instability from earlier, Thane's adrenaline kept him poised. As the flames faded, he ran to the monster and completed his kill with four more thrusts. Satisfied that the salmon-skinned mage was truly dead, Thane sheathed his blade and rushed to Zeere, hoping that he had survived.

"Not good," Zeere confessed with a choked breath. Red covered his neck, and Thane couldn't figure out how to cover the wounds on his neck and chest to stop more blood loss. The sword wound was too wide.

Thane's heart pounded as he struggled to come up with words to say. "Our attacker's dead now," was all he could say. Zeere was alive for now but bleeding out, and they had no medical supplies.

"Sludge," Zeere wheezed. Thane wasn't sure if the suggestion would save the Lucidian's life or if it was just a desperate idea. He dipped his hand into the mud and scooped out a handful of what looked like golden feces.

"Even if this works, your wounds will probably become infected," Thane warned.

"One problem...at a time... Look—the Savager was searching for something close by. Find it."

"Stop talking, or you'll bleed out faster," Thane snapped. He applied the mud to Zeere's neck and chest, then spread it. Grabbing Zeere by the arms, he dragged him to a nearby dead tree. Using some of Zeere's existing bandages, Thane reinforced the dressings before sitting on one of the giant roots to wait. The sun might bake the mud and seal the wounds by nightfall, but the real question was whether Zeere would survive that long.

The sludge patching his injuries likely contained poisonous spores, rotting fungi, or another manner of toxin that Thane couldn't even begin to imagine. Even if the wounds sealed, the full extent of what would linger beneath his skin remained unknown.

Returning east to seek a healer was too risky, especially since the guards were searching for them, and Sky Tower Coast was days away. They were already halfway to the Lucidian Enclave, but that wasn't an option either. With no other choices, they had to manage Zeere's wounds themselves, but Thane struggled to think clearly.

He was still in shock from what the Savager Mage had done. Zeere had identified the Lucidian's type at first sight, but he had never mentioned that Lucidians could possess multiple powers. It remained unclear why it had been foraging around the Lowland Graves. Thane had countless questions, but Zeere could no longer speak or provide answers at the moment.

Thane let his friend rest as he walked over to the brush where they'd first heard the crazed man sloshing behind the wall of grass. There, he found a small body of liquid, no more golden or wider than the surrounding pools. Thane squatted in the sludge, where the Lucidian's knees had left imprints, and reached into the water where the Savager had been searching. The pool was lukewarm, with the consistency of old bone broth. A layer of wheat-colored moss covered its surface, making it murky beneath. What had the man hoped to find within the muck?

His fingers reached deeper into the murky water, submerging his entire arm until they brushed against the squishy sludge at the bottom. He felt around, searching for what the Savager Mage had sought. His fingernail grazed something solid, prompting him to reach further.

He gripped the object, its surface smooth yet weighed down by decades of grime. With his arm still submerged, he squatted and used his entire body weight to pull it free. The effort sent him sprawling backward, landing with a thud on his rear. Examining his find, he saw a somewhat intact ribcage. Lucidian skeletons looked identical to human ones. The sight of the gore surprised him but didn't inspire fear; years among the Loyalty Circles had dulled his sensitivity to such sights. The recently deceased disturbed him far more than those long dead. Whoever had met their end there must have perished ages ago, but why would a blood-drinking mage take interest in what was essentially a graveyard?

No, the Lucidian wasn't after the body itself, but perhaps the former warrior had carried something important before they'd died. Thane reached again into the pool, resolved to uncover more secrets.

Five minutes later, he emerged with a handful of trinkets: a tarnished copper ring, a reddish-purple amethyst, some coins, the tip of an arrow, and a small broken chain that might have been part of a bracelet. None seemed significant, but he carried them over to where Zeere lay resting against a tree. Hovering his hand slightly above Zeere's nostrils, he checked for breath—and detected shallow, uneven breathing. He was still alive, just sleeping.

Next, Thane approached the Savager Mage's body and searched the pockets of his sludge-colored tunic, but found nothing—no knife, no supplies. Even with magic at their disposal, no one would travel without provisions. The Lucidian must have had a nearby camp with more answers.

Starting from the bones and trinkets, Thane walked in a spiral pattern to search in all directions among the swampland trees. His method ensured he'd eventually locate where the Savager had come from—Thane only hoped it wasn't too far away. He didn't want to leave Zeere alone for very long.

As dusk turned to nightfall, the foliage took on a darker shade of gold. Thane spotted what he was seeking: a small tent nestled against a tree trunk, beside a satchel and an axe. Though modest, the campsite confirmed his suspicions that the Savager Mage had been traveling alone.

He searched the bag and found a canteen of water—thankfully not blood, as he'd expected—along with dried peaches and a notebook. Every page, front and back, displayed the phrase "FORGIVE ME, ASURA", which appeared to be either a therapeutic exercise or an obsessive prayer. Thane kept the canteen and axe and discarded the tent, satchel, and remaining contents into a nearby sludge pool.

Having circled the area, returning to Zeere was just a short walk. The Lucidian remained at the tree's base, his flame-colored eyes standing out vividly against his pale gray skin.

"I found his camp; he was traveling alone," Thane announced, squatting beside him and offering the canteen of water. "I retrieved his supplies as well. Nothing else on him seemed important, so I hid the rest of his belongings."

"It's smart to cover your tracks," Zeere grumbled. "Feiir, you need to run—don't wait for me. The Enclave hunts Savager Mages, and their Sentinel Mages and guardians won't be far behind."

"There's not enough light for anyone to find us out here," Thane countered. "We should rest tonight and decide in the morning whether to continue forward or move backward. You need a proper healer." He wouldn't abandon his only ally.

"New Ginstown is located south. Going there is closer than the Sky Tower."

"And that's our best option, you think?" Thane had never heard of it, but if it wasn't in the Enclave, it must belong to the Darian Kingdom. Even if nobody recognized him in New Ginstown, Zeere's presence would still be too noticeable, and stopping so close to the Enclave posed a risk. At least no one was looking for them there.

The Lucidian sat up against the tree. "If we meet anyone, give them gold to keep quiet about us," he instructed. He broke out into a coughing spree, ending with a coarse spit of blood.

"Here," Thane said, holding out the deep purple-red gemstone he'd found to Zeere. "I believe this may be why the Savager Mage came here—it must be worth a lot of gold."

Thane wished it were a Tear of Asura, but the amethyst was larger and more irregular than the stones Bios Auras had thought were genuine. Still, at about the size of a plum, it would sell for a good price.

"Where did you find that?" Zeere exclaimed.

"Near a dead body in the swamp's water. This rock is from the war, I think. Maybe it's a family heirloom."

Zeere straightened himself against the tree. "Let me examine it, please."

He handed him the purple-red stone, and Zeere nearly dropped it as his fingers closed around it. "I've always suspected…"

"Save your voice," Thane warned. "You need to let your neck heal first." But Zeere seemed too excited by the discovery to listen.

"It's too important," the Null Mage said. "I need to explain it to you in case I don't survive." He took a deep gulp from the canteen. "When Lucidians use magic, it feels amazing, like accomplishing something great. The sensation is so intense that some become addicted, despite it draining their blood. The craving for more becomes all-consuming, overshadowing everything else in their lives."

"So that's why he—"

"An addiction to casting magic, even without purpose, driven solely by pleasure, renders them no less primal than a common animal," Zeere said. "The Enclave usually executes them, but occasionally, some escape and become killers."

"They are powerful murderers," Thane said, "and terrifying. That one had more than a single ability."

Zeere paused as he recalled the fight. "I've never seen it before—a cross between a Scarlet Mage and an Enforcer. That's why I want you to dissect the Savager Mage. I need to understand what we're dealing with."

"What? Why would we do that?"

Zeere left little opportunity for him to argue. "I've heard every

Lucidian possesses two hearts—one much like a human heart, while the second converts magic from blood. Magic use might have resulted in the processed blood, making the stone you found. Tell me, how many hearts did the Savager Mage have inside him?"

His bizarre request brought to mind the strange conversations Thane had long ago with the Elders, during the time his father conducted sacrifices at Zann-Xia-Czul's command. Blood was the essence of magic, and even dragons needed to use it for their abilities. The mystery of how one could harness another's blood was likely what drove Zeere's current desire to uncover its secrets.

"I understand your curiosity," Thane said. "If you solve this, you'll learn how it works."

"Yes, that's the goal," Zeere responded. "The Enclave goes to great lengths to keep ordinary people unaware of the details of our internal anatomy. They even remove the dead before the funeral can happen. Will you help?"

Without Zeere, Thane's mission for Somnius could have ended either at Sky Tower Coast or during his encounter with the Savager Mage. Though he owed him a debt of gratitude, Thane found himself equally curious about the request, despite its gruesome nature.

"As long as you rest for now," he said, "then I'll search his body."

"Then we've reached a suitable arrangement."

THANE GRIMACED AS HE EXAMINED THE SAVAGER MAGE'S CORPSE, knowing the gruesome sights and smells were necessary to find answers. Two more amethyst stones clung to the man's ribcage, encased in a crusty white substance. With a firm tug, Thane pried the jewels free and hurried back to the tree where his companion rested and waited.

Upon seeing the stones, Zeere wheezed, "You found two of them," he said. "One from each power, perhaps? But no extra hearts."

"They match the one we found among the war remains," Thane replied grimly, placing the crystals beside him on a clump of mud. The similarity between the two here and the single one they'd discovered earlier was troubling. Why had two crystals formed inside this Savager Mage instead of one? Were they the result of separate abilities—or something else entirely?

"The implications are endless," Zeere breathed after a series of dreadful coughs. "This is a clue involving a larger mystery!"

As night fell over the swamp, Zeere lay down to rest his injured throat. Thane kept watch from a nearby log, his mind reeling with questions. Were more Savager Mages lurking in the darkness around their small camp? If another Savager Mage appeared while they remained vulnerable there, they would be in deep trouble.

Thane's experience was with human combat, but facing an enemy like the Savager Mage, who wielded magical powers, was a terrifying awakening to just how dangerous the world outside his motherland could be. He needed to adapt his fighting tactics urgently to survive future battles against magic users.

He couldn't help thinking about the broader world. What if the Lucidians entered the war between the Throatians and Darians? To which side would they be more likely to offer an alliance? How did the Enclave react upon learning of Princess Lydia's murder at her wedding? What if Grimm Kathaar sent a message to the Lucidians, urging them to join forces?

His eyes drooped and his head bobbed as he stared into the swamp's eerie gloom. He dozed off for a moment or more, then snapped awake again when footsteps squished through nearby sludge.

Morning had arrived, and several people were approaching…

THE MORNING SUNSHINE PENETRATED THANE'S EYES, AND HE immediately understood why. His sword, which had been at his side, now dangled barely out of reach, blazing reflected rays into his face. Just as Zeere had feared, there stood a Lucidian Enforcer Mage who'd been tracking the Savager.

Thane glanced over at Zeere, who was leaning against a tree trunk. Before he could evaluate his friend's condition, a stern voice cut through the pungent air.

"Don't move! If you do, I'll rip every bone from your body!"

A gray-skinned man emerged from the underbrush, hiding his eyes under a wide-brimmed straw hat. His brown suit blended with the terrain and a massive scythe hung across his back. The weapon would have been terrifying had Thane not already seen the warrior's telekinetic abilities.

"We have nothing valuable with us," Thane tried, but his wavering voice revealed his fear.

"Quiet!" the Enforcer Mage warned, his face frozen as if listening for something. Then, he pressed two fingers to his lips and let out a sharp whistle.

Another Lucidian came from the foliage, her skin as dark as deep ocean water. "She didn't tell you it's not him?"

"The trail goes cold if it doesn't end here," the Enforcer Mage replied.

"I sense nothing from either of them," the second Lucidian said. "This isn't it."

Thane suspected they might have been searching all night. "You must be a Sentinel Mage," he ventured. "The one you seek is already dead."

"Impossible!" the Enforcer Mage exclaimed, still levitating Thane's sword. "A mere pair of humans couldn't possibly accomplish such a feat!"

"It wasn't an easy fight," Thane confessed grimly. "My friend paid a heavy price for our victory. Could you spare some supplies for him?"

The Sentinel Mage scoffed. "How dare you! We ought to gut them now, but she's ordered us not to yet. They might have seen something."

Cooperation was his best option, as he was aware of his own limitations against the Enforcer Mage's formidable magic and did not know the Sentinel Mage's abilities.

"I can show you the Savager's body," Thane offered, hoping to negotiate a deal. "We'll help you but request your assistance. We just need to tend to my companion's wounds, and then we'll be on our way."

Suddenly, an invisible force seized Thane by the throat and lifted him off his feet. His arms flailed as he gasped for air. The world blurred around him as he teetered on the brink of suffocation.

But just as suddenly, the magic faded, causing Thane to crash back onto the muddy ground, giving him a mouthful of foul swamp water. As he struggled to stand, his lips pressed so tightly together they ached from the strain.

"Don't speak unless spoken to, human," the Enforcer Mage

warned coldly, tossing Thane's sword to the dirt. "I have my orders, but even orders can be defied."

Thane nodded in silent surrender. Even a single Enforcer Mage would be far more dangerous than any opponent he had ever faced in combat, let alone the Savager Mage. Even Bios Auras, the crimson knight who seemed impervious to death, might struggle against these formidable Lucidian warriors.

"We're instructed to bring them to Camp One," the Sentinel Mage announced.

"You're taking me for a fool," the Enforcer replied.

"She wants to know what they've encountered in the graves and how they defeated Savager 1836."

The Enforcer sighed heavily. "A waste of time, but if she insists, so be it. We'll go now."

Suddenly, Thane felt a searing pressure on his jawline, like the sharp sting of a bee. When he instinctively slapped at the spot, he realized with growing helplessness that this wasn't an insect—it was the Lucidian's magic holding him in a merciless grip again.

Unable to resist the mages, Thane's eyes closed as the surrounding swamp dissolved into darkness, and he lost consciousness.

14
KAINE - THE FOREIGN PRINCESS

Still in Orin's shack, Kaine's blade trembled as its tip pointed at the Lucidian in front of him. His right hand remained bound in a sling. He knew not to underestimate the purple-skinned creature before him, whose unassuming appearance hid her true magic. She could unleash fireballs or consume the shack in shadows with a single thought. Her power, whatever its nature, was likely too dangerous to wait to learn more.

He poised his right leg, preparing to charge.

"Stop it!" she gasped, raising her hands. "I promise—I mean you no harm!"

Perhaps she was telling the truth, but it could also have been a trick. Kaine perceived her as a harmless elderly woman, but the unusual hue of her violet skin betrayed her true identity as a Lucidian. Their magic was unpredictable, and she might cast a spell at any moment. Maintaining his advantage was crucial.

Despite the wavering of his sword, he kept it directed at her. "Prove it," he demanded.

She maintained both her hands raised without casting any magic. "I was looking for Orin," she said, though she still seemed suspicious. "It's just a coincidence that you happened to be here. I have no weapons, and my power is harmless unless I touch your head."

Her raspy voice strained to portray confidence, and Kaine could sense a shaky fear beneath it. Her advancing age may have weakened her powers, or perhaps her abilities required too long to summon. It wasn't clear if she was bluffing, but she likely would have acted already if she could have.

"Sit down for now," Kaine ordered, gently nudging the tip of White Oath toward the table. Seated, she'd have less chance of surprising him.

She pushed her chair against the wall and asked, "Why did you steal from Elder Orin?"

Kaine's grip tightened on his sword. "I wasn't stealing anything—I was returning it to its rightful owner."

Her eyes flickered toward the letter on the floor. Did she know what it was?

"I understand it now," the woman said. "Digging up the past will disappoint him."

"So, you must be Zelia," Kaine concluded. The God Stones likely reacted to her presence, explaining their intense glow when they first arrived in the village. Zelia might be not only the princess of the Lucidians but also the original owner of the God Stones.

"The princess? No, I'm not her. Zelia died many years ago. My name is Celeste, a Mind Mage."

Kaine sheathed his sword. Celeste was hiding more than she revealed. "I'll trust you now if you tell me what you know about her," he said.

"I accept your offer," Celeste replied, her purple eyes meeting his. "She once came to our village to meet Orin, but soon after, she died unexpectedly."

Orin Axemonger, King Ether, Queen Blanche, and Princess Zelia shared a history, but their connections remained unclear. Celeste's words, combined with Kaine's own discoveries, left him sensing that a crucial detail was just beyond his grasp.

"Did you know Lily von Stonewall?" he tried.

"I did."

"Was she a Lucidian?"

"What? No." Celeste gawked at the apparently ridiculous question. "The Darian queen lived in Gale Village. Besides, she doesn't share our skin color, nor does she possess our powers. She's no different from any other human."

Before Kaine could press further, the door slammed open. Orin stormed in, his face redder than ever. "Thieves and liars, the lot of you!" he bellowed. If he'd had an axe in his hand, he probably would have hurled it at him.

Kaine brought White Oath back to chest level. "The same could be said of you, Orin!"

Merdel, Xander, and Kira entered the room, and the princess let out a startled gasp at the sight of the lilac-colored Lucidian. It was unclear how Orin had reached the small shack first. Kaine assumed Merdel had stopped to talk to the children and prepare them for what they might encounter inside. However, none of them could have expected to find an enemy of their kingdom there.

Orin's scowl added twice as many wrinkles to his forehead. "Celeste," he commanded, "bring me my cane. I need to teach our guests some manners..."

Merdel slid his arm in front of Xander and Kira to shield them from Orin's threat. The Darian Master of Foreign Relations' plan had backfired, and the consequences of his scheming were inevitably unfolding before their eyes.

Kaine reluctantly let Celeste rise from her chair as he kept his eyes fixed on Orin. "Zelia entrusted that letter to you in confidence, but you never passed it on to King Ether," he accused, keeping his words vague to avoid revealing too much to Xander and Kira.

Merdel gave Kaine a puzzled look, unaware that the letter was from Princess Zelia. Possibly, they also kept King Ether in the dark about its true meaning.

Orin leaned on his cane, his grip tightening as he met Kaine's gaze. "Many years have passed," he said steadily, "but I still stand by my decision to keep that letter here. Your actions, Kaine Khalia, are another matter."

Kaine resented the elder's judgmental tone. He reminded himself that since they were strangers, Orin's opinion carried little weight. "You have no right to judge me," Kaine retorted. "Especially since you've been harboring a Lucidian."

Merdel stepped forward, his expression solemn. "I asked Sir Khalia to retrieve the letter," he admitted. "But you were wrong to withhold what rightfully belongs to the king."

"The same king who lied to you about why you're really here," Orin spat. He turned to Xander and Kira, whose wide eyes showed they were taking it all in. "We should send the children away; they don't need to hear this."

Kaine agreed, sheathing White Oath. "Xander, Kira, please wait for us at our shack."

Kira nodded and moved towards the door, but the prince didn't budge.

"I think we should stay," the prince said. "One of you is in the wrong here, and I don't like how you're talking about my father."

"We'll remain civil," Merdel promised. He muttered to Orin, "Won't we?"

"Xander," the princess warned. "We should listen to them."

"Why is a Lucidian here?" he demanded. "They were my father's enemies—and yours as well, Orin. Explain why you're keeping them here."

The elder gave him a slight bow. "In time, Your Highness, everything will become clear. In the meantime, I assure you that Celeste won't harm any of you."

"It's still treason regardless," Xander said. "You deserve an immediate beheading."

"Xander!" Kira yelled, stepping away from the doorway. She marched over to her brother and slapped him hard across the face. The prince gasped, and Kira seemed startled by her own force. Time froze for a moment, neither of the siblings making the next move until finally Kira said, "Orin's been like a grandfather to us. Don't say things like that!"

The prince's anger was justified. Orin had kept far too many secrets over the years despite having sworn an oath of loyalty to the Darian crown. Withholding a personal letter from the king, concealing dangerous magic users responsible for countless deaths, and likely stealing a God Stone—all those actions warranted severe punishment. There must have been a greater reason for his decisions.

Still, Kaine intervened, keeping his voice as calm and reassuring as he could muster. "We'll get this sorted out soon, Xander," he said. "For now, let's allow the adults to handle things on their own."

The prince hesitated before reluctantly nodding. "Fine. But once you're done, you must explain yourselves to me. I am the Darian Prince, and my subjects should not be scheming behind my back."

As Xander and Kira left the shack, Kaine turned to Orin. "We need to make this right," he said. "Before it's too late."

Merdel nodded in agreement. "With any luck, we'll have all the secrets out in the open soon."

THE TENSION INSIDE THE SMALL, DIMLY LIT SHACK SHIFTED ONCE Xander and Kira had left and were out of earshot. Inevitably, they would discuss something the elder didn't want the prince and princess to overhear. Orin's temper had cooled, but his watchful eyes turned back to Kaine. "So," he rumbled, "did you peruse the whole letter while you were snooping?"

"I've read everything," Kaine replied, "but I still don't understand every detail. Why did you prevent this message from reaching King Ether? And how does it connect to the God Stones?"

From what Kaine had observed, the king didn't seem inclined to be unfaithful to Lily, but he might have had a prior relationship with Zelia before marrying her. If Ether and Zelia, despite them being fierce enemies in the war, were actually former lovers, that would explain why Orin was the first to suggest that Xander and Kira leave the conversation. Something was amiss, and he seemed to hold the answers.

"It didn't happen like that," Orin said, "and I don't owe you an explanation."

"Elder," Merdel warned, taking a cautious seat next to Celeste after looking her over, "I thought we agreed that our discourse would be civil."

"Notice that I don't have an axe in my hand," Orin said. "Believe me, this is a civil conversation."

Merdel straightened up in his chair. "Kaine," he said, "what exactly did the king's letter to the queen say?"

"King Ether did not write it to Lily, as you thought," Kaine said, swooping up the paper from the ground. "It was from the Lucidian princess Zelia to Ether. Here—read it. It doesn't make much sense."

"Such a message would be from the time of the war, no doubt," Merdel declared as he took the paper. His eyes skimmed the text, and his mouth dropped open in befuddled astonishment. Reaching the bottom of the page, he returned to the top and reread Zelia's words, this time with closer analysis.

"I-I stand corrected," the Master of Foreign Relations said. "My apologies, this is unprecedented. Black Sands, Orin... Were the Darian King and Lucidian princess lovers? What else do you know of this?"

Merdel had likely noticed Zelia's mention of five God Stones, one of which was missing. His deliberate shift to the relationship topic raised Kaine's suspicions—he might have been stalling to process what he'd read or avoiding it for reasons tied to the prophecy referenced in the letter. There was more to discuss with him privately later, but for now, it was better to gather as much information as they could from the elder.

It appeared the document was evidence of a major scandal to the von Stonewall name. Perhaps Orin, bitter about the king, had held the envelope over him out of spite. Perhaps the elder of Gale Village himself wrote the letter. It was even possible King Ether had lied to Kaine and Merdel regarding the details in order to keep his integrity.

"It doesn't matter anymore," Orin said. "Zelia isn't coming back, and I don't owe Ether's servants an explanation for what happened decades ago."

"Elder," Celeste interjected. "The Darian King sent two people here this time, attempting to bring peaceful negotiations. If they return to Last Hope, they could expose us, and Ether won't tolerate knowing people like my kind are here. Tell them what they need to know and ask them to keep our secret from the king. As you know, Zelia is gone—Ether must have discovered the letter's existence and is seeking clues."

Orin snorted. "Peaceful negotiations, huh?" He laughed. "Why did the man who was once my best friend send him here of all places?" He pointed at Kaine. "This one killed my son. Kaine Khalia shouldn't even be here. He undoubtedly sent him to torment me with painful memories and remind me that my son's murderer escaped punishment."

"What?" Kaine exclaimed. Orin's accusation was the wildest deflection he'd ever heard in a conversation.

"My son is dead because of you. Since your arrival, I have had many opportunities to avenge his death. You are fortunate that I have chosen, so far, to contain my anger."

"Kaine," Merdel said, looking up from the table. "Is what he says correct?"

"I don't know what he's talking about!"

It was true Kaine had slain several people, mostly slave traders in the Silent Deserts or Throatian soldiers during the battle to retrieve Lydia's body. Unless Elder Orin's son was involved in either of those groups, he must have been mistaken. Kaine had killed no one else except in one situation years ago, and that wasn't his fault.

"I wasn't aware you had a son," Merdel added.

"Axis Axemonger was his name," Orin said, "and I know for a fact that you murdered him, Kaine—and now I've caught you stealing from me, ruffling through my private things. You—"

"I didn't do it," Kaine said. "Not unless he was a slave master in the Silent Deserts or a Throatian."

Orin's face turned red. "And you've apparently forgotten him, too. How disrespectful. You can't even remember the name of the young boy you killed all those years ago."

"I still don't know what you're talking about!"

Across the table, Celeste's astonishment revealed she was also unaware of Orin's accusations. The elder must have been trying to distract them from the fact that he'd hidden King Ether's letter. If not that, perhaps his age clouded his memory, causing him to mistake Kaine for someone else.

Merdel stood and raised his chest. "Orin, you are making a serious accusation. Do you have proof that Kaine was responsible?"

"Of course. It was the queen who told me."

"The queen? But that alone doesn't prove anything," Merdel said. "Lily von Stonewall can't speak for herself anymore. Do you have any other verifiable evidence? If you don't, I'm afraid I cannot accept your word by itself."

Small beads of sweat began dripping down Kaine's forehead. The incident from so long ago had been an accident, not a murder. Could that boy have been Orin's son? If yes, then there was only one way Orin could have figured out the truth.

When Princess Lydia secretly used the Memories Stone to read into Kaine's past, she witnessed everything he had lived through—both the good and the bad. Despite his history in the Leila Kingdom, she deemed him to have a moral character and vouched for him to her father. Had she shared everything with King Ether—and had King Ether, in turn, revealed it to Orin? Had his buried secret spread beyond its original confines? The incident and the dark memories threatening to resurface—Kaine had repressed them deep for a reason. The past was meant to remain buried, and it had to stay that way.

Kaine tried to calm himself, telling himself that it was unlikely Orin knew the truth. But a nagging doubt remained. What if Orin wasn't bluffing?

"No, not Queen von Stonewall," Orin stated. "It was Queen Blanche who revealed Kaine's involvement in the fate of my son."

"I don't think what you're saying is possible," Merdel said. "At the very least, Queen Blanche must be mistaken. Kaine isn't a common brigand. He's not the type to be a murderer."

"Elder," Celeste replied calmly. "Despite these circumstances, I sense it as well. Kaine is far from cold-blooded. You're absolutely sure that you have all the facts?"

"I...I don't know what you're talking about," Kaine muttered. He already knew it was pointless to lie, but the words had leaked from his lips. What if Orin was right? Did he understand what he was speaking about?

The elder scowled disapprovingly. "Pity. While you were ransacking my home, you looked through the letter that you weren't supposed to read. Did you also unfasten the leather satchel that you tore from my armoire?"

"I didn't do that. I opened only the letter."

"Go on, then," Orin snapped. His knuckles whitened as he gripped his cane. "Open the bag, and you'll remember my son's face."

Reluctantly, Kaine approached the leathery case lying on the floor. Earlier, he had dismissed it as unimportant, but as he opened the flap, memories from ages ago reawakened from the darkest depths of his mind.

The memory itself was blurry, composed of reconstructed pieces and additional details he'd remembered every time he repeated the evening in his mind. The memory resurfaced of the time he was dedicated to the ambition his parents set for him: the Purple Guard. That same night had set him on the path toward leaving the Leila Kingdom and becoming a merchant.

One aspect Kaine had always remembered was the painting he'd recovered for the queen. Inside the satchel, there it was again—rolled up in a scroll, the same as it had been the evening when Orin's son must have died. Kaine didn't need to unravel it all the way to know that's what it was, but he did so anyway, to confirm that the artwork was just as beautiful and unsettling as it had been all that time ago.

Kaine swallowed as he took in the details. The canvas depicted a hand, not quite human, with its seven fingers stretched out against a night sky filled with stars. Each fingertip held a glowing orb, pulsating with magical lights—emerald, ebony, blue, silver, gold, crimson, and white. Small hieroglyphs intertwined around and between the fingers, their meanings open to different interpretations.

The emerald sphere drew his eyes. A man stood amid black dust, his hands clutching his head. Was it despair he felt, or perhaps madness? What were the black dots supposed to symbolize that could have been so painful?

Moving on, he examined the ebony sphere. Another man knelt helpless as a figure with irregular lines like worms stepped onto his back. But what had conquered the first? Was it even meant to be interpreted as something aggressive?

Near the blue sphere were two women. One reached out, her hand resting on the other's head. A transfer of power? Or perhaps sharing her knowledge?

His eyes shifted over to the silver sphere. The sun and moon rotated around it, hinting at a cycle between light and dark. Of the hieroglyphic images he'd seen so far, the sun and moon were the most straightforward in their meanings.

Beside them, a full-grown tree and a sapling occupied the area on the page beside the golden sphere. It must have represented natural growth, but also the bond between the past and future.

The crimson sphere held a man connected to another by lines, symbolizing influence or perhaps connection. It was another aspect of the hieroglyphics he could not even begin to understand.

Finally, his eyes fell upon the white sphere. Another figure walked through an archway into the stars making up the rest of the painting's background.

Though it was a beautiful painting, why was it here? What did it have to do with Zelia's letter and that night so long ago? As for him, why did it have to pull him into that time again? There were several aspects he didn't understand when he was younger, and he understood even less at that instant, after all the years that had gone by.

"Do you remember my son now, Kaine Khalia?"

Although the memory was painful, Orin was right: Kaine had killed Axis Axemonger. He had never known the name of the victim, and it had happened so long ago. The events leading to that moment had seemed unrelated at the time, but now, he could no longer deny the truth. It was best to explain everything, even though it wouldn't change any of it. At the very least, perhaps it would help Orin, Merdel, and Celeste understand.

"It would be dishonorable to completely forget," Kaine admitted, ignoring Merdel's gasp, "and I can tell you why he died."

15
KAINE - THE FIRST SCAR

Back before he'd become a merchant, Kaine Khalia had been far more naive. The wealth from his parents' stallion racing business had placed him among the upper ranks of the Leila Kingdom's City Guard. Despite his youth and lack of combat experience, he had already achieved a prestigious position with significant potential for success. Kaine was blessed with many privileges because of his family's wealth, connections, and the countless people who owed his father their gratitude for past favors.

The kingdom lacked a powerful military, so it relied on the City Guard to protect its people and maintain order. The guard handled brigands, local criminals, and anyone else who disrupted the peace. A promotion to the Purple Guard, however, would offer greater safety. Those elite knights lived a life of luxury within the Queen's castle, indulging in fine wine and counseling her on matters of their kingdom. Their swords, their purple-hued armor, and their sense of superiority—all of it was just for show. Kaine had never heard of them engaging in battle or patrolling the streets where ordinary people dwelled.

The Leila Kingdom had no enemies outside of their border wall; they only had an older brother, the Darian Kingdom, and no Lucidian would dare break the peace in Yaenia again. Kaine felt confident pursuing the highest position he could attain, second only to Queen Blanche—a goal that would also earn his parents' approval. Until that day would come, however, Kaine was just a city guard. However, that night, everything he believed about his future would change.

Kaine idly gripped his empty mug as he waited among the laughter and chatter of guards and trainees. The scent of barley dominated his immediate surroundings, and he couldn't ignore the faint sourness lingering along with it. He noted the guards' unusual preference for drinking diluted beer in large tankards—unlike the stronger ales served at Miner's Kitchen and elsewhere in the city. Though weak for a drink, the brew did the job once he'd had enough. Tapping his foot impatiently, he scanned the room, waiting for the queen's messenger.

He frequently visited the canteen to enjoy the free meals and the calming atmosphere. Lower-ranking guards avoided him due to the Dandelion-ranked band on his arm, knowing he could reprimand them if they became too drunk or rowdy. Closing his eyes, he savored the tranquil setting as cutlery clattered faintly in the background.

Next to him sat Ilya Oleanne, the only lower-ranked guard daring enough to join him at his table. The two were close companions, but around other City Guards, they maintained a neutral demeanor. Kaine outranked her by several levels, and to avoid suspicion, their relationship remained private, leaving no room for questions about whether their imbalance of power allowed him to take advantage of her or her of him.

"So, tonight's the night," Ilya said. "Are you ready?"

"I was born to join them," Kaine replied confidently.

Within the hour, he would meet Queen Blanche alone for the first time. She had invited him to her private chambers for evening tea, instructing him to prepare for a discussion about his future. He suspected his father's influence had peaked, and now she planned to recruit him into her Purple Guard. If true, this oath would chart his destiny—secure and unchangeable—and demand absolute commitment. For hours, he'd rehearsed possible scenarios, reciting answers to the questions she might pose.

"Your confidence shines brighter than the Black Sands of Tornaa burn," Ilya whispered back. Brushing her flame-like hair over her shoulder, she glanced around the canteen. "How much longer do you think you'll serve in the City Guard before joining the Purple Guard in Aeon Eve?"

They kept only five members at a time, and each member held their position for life or until retirement, so Kaine would not replace another guard for some time. He had heard rumors one guard was struggling with a bad knee, which might explain why news of an opening had circulated among City Guard members. If so, Queen Blanche might be searching for a successor to the knight.

"It could happen tomorrow or in a few years," Kaine said. "There's no official word yet, but I'm sure the queen has a plan."

He glanced at his half-eaten eggs and hash browns, now cold. Time had slipped away quickly while he was lost in thought. Ilya, engrossed in her poetry book, didn't mind his thoughtful silence. Their bond thrived on unspoken words.

"My time will come too," she said. "Won't it be nice when we're both living in the castle?"

"Nobody else deserves it more than we do."

He wasn't certain whether Ilya could realistically secure the coveted role, but he genuinely hoped she would succeed, eventually. Ilya, a former Shadow Walker, was a child of the streets. For many like her, joining the City Guard was one of the few ways out of poverty. Throughout her childhood and teenage years, she had committed crimes to survive, with stealing food being the least of her offenses.

Ilya used her choices to escape her circumstances—while most Shadow Walkers remained trapped by choices that could have freed them. Joining the City Guard provided her with stability that would have otherwise been unimaginable. She had no assets or advantages aside from those she'd built on her own. Her determination and positivity—her most admirable traits—were why Kaine took an interest in her.

"The queen rarely receives visitors after sunset, I've heard," Ilya remarked. "How did you get an invitation and for so late at night?"

The most likely explanation was a recommendation from his father's connections. All he needed to do was prove himself worthy — and his role in the Purple Guard would be secured. In the Leila Kingdom, the upper class followed unwritten rules: nothing came for free, not even in a commoner's market.

"I'm not sure of the reason," Kaine said. "I've been working hard on my swordplay and helping others train. There's also been a few delicate escort missions to Sky Tower Coast, protecting diplomats from bandits and other hostile groups." It was the truth, just not the entire truth. There was no need for Ilya to learn his father had been involved, if he even had been.

Ilya concluded, "You've built a reputation that speaks for itself, and you're the top-ranked of knights."

"Don't congratulate me just yet," Kaine said. "Much remains to be done, and I haven't finalized anything."

In reality, becoming a member of the Purple Guard meant far more than only being a knight—it was the highest political rank in the kingdom, only below the queen. His family's influence would double, and he'd no longer need to worry about living up to his parents' expectations.

"I'm sure you'll get it," Ilya replied.

"Thanks for putting your faith in me."

Ilya scanned the bar, searching for the messenger. "Hopefully, your escort will arrive soon," she said. "I must go now—I still have to run a few errands before the day ends."

He gave her a casual nod to conceal their relationship as she stood to leave the canteen. As he continued waiting, he ordered a drink despite his dislike for watered-down beer, and then another. Just as he was about to order a third, the messenger he waited for appeared. She wore a purple tunic with golden trimmings and a matching round hat—the uniform of Aeon Eve's servants.

"Sir Kaine Khalia?" she asked as she approached the table.

"That's me."

She peered down at his empty tankards. "Are you still suitable for meeting the queen?"

"Quite so," Kaine said, leaving behind his finished pints and wiping his mouth with his sleeve. "Lead the way."

The servant led him from the canteen through the Leila Kingdom's city to the palace. The walk lasted only ten minutes, but during that brief period, a sudden rainstorm appeared out of nowhere and showered them both.

Kaine scowled at his soaked uniform. "Perhaps I'm no longer suitable for meeting her after all," he muttered as they entered through the gates.

"Apologies, Sir Khalia," the servant replied as if she had summoned the cold water herself. "If you'd like, you can dry your clothes by our large indoor fireplace, or I can have someone bring you fresh garments right away."

He couldn't predict the clothing they'd offer him—servant rags, or a shirt made of gold—but his formal soldier uniform would best portray his authority and abilities, even if it was drenched.

"On second thought, I prefer not to keep the queen waiting."

"A wise decision, sir. Come—her chambers are this way."

SHE TOOK HIM THROUGH AN EMPTY, DARK THRONE ROOM, WHERE THE servants had already extinguished all the torches for the night. At the rear was another doorway, leading to a hallway lined with paintings. Each painting depicted scenes of nature, but Kaine recognized one location among them: the towering structure of Starlight Beach University, rising above the seaside cliffs.

"Did the queen paint all these?" he asked.

"She collects them," the servant answered. "Upstairs, there's an entire collection filled with rare artwork collected by Her Majesty."

They navigated through a series of corridors until they reached a spiral staircase lined with maroon carpet trimmed in gold along each step. Finally, they ascended to another level, where an art gallery held priceless artworks that seemed far more valuable than the pieces scattered throughout the common areas below.

"Presenting Soldier of Rank Seven Kaine Khalia of the Dandelion Division," announced the servant as she opened the door.

"Send him in," commanded the stern voice belonging to none other than Queen Blanche herself.

He stepped into the queen's chambers, amazed by the indigo fabric that cascaded from ceiling to floor. Tables surrounding him displayed gleaming trinkets and what appeared to be ancient antiques. Bronze bowls of steady flames hung between tall white marble columns, and Kaine marveled at their persistent burn. A lavender scent permeated the air, leading him to believe it came from a grassy field painting. However, he soon noticed an enormous glass lion across the room, its nostrils emitting wisps of incense smoke.

"Welcome, Kaine Khalia," the queen greeted.

She emerged from the vicinity of one of the large white marble pillars, her presence commanding yet elegant. Water from the relentless downpour outside drenched the large balcony behind her and seeped into the room. The queen seemed indifferent to the rain's intrusion.

Kaine dipped to one knee and bowed his head. "My thanks, Your Majesty," he said. "It is a true honor to be here."

"We've met a few times before, if I recall," Blanche continued. Her voice carried a hint of smugness. "At a soldier rally, a lengthy dinner with the nobles, and at the stallion racing courses."

Kaine only recalled the last two events but decided not to correct her, considering it a minor detail. "I'm surprised you remember me."

"How could I forget you?" the queen declared, settling into her seat. "The lonesome Khalia boy, someone called you… It compelled me to wonder why the son of Roderick and Isabel Khalia, known for their charisma, would be so unlike them in every way."

"I am not sure what to make of it," Kaine said, struggling to slide his unexpectedly heavy chair under the table.

"Make of it what you will," Blanche said dismissively. "I've only summarized what I've heard. Hearsay won't taint my opinion of you, but if that's the case, then that's the way it is."

"I do prefer solitude sometimes," Kaine admitted. "Is that a matter of concern?"

"Do you already know the reason for your invitation here?"

"No one told me the exact reason," Kaine said, "but I have my own suspicions."

"The coveted role of the Purple Guard," she answered, speaking for him. "You, along with countless other knights, soldiers, and guards, seek to serve by my side as both my shield and sword—is that not your wish?"

His speculations had been correct—she had invited him to grant him the title and its responsibilities. His parents would be proud that he had achieved this distinction after only one meeting with the queen, especially since he had yet to experience true combat. Kaine was born in Year 432, just under ten years before the outbreak of the First Great War. Like many others during that time, his family had fled the chaos and famine to Southern Yaenia. Children of his age might have gone to war, depending on their circumstances.

He'd grown up in Sky Tower Coast and naively played with swords beside the water for fun, unlike others who'd faced the realities of the war. As an only child, Kaine was unaware of the dangers his parents had protected him from by settling near the sea, where the Lucidians had little interest in conquering. Though he had wanted to fight—fighting seemed the honorable choice—his father had forbidden him from joining the war. Just as Kaine had almost convinced his father to let him go, the conflict abruptly ended. All along, his family had used their wealth and leverage to isolate themselves from the problems of the wider world.

Kaine was seventeen years old when the Leila Kingdom was formed. After his family migrated there, his father, Roderick Khalia, encouraged him to join the City Guard and build influence. Roderick saw the kingdom as a promising opportunity—it was still young and thriving. Joining the Purple Guard, the queen's personal guard, was both an honor and an investment. As the Leila Kingdom grew, so too would his family's power.

"I would gladly serve you for the rest of my life," he exhaled in one breath.

"That's the bare minimum of it—becoming a member of the Purple Guard demands more than serving me; it entails serving our entire kingdom."

"Of course, Your Majesty," Kaine said. "I can do it. My records in the City Guard are flawless."

She sipped her tea and crinkled her nose. "Can you truly move forward? You understand that becoming one of mine practically makes you a king? Are you sure you can handle that weight and responsibility?"

"Absolutely," Kaine replied. The questions appeared almost too easy to him.

"But for someone who prefers solitude, are you able to care enough about others to place their well-being over your own interests?"

"I-I don't understand what you mean." Where was she heading with that statement?

"Being a lone wolf brings a sense of serenity when you're alone, doesn't it?" the queen said. "To meander in your private thoughts and patterns offers an escape from society, but isn't it also somewhat selfish to ignore the rest of the world around you?"

Her words were obscure and difficult to decipher, as if she were trying to confuse him on purpose. He repeated her words in his mind before responding.

"I don't turn my back on society," Kaine said. "Therefore, I wouldn't call it selfish. I would do everything in my power to help everyone if I could."

"But when you sidestep mundane conversations, you miss out on important opportunities to build relationships," the queen went on. "Casual talks at gatherings, such as those your parents often host, act as the foundation for understanding those around you. If you dismiss their stories and perspectives, you cannot truly serve them. Do you understand why you must level with them now, Lone Wolf?"

Her explanations came across as unnecessarily insulting, yet her calm tone softened her words, making her approach seem more advisory than reprimanding. Despite this, she'd made many assumptions about his character, and not all of them were true.

"So perhaps you've analyzed me based on gossip alone after all?" Kaine asked.

"Far from it," the queen said. "People forget that before I became a monarch, I was a soldier. Though no longer in physical condition to fight battles, I know how to add two and two together thanks to my secret visits to see my knights' morale. That's how I've come to understand you. The best way to judge someone's character is by observing them when they are unaware they're being watched."

His patience was running out. If she was so well-attuned to her subjects' traits, why was she dragging him through her decision-making process? Had she not already chosen what she wanted to do with him? Despite his frustration, she held the power to shape his destiny. Cooperation was necessary.

"Your disguise must have been remarkable; none of us realized you were among us," Kaine commented, though he was unsure how she'd pulled it off.

"When nobody is looking for you, it's admittedly easier to hide," Blanche grinned. "Still, that is beside the point. My thoughts are these… I'm not sure whether you're ready to become a Purple Guard yet. I want to see you interacting more with your fellow soldiers and forming bonds. Then, do the same with ordinary Leilan people. It's crucial that you build—"

Her words trailed off and he realized something was very wrong. Instinctively, he seized the bronze teapot, gripping it tightly though its metal burned his palm. He threw it with all his might across the room.

The teapot crashed to the ground, spilling boiling water everywhere, and a man hidden behind one of the marble pillars howled in pain. Kaine stood, reaching for his weapon at his waist, only to realize he hadn't brought his knife.

"What in the Black Sands of Tornaa are you doing?" Blanche yelled. "You just threw that at one of my servants!"

"I'm sorry!" Kaine said. His earlier alcoholic drinks must have impaired his senses. "I just felt that—"

"You felt what? Like raising a storm on your way out?" the queen scowled. He'd be lucky not to be hanged by the time he left the castle.

It had been a reckless mistake. Why had he grabbed the boiling teapot and thrown it on a hunch alone?

"No—I just—something didn't feel right," Kaine stammered. He looked over where he'd thrown the teapot but saw no servant.

Then a dart flew toward them. Kaine shoved the queen out of her chair, and they toppled to the ground, huddling behind it for cover. The dart buried itself in the purple curtains.

"Okay, now I agree with you," Blanche said almost too calmly. Her voice was unexpectedly composed, as if assassins routinely visited her bedchamber. "So, do you have any weapons?"

He had come empty-handed, believing it was forbidden to carry anything sharp into the queen's bedchamber. Still hunched over, Kaine rushed to the curtain and spotted the glint of the assassin's projectile. It was better than nothing.

A thin layer of greenish oil coated the dart's tip—likely a sort of poison. Even without a way to shoot it back, simply pricking the owner's skin would suffice.

"I have one now," Kaine whispered, also grabbing a golden platter lid as a makeshift shield.

He glided through artwork and trinkets, blocking another dart with his lid. He scanned for a better weapon but found nothing more useful than what he was already holding.

Opposite the pillar where he'd started, Kaine spotted his first glimpse of the assassin—a short, slender figure cloaked in black cloth that hid their face. Through narrow slits for eyes and nose, Kaine noticed the attacker was male, likely no older than eighteen.

"Stop right there! You're already caught!" Kaine yelled, hoping to intimidate him into surrendering.

The young assassin had other plans. In a split second, he dashed for the nearby balcony. Kaine desperately threw his salvaged dart at him, but it missed by a long shot as the young assassin disappeared outside into the pouring rain.

"Catch him alive if you can," Queen Blanche commanded firmly. "I want to know who sent him."

Between breaths, Kaine sprinted, muttering, "I will."

OUTSIDE, THE ASSASSIN LEAPED FROM THE BALCONY LEDGE TO THE rooftop below. A dark satchel bounced behind him as he ran. From the uppermost tower, the distance to the rooftop was dangerous. If the attacker could make the jump, so could Kaine. The ledge's smooth stone surface was slippery, but Kaine kept his balance and jumped to the nearest rooftop.

Every shingle crunched as he landed clumsily compared to the boy ahead. The roof's steep slant made movement awkward. Kaine ran, balancing himself by extending his right arm. Three stories above the ground, the assassin headed toward the castle wall.

Rain poured over them as Kaine sprinted forward, jumping rooftop after rooftop. He slipped several times on the clay shingles covering the roofs. After an agonizing minute, Kaine closed in on the assassin and grabbed his shoulder, punching him in the face. His fist snapped back as he dropped the lid. He hoped the queen wouldn't notice as it tumbled off the roof into the dark alley below.

Though it surprised Kaine how little he used his feet, the assassin's facial coverings did not hinder his ability to trade blows. A skilled fighter would have bent their knees more, shifted their stance for an advantage, or thrown a kick, but the assassin did none of these. He seemed more focused on escaping the fight than winning it, or perhaps he was an amateur. Kaine couldn't let him get away—his entire future as a Purple Guard member depended on it.

He slammed his knee into the assassin's chest, knocking him off balance. His foe stumbled toward the roof's edge, nearly falling. As Kaine grabbed the assassin's arm, his opponent twisted free and lunged—not to punch, but to grab. His fingers clawed at Kaine's sleeve, seized the fabric, and yanked hard. Kaine's boots skidded on the wet shingles until he lost his footing and tumbled over the edge. Desperate to stop his fall, Kaine flailed for anything he could grab to save himself. His fingers caught the assassin's satchel strap and pulled.

They both fell. The ground rushed toward his eyes, and seconds stretched into what felt like minutes as Kaine wondered if either of them could survive the impact. His world went black with a squish, thud, and crackling noise, though none of the sounds came from his own body.

Through Asura's blessing, Kaine landed in a hay pile left out in the rain by a farmer or merchant. He hit the cart's wooden bottom, but the crash was as if he'd fallen out of a chair. Rain poured over him as he climbed from the golden straw pile. Just ahead were the assassin's remains. The boy was dead, but Queen Blanche would still want to investigate who'd tried to kill her. Moving the body back to the palace wouldn't go unnoticed, even though the storm had emptied the streets.

"This isn't good," Kaine muttered. Steam gushed from his nostrils and lips as he scanned the area to check whether anyone had seen them fall. He was unsure whether the lack of witnesses was a blessing or a curse. Without someone to vouch for him, anyone finding him and the body would assume he was a murderer. Who would believe his claim that the dead boy was an assassin he'd chased from the queen's bedchamber? The safest course of action was to return the assassin to Queen Blanche discreetly. She would confirm the boy had posed a threat, clearing any doubts about Kaine's intentions.

Kaine clumsily patted the cart's contents, hoping the rope bag held enough to spare him trouble. He dumped the excess ropes onto the hay pile and dragged the empty sack beneath the roof's edge—the exact spot where the assassin had fallen. Averting his gaze, he clutched the cooling body and lifted it into the sack. Despite the bloodstains, he slung the boy's satchel over his shoulder, planning to examine its contents later when no one else was around. The clues about who sent the assassin were likely inside, but he needed to return to the queen before anyone noticed.

Kaine wrapped the sack around the boy's body, then lifted it over his shoulders and walked toward the queen's castle. Moonlight reflected off the rain-drenched cobblestones and Kaine knew the assassin's blood had already washed away. Only the missing sack from the hay cart remained—a single clue to the violence.

He'd been too afraid to trust anyone's perception of him carrying a corpse. With the queen's men and any other bystanders potentially watching, it was safer if no one saw him. It would be easier if he didn't have to explain himself, for on that night, Kaine suspected his luck had already run out.

Two figures emerged from the road's far side after a few minutes. The narrow streets, lined with three-story villas, left Kaine no room to turn. Pressing forward, he pretended the heavy sack was his only burden. He shifted the body's weight, but his hands trembled with anxiety.

As the two individuals drew closer, it became clear they were boys, no older than eleven or twelve. Their battered and patched tunics, gray and worn, marked them as the city's beggars, Shadow

Walkers. Kaine sighed in relief, thankful they appeared harmless. Why hadn't the rain prompted them to seek shelter somewhere?

With his head bowed, he crossed paths with two boys who paid him no mind, absorbed in their own conversation.

"Not even any chicken or meat," one of them muttered to his friend.

"Or alcohol!" the second exclaimed. He inhaled, then spat phlegm. "Privileged bitch. She must've kept that for herself."

Kaine hurried ahead, putting more distance between himself and the two boys. The castle gates were almost within reach. As he strode forward, he spotted a pile of discarded scrambled eggs and hash browns—identical to the meal he'd eaten in the guard's canteen—lying near the path. He had no time to question why the food was there; instead, he scanned the area for observers. Minutes stretched as he moved, but soon he reached the castle gates.

On a clear day, Kaine would have stopped to admire the castle's massive violet stone gate. Carved with intricate flower shapes, it resembled a well-tended hedge. Though delicate in appearance, its sturdy thickness revealed formidable strength—built to withstand an army of battering rams. Likely the queen's design, it combined her warrior instinct with her refined taste for beauty and art.

"State your business," the guard at the main gate blurted, shielding his forehead from the pouring rain. Kaine didn't recognize him, and the guard gave no sign of knowing Kaine. The man who'd admitted him earlier had long since finished his shift and was surely asleep.

"I'm Kaine Khalia," he replied. "I was... in here earlier, but I needed to... fetch something for the queen."

"Khalia, you say?"

"Kaine Khalia."

"You're expected?" He seemed unaware that his queen had narrowly escaped assassination.

Why had Queen Blanche not summoned every guard at her disposal to help find her potential killer? Getting into the castle was important; telling the truth about what had happened would sound too mad for anyone to believe. She hadn't acted, so there must have been a purpose. Kaine decided to remain discreet, whatever the reason.

"Of course," Kaine said, speaking with casual ease. "Why else would I be hauling these overpriced carpets in this awful weather if not for a direct order?"

"It's a shame even Dandelions have to do pointless tasks on a whim."

"It doesn't matter; my pay remains the same regardless," Kaine said, staring beyond at the dry entryway. "So, may I proceed?"

"In due course," the guard replied with a light bow. "May this be the last of the rain you face tonight."

Kaine thanked the man and continued, the assassin's body still strapped to his back. The weight made the return journey to the throne room grueling, but he pressed on. As he approached the oak doors, he realized someone had locked them for the night. The castle hallways were empty, with no guards in sight—an odd sign.

He followed the flickering torches down the cold corridors. The path led nowhere familiar. Everything seemed like a maze. Kaine, who had never received a formal tour, struggled to navigate its halls. Each corridor looked identical to the last until he recognized a portrait of a bearded man and turned left.

Approaching the stairs to the queen's room, he listened for movement but heard only the echo of his footsteps. Taking a deep breath, he knocked on the door, praying everything was okay.

The door creaked open, and the queen, sitting alone in her chair, nodded in approval. "So you had to go all the way. I wanted you to keep him alive, Kaine Khalia, but I understand it's not always possible. Don't worry about that."

She beckoned him inside. The room was in disarray from their earlier struggle, with no guards or staff securing the area or cleaning up.

"Are the Purple Guards searching the city for him?" Kaine asked, lowering his voice as he stepped around the violet rugs. "Perhaps you can tell them to stop now."

"I didn't summon anyone," Blanche said.

"An assassin tried to kill you, Your Majesty. Pardon me for speaking plainly, but everyone should be working to protect you."

"See this?" the queen said, holding out the dart. Kaine hesitated, and Blanche said, "I've already removed the poison. It won't harm you."

Kaine examined the dart to see if it was the same one used earlier. Its bamboo handle was dark green, almost black in certain light. The tip—a small, warped wooden twig—had been cleaned, as Blanche had noted. He had to trust she had identified the poison on it.

"The dart seems generic," Kaine said. "Possibly made by an amateur. Can we identify who did this to you based on this alone?"

"This weapon is for incapacitating rather than killing. It's clear the assassin relied on stealth to get close to me. I suspect I know who the intruder is. Please confirm my suspicion."

Kaine uncovered the body, his heart pounding as he revealed the boy's face. The moment the queen saw it, she collapsed into a nearby chair.

"So it was him…" she said under her breath. Rubbing her temple, she added, "We weren't dealing with an assassin—we were facing a thief."

Kaine re-wrapped him in the bag. "I'm sorry about his condition," he said. "He fell from a three-story rooftop. I didn't mean—"

"I saw my share of dead bodies during the war," Blanche interrupted. "It's not the carnage that shocks me—it's who this is. He is the son of an old friend, and I can't understand why he'd betray me."

Kaine offered her the leather satchel. "He was carrying this bag. Maybe its contents will offer a clue to his motives?"

The queen stared at the worn surface as if recognizing it. "I don't know how any of this happened, but since the boy is dead, salvaging my relationship with his father seems impossible now," she said. Her voice sounded different. Regardless of who he was, she clearly knew him well.

Kaine pulled a handful of darts and a scroll from the satchel as he spoke. "He fell from the roof by accident," he said firmly. "I'd only meant to capture him, not kill him."

"I believe you," Blanche said. "The storm outside is unforgiving. He slipped while you were chasing him across the rooftops, didn't he?"

Everything had happened so fast. Kaine had never intended for the boy to die.

"We both lost our footing," Kaine said. "But I was the lucky one, landing in a hay cart."

"None of this would have happened if he hadn't snuck in here," Blanche said as she rose from her chair and knelt next to him. "Now, what's in this scroll that you recovered?"

The scroll, which Kaine had expected to be a map of the queen's castle or detailed instructions, was simply a piece of artwork. It depicted a large, seven-fingered hand against a dark starry backdrop, surrounded by hieroglyphics and small images. Though abstract, the painting seemed unremarkable to Kaine, but he knew the queen valued it for reasons he couldn't understand.

"It must have been worth a lot of gold for him to sneak into the castle for a single artwork," Kaine commented.

The queen rubbed her fingers on the fabric of her dress before taking the scroll from him and unrolling it. Her trembling hands examined the paper, edge to edge. "I kept this in a drawer in my chamber, not for display. It seems my friend wanted it and had the guts to take it without asking."

"And the painting's condition, is it okay?" Kaine asked. He couldn't see if any rainwater had seeped onto the parchment's surface, and the dark strokes made it hard to tell if it was damaged.

She stood in silence, gazing at the starry night and hieroglyphics, as though the sight of them triggered a flood of painful memories from years ago. "It's fine," she muttered.

"My queen, are you alright?"

Blanche looked up, rolled up the art, and said, "Apologies, Kaine. I'm sorry you had to get mixed up in this."

He gave her a slight bow. "Protecting you is my honor. The city guards are sworn to—"

"I know your oaths," Blanche said, "and I thank you for them. I'm deeply grateful for all you've done for me tonight, especially your discretion in bringing him back. No one else knows what you've brought here, do they?"

The queen's desperate plea hinted at her guilt over her friend's son's death. Even if she offered Kaine a hefty sum for his silence, he would refuse. Exploiting the situation was out of the question for him. Having already played a part in the tragedy, he felt it was best not to involve himself any further. Whatever the queen decided to do next, he would leave it in her hands—unless she specifically requested his help.

"A few people saw me carrying the bag, but no one should suspect it held a body."

"Please, Kaine, keep this incident private between us. It's a personal matter to me. I'll handle the boy's father, but I need everyone else to remain unaware of these events."

"I promise, as one of House Khalia, that I will not reveal any details of tonight's events to anyone," he assured her.

The queen quietly studied him before responding. "I appreciate your sense of honor, Lone Wolf Khalia. A vacancy shall soon arise in my Purple Guard. If you honor your oaths and can strengthen relationships with others as we discussed earlier, I will ask you to fill that position. Your family will be proud."

"My family's reputation is important, but I would only accept such a role to serve my kingdom," Kaine replied. "Nothing less."

"And my expectations are nothing less than what I've told you. Thank you for coming tonight, Kaine Khalia. I have more matters to attend to." She glanced at the boy's lifeless form.

"What will you do with him?" Kaine asked.

"A bird will deliver the news to his father's town, a servant will clean the boy and make him presentable for the journey, and a substantial amount of gold will ensure everyone involved remains silent," the queen explained. "This boy isn't important in the grand scheme of things, except to those who knew him well. I don't want the news of his death to become public. I wish he hadn't died, but—"

"Sometimes, everyone falls," Kaine finished for her, "and some must continue living. That I understand."

"Indeed," the queen said. "Don't dwell on this. The boy shouldn't have stolen from me, especially tonight."

"I'll do my best not to think about it," Kaine said as he stepped toward the door. "I've heard that it's impossible for a warrior to forget their first kill, though this one was an accident."

"Only a dishonorable knight forgets the faces of their defeated foes," the queen warned. "Remember this."

Guided by newfound wisdom, Kaine left the queen's bedroom, his thoughts still swirling from their intense discussion. The poorly illuminated corridor extended before him, offering a safe space where he could briefly lower his guard. He leaned against the wall, closing his eyes and exhaling deeply.

The fall from the roof replayed vividly in his mind like a haunting, never-ending song—the desperate struggle with the boy, the sickening thuds as their bodies hit the ground. Could he have reached and saved him in time, or had they both lost their balance amid the chaos of the fight? The uncertainty ate at him; each possible outcome of that night sank its teeth deeper into him.

He pushed away from the wall and walked down the hallway, his footsteps echoing. Kaine couldn't shake the uneasy feeling in his chest. Fate should have let him capture the boy and put him on trial, not wrap him in a bag and leave him dead on the queen's floor. Stealing from her demanded consequences, but was the result a genuine justice? Destiny was too often cruel in multiple ways.

He stepped out into the night, finding relief in the cool air after the stuffy castle. The rain had slowed to a trickle, leaving the streets slick from the downpour. Kaine made his way home, his mind still processing the night's events.

As Kaine approached his villa, he noticed two cats nibbling on the discarded eggs and hash browns he'd passed earlier. Unlike the boys, who'd complained about the mess, the cats appeared content with their free meal. He watched them for a moment as they purred over their newfound feast.

After his parents had upgraded to a larger villa, they gave Kaine one of their older properties in a prominent area of the Leila Kingdom. Delicate vines with pink flowers cloaked the outer walls of both levels. The rich golden-brown bricks beneath the overgrowth were hard to see, and Kaine hadn't seen the stones since his childhood.

Most city guard members lived in the barracks, but Kaine was among the few who did not. He often stayed at his villa only from late at night until just before dawn, when he had to return for duty. Though the villa was large and multi-leveled, it was nothing more than a grand residence for his bed, the only luxury he ever used.

At the large oak front door, he inserted his key into the polished doorknob, but it turned too easily. He examined the doorframe for scratches and signs of someone tampering with the lock, but everything seemed in order. Perhaps he'd been nervous about his upcoming meeting with the queen and forgotten to lock it behind him earlier that morning, or perhaps Cedric, the head servant of the property, had overlooked it.

He stepped into the entryway, where a painting of the Khalia family hung on the opposite wall. In the painting, young Kaine, around ten years old, posed between his mother and father, who had recently purchased a field that would become their horse racing track. The painting failed to capture the high expectations his parents had for his future. Though Kaine had inherited the villa, he never had the courage to remove the portrait, or even to change any of the other decorations inside. If his mother and father visited and noticed any changes, he feared it might prompt unwelcome questions during their stay.

He took off his boots upon entering and shut the door behind him. Four torches flickered in the dim room, almost spent for the evening, but he was too tired to replace them. Sleep was what he needed most to clear his mind. He moved up the stairs, which forked in two directions at the top, and took the leftward one leading into the master suite.

To his surprise, he found Ilya sitting in his room, a book in her lap. "What are you doing here?" Kaine exclaimed at the unexpected sight. Nobody but Cedric should have had access to his villa.

She fidgeted with the hem of her shirt. "I-I needed someone to talk to. I'm sorry for picking your lock, but you took too long to come home from your meeting, and nobody answered the door."

Kaine sat beside her on the bed, his mind still on the night's earlier events. "What's going on?" he asked, feeling more awake instead of calm.

"I don't even know where to begin," she muttered.

Kaine put an arm around her shoulders, offering whatever comfort he could, despite his own inner turmoil. "I'm ready to hear it."

She inhaled deeply, her words tumbling out in a streaming rush. "There's a secret I've kept for weeks. Kaine, growing up on the streets was harsh. The Shadow Walkers were my family when I had none. For weeks, I've risked everything to bring them meals from the barracks' kitchens. On some nights, a full meal can mean life or death. But it wasn't worth it. I shouldn't have."

Kaine's mind flashed back to the spilled food he'd seen earlier—discarded eggs and hash browns meant for someone else. Stealing from the kitchens could get Ilya removed from the City Guard, or worse.

"So, you stole food to feed the needy? I noticed some on the ground earlier. Did you accidentally drop it?"

Ilya scowled, her frustration clear. "I realized tonight that some people don't deserve my help. The Shadow Walkers, some I've known my whole life, were ungrateful for what I gave them and even threw away the food I'd brought. That must have been what you saw."

Kaine's heart ached for her—for the ramifications of her secret and the pain it had caused. "Fate does not pick and choose who it helps and hinders; it exerts its gravity over anyone, showing no preference or prejudice. Life will collect its payment for their disrespect to you."

Ilya's face twisted in surprise and disbelief, as if she didn't recognize him. "What in the black sand happened to you tonight that's got you so gloomy? Did the queen not let you into the Purple Guard?"

"Gloomy? I'm not gloomy," Kaine protested, but even as he said the words, he knew they were a lie.

"So, she did not offer you the seat?"

Kaine took a moment, searching for the right words amidst his tangled thoughts. "She implied it's mine if I bond with more members of the City Guard. But now, I'm no longer sure that becoming a member of the Purple Guard is who I'm meant to be."

"What? But why?"

Though he trusted Ilya to keep a secret, he didn't want to reveal the full details of what he'd experienced. The thought of Ilya thinking differently of him if she wondered whether he'd purposefully killed the boy was unbearable. It was better to explain everything hypothetically.

"The queen and I discussed the duties and responsibilities," Kaine said carefully. "And I realized I don't want to live with the decisions of whom I may have to execute on behalf of the crown. There's too much room for second-guessing, killing someone who should have lived, or sparing someone who should have died. If I encounter an enemy, they'll be a stranger—I can't be sure if my actions with my blade are right or wrong."

Ilya moved closer, her warmth soft and reassuring. "It takes time to learn how to make those decisions well," she mumbled. "And even then, you cannot achieve perfection. Nobody expects that of you."

"I know that... and I don't want a trail of innocent lives behind me," Kaine said.

Ilya's eyes widened. "And you're going to give up? You're almost there! The queen knows your name and invited you to discuss matters in her bedchamber! Her bedchamber! I'm not recognized by senior officials yet!"

She was right. Kaine would give up everything his family had invested for his future, but it wasn't fair to her. Ilya had no prestige, no family reputation or perks. She possessed great combat and decision-making skills, but being a nameless member of the City Guard weighed her down and made her unknown to those who mattered in deciding who would advance in rank. Why couldn't it have been Ilya who was being considered for the Purple Guard?

"I'm not giving up on this," he told her. "My goals have only changed."

"Being a Purple Guard is more than being a City Guard," Ilya said. "You shouldn't stop. Remember our promise? We're supposed to move forward together."

"You should do your best to become a Purple Guard," Kaine lamented. "You're a better fit to succeed. This has made me realize I'm not meant to be any kind of guard. I don't know what I want to do yet, just that this isn't it."

Kaine realized he could use his own influence to help her. Tomorrow, he would request another meeting at the castle. He'd vouch for Queen Blanche to select Ilya as the next member of the Purple Guard instead of him. Whether it was his birthright or something he'd earned, Ilya had already made it so far on her own. She deserved it and seemed willing to bear the weight of the decisions Kaine didn't want to carry.

"I want to support you," Ilya continued, "but I think you're making a terrible mistake. You should rest and reconsider everything in the morning."

"Maybe," Kaine said, but he had already decided. Ilya would join Queen Blanche, not him.

"It's your destiny to become a leader, Kaine. A hero. We weren't alive during the last war, but I know the Lucidians will return to take their revenge on the Leila and Darian Kingdoms. There's no ambiguity—it's when, not if, they will come."

Even if all the Lucidians were defeated, there would still be other humans who'd oppose or violate the crown's will. It was impossible to predict what the future might hold. He didn't want to argue with her anymore.

"Thank you for believing in me," he said. "But I feel like this evening showed me I can no longer be part of this future. I don't know where to go or what to do, but I know this path isn't meant for me. I need to find my own way now."

16
BIOS AURAS - THE OCEANSONG BLADE

The cart creaked and groaned its way southward, its wooden wheels wobbling unevenly on the rough terrain. In the back sat Bios, his crimson armor hidden beneath a brown cloak that disguised him as a peasant. He watched the landscape unfold before him, where the dark silhouettes of black peaks and volcanoes dominated the horizon.

Beyond the desolate terrain rested Wargonne, but the natural barriers—mountains, rivers of lava, and toxic fumes—made hiking the shortest path impractical. Rather than risk the treacherous terrain above ground, the People's Army had arranged for them to approach by sea. For now, their immediate goal was to reach the harbor at Starlight Beach.

His new companions, three knights, shared his mission, and like him, they had just been assigned to the Equity Guard that same day. The closest to him, a woman with hair as light as silver bundled into a braid, turned to him.

"Alright, everyone," she said, her voice filled with youthful enthusiasm. "We're all thinking it: how difficult do you think it will be to sneak into Wargonne?"

"There won't be any challenges—only opportunities," Bios replied, his eyes still fixated on his boots. It was reassuring to him that they were opening up to him and revealing their inner workings.

The knight with a scar running down his cheek nodded solemnly. "This is our chance to strike back at those who have oppressed the common people," he said. "But this mission will not be easy. Many have tried before us and failed. If we misstep, we will be doomed. Have any of you done work like this before? I must admit I haven't, but I'll give you my best efforts. To that end, I am Ambrose."

"My name is Cassia Blacksand," the final knight declared, her green eyes blazing with determination. "And I won't let us fail. My blade belongs to the three of you as much as it does to the Common People."

Cassia's family name, Blacksand, revealed she was not from a family—it was the name of slaves from Tornaa. By keeping her birth title, she remained connected to her past, a choice that likely meant she was purchased by the People's Army or lent by her master for payment.

"A Blacksand is with us?" Ambrose exclaimed. "How interesting!"

"So be it," the other woman said with a sharp tone. "In that case, since we're introducing ourselves, my name is Alina Oceansong."

She was also a slave or former slave from the Silent Deserts. Oceansong, as a name, revealed she came from the Salt Heart, a flat beach rich in resources. But why were the two of them in Yaenia? They must have been acquaintances at the very least; otherwise, it would be too much of a coincidence. Bios wanted to examine their forearms for any marks that might reveal more about their past, but both wore gauntlets that covered the areas where such information would have been inked.

Alina's calloused hands had cracked skin from long hours in the sun handling seawater. Her fingernails, yellowed and thickened from years of scraping dried salt off metal, suggested she had left the Silent Deserts recently. When he glanced at Cassia again, her palms bore similar signs of labor.

"You've journeyed far from home," Bios said, testing how much they might reveal. "Why join the People's Army?"

"We can make a greater difference in Yaenia than where we came from," Alina replied. "If you recognize our names, then you're already aware of the injustices in our homeland."

"How did you know they came from the Silent Deserts?" asked the scarred knight named Ambrose.

"Their names reveal their origins," Bios said. "Where are you from?"

"I am Sir Ambrose Lyren from the town of Emil," the knight answered. "Though I may lack the worldly experience of the rest of you, I will earn my place here. I have a strong sense of justice, and I am honored to work alongside you in the People's Army."

"And how long have you been with the People's Army?" Bios inquired.

"Six long months now," Ambrose said. "And it's been a path of redemption for me."

"And you two?" Bios asked, gesturing toward Cassia and Alina, his voice probing.

"Three months," Cassia said, glancing at Alina. "It's given us reassurance this is the right path, after all we've been through."

Alina nodded, even though her eyes suggested there were still deeper stories from them left untold. "We've learned and grown stronger since then. The People's Army holds great power, and we're all part of something greater than our pasts."

The information settled into Bios's mind as though he were scribbling it onto parchment. "I also hope to make a difference in the world."

"You never told us anything about redemption," Cassia said to Ambrose.

"I was ashamed of my past until recently," the knight replied. "However, since we'll be working together from now on, I suppose I can share it with you."

"We all have our secrets," Alina admitted. "Say what you will."

"Before joining the People's Army, I owned several homes," Ambrose said. "People paid me each month to live in them, but one man failed to pay for multiple months. He'd encountered difficult times, and I let him continue living there longer than I should have. His debt grew, and despite promising to settle it, he always found new excuses. The night before I was going to forcefully remove him from the home, I smelled smoke. My home was near his, so I knew something was amiss. The house was on fire!"

"Was he okay?" Alina asked.

Ambrose continued recounting the event. "He fled safely, but flames engulfed the house and its contents. Amid the chaos, I seized him by the shirt, demanding all the gold he possessed. When he revealed his coin purse remained inside the burning house, I threatened him to retrieve it or face the consequences. Driven by my demands, he ran back into the inferno and never returned. The event shook me deeply and exposed a darker side of myself."

"So he... died?" Cassia gasped.

"A pointless death," Bios commented.

"It opened my eyes," Ambrose said with woe. "I had been more concerned about my gold and house than his life and what he'd lost. His bones were in the ruins, so I know he didn't escape. What pains me most is not knowing whether he found his coin purse—or if my words caused him to stay inside."

Ambrose seemed to have become a better man, but Bios doubted his future usefulness. The noble knight held too much light in his heart and not enough darkness. Faced with a difficult situation, Ambrose would hesitate—or even refuse—to follow Bios's orders.

"You seek to fight against greedy landowners," Alina concluded. "Those who are like how you once were."

"People can change. I am proof of that," Ambrose said. "But only if they're willing to let go of greed. Asking for payment isn't wrong, but when does it become exploitation?"

"Slavery follows the same patterns of inequities," Cassia remarked.

"The masters are often the worst kinds of people," Bios said, choosing his words carefully to gain Alina's and Cassia's trust. "Were you sold or freed from your former master? In either case, it is justice knowing you're now doing as you wish."

"Cassia and I escaped together years ago," Alina explained.

"Escaped?" Bios asked, narrowing his eyebrows. "Nobody escapes the Silent Deserts. The masters are too cautious to let anyone slip through. And Cassia—she's from the Black Sands of Tornaa, isn't she? There's nowhere to run but to the sands."

"It's a complicated tale," Cassia said, "but we owe our lives to two merchants—Lionheart and Khalia. I'll never forget their names."

Bios wasn't familiar with them, but her tone suggested she wasn't divulging the complete story. If they were still slaves, they would still have a master, but the real question was whether there was someone looking for them.

"So, you've been in Yaenia for many years now," he started, attempting to steer the conversation toward another angle to uncover their complete histories.

"It's been different here," Alina said. "In the Silent Deserts, we harvested salt for our master, and in Yaenia, we chopped wood. But even with wages, we remained trapped in an endless cycle of servitude. Freedom and security, not payment alone, is what truly matters."

"We sometimes argued," Cassia added, "that as slaves, we didn't have to worry about money or the future. Our former master provided everything necessary for survival. In Yaenia, however, we had to work, and there was no guarantee we'd always have enough coin to support ourselves."

"But here, we have the freedom, choice, and responsibility to shape our own futures," Alina said. "The People's Army is the key to balancing those who serve and those who are served."

"By redistributing the wealth, I assume," Bios Auras concluded skeptically.

"When the People's Army seizes control of Yaenia, all resources will be distributed fairly to the workers based on their contributions," Ambrose declared. He wasn't lying—or perhaps he truly believed his own words. People like him clung to any ideology promising salvation or a perfect world. Believing in idealistic outcomes often characterized those who hadn't yet been disillusioned by actual politics and social dynamics.

As for Alina and Cassia, they spoke as though they'd rehearsed their lines countless times. Their words lacked depth, as if they were parroting phrases from the Hierophant or the Hanged Man instead of sharing their own thoughts. Did they truly believe what they said?

Alina's eyes held a flicker of something more, perhaps a bit of doubt or a trace of uncertainty beneath the surface.

"The freedom to shape one's future is a powerful motivator," Bios said, nodding as if to endorse their ideals.

She smiled at him for the first time, pleased to have another believer nearby. "Exactly," she said firmly. "We're fighting for a world where everyone has the chance of equal opportunity."

"And an equal outcome," Ambrose added, though his words made Cassia's lips twitch. "One country, one fate. This is what the Darian Kingdom should be."

Alina and Cassia exchanged a glance. "We've seen what happens when power is concentrated in too few hands."

"Yes," Cassia chimed in forcefully. "The rich control the weak."

"Much of the time, that is true, but not all control derives from one's pockets," Bios warned.

"Of course it does," Ambrose said. "Gold gives one more opportunity than not."

"If you say so," Bios replied, not caring enough to continue the conversation. He glanced to the front of the cart, where another member of the People's Army drove. He wondered if the man was listening, and if he was indoctrinated like Ambrose or just pretending as he, Alina, and Cassia seemed to be.

The two women of the Silent Deserts had their reasons for being there, but what did they truly seek? Having endured slavery and escaped its bonds, they should have known better than to trust the hollow promises of the Hierophant or the Hanged Man. The Silent Deserts were no land of hope; harsh realities shaped everything there.

Maybe Alina and Cassia, unaware of life beyond their desolate homeland, couldn't recognize or resist the appealing ideas proposed by the People's Army. Ideals like equality, fairness, and freedom were unattainable—humanity was flawed, resources scarce, and yearnings endless. Diversity of thoughts led to diversity of desires, and desires were limitless. Conflicts and struggles for power were inevitable and would shatter any false beliefs that order could prevent chaos.

"You just joined the People's Army today, you said, yes?" Ambrose asked.

"That's correct," Bios replied.

"You'll come to understand everything it offers soon," the knight promised. "I'll teach you our ways."

Bios looked into Alina's eyes as he responded. "I realize I've only breached the surface of the truth so far. The People's Army seems to have more layers to it than I thought."

WITHIN THREE DAYS, HE GREW TIRED OF THE CART AND, EVEN MORE so, of Ambrose. The journey from Hillside Reach's Golden Mare to Starlight Beach would take more than two weeks. From there, the voyage to Wargonne by ship would take an unpredictable number of days, and Bios could no longer endure Ambrose's endless preaching.

The knight rambled on, his voice like a mosquito singing within the confines of the cart. "An ideal world," he mused, "would be one where every man, woman, and child has equal claim to the fruits of their collective labor."

Bios shifted uncomfortably in his hard seat, growing annoyed by Ambrose's words. His patience was wearing thin. He contemplated using the Teleportation Stone to dump Ambrose into the ocean, but such an action would raise too many questions. For now, Bios Auras let a silent rebuttal simmer inside himself—shared wealth was an illusion leading only to hidden poverty.

Ambrose, oblivious to Bios' irritation, continued, "The common good of the people must come before individual greed. Imagine a kingdom without classes, castes, or hierarchy—a realm where the chains of ownership are abolished."

Next to him, Alina raised an eyebrow and failed to hide her condescending grin. "Is that even a kingdom at all? Someone needs to take charge and lead it."

Bios recognized Ambrose's ideas for what they were—childish fantasies. Humans were inherently unequal in their abilities and desires; ignoring it was delusional. Attempting to control such inequalities would only lead to resentment and death.

Though Bios often considered rebuking the knight's naive rants, he dismissed the idea, realizing it would be futile—as fruitless as explaining the nature of the universe to a dog. In reality, those responsible for redistributing wealth would merely hide inequalities in the end, but Ambrose's short-sightedness prevented him from recognizing this.

Ambrose remained oblivious to Bios' silence as he carried on. "If the People's Army can restructure our society so that even the smallest tasks are acknowledged and benefit everyone, we can build a future based on cooperation."

Cooperation? Bios nearly scoffed out loud. The same cooperation that led to backstabbing in royal courts? The kind that turned brother against brother for the sweet taste of power? Bios had seen too much throughout his time to believe in such simplistic solutions. Perhaps a visit to the Throatian island would enlighten Ambrose—there, gold was as meaningless and worthless as his dreams.

Bios stared across the cart with both pity and disdain. Despite owning houses where people paid him gold to reside, the knight lacked understanding of true power. He didn't realize that even in a world without wealth, people would always seek control and power —men like Bios himself. The vision Ambrose envisioned would never come to be so long as free will persisted. Bios couldn't take it anymore.

"And what of leadership in this ideal world?" Bios interjected with feigned curiosity. "Who would decide what's best for the people if not an individual or a group?"

Ambrose smiled, seeming pleased with the question. "The leadership would be based on communal agreement, with decisions made collectively to ensure every voice is heard," he said with conviction.

The notion of "every voice" shaping the future was laughable. How could true consensus ever emerge among people with such varied dreams, opinions, and fears? Ambrose's greatest flaw was assuming everyone thought like himself and that people were inherently genuine. He failed to see the differences between people and cultures. If "every voice" truly shaped the future, such a reality would devour any chance of peace. Order inevitably led to chaos, and chaos to order.

Someone had to make decisions a total consensus could never reach. The world needed a god to guide it, even if forcefully. Asura was the answer, but groups like the People's Army would never acknowledge it. Instead, they clung to their political ideologies the same as a religion, even if they might deny it.

Without a unifying force, the world would remain trapped in endless power struggles, ruled by flawed mortals destined to fail at stabilizing it. Without a god, nothing could be trusted to last forever. It was Bios's duty to save the world, even if it meant destroying many along the way. By claiming the God Stones and mastering Asura's power, Bios Auras would become the force needed to make them bow to Asura.

"It truly is best for everyone to take part in making decisions," Ambrose continued. "I hope you see the truth of the matter."

Bios saw the truth—a different one than Ambrose wished him to believe. "I can see it now, a greater world," he said through gritted teeth. "The People's Army truly has noble ambitions." And they were all either lies or foolish.

"Your eyes have been opened," Ambrose said, extending his hand. "It's a pleasure to serve alongside you, my new brother."

Bios Auras had no siblings and never would. He shook Ambrose's hand with a faint smile, maintaining appearances for now. Though Ambrose was unlikely to succeed as an ally, he might serve a purpose down the line.

"May our quest to Wargonne come with great success," Bios Auras said.

As nightfall approached, the wagon ground to a halt, and the group began setting up camp. The mysterious driver, who barely spoke unless spoken to, kept to himself and passively refused to help gather wood or prepare their tents. If not for his driving them further, Bios would have demanded his help. The driver kept to himself, insisting his sole purpose was delivering them to Starlight Beach. Unlike Ambrose, whose mouth never stopped moving, the driver didn't join their meals or interject himself into their conversations.

To Bios's disappointment, he and the talkative knight needed to share a tent. Even well into the night, Ambrose kept talking until his snores finally overtook his words. After an hour of failed attempts to rest, Bios slipped out of the tent with a tired sigh.

He approached the dying fire, where the last embers flickered in a faint orange glow. Alina sat perched on a rock, her gaze fixed on the dying flames. She didn't startle as he came near, and her blade rested close by.

"It seems Lady Oceansong can't sleep tonight either," Bios said, settling beside her on a nearby rock.

"Sir Hellvar," Alina greeted softly. "It's fortunate we can finally talk alone. It's hard to find rest among such... enthusiastic company."

Bios smirked at her choice of words. "Enthusiastic is one way to describe it," he said dryly.

She looked at him, eyes piercing through his crimson armor. "You don't believe in their cause," she accused. "You may fool Ambrose, but not me."

"And you?" Bios whispered. "I sense you're merely following their lead, the same as me. Do you truly share their worldly ambitions?"

Alina's eyes shifted back to the dying embers. "I believe in freedom," she said after a pause that Bios sensed was hesitant. "My experience has shown me that true freedom isn't granted by those who promise equality with one hand while gathering power with the other."

"A wise observation," Bios applauded quietly. "But if you don't believe in the People's Army, why are you here?"

He studied her as she contemplated her response. "Cassia and I plan to climb through their ranks," she said. "If we can gain enough influence within the People's Army, we can guide them toward a just cause. An achievable cause."

He tilted his head slightly, feigning intrigue. "And what cause would that be?" he prodded, already piecing together her intentions from their earlier conversations.

"The Silent Deserts," she answered. "The slavers there have held control for too long. They thrive on the misery and suffering of others. If I can command the People's Army, I want their world to collapse. People have a right to be free."

Bios leaned back, contemplating the depth of her ambition. Unlike Ambrose, Alina had a practical goal that aligned with the stated ideals of the People's Army. Yet Bios understood the immense challenges of conquering the Silent Deserts—an army alone could only achieve so much while also facing a naturally harsh environment.

"And you believe the Darians will follow you on this personal crusade?" Bios asked, his tone betraying some of his skepticism.

Alina met his questioning stare. "The Common People should despise slavers just as much as the wealthy who hoard their riches. They claim to act for the common worker. What better way is there to prove their commitment than by freeing the chained people in the Silent Deserts?"

Her logic was sound—Bios couldn't deny it. The prospect of using the People's Army to dismantle a system infested with slavery was bold, yet it presented an opportunity for him as well. If Alina succeeded, it would create chaos—a fertile ground for someone like him to exploit later.

He nodded slowly. "Your plan has merit," he acknowledged. "But you'll need more than just a noble idea to persuade people to follow you."

"I know," she said, her eyes steely with determination. "First, I must earn their trust and build my influence. Only then can I strike at the heart of my motherland."

Bios watched Alina's profile, illuminated by the remnants of firelight. Her dedication might serve his purposes—or it could become an obstacle to his goals. For now, this alliance—and her ambitious dream—would serve him well.

"Then let us hope your rise is swift," he murmured. "For your sake—and for those you seek to liberate."

"Even if I cannot succeed at this," Alina continued, "I must one day return to my motherland and atone for my mistakes."

"Whatever do you mean, Lady Oceansong? You escaped to Yaenia and are free now, aren't you? You're a strong-willed and clever woman—that much is clear. What mistakes could you have possibly made?"

Alina shook her head solemnly. "I cannot rest until my former master is dead."

"I see—I should have expected that. Tell me about your master—why does he deserve to die?"

"My former master," Alina corrected him sharply, "was Klein Pene, and he is the worst kind of man. Whatever terrible thing you can imagine a slaver does to their slaves, he has done to me."

"Klein Pene," Bios's lips curled into a smile. "I know of him."

Alina looked up sharply. "You do? How?"

"I don't know him personally," Bios said, lying, "but I've been to the Golden Bay Market many times. I often needed some illegal spices that were only available there. Klein's name often came up among the stalls as someone to visit if I ever needed help carrying my goods."

"So, you've never traded people?"

"Of course not," Bios insisted. "I'm corrupt enough to trade in illegal spices used in pain-reducing recipes, but trading for human lives is too far."

"I see," Alina said, her shoulders relaxing. "Would you fight against someone like Klein if you could, Sir Hellvar?"

"When the time is right and success is likely," Bios promised. Now he held the power to control Alina or use her as a bargaining chip to influence Klein if needed.

Alina's fair and thin face softened. "Thank you, Sir Hellvar, for understanding my situation," she said, her features illuminated by the moonlight. "But what of you? Why did you join the People's Army?"

Bios Auras tilted his head, the crimson shine of his armor reflecting in the dying fires. "I am in search of information," he confessed with a hint of controlled reluctance, "about certain magical artifacts of great importance to me."

"Magical artifacts?"

"Yes," Bios continued, measuring her reaction. "You see, I was born different from most people as a half-human, half-Lucidian." He paused, letting his lie settle. This false explanation would account for his magic without revealing the God Stone within him. "Such a lineage brings unique abilities," he added.

"You're able to use magic? Truly?"

"Yes, I possess powers that could make our missions easier." His voice was low, concealing how much information he had withheld from her so far.

"I didn't realize half-Lucidians existed, especially ones with magic."

"I've been cautious about revealing this," Bios admitted, his eyes locked on hers. "Men like Ambrose... when they see such power, they set aside their ideals and seek to control it for their own ambitions. They disregard the wills and wishes of those who carry the burdens."

She nodded slowly, absorbing his words. "I understand your hesitation," Alina said. "Your secret is safe with me, Sir Hellvar."

"As you've likely deduced, I also aim to use the People's Army for my own purposes," Bios said. "But I need allies who will follow my orders without question. Might we work together to achieve our goals?"

"Asking someone to follow orders without question," Alina commented, "sounds like something a slave owner would say."

"Alina," Bios began, his voice carrying a heavier weight than hers, "I have seen the strength in your conviction and the nobility of your purpose. With my magic and your dedication, we could reshape this world as we see fit. But the path I walk is one of both light and darkness. I cannot have allies like Ambrose who'll hesitate when their morals are tested. I harness darkness for the greater good—it's the only way to defeat what stands in my way. The world is unforgiving to those who hesitate, and time waits for no one. I need you to follow my commands without question, even if they conflict with your beliefs. You'll have my respect, and I won't consider you a slave by any means."

He paused, letting his words linger. The night was silent except for the distant rustle of leaves in the nearby trees. She would soon surrender to him, just like Cereene had pledged herself.

Alina's face shifted between disbelief and consideration. "I didn't flee Klein to be enslaved by another master."

"But such an undertaking requires more than mere agreement," he continued, his tone insistent and soothing. "It demands unwavering loyalty—to each other above all else. I'll stand by you with my magic and sword. If you wish, we can one day kill all the slave owners, using darkness to bring forth light. I wouldn't hesitate to do that for you. Help me earn what I want first, and I will aid you in return."

He watched as Alina weighed his proposal, her expression

unreadable in the dim light. How long would it be until she would commit to him?

"If I pledge my loyalty to you," she began, "how can I trust that you'll keep your word? You could easily betray me once your goals are met."

Bios offered her a half-smile, holding both promise and mystery. "Because, Alina Oceansong," he said, saying her name in full to emphasize his sincerity, "our goals are now connected. The People's Army is a means to an end for both of us. Our shared goal is a greater world. Order cannot come without manipulating chaos."

He extended his hand toward hers, palm open and inviting, an offering and a trap together.

"Join me," Bios urged softly. "Pledge your loyalty to me alone, and I will lend you my power. Together, we will bring the People's Army into the Silent Deserts and beyond."

Alina hesitated only a moment longer before placing her hand in his. "My blade is yours," she said. "We will free the slaves and grant them the freedom to live their own lives."

"Whatever I may ask of you in the future will be for a greater light," Bios said with a firm shake. "I promise."

17
EISENBERN - THE PRISONERS OF SKY TOWER COAST

Within ten minutes of reaching Sky Tower Coast, Eisenbern, Ilya, and Gustav found themselves at a lively tavern called The Lucky Fish Hook. Their appetites prompted them to order the heartiest meals on the menu: a platter of freshly caught fish, oysters smothered in a tangy garlic-lemon sauce, and a sweet wine that Eisenbern declared the finest he'd ever tasted. Unlike the suspicious inn they'd encountered in Hillside Reach, The Lucky Fish Hook felt legitimate, evoking memories of Miner's Kitchen back home. Each bite and sip compensated for their previous meal at the Golden Mare, and Gustav seemed to have forgotten his earlier complaints about the rat meat.

"Eat up, both of you," Eisenbern encouraged. The road beyond them would be mostly wilderness, with no towns or settlements for half a month. "We have a long journey ahead of us, and this could be our last proper meal for some time."

Gustav slurped down what might have been his fifteenth oyster from its shell. "These are the best I've ever had!" he said. "How many days do you think they'll stay fresh if I bring some along?"

Ilya rolled her eyes. "Not even long enough for you to get hungry again!"

Eisenbern stood up. He needed to send the letter to Renato so he could investigate further while he, Ilya, and Gustav traversed the northern wilderness. He'd recorded every detail about their encounter at Hillside Reach and the Golden Mare inn: the knight in crimson armor who had demanded the Strega Generatrice, the hundreds of people who had vanished as suddenly as they'd appeared, and the bartender who seemed overly friendly—and therefore suspicious.

"I'm going to send that letter to Renato now."

Alone, Eisenbern navigated the winding streets, passing the market and heading toward the roost tower where the city's birds were housed. The musty barnyard scent filled the air, and flies buzzed around his face. In the center of the room, a ladder led upward into the structure, though some birds nested along the roof beams. Across the dirt floor, a birdkeeper's apprentice climbed up and down the ladder, transporting message scrolls.

When his turn came, Eisenbern stepped up to the desk and handed over the scroll intended for Renato. "I need to send this to Aeon Eve, please," he said. The man gestured to a row of posted signs showing the costs for sending correspondence to various locations. Curiously, mailing a letter to the distant Emil required less money than sending one to Last Hope. Eisenbern guessed the lower cost might have been because of birds naturally favoring that route or perhaps fewer messages being sent there overall. Either way, Renato would receive his message.

He passed the necessary coins and the letter over the table sitting him and the worker. "Can you check for messages for me?" he asked.

"I can," the birdkeeper replied bluntly. "Your name or affiliation?"

"Rufus Merdel's store," he said. "For anything to the attention of Jarret Eisenbern."

"Hold on."

The birdkeeper scribbled a note and passed it to his apprentice. She vanished through a hidden trapdoor into the tower's basement, a place Eisenbern hadn't noticed until now, and returned moments later with a thick letter.

"Is this yours?" she asked.

He glanced at the title and saw his own name. On the back was a seal depicting Asura's spear piercing two interlocked loops, symbolizing balance and continuity. It was from the church, meaning Ophelia had written to him.

"It is mine, thank you," he said, his heart sinking as he opened the envelope and read the opening lines:

Dear Jarret Eisenbern,
It is with heavy hearts that we write to you today.

Ophelia, a dear friend and cherished member of our community, has passed away. Her untimely demise was caused by the cruel fate of illness, specifically her Scarlet Cough, at a time when she was perhaps still in her prime. Her loss leaves us all deeply saddened.

We have honored her memory and her service to our church community by burying her in our church's graveyard. This way, she can remain close to us and be remembered for all eternity. We have arranged for her body to be laid to rest with the honor and dignity that she deserves, as per Asurian traditions. Her burial will be a time of quiet reflection and remembrance for our community.

Please know that Ophelia was an incredible source of light for our church. She was a person of immense faith, wisdom, and kindness. Her presence in our community was a true blessing, and her spirit will forever guide us. In her last moments, she spoke highly of you and expressed her deep love for you.

May Asura provide you with solace and peace during this difficult time as you mourn the loss of your companion, Ophelia. We extend our deepest sympathy to you.

Sincerely,
Members of the Seventh Church of Asura

His tears came slowly. Eisenbern read the letter twice more before he could accept that it was real. His legs turned to stone as he stood there outside the bird's tower.

"Ophelia," Eisenbern gasped. "I should have stayed with you."

He recalled what he'd told her before leaving: Asura would call on their lives to end when they were meant to conclude, and not a moment sooner or longer. One could only wonder if they would be ready when the occasion came.

Had Ophelia been ready? He sank to the ground, leaning against the nearby stone wall to stop himself from lying down.

There hadn't been enough time.

There just hadn't been enough time...

Shortly after regaining composure and suppressing his emotions, Eisenbern found solace in the belief that Ophelia's departure was part of Asura's grand design for him. Her slow walk toward her fate had been like an inevitable sunset, but now that it had come to pass, a chilling numbness overpowered him, as if he were waking from a terrible nightmare.

He had prayed every day for Ophelia's recovery, but Asura had not spared her. There must have been a reason for it, a purpose his god had chosen not to restore her to health. The pain was unbearable, yet he forced himself to trust that what had happened to Ophelia was for the best, even though he could not fathom why. He reasoned that Ophelia's farewell was meant to alter his destiny, as she had foretold, and they were never supposed to be married. He could only hope that she had finally found peace after all the pain she had endured in her final days.

His thinking and pondering were short-lived, however. When he returned to the Lucky Fish Hook, Ilya and Gustav offered him drinks and support, but an interruption soon came. The entryway door burst open and a scrawny boy, no more than twelve, ran into the tavern, leaping onto a stool and waving his hands wildly. "They found them! All four of the blood lickers!" he shouted.

"Four now, you say?" the bartender asked, his excitement barely concealed. "Go on ahead. I'll join you there." The boy vanished as quickly as he'd appeared, and the bartender glanced around his establishment. "The city guard has captured the Throatians everyone's been searching for," he announced. "I'm closing up to watch the executions. You can finish your meals, but no new orders until I'm back."

The news sent a storm of panic among the locals, who rose from their seats in a chaotic scramble, grabbing what food and tankards they could carry. The bustle of people leaving suddenly left Eisenbern, Ilya, and Gustav confused and alone.

"Am I going mad, or did he say they caught Throatians?" Ilya blurted out.

It was impossible. To reach Sky Tower Coast, the Throatians would have had to sail through their own storm wall, navigate past the Darian fleet, cross to the southeastern Yaenian coast, then travel north along the heavily guarded coastline of Wargonne, and continue further west to their destination. Sneaking into the country via the northern shores would have been their only chance for a subtle approach, but the endeavor was both time-consuming and dangerous.

Like the other patrons, Eisenbern, Ilya, and Gustav wanted to see it for themselves to uncover the truth. "It confuses me how they ended up here," Eisenbern said. "We should check this out," he suggested.

"Maybe the Throatian island's storm was a distraction all along," Ilya proposed as they jogged down the streets, following the crowd. "They must have another means of entering and exiting the island. The dragon flew them in, perhaps?"

"That or left people here before the Wedding of the Torn Rose," Gustav said. "They might have been hiding in Sky Tower Coast for months."

"You're probably right," Eisenbern replied. "Everyone's been so focused on breaking through the magical barrier on their island that we never considered enemies may still be here from before. We must investigate this."

WEAVING THROUGH THE STREETS AND ALLEYS, THEY FOLLOWED THE crowd, as the entire city was eager to attend the event. The crowd parted, revealing the distant town square. Between Eisenbern and a large wooden platform stood numerous vendor carts, now overwhelmed by the growing sea of spectators. At the top of the platform waited a lone man, almost as tall and imposing as Gustav. Beside him lay a massive axe, its handle resting in his hands. A dark, blood-colored hood hid his face.

"It seems the locals were searching for the Throatians for some time," Eisenbern muttered. "I wonder how long they stayed and why they came here."

"Maybe they are defectors?" Gustav suggested. "Not all Throatians serving the Asche family may have agreed with the murder of Princess Lydia. There's a chance they could be innocent."

Eisenbern scratched his beard. "Though I wish that were true, they were likely up to no good. If they were wise, they would have either surrendered to King Ether von Stonewall with information or kept a low profile to avoid attracting attention."

"There they are!" Ilya announced.

A group of city guards led four hooded captives up the wooden stairs to the platform. The crowd erupted in cheers; the blue-robed judge behind the captives raised her arms to call for silence.

"Citizens of Sky Tower Coast, I bring good news today," the middle-aged woman said. "Asura has sent us four foreigners whose presence threatens our community. Today, justice must be served. I, Sigrid Var, promise you that justice."

She motioned toward the Throatians. "These are the four individuals—two men and two women—who stole food from our traders at the docks. But they are not mere thieves; they are Throatians, a fearsome breed of animal that drinks human blood and kills without hesitation to satisfy its cravings. Shall we offer these enemies of Asura even a single drop of our own?"

"NO!" the crowd screamed in unison.

"Should we not spill the cups of the blood drinkers?"

The executioner approached, positioning himself before the four prisoners. They stood silently, their heads covered, though likely still able to hear. Even if they had a trial, the ropes around their mouths probably prevented them from speaking. Throatian magic remained a mystery, and as a precaution, the prisoners' tongues and lips were likely kept immobile in case their powers required spoken incantations.

"Throatian Male One," the judge barked. "Step forward and position your head on the executioner's block."

The man nearest to it walked calmly toward his fate, escorted by the executioner. One of the female Throatians turned away, her legs buckling under her. She fell to the ground, landing on her knees, then fainted, her body going limp across the stage. A guard rushed to her side, hoisting her upright beside him.

Sigrid Var, the judge, ordered the event to continue. The executioner tightened his grip on the axe. Eisenbern counted to three, and with a swift motion, the blade fell, ending the first prisoner's life.

The guard then lifted the unconscious woman and placed her on the chopping block.

"Something isn't right," Eisenbern commented. "Do either of you feel it?"

Why weren't the prisoners' faces revealed? He found it peculiar that the Throatians didn't have to face the people they'd wronged, even though it was common to cover a prisoner's head during an execution. Maybe the population of Sky Tower Coast had their own softer approach to handling such matters and didn't force the public to see the criminals at their final moments.

"It's an execution, after all," Ilya said, "but it's surprising how many spectators came to watch."

Blood dripped from the man's axe as he raised it once more. The woman had spared herself the terror of approaching the platform and awaiting the blade's fall. Still, Eisenbern couldn't help but feel sympathy for her—even as a Throatian, she would die, and nobody there would know or remember her name.

As the second execution concluded, the crowd erupted in more applause and cheering. Eisenbern watched the audience before him, their faces turned toward the spectacle. Death was an inevitable part of war, even when the enemy was unarmed and anonymous. Prisoners of war had to be executed, especially if they'd harmed innocent civilians. He recalled the slaughtered horses in the forest and the screams of those prisoners burning aboard the Throatian ships —the horrors committed by the Throatians were as unforgettable as they were unforgivable. Their religion and its followers were evil; neither could be permitted to survive.

He clenched his fists, and his heart pounded, but a growing uneasiness fluttered within his chest. The judge had declared them guilty, though the specifics of their crimes remained unspoken. Bringing the Throatians to answer for their people's crimes was the right action. But as Gustav suggested, perhaps they were defectors, not wanting to be associated with their own culture. What if they weren't as bad as the rest?

He silenced his thoughts, trying to dismiss his growing emotions. As a Purple Knight, Eisenbern should have trusted the judge's process, but what would Ophelia have done had she been in his place? Redemption, forgiveness, and grace were the answers, but could they apply to people as sinful as they were?

The cheering of the crowd dominated the background as the third prisoner, the second woman, neared the chopping block. In the strange silence, multiple possibilities circled through Eisenbern's mind. Everything depended on one simple, absurd condition: the Throatians needed to be spared. They needed another chance at life so they could confirm their own wickedness or choose to walk the path of light. Ophelia would have confronted them, giving them a final opportunity to repent. He should do that much in her memory—it was what a Holy Knight should do.

"Stop the executions!" he yelled.

"Eisenbern!" Ilya exclaimed, spinning toward him. "What are you saying?"

"I need to stop this. If anything goes wrong, I don't want either of you involved. Neither of you knows me, do you understand?"

"What do you see?" Gustav asked.

"You said they could be defectors," Eisenbern retorted. "There's not a moment to lose—I have to go!"

He abandoned Ilya and Gustav and forced his way through the crowd, yelling for the executioner to stop. Commoners gaped in disbelief, as though he were a crazed heretic or a fool. The crowd was too thick for anyone on the stage to hear him. As Eisenbern reached it, the last prisoner was already approaching the chopping block. This was his last chance.

"Stop the executions!" Eisenbern yelled for what may have been the hundredth time.

The judge heard him but showed no concern for the prisoners. "Guards!" she shouted. "Stop the man in purple armor!"

Eisenbern moved up the small set of stairs to the platform. As the judge's knights blocked his path, he raised his hands from his waist, signaling he wouldn't draw his sword. "I'm Jarret Eisenbern, leader of the Leila Kingdom's Purple Guard," he declared. "I need you to stop this execution immediately."

Judge Var glared at him with suspicion and bewilderment. "You have no authority here, Leilan. Step down before you get yourself hurt."

"The Throatians may possess information vital to the war," Eisenbern yelled. "Surely someone as well-educated as yourself has heard of the storm curtain surrounding their island?"

The woman stammered, clearly surprised by the news. "You need to leave, sir. This event doesn't concern you. We've already checked—they know nothing." She turned toward the hooded man. "Kill the last Throatian now."

"HOLD YOUR AXE!" Eisenbern yelled, charging through four

guards. Their swords clanged against his armor as he fought forward, but the executioner had already repositioned his axe. Now, he raised it overhead, ready to strike Eisenbern instead.

"Step down, Leilan," the judge warned. "This is your last chance."

"There's something important I need to discuss with your prisoner," he said to the guards. "Please let me speak."

"No," the executioner snarled. He bent his knee, preparing to charge forward with what would likely be a horizontal swing.

The situation was getting out of hand and could become a point of strife between the Darian and Leila kingdoms if he escalated the situation any further. However, there was a crucial question he needed to ask the last surviving Throatian prisoner, one whose answer held profound implications: If the Throatians entered Yaenia after the war began, how did they pass through the storm, and if they arrived before the Wedding of the Torn Rose, how many Throatians remained behind? Above all, could they turn away from their god and toward the light of Asura?

"I need to know when and how they got to Yaenia," he explained. "That is all."

"You're not entitled to that information," the judge said. She looked over at her guards, then pointed back at him. "Arrest this crazed man immediately."

"Fine! But we're arresting him too!" Ilya interrupted, her voice sharp and decisive. She had snuck up the rear of the stage and positioned herself behind the Throatian. With her knife against his throat, she smiled at the judge.

The woman snapped, "I don't care if you kill the blood drinker." Meanwhile, the executioner lowered his axe from Eisenbern and swung it toward the final prisoner and Ilya.

"Your opinion doesn't matter," Ilya shot back. She yanked the hood off the prisoner and slashed her blade upward, cutting the rope bound around his mouth. The man, trembling and sweating, let out a shaky sigh before speaking.

"We're not Throatians!" he exclaimed. "Judge Var is corrupt! She knew my brother had discovered her secrets. She abuses her power and steals and cheats and—"

"Kill him now!" Judge Var roared. "I won't tolerate the lies spewing from this foreigner."

Eisenbern stepped forward. "You've got some explaining to do," he said. "Ever since my friends and I arrived at this grand display in the town square, something felt off. Despite what you might say, I believe the man when he says they aren't Throatian."

Before he could continue, the executioner moved toward Ilya and the prisoner, readying his axe to strike again. Ilya stepped back, pulling the captive with her as she cut his hands free.

"Come with us," she offered the person she'd just freed, "and we'll help you."

"No!" the prisoner yelled. He ran to the side, putting distance between himself and both her and the executioner.

Suddenly, four city guards advanced toward Eisenbern. One swung first, but Eisenbern leaned aside and drew his blade. "I really didn't want to fight you all," he said. "Can't we just pull up some chairs and have a nice, calm talk over a drink?"

Inevitably, they fought. As Eisenbern held his own despite being outnumbered, he glimpsed Ilya taking on the executioner, armed only with her knife. Chances were that Gustav, wherever he was, had the Shadowstone spear and was preparing them a means of escape. Meanwhile, Judge Var was screaming and summoning more guards. Time would run short if they didn't hurry up and get out of there.

Eisenbern's sword poked the city guard in the shoulder. "Sorry," he said. The guard grunted but didn't back down, so Eisenbern punched him in the face and then kicked him in the leg. "Really sorry," he added.

Taking advantage of the downed man, Eisenbern leaped over him toward Ilya and the executioner, who were engaged in their fight. Neither had landed a hit yet. The axeman was strong but slow while she was fast, though her knife's limited range kept her at a distance. Luckily, the person in charge of the executions wasn't wearing armor that day, leaving himself vulnerable if Ilya could overcome the length of his weapon.

"I told you not to get involved!" Eisenbern scolded in her direction.

"As though you wouldn't have called for help five minutes later, anyway!" she called back.

Ignoring the guards behind him, he charged at the preoccupied executioner and executed a roll. As Eisenbern had hoped, the axeman hesitated and balked, leaving an opening. Landing low, the Purple Guard's leader swept his blade horizontally, cutting near the executioner's calf.

Eisenbern hurriedly apologized. "Sorry about that. Just let us talk to the prisoner."

"Eisenbern! Stop saying sorry whenever you hurt the enemy!" It was Gustav's voice, and he was out of sight somewhere off the stage. "They won't feel any guilt for hitting you!"

The ground trembled, nearly toppling Eisenbern. The beer he'd drunk earlier might have been affecting him. Regardless, the axeman's time was running out. With his leg injured, the large man struggled to bear his weight fully. Ilya, sensing this, lunged forward with a feint, forcing him to waste energy and lose his balance. She now had the upper hand, prompting Eisenbern to pivot right and shift his focus back to the guards on the opposite side of the platform.

The man he had stabbed earlier had retreated off the stage. Now, he pointed his sword's tip at the three remaining. "We really don't have to do this, you know."

They charged, baited into the trap, as he observed them. As they neared, he executed another calculated roll, tripping two guards into each other and brushing his blade against the third's side. Just when he thought he had them defeated, clanging metal boots echoed across the wooden platform, and twelve more guards appeared.

"Ilya!" Gustav's voice yelled from the sidelines. "A present for you!" He tossed the Shadowstone spear to her. She caught it, twirled it, and watched as Gustav disappeared onto the other side of the stage once more.

"Follow me, Throatian," she said, as the prisoner behind her shivered. With her long new weapon, she made quick work of the executioner, piercing his armorless, wide openings. With two quick thrusts to both shoulders and a final blow to his hip, Eisenbern felt the man's massive body thud to the ground.

Immediately after, Ilya dashed to Eisenbern, pointing her spear at the oncoming guards. "How much trouble are we in if we win?" she asked.

"Too much trouble, win or lose," Eisenbern said. Judge Var had fled and was probably gathering more reinforcements. "None of this went as I'd planned. We're better off running at this point. Where's Gustav?"

"I imagine he's nearby, planning an escape for us. If we can hold on until then, we'll be okay."

They engaged the twelve soldiers, with Ilya handling most of the combat. The guards' swords posed little threat against the Shadowstone spear. Despite her smaller stature, Ilya used her weight effectively, driving the spear's tip through their thin armor. She impaled one guard in the gut while Eisenbern dealt with the better-trained guards who had flanked them and were trying to surround them.

The ground shook again as the stage collapsed sideways, causing Eisenbern, Ilya, the prisoner, and the guards to tumble and slide toward the executioner's motionless body. At the corner of the demolished stage, Gustav stood, frowning as he massaged his clavicle.

"There's no time to waste," he said, plucking the prisoner from the pile of fallen people and hoisting him onto his shoulders.

Eisenbern and Ilya rose from the ground and followed him through the crowd. Though Gustav had knocked out one of the stage's legs, Eisenbern hoped he had a plan for what to do next. With hundreds of witnesses in the town square and Judge Var clearly furious, the entire city guard would soon be searching for them. The three of them, along with their new prisoner, needed to hide.

"Let go of me!" the prisoner shouted, slamming his fists helplessly against Gustav's armored back.

"Where are we going?" Eisenbern yelled over the commotion. Surprisingly, the crowd let him pass without resistance. He couldn't tell if it was out of fear or support. Then again, Gustav was large enough to break his way through anyone who would stand to block them.

"Just follow!"

Gustav led them through the crowd until it began to thin near an alleyway. As they trudged through, Eisenbern constantly glanced back, checking if anyone was following. Everyone else was likely close behind. Since so many civilians had seen them leave the stage, they knew the guards would soon catch up to them again.

They turned right at the next block, then left. Carrying the prisoner, Gustav freed a hand to open the first house door and carried him inside. Ilya followed while Eisenbern scanned the nearby streets. People nearby gawked at the large man hauling someone over his shoulders into the house.

"He drank too much!" Gustav tried.

The home inside was small but cozy, although they risked discovery at any moment. Fishing poles lined the walls, clothes dried by the fireplace, and a layer of dust covered every surface. Whoever lived there must have been gone.

"Whose house is this?" Eisenbern said, entering and shutting the door behind him. When he attempted to lock it, he realized Gustav had already smashed the mechanism.

"I don't know," he said, setting the man down. "We're just borrowing it. I stored our stuff upstairs. Do what you must, and then we need to move on."

"IN HERE!" the prisoner yelled. "WE'RE IN HERE!"

Ilya slapped him hard on the head. "Shut up, you idiot!" she snapped. "The three of us just saved your life!"

The man glared at the three of them, his face bearing a fresh red mark as he rubbed it. "Saved me from what?" he demanded. "I watched them kill my wife, my brother, and my sister-in-law. You should have let them kill me too. It isn't fair that only I should live, especially after what happened!"

Gustav motioned for the prisoner to take a seat on the bed and then sat down beside him. Surprisingly, the man cooperated.

Eisenbern went to the windows, checked if anyone was listening, and closed the curtains. "The thing is, we need your help," he said. The owner was likely returning from the town square and would be back soon. "Are you a Throatian?"

"I already told you, none of us were Throatian," he said.

"You have the perfect accent for it," Ilya replied with a confident smile.

"Actually, he doesn't have it," Eisenbern stated. He recalled the sharp, almost melodic style of the Common Tongue the Asche family had used during their wedding speeches. The man before them was likely from the Silent Deserts or another distant region. "Even if you're not Throatian, you were still accusing Judge Var of corruption. Explain yourself and why they arrested you. She wanted you silenced as soon as you began speaking out earlier. You must know something important, don't you?"

Judge Var's claim that the prisoners were Throatians must have had a reason behind it, but what?

"There's nothing you can do to help me now," the man said coldly.

"Try us," Ilya spat, brandishing the spear at him.

"You need to calm down," Eisenbern said. "Go watch the windows and make sure nobody's coming." He sat in the chair, his arms resting on the armrests. "Now, sir, we went through a lot to bring you here, and we meant to do you good. Reveal what you know, and we'll let you go."

"My life isn't worth living anymore," the man sobbed. "Everyone I cared about has died. Can't you see?"

Eisenbern gave him a stern, solemn nod. "What happened at the town square wasn't right. We both agree on that. It's no coincidence we've met today, or that you've survived this far. Now's your chance to make it matter. We'll help if we can, but we need the truth."

The prisoner avoided eye contact, his gaze fixed on his feet, before speaking. "Fine. I'll tell you what I know, but you must let me go afterward."

"Very good!"

He took a deep breath. "My brother, the first one they killed, was Judge Sigrid Var's bookkeeper. Recently, a Throatian was involved in a disturbance at a bar. He claimed to be from the Silent Deserts but couldn't provide simple information about it. After he escaped, Judge Var ordered his arrest. She raised taxes by four percent to hire more guards and search for enemies within the city. However, the guards found no others, and my brother discovered she was funneling over half the new tax revenue into fake businesses she controlled. He planned to expose her, prompting her to retaliate by arresting the four of us. By accusing everybody of being Throatians, she could eliminate loose ends and conceal what my brother had uncovered."

"Politicians will never let a crisis go to waste," Eisenbern muttered. "I'm so sorry about your family."

"Can I go now?"

"But what will you do?" Eisenbern asked. "You're still wanted."

"I don't know. This ruined my life. Just leave me alone. Don't save people who don't want to be saved." He stood up from the bed and headed toward the door, but Gustav slid in front of him and blocked his path.

"If we're clear of guards outside, let him go, Gustav," Eisenbern said, avoiding eye contact with the prisoner. "We've troubled him enough."

Ilya peeked through the curtain and gave them a silent nod. Gustav let the man out and strode upstairs to grab their belongings. Upon returning, they quickly divided their things and organized their bags. They then removed their distinctive purple armor and hid it, leaving them in simple tunics that made them less recognizable to those who had witnessed the commotion in the town square. However, Eisenbern still worried that the Shadowstone Spear and Gustav's imposing stature might give them away.

"What about the horses?" Ilya asked as they returned to the street, scanning for guards. Earlier, they'd tied their horses a few blocks from the bar, but it was far from the home they'd hid in.

"We'll go back for them later," Eisenbern said. "We should book another inn and lie low there for a while."

"A wise choice, sir," Gustav said. "The city's exits are likely filled with patrols searching for us. A day or two will allow the dust to settle."

Eisenbern shook his head. "We'll need at least seven days for that."

"A whole week?" Ilya blurted. "Why?"

He glanced around to verify no one was following as he led them down an unfamiliar street, moving away from the town square. "It's for the same reason Gustav mentioned," he said. "I want the news involving us to be drowned out by something else. People obsess over the latest story, and if they forget our faces, it'll make things easier. Plus, I need to send a letter to the queen—to inform her of my error, why we acted as we did, and what the prisoner revealed. This might be our last chance to send a message for a long time. We must ensure whoever delivers it, whether a bird keeper or a courier, doesn't notice us."

They stopped at the first inn they found and sent Ilya in to book a room, as she was the least likely to attract attention without her armor. Several minutes passed as Eisenbern and Gustav waited nervously outside, hoping the innkeeper wouldn't recognize her from the stage and that no one on the street would notice them. Soon she returned, grinning and holding a key.

She whispered proudly, "I secured the lodgings. Seven days, paid in advance. It's the first on the left side upstairs."

"Thanks for your discretion," Eisenbern replied. "It's time to hide."

WHILE GUSTAV VISITED THE LATRINE, EISENBERN AND ILYA CARRIED their belongings upstairs to a modest room. The room featured two single beds, a table, and a vanity mirror—cozy accommodations that would suffice for their stay in hiding.

"Choose whichever bed you like," Eisenbern said. "I'll give the other to Gustav."

"I don't mind sleeping on the floor," Ilya said. "Wooden flooring is better than lying on dirt or waking up with pebbles in your back."

"I insist," Eisenbern replied. "The two of you really helped me earlier. I made a fool of myself by trying to be high and mighty."

"What do you mean by that?" Ilya asked. "Those were innocent people being killed!"

He shushed her. "Don't raise your voice about that. The walls may be thin here."

"Sorry, but we swore an oath to protect the people. There's no guilt in trying to save them," she said.

"The oath was to shield our own people, the Leilan people," Eisenbern corrected. "Today, I overstepped. The judge we saw might have been corrupt, as the prisoner had claimed, but she was right about me. It wasn't our place to judge him without knowing all the facts. We may have caused more problems than we solved."

Ilya took a moment to contemplate his words. "Both can be true. We hurt a lot of guards, yes, but we still saved the prisoner from a wrongful death."

"There were many better ways today could have gone," Eisenbern said, his voice heavy with regret. "I thought he was a Throatian and might deserve a chance to repent for his actions. I was naïve, but with my newfound understanding of the truth, it may have been more merciful to let him join his family in death. Left alive, he must endure the memories of today's events and the consequences. Perhaps we shouldn't have interfered."

Ilya gave him a brief, consoling hug, then said, "At least now, that man has the opportunity to do whatever he wants with his life. You've given him the chance to shape his own destiny, rather than suffer the fate Judge Var imposed on him because of his brother's actions."

Eisenbern began unloading the first of their bags, placing each piece of armor onto the room's only table. Each piece clanged as it hit the surface. "I fear I've doomed that man to a lifetime of wondering why he was the only one in his group to survive. Knowing they were innocent Darians used as political pawns makes my gut churn," Eisenbern said.

Ilya followed suit, emptying another bag containing flint, spare clothing, a map, a pot, and various vegetables. "You're being too hard on yourself—you didn't know the truth at the time. What if those people were guilty of the terrible things you told me about the Throatians? You can humanize the enemy all you want, but they were still responsible for murdering Princess Lydia, burning children alive, and needlessly slaughtering horses. Anyone who follows a religion with those practices must bear the consequences. Their executions would have been justified."

"True, but you're talking hypothetically," Eisenbern replied, sitting on the floor near the end of a bed. "In truth, a man lost his family, and sparing him from death was a curse."

"The grace you gave him counts for a lot, even if he doesn't realize it at first," Ilya countered. "Sometimes, not everyone who wants help needs it, and not everyone who receives it deserves it. We just have to do the best we can to know the difference. Don't linger on this."

He inhaled deeply and exhaled slowly. Ilya was right—no matter how much he wanted to do good, he couldn't have all the facts. Every well-intentioned action risked unintended consequences. The best he could do was to continue doing what a Holy Knight should do, every time, whether he knew everything else or not.

"Thanks, Ilya," he said. "Of all the members of the Purple Guard, you're the speediest and mightiest with the Shadowstone spear. You're equally wise."

"You flatter me," she said. "But it was your choice and a decision you can live with in the future. That's all any of us can hope to bear."

18
BIOS AURAS - THE ASSASSINATION

As dusk painted the sky in waves of orange and purple, Bios Auras spotted the ocean and the faint outline of Starlight Beach against the horizon. Relief washed over him. After a grueling journey in the bouncing cart, Alina's assurance that Cassia was fully committed to their mission finally gave him something to be grateful for.

From his observations, Alina had the stronger leadership qualities of the two women from the Silent Deserts. This realization strengthened Bios's confidence that their partnership would serve him well. Seeing both women committed to freeing their people, Bios revealed his magic to them, reducing the chances of any future betrayal.

The complication was Ambrose, who remained oblivious to the group's evolving dynamics. For now, Bios Auras waited patiently—outwardly calm but inwardly preparing for what lay ahead. It was time to speed up the mission on his own terms, without distractions or delays. Most satisfyingly, he would finally stop Ambrose's tiresome political ramblings.

"Are you both ready?" Bios muttered under his breath to Alina and Cassia, careful not to draw Ambrose's attention.

"Isn't Starlight Beach quite the spectacle?" Ambrose chimed in. "Though it's hard to see from here, that tower belongs to the university, which attracts minds from all corners of the realm in pursuit of knowledge and wisdom. I've heard the view from up there is truly unparalleled."

Bios rolled his eyes. Ambrose's incessant comments were unnecessary and distracted from the seriousness of their mission.

"Ready to go," Alina responded.

"Ready," Cassia echoed, her face set with determination.

"Oh, I don't think we'll have time to visit there," Ambrose continued, oblivious to the true meanings behind their words. "The ship smuggling us into Wargonne will depart soon. We need to check in at the docks."

Bios's voice broke through Ambrose's chatter. "Stop the cart! Everyone out."

The wooden wheels sank into the muddy path. The driver, a stocky man with an unkempt beard, brought the cart to a halt with a creak. Confused, he turned back to face the passengers.

"What's wrong?" Ambrose asked before the driver could speak. "Why do we need to stop?"

Bios jumped down from the cart, landing on the ground. Despite the weight of his armor, his movements were graceful. "We'll walk to Wargonne from here," he said as he turned to the driver. "Proceed to Starlight Beach and tell the ship to leave without us. Our mission will continue on foot."

The driver nodded, but his expression remained unconvinced. "Very well, Sir Hellvar," he said. "I advise you to follow your quest giver's instructions, but ultimately, the mission's success depends on you."

With that, the driver urged the cart forward, taking their supplies with him. Ambrose stood frozen for a moment, his mouth wide in disbelief.

"What in the Black Sands are you doing?" Ambrose exploded, his voice trembling with panic. "We can't just walk to Wargonne! The journey is dangerous—volcanoes, black mountains, and air so scorching it's impossible to breathe! It's madness!"

Ambrose realized he had used Cassia's name as a curse and apologized to her, his crimson cheeks overcome with embarrassment.

Bios turned to the three knights with him, but kept his eyes fixed on Ambrose. "Our mission is to assassinate Councilman Conan in Wargonne. The ring on his finger will serve as proof of his death."

Alina nodded, her eyes nervously meeting Bios'. Cassia stood beside her, her loyalty promised, though unproven.

"Now," Bios continued, turning back to Ambrose, who was still spluttering in protest, "I'll show you my true power."

He closed his eyes and focused on Wargonne, the daunting

fortress with its many towers reaching for the heavens. From a particular rooftop, he recalled, he could take in a greater view of the surrounding area. The roof's tiles, though decades old and weathered by time and sun, remained sturdy enough to support him.

The air shimmered before them and an invisible portal blinked open. Cassia's green eyes widened as the portal swallowed her.

Ambrose barely had time to process what was happening before Bios grabbed him. His protests died in his throat as he pushed him toward the portal. The ground gave way beneath him, and he stumbled forward, falling through the portal and emerging onto the rooftop Bios had remembered from years earlier.

Finally, it was just Alina and Bios remaining. Her eyes revealed she admired him yet also feared his power. What Bios could do was unlike anything she'd seen before.

"Are you ready?" he asked as his heart beat faster.

Alina nodded once, her stance refined for battle as she gripped her sword. She took a deep breath to steady herself and stepped forward.

Seconds later, the four of them stood undetected on the rooftop. Ambrose staggered, his attention switching between the shock of seeing the courtyard and Bios Auras. Alina and Cassia were amazed but more restrained, already knowing what was coming next.

"How did you—" Ambrose gasped. "How did we get here? Are we really in Wargonne?"

He regarded the knight with a half-smirk as pride lined his lips. "I wield power others can only dream of."

"But surely you can't just—" Ambrose protested, but Bios silenced him by raising his forearm, where the God Stone rested hidden beneath his skin. Another portal opened silently beneath Ambrose's boots.

Without warning, Ambrose fell through the ground and reappeared in the deserted courtyard below. He landed inelegantly on the cobblestones, scrambled to his feet, then looked up at Bios, who stood high above, stark and distant.

"Now, Lady Oceansong," Bios commanded. "Do as we practiced."

"I'm ready," she declared, drawing her sword.

He opened another portal, this time underneath Alina. With a series of quick manipulations, he dropped her through the air. Bios rotated her mid-flight, guiding her onto the precise trajectory he had envisioned. Alina emerged directly above the knight, her blade aimed precisely at him. Gravity lent her strength as she descended with a hawk's grace, her strike swift and deadly. Ambrose had no chance to react before her sword ended his life.

A metallic thud echoed through the courtyard as Ambrose's body collapsed. Alina vanished through another Teleportation Stone portal as swiftly and silently as she had arrived.

Bios smiled, not only because he would never have to endure Ambrose's political lectures again but also because Alina had proven her loyalty and passed his test magnificently. She'd killed Ambrose for him, and without question.

Alina landed on the roof next to Cassia and sheathed her blood-stained blade. As a skilled assassin, it was clear why the People's Army had chosen her for the Equity Guard.

"A clean execution," Bios complimented. "I couldn't have done it better myself."

Despite his own trail of sins, all evil would vanish once he collected the remaining stones. Having Ambrose killed would ultimately be irrelevant, as the knight would serve a higher purpose.

Cassia lowered herself onto the uneven tiles, crossing her arms. "Now we wait," she said, her tone revealing her impatience.

The minutes stretched by endlessly as they watched the courtyard below. At last, a guard emerged around the corner, his idle whistles echoing off the stone walls. Upon spotting Ambrose's body, he paused. "What happened here?" he muttered under his breath.

The soldier approached with caution then stopped to inspect Ambrose's remains. His eyes widened in shock upon noticing the pool of blood near the knight's chest. "Did he die by his own sword?" the soldier muttered.

Another soldier emerged in response to the first guard's urgent call for help. "What's going on?" the second guard asked, rushing over to his comrade and the body.

The first guard shook his head. "It seems someone killed an intruder. He's not one of ours." Frowning, he asked, "How did he get in, and who killed him?"

He unsheathed Ambrose's sword and inspected it. The blade was clean, showing no signs of recent use. "Something's off here," he muttered, scratching his beard. "This doesn't add up."

More guards arrived, responding to the disturbance, and an older knight emerged, a grizzled veteran with a thick beard and piercing eyes. "What's happened here?" he barked as he surveyed the scene. Crouched beside the body, he examined Ambrose's armor closely. "He's not from our ranks," he declared. "But how did he get in? And who killed him?"

One of the younger guards spoke up. "Perhaps a patrol defeated him, sir. But why leave the body here?"

Another guard dropped to one knee beside the senior knight. "Examine this wound," he said. "It's as if the blade was driven through from above."

The senior knight frowned, tracing his fingers along the edge of the sword wound. "Indeed, this is peculiar. Summon the councilman. Perhaps he can identify the man or his armor."

Bios watched from above, a grin spreading across his face. His plan was unfolding perfectly—he had used Ambrose's body as bait, a wise act on his part. Wargonne's layout was massive, but by drawing Councilman Conan to them, they could bypass navigating the fortress's labyrinth-like halls.

Cassia shifted uncomfortably beside him. "How much longer do we have to wait?"

Alina remained silent, her eyes fixed on the courtyard below. Meanwhile, Bios sensed her unease but knew it wasn't the moment to address it. They needed to wait just a few minutes more.

The senior knight gave his men orders. "Search for anything else out of the ordinary while we wait, but remember, Conan will want the area untouched."

The three of them waited on the rooftop for Conan to appear. Many years ago, Bios had seen the man from a distance. Even now, the soldier was easily recognizable as the Darian Kingdom's Master of Defense and War. Conan stood at attention, his hands folded behind his back, as the evening sun beat down on him. His aged skin bore the marks of time spent fighting the Lucidians and patrolling the kingdom.

Conan's polished silver armor, accented with gold edges, made him stand out even among his peers. He carried an imposing presence, towering over others, yet his watchful gaze over those around him was that of an older brother. Known for his kindness, his frequent smile brightened the fortress as he performed his duties and served the people of Wargonne. His reputation for both compassion and strategic cunning in battle was renowned throughout Yaenia.

Bios watched the knight below as Alina and Cassia analyzed the soldiers gathering. Noticing a gold ring on Conan's hand, he wondered if it was the one they sought.

"Can either of you tell if he's wearing the ring we're looking for?" Bios asked, squinting.

Alina shook her head. "That's a ring, but is it the right one?"

Cassia scoffed. "You two must have lost your sight. It's clearly the ring we need—a sun emblem on a maroon background. There's no mistaking it."

Bios dismissed the comment as he brushed the hair from his eyes. "We'll confirm soon enough. Defeating Conan is our priority. Once he's defeated, the news will spread. The People's Army cannot ignore our success, ring or no ring. Are you both ready for the next step?"

"Yes," said Cassia, tightening her grip on her steel blade.

"Ready," confirmed Alina.

"Remember, Conan is mine, and the guards are yours," Bios said, focusing his concentration on his right arm. He dropped from the rooftop, as he had done with Ambrose earlier, but this time, only Conan would be surprised.

Bios stepped through the Teleportation Stone's portal, sword raised, poised to strike Conan from behind. Conan stumbled forward but barely dodged as Bios materialized behind him. The master of defense and war drew his massive, surprisingly light broadsword. But Bios didn't care about the weapon—he was confident he had the skills to defeat Conan no matter what he wielded.

"Who are you?" the Master of Defense and War demanded, his voice booming with authority as he readied himself for the next attack.

Bios lunged, only to parry a wild swing from the veteran knight. They exchanged more blows, their weapons clashing and echoing through the courtyard.

"My name is irrelevant," Bios panted. "I'm a Throatian here to avenge Harkbin Asche."

Conan's brow creased as realization dawned on him. "Wait… You're the knight King Ether mentioned—the one in crimson armor, with blond hair, and that twisted grin. You were there when they killed Princess Lydia! Guards, arrest him!"

Bios roared, his eyes blazing with fury. "Your memory betrays you—though great, it will be your undoing." Now, he needed to eliminate any witnesses to prevent the news of his appearance from reaching Somnius.

"No," Conan stepped forward, his voice steady and indignant. "It is you who owes a debt to the Darian Kingdom. We haven't forgotten what you Throatians did to our princess on her wedding day."

The other soldiers were engaged in battle with Alina and Cassia, unable to hear Conan's calls. In doing their jobs well, they allowed Conan and Bios to face each other alone. This was Bios's moment to achieve the purpose he had joined the People's Army for. With Ambrose gone, he no longer needed to hide his true intentions from Alina and Cassia. He could kill them, too, if they ever betrayed him.

Bios shouted, "King Ether has hidden the God Stones here!" Though uncertain if it was true, he knew he had to capitalize on the moment. "Bring them to me now!" he ordered.

Conan's face paled as Bios's words hit their mark. "I don't know how you found out about them, but they're not here."

"Lies!" Bios shouted with a swing of his sword. With a flick of his wrist, he opened a portal beneath Conan, sending him plummeting from six feet above to the stone ground.

Conan's armor clanged as he collided shoulder-first. The impact knocked the breath from him, but he quickly regained his footing and adopted a fighting stance again. Sweat trickled down his face; the Teleportation Stone's magic was unlike anything he'd faced before in battles against the Lucidians.

"So you already possess one stone," Conan stated, fear growing in his voice —an emotion his guards had likely never seen from him before. Many wouldn't see his defeat; Alina and Cassia were defeating their nameless other opponents as fast as each wave came.

Bios declared, "I want all of them, and I'll crush anyone who stands in my path. Hand over the God Stones you're safeguarding for the king, and I'll spare you and your men."

By now, the commander surely realized there was no escaping this assault. If he surrendered to Bios' false promises, he might reveal what he knew. Either way, Conan's fate was sealed.

"It's true you have the advantage," Conan replied, "but lacking the God Stone, you're nothing but an ordinary man. Fight me with honor—if you can even fight without your magic! Prove to me you're more than just your trinkets."

Bios couldn't blame Conan for trying to disarm him with words alone, but it wouldn't work. Honor and vulnerability were interdependent sisters—distractions he couldn't afford, especially after what had happened before with Somnius.

"Greater weapons win battles, not greater honor," Bios said. "Let me show you."

Immediately, he lunged forward, opening a portal in front of him. In a flash, he soared over Conan, his weapon aimed at the councilman's shoulder.

Conan darted left, evading Bios's strike and countering with a horizontal slash of his blade. The attack landed with a grisly crunch, causing Bios's sword to clatter to the ground as his left arm gave way. Pain surged through him, hot and intense, but he clenched his teeth, forcing himself to remain conscious.

As Bios attempted to open another portal, Conan swung again with rapid precision.

Bios raised his limb, mangled though it was, to absorb Conan's blow. The blade burst through the gap in his gauntlet, piercing the skin and severing his forearm from the elbow.

Alina screamed, "Hellvar!"

Bios's fingers gripped the stump of his arm, blood pooling beneath his stump. Fortunately, Conan had severed Bios's left arm instead of his right, leaving the Teleportation Stone still inside his body. However, if Bios lost too much blood from his open wound, he would faint until he recovered, making him vulnerable to capture. Although Conan had bested him with that strike, it made little difference—Bios Auras knew he would never die.

"I'll never betray Ether's trust," Conan announced. "Stay down and yield, you Throatian scum."

Kneeling, Bios picked up his severed limb as if to block another blow and keep Conan guessing for now.

Despite his pain, Bios found his lips curling into a sinister smile. "Your honor cannot save you."

The Master of Defense and War raised his sword, its steel cold in the night air, as he prepared to deliver a final blow against Bios Auras. The crimson knight, though tormented by searing pain in his stump, redirected his focus to his enemy's right arm.

He narrowed his eyes, examining each muscle of Conan's appendage until he found the spot. Then, Bios Auras summoned the smallest portal he had ever created, only six inches wide, at Conan's biceps. The Teleportation Stone's magic hummed softly as he opened a tiny bridge, just as usual, but this time with a different purpose in mind.

Conan's broadsword clattered to the ground as the portal severed his arm—all while a scream tore from his throat.

Bios Auras smiled gleefully. "Thank you," he said to the kneeling councilman. "Thank you so much for your inspiration."

"My arm..." Conan groaned, clutching the stump where his arm had just been.

Bios strode forward, snatching Conan's sword and flinging it to the side like a child's toy. "This is your last chance," Bios declared, brandishing his weapon. "Give me the God Stones or die."

"I don't know where they are," Conan insisted. "They aren't here. I swear on my life, King Ether hasn't told us where he—"

Bios Auras interrupted, his voice cold and echoing through the courtyard. "This fortress is the safest place for what could be the most powerful magical weaponry in the world. You claim the king never entrusted you, his Master of Defense and War, with them?"

Conan pleaded, "He didn't! The King always kept the stones nearby wherever he was!"

Bios Auras pondered, unsure whether to trust him. If King Ether hadn't given Conan the stones, where else could they be but in Serenity Keep? However, the Asche family had searched the castle and surrounding areas thoroughly before Prince Thane's wedding and had only uncovered counterfeit stones. Before acting further, he needed to confirm that Conan was unaware of anything else.

"So you have nothing for me?" Bios Auras snapped, his sword pressed lightly against Conan's shoulder. "Nothing that could save your life?"

Conan swallowed hard, his eyes wide with fear. "There are hermits—mountain people living northwest of New Ginstown. My men heard rumors of strange voices echoing through the mountains, warning intruders to stay away. But the voices weren't spoken aloud—they sounded from within their own minds. It must be magic. They are called the Whisperers. Maybe they are using the stones."

Bios Auras contemplated the information and realized he needed to investigate, regardless of whether Conan was telling the truth. If he wasn't, it was a well-crafted lie that was too specific to ignore. The mention of mental voices suggested a dragon, perhaps similar to Zann-Xia-Czul rather than the God Stones. Another dragon, if that's what it was, would complicate everything further.

"We don't have proof," Conan continued, "but we suspect it's so. King Ether may have entrusted the stones to someone there. Take it as you will. There's something magical in the forest."

"Mountain hermits," Bios Auras mused. "I pray you aren't lying."

"It's the truth," Conan insisted. "I only hope I'm wrong; otherwise, I would have betrayed my king."

Bios sheathed his blade with a soft click and nodded faintly, not to Conan, but as a signal. Alina, the lady of Oceansong, understood and stepped forward, her sword still in hand.

"I apologize, Councilman Conan," Alina announced, her voice steady despite the circumstances. "You may have struck a deal with Hellvar, but not with me. My purpose here is to fulfill my mission. This is nothing personal."

Before Conan could react, Alina struck and ended his life—concluding the conflict. Bios Auras instantly teleported Alina, Cassia, Conan's body, and himself to the rooftop. There, they removed the Darian-sigil ring from Conan's body and sent the councilman back down to the soldiers. They completed the mission exactly as planned, thanks to the Teleportation Stone, which accelerated their progress by weeks. Their contact in the People's Army would be shocked by their early return—especially with Conan's ring in their possession. Smiling at the chaos in Wargonne, Bios Auras opened a final portal, safely transporting the three of them to Hillside Reach.

THE BACK ALLEY BEHIND THE GOLDEN MARE REEKED OF ROT AND dampness, a concoction of alcohol, vomit, and mud. Crates and barrels along the walls were the only witnesses to what would soon unfold. Cassia's breath was visible like a ghost in the chilly night air as she spun to face Bios and shoved him hard. "How could you do that?" she demanded.

Bios was surprised and stumbled slightly, but he soon regained his composure. He raised an eyebrow, his controlled demeanor hiding his true shock. "What difference does it make now? The job is done."

"You could have killed Conan as quickly as Alina murdered Ambrose," Cassia stated. "Instead, you toyed with him first. It was cruel and unnecessary!"

Alina stood close by, her arms folded, also surprised by Cassia's outburst.

"Lady Blacksand," he began coolly, "Conan might have known the God Stones's location. I couldn't risk killing him without learning what he knew. You have no right to lecture me on matters of morality when you were perfectly fine with letting Alina kill Ambrose."

Cassia turned away for a moment, and then back to him. "You played with him!" she accused, her voice rising. "The man was on his knees, pleading for mercy."

Even though they were alone in the alley, Cassia risked attracting unwanted attention to their group. It would be better to calm her down than to try changing her mind.

Bios raised his hand. "This is the reality we live in. I had to make a choice, and I had to act," he reasoned. "The God Stones are what I've been searching for all along. That is why I needed him to talk, even if by force. Besides, he cut my arm off first."

Cassia crossed her arms, her body language defensive, and shook her head in disbelief. "It doesn't matter," she muttered. "How could you be so cold? You promised to spare his life."

Bios frowned, his expression stiffening. Maybe convincing her was the better path after all. He felt no guilt, but revealing deeper truths might appeal to her emotions. "I did what was necessary to force his hand," he replied. "I must do whatever it takes to get those God Stones, even if it means leaving a trail of blood behind me. The truth is, I am the instrument of Asura's will, and I will carry out my mission to purge the world of evil, regardless of the cost."

Cassia let out a harsh, bitter laugh as her eyes flared with anger. "What kind of man are you?" she accused. "You commanded us to use Ambrose as bait and kill him, then you—"

"The three of us had an agreement," Bios interrupted calmly but firm. "Didn't we determine Ambrose was a liability to all our goals?"

As Cassia began to speak, Alina stepped forward. "That's enough," she interrupted. "It was I who withheld mercy from Conan. What Hellvar did is understandable now that we know of his additional intentions."

"You're siding with him?"

"I'm siding with the mission," Alina affirmed. "Having seen what I saw, I believe we couldn't have completed our goals in Wargonne if not for Hellvar's magic. If he needs anything, we should help him—our future successes depend on what he can do for us."

"The two of you swore to obey me without question," Bios reminded them. "Your ability to uphold your oaths to me is the only way I can lead us to our goals, including freeing the slaves in the Silent Deserts."

Cassia crossed her arms, her tension finally easing. "You need to do… less questionable actions along the journey. I'm not opposed to killing on your behalf, but it should be done with more respect. Shouldn't a so-called chosen one of Asura live their life by such a creed, if that's what you even are?"

Bios nodded, opening his palms. "Believe me, I try not to kill anyone. I understand the value of life, but sometimes we must sacrifice for the greater good." What he didn't mention was that he preferred not to take lives directly to avoid losing control of the God Stones. Without that constraint, he would have had no objection to making his own kills.

To his surprise, Alina spoke up in support again. "Hellvar is right about everything. He's the chosen one of Asura." Her voice trembled, and her face betrayed a hint of astonishment.

Cassia turned to her. "You believe his claim? How can you be so sure?"

"There's no denying it; Hellvar is special," Alina replied. "Look at him."

"Look at what?" Cassia exclaimed, her confusion clear.

Then, she saw it. Bios flexed his healed arm, feeling the familiar surge of strength return as he moved his fingers. Following the chaos of teleporting out of Wargonne, his limb had instantly regrown where it had been severed. Though his gauntlet was unfortunately gone, he would retrieve a spare from one of his stashes in the Silent Deserts sometime later. Meanwhile, Cassia gazed at him in awe, her eyes wide with astonishment.

"How is that possible?" Cassia gasped. "Your arm was completely gone! How did you…? Is it even the same one?"

Bios offered her a mysterious smile. "I am Asura's chosen one," he declared. "My body serves as a vessel for the divine power coursing through me, granting me the ability to endure and recover from any injury."

"I've never heard of such magic coming from Lucidians," Alina exclaimed, "so it must be you're not a half-Lucidian after all."

Bios shook his head. "I'm not," he admitted. "But Asura has chosen and blessed me for a reason. I will be there to help you both when the time comes, using my abilities. In the meantime, you need to trust me without question."

Cassia exchanged an uncertain glance with Alina. "Are we sure about this?"

Alina placed a comforting hand on Cassia's shoulder and replied, "The three of us crossed paths for a reason," she said. "Our cause is just, and we must use every advantage to achieve it. If we won't cross certain lines, then we're no more realistic than Ambrose."

Bios gave them a single nod of agreement. Now, he had them both. "I will do whatever I can to help you both," he promised. "But for now, let's focus on our missions. We still need the People's Army for information and influence."

"That's true," Cassia admitted. "I'm sorry for how I..."

"There's no need to apologize to me," Bios said gently. "I find solace in your realization that there's more to saving this world than clinging to a single set of ideals."

"Thank you for your insight, Hellvar," Alina said. "It is clear Cassia and I both can learn a great deal from your... divine knowledge."

"Please," he replied. "You may now call me by my real name, Bios Auras. Hellvar was the false name I used when joining the People's Army to hide who I really was. Together, we will remove every evil in this world—I promise."

INSIDE, THE GOLDEN MARE BUZZED WITH ACTIVITY, THE AIR RICH with scents of sizzling meat, sweat, ale, and smoke. Patrons laughed and chatted, their faces flushed from warmth and drink. At a nearby table, a group of squires shared tales of their exploits, their laughter echoing despite the modest steaks on their plates. Bios gave them a passing glance; only those in purple armor would have caught his interest. He scanned the crowd for any Leilan Knights but found none, a fortunate relief. As he, Alina, and Cassia approached the bar, the grizzled bartender with a bushy beard looked up, his eyes blinking with startled surprise.

"Well now, if it isn't your lot again," he said. "You're back so soon. Did something happen on the way south?"

Bios leaned casually against the counter, a smirk on his face. "We've completed our mission." He produced Conan's ring and laid it down in front of him.

The bartender gaped as he examined the dead councilman's accessory. "You really did it?"

Alina nodded. "There's your proof."

"I… I don't understand," the bartender stammered, still in shock. "That's not possible! You left less than a week ago…"

Bios leaned in close to whisper. The bar buzzed with noise, but he kept his next words private.

"The news of his death is going to come soon," Bios assured him quietly, "and it will confirm our success."

"But how? There wasn't enough time…"

Bios's eyes glowed with amusement. The Teleportation Stone's magic had always enabled him to move faster than birds and their letters. "We have our ways, and as long as we're not exposed, all's well." He flashed another cryptic smile before changing the subject. "But for now, shall we raise a toast?"

"A drink would be nice," Cassia chimed in. "Hellvar makes it seem easy, but it was far from simple. Guards heavily guarded Wargonne."

The bartender nodded slowly, his approval apparent as he poured them three large tankards of ale and shots of something stronger. "To many more surprises like this one, and to the benefit of the Common People," he toasted quietly before downing his drink in a single gulp. Bios raised his mug, catching Alina's eye as she finished her shot in a single swallow.

"Well done on our first mission together," she said. "I look forward to whatever comes next on this path we walk toward a brighter future."

Cassia nodded, choosing to sip her drink instead of indulging in it fully. "Remember, our work is far from over."

Bios raised his mug again. "To interesting adventures," he said. He was usually alone when he drank, so the chore of giving a toast caught him off guard.

"One last thing," the bartender added as he leaned closer. "I already suspect I know what happened, but Ambrose didn't make it back?"

Bios met his curious gaze. "He fell to the guards, and we couldn't save him."

The bartender nodded. "It's surprising that three of you survived. I'll speak with my guide and assign another mission to you. Until then, you can stay in the rooms upstairs."

Bios's eyes narrowed at the proposition. Was the bartender's offer genuine, or did he intend to detain them at the inn until their next assignment?

Alina overlooked the hidden motivation behind the request. "A chance to breathe is always welcome," she said.

"A bed, too," Cassia added wearily.

Bios leaned forward. "So, who should we thank for arranging these accommodations? You've never told us your name before."

The bartender smiled. "Most people know me by another name," he said, "but those loyal to the Common People call me... the Magician."

Bios raised an eyebrow. "An interesting title. One I won't soon forget."

As they made their way upstairs, Bios couldn't shake the impending sense of danger. He realized someone would inevitably ask how they'd defeated Conan so quickly, and he needed to have an answer prepared. For now, though, success was theirs, and he intended to savor it.

Even if the People's Army wanted him to stay at the Golden Mare until their next mission, Bios knew he could come and go as he pleased. He took pride in his ability to manipulate everyone around him for his own ends. No one—not even the People's Army—could stand in his way.

19
THANE - THE HIEROPHANT'S INQUIRY

The wagon's squeaking wheels confirmed the Lucidians had spared his life. As he regained consciousness, his eyes opened, registering the uneven path beneath him as the wagon jostled him. Darkness had settled, but Zeere's bandaged face was still visible in the cramped cart.

"What happened?" Thane muttered. His fingers traced the spot on his neck where the Enforcer Mage had rendered him unconscious using a magical pinch.

"We're heading south," Zeere said softly. "You should have left me behind, Feiir."

Despite the bandages concealing his companion's face, Thane could sense the weariness in his every spoken word.

"They haven't tied or constrained our hands," he whispered back. "We might find a chance to escape this."

Zeere let out a hollow laugh. "Feiir, you don't realize what we've gotten ourselves into," he said. "The Enclave has thousands of warriors, each with magic far greater than the two who captured us. Many harbor deep prejudices against humans, so we are already as good as dead. Wherever this cart is going will be our final stop."

"I'm sorry for falling asleep," Thane said. "I'll find a way out of this mess I've made."

"Whether you were sleeping or awake last night, it wouldn't have mattered," Zeere lamented. "Few can escape an Enforcer Mage. Your enthusiasm is as heroic as it is foolish."

Thane refrained from responding further. He wondered if

Zeere's pessimism was justified or if his own fear of being sent back to the Enclave was causing his morale to plummet. Regardless, Thane's mistake had resulted in their capture. It was his responsibility to undo it.

As dawn broke, the Enforcer Mage tossed them bones for breakfast and half a cup of water to share. Thane followed Zeere's advice, remaining silent and ignoring his captor's mocking words, and didn't touch the skeletal remains. Meanwhile, Zeere's health had improved since the previous evening. The Null Mage sat up straighter, appeared more alert, and, during brief breaks from the wagon, could even walk despite his neck and chest wounds.

"It's a miracle you survived what the Savager Mage did to you," Thane remarked as they returned from relieving themselves in the bushes.

"A Grace Mage at one of their checkpoint camps healed me while you slept," Zeere replied. "It wasn't out of kindness, though. Something big is happening—I'm certain of it. I haven't seen so many Lucidians outside the Enclave since the war."

"They were preparing for what would happen when they found the Savager Mage," Thane speculated. "Their goal was to capture him."

Zeere shook his head. "No, I suspect something more sinister was at work. The Enclave wouldn't send a great number of people outside for just one Savager."

He leaned in closer. "How many were at the camp you spoke of?"

"They blindfolded me as we came to the Grace Mage," Zeere said, "but I could still hear the chatter. Crowds were gathering nearby, enjoying the evening. Something was happening but I couldn't tell what."

"It must have been an army," Thane said. "With the Darians focused on the war against my people, the Lucidians likely saw this as an opportunity to strike. If they're not in the Enclave, they've probably headed east toward Last Hope."

"Perhaps," Zeere said slowly. "But Lucidians don't fight straightforward battles. They won't simply appear at your border with an army—they'll find a way inside your walls and attack only when the timing is perfect."

Thane tilted his head slightly to the left. "Why would they resort to complicated tactics and striking from the shadows? A single Enforcer Mage could conquer an entire city."

"But what happens if two Enforcers fight each other?" Zeere

countered. "That's why their civil war was so prolonged, which taught them not to underestimate notable foes like King Ether von Stonewall."

Thane failed to see the connection between the Darians and Enforcer Mages, but Zeere must have been alluding to a part of history he didn't know.

Though Thane was uncertain, he tried to envision what Throatians might do if they had left their island without intending to wage war. The most probable reason for their departure could be religious—perhaps they aimed to convert others to the worship of Zann-Xia-Czul. Another possibility was that they were on a diplomatic mission, or at least pretending to be. The other chance was that they were rebels. Which was most likely for the Lucidians?

"Are there any groups that might defy the Enclave's rule?" Thane asked.

"None whatsoever," Zeere said. "The Enclave has no rebellions that last beyond their infancy. The only people you'll find outside the border are stragglers like me, who never returned from the war. Regardless of who apprehended us, we are still in grave danger."

He was probably correct. The Enforcer Mage and Sentinel Mage who had captured them seemed to embody the very tyranny Zeere had described as ruling the Enclave. They were unlikely to be part of a noble rebellion of warriors resisting their homeland.

Their cart continued onward for several more hours before stopping again to allow their captors to water the horses. After a brief rest, they resumed their journey, but Thane noticed they had changed direction—they were now heading south along the Enclave's border instead of west toward it. Zeere confirmed they had already passed New Ginstown and were moving parallel to the wall.

After a few more days of travel, someone blindfolded them again and led them from the cart. Voices in both the Common Tongue and Lucidian echoed around them. When their blindfolds were removed, they found themselves in a jail cell. Once settled, a human —rather than a Lucidian—greeted them with an ominous warning: "The Hierophant will see you soon."

"Who is the Hierophant?" Thane asked Zeere once their warden was out of sight and earshot.

"I've never heard of that name or rank," Zeere answered, "and I suspect meeting them is not in our best interest."

Thane examined their cell. The walls were stone, though dry.

Though Thane wore his white armor, both he and Zeere were unarmed and carried no weapons that might be of use for escaping.

Thane couldn't help but remember when he and Hrodspire had been behind bars at Grimm Kathaar's command. What hurt his heart wasn't entering the prison, but leaving it. After their release, they faced the Reminders of Suffering in a trial, the Throatian ritual of single combat to prove loyalty to Zann-Xia-Czul. To survive, Thane had killed an innocent armorer, Hrodspire, and almost Cereene. His deal with Bios Auras saved both him and Cereene that day. Seeing a jail cell again reminded him of that time and the pain it caused him. Now, Thane wondered if the Lucidians' cruelty would match Zann-Xia-Czul's and Bios Auras's.

"We need to find a way out of this," Thane said, his voice steady despite the fear growing inside him. "At least they didn't lock us in with magic."

"Cells in the Enclave are specially constructed to contain magical prisoners," Zeere explained. "Since this is an ordinary human cell, it confirms we're still in their territory. However, a prison remains a prison, and even beyond the bars, our foes possess magic we do not."

"So, if we can escape," Thane said, his voice hardening with determination, "then there's still hope. We'd need to reach a place where the Lucidians wouldn't want to draw attention to themselves." He offered a small smile.

"Your foolish optimism is starting to wear on me, Feiir," his companion growled.

* * *

"I've brought the first prisoner," the Enforcer Mage announced. Time had run out, and they couldn't investigate further.

"Uncover his eyes," a harsh female voice commanded, "and then leave us."

The veil over Thane's face vanished, revealing a woman wearing a golden owl mask that hid her identity. She leaned back on her throne, which appeared to be made of obsidian. The dimly lit brownish tent held only a single candle on an empty table to her right. The Hierophant offered no introduction before the Enforcer Mage bowed deeply and left.

"Which of you defeated Savager 1836?" she asked.

"It was I who gave the final blow," Thane answered.

"That is unsurprising," the Hierophant replied coolly, "given your companion's condition. Tell me, great warrior, where did you obtain this magical armor?"

Thane hesitated as the Hierophant narrowed her eyes, waiting for a reply. He couldn't reveal the truth about Somnius or his mission. His ivory suit, glowing with emerald light along the edges, left no doubt of its uniqueness. As he had done throughout his time in Yaenia, he chose to hold back the truth.

"I'm a mercenary from the Silent Deserts," he said carefully. "I purchased it there."

The Hierophant tsked behind her mask. "More lies," she concluded coldly. She then rose and circled him.

"It's the truth," Thane insisted, turning his head to follow her. "I came to retrieve the Savager Mage's body. A client in New Ginstown hired me for the task."

A faint sneer echoed from behind the golden mask. "Even more lies," she snapped. "You leave me no choice."

Her voice sounded in his mind without moving her lips. Thane froze; only Zann-Xia-Czul had ever spoken directly into his thoughts. Whisperers were the only ones credited with such power, and Zeere had claimed Lucidians lacked this ability. Just who was she and how was she doing it?

"WHO ARE YOU?" the Hierophant's voice boomed inside him.

Thane remained silent, unwilling to reveal more. He knew from experience that speaking his true name was dangerous—here, as in the rest of Yaenia, he couldn't risk it.

The Hierophant circled him again, her presence surging with power and menace. "DO NOT LET YOUR MIND WANDER. ANSWER ME."

"I am Feiir," Thane said aloud, echoing his earlier words to Zeere. He hesitated to ask if she was a Whisperer directly, for it would reveal too much of his own knowledge. Instead, seeking to avoid suspicion, he asked, "Are you somehow a dragon?"

"Feiir the fool," the Hierophant snapped with disdain through her mask. "I am a Mind Mage—tell me your real name."

Thane bit his lip, resisting her mental intrusion. He couldn't yield—he had to protect himself and Zeere.

"YOU WILL ANSWER ME," she forced into his thoughts again, this time with a power that made his body shake. "ANSWER ME TRULY."

The room faded into darkness as the words repeated. Then, a new truth dawned on him: perhaps the Hierophant meant no harm. Perhaps she could protect him from the Enforcer Mage and anything else that could harm him.

Maybe he could trust her with the truth.

Maybe she was an ally—his ally. Yes, she could become an ally.

She had not ordered their deaths. The Hierophant had instructed the Enforcer Mage to bring them to her. She had already spared their lives.

The Grace Mage had saved Zeere's life under the Hierophant's orders. If Thane had been the one gravely injured by the Savager Mage, she might have saved him as well.

She deserved his thankfulness. He should answer and tell her his real name.

She was an ally, after all.

The Hierophant was an ally. The Hierophant was an ally. The Hierophant was an ally! The Hierophant was an ally! The Hierophant was an ally! The Hierophant was an ally! The Hierophant was an ally! The Hierophant was an ally! The Hierophant was an ally! The Hierophant was an ally! The Hierophant was an ally! The Hierophant was an ally! The Hierophant was an ally! The Hierophant was an ally!

"My name is Thane Asche," he blurted before he could stop himself.

The room brightened again, and Thane's heart sank, realizing what a terrible mistake he'd made in revealing his true identity to this powerful stranger. What had she done to him?

The Hierophant sighed. "You've lied to me again. The Throatian prince is long dead." Though she had wielded her Mind Mage abilities, perhaps they were not as all-knowing as Zann-Xia-Czul's magic.

"You asked me to answer you truthfully," Thane replied quietly, "and I have." It was fortunate she still didn't believe him.

"Your name and where you acquired your suit doesn't matter," the Hierophant conceded. "There's something unique about it, and I want it to belong to me."

Darkness overcame Thane's vision once again as she penetrated his mind.

The command "GIVE ME YOUR ARMOR" echoed hundreds of times.

"Why do you want it?" he asked, stalling for time. "I can't give it to you—I need it."

Thane's thoughts jumbled with memories of Somnius's words from that day long ago: "Though white armor cannot protect you from a black storm, armor of light will help you defeat the darkness."

"GIVE ME YOUR ARMOR. PROTECT ME, AND I WILL PROTECT YOU."

Though Thane knew her magic was manipulating him, his mind was tormented as she exploited his deepest fears. His armor, which could protect him from human enemies, was powerless against Lucidian magic. Surrendering it to her might spare his life, offering protection far beyond the threat of human weapons.

He unbuckled the straps and laid the pieces out one by one on the table, leaving only his simple black clothing beneath.

"VERY GOOD, FEIIR THE FOOL," her voice echoed in his mind. "THANK YOU."

A bell rang outside, and the Hierophant ordered the visitor to enter. The darkness faded from Thane's eyes as a woman entered—someone he hadn't seen before.

"Excuse me, but we've received word from the Magician," the messenger said. "The mission at Wargonne succeeded. Conan is dead."

"Already?" said the Hierophant.

"The news is spreading throughout the kingdom," she said. "We only have a few days' advantage before the next phase begins."

"Return this prisoner to his cell at once," the Hierophant ordered. "Store that armor in my tent—I'll finish questioning him tomorrow after I've had time to study it further."

Blindfolded again, Thane was led away from the Hierophant's presence and back into the depths of the Lucidian camp. He couldn't shake the feeling that he'd made a terrible mistake by succumbing to her. The Hierophant had used her mind magic to manipulate him, and now she held his only real protection against the dangers ahead.

As they walked through the dark corridor of the dungeon, Thane tried to push down his rising sense of dread. He needed to stay strong for Zeere's sake as much as his own. They were in this together—two people lacking magic facing forces as powerful as they were brutal.

Someone ripped the blindfold from his eyes, leaving him disoriented as he stumbled to the floor at Zeere's side. The guard's echoing boots retreated into the silence, but Zeere's sharp voice took over his attention, despite his vision remaining blurred.

"What happened to you? You look dreadful."

He longed for sleep;, the residual effects of the Hierophant's magic lingered, making him unable to form coherent thoughts. His head throbbed painfully, as though he'd just slammed it a thousand times against the wall and spun in circles a thousand times more. His thinking was sluggish and muddled.

"The Hierophant is a Mind Mage," he whispered, his words barely intelligible. "She made me tell the truth and took my armor."

He fumbled with his neck, relieved to feel the necklace Cereene had given him still secure. At least that remained safe. Without that, he had nothing else left of her aside from distant memories.

"But what did you reveal to them?" Zeere pressed urgently.

Before Thane could answer, dizziness overtook him, and he slumped onto the straw, his body trembling uncontrollably as he went horizontal.

"Feiir!" It echoed from somewhere ahead.

"Feiir!" Closer now.

"Thane! That's long enough!"

His eyes jolted open, and he sat up, soaked in sweat but less disoriented than a moment ago. Although it must have been longer than a minute. How long had he been unconscious?

"What did you just call me?"

"You're the Throatian Prince. Your true name is Thane Asche."

Thane pushed himself upright, fixing his sharpening gaze on Zeere. "How do you know that?"

"The warden and guards talked while you were out," Zeere explained. "They ridiculed you but referred to you by your true name. Do you notice the smell of beer all over you now?"

Thane sniffed and realized the stench of alcohol, not sweat, soaked his clothes. Their captors mocked him, tossing drinks through the bars.

Zeere nodded. "I figured it out. The Hierophant forced you to answer her questions, but she didn't trust your words. That's why nothing has happened yet—everyone thinks you're just a fool. But I realized the truth, even though they don't acknowledge it. That doesn't mean we're safe, however."

"I lied to you to protect myself," Thane admitted. Zeere had proven himself trustworthy so far, and there was little purpose in continuing to hide the truth. "In Yaenia, many would betray me to King Ether von Stonewall for gold or honor. That's why I took my twin sister's name as a disguise."

"I'm no stranger to using false names since the Enclave is after me too," Zeere said. "But let's save our stories for later. I have an idea of how to escape this place."

A flicker of hope finally graced Thane's heart. "How?"

Zeere stood and moved toward the cell door. "I can open the lock, but I don't know what's beyond."

"It will be a blind run either way," Thane said. "However, you're correct that we'll die if we stay here much longer. Running still offers a better chance than waiting for the Hierophant."

"I'm willing to run if you are," Zeere said. "But I must warn you that once we move forward, it will take time before I can wield this magic again. No matter what happens outside this cell, we must remain together."

Thane raised an eyebrow. "Magic? You said you were a Null Mage. Was it a lie?"

"Finding strength to endure suffering is a different kind of magic," Zeere told him.

Thane scoffed. "In my country, we did a rite called the Reminder of Suffering. There were only skill and luck involved during the battles to the death. No magic—only unforgiving reality."

"Charming," Zeere said. "But results speak for themselves. Shall I free us from this prison, and then you take the lead?"

Thane nodded. "Let's go. The sooner we're out of here, the better."

His companion took a deep breath and moved to the outer edge of their cell, near the large padlock that sealed them inside. Thane initially thought Zeere might try to pick the lock, but his companion surprised him by taking a different approach altogether. He slid his hands between the bars and reached into the torch's mounting chamber. Though Zeere flinched and grunted, he grabbed the flaming torch and moved it to the inside of their cell.

"Have you gone mad?" Thane exclaimed. The flames were

burning through the bandages over Zeere's hands and scorching his skin.

His companion only said, "Trust me," as he clutched the fiery mass closer to his chest.

Thane fell speechless as his companion held it steadily on the lock. Was the flame hot enough to melt the shackle?

"I just need a little longer," Zeere hoarsely strained through the pain.

"How are you doing that?" Thane gasped.

"It's as painful as you'd expect. But it's not the first time I've done something like this."

As the lock glowed orange, Zeere tugged at it, holding the flaming tallow. His entire body weight pulled until the weakest point of the padlock bent enough to break free. It snapped, and he dropped it and the torch's flame to the ground.

"There," Zeere groaned, "we're finally free."

"Are you okay?" Thane asked, wide-eyed.

"I'm injured, but far from dead," Zeere said. "Let's go now. Worry about me later. We're free."

AS THEY CREPT OUT AND SAW THE NIGHT SKY OVERHEAD, THEY realized their prison had been a watchtower, not a dungeon as they initially believed. Nearby stood a large tent, spacious enough to accommodate over a hundred people. The sound of chatter drifted from within, though it was unclear how many were still awake. Two smaller tents sat to one side, likely serving as guard quarters. Though nobody was in sight, Thane suspected someone was keeping watch from atop the very tower they had just escaped. He pointed upward toward his eyes, warning Zeere of the danger above.

The Null Mage looked up, curious, then nodded. As Thane crept toward the tents, Zeere grabbed his shoulder, stopping him. "What are you doing?" he hissed.

"We need weapons and armor," Thane whispered. "It's probably in the Hierophant's tent, which must be one of these two."

Zeere scoffed, his concern clear despite his wrapped face. "There will be chances to find more of those later," he said. "We should get out of here. Now."

But Thane was determined. The magical armor given to him by Somnius was too powerful to risk falling into the wrong hands. Knowing the Hierophant had stolen it compelled him to retrieve it at all costs.

"I need to correct what happened earlier," Thane clarified. "The armor is magical, and we can't let a Lucidian get their hands on it. I know it's risky for us to go into the tents to check, but we should try."

"Sneaking in on her while she's asleep isn't wise," Zeere cautioned.

"If she's asleep, even better," Thane countered. "We don't want to fight her—there's no point in risking a confrontation."

The Null Mage hesitated for a moment, considering Thane's words. "No, I suppose not," he conceded. "But let's not take any more unnecessary risks."

As they approached the smaller tents, Thane glanced toward the watchtower overhead. The flickering orange light from a torch revealed that there was indeed a guard on watch, scanning the horizon. He hoped not to be spotted as they crept closer to their target.

Suddenly, something massive caught Thane's eye, casting a dark silhouette against the moonlit sky. A round boulder, as large as two carts combined, rested in the open field before them. Its shape was too perfect to be natural, and there were no other rocks or mountains nearby to explain its presence. Thane wondered if someone had dropped it from the watchtower above.

"Did a Lucidian carry that big rock here?" Thane whispered as they continued onward.

"It's possible they brought or made it," Zeere said.

"Made it?"

"An Enforcer Mage must have been training—maybe they were collecting bits of dirt and rock and compressing them together. Magical abilities are like muscles."

There was no time to speculate further. They needed to focus on retrieving Thane's armor and escaping the camp before anyone discovered them. As they approached the first tent, which had two flaps forming the entrance, Thane tiptoed, and Zeere did the same.

Thane listened before moving his face closer to the small gap that let him see inside. A pair of candles hung from the canopy, lighting the interior and showing their only bit of good luck in days. A large table held various unsorted items, along with swords, boxes, and unfamiliar trinkets that might be useful. Behind it was a large chest.

"What are all these things?" he whispered with a quiet murmur.

Zeere picked up a golden teacup, admiring it with a grin. "A random assortment, indeed," he said, "but look—my satchel with the amethysts is here, and my smoke pellets too!" He set the cup down, securing his bag and snatching a sword and a gray leather vest. "Prisoners' belongings, maybe?" he wondered, "or artifacts?"

Thane helped himself to his original weapons, but when he approached the chest at the rear of the tent, he found it secured tight with a thick lock that was even bulkier than the one that had kept them in their prison cell. Unlike the first lock they'd successfully broken through, he suspected melting the shackle wouldn't be an option this time.

"My armor must be inside this treasure chest," Thane said. He kicked it to test its weight, but it felt immovable.

"Somehow, I doubt the key is nearby," Zeere said.

"We still should search for a moment, just in case it's here," Thane pressed. "We can't let them use it. Or can you help me lift the chest? Maybe we can drop it and break through."

Zeere stepped over and examined the box. "That wood is thick and coated to resist fire. We aren't going to break it or burn through. As much as I hate to admit it, we—"

"Let's steal the whole chest, then," Thane said. He tried to lift it from one side and discovered that idea was fruitless as well.

"You have everything you need but the armor and helmet, yes?" Zeere asked.

"I do."

"Then leaving is the better option. Even with your armor, we aren't capable of defeating Lucidians."

Thane swallowed hard. Somnius had created that armor for him with her magic. Was there any chance she could make it disappear just as well? He conceded Zeere was right; the armor gave him a major defensive advantage over humans, but very little against magical attacks.

Before they could decide on a course of action, a sharp trumpet blast echoed through the night, reverberating loudly. Thane and Zeere froze, their eyes snapping toward the tent entrance.

As they neared the tent's entrance, a sudden, resounding cackle erupted from the other side of the flap. Thane's heart skipped a beat as he recognized the voice. It was the Hierophant.

"Oh my," came the taunting voice, followed by a low, mocking giggle. "I do love it when plans that have come together so perfectly suddenly drop dead."

The tent flap swished open, revealing the Hierophant as she stepped into the dim light. Somnius's magical armor was ill-fitting on her, slightly too large, but the Hierophant seemed unbothered by it. Thane knew all too well that whatever material the suit was comprised of, it was featherweight compared to traditional metals.

"Black sand," Zeere muttered.

Thane was speechless. There was no possibility of getting the armor back now.

"Run!" Thane yelled, but the Hierophant raised her arm in a warning to block them. She stepped forward and the white dress underneath her new acquisition swayed.

"The Prince Thane imposter," she purred, "and your little friend who wraps himself in bandages from head to toe. I must admit, your determination is commendable, though your cleverness seems... lacking."

As Zeere tightened his grip on the sword, Thane's voice faltered, unable to find the words for a taunting remark, an intimidating display of power, or even a desperate plea for mercy.

"Well, well," the Hierophant said. Her golden owl mask seemed to mock them and her eyes pierced Thane with a mischievous gleam. "It appears we have quite a situation, don't we? Thieves caught red-handed. Perhaps I should summon the Enforcer Mages to return you to your cells, one limb at a time."

She reached out, her delicate hand lightly touching Thane's cheek. Her command assaulted his mind: "OR PERHAPS YOU SHOULD JUST TAKE YOUR NEW WEAPONS AND STAB YOURSELVES."

Her confidence matched her anger, and her mental command forced itself through the air like a battering ram—too direct and harsh to truly influence him. Yet, in that moment, Thane sensed a vulnerability beneath her assured exterior: her pride—she underestimated them. The Hierophant's arrogance was her weakness. If they exploited this blind spot, they might turn the confrontation in their favor.

He remembered the tactics of the Loyalty Circles, where feinting was key. Tonight, he would feint surrender, using the dagger at his side as an unexpected weapon.

"You win," Thane said. "We'll return to our cells quietly. Just spare our lives."

The Hierophant's laugh echoed, a sound that would have annoyed him if she weren't so terrifyingly vicious. "I pity you," she cooed. "You have no idea what I'll make you do to yourselves later when I'm no longer busy."

Before she could finish, Thane lunged forward, his eyes locked on his target: the Hierophant's neck. His aim was true, but the Hierophant shifted with unprecedented agility, her movements swift and fluid. He adjusted his stance, trying to compensate for her sudden change in position.

The Hierophant's piercing shriek echoed in his ears and mind. Thane staggered, the force of sound and mental pressure disorienting him. He struggled to stay focused, his grip tightening on the dagger. As the Hierophant moved, Thane's reflexes kicked in, but too slowly. Before he reacted, Zeere's hand grounded him, snapping him back to the present.

"Don't!" his companion warned.

A crack sounded beneath his feet, and white smoke erupted from the ground. Zeere yanked him backward, pulling him away from the Hierophant. The tent filled with thick, swirling fog, the same as the one that had aided their escape from the bar in Sky Tower Coast. It was disorienting, but Thane trusted that Zeere knew what he was doing.

They moved toward the rear, and Thane fumbled with the dagger to cut a flap in the thick fabric. The blade tore through the cloth with a ripping sound and they slid through the narrow opening, exiting into the cool night air. Layers of fog dimmed the stars above.

The Hierophant's enraged screams echoed behind them as they darted out, sprinting into the darkness. Thane's lungs burned, his heart pounding so rapidly he feared it might give out. He caught glimpses of flickering torches growing brighter and distant shouts rising from the camp.

"CATCH THE PRISONERS!"

"Keep running," Zeere said. "They won't concede easily."

The farther they ran from camp, the harder it was to see the ground beneath them. Twenty minutes later and surrounded by complete darkness, they slowed their pace to a cautious walk, afraid of twisting an ankle in the pitch-black night. The treacherous terrain made it impossible to move safely without a light source, but even a small lantern would have been too risky to light, as the Lucidians would have spotted it immediately.

"We need to change course," Zeere urged. "They'll track us if we stay predictable."

"Can they see in the dark?"

"They can't," Zeere confirmed. "But that doesn't mean they won't have other ways of finding us. The Sentinel Mages are likely spreading word of our escape. If we encounter any settlements, we must verify they are Darian, not Lucidian. I never imagined entering a Lucidian camp outside the Enclave—it's unheard of."

It seemed just as odd as discovering a Savager Mage in the Lowland Graves. What could be happening?

"I'd also never considered I'd somehow feel safer in King Ether's company," Thane admitted.

"As someone who has been on the run for years, it's not surprising to hear you say that," Zeere replied.

Thane's gaze drifted to the shadows ahead, and a new thought struck him. "Is it possible for a Mind Mage to control several people at once? Maybe the camp wasn't all Lucidians. Maybe the Hierophant was controlling some humans with her magic. Maybe she was even controlling me after we escaped. You were right from the beginning—we shouldn't have gone searching for supplies and the armor. In hindsight, it was foolish of me to suggest it."

Zeere paused as he analyzed the possibilities. "We're both just tired and not thinking clearly," he replied, continuing to walk. "The Hierophant couldn't have manipulated you—or anyone else—that way. Her control over you was limited, and without a constant blood supply, her influence would have faded quickly. The people at the camp were there willingly—but why?"

"After escaping our cell, the Enforcer and Sentinel Mages who captured us had already left the camp," Thane said. "That's why we escaped. There must have been humans with the Hierophant, or she would have sent Lucidians after us."

If he was right, then the Hierophant, despite being a powerful Mind Mage, was far weaker in magic than Zann-Xia-Czul. Though their powers differed, she was still dangerous. She or her people would pursue them at first light.

"I would hardly call that a simple escape," Zeere said, "and we must keep our guard up. No place is safe for either of us."

"You're right—nowhere is safe," Thane said. "But I've made a promise to something greater than myself. We'll find our way back to the Whisperers, no matter how long it takes. For now, let's figure out where we are."

20
KAINE - THE SYMPHONY OF CROWNS

The flickering candlelight on Orin's table had almost gone out when Kaine finished his story. The room was nearly dark, filled with scents of fading candles and the faint mustiness of old, smoky wood. Kaine's throat was dry because he had talked for hours. No one had interrupted him or asked questions. Everyone seemed too shocked or too interested to break his speech. Kaine couldn't help including even the smallest details of his story involving Ilya. Although it was painful to recall, he'd shared his raw account of the events and his thoughts from that night in the Leila Kingdom.

"That's everything, and I'm sorry that your son died," Kaine said to conclude his tale.

The elder of Gale Village clenched his black cane, resting it on his legs, thinking from the other side of the table. Faint reflections of tears glistened beneath his exhausted eyes.

"I always wondered if it was my fault for sending him," Orin muttered. "Blanche insisted it was all an accident, but I suspected she said so to diffuse the tension at the time."

Merdel looked up from the parchment, scribbling notes as his quill scratched the silence. "And now the truth has hopefully reduced the strain of today's tension, too. Can we agree that Kaine's involvement in Axis's death was coincidental, not intentional?"

The elderly Lucidian woman named Celeste was frozen to her chair. Her eyes were open, but Kaine suspected she'd fallen asleep or into a deep trance. He flinched when she said, "I sensed Kaine's burden as he spoke. The event was his first scar."

"My first scar?" Kaine asked, one of his eyebrows raised.

"The first on your soul," the Mind Mage said, her voice reverberating within the cramped room.

Orin's body softened as he propped the bottom of his cane on the smooth surface of the floor. "I am familiar with those lines of questioning, wondering whether anything could have happened differently and for the better. Struggling to understand true justice haunted my conscience when I killed my first Lucidian. My son was the first person you'd ever killed. Perhaps you and I weren't so different in our younger years after all."

"Kaine gave up his future of becoming a Leilan knight because of it," Merdel said. "Blanche and I had talked about this before, though I hadn't known the full details."

"I—I didn't want to admit it before," Kaine said, his voice trembling, "but you might be right. It wasn't so much because I despised the upper class that my family involved themselves with. Don't get me wrong—I still don't like the politics or the shallowness, but maybe I could have tolerated it on my original path toward becoming a Purple Knight."

"Do you believe his story, Orin?" Celeste asked.

"I do," Orin replied with a single nod.

"And?"

"It won't bring my son back to life," he admitted, "but I can at least know he wasn't murdered in cold blood as I imagined."

"Everything I've learned tonight challenges the most common songs," Merdel commented, his eyes narrowing in thought as he set down his quill. "Ether the Stone Wall, Blanche the Silver Wolf, and Orin the Relentless were inseparable. Even the most beautiful melodies can hide shades of discord. Now, each of you sits on your thrones, cursed to reflect on those truths you knew all along."

Orin nodded, considering the councilman's words. "Indeed, Merdel. A symphony of crowns is nothing more than a collection of deceptions and dreams. Nobody wants to hear that song when they realize most of those delusions are self-inflicted."

"Again, I am so sorry about what happened," Kaine continued. His throat itched, but there was no water to drink. "I wish I could have just captured your son and let the queen question him. He didn't need to—"

"I forgive you," Orin stated firmly. "Like Celeste sensed, I acknowledge the pain this brought upon you. This might have been my fault for sending him to the queen's bedchamber to begin with. I'd often wondered, but now I know."

Celeste rose and drifted over. She said, resting her hand on Orin's shoulder, "It's better not to mourn him this way. Celebrate the meaning Axis gave you while he still lived."

The elder inhaled and released a shuddering breath. For the first time, Kaine recognized the human behind the mask of a bitter old man. "You're correct, old friend," Orin said. "We lack the years left in our lives to waste pondering events we can't change."

"I feel it too," Celeste said with a hint of woefulness. "The sun and moon will rotate for us only so many more times. We mustn't lose sight of what is good."

The candle on Orin's table fizzled out, casting the room into darkness. Celeste retrieved a replacement, her movements slow and precise because of her curling spine. Despite her age, Kaine expected her to flick her fingers and spark a flame with her magic, but she used an ordinary flint instead. A faint light filled the shack, revealing the outlines of everything once more.

"Please accept my apologies, everyone," Orin said. "I've steered our conversation astray. It's no coincidence you've arrived here and brought out Zelia's letter and Blanche's old painting. Everything is intertwined. Perhaps we're meant to be allies in the coming war."

"The coming war?" Merdel said, perplexed. "You mean to say you'll join the fight against the Throatians?"

"He means the greater war," Celeste replied, suddenly energized. "The one foreseen by the Lucidian Princess Zelia. She believed the painting was connected to the future, but she died before she could explain it."

"I suspected the artwork was important," Merdel said, "but its history eludes me. Why did Blanche have it, and why did you send your son to steal it? Couldn't you have just asked her to let you look?"

The fabric rustled as Orin rolled it up, concealing the hieroglyphics. "Blanche had received it as a gift," he explained. "Zelia knew, but I couldn't see it myself. Of all the artwork and trinkets the Leilan queen hoards and displays in the halls of Aeon Eve, the one I wanted was hidden in her bedchamber. After the war, Blanche, Ether, and I weren't on good terms. I dared not ask her to show me the painting without raising suspicion about my true purpose here.

That's why I sent my son—he had to steal it. It was the only way for us to study its symbols."

"I understand the complications and delicacies between the three of you now, but what were you doing here?" Merdel asked, leaning forward. "Besides hiding Lucidians."

"That, and nobody else outside of Gale Village knew of Zelia's return," Orin said. "It... wasn't a good time to let Ether or Blanche know what was happening. The princess needed my help, but..."

Orin stopped as though he'd remembered something painful from all those years ago. Kaine surmised Orin had not wanted to leave his shell, the isolated Gale Village, even if it meant having to solve some problems without his former greatest allies.

"By that time, Zelia's madness had appeared," Celeste said. Her eyes were distant.

"Madness?" gawked Merdel.

"Most of the time, she was perfectly coherent," Orin continued, "but it was clear her use of the God Stones was creating cracks in her sanity. Some days, she would respond to me as though we were having an entirely different conversation."

"A side effect of the Time Stone or the Memories Stone, perhaps," Celeste said. "She would lose track of when and where she was because of how much she'd seen."

What had been Zelia's goal? Had she been unable to master the God Stones, or was it a fruitless venture for a Lucidian? Had the God Stones caused Zelia to give up her life for the greater good, as Lydia had done? Had Zelia confided in Orin the same way Lydia had confided in him?

"Zelia knew she was losing herself," Kaine speculated. "Her letter to King Ether explained that much."

"The letter was one way she was trying to connect us to the future," Orin replied. "The painting was the other."

"And the third piece is the most intriguing," said Merdel, his curiosity clearly piqued.

"The third piece?" asked Kaine, leaning forward.

"Zelia's claim that she and Lily von Stonewall were of the same bloodline," Merdel said. "I find it hard to believe a Lucidian and human share the same ancestor. If true, that would have made Lydia, Xander, and Kira Lucidian royalty, not Darians. It cannot be so."

"That's because it's impossible," Orin said, shaking his head. "It must have been one of her hallucinations. Zelia could see alternative histories and other ways of how the war might have gone. That may have confused her, I think—maybe she misunderstood or concluded that anyone who could use a God Stone should have also been Lucidian. It cannot work out that way in reality. You know it's impossible for the von Stonewall family to be Lucidians."

"It's reasonable to hold doubts about it," Merdel assured. "But you believe in the painting's importance, correct?"

"There's one thing I still don't understand," Kaine said to Orin. "I prevented your son from stealing the queen's painting, yet you have it here, anyway. How?"

The elder gave him half a toothless smile, his first hint of genuine friendliness since the group had arrived in Gale Village. "Blanche and I reconciled after Axis died, though I couldn't accept that his death had been an accident. She apologized profusely to me and offered the painting in good faith. It restored our friendship, and we became open with each other again."

"Well, in any case, I'm glad we could put our past misunderstandings behind us," Merdel said, stretching his arms. "The hour grows late and dawn draws near. Perhaps we can continue this conversation after sunrise? There's still much left to discuss."

"Say no more," Orin replied. "You're both welcome to stay here as long as you wish. We can continue trading information once we've all rested."

"Tomorrow, then," Kaine said. "We would like to learn more about the letter and painting. Xander and Kira will need to learn about the circumstances, too."

"You will learn of everything we know," Orin said gravely, a hint there was still much more to his story, "but alas, such knowledge will ensnare you with the burdens of their own mysteries, mysteries that Celeste and I still haven't yet solved."

Xander and Kira slept peacefully as Kaine and Merdel entered their shared shack in the dead of night. Despite the matching shadows under his eyes, he couldn't help feeling uncertain about whether sending the von Stonewall children to bed early had been right.

Celeste seemed trustworthy, but it was clear other strangers who were Lucidians lived in Gale Village. Forgetting they were potential enemies of the Darian Kingdom and a threat would be unwise. At the present time, Xander and Kira were secure, but leaving them alone, especially for a large portion of the night, was a bad idea. If other Lucidians had found them unprotected, the consequences might have been dire.

He sighed as he pulled up his bedcovers. With any luck, he could garner two or three hours of sleep. Despite that, Kaine squandered the time, trapped deep in his own thoughts. The musty smell of Orin's shack lingered in his mind as he contemplated everything he'd uncovered since reading Zelia's letter. Each of the past stories he'd heard about King Ether, Princess Zelia, and Orin gave a new perspective on his version of events.

The Lucidians seemed to have had a greater role in history than Kaine had previously known, including with the God Stones. Why had Zelia given King Ether, the enemy of her people, such a powerful source of magic? Beyond that, how was it that Lydia could wield such magical powers? Was the prophecy mentioned in Zelia's letter truly the reasoning behind everything?

As soon as Kaine fell asleep, he heard Kira cry, "Xander, wake up! They're back!"

As the princess jumped onto the foot of his bed, it creaked and wobbled so much he worried it might collapse. "Is everything okay between you and Elder Orin? Is the fighting done?"

Kaine opened his eyes, reluctantly letting the blinding sun overtake them. "We've reached an understanding," he said, "but the night went by fast, and we didn't finish discussing everything we needed."

"Did you at least learn why there are Lucidians here?" Xander asked.

Across the room, there was a rustle of blankets as Merdel rose from his bed and started folding them into a neat pile. "Not yet," the councilman said. "From my perspective, our conversation led to more questions than resolutions. Orin still owes us a lot of information. We'll remain here until we uncover the truth of it all."

For the next while, Kaine and Merdel recapped their discussion from the previous evening, discussing Kaine's involvement with Queen Blanche. Surprisingly, both the prince and princess understood the dilemma he'd faced long ago, and Xander commended his "accomplishment".

"So how old were you when you made your first kill?" Xander asked.

"Probably around twenty," Kaine replied. "I was still just a boy. It's not something to boast about."

"But Axel might have killed you had the fight gone the other way. A victory is a victory."

"Xander!" Kira exclaimed. "Mind yourself!"

Kaine observed a pattern: Xander, unaware of his tendency to overstep boundaries, often came close to being provocative. Each time he did so, Kira would promptly correct him. Kaine hoped their interactions would foster mutual mindfulness. Xander needed to restrain his words during kingly meetings, while Kira should address him only privately.

"Remember," Kaine said, "that above all else, you are siblings. Avoid aggravating each other too often. Mind your appearance."

"What appearance?" Kira asked. "I didn't do anything wrong. But Xander, he—"

"The prince has his own lesson to learn," Kaine continued, "and you must support your brother in diplomatic situations. Appear united in public; otherwise, others will use your discord to divide you further. Don't show your conflicts except in private if you can help it."

The princess's mouth hung open in silent awe. "I'll think about it. Thank you, Kaine."

"And Xander," he continued, "your curiosity isn't wrong, but you must be mindful of how others feel about your questions and comments. Think before you speak, or else those around you won't be comfortable sharing their true worries and secrets."

"Fine." The prince scowled but seemed to take the words seriously. "I'll be careful."

Meanwhile, Merdel let out a playful chuckle. "You're both on great paths. Someday, your time for power will come! Kaine's lectures lack embellishment now but trust me—he's given you some genuine wisdom."

A knock sounded from outside, and the councilman rushed to answer. As the shack's door opened, the man named Finnegan offered them a large platter of biscuits, chicken, fresh eggs, and a berry jam. He smiled widely, speaking in few words:

"After breakfast, Elder Orin has requested you join him for tea at the mountaintops."

"Finn," Xander said. "I have to ask you something."

"Yes, my prince?"

"I must know. Have you been a Lucidian all this time? Why isn't your skin purple or another odd color?"

The man smiled, his wrinkled and sun-tanned face failing to conceal a prior lifetime of hardships. "I'm as much of a Lucidian as the chickens I tend. You needn't fear the handful of their kind living here. Most of the Lucidians in Gale Village were only supporting roles during the war—healers and whatnot. We had a fire magic user once, but she passed away a few years ago. Those of them left only wish to live out the rest of their lives in peace and solitude."

Now that their secret was out, Finn seemed more open and talkative. Perhaps he had loose lips and someone had warned him to keep quiet while visitors were present. Whether what he said was true remained to be seen. To Kaine, something felt off. Why would the Lucidians hide in Gale Village instead of returning to the Enclave with their people? The Enclave was large enough to hold them all and would provide better protection. He'd ask Celeste later.

"What were you saying about tea?" Kira asked.

"Our climate features nearby geysers and hot springs," Finn said. "Among Gale Village's luxuries are amenities unavailable elsewhere in the Darian Kingdom. Elder Orin has invited you to enjoy them and partake in drinks."

"Can we go?" Kira pleaded. "Please?"

"Can everyone maintain their composure if we go?" Kaine warned the children. "There may be some tough topics in the discussions."

"We'll try our best," Xander promised.

"In that case," Finn said, "come over to my barn after you're done eating breakfast. I'll have a cart waiting." He brushed off his light blue buttoned shirt and returned through the door.

"What is your opinion of all this? On everything?" Kaine whispered to Merdel once Finn was far enough away from their shack. Meanwhile, Xander and Kira were busy gobbling down as much chicken and eggs as they could get away with.

"Where to begin? While there's much to consider, at least your mission from King Ether succeeded," the councilman replied, brushing some biscuit crumbs from his mustache. "Now that the farmer has spoken, I understand Gale Village better."

"How so? What's changed?"

"I never guessed there were Lucidians here, but given Orin's demeanor, I suspected those who chose to live here were deserters or refugees. Orin welcomed them, and they had some sort of understanding. I don't know the details, yet there must be peace for humans and Lucidians to live together. They would have exiled all violent offenders from both sides. That's the only way a place like this could survive."

Merdel was possibly right. Isolation from the rest of the Darian Kingdom came with benefits. They were too far away from the larger towns and cities for anyone to control them. Adding in the personal tension between Ether and Orin would leave him as a small king of their quaint village. The distance, both physically and emotionally, was the only way Orin could succeed at allowing Lucidians to live there despite technically being inside the Darian Kingdom.

Merdel had discovered something about the secret inner workings of Gale Village, but a more pressing issue remained. Despite Orin's openness, there was a detail from Zelia's letter he hadn't mentioned—one that might be the most crucial fact of all.

Kaine glanced at Xander and Kira to ensure they weren't listening. They had finished their breakfast and were now chasing a beetle on the other side of the shack. Speaking plainly, Kaine asked Merdel, "Did you notice that Zelia's letter mentioned five God Stones, but King Ether only had four? Do you think Orin kept one of them? That could explain why he hasn't delivered the letter to the king."

"I also noticed the discrepancy in the note," Merdel said, "and it was wise to avoid discussing it. I've been thinking about what might have happened. Since you found Orin's hiding spot in his armoire, if he had stolen the fifth stone, it would have likely been in there with the rest. Alternatively, perhaps Ether had the fifth stone but gave it to someone else. However, telling Orin that Ether only had four stones could reveal too much. There's more to this that we don't know. We should observe what Orin says today and see if we can gain more insight."

"The key question is whether he actually gave Ether all five God Stones," Kaine said, before swallowing a mouthful of chicken. "I'll check if that's true later today. We need to figure out where the missing God Stone is."

"I too will try to steer the conversation in that direction. Orin's cooperation has definitely improved since you told your tale about what happened with his son, but I still think he might not be showing his entire hand to us."

Kira screamed as Xander had apparently stepped on the beetle and crushed it. The children then ran outside and chased each other around the shack. Normally, Kaine would have scolded them and sent them back inside, but his conversation with the councilman preoccupied him.

"Negotiations are your specialty, Sir Merdel. Do you know any eloquent political dances that could make him open up?" Kaine asked.

"I have my ways of making people reveal their secrets," Merdel said. "Time and patience are the best of them."

Kaine chuckled softly. "I was going to suggest beer."

21

EISENBERN - THE DRAGON MAR

Gustav returned hours later, carrying fruits, nuts, bread, and other provisions. For five days, they stayed in the room, tiptoeing to the hallway only when they needed the latrine. They kept their voices low during the day and played cards, hoping the innkeeper would believe they had left. Ilya frequently peered through the window, scanning for city guards who might be searching for them. Beyond occasional patrols roaming the streets, little indicated they were still being hunted. Still, Eisenbern insisted they remain in the lodgings for the week Ilya had already paid. Remaining hidden would delay their journey to the Black Moon Tribe, but to him, reducing their risk was more important.

In his first three days of self-confinement, Eisenbern spent most of his time drafting a letter to Queen Blanche. He updated her on everything that had happened but struggled to articulate the complexities of their situation. Four times, he crumpled his paper and started over, fearing how Judge Sigrid Var's reaction to the events at Sky Tower Coast might have caused trouble for the queen. Finally, he decided to stick to the facts, omitting his personal speculations. He concluded by apologizing and promising the queen they would be more discreet in the future. Many of their current issues could have been prevented if they hadn't worn their armor and announced themselves as the Purple Guard.

By week's end, they packed and left the inn uneventfully. Dressed in plain dark tunics, they re-entered the city, taking one last breath of the fresh sea breeze and feeling the sun dry the nervous sweat dripping down their faces. Eisenbern approached the nearest bird tower with the sealed letter in hand. Instead of mailing it directly to the Leila Kingdom, he sent it to Merdel at the Darian Kingdom's castle. Merdel would understand that he needed to forward the message securely to Queen Blanche and ensure no one intercepted it.

After making a final solo trip to retrieve their horses, Eisenbern, Ilya, and Gustav were ready for the next leg of their journey. Upon reaching a quarter-day's travel west of Sky Tower Coast, they dismounted and gathered around Gustav, who unlatched the largest of their bags and placed it on the ground.

"Finally, we can ride with our true colors again," Gustav grunted, reaching into the bag and pulling out Eisenbern's pieces of armor. "You go first, sir."

Eisenbern sat on the grass and pulled on his leggings. After securing them, he wrapped the armor plates across his chest and back. As he reached for the bottom straps, Gustav approached to help fasten them.

"Thank you, friend," Eisenbern said. "You've really stuck your neck out for us this week, handling so many errands."

"They were simple tasks, really—no need to give me too much credit," Gustav said. "A beer will do whenever we get the chance."

"Just not the Golden Mare's beer," Ilya chimed in as she dug through the pile for her armor pieces.

"Agreed," Gustav said. "I'll never set foot in that place again, even if it's my last day alive and I need a drink to ease my suffering into death."

"Very well—I correct my previous statement," Eisenbern said, patting his chest plate. "I promise to buy each of you the next quality beer we encounter and to avoid causing any new side adventures."

After suiting up, Eisenbern stepped forward and pointed north. On the horizon, shrouded in white fog, the black mountains waited. Somewhere near the base of them was the entrance to the underground city where the famous tribe resided. The journey would take half a month.

"It's a long road ahead," Eisenbern said. "Is everyone ready?"

"Ready!" Ilya shouted cheerfully, mounting her horse and adjusting the spear at her back.

"Let's do this," Gustav grunted. "I want to learn how to kill dragons."

For over half a month, Eisenbern, Ilya, and Gustav pressed northward. Their tanned, sweat-soaked faces showed their determination, even as their horses grew weary of the endless path. Each morning, they raced the rising sun to avoid the midday heat, and each night, their skin remained sticky from the day's journey. Water was scarce; they had carried enough to drink but not to bathe or wash.

Dusty roads followed with the mountains on the horizon, but the expedition was anything but leisurely. Most people in Southern Yaenia were refugees from the north or descended from them. The northern lands were mostly uninhabitable, except for small patches unscathed by the Umbral Rot. Now, only a few settlements of humans and Lucidians remained, bound by tradition or too stubborn to abandon their homelands.

Renato had once explained that Umbral Rot had been an ultimate weapon in the Lucidian civil war. It destroyed nearly everything, spreading like a rash over the land. When the sickness reached the human settlements, their crops, livestock, and wildlife died first. Without farms, the food supplies dwindled, and the rivers and lakes faded to dust. Most cities fell within weeks, and those who drank the cursed water suffered ashen lungs and a deadly contagious cough. Lucidian magic had turned once-beautiful fields into desolate wastelands. Only a few settlements in the far northeastern corner of the continent remained unscathed.

Staying alive meant moving south, to the lands saved from the Rot. Eisenbern, an infant at the time, had no memory of the journey. His family's dedication ensured his survival, and they reached the land that became the Leila Kingdom. Growing up there, Eisenbern heard stories of his family's hardships during the recent war. These tales painted a grim picture of a world where life was precious, and each day might be the last. Despite the chaos, their sheer willpower had forged a new home for them in the south.

Now, years later, Eisenbern was returning to the land his family had once fled. His emotions were high, knowing he was walking the same path his ancestors had once taken.

"We're close to Shield Haven," he said. Despite its name, Shield Haven wasn't a place for physical shields. It was an area of dead terrain, scorched by fire and covered in a clay-like substance. Its sole purpose was to halt the Umbral Rot's spread southward. It stretched from the coast, across the border, to the rocky mountains, forming a barrier of dormant land where the Rot could not pass. Of the Enclave's actions, creating the area was its only redeeming accomplishment, even if it had been self-serving.

"Neither of you has been here before, right?" Gustav asked as they passed through the abandoned settlement in Shield Haven known as Haventown.

"I've heard more reasons to avoid this place than to go," Eisenbern replied. "Learning how to kill dragons is the first reason to ignore all the warnings I've been told because we can't find what we need in books."

Later that day, they passed through the far end of Shield Haven and headed northeast. Finding the entrance to the underground city proved far from easy. They had only a rough map marker indicating the Black Moon Tribe's likely location.

"Since the Black Moon Tribe defeated the last dragons long ago, what do they do now?" Ilya asked, her fingers stroking her pony's mane.

"Renato told me their society became reclusive after going underground. Historians lost interest when the novelty of their accomplishment faded," Eisenbern said. "We need to stay alert for anything unusual, something invisible to a dragon yet subtle to humans."

The Black Moon Tribe's history mixed legend and fact. Dragons once enslaved humans, forcing the tribe to take refuge underground. After many years of strife, they built up their forces and eventually tracked all the dragons down. While the details varied, the central narrative remained the same: dragons once existed, and the Black Moon Tribe handled their eradication.

"I've read that they used specially trained assassins to kill the dragons," Ilya replied. "Small groups of special archers tracked and eliminated them one at a time, targeting females first to prevent further breeding."

Eisenbern had heard of this strategy before but had since forgotten. "I hope they're willing to share their history," he said. "If the Throatians do have a dragon, we must learn how to defeat it."

"A single dragon shouldn't be a problem for them," Ilya said.

Gustav added, "None of the current tribe members may have

seen one of them. After so many years, only their elders, if anyone, would have witnessed it."

"It's easy to forget how recently the dragons all died," Eisenbern said.

After hours of travel, they entered a narrow valley where towering black mountains blocked the fading sunlight, signaling the coming night. They needed to reach the city's entrance before darkness fell. The hollow contained dry, non-decaying trees whose wood was brittle and highly flammable. Eisenbern feared that even a small fire could ignite the entire hollow.

More concerning, their water supply was dwindling. They had found no sources in days, and Eisenbern calculated how long it had been since their last refill. At home, the volcanoes provided steam for drinking water, but the central Yaenian mountains offered no such resources.

"We'd best hurry and find a way into the city," Eisenbern said. "Time is running out. We must conserve our strength and stay alert—someone could be watching from the cliffs."

The valley was eerily quiet, devoid of natural sounds. No wild animals or insects were visible, and the land was dry and desert-like.

"I'll scout ahead if there are no objections," Ilya said.

"We've stuck together this long; there's no point in splitting up now," Eisenbern said. "We're right where we should be—in the mountains. It's safer to watch each other's backs."

The land was unfamiliar, and its essence seemed to hold nothing but death. Had the deaths of former dragons cursed the area, or had the creeping effects of the Umbral Rot sapped the land of its life?

"If the entrance isn't in this valley, we'll need to circle the mountain perimeter," Gustav said. "It makes sense for them to make the doorway small enough to prevent a dragon from sticking its head inside."

"Good point," Ilya said. "But they'd also want to avoid flooding. The doorway must be at least a little above ground."

"The Black Moon Tribe is clever, and so will be their hiding place," Eisenbern replied. "We must search everywhere, high and low."

They wandered throughout the valleys for another stretch with no luck. The dwindling water supply and the eerie atmosphere made Eisenbern sense something was amiss.

"Say, Gustav, how about a song?" he proposed. "We could use a little entertainment."

Gustav hesitated, glancing around nervously. "Won't that announce our presence?"

"If they like the sound of your voice, maybe they'll come out and give you a coin or two," Eisenbern said. "Besides, it might be better if they found us."

"I could go for a song," Ilya said.

"What do you want to hear?" Gustav muttered, but he agreed.

"The Fall of Zaal," Ilya piped.

"Very well. Eisenbern, you owe me another drink for this one." Gustav cleared his throat and sang:

Back in the years of wars with magic,
Blanche Voussoir was a lady of gall,
Strong as the roads she marched on,
Until she met Zaal's fiery goal.
Zaal the Broiler, with flames so bright,
Had burned down many, a fearsome sight.
"Do not face him," Ether von Stonewall warned,
"His hands breathe fire with orange light."
But Blanche, with heart and mind combined,
Matched Zaal's threat, though not with a fight.
Beneath the forest's eyes, she sought her place,
To hide, to plot, to dig a fatal plight.
Just outside the enemy camp,
Shovel in hand, she made her trap,
Fooled him from his shadowed reign,
To stumble, fall, and end his name.
Blanche proved all wrong, her cunning clear,
Without a blade, she conquered fear.
She had buried her swords, but not her pride,
And felled the beast in a pit of steel.
Back in the years of wars with magic,
Blanche Voussoir, a lady of gall,
Defied the odds with a mind so sharp,
And brought Zaal the Broiler to fall.

Though Eisenbern chuckled at the song, something pricked his neck. He instinctively slapped it and noticed the insect's thick, gray shell. It was half an inch thick and twice as long, far larger than any mosquito. On his palm rested a small smear of blood.

"Asura's ass indeed," Eisenbern yelled. "Some fat bug just bit me!"

"It's at least a sign of life," Gustav said. "Insects gather around food sources. There must be some water nearby. Let's search more carefully."

"OW!" Ilya shouted. "One got me too! Let's get out of here! I hope they aren't poisonous!"

"Fair point," Eisenbern said. "We should turn back for now and return to this area tomorrow once we've better protected our skin." His neck itched, and he resisted the urge to scratch.

"Was it some kind of beetle or a bee?" Gustav asked as they retreated. Grabbing more clothes from their bags, they covered their necks, heads, and faces.

"It was probably a wasp," Eisenbern grunted, blinking as he felt tired. "I think it had a numbing effect. I feel a slight tingling in my face."

"Same here," Ilya said. "We should set up camp away from the bugs; I'm exhausted after today."

There was no time to find a better place to settle for the night. The insect prick depleted Eisenbern's energy. The ground would offer them rest, and though the exposed valley was a dangerous choice, there was no other option.

"Dismount for now, Ilya," he called as he realized. "The bite... It's—"

Before he finished, Ilya slid off her horse and rolled sideways. Her small body had made her more susceptible to the poison. She thudded to the ground, and the Shadowstone spear snapped the strap that held it strung around her back.

"Hey! Are you okay?" Eisenbern shouted, jumping off his horse and running to catch her. She was still awake but clearly disoriented.

"No."

"Black sand..."

"Gustav," Eisenbern said. "They weren't bugs. They were darts."

"What?"

Gustav dismounted and stumbled over the grass. Eisenbern looked up at the mountains, expecting to see archers, but there was no one. So where did the darts come from?

Eisenbern felt his legs waver as he laid Ilya down. "The Black Moon Tribe found us before we could find them. I hoped your song could save some time, but..."

"I'm as good as gone, unfortunately," Gustav replied, moving down to one knee. "They got me twice."

Then, Eisenbern noticed the mountain's walls had eyes. A woman, camouflaged in paint the same gray tint as the ridge, stepped from her hiding place. She held a pipe, which she slid somewhere near her waist. Her clothing was simple—a cotton shirt and trousers—without armor or other identifiable accessories. Proficient in stealth, she didn't appear prepared to take down a dragon, but she had been ready to dull their senses.

"You there!" Eisenbern called out. "I understand why you shot us, but we come in peace. We're looking for the Black Moon Tribe. We need their aid. Can you help?"

The woman painted from head to toe maintained a neutral expression. Her brown eyes stared right past them, her mouth slightly open, as if something was wrong. Had she accidentally pricked herself with one of her own darts?

Time was running out. He had to explain himself before he got any dizzier. "We're from the Leila Kingdom," he said. "My name is Jarret Eisenbern, leader of the queen's Purple Guard. We mean you no harm. Are you part of the Black Moon Tribe?"

She stood motionless. Eisenbern saw six others approaching—camouflaged to blend into the mountains, just like the first woman he'd seen. They carried swords and spears, their faces blank and expressionless. Eisenbern suspected they had hunted in the valley for days without sleep.

"We've come as friends," Eisenbern said. His vision blurred as he scanned the group, trying to identify their leader, before collapsing onto one knee—not a gesture of submission, but because his leg had gone numb.

"We come in peace from the Leila Kingdom of southern Yaenia," he tried again, this time collapsing into the dirt. Each breath grew harder, as though his lungs were hardening into stone. As he lay on the ground, he saw the first warrior's leather shoes enter his line of sight.

"Who are you?" Eisenbern gasped, his final breath escaping as he whispered the words.

He heard echoes through the ringing in his ears as more footsteps crunched the dirt near his face.

"I am Somnius," they all said in unison.

THE CAVERN WAS CHILLIER THAN ANY DUNGEON EISENBERN HAD known, and for the first time, he was on the wrong side of the bars. Every wall glowed with a mysterious luminescence from a cluster of fungi growing in the farthest corner of the ceiling. The light was an unsettling shade of green, much like spoiled milk, although the air lacked the same foul odor.

Eisenbern lifted his groggy head from the cold ground and tried to focus on the blurred shapes of Ilya and Gustav, who lay next to him. Both were still breathing, though the sedative's effects lingered. Knowing they were still alive and that they still had their weapons offered some small comfort. Ilya clutched the Shadowstone spear, capable of sliding through the bars. Surely the Black Moon Tribe hadn't been foolish, and that hinted that prison might have been a formality, a temporary measure until they could fully explain themselves. Eisenbern considered how far underground they were and what they would confront if they tried to escape.

He pushed himself up and surveyed the room. A small wooden table for two stood against the wall, probably meant for a guard. Their cavern was too cramped to contain other cells, and a large opening led to a rocky hallway that likely branched off to other parts of the prison.

"Is anyone awake?" he whispered to Ilya and Gustav.

The large, bear-sized man grunted. "Where have they taken us?"

"We're underground inside the mountain, I think," breathed Eisenbern. "Have either of you seen our captors or found out anything about them?"

"There were two women—one of them shot us," Ilya replied.

"Did they look friendly?" Gustav asked.

"Quiet," Eisenbern hissed. "Something's coming."

The woman with the trance-like gaze appeared at the entrance, now cleared of her facial paint. Her clothing was dark gray and matte, with a texture that seemed both firm and bendable, like a flexible metal. Carved into the armor was an emblem of twisting, overlapping lines, resembling a complex yet elegant knot. Eisenbern had never seen protection such as this and couldn't help but wonder about its design.

The woman approached the cell, close enough to study them but out of their reach. Her viridian eyes, faintly illuminated by the fungi, appeared almost blind, as if years underground had affected her vision.

"We came in peace," Eisenbern said, breaking eye contact. "Do you speak the Common Tongue?"

"I do," she replied, her voice soft and emotionless, though she seemed distracted.

"I'm Jarret Eisenbern," he continued, meeting her gaze again. "We traveled from the Leila Kingdom searching for the Black Moon Tribe. Have we found them?"

Her stare was unsettling in its intensity, as she examined every detail with unyielding attention.

"Why are you here?"

"We must learn how to defeat a dragon and its magic," Ilya said.

The woman's face tightened into a stone-like expression again as she glared at Ilya. Just as Eisenbern thought she might leave the room without saying another word, she spoke.

"For what purpose?"

Her questions were brief, but they revealed the answer Eisenbern had been hoping for. With any luck, they would be out of the cell soon.

"I'm not sure how fast news spreads from Southeast Yaenia to here," he said, "but recently, Princess Lydia of the Darian Kingdom was engaged to Prince Thane of the Throatian Kingdom. Instead of marrying her, as they should have, Thane and his family murdered her. It's unclear why, but it involved blood magic. A massive wall of rain soon appeared, surrounding their island. We think a dragon might be the cause."

"Were you there during the battle at sea?" the woman asked. "Did you see the great storm?"

"I witnessed most of it," he replied. "I was the one who captured Harkbin Asche and handed him over to King von Stonewall. He—"

"Then, I know who you are now, Sir Eisenbern," she said. "I too was at Princess Lydia's wedding and saw you there."

Eisenbern's face turned scarlet. He had never seen her before, but he would have remembered someone as beautiful as she was, even with her unconventional attire.

"I suppose the more interesting point is I don't recall having met you," he said.

"We haven't introduced ourselves yet," she replied. "But I'm relieved to see that everything you've done since the wedding has been according to my expectations."

"What's that supposed to mean? How do you know what I've been doing?"

"Come," the woman said, taking the key off the wall. "We have so much to discuss."

THE WOMAN IN STRANGE DARK ARMOR LED THEM THROUGH A MUSTY corridor within the cavern. Water dripped from the ceiling, forming puddles at their feet. Pale green mushrooms, faintly glowing, provided their only light as they navigated the winding passages. Since the toadstools were spaced farther apart than torches in a typical castle, Eisenbern wondered if the Black Moon Tribe had planted them or if they grew naturally in such a pattern.

As they moved further from the prison cell, the glowing caps multiplied, providing a mysterious aura as the cavern's walls gradually widened out. Some mushrooms pulsed as though they had heartbeats. He carefully stretched out his finger, bracing for something harmful, but the Black Moon Tribe warrior's inaction gave him a feeling of safety. The surfaces were cold and damp, contrary to the subtle hotness he'd expected them to have within. Apart from their glow, they resembled ordinary mushrooms.

The silence inside the caverns gave him ample opportunity to pose questions, but his gut told him to hold his tongue and observe everything around him. He could question more later, and there were more important matters to ask once they reached wherever the warrior was leading them. For now, he couldn't tell where that might be.

A unique entryway fortified by metallic frames linked each cavern room instead of conventional doors. These entryways branched into short, S-shaped sub-hallways that wound around for privacy. As they passed several openings, Eisenbern realized the underground city was a vast, dark maze, and no one in the Black Moon Tribe likely knew every detail.

Their pathway opened into a large circular room, with five corridors branching in from different directions. A round table stood in the center, its glass platter glowing with a welcoming golden light, overflowing with mushrooms similar to those he'd seen earlier. Plucked from elsewhere, these proved to be a suitable alternative to torchlights and candles. Next to the crystal tray of mushrooms sat a massive silver goblet filled with wine. The woman gestured for them to sit and took the farthest seat for herself.

"First things first," she said, ignoring the goblet of alcohol in front of her. "My name is Somnius, and the body you see isn't mine. The woman before you is called Herja, and she willingly lets me control her. She leads the Black Moon Tribe and has kindly permitted me to command her people during my stay here."

"Are you..." Ilya blurted, "are you a Lucidian? How are you doing this magic?"

"I am not from your world," a voice echoed from a connecting tunnel. Another warrior approached their table—a middle-aged man wearing unusual armor similar to Herja's, fitting his muscular frame. His powerful build suggested he could brawl with a dragon if needed. Across his back was a broadsword almost as tall as he was.

"This one is named Ragnar," Somnius said through his lips, "and I also have control over him."

"How are you doing this?" Eisenbern repeated in place of Ilya.

"I came from another world," Somnius announced once more, "and though my supplies are dwindling, I possess a potion that enables me to control others while my body rests."

He wondered if Somnius intended to take control of their bodies as well. While Eisenbern didn't trust Somnius, he realized that if Somnius had wanted to force them to drink the potion, she could have done so previously when they were first captured.

A momentous event was unfolding around them, though he couldn't grasp its magnitude or nature. He sensed it, yet its scale was beyond comprehension. Somnius spoke in a cryptic way, as if they already knew everything. Despite how outlandish their words sounded, the expressionless faces of Herja and Ragnar confirmed their truthfulness. The real question was: Why? What motivated it all?

"You came to the Black Moon Tribe, meaning you must desire to defeat a dragon," Gustav deduced. "But being present at the Wedding of the Torn Rose, and from there concluding a dragon is involved, hints you're in the middle of everything."

"Your insight is formidable," Herja's body said. "Similarly, you three, and Kaine Khalia, can be described the same way."

"What does Kaine have to do with it?" Ilya asked.

"Everything, if my calculations are correct," Somnius said through Ragnar. "This is about more than a dragon. The war is as complicated as it is delicate."

"And controlling the Black Moon Tribe's bodies?" Gustav pressed. "That seems like a strange complication, perhaps even forced."

Ragnar approached the table, grabbed the massive goblet, and took a swig of the wine inside. He paused, his shoulders relaxing and his posture drooping until he seemed like a man instead of a wooden soldier. Eisenbern's fingers rubbed his chin as he concluded the goblet's contents must have been an anti-potion.

"It's because of the prophecy," Ragnar said. This time, his voice sounded deeper and more like the warrior's tone Eisenbern had expected.

"What prophecy?" said Eisenbern.

"I have released him from my control," Somnius announced through Herja. "Ragnar, please lead them to me at the end of this week. I will let them see the rest of the truth then. For now, show them how the Black Moon Tribe fought the dragons. Teach them your ways so that they will understand the next steps."

"You trust them that much already?" Ragnar asked Herja.

"Now that I comprehend their identities in this timeline, I know they are among the few I can."

"Very well, Your Grace," Ragnar said with a rough nod. "Likewise, my faith grows as fully as yours."

"What do you mean by timeline?" Eisenbern said, frowning. "I don't understand."

Ignoring his question, Herja picked up the goblet and drank some of the anti-potion. Like Ragnar before her, the wine-like drink released her from Somnius's control. Her body stiffened then loosened as the potion took effect.

"My apologies, Sir Eisenbern," she said. "There will be time for questions later when you meet Somnius. For now, I am Herja, the Dragon Mar of the Black Moon Tribe. Though I have not yet faced one of the legendary beasts, I have spent my life preparing for this war. Follow me, and everything shall become clearer soon."

22

KAINE - THE GRACE MAGE'S GIFT

As Kaine trudged up the charcoal-dark mountain trail, the sling around his arm tightened with each step. Beside him, Finn, sweat-soaked and focused, pulled the rickety cart carrying Xander and Kira. Though both children could walk the path to meet with Orin in an area secluded from the rest of the village, Finn insisted on carrying them up the mountain. The route wound its way deeper into the heart of the Shadowstone Mountains. Finn didn't complain about the heat, but Kaine still wondered if the climb was too strenuous for him.

The combined weight of Xander and Kira was unremarkable, but the cart appeared far bulkier and heavier than the children themselves. The upward slope only added to the difficulty of the task. Kaine wished he could trade places or assist their host in some way but the wrappings around his arm prevented him from doing so, leaving him to offer occasional words of encouragement instead.

Trailing behind them, Merdel gazed at the distant orange-capped volcanoes in awe. "It must be dangerous living so close to them, don't you think?" he inquired.

"It's true that eruptions happen often," Finn replied, "but they are far enough away that their fires and magma cannot reach us. On smoky days, we cover our faces and stay inside until the air clears."

"Wouldn't the hot springs be too close to the volcanoes?" Merdel continued.

"Not nearly," Finn said. "I promise you'll be safe where we're going today."

He led them along a trail for half an hour until they reached a large wooden structure perched between two hills. Surprisingly, it was in far better condition than any of the other structures in Gale Village. A faded red pagoda with tiered roofs stretched across the hillside, its overlapping curved tiles painted in pale green. Though not as recently constructed as the remaining buildings farther down the mountainside, it held a distinct design that set it apart. The group arrived at a vast, striped doorway. Xander and Kira climbed out of the cart and entered through the door. As they moved forward, Kaine realized the structure wasn't a building but a passageway with three walls opening onto a terrace overlooking a large hot spring.

On the other side of the walkway stood a lone wooden shack, like the others in the village. It perched forty feet from where the water met the smooth black stone, and its mossy, warped boards suggested great age. Kaine assumed it served as a storage cache, not a residence.

A wall of interwoven twigs separated the steamy hot spring into two private sides, spanning the enclosed basin while allowing water to flow through. Though the spa could hold thirty people on each side, Kaine suspected few visited at once because of the hike's difficulty from Gale Village.

On one side of the partition, Elder Orin and Celeste were already in the water. Both wore strange plum-colored suits, long and high-necked, with sleeves covering their arms from shoulders to wrists. Their attire seemed modest for a shared bath, perhaps overly so. Even if not, steam rose from the water's surface, forming a thin white veil.

Kira scrunched her face in disgust as she stared at the water. "We have to go in there? Together?"

Xander shook his head, also looking uneasy. "I thought each of us would have our own pool."

Kaine and Merdel exchanged bewildered glances. Finn had mentioned "hot springs," and they assumed this meant there were multiple water bodies. Even if there weren't enough for each person to have their own private bath, the idea of gathering into a single large pool seemed unusual—especially with a Lucidian among them.

Thankfully, Orin was too far away to hear their protests. "Good morning, everyone! The water is perfect today! Come on in and let the natural salts revitalize your body and soul!" he called out with enthusiasm.

Finn nudged Kaine on the shoulder. "I'll be back later this afternoon to pick you up. Enjoy your time here," he encouraged. He then returned through the entryway and resumed hauling his empty cart.

"We will," Kaine said as he unbuckled the brown leather belt from around his waist.

"Whoa there, Sir Khalia," Orin called out as Celeste chuckled from across the water. "You've never been to a hot spring before, have you? Let me explain the proper etiquette. You don't simply undress and jump in like a child at the ocean! Instead, go to the shack over there and knock. Sen is in there, but once she's done, she'll provide you with a robe to change into."

Kaine's face flushed red. "My apologies, elder. You're right; I've never been to a place like this."

Merdel let out another loud laugh. "He was only one step ahead of me in fully undressing!"

Meanwhile, Kira stared at her feet, grinding the edges of her shoes into the black rock surface of the patio. "I really don't want to get in," she muttered.

"Perhaps you could sit on the edge and just dip your legs in?" Kaine suggested. Given her age and royal status, it seemed inappropriate for her to enter the water in front of everyone else. She likely felt the same way.

"Maybe."

"Do whatever you feel comfortable doing, my princess," Kaine said. He swore he saw her sigh with relief.

"Thank you."

"I don't want to go in there either," Xander said, then lowered his voice. "Especially not with a Lucidian."

"You should go in, Xander," Kaine said. The prince would be the king someday, and if taking a shared bath with Orin and Celeste would ease tensions with the Lucidians of Gale Village, it was worth the awkwardness and uneasiness.

"Why do I have to go into the water, but she doesn't?"

"You're the future king, and Gale Village's culture calls for it," Merdel explained. "It's not something we would normally do, but think of it like pouring a fine glass of wine for your guests. Wouldn't you be insulted if they spat it out and complained it was too sour?"

The prince winced. "If the wine were so sour due to its inferior quality, I wouldn't be drinking it."

Before they could argue further, Orin called out to them again. "Are you all deciding who'll change first?"

Kaine smiled, relieved the elder and Celeste couldn't hear them. He took a deep breath, determined to lead by example. "I'll go first!" he shouted across the pool.

The princess gazed with admiration at Kaine as he approached the small shack. Meanwhile, Xander sought guidance from Merdel, contemplating his next move. From behind Kaine, the councilman muttered, "There's no way out of this for either of us." Chuckling, Kaine knocked on the shack's door.

"Just a moment!" a woman's unfamiliar voice sounded through the door.

The shack's door creaked open, and a Lucidian woman presented herself. Though wrinkled, she was still younger than Celeste. She wore a tan robe that reached her slender periwinkle-shaded ankles. Who was this woman, and would she join them as well?

He glanced back toward the water and noticed both Kira and Xander staring curiously at the newly appeared Lucidian.

"What happened to your arm?" she squeaked. It was an unusual question to ask during a first meeting; Lucidians were odd people.

Kaine glanced down at his sling and shrugged his shoulders. "Months ago, a war hammer smashed my arm. It will heal someday."

"I can heal it now for you, if you'd like," the Lucidian offered in a tone that seemed too kind and enthusiastic to be genuine.

His arm was already useless, and her magic couldn't worsen it. Despite her abilities, he doubted she could mend his broken bones. Lately, Kaine had felt uneasy, suspecting his arm had partially healed on its own but had set improperly. The natural healing that had already occurred might have advanced too far for her to correct.

Being near magic users made him feel the same nervousness he'd experienced around royalty. Their power, both explicit and implicit, could change his life instantly. If she were honest and her magic as powerful as he imagined, healing his arm would be an unexpected but welcome outcome.

"If you're truly capable of healing my arm," Kaine said, "then I'd be deeply grateful. But are you certain your magic can do this?"

"Of course! I'm Sen Zorra, a Grace Mage."

"I'm Kaine Khalia. Thank you, Sen. Pardon my skepticism, but I'm not used to… encountering magic users."

Sen stepped further out of the shack and gently touched his sling. "The pleasure is mine. This arm won't be a problem. Go and change first. There are plenty of robes inside there you can use. I'll wait outside for you."

As Kaine stepped into the shack and closed the door behind him, he realized how incredibly cramped it was. In the center of the room stood a footstool, inches from a shelf holding linen cloths. Everything else seemed ordinary and expected except the second shelf beside it, which held an assortment of strange items. Jars of pickled mushrooms, dried herbs, and mysterious substances lined the shelf. Were these meant for the hot spring, or were they medicines? Was this Sen's home?

He removed the sling's wrappings and held his arm close to his chest as he took off his shoes and shirt. For what he hoped would be the last time, he struggled to unbutton his pants and undergarments before selecting a suitable robe. With his bare feet, he pushed his footwear into the corner and then piled his clothes into a messy heap. He hoped the others would understand he couldn't fold them yet. He looked forward to the day when he could manage it on his own, and if Sen's promise was genuine, it would be soon.

As Kaine stepped out of the shack, he heard Merdel's laughter echoing as he conversed with Orin and Celeste by the water's edge. Nearby, Kira and Sen discussed their journey from Last Hope, while Xander stood motionless, his arms crossed.

"I'll go next," the prince muttered as Kaine approached him. He stepped shakily past Kaine and towards the hot spring shack. The prince would feel more at ease once he was in the water.

As Sen drew near with Kira, her long violet hair flowed through the mist. With a gentle smile, she admired Kaine's exposed right arm. "Thank you for removing the sling—I forgot to mention earlier that I needed it off. So, you've already helped me. Let me begin."

"Will this hurt?"

"The experience may feel unfamiliar, but it won't cause you any discomfort. Please don't move—I'll let you know when it's finished."

Sen rested her dark fingers against Kaine's forearm, her grip tightening until it was firm enough to be certain. Kaine winced, uncertain why the hold felt so restrictive. Her other hand hovered over the healing spot, and Kaine couldn't help but tremble. A warmth like summer winds spread through his body as her palm glowed with a faint purple light, matching the exact hue of her skin. Then, wriggling sensations began beneath his skin—like worms crawling from his elbow toward his fingers—but it was only a sensation. He wondered if magic could conjure such things within him. Were they actually mending his arm, or was it just the feeling? Before he could respond, the sensation faded, leaving a gentle, rhythmic squeezing throughout the injury. Sen's hand remained still against his skin, its faint purple hue unchanged. It seemed her magic was working!

"How many arms have you healed before?" Kaine asked, though it was too late to turn back, even if he wanted.

"Too many to count," Sen said. "Legs too. Granted, I can't regrow lost limbs or add ones that weren't there from the beginning, but I've learned that healing essentially means restoring people to their natural order."

The pulsing sensation faded from his arm, and he felt the blood surge again toward his hand. An imaginary tightrope seemed to have loosened around his wrist.

"A person's natural order… so I'm guessing you can't bring someone back from the dead?"

"If only I could do that… My power is suitable for several physical ailments, but not everything. For instance, I cannot restore what was lost, such as Orin's eye. Lucidians vary in the gifts they bear. Sometimes, magic is inconsistent."

"That's still amazing!" Kira said. "I wish I could do what you're capable of. Imagine how many people you could help!"

"But there must be limits," Kaine said.

"There are, but perhaps we can discuss them later," Sen said. "Your arm has now healed."

For the first time in months, Kaine's right arm felt normal. It had taken him so long to adjust to wearing a sling, and as his recovery kept being delayed, the sling had started to feel like a permanent part of him. He grinned, realizing he'd never need it again.

"That was fast!" Kaine said, gently testing his arm's mobility. Everything was painless.

"This experience may feel unfamiliar," Sen explained, "but it won't cause you discomfort. Be patient as your muscles naturally regrow and regain strength. Exercise and stretch before attempting to lift heavy objects with both hands. Currently, your left arm is stronger than your right, and this imbalance will take time to correct." Sen's knowledge was impressive.

"How can I ever thank you?" Kaine exclaimed. "You've given me my life back."

Kaine had waited so long for this moment that he'd stopped

counting days since Urith Asche's war hammer struck him. He almost believed it wouldn't come.

"It's but a small ordeal for me," the Lucidian replied. "I only ask that you keep my people hidden in Gale Village."

"Consider it done!" Kaine said, extending his healed arm to shake her hand. Sen smiled gently, and they completed their agreement.

The shack door creaked open again as Xander emerged, wearing a tan robe similar to the others. He gripped the edge of his own tightly as he approached them. "What happened?"

"You missed it!" Kira yelled. "Sen used magic to heal Kaine's arm!"

"Interesting," the prince replied. Perhaps even miracles could not ease his discomfort about entering the hot spring.

"So shall we enter the water now?" Kaine asked him.

"If we must."

As Kaine and Xander approached Merdel, Kira and Sen moved toward Celeste. The princess watched Sen, curious whether she too would enter the pool.

"You aren't going in?" Kira asked.

"I shouldn't now," Sen said. "The saltwater will make me too lightheaded. I'll wait until tomorrow morning, after I recover some."

"Recover? What's wrong?"

"Magic costs blood," Sen explained. "Like humans who've suffered a wound, I've lost some of mine. It will return eventually, but no Lucidian is limitless in that regard."

"When I was a merchant, I learned nothing comes for free," Kaine called over to her. "It seems the same holds true for magic. Now that I understand this, my gratitude toward you grows even greater."

The Lucidian offered him a gentle smile as she settled by the water's edge, dipping her legs into the steaming surface. "Losing blood through magic is like feeling sleepy or hungry—it's a natural course. So long as I don't overuse my abilities, there is little discomfort or harm in healing others."

Sen's explanation clarified the boundaries of the Lucidian's powers. Was this what the Throatians had aimed for in killing Princess Lydia—trying to harness her blood for their own purposes? Were their ambitions rooted in a hollow faith, or was there some validity to their plans after all? As long as they never created magic that could rival the Lucidian's, he hoped the beliefs of the Throatian people would remain irrelevant.

"I really wish I could do what you do," Kira said, sitting next to Sen at the edge of the water.

The hot springs were intimate yet comfortable. For political discussions, Orin's choice was shrewd. Kaine wondered if Sen's presence and the offer to heal his arm had been a calculated gesture of goodwill. Either way, the tensions since arriving in Gale Village were fading. Hopefully, the next step in uncovering the truth about the painting and the God Stones would be fruitful.

A loud splash echoed as Xander jumped into the hot spring. Water spilled over the edge, drenching Kaine's toes. The warmth, feeling like nearly boiling water, soothed his feet. Entering the pool with the others no longer felt like an awkward idea.

"This is your first time at a hot spring, isn't it?" Orin called out to him from where he sat in the water.

"It's not my fault we've never been here before," Xander said after wiping his eyes. "After all the times we've visited." He waded through the water and took a seat nearby. "Aren't the rest of you coming in?"

23

KIRA - THE DEMISE OF A GOD

By the edge of the hot spring, Kira felt out of place and self-conscious in the intimate setting. Around her, Kaine, Merdel, Xander, and Elder Orin lounged comfortably in the steaming water.

Her cheeks stayed a deep pink as she imagined changing into one of the strange robes. While communal bathing appeared to be a common practice here, it felt strange to her. She fidgeted with the hem of her dress, struggling with her shyness. Was it really expected that she should join them?

Her father had visited the hot springs on previous trips, but this was her and Xander's first time traveling beyond the village's main areas. She wasn't sure whether Lydia had ever joined the group in the water and whether it was proper to bathe with them or politely decline. If only she could have asked Lydia for advice right then.

"Are you coming?" her brother called.

"Um… I'm not sure," Kira hesitated. She bit her lip, torn between hesitation and desire. The hot spring beckoned invitingly, its steam curling upward and carrying the scent of minerals and herbs, more soothing than her usual bath at home. Her muscles ached from days of travel, and she hadn't felt truly clean in ages.

Kira took a deep breath, trying to steady herself. This was her chance to connect with others—to prove she wasn't afraid or uptight, as others may have perceived her.

"It's not that bad," Xander said.

Kira rolled her eyes. "You're only saying that because you refuse to admit how hot it truly is."

"Prove it by coming in then," he taunted.

Sen returned from the shack with dark red tea for everyone and offered Kira a small cup.

"It was a pleasure to meet all of you, but I have duties I must attend to," she said, after serving them tea. She exited through the tower entrance.

The sudden departure distracted Kira, and she wondered about Sen's true nature. The Lucidian's healing of Kaine's arm directly contradicted the magical demons described in her childhood stories. Celeste seemed kind-hearted, too. Why did they differ so sharply from the accounts of her father's struggles when he founded their kingdom? Kira realized entering the hot spring presented a far less daunting challenge than the trials her father had faced at her age—or all that Lydia had endured. She needed to become braver, and this step could mark her first attempt. Though Kaine or Merdel might scold her afterward, the consequences would be minor.

"I'm coming in," she announced while marching toward the shack.

After changing into her robe and returning to the water, the steam thickened around her, enveloping her in warm mist. The air carried the earthy scent of sulfur, likely from the nearby volcanoes. As she waded into the spring, the hot water soothed her aching muscles. With a smile, she knew she had made the right choice, if only for this moment of relief.

Orin, who sat apart from everyone, seemed unfazed by the overpowering odor of sulfur. He cleared his throat and began their discussion as Kira submerged herself deeper into the water.

"Now that everyone is settled," Orin announced, gesturing toward her and Xander for emphasis, "let's get down to business. I assume the children have been informed about everything we discussed last night, including the God Stones?"

Kira was unable to sleep the night before, tormented by what Kaine and Merdel had revealed. The Throatians hadn't just killed Lydia for her blood—they had also sought her father's magical God Stones. Despite everyone's efforts to stop Prince Thane and his family, they failed to save Lydia. Kira couldn't help wondering why this had to happen and how the Throatians could commit such a cowardly act. Magic was important, but Lydia was irreplaceable.

"We covered the details," Merdel confirmed. "The royal children now realize more is happening and at stake than they knew."

She wished her father had shared the truth about the God Stones from the start. Magic was so powerful it couldn't be kept secret, especially since it invited danger.

"I always thought they were just valuable gems," Xander said.

As children, they had once seen their father's secret, though they didn't fully understand its significance. He introduced them to a game with glowing stones, presenting it as a fascinating puzzle. Little did they realize at the time that this was their first introduction to magic. While Kira and Lydia quickly mastered the stones' glow, Xander struggled and eventually accused their father of cheating. The game was played only once and never repeated.

"He tested us without us realizing how important it was," Kira said.

Orin placed his tea on the black stone surface near the water's edge. "Your father was right to test you," he said, "but wrong to keep you unaware of the consequences. Understanding the significance matters more than what you might have otherwise done."

Kira hesitated, torn between agreeing and disagreeing. Her father must have had his reasons for keeping everything a secret, and she hoped those reasons were good. However, keeping everything that way, even now, didn't feel right.

"King Ether's caution was justified—the danger is real," Merdel said, as Kira glanced at Celeste. "The God Stones' powers exceed those of a Lucidian. Orin, what do you know of the God Stones, and what does the painting from Kaine's story signify?"

She hadn't seen it herself. Kaine described the painting as rough sketches filled with abstract symbols, though he didn't know who painted it or what it meant.

"Zelia believed Blanche's painting is connected to the God Stones," Orin explained. "While the artwork doesn't explicitly reveal their powers or origins, the symbolism suggests there's more to uncover here than we know. But there was something intriguing about it. Scrawled on the back were words—a prophecy. Zelia had entrusted me with her letter and the God Stones, while Blanche found a prophecy attached to the painting. Each of us holds a key piece of the puzzle."

"A prophecy written on the back of the painting?" Kaine exclaimed. "How can you be sure it's not a poem?"

"It's certainly a prophecy," Orin declared. "If King Ether had known about it, he would have told you."

"We don't know anything about it," Merdel admitted. "But if you could enlighten us, we'd know for sure whether the God Stones are related to it."

"The God Stones are a fascinating puzzle," Celeste added. "If we can figure out how everything connects, our questions will be answered."

"Celeste and I agree that everything is interconnected," Orin reaffirmed. "The Prophecy of Tears and Sacrifice is this: a god will die, and a false god will replace them. After a great sacrifice, a hero will appear, one who will use the God Stones to rid the world of corruption forever. What do you make of it?"

The hot spring fell quiet as Kaine, Merdel, Xander, and Kira grasped the prophecy's implications. A crow cawed ominously nearby, as if to warn them to forget everything they'd just heard.

"So," Xander began, crossing his arms. "The dead Lucidian princess, the God Stones, the painting, and this prophecy are all connected." Kira scowled at his bluntness.

Orin repeated the words, "a god will die, and a false god will replace them. After a great sacrifice, a hero will appear, one who will use the God Stones to rid the world of corruption forever."

Kira pondered at the words, a stray thought surfacing as she mumbled aloud, "Perhaps Princess Zelia was meant to be the hero—but she died. It seems the prophecy didn't account for that outcome. Maybe it wasn't true after all."

Merdel added, "The prophecy and the God Stones' preference for certain individuals might be connected. Kira, you might be next in line to wield the God Stones, as Zelia and Lydia did before you. This could be dangerous."

Kira's eyes widened at Merdel's suggestion, her heart pounding as she realized the truth. There was a reason the God Stones responded to Zelia, Lydia, and her, unlike others. The magic was both powerful and deeply disturbing. Just because she could make the stones glow during her father's test didn't mean she should push herself further.

"Princess Zelia was wise until her last breath," Celeste said in her hoarse voice. "She entrusted the stones to the von Stonewall family, foreseeing what others could not. In her letter, she hinted that Lily von Stonewall might be the next step in fulfilling the prophecy. Maybe that indirectly meant her children."

"Maybe it all comes down to bloodline," Merdel said. "If the prophecy is tied to blood, then Kira may be the one chosen to fulfill it. But if magic is inherited, why can Zelia, Lydia, and Kira wield the God Stones while Xander cannot?"

Kira's face flushed red as they spoke of her as if she weren't there. She, along with her siblings Lydia and Xander, shared a physical resemblance; Kira looked like a younger version of Lydia, who also resembled their mother. It could have been the God Stones only worked for girls, leaving Xander unable to use them despite being of the same bloodline.

"Xander is certainly Lily's child, isn't he?" Celeste mused. "So why was he unable to use the magic? And Zelia has no relationship to the von Stonewalls. There must be something deeper at work beyond mere bloodlines."

"Of course I am my mother's son!" Xander snapped, annoyed. Kira too, grew increasingly frustrated with the suggestion that their family wasn't legitimate.

"I witnessed his birth and watched him grow up," Merdel said. "The young man with us now is the true Darian Prince—not a bastard, not exchanged at birth, or anything of the sort."

Kira mouthed her thanks to the councilman. Though Xander looked more like their father than she or Lydia, it was reassuring for the confirmation that he was her brother. Kira hoped Celeste was being thorough rather than trying to sow doubt.

"Who can say whether using the God Stones signifies anything?" Orin asked. "Perhaps those who wield them possess an inherent connection to their power. However, when it comes to the gods and the prophecy, that aspect is much more difficult to verify or disprove."

"A god will die, and a false god will replace them," Kaine repeated. "The words resemble an ominous beginning of a dark fairy tale."

"Think about this," Orin said. "Believing in a god doesn't make it real. For the prophecy to hold true, the false god must be something alive. The Throatian god might be the false god mentioned there. Their god supposedly granted them magic, leading them to murder Princess Lydia. But none of it accomplished anything. Their god isn't a god, as you've explained."

Xander pondered, "What if a god existed but is now dead?"

His question might have seemed odd, but Kira knew what he was considering. Years ago, their father had taken them to church to pray to Asura. Lydia was more devout in her faith than her siblings. While Kira believed in Asura and his teachings, Xander quietly revealed that his faith was weaker. Kira had heard about the Dead Asura Theory before. One day, while their father spoke with another church visitor, Xander had whispered about a secret belief shared by some, including himself. They claimed the god Asura had abandoned the world and taken his own life.

Kira had asked Lydia whether Xander's story could be true. Her sister replied that Asura was still alive, wandering the world in human form, waiting for the right moment to purify it. Kira agreed with her sister's belief—if Asura had died, why would so many people still worship him? It made no sense for a god to abandon the world so selfishly.

Following the incident, Xander never again mentioned his religious beliefs. Kira suspected that Lydia had spoken to Xander about his views and corrected him. Kira never asked him whether his opinion had changed, because the memory was still uncomfortable for her.

She felt tears forming in her eyes. Though she told herself it was only steam, it made no difference—the conversation continued without giving her a chance to speak her concerns. Why couldn't she have agency in her own life? Did anyone there care about what she thought about this?

"If Asura is dead and the Throatian god isn't real, then the first part of the prediction would already be fulfilled," Kaine suggested.

"Zelia was so close to solving the mystery," Celeste lamented. "The God Stones were tied to the prophecy, but their use exhausted her mind, leading to her death in her sleep. If only she had lived another day, she might have provided more guidance."

"They've made their guesses," Orin said, shifting his gaze between Merdel and Kaine. "Celeste and I have our own ideas of what's true. Come. Follow me. Our skin will wrinkle if we stay here too long."

The elder led them out of the water. After changing, Orin guided them from the hot springs down a winding path that Kira hadn't traveled before.

"Look over there—you can see part of the fortress at Wargonne," Orin said, pointing toward the horizon, "It's not something you can see from even the highest tower at your home."

Kira squinted in that direction but saw no sign of the fortress. "Where is it?" she muttered.

"Between the shorter and taller mountains," Orin insisted, "lies a fortress with gray walls, not black. That's where your father should have established his home once the war had ended. Wargonne is the safest place in Yaenia. The name even fits."

Kira attempted to find it, seeing a shape that might be a rock or the fortress Orin had described. Though unable to identify it from afar, she knew the war would inevitably lead her in that direction. She wondered how long it would take before she needed to travel there.

"I don't see it," Kira said. "Could I go back to the village for a while?"

"It's best that you do not return to the shack alone," Kaine said. "Stay with us so we can watch over you. There's no telling what might be lurking on the mountainside."

"You also wouldn't want to twist your ankle or anything," Merdel added.

Kira smiled, though her eyes remained watery. Everyone saw her as a child who needed protection, yet their words suggested she was meant to shoulder responsibilities far beyond what they were obligated to handle.

A sensation stirred within her—something she couldn't name, define, or act upon. She was older than a child, yet they still spoke to her as if she couldn't speak for herself. They were making plans for her future, treating her as an object of care while ignoring the truth: she was the one who needed to grow to meet the expectations they placed upon her.

For a moment, Kira chose the path of independence. She needed to reject their help, their safeguarding, and their coddling. Would she ever have the power to make her own decisions if they never gave it to her? How could she grow if she lived without ever being hurt? It was a weakness to let others shield her, if not laziness. Kira needed to grow without them protecting her.

But then looking forward, she realized her father couldn't have succeeded without help. He'd become the king, not by forging a crown and placing it on his head, but because his friends and allies had bestowed it upon him.

To make her own decisions, Kira didn't need to dwell on whether she should be alone; she just needed to learn to speak her mind as often as she listened to the others. This, she suspected, would be the first step toward overcoming everything else.

24
THANE - THE VALLEY OF THE WHISPERERS

Zeere and Thane traveled through the night until the first hints of sunlight appeared. Using nearby mountain landmarks, Zeere realized they were near the town of Emil. They changed course, heading to the town to restock and rest before continuing north toward the Whisperers' rumored location.

As they approached Emil, the town nestled at the foot of a mountain revealed itself as a quaint sanctuary. To Thane, it resembled Hillside Reach but with a unique charm that set it apart. The town's well-tended gardens hinted at a community proud of its surroundings. Even the chickens strutted around freely with an aura of self-importance. It appeared the town had been painstakingly groomed to showcase its cultural depth. Cleanly painted rows of cottages arranged in neat clusters displayed an elegance finer than the rugged stone huts of Thane's homeland.

As they entered the heart of Emil, the main street bustled with early morning activity. Freshly baked bread's pleasant aroma filled the air, and distant chatter and bargaining could be heard. Emil's market was busy and lively, but smaller than the markets Thane had seen in Starlight Beach and Sky Tower Coast.

After browsing the stalls to find a suitable vendor, they stopped at one specializing in furs, leathers, and textiles. Zeere sold one of his amethysts, accepting a fair but less-than-optimal sum to avoid attracting attention.

"The one bright side of our blunder in the Hierophant's tent is that at least now we have money," Zeere commented.

With their gold coins in hand, they headed to one of Emil's cookery lanes for breakfast. As they sat outside enjoying their meat pies, Zeere expressed his intention to keep the remaining two amethysts, believing they held the key to unlocking Lucidian magic.

"You're welcome to keep the other two jewels for yourself," Thane said, leaning back in his chair. "We survived, and now we have something to show for it. I only wish we'd been able to retrieve my armor as well."

"Life is unfair like that sometimes," Zeere said. "But as long as we don't have to fight her again, her having the armor is not our problem."

"Anyway, let's leave town now," Thane said, "I don't know whether the Lucidians are following us, but I don't want to wait around and find out."

His companion replied, "The merchant said they wouldn't be ready until midday," referring to the transport they had arranged earlier that morning in Emil's market.

"A tad bit more gold will make them prepared sooner," Thane said. "The cost of our concealment is the cost of our survival."

"You're right, I guess."

"It's not cheap," Thane admitted, "but traveling privately greatly improves our chances of reaching the north undetected. Delaying our departure only works against us."

"Very well," Zeere said, "but again, please let me keep the other two jewels we found. I have no objections to spending our money as long as we don't squander it."

"It is better to be free with empty pockets than rich and under our enemy's thumbs," Thane said. "Gold won't be much help for us once we are in the wilderness, anyway."

They returned to the market square and approached a merchant's stall where three carriages were being loaded with vegetables, linens, and crates of supplies destined for sale in New Ginstown to the north. Nearby at his stall sat the same bodacious man they had spoken to earlier, double-checking his ledger.

"Ah, you're back," he said. "I already mentioned I wouldn't be ready to move until midday."

"We were hoping to persuade you otherwise," Thane said smoothly. Zeere reached into his belt pouch, pulled out several gold coins, and offered them to the merchant.

The carriage owner's eyes widened slightly as he took in the sight. "Well now," he said slowly, "I could work a bit faster if you're willing to pay extra. Something urgent happening in New Ginstown?"

"We're heading to a wedding," Thane lied. "But there's an angry woman searching for me here."

"Your predicament is understandable, my friend," the owner said, pocketing the coins and turning back to his ledger. He marked his spot with a feather from his cap and closed the book. Within half an hour, their cart and the other two of the caravan were ready to depart.

They boarded a covered cart and settled among sacks of flour, which served well as pillows. Neither of them had slept the previous night, so they were both eager to rest. Once they were on the road outside Emil and certain they weren't being followed, Thane and Zeere took the chance to sleep. Even if the Hierophant or Enforcer Mages were searching for them now, they'd be much harder to find there.

Thane slept for hours, despite the rhythmic clomping of hooves against the dirt road. When he woke, his senses were instantly alert. Opening his eyes, he confirmed he was still in the cart. Sunlight filtered through the cloth-covered doors at the back, reassuring him he had rested most of the day without being captured. His legs stretched out to the far end of the cart where Zeere sat opposite him, his head resting against the wooden panels. The Null Mage had unraveled the bandages around his hands and wrists and was examining them carefully.

"Your hands must feel terrible after holding that fiery grease ball," Thane said.

"Sooner or later, they'll heal," Zeere grunted, "but I wish there was a Grace Mage here to speed up the healing. Still, this isn't the first time I've suffered this."

He gave the Lucidian a perplexed stare. "How many times have you grabbed fire from torches exactly?"

"Just once, when we escaped our cell," Zeere replied, "and perhaps now is a good time to tell you why I'm wrapped from head to toe in bandages. We've got a long journey ahead of us."

Zeere suddenly laughed so hard that Thane was caught off guard and instinctively reached for his sword. The laugh seemed inappropriate, given that Zeere was about to reveal a secret he'd kept hidden for so long. Thane suspected his companion's bottled-up emotions had caused the unexpected outburst.

"It's not easy for me to say why I wear the bandages because it's… as humiliating as it is sad."

Thane chuckled nervously. "It can't be more humiliating than having the Hierophant force you to reveal your secrets and give away your armor," he said. "Nor can it be more shameful than murdering your wife on your wedding day." He paused. "Come now, what's happened to you? Why do you wear bandages?"

Zeere's laughter faded into a neutral expression as his eyes met Thane's. "Have you ever done something so stupidly cowardly yet clever that it saved your own life?"

Thane frowned, considering the question. "A stupid decision somehow saved your life? I don't understand."

"There are many ways to survive a war," Zeere replied bitterly, "but some methods are both foolish and effective." He gestured toward his bandaged face. Thane noticed the uncertainty in his eyes. It seemed as if he were about to remove the mask—revealing that he'd been unharmed all along—and finally expose a sick joke.

"Whatever you've done, I've done worse," Thane offered.

"I told you earlier that I'm a mortician who faked my own death to escape the war. Though I wasn't present at the Lowland Graves the day everyone else died, I was close enough to witness it from afar."

"Well, it worked out perfectly then," Thane said, attempting to lighten the mood with a weak smile. "You survived because you fled. That sounds like good luck to me."

Zeere's expression darkened as he looked away toward the cart's rear. "Watching so many friends die while the corrupt leaders remained safe behind their walls was unbearable. We gave everything to our government, and for what? To force the northerner Lucidians to follow our laws and customs? The price was too high, and I couldn't pay more. Escaping the Enclave's influence is no easy task, as you know."

Thane nodded, observing the tears streaking Zeere's bandaged face. "Of course not," he responded. "It appears that your kingdom thrives by monitoring everyone closely. How do your injuries fit into this? Did the Enclave catch you, or was it the Darians?"

Zeere shook his head, though the rest of his body remained still. "Neither group tracked me down," he said softly. "When I planned my escape from the war, I devised a permanent means of staying hidden—ensuring that even if the Enclave found me, I would be unrecognizable. So I..."

He paused, his voice trailing off as memories of his pain resurfaced.

Thane pressed forward. "You hid yourself how?"

Their eyes locked, revealing the calculating yet weary man beneath the bandages. "I taught you that Scarlet Mages wield fire magic and Grace Mages have healing abilities," Zeere reminded him. "For hours, my confidant, Hizarra, cast flames upon me, while my friend Sen tended to my wounds. Destroying and healing my body at the same time corrupted the very essence of who I am... By Lucidian standards, I was once a handsome man, but I had to give that up—I destroyed every part of myself to ensure no one could recognize me. Now, even Sen's powerful magic can't restore my former self, though I regret my decision. Though unnecessary to hide my identity, I wore the bandages to cover my shame."

Thane took a moment to process what he'd just been told. The magnitude of what Zeere had done to himself sank in slowly, leaving him momentarily speechless. What he had inflicted upon himself hadn't been right.

"To go to such lengths to hide your identity seems not only overly cautious but also reckless and mad. There must have been something else... some other reason you did it."

Zeere shook his head. "I had justifiable reasons then, but I went too far. I knew it then, and I know it now."

The distant sound of horses' hooves broke the silence, drawing their attention. Another carriage approached from the opposite direction, carrying what appeared to be another traveler who paid no mind to their caravan. As they faded off into the distance, Thane continued the conversation.

"The years of being on the run must have changed you," he suggested. "One doesn't go from running from authority to wanting to eliminate it in a single day."

Zeere turned his attention back to him. "That's how it went," he said. "Though hiding was necessary, the cost was too high. At least my scars give me the freedom to move freely in Yaenia as I gather information. One day, I hope to overthrow the Enclave. Not all Lucidians are like their leaders—I must save those people before the

Enclave tries to conquer Yaenia again, just as you seek to save the Throatians from Zann-Xia-Czul."

Thane's hand tightened at the mention of his own struggles. "We'll find a way to stop them," he promised. "If you explain your cause to Somnius, I'm sure she'll support you. The Enclave is just as great a threat to the world as Zann-Xia-Czul."

Zeere's eyes drifted toward his feet, staring distantly as if foreseeing future conflicts. "As much as I hope you're right, I don't believe she's a goddess from another world," he replied. "Are you sure she can be trusted?"

If only Somnius could have provided more information—a sign, a message through a bird, or anything else. Thane suspected that something greater was happening far away, and that she was dealing with problems far more complex and dangerous than their own issues.

He nodded reassuringly and said, "Though I didn't travel with her for long, I believe she is truly divine. She's also merciful, especially to someone like me, who she had every reason to kill."

"I'll give you the benefit of the doubt for now—and make my final judgment if I meet her someday. For now, I have less trust in the Whisperers you so eagerly want to meet. The powers you described them as having seem awfully similar to those of the Hierophant. I hope they are not one and the same."

"Who can say what we'll encounter next?" Thane said, his voice firm though he felt uneasy. "If retrieving the horn from the Whisperers can help the goddess, I want to do it. The only question is how difficult it will be, especially without the armor I was given. But it seems to have been our destiny to have come this far and still be alive."

Still, he couldn't shake the feeling that their next destination would challenge them in ways they couldn't even begin to fathom.

AFTER A WEEK AND A HALF, THE MERCHANT'S CART ROLLED INTO NEW Ginstown with a creak. Thane and Zeere quickly disembarked and headed straight for an inn, seeking privacy from prying eyes. The inn offered a warm embrace, with inviting fireplaces and the mouth-watering scent of roasted pig. Over the next day, they restocked, haggling with merchants for fresh provisions and new swords that felt better balanced than their old ones. Under the cover of darkness on the second night, they slipped away, heading northwest. Guided by the faint glow of the distant mountains rumored to be the home of the Whisperers, they moved stealthily, their ears alert for any sign of pursuit by the Hierophant or any others who might have taken an interest in following them.

They navigated the plains while purposefully straying away from direct roads, relying on the sun and the towering hills to find the way. Thane couldn't help wondering about the Whisperers after what Zeere had said earlier in their journey—were they friends or foes? Zeere mentioned the Enclave was further west, and his jeering tone revealed his opinion of them.

"When your neighbor is the Enclave, it is suspicious," Zeere had commented with a sneer. "There must have been some purpose in choosing to live so close to them. I only wonder at the reason."

As they ventured deeper into upper southeastern Yaenia over the next few days, the landscape transformed. The ground grew darker, the soil richer and stiffer underfoot and shrouded in mist. Thane sensed they were moving farther from civilization with each step. After hours of climbing, they reached a mountain pass where the switchbacks wandered into a hidden valley below. The trees there were ablaze with autumn color, their leaves a deep crimson that seemed almost magical against the stark backdrop of the mountains. It was beautiful yet foreboding. The mountains differed from those he'd viewed from Hillside Reach; not made of Shadowstone, but with a distinct aura both ancient and somber.

Dusk approached as they worked their way down, and Thane noticed an unexpected sight beneath the canopy of red leaves—a pale green light, unlike any fire or torch he had ever encountered. It seemed almost otherworldly, an ethereal glow. He inhaled the crisp air, detecting only the fresh scent of evening and the natural aroma of the forest. There were no hints of smoke.

"Looks like we're heading into Whisperer territory," Thane said, peering lower into the valley. "Let's see if we can make it down there before complete nightfall. Maybe we can set up camp at the base of those trees."

As they approached the valley's glowing center, Thane noticed the light came from clusters of luminescent mushrooms scattered across the forest floor. Their soft, eerie glow cast an emerald hue over the surroundings. Curiously, wherever these mushrooms grew, the bases of the trees appeared dead, their bark as white as bone. The soft light spared them the need for a campfire that evening. They skipped cooking and ate buttered bread from their supplies. The loaf seemed almost magical in the green light, and Thane savored each bite, enjoying the simplicity of the meal amidst the unnatural setting.

"The fungi are feeding off the trees," Zeere observed, bending to examine a mushroom closer, but not courageous enough to touch it.

Thane nodded. "Perhaps they are dying because the mushrooms are toxic."

The Lucidian watched through the night, giving Thane a few hours to rest before dawn. After allowing Zeere a turn to sleep, they packed up their belongings and resumed their trek just as morning broke. As they traveled deeper into the forest, the trees grew whiter, perhaps having been dead longer than those along the outer perimeter. All around them, the silent trees offered no hints as to why life had been drained from the forest. However, Thane and Zeere were not alone.

An unknown voice suddenly filled their minds, much like the way Zann-Xia-Czul and the Hierophant had communicated without words. Her voice was as firm and sharp as steel: "LEAVE THE FOREST NOW, BEFORE THE LAND CLAIMS YOU!"

Thane tightened his grip on his sword. He glanced at Zeere, who stood vigilant, his eyes already scanning their surroundings for the source of the telepathic intrusion.

"Is it a warning or a demand?" he murmured, to himself more than to Zeere. He sheathed his blade, hoping to calm the situation.

As the voice echoed again, louder this time, it declared, "THE LAND CLAIMS ALL WHO DWELL TOO LONG. LEAVE NOW, OR FACE DEATH."

"We seek the Whisperers!" Thane shouted to the dead trees around them. "I've come to retrieve the dragon horn."

A stillness settled over the forest as the speaker pondered his words.

"THE DRAGONS ARE DEAD," the voice returned.

"Not all of them," Thane insisted. "One still lives."

"AND WHO ARE YOU TO DARE SUMMON IT?" the voice boomed.

Thane and Zeere shrugged at the question. It wasn't clear if the Whisperers could be trusted with the entire truth yet, but one fact was certain: they couldn't turn back empty-handed now.

"The dragon is my god," Thane said deceptively. "I seek the horn to prevent others from misusing its power."

"And I am a Lucidian Null Mage," Zeere announced. "I've come to learn how you speak like the dragons."

Thane futilely covered his ears as booming laughter erupted in his mind.

"YOU DO NOT KNOW THE COST OF WHAT YOU WISH FOR. YOU FAIL TO SEE THE SACRIFICES YOU MUST MAKE."

"Let us talk to you—face to face," Thane said. "We can explain ourselves."

"MORTALS HAVE NO PLACE HERE AMONG THE ENLIGHTENED ONES. LEAVE NOW, OR THE FOREST WILL CONSUME YOU. YOU WILL DIE THE SAME AS THE DRAGONS."

Drawing his sword with a determined swing, Thane said harshly, "I'm not leaving without the horn."

He heard a rustling in the close trees, but nothing moved in that direction. Had it only been the wind?

"YOU WOULD THROW YOUR LIVES AWAY FOR RELICS AND MAGIC?"

"We'd prefer to continue living, of course," Zeere said, "but you have something we need, and we have gold we can trade you for what you have."

"GOLD IS AS WORTHLESS AS THE FLEETING SUN. TRUE POWER CANNOT BE PURCHASED. YOU ARE UNWORTHY OF WHAT WE HAVE ACHIEVED."

"We need the horn to defeat the last dragon," Thane admitted.

"YOU WOULD KILL THE VERY GOD YOU WORSHIP?"

"I would explain everything to you if we could just—"

"YOU KNOW NOTHING OF DEFEATING DRAGONS IF YOU THINK SUMMONING ONE WILL HELP YOU KILL IT."

"I know we must destroy Zann-Xia-Czul," Thane said. "His tyrannical reign over my people must end. The deaths, the lies, the suffering—they must all stop. The horn is important to it all."

"PROVE YOURSELF. PROVE THAT ZANN-XIA-CZUL LIVES."

"I am Prince Thane Asche of the Throatian island," he declared. "I must defeat the last dragon and reclaim my homeland." He removed the necklace from his neck, holding its charm in the air to reveal the single Throatian character engraved upon it. "This mark bears the name of the false god, proving I am here to fulfill my destiny!"

Another round of silence came, followed by rustling leaves. Suddenly, a woman emerged from behind a cluster of nearby trees. Her ragged purple robes were covered in black soot, as if she'd rolled in a pile of charcoal. She appeared frailer than her wrinkleless face suggested, as if she'd carried heavy stones for miles.

"Who are you?" Zeere shouted at the approaching woman who seemed both young and old.

"SHE IS OUR KEEPER, BOUND TO SILENCE EXCEPT TO US," the voice rang inside their minds. "SHOW HER WHAT YOU HAVE BROUGHT TO ME."

The keeper greeted them with a wide, enthusiastic smile, while also revealing her missing tongue. She motioned for the necklace and, reluctantly, Thane handed it over. The woman inspected it, scrutinizing the silver amulet with the cerulean jewel at its center. She let out a gleeful cheer, then nodded wordlessly at the trees, confirming the necklace's authenticity.

"DO YOU UNDERSTAND THE DRAGON TONGUE?" the voice asked in Thane's mind, speaking now in Throatian instead of the Common Tongue it had used before.

"Yes, but how do you understand Throatian?" Thane asked back in his native speech.

But then a stark realization struck him: Throatian might have originated from the language of dragons. A young girl in Last Hope, Ursula Frost, had once claimed that the character on Thane's necklace was of dragon origin, but he dismissed her claim as improbable. Now, however, he realized she might have been right all along. Throatian and dragon speech might have shared a common history.

"THOUGH BROKEN, YOU SPEAK DRAGON TONGUE," the Whisperer's voice confirmed. "COME. WE HAVE USES FOR YOU. FOLLOW THE KEEPER."

"What are you talking about?" Zeere asked Thane, startled because he had never heard him voice anything but the Common Tongue.

"Apparently, Zann-Xia-Czul has been teaching my people to speak like dragons," Thane replied. "But we speak it aloud with our mouths, unlike them—dragons communicate through their minds."

"How is that possible?" Zeere asked. "I thought dragons could only roar. What you're saying sounds more like strange singing—not the kind of noise I'd expect from a dragon."

"I'm just as confused about this, but perhaps the Whisperers will explain," Thane said, as hopeful as he was perplexed.

They gathered their bags and followed the keeper through the dense forest. During their walk, they remained silent, as the keeper seemed unable to communicate telepathically, unlike the other Whisperer they had spoken with previously.

For fifteen minutes, they moved deeper into the valley, descending a slope previously hidden beneath the trees. The white-barked trees grew taller here than elsewhere, though they were less dense.

They reached a clearing where a rickety house, constructed from the same dead trees, stood. The keeper beckoned them toward the residence. Gingerly, she opened the unlocked door and led them inside, where they were met with an overwhelming number of crates. Each crate, like the house, had been made from cut pieces of the ghostly white trees.

"YOU HAVE ENTERED THE KEEPER'S STUDY," announced the Whisperer's voice, now speaking in the Common Tongue. "SHE WILL TEST YOU ONCE MORE."

The woman gestured toward a pair of chairs that seemed constructed from bones. With wrinkled, trembling hands, she fiddled with an inkwell and quill. Then, she crossed the room and handed the paper to Thane.

Cautiously, he unraveled the paper without crumpling it and read a single familiar phrase:

Shivanna Adul

The phrase was a common Throatian greeting, commonly translated as "to be at peace" or, as a question, "are you at peace?" Thane found it peculiar that such a simple sentence would be written on an entire scroll. It was more unexpected to see his native tongue outside his homeland.

"What does it say?" Zeere asked.

"It only says hello," Thane said as he turned back to the keeper. "Why is this important?"

The keeper smiled and wrote another message. This time, the words were more numerous, and Thane struggled to understand their meaning. They seemed to have been written in an archaic style filled with idioms that he could only grasp after reading them multiple times. He read aloud:

> *Where dragon eggs rest, unbroken and cold,*
> *Life's promise in ruin, tales never told.*
> *Reminders of suffering and death, in darkness unfold.*
> *Potential, like their embers, forever grown cold.*

Had Cereene been there, as a Son See'er Vrai, she would have been far more adept at deciphering the older tongues. The text he read was Throatian, poetic, and grim, but he was too preoccupied to ponder its meaning deeply without additional context. Still, the references to the "Reminder of Suffering" and "Reminder of Death" clearly originated from Throatian traditions.

"I don't understand it," Zeere remarked. "What does reading these scrolls prove? That Thane can speak the words of a dragon?"

The keeper smiled approvingly, then looked up, seemingly communicating her thoughts to the Whisperers, who, though elsewhere, awaited her conclusions.

"WELL DONE. WE WILL AID YOU IF YOU AID US," the voice said, now more enthusiastic than ever.

"So, you'll give me the dragon horn if I read more scrolls?" Thane asked.

"TRANSLATIONS ARE NEEDED. TOO MANY WORDS REMAIN UNKNOWN TO US. YOU MUST CONVERT THEM INTO THE COMMON TONGUE. THIS WILL REQUIRE SEVERAL WEEKS."

It would be a tedious ordeal, something Thane would not have chosen voluntarily under other circumstances. Still, it was a safer obstacle to overcome compared to the challenges he had faced on his journey so far.

"Your terms are acceptable," he said.

"And would that include teaching me how to communicate directly with others' minds?" Zeere asked. "Are you Mind Mages?"

"WE ARE ENLIGHTENED. WE HAVE MADE THE NECESSARY SACRIFICE."

Thane sensed their deception and deduced that their claim of being "enlightened" might not have ruled out that they were Lucidians. However, it felt unlikely for a Lucidian to have learned Throatian so thoroughly. Therefore, whatever the Whisperers were, they seemed to be a blend of Throatian, dragon, and Lucidian characteristics, though Thane couldn't understand how or why.

"Take us to them," Thane told the keeper. "If we are to help each other, we must meet face to face."

The keeper looked up at the roof and waited. Suddenly, the voice returned.

"YOU WILL AID US COMPLETELY, AND THEN WE WILL AID YOU. COME NOW. LET US OPEN YOUR EYES."

25
EISENBERN - THE MARKET OF TWILIGHT HAVEN

From the room where Herja and Ragnar drank the potions to release themselves from Somnius' control, Herja led them through winding underground corridors. Each hallway seemed identical until they emerged into a vast cave resembling a marketplace. Above stretched a ceiling of glowing mushrooms, a wonder more numerous than Eisenbern ever imagined. A greenish-yellow light bathed the area and there was no sign of the sun. How deep underneath the surface they were, Eisenbern could not guess.

"Where are you leading us?" he asked.

"As the goddess requested," Herja replied. "To show you how we fought the dragons and to train you to do the same. There's no time to waste."

The market appeared vast at first glance, with rows of stalls, barrels, and crates. Yet the square was eerily empty of people and goods. Had nightfall come above the surface? The steady glow of the mushrooms obscured the time of day.

"How do you keep track of time underground?" Gustav inquired.

"We had scouts who traveled to the surface to track the sun's position," Herja explained.

"Had?" Gustav echoed. "So, you don't check anymore?"

Herja hesitated, brushing her fingers along her waist. "The market is empty and lifeless—do you understand why?"

"Is it because it's nighttime?" Ilya asked, just as unaware of the time as Eisenbern.

"Herja," Ragnar cautioned, "are you sure you want to say?"

"I already suspect what Somnius will ask of them," she replied. "They'll understand the truth because of this. There's no point in hiding it."

"The truth about what?" Eisenbern pressed.

"Of Twilight Haven, our city," Herja said, sweeping her hand toward the empty marketplace. "Once, despite the dragons taking many of our people, we kept a population of thousands. After defeating the dragons, the Black Moon Tribe fell into decline. Few remember our traditions now, and fewer still care. Our numbers have dwindled to under forty."

"Forty?" Eisenbern exclaimed. "You only have forty people left in your entire tribe?"

He had expected thousands, perhaps more. Though the dragons were long gone, it was strange that the entire civilization had vanished over the years. What had become of Herja's kin? Had the Umbral Rot triggered a famine, as it had in the towns and cities above?

Dirt clouds rose from Ragnar's feet as he trudged alongside Herja and Ilya. As he moved, Eisenbern observed the resemblance between Ragnar and Gustav—not only in their stocky builds but also in their calm, precise mannerisms.

"Twilight Haven was the perfect refuge during the Scourge of the Dragon Slavers," Ragnar said, his voice steady yet marked with a growl. "Once the dragons fell, few wanted to stay underground, especially with the Umbral Rot's lingering threat above."

Eisenbern realized the Umbral Rot had affected them worse than those towns and cities on the surface. Underground, options for growing food or raising livestock were scarce. They survived on what little could grow in the darkness or traded with others. Many of Herja's people would have starved if their food supply had been cut off.

"So, they left for southern Yaenia, the same as Darians and Lucidians," Gustav finished.

"They left for the south," Herja confirmed, "and the tribe's culture faded with them. After their departure, we no longer considered them members of the Black Moon Tribe. They were Fallen Stars—all of them."

The marketplace they passed now told a desolate tale. Dust and debris blanketed every table, cart, and stall. People had abandoned Twilight Haven, leaving behind their resources because it wasn't worth carrying them to the surface or on their journey to southern Yaenia.

Invisible ghosts filled everywhere nearby, and the descendants forsook their ancestors. Eisenbern imagined the once bustling marketplace, crowded with people bartering for simple goods that were a luxury underground—a potato, steak, or fish. What would those have been worth to someone who couldn't venture above because of the dragons and Rot?

With the city mostly abandoned, Herja's struggles as the leader of the Black Moon Tribe became clear. Their former glory was nearly gone. The dragons' absence had caused their purpose to wane. With so few people remaining, Herja and her people became scavengers in their own homeland.

"Now that we're certain there's a dragon on Throatian Island, some of your people might return home," Ilya said.

"It's too late for that," Herja said. "Even if hundreds of dragons rained from the sky, as said in our legends, there are too few who know our ways. To join the Black Moon Tribe, one must understand its lore, creed, and heart, not to mention our fighting techniques."

"Between knowing how to kill dragons and preserving your culture, which matters more for rejoining the tribe?" Eisenbern asked.

"Both equally," Herja said. "Everything we once were is nearly gone, and what remains is too little. I must save what's left and somehow restore the Black Moon Tribe to its former power."

To their right rested an empty forge, ancient and covered in soot and copper rust. At its base lay chunks of charcoal and rotted wood. Nearby sat an anvil, mostly intact except for a thick mat of moss covering half its surface. The grinding stone was split into three pieces, and the fallen rock that had caused the break lay nearby. A large workbench, bearing spears, leather strips, and miniature harpoons, occupied the remaining space.

"My grandfather was the last blacksmith here," Ragnar told them. "He died of Scarlet Cough."

Eisenbern froze, reminded of Ophelia. Like him, Ragnar must have known the pain of losing someone to it.

"He hadn't gone above the surface very often, had he?" Gustav asked.

"Never," Ragnar replied. "My father always said he was most needed underground. He worked in this forge every day until the coughing forced him to stop."

"Over time, Scarlet Cough killed more of our people than the dragons did," Herja explained. "The moisture in our caves—likely from the Umbral Rot on the surface—caused it. Once someone's lungs became infected, death was inevitable."

"It pains me to hear that your tribe suffered so much from that illness," Eisenbern said. "I always imagined you as all-powerful warriors facing dragons as your only threat. I didn't realize life underground came with so many other challenges."

"Despite the quiet, slow-moving threat, the Scarlet Cough here is far less deadly than the Umbral Rot up there," Herja said. "You Yaenians lost more than your lives to the disease plaguing the surface world."

"Umbral Rot causes Scarlet Cough—I'm certain," Eisenbern said. "Someone important to me died from the sickness. My thoughts are with your people."

"I can sense your earnestness, and I appreciate it," Herja replied as they passed another row of empty stalls coated in dust and grime. "Neither Ragnar nor I enjoy political pleasantries and empty well-wishes. We are straightforward when we can be."

Eisenbern gave a heartfelt laugh. "That makes two of us! Tell me, Dragon Mar—do you have any beer down here? What do the Black Moon Tribe's people drink when they celebrate killing a dragon?"

"Our victories traditionally came with moonshine," Herja said, a soft smile breaking through her serious expression. "Once we defeat Zann-Xia-Czul, I can share some with you, and you'll find out."

"As long as it's not the same drink that lets someone else control your body, okay?" Ilya asked. "That would be too strange."

"It's not," Herja said. "However, our alcohol is a bit too strong for one as slender as you. One sip will send you straight to bed."

"I'm tougher than I look," Ilya said, accepting the bait. "Might we have a practice duel later to see how the Black Moon Tribe fights?"

Ragnar laughed for the first time. "Perhaps Lady Ilya does not know what she's asking."

"And what are you implying? That I can't fight?"

"We train to fight in the air," Ragnar said, turning to face her. "Our equipment allows us to glide through the clouds and shift direction as needed. You wouldn't last a minute against Herja. With some training, however, you might survive two."

"How does the flying work?" Gustav asked.

"Our greatest tool is the spring," Herja explained, her voice filled with pride. "Springs propel our warriors into the air, expand our wings for flight, and fire our cables like arrows, allowing us to change direction at will."

Eisenbern struggled to fathom how complicated it must have been to fight with such contraptions. The three of them would need to learn the style to battle a dragon. Even though there were hardly any warriors left in the Black Moon Tribe, their knowledge remained valuable.

"I want to learn it," Ilya said.

"Then I will teach you," Herja promised as they reached the crumbling stone archway, which marked the end of the marketplace.

"How do you train in the sky?" Eisenbern asked. "Wouldn't that have revealed your location to the dragons?"

"We have large caves down here suitable for practice," Ragnar said. "Our only rule is not to pierce the walls. There's a risk of causing the chamber to collapse."

"Fascinating!" Ilya grinned like a child who had just been told she could ride a horse for the first time.

Leaving the market behind, they entered another series of tunnels. These paths slanted downward, so steep that Eisenbern had to balance himself to avoid falling into Herja. The ceiling also lowered, forcing everyone but Ilya to adjust their posture. Gustav became frustrated and adopted a low squat, making him look like a monkey.

"Who is Somnius, anyway?" Ilya asked. "I heard what she said earlier, but I still don't understand how she can be from another world?"

"Your religion is to worship Asura, is it not?" Ragnar asked, joining Gustav in the squat-walk.

"Faithfully," Eisenbern said. "Asura's existence dates back further than any other false deity in the world."

"I don't mean to cause discord, but everything you believe is wrong," Ragnar said. "You need to stop following him. The world is different from what the churches want you to think."

Ragnar must have believed in the Dead Asura Theory, but it was impossible that Asura had taken his own life and abandoned the world.

"I've been told I was wrong before," Eisenbern said. "It doesn't matter. Faith is about trusting in something beyond human proof."

"But what I'm about to say is provable," Ragnar continued. "Somnius, a goddess from another world, came to save ours. Asura has not."

It was a bold claim, and this one seemed too much to accept at the Black Moon Tribe's word alone. How could he prove Somnius was a goddess if there was no proof of Asura's existence?

"I've never heard of her until we arrived here," Eisenbern said. "Has she always been the deity of the Black Moon Tribe?"

"We only learned of her recently," Herja said. "Our people traditionally believed in the life force of our world. When Somnius arrived and proved herself to us, we abandoned our old ways and pledged our allegiance to her instead."

"But how did she convince you she was a real goddess?" Ilya asked. "It's hard to believe."

Herja and Ragnar sounded like fanatics, drip-feeding claims and information without offering proof. Though Somnius appeared powerful and knowledgeable, she still didn't seem like a genuine goddess.

"Her explanation of the World Veins convinced me," Ragnar said. "She explained them in a way that finally made sense."

World Veins, the portals supposedly enabling travel between distant locations, likely never existed. People described them as invisible and constantly shifting, which conveniently explained their absence. Ragnar appeared to be a formidable warrior, but perhaps his skepticism wasn't as sharp as his great sword.

"Somnius will prove herself to you, I promise," Herja said. "There's too much to reveal in one conversation. We would seem indoctrinated if we piled everything on you at once."

"I trust you on many things, but I doubt I'll ever be convinced she's a goddess," Eisenbern declared bluntly. "Having personal theories about the universe doesn't make someone a god." If that were true, then every time he'd gotten drunk at Miner's Kitchen and accurately predicted the Khalia Stadium horse race results, he'd be one too.

"It's understandable that there's a lot to take in," Gustav replied, shifting the topic. "But have you actually seen this goddess, or does she only appear when you drink her magical potions?"

"Somnius sleeps in our deepest chamber," Herja said. "We've seen her, and she looks as human as any of us. As we mentioned, we have to protect her. That's the purpose of everything."

Inside the narrow tunnel, Ilya trailed behind the warriors in single file. "I still don't understand why a goddess would need bodyguards," she muttered.

"She needs our help," Herja said. "Protecting her was our reason for allowing her to control our bodies and use our eyes. Someone evil and powerful is searching for her, and we must ensure they haven't discovered that she's hiding here. She's bringing the other tribe members to Twilight Haven now. Once everyone returns, she will awaken, allowing you to converse with her directly. That's why you won't be able to see her until later this week."

"That is a powerful potion," Ilya said. "I can't even imagine what it must be like to control forty bodies at once—especially while asleep."

"She brought the magical potion from her own world, which is beyond ours in every way," Ragnar said. "Believe me that Somnius is here to save our world from those who would destroy it. You'll meet her soon, we promise. For now, let us begin your training."

26
KIRA - THE SEVEN STONES

After a brief stay at the hot springs, the elder led the group to a campsite. There, they found a box of large mushrooms —likely prepared by Finnegan or Sen—and a pot of fresh water. Orin boiled the mushrooms in water until they were tender. They sat in a circle, using flat rocks for seating and tables.

"I've eaten this kind of mushroom before," Kaine commented. "They're as satisfying as venison."

Kaine had apparently never tasted venison. To Kira, the toadstools lacked flavor, tasting like thick-skinned fish.

After serving his guests their food, Orin said, "Celeste, would you explain the problem we found with the prophecy?"

The Lucidian leaned forward in her stone seat. "The God Stones, painting, and inscriptions on its back are ancient artifacts. Orin cited the text written in the Common Tongue. The Lucidian scholars had an older version of the prophecy."

"Are you suggesting that everything originated from the Lucidians?" Kaine asked.

Celeste shook her head. "I'm not a historian, but our language has evolved over the centuries. What Blanche and Orin got is likely a translation of a translation, meaning the original meaning may have been lost or altered. I believe the Lucidian version of the prophecy predates the Common Tongue version."

Kira shouldn't have found her latest revelation surprising. Princess Zelia had previously used the God Stones before passing them to her human father. Since Lucidians were the only beings capable of magic, it made sense that any prophecy involving the stones would have Lucidian origins. What truly confused Kira was the stones' existence. She wondered whether the ancient Lucidians had created them or only discovered them. It seemed odd that Lucidians would create stones allowing humans to match or surpass their magical abilities.

"Where did the God Stones come from?" Kira asked. "Before Zelia had them?"

"None of us knows," Celeste replied. "The Enclave claims the God Stones are Lucidian, but the Silent Desert's texts mention them —hinting the Enclave might be lying. This isn't the first time they've rewritten our history to serve their agendas. Also, the God Stones were originally called the Tears of Asura, a name associated with a non-Lucidian religion. This further supports my belief that the God Stones didn't originate with our people; we never worshipped Asura."

Kira wanted to ask Ursula at Serenity Keep about it. Ursula's mind held a vast library of knowledge—likely every book ever written. Ursula would know any useful historical fact.

"As pompous as the Enclave may seem," Orin remarked, "we suspect their archivists either made errors or intentionally changed meanings during the Common Tongue translation. Lucidians have a history of reinterpreting texts to align with contemporary social values and of revising past stories and legends to meet current needs. Some clauses might have been reversed in earlier translations."

"Reversed?" Merdel replied. "A language's evolution shouldn't lose meaning."

"Lucidians continually add and subtract words from our language," Celeste said. "Phrases once common are now declared unacceptable, replaced with similar alternatives. Languages and history change, for better or worse."

"We suspect a translator took the liberty of imposing what they thought was a more logical word order," Orin said.

A god will die, and a false god will replace them. After a great sacrifice, a hero will appear, one who will use the God Stones to rid the world of corruption forever.

It was hard for Kira to believe anyone could have mistranslated that. The hero, whoever he or she was, would defeat the false god, restoring balance and purity to the world. It was straightforward and impossible to lose the meaning unless someone intentionally distorted the words.

"Consider this," the elder continued. "After a great sacrifice, a hero will appear, one who will use the God Stones to rid the world of corruption forever. A god will die, and a false god will replace them."

"It's the same result, isn't it?" Xander remarked.

"I understand now," Kaine said. "You suggest the hero must kill the original god instead of the false one."

Kira was confused. The prophecy had suggested that the hero would defeat the evil god. Why would someone kill a god only to let a false one take its place?

Merdel seemed puzzled by the story's sudden change in direction. "So, the ending should have a false god surviving?" he questioned. "That feels unsatisfying. Your earlier account of the prophecy seems more fitting."

"That's exactly it!" Orin exclaimed. "So could it be that the hero ends up as the false god?"

Kira's eyes widened. His suggestion was dark, twisted, and almost sinister.

"That's an interesting take," Kaine said. Only then did Kira realize how many years Orin and Celeste had probably spent interpreting the prophecy.

"I'm confused," Xander chimed in. "Why would a hero become a false god? Why would they kill a real god, and how could they even achieve that?"

"Consider the implications of the God Stones," Orin said. "They grant god-like powers, leading to corruption. Even a noble hero would struggle to resist such temptation indefinitely. The prophecy might not foresee a desirable outcome. Instead, it may serve as a cautionary tale rather than a goal."

"You are correct about human nature, but you're making some bold assumptions," Merdel said. "Still, I understand where you're stuck."

"You do?"

"Everything depends on the God Stones," Merdel explained. "According to the Common Tongue prophecy, the hero must gather the stones to save the world. However, if the prophecy is a warning, as your theory suggests, our goal changes. Instead of collecting the God Stones, we should keep them apart, ensuring the so-called hero never gathers them all."

Kira's eyes widened in disbelief. Merdel's idea seemed outlandish but might have held some truth. Could the God Stones be inherently evil? Or had Orin and Celeste misinterpreted the prophecy? The uncertainty left her questioning everything.

"I'm not convinced by this idea," Kaine stated. "Do you find it possible you've been seeking purpose in the void left by Princess Zelia's death, while grieving over her loss? I'm sorry if the question offends you."

"No insult is taken, Sir Khalia," Orin replied. "Both can be true. We've worked on this for years, not from boredom in these mountains, but because Celeste and I vowed to complete what Zelia started or at least understand it."

Kaine smiled and leaned closer to the fire pit at the center of the gathering. "There's still one way we can investigate this," he said, "since you've likely kept your theories to yourself all this time."

Orin nodded appreciatively. "What do you suggest we do to unravel the truth?"

"We must consult Queen Blanche," Kaine said. "She has valuable insight into the painting's history and whether the prophecy requires deeper investigation. She met Princess Zelia before her death, just as you and King Ether did, correct?"

"Blanche and Zelia crossed paths," Orin confirmed, "but it's not worth pursuing. We should focus on understanding the God Stones. Each stone contains tremendous magical power, and beyond what Zelia and Lydia showed, we don't know what other powers they might hold. The painting shows seven stones, but so far, we've only found five."

"You're referring to the same five stones you gave King Ether?" Kaine interrupted. Kira found the question odd; the conversation had grown confusing enough already.

"Yes, I gave King Ether the same five stones Zelia gave me," Orin replied with a raised eyebrow. "Since the king has five stones, two are still missing. They are likely with people who can't use magic; otherwise, we would have noticed."

Prince Thane and his family had gone to great lengths to gain access to Serenity Keep—a process that was terrifying. Now, with no one to trust, her father had likely hidden the God Stones somewhere new within Last Hope. If all were right, the stones would be safe from both the Throatians and anyone else who might attempt to steal them.

"In fact, Orin, your idea that the stones should remain separate might be onto something," Merdel commented, helping himself to another bowl of mushrooms from the communal plate. "Why create seven God Stones with unique powers if their ultimate purpose is to be reunited?"

The Elder responded, "I had a similar thought. Dividing the stones into seven likely maintains the balance of their power or prevents any single person from wielding their full magic unless they possess all seven. Zelia explained, and you observed with Princess Lydia, that someone can use each stone independently. Together, however, all seven could trigger the next phase of the prophecy. I don't know for certain, but that's my guess."

"Perhaps one of the Lucidians hiding among you knows the answer?" Xander retorted, accusatory. Kira scowled at him, her frustration clear. Moving forward was better than risking their hard-won trust and cooperation.

"We've exhausted our theories and knowledge," Celeste said calmly, ignoring the slight. "Princess Zelia was our only hope, but we didn't have enough time."

"And that's where you come in, Prince Xander, Princess Kira, Sir Khalia, and Sir Merdel," Orin said. "King Ether needs to help finish what Zelia entrusted us with."

"And what is that, exactly?" Xander asked.

"Find the remaining two God Stones," Orin said. "Ether has the most resources for the search—soldiers, gold, ships, influence, and eyes. We also need to locate Zelia's mentor. Ether has prior knowledge of her, though I don't know her name. Kira, with the aptitude, could learn to harness the magical powers, though I'm uncertain if she should wield all seven stones."

"But I..." Kira sank into her rock chair. "Is this really my purpose? Killing a god feels neither right nor possible. I don't want to lose my mind or life, or to bring others to death. Even if I did, I don't even know where to begin."

Celeste rose and approached Kira, her purple, wrinkled hand resting gently on her shoulder. "No one knows the right path for you," she said. "Learning to use the God Stones is just one path among many. But those doors will remain closed unless you open them first."

Understanding the God Stones would unlock many opportunities—this was undeniable. Yet if Orin were correct and the prophecy served as a warning, seeking them could be a mistake. What if fulfilling the prophecy's ambiguous message led her to commit some dreadful act? Was this the reason King Ether had kept their magic hidden from her and Lydia?

As Kira looked at Kaine, who was engrossed in thought, she felt her mouth growing numb.

"Does she even want to go through with this?" Xander asked, glaring at Celeste. "You said Zelia went mad and died while trying to use the stones' magic. Gather them if you must, but don't let Kira meet the same fate. Destroy them instead—throw them into one of your volcanoes or something."

"The prince has a good idea," Merdel said, glancing at Orin. "Why don't we destroy the God Stones?"

"We discussed this with Zelia," Celeste said. "The God Stones cannot be destroyed. Even if placed in a volcano, they would only become temporarily inaccessible. Eventually, they'd be rediscovered, even if it took thousands of years."

"Then perhaps the best approach is to throw them in there," Xander said. "That way, they won't fall into the wrong hands during our lifetimes."

"We need all seven stones to make the plan work," Orin replied. "If we discard the five we already know about, the remaining two could still pose a threat if in someone else's possession. Even if just one God Stone remained, you'd still need your own to protect yourself. Collecting all seven is necessary to try destroying them, but then that would also fulfill the prophecy."

Orin's words flowed effortlessly, as if he'd waited years to share his ideas and answer questions. Kira could tell it had been a long time since he last discussed his strategies; his enthusiasm was the highest she'd ever seen.

Merdel stretched his arms and flexed his shoulders, preparing himself. "Non-von Stonewall persons can wield God Stones—Zelia proves it. Currently, we have Kira. If we gather the stones and she resists their magical temptations, she could influence the prophecy's course. If she controls both herself and the stones, the prophecy's sequence might not matter."

"I understand," Kaine said. "Winds shift, but if Kira is our ship's sails, she can guide us right when needed. I trust her judgment, yet she's too young for such responsibility. I'm also uneasy about acting without the king's knowledge. After all, Kira is his daughter; we should seek his approval before doing anything else."

"Ether will not budge," Orin said. "This has to be Kira's choice alone."

"Mine?" Kira exclaimed, but neither he nor the others seemed to hear her.

"From what I gather, he'll forbid her involvement in magic," Kaine said. "We lost Lydia because of the God Stones, and he won't risk losing his other daughter, even if she protests."

Orin exchanged a disappointed glance with Celeste, then turned to face Kira. He opened his mouth, but the princess interrupted. It was time for her to tell them the truth.

"Destiny has given me this gift, and I shouldn't squander it," she said. "If I master the God Stones, I can make this world a better place. The prophecy foretells ending this corruption, whatever form it takes. I hope that's what it means. But even if my father agrees, can I truly do this?"

"I want to avenge Lydia, but I don't want to risk your safety," Xander said. "Prince Thane remains in his homeland, hiding in the shadows after betraying our family. We can find a way to defeat him without magic."

Kaine nodded, but his unreadable expression hid his lingering unease. "My princess, if you take this path, you may face demands to use any magic you learn for the kingdom's benefit. Unfortunately, it could also mean enlisting you in the war effort. Your skill with the sword is praiseworthy, but I must stress that it will require time before you are ready to become a knight, even with God Stones as a second weapon."

Kira spotted the fortress on the horizon, just as Orin had described. Once she saw Wargonne's imposing gray walls, she knew avoiding them was impossible. She would board a ship from there and sail to the lands where her sister's murderers awaited, confronting them herself or ensuring her father's soldiers had the chance.

"The Throatians are terrible people," Kira said. "Though I don't want to kill anyone, I must do all I can to help our kingdom create a better future—that's the promise I made to my mother."

Would either her mother or Lydia be proud if Kira used the God Stones, or were they pleading with her from the afterlife to resist the magic that risked leading her down a dark path?

"Kira, before your visit, I was unaware of your ability to wield the stones," Orin confessed. "I deeply regret involving you in this matter. I never intended to mention it during your stay. Kaine's search of my shack revealed new information, and Celeste and I found another crucial piece of the puzzle that has haunted us. You must decide whether to bear the God Stones, but I'm relieved. You are someone I trust implicitly with such power, even if you're not ready. In the end, you may be the one destined to set everything right."

"I hope I can make it all better," Kira said, "but I don't know what this all means or where it will lead."

"And what about your father?" Merdel asked.

"Orin needs to convince him," Xander stated.

Kaine extended his palm toward the Elder. "You were central to everything during Zelia's time. The king won't listen to Merdel or me unless you reconcile with him first."

"Who said the king has a problem with me?" Orin retorted.

"If the prophecy is as critical as you claim, there's no room for superficial distractions," Kaine continued. "Convincing Ether requires everyone's full effort, including the Lucidians you've been hiding. Don't you agree?"

Orin's face paled, and Kira could swear the ground trembled beneath them. "I'll… I'll consider it."

Merdel declared respectfully, "Kaine is right. To locate the God Stones and ensure Kira can wield them safely, we need to unite all our minds—Ether, Blanche, their councils, and everyone assembled. Given that the war with the Throatians is likely tied to this prophecy, events beyond our control are already unfolding. We must act swiftly and remain vigilant for signs."

Kira swallowed, realizing she had barely touched her mushrooms. Despite their differences and past conflicts, each person seemed willing to unite around her. Would her father do the same if they asked him? She needed more time to think but would speak her mind for now.

"Thank you, everyone," she said, knowing her words would bring them hope. "I'll use the God Stones for everyone's good and save us from the greatest evils."

27
BIOS AURAS - THE RIVER

Finally alone in the quaint room of the Golden Mare, Bios collapsed onto the bed, exhausted from his battle. Conan's revelation of a possible God Stone in the mountains lingered in his mind. Could the councilman's words have been true? A dragon, a God Stone, or both hidden in the forest? He closed his eyes, letting his mind wander to calm his nerves. After a few minutes of sleep, a creak from the door jolted him awake. Though he reached for his sword, he lowered it when Alina slipped into the room unannounced.

"What do you want?" he asked with more than a hint of annoyance in his voice. He couldn't help wondering whether he should have bolted the door. Being invulnerable, he'd never feared someone murdering him while he'd slept, but she'd shown no regard for his privacy.

Inside, Alina paced across the room as she searched for the right words. "I've been thinking about what Cassia said when we returned from Wargonne," she began hesitantly. "She overstepped by criticizing you without understanding your reasons, but she wasn't entirely wrong either."

Bios raised an eyebrow, intrigued by her unexpected introspection. "And what do you think of what I did?" he countered. "Conan took off my arm first, and I only did to him what he would have done to me. Does it matter how he died? We were going to finish him anyway."

"But your arm came back—somehow," Alina retorted.

"He didn't know it would happen," Bios replied evenly.

Alina paused, letting the words settle. "You said you use chaos to bring about order," she stated, her tone still accusatory. "But how can that be justified? Aren't peace and stability better achieved through less violent means?"

Bios realized she was no longer referring to Conan. Her expression conveyed remorse for how they had betrayed Ambrose and used him as bait. He simply nodded. "As I've mentioned before, Alina, everything I do serves a greater good. Humans are as temporary as their mortality allows them to be. Our eventual results will be permanent."

"A greater good is the goal, yes," she replied. "But why should it be an excuse to do what some might consider evil?"

"The grand scope of time forgets the sins of its people after enough years have passed," Bios explained. "If people must die for the sake of lasting change, then they will have served a greater purpose than they ever could have achieved on their own. Ambrose died sooner than he might have otherwise, but what greater good could he have served if he hadn't brought Conan into the open? How much potential do you think humans waste on their trivial pursuits?"

Alina frowned as she studied him, clearly still unsure. "But in that regard, Ambrose was still innocent, even if he wouldn't amount to anything greater than being used by us. Was it our right to decide his fate? We could have found Conan without killing Ambrose—so wouldn't that make Ambrose's death unnecessary?"

"His death was a path to order," Bios corrected. "It brings chaos and upheaval—but that is part of the inevitable cycle. Remember, Alina, there are no innocents in this world. My responsibility is to confront and manage chaos and suffering—even if it means causing temporary pain. Everyone has a role in this, chosen or not. Sometimes, the only path to true order is through chaos."

"Is this what the god Asura taught you?" she asked. "I still don't understand who you are or what you believe. You don't seem entirely human to me."

He moved to a chair at the small table in the corner and sat. "I'm protected by Asura and can use the tools he gifted me, but otherwise, I'm human as far as I know. Human but chosen, someone powerful once told me."

She followed him, though he could sense the faintest tremble in her steps. It wasn't fear—Alina was beginning to revere him. Her questions differed from Cassia's; Alina sought to understand the truth, not to make him feel guilty or change him.

"But how can you be certain you're Asura's chosen one?" she asked. "The churches claim he died long ago, before either of us could have been born."

"Born," Bios said bitterly. "Ha."

Alina shivered and asked, "What do you mean?"

"I have no mother—or, if I do, I cannot remember her."

There was a river. He'd nearly drowned in it. His first memory was waking up with water all around him, sunlight far above the surface. Whenever he thought back, his mind filled with black fog, blocking anything before that memory. Now, he could only move forward.

"I never knew my mother either," Alina said. "But everyone was born somewhere. Still, it's hard to feel so… alone."

"I… I wasn't alone. Let me show you."

Bios closed his eyes, and instantly, the surrounding room dissolved into a swirling vortex of light and shadow. Alina gasped as the magic of the Teleportation Stone enveloped them, the air rushing past their ears. When the world steadied once more, they found themselves at the edge of a vast river, its waters reflecting the moonlight.

The riverside was serene yet solemn, its gentle flow providing a haunting contrast to the simple memories that had brought him there. The trees, overcome by shadows, appeared almost purple, and the light and darkness shining through them remained trapped in an infinite struggle. Their leaves rustled as if greeting him finally after his long absence.

He had returned to the river's edge countless times whenever he needed to reimagine his purpose. The river had always offered him solitude. Now, it was only a source of irritation and anguish. He would show Alina, but even that brief act would feel like a waste in a location that had lost all its former meaning.

Alina gazed around, her eyes wide with wonder. "This place feels… ancient," she murmured. "Where are we, and why are we here?"

Bios turned to her, somber yet reflective. "I was found here," he said, staring into the steadily flowing waters. "With no memory of who I was."

He could still recall the rushing waves, the sensation of being pulled under their surface, and the warmth of Somnius's arms wrapping around him. She had saved him.

"Maybe you died and were reborn through your healing abilities?" Alina suggested.

"I don't know," Bios murmured. "I've never died before—I always heal. It was Somnius who rescued me from the river. She was a goddess from another world, sent by Asura to guide me on my quest for the God Stones. She betrayed me."

Alina looked at him curiously and asked, "Are you sure?"

Bios paused, remembering their past encounters. He recalled Somnius's initial kindness and her wisdom, but he also noticed subtle shifts in her behavior and hidden agendas that had revealed themselves over time. She wasn't the light she claimed to be.

"At first, I believed Somnius was my savior, my guide," Bios continued. "But as I journeyed further, I began to notice changes within myself. Imperfections I had never known began to surface. I found myself drawn to the darkness, the forbidden, and the corrupt."

"You mean... you were tempted by chaos?"

Bios nodded. "Exactly, and it was a struggle to accept until I realized that both darkness and light are necessary to defeating the evil in our world. I came to see good and evil not as opposing forces but as tools to be used toward a higher purpose. Order and chaos, darkness and light, the right hand and the left hand all are as necessary as they are connected. The responsibility and the burden of using them for the greater good fell onto me."

Alina paused thoughtfully before asking, "If the one who saved you was a goddess, how could she have been wrong?"

"I don't understand why or how. It's clear that gods and goddesses aren't always perfect or right," Bios said. "Perfection is relative. Morality is relative. A goddess is simply a higher being, possessing her own opinions and objectives."

"But you said she was helping you collect the God Stones."

Bios let out a breath, and the coldness of the night revealed its greater depth. "She was helping me find them, yes. But as we journeyed together, I began to suspect Somnius was not as she seemed. There were too many lies, inconsistencies, and accusations."

"She disagreed with your ways," Alina concluded. "Or perhaps she simply desired the power for herself."

"Both," Bios said. "I no longer needed her guidance—in fact, she had become a hindrance to me. I confronted the shadow within myself and overcame it alone. Now, I embrace it. It serves me, and I am at peace."

His right hand warmed and glowed like the sun for the first time in years. With a swift jerk, he thrust his palm forward, launching a light spear toward the river. The spear pierced the surface with a sizzling splash, vanishing instantly. His jaw clenched as he sent five more light spears into the water in a fitful rage.

Alina rose from where she'd been watching and turned to him. Though the moonlight illuminated her face, Bios could still sense the growing darkness within her.

"What is that magic?" she shouted over the commotion. "And how are you doing it?"

He paused, watching as the water gradually calmed. "Besides my immunity to death, Asura granted me a power matching his own," Bios replied with a closed fist. The ability to conjure spears of light was another innate talent of his—unlike the others, it didn't require a God Stone. However, it drained his physical energy. After firing around twenty bolts, he'd need to rest for the day to avoid falling unconscious.

"Isn't it clear this power is meant to be destructive?" he continued. "Somnius never understood why I'm meant to wield my abilities this way. She never grasped that order alone isn't enough to save the world."

Somnius had never seen the snowy Temple of White in the future he had described to Cereene. As far as Bios knew, the goddess was unaware of the impending destruction—a future foretold by a man cloaked in robes marked with the sigils of the sun and moon, who had warned him of what was to come.

"I might understand your point of view," Alina said. "Before Cassia and I fled the Silent Deserts, I tried organizing a resistance against the slavers, but few were willing to join. They argued it was wrong to defy their masters, but in truth, they were afraid of the responsibility that success would bring. Defeating slavery won't come without bloodshed—the masters will have to be removed. As you've said, chaos will be necessary to bring about order and peace."

"It's perplexing why a slave would believe it's wrong to break free from their master," Bios said.

Alina explained, "The relationship between masters and slaves is more complex than simply that of oppressor and oppressed. Wise masters understand the value of keeping their slaves healthy and happy. It's surprising how many people are willing to give up their freedom for such stability."

"And yet, even offering freedom and stability, you couldn't inspire them to turn against their rulers?" Bios asked.

"I wish I could have done so," Alina said. "When a culture remains stagnant for too long, its people lose sight of its flaws. Some refuse to see alternative futures, even when shown them. I suspect your goddess from another realm closed her eyes to your ideas as well."

Perhaps this would be his final visit to the waters. He'd come many times, reflecting on whether he'd made the right choice by turning against Somnius as she'd turned against him. There was nothing else left here to think about or learn from. Now, the river was just a river—its surface changed only by the occasional ripple from a fish underneath.

"She kept her eyes closed to what I discovered," Bios nodded approvingly. "And like it or not, Somnius will eventually have to see the world for what it truly is."

28
KIRA - THE QUEEN'S GRAVE

After the long day of discussions, they returned to the heart of Gale Village. Kaine and Merdel ventured off to locate Sen and ask her more about her healing abilities, leaving Kira and Xander with a moment of peace within their shack.

Once inside, Kira collapsed onto her bed near the doorway, weary from the day's events. She closed her eyes, hoping to nap, but her mind refused rest. Soon, she gave up and joined Xander at the small table as he sketched a deer.

"Couldn't sleep?" her brother asked, not looking up from his drawing.

"I wanted to, but you know why I couldn't."

Xander guided his quill over the paper while Kira picked up her mirror and brush, running her fingers through her long, chestnut hair. Her reflection revealed the exhaustion in her eyes. She brushed repeatedly, hoping to distract herself from the various thoughts and ideas overwhelming her mind. Despite her efforts to push them aside, the prophecy, the God Stones, and her role remained impossible to escape.

"Xander," she spoke up. "Do you think... do you think I'm ready for this?"

Her brother snapped up from his drawing, anger and frustration overtaking his face. "You shouldn't do it," he warned.

She sighed, set her brush down, and leaned back in her chair. "I must if I'm meant to do what they said. I need to become better at everything I do."

"They discussed it for hours, but it might not amount to anything in the end," Xander said. "It could simply be a painting with a poem, nothing else."

"Do you really believe that?"

"I don't know what to believe anymore," he admitted, setting down his quill. "I've always been skeptical of the stories and gossip from church. Now, I'm more certain. As for Asura... I don't think he ever existed. Or if he did, he's long gone."

Perhaps Lydia had failed to talk sense into their brother after all.

"Asura will reveal himself," Kira said. "We must believe in him."

"The day you were born, Mother died, and on Lydia's wedding day, they killed her. What kind of god would allow that if truly real?"

Kira lowered her gaze. They'd already learned the answer to that question many times. Asura believed in letting everyone make their own decisions and learn from their mistakes. In other cases, suffering was a test of faith or stemmed from a lack of understanding of the greater purpose. Had Xander forgotten those teachings, or had he deliberately rejected them?

"I wish they were still alive too, but we have to continue believing in the grand nature of the world," she said. "There are many things we can't comprehend."

Xander sighed, his voice quiet. "I don't know if I can keep pretending everything will be okay. The world is cruel, and hope is just a way of coping with the inevitable. That's what you don't understand. It's simple once you realize it."

Tears welled up in her eyes. "Don't say those things!" she pleaded. "We have to try! We can't just sit and do nothing!"

"You'll die too if you listen to them," Xander warned, clenching his hand into a fist against his waist. "I cannot let that happen. Even if what they said is true, the Lucidian princess went mad and died. Don't get involved. Just don't."

He trembled, but seemed unaware of his own trembling. Kira's green eyes met Xander's blue gaze, and she embraced him gently.

"You're afraid because you care, but that fear doesn't mean we can't overcome this together," she explained.

His shoulders relaxed, but his back remained stiff like the wooden planks of their shack. "I still don't know how this can possibly end well."

Kira's mouth froze as she finally understood Xander's fear. Had she known about Lydia's danger on the eve of her wedding, Kira would have done anything to prevent it and protect her sister. At that moment, her brother was trying to do the same for her.

"You're right to worry about me," she said. "This won't end well, but doing nothing could make it worse. If I can master a fraction of the God Stone's power, I can improve things. I'll stop if it starts harming me or if I begin losing myself to its influence."

"But what if you can't?" Xander said, pausing. "Father didn't want us involved because he knew the consequences—I'm sure of it now. Don't use or collect the stones. If the prophecy is real, it can't happen without all seven God Stones. We should go home, and it will never come true."

She picked up Lydia's mirror and resumed brushing her hair. Orin, Kaine, and Merdel appeared to share her father's opinion on the matter. Was it possible she might be wrong and everyone else right to keep the stones hidden? If their father had intended for them to use the stones, he would have let her and Lydia learn from the beginning.

But there had to be more to it than that. Even her sister had faced challenges in using the God Stones by inadvertently creating a monster. Nobody seemed to understand why that had happened, but there must have been some purpose or meaning in it. Lydia wasn't naïve or foolish, so why had she tried using the God Stones? What had she known?

How much of a coincidence was it that Lydia had started using the God Stones just a few days before her wedding? Kira's face scrunched at the thought. It couldn't have been an accident—Lydia must have had a reason to try using the magic, especially since she also ran into the forest just before the Throatians arrived in Last Hope from overseas.

In hindsight, Lydia may have been saying goodbye. Just hours before the ceremony, Lydia had woken Kira and invited her to Lydia's room. That had been their last significant conversation.

Kira's face went white as she looked at her brother. "Xander," she said, "do you think Lydia knew the Throatians were going to kill her?"

"Nobody knew what the Throatians were planning until it happened," her brother said.

"There wasn't enough time," Kira concluded. "Maybe Lydia knew they would betray her, but she discovered it too late—why she used the God Stones and fled before the wedding."

"Stop it, Kira," Xander said. "Nobody knew it was coming!"

"The monster in the forest," Kira continued after swallowing hard. "She couldn't control the God Stones. She didn't have enough time to learn how to use them and fight the Throatians, but I do... I do have the chance at studying them. I have some time. I—"

"You can't do it—or maybe you can. Either way, you shouldn't," Xander warned. "Remember what happened to Zelia?"

"The others were right," Kira said. "Maybe it is I who should figure out how to use them. What if I am the only one who is supposed to learn properly? That might be why Zelia couldn't."

"We have to ask Father first," Xander said, "before doing anything. While I desire revenge against the Throatians, I don't want it to come at the cost of you."

No, Kira thought as she stared into the mirror and could only see Lydia's face instead of her own. Everyone was right that her father would likely reject the idea of her learning to use the stones. Instead, she would have to ask her mother what to do next.

The next morning, Kira and Kaine walked along the dusty stone path, retracing the familiar trail they had hiked with Merdel. They noticed the rock where he had stumbled and hurt his ankle. Every part of the landscape seemed frozen in time, still and quiet except for the gentle sounds of the breeze.

She strolled with her face toward the ground and shoulders slumped, unsure of what to say. The previous night, she tossed and turned, questioning whether Xander's reasoning was true. His words wouldn't leave her mind, and she felt more uneasy than ever about asking their father for permission to use the God Stones. The danger was undeniable, and in that, both she and Xander agreed.

Kaine walked beside her, his calmness undermined by the tension in his shoulders. His eyes scanned the mountainside, watchful for any sign of hazards. Kira wished she could read his thoughts as effortlessly as she sensed his unease.

"Thank you for bringing me back," she whispered, breaking the silence.

Kaine glanced at her, his soft eyes offering reassurance as always. "It's no trouble, my princess," he replied. "We were sent to visit the queen after all, and we've done that. Though I must admit, things have taken an interesting turn."

Kira's eyes met Kaine's, seeking answers. "I didn't know about your history with Queen Blanche," she mumbled. "I'm sorry."

Kaine's smile faded into a thoughtful expression. "No need for apologies, Princess. It's a part of who I am, even though it's caused me pain over the years. But tell me, how are you holding up? You carry a heavy burden, and we've faced many unexpected twists and turns on our journey."

Then, Kira confessed her fears. "I'm afraid," she admitted. "What if I'm not prepared to make the correct choice? What if I have power, but don't know how to use it?"

"About using the God Stones?"

Kira nodded solemnly. "Do I even have a chance of living up to everyone's expectations?"

Kaine's next honest response startled her. "You're still young, Kira. You're unprepared for battle or war. I don't want to see you thrown into combat against the Throatians. Those people committed terrible acts, including against children younger than you. The God Stones might be our only hope, but at what cost? What will using them require you to do? That's what I'm unsure of."

As they hiked higher on the hill, Kira persisted, seeking insight and answers from her retainer. "And the prophecy?" she asked. "Do you believe it's true?"

After a moment of introspection, Kaine replied, "I've witnessed enough to believe the prophecy is real. My only fear is not understanding why it's real, or how it will unfold."

His words perfectly articulated what she had struggled to express. As with everyone else, he likely believed she was the chosen one destined to wield the God Stones. Like her, he didn't know how to come to terms with it.

"Kaine," she called out softly.

"What is it?"

"I... I don't know. Something's not right."

"Something hasn't felt right for a long time now," he replied quietly. "Our world is changing."

She finally asked her most pressing question, a question only he might answer: "Do you think Lydia knew about the prophecy? Did she sacrifice herself to protect me and my family?"

She'd just asked Xander the same question earlier, but had realized Kaine was better positioned to speak the truth rather than speculate—having been present before the wedding and during the confrontation with the Throatians. He'd consistently proven trustworthy to her, and it was likely he'd at least considered the possibility.

Kaine studied Kira's expression. His cheeks drained of their color as he wrestled with what to say.

"Even if Lydia knew she would die," he said uncertainly, "it wouldn't change anything. Your sister used the God Stones, but the outcome was the same as if she hadn't."

She felt his pain as if it were her own. Perhaps she had overanalyzed the situation, causing him to follow along with her.

"I'm sorry again," she mustered.

"There's nothing for you to apologize for, my dear princess."

They continued up the hill to Gale Village's graves, nestled at one of the peaks. Upon reaching the summit, Kira's eyes lingered on the scattered stone hedges that marked the resting place of the former villagers. The breeze drifted around them, carrying the scents of the volcanic ash and smoke. Even though they buried her mother there, Kira wondered if she would have been better off in Last Hope, at her rightful home in their family crypt. Lydia was there, after all.

"I'll need a moment," Kira whispered, approaching her mother's grave.

As the breeze enveloped her, a chill of emptiness and loss settled over Kira's body, echoing the same numbness she'd felt when she'd first heard about Lydia. The gravestones before her seemed to mock the life she'd left behind. Her mother was gone too—returning here held little purpose. Neither of them could hear her cries. So now, what could she do?

Before she could gather her thoughts, the ground shifted beneath her feet, and her mother's gravestone slid sideways as a low rumble reverberated through the hills. Then Kaine's sharp voice cut through the chaos.

"Kira!"

She stumbled hard as a towering plume of dark smoke burst forth from the mountainside: the volcano was reawakening.

"Kira!" Kaine shouted again, now closer.

She longed to be with her sister again, but it was impossible. Her mirror was back at the shack, and she wished she had brought it along. Though it wasn't Lydia's, seeing her reflection brought her comfort. Their faces were similar enough that she could almost see her sister alive again. She told herself that letting go would bring her peace, but it wouldn't be easy.

As the earthquake subsided, Kira was caught in Kaine's arms. Despite holding her tightly, his body radiated fear.

With red, teary eyes, Kira looked up at Kaine and whispered her confession softly: "I don't think I can do it or be what they want me to be."

"I'm not Lydia," she couldn't say, though she longed to. All she could think about was her sister's mirror, and how it reflected only Kira's face.

Thankfully, Kaine pulled back just enough to meet her eyes. "The choice must be yours, Kira. Not your father's, not mine, not the kingdom's. No one can force you to take this burden. If your heart isn't true to yourself and what you must do, then you cannot succeed."

29
KAINE - THE MIND MAGE'S POWER

Kaine's group stayed in Gale Village for another week, with each day stretching on. This allowed Orin extra time to reflect on his relationship with King Ether and the Prophecy of Tears and Sacrifice. Meanwhile, Kira and Kaine wandered the winding mountain trails, noticing the faint scent of smoke in the air. Despite occasional tremors creating a lingering sense of unease, the black and green mountains remained mostly peaceful. Orin explained the earthquakes were common and harmless, reassuring them that Gale Village was far from the magma paths and splitting grounds, ensuring their safety. Nevertheless, he gave them a map highlighting specific routes and switchbacks to avoid.

While Kaine and Kira ventured through the mountains in search of scenic beauty, Xander opted for a more leisurely routine, spending his days idly snoozing in the modest confines of their shack. Kaine vowed to encourage Xander to resume sword training once they returned to Last Hope.

Meanwhile, Merdel devoted himself to recording the stories of ten Lucidians who had fled their Enclave's oppressive rule and found refuge in Gale Village. He believed that presenting them as refugees rather than former soldiers might persuade King Ether to consider an alliance, though he doubted whether this approach, along with Orin's influence, would be enough.

Orin's preparations for his meeting with the king worried Kaine. For the past week, Orin had been fasting, spending his days alternating between the hot springs and his shack. Kaine couldn't determine whether Orin's reclusive behavior stemmed from anxiety about seeing King Ether or was just part of his usual routine. When Kaine asked Merdel for his opinion of the elder, the councilman dismissed his concerns.

"I'm a politician, not a relationship counselor," Merdel replied. "Orin needs to confront his unresolved issues from the past. Only he can find the right words."

With only three days remaining before they had to return to Last Hope—regardless of whether Orin joined them—Merdel repeatedly complained about the lack of birds traveling in either direction. Each additional day spent in Gale Village meant more time without news from the outside world, and the king was likely growing increasingly concerned about their prolonged absence. It seemed wiser to leave sooner rather than risk being presumed missing.

Despite the worries, their extended stay brought a subtle blessing: isolation. As the evening wore on, Kaine began to understand why Lily von Stonewall might have chosen Gale Village over Last Hope for her burial. Here, the war against the Throatians felt distant, and he wondered if the late queen had wanted a similar sense of peace during her time in this place.

Before he could think further, Xander's bloodcurdling screams broke the silence.

"LYDIA! LYDIA! NO!"

Kaine bolted upright, instinctively reaching for White Oath. Kira was already by her brother's side, trying to wake him.

"It's just a dream," she urged. "It's just a dream."

Meanwhile, Merdel continued sleeping peacefully, unaffected by the commotion.

"Sorry about that," Xander replied as the blankets on his bed shifted. "I can't keep doing this."

"It was the same dream again, wasn't it?" Kira asked.

"Yeah. The same dream."

Kaine had seen Xander yell out in his sleep multiple times since leaving Serenity Keep. Xander often dreamed of saving his sister but failed every time. Accepting the nightmares as they were was easier said than done. Kaine knew this was the solution, but he didn't know how to help the prince achieve it.

"Perhaps some fresh air would benefit us all," Kaine suggested. "Would you two like to take a midnight walk around the village?"

"It wouldn't hurt," Xander muttered. "I just feel so cold... and empty."

"Pack a coat, then," Kira chimed in.

In silence, the three of them prepared and exited, leaving Merdel unbothered and asleep. The large moon glimmered through the smoky fog, providing barely enough light to navigate the dirt roads. They walked without saying a word until Kaine finally spoke.

"What happened to Lydia still haunts me," Kaine admitted. "I'm not sure any of us will ever find peace with it. She was your sister, and I can't begin to imagine how hard this must be for you. I wish I knew how to help, but at least I know I can adequately protect you again." He patted White Oath at his waist.

Neither child responded as they walked on. Kaine wondered if he had been too blunt. Should he have assured them everything would be okay in time? The children likely heard such assurances often at Serenity Keep, but he knew better than to promise a happy ending. At least he was giving them the truth, though it was painful.

The princess was not yet eleven, but her life forced her to face trials unfair for a child. Despite her father raising her more level-headed and mature than any children Kaine had seen her age, the expectations on Kira's shoulders were exceptionally high, even for an adult. Kira was younger than Lydia, yet bore many of the same burdens cast on her older sister if not more.

"Now is a good chance to take a rest," Kaine added, acknowledging the sharpness of his previous words.

He led them to sit down on a nearby rock, and the cool stone beneath them provided some comfort. The silence stretched out between them again until Xander broke it.

"Why couldn't it have been me?" he blurted out. "Why wasn't my blood magical? I'm supposed to be the next king!"

"Even if we knew why, it wouldn't change anything," his sister said.

"It should have been me learning to use the God Stones," Xander continued. "You're already better at swordplay, archery, and everything else—and now you'll master magic as well! I don't even have a chance to help in any way. Why can't I be useful?"

The nightmares had caused the young prince to feel inadequate and likely overshadowed by his sister. He needed reassurance that there was more to his potential than being compared to Kira's talents.

"You're not useless," Kaine said. "One day, my prince, you are going to become our king. You must grow into a wise and selfless ruler whose dedication will benefit his people. This is far more important than raw talent alone. Nobody can be born with the integrity to persist at hard work. Dedication is made, not given by fate."

"Hard work alone isn't enough to solve everything," Xander growled. "Who will bring justice for my sister? The Throatians must be defeated."

Kaine replied calmly, "It's not your duty to do this alone. The Darian Kingdom stands with you—we might not be there the moment Prince Thane is captured, but we'll be there for the final judgment."

"If I can learn how to use the God Stones, I'll make everything right again," Kira promised.

"You can't do it!" her brother cried. "We already talked about this —the risk is too great, and the magic will kill you!"

"But there's nothing else I can do! Aren't I destined to become the heroine Lydia never got the chance to be?"

Kaine inhaled deeply. The children were overwhelmed and clearly strained. He opened his mouth to tell them to pause and soften their words, but the scent of lavender and a familiar raspy voice interrupted him.

"Good evening!" Celeste's voice rang through the darkness. Kaine turned toward one of the nearby shacks, whose single window glowed faintly with an orange light. The shack was noticeably larger than Orin's, but in similarly poor condition—on the verge of falling apart. In the doorway stood the light-skinned purple Lucidian.

"Sorry about the noise," Kaine said. "It's been a difficult night, and I hope we didn't wake you."

"You didn't," Celeste said. "I'm quite busy, in fact."

"You couldn't sleep either?" Kaine asked.

"I chose to remain awake," the Lucidian stated, beckoning them closer. "When I can't sleep in the evenings, I craft lanterns for the offerings. Would the three of you care to join me? I have plenty of supplies for everyone and can teach you."

"Are these the same lanterns you release into the sky?" Kira asked.

"Okay," the prince said, clearly uninterested, but perhaps trying to be polite anyway. "Let's go make lanterns, then."

Celeste's shack, much like Orin's, was hardly furnished, containing only the bare necessities—a bed, an armoire, and a few scattered possessions. The only notable difference was a large, sturdy table placed in the center of the room, surrounded by six well-used wooden chairs. The table's surface was littered with stacks of pink and red paper, where not even one was perfectly smooth. It was apparent that Celeste had spent a long time crafting each of them by hand.

Kira approached the table, her curiosity evident. "How do you fold these papers into lanterns?" she asked as she reached out to touch one of the thin papers.

Celeste smiled indulgently, taking the paper and demonstrating the precise folds and creases to form the basic frame. "It takes practice," she explained, her wrinkled fingers moving with a practiced rhythm. "If the frame is too loose around the twig, the hot air won't lift it. If it's too tight, it might tear or catch fire in the slightest breeze."

Constructing the lanterns was a delicate process, but Celeste found it a good way to pass the time on nights when sleep eluded her.

"The other night, we thought you were letting fireflies go," Kaine said. "I'm surprised to see you're using lanterns instead."

"We use both," Celeste explained. "While lanterns are traditional for Asura's worshippers, we often struggle to obtain the materials required for the rituals. Fireflies help conserve our supplies since they always return to us."

A snort came from Xander, who was leaning against the far wall with his arms folded. "All this effort for a few candles in paper? That's an overly laborious process, if you ask me."

"Loyalty to Asura demands that we make the most of what we have," Celeste said. "It's more than just words; it's about sacrifice and dedication, even when the results seem small or unimportant to outsiders."

Xander, like Kaine, appeared surprised, startled that a Lucidian would share the same deity as most Darians. Had Orin converted her? As far as Kaine knew, Lucidians didn't worship Asura, and he remembered Celeste mentioning as much before too.

Kira frowned, clearly troubled. "Celeste, I don't mean to pry, but how do you worship Asura? I thought Lucidians were prohibited from believing in gods."

"The Enclave forbids religion in favor of only allowing loyalty to the country," Celeste affirmed. "But I am no longer of the Enclave."

An awkward silence descended over the shack, broken only by the soft crackle of the candles' flames.

"I didn't mean to offend you," Xander hesitated, "but everything I said about the lanterns was true."

"And I have agreed with you it's accurate," Celeste confirmed. The paper crunched as she folded it into what would become the base of a lantern. Ten slow seconds passed before anyone spoke again. "My young prince," she said, "you're still hurting inside, aren't you?"

"What?"

"Both you and your sister are in pain," Celeste said. "Though Kira is less burdened with what happened to Princess Lydia. Kaine holds many painful memories inside him as well."

"We do?" Kaine asked skeptically. She was correct—everyone had sad memories, but it wasn't as if she could see them.

"I'm fine," Xander insisted. "There's nothing out of the ordinary about what I'm feeling."

"If you say so, perhaps it's true," the Lucidian replied. "I just realized I never told you about my power as a Mind Mage. I sense a stronger shadow within Kaine. Perhaps I can help him."

A shadow? Kaine was amused. "What kind of magic do you wield, Celeste? What is this darkness you speak of?"

"During the war, soldiers witnessed unforgettable, haunting, and cruel things. They witnessed friends and family die or committed acts so terrible that guilt consumed them. I, a Mind Mage, healed those wounds. Not in their bodies, as Sen does, but in their minds. I can sense their trauma and the darkness within. I heard your story, Kaine, and before you even spoke of it, I already knew the heaviness of your burdens. Many shadows ache your heart. I've sensed this since we first met each other in Orin's home."

When Kaine first encountered Celeste, he couldn't deny his fear. Since childhood, he'd been warned to be cautious around the Lucidian people, and that day marked his first encounter with one. His fear was understandable—not only was he facing a Lucidian, but he had also just been caught rummaging through Orin's home.

Perhaps Celeste referred to his story about accidentally killing

Axis Axemonger. Or maybe it was something else altogether. Did her ability genuinely allow her to sense his feelings, or did it enable her to peer deeper into his heart?

Kaine couldn't dismiss the possibility. Celeste wouldn't have been the first person to reach inside and see his inner self. Long ago, Princess Lydia had used the Memory Stone to absorb all his past memories, witnessing his lingering pain in vivid detail. Could Celeste sense his struggles without knowing their specific causes? More importantly, did she truly have the power to heal them?

"Your power is to lift someone's spirits, isn't it?" Kaine asked.

"In the end, that's right," Celeste said. "My magic allows me to erase memories, helping people let go of what no longer serves them and focus on what truly matters. Cleaning the mind revitalizes it, offering a fresh start—a re-roll of life's dice. Whether it's good or evil depends on the scars within the person I touch. Some might choose to forget their old pains if given the chance. I believe I can help you, Kaine."

Her role in the previous war made perfect sense. An army without trauma was more effective than one haunted by past actions. How could a soldier stripped of their past function in the world beyond the battlefield? Surely, erasing memories came with unforeseen consequences and limitations.

Kira too had similar questions. "But how can you know which memories you should erase? How can you be sure it's right?"

"When I erase someone's memory, almost everything disappears," Celeste clarified. "Though it's hard to understand, I keep the important aspects of their life written in my velvet book—their loved ones, cherished memories, and passions. These guide them back to a happier path, a world unburdened by the previous traumas they carried."

"So, you erase everything and help them remember what was important," Kaine commented. "There's no picking and choosing what to let go. How can people return to normal lives with their memories removed?"

"I have remarkable experience in helping people restore key parts of their past lives," the Lucidian said. "Carrying trauma can negatively impact what they value. Our lives are too brief to bear so many heavy scars. Releasing these pains offers a solution when individuals struggle to overcome their sorrow and distress. That's why I intervene. A purified mind can return to normalcy within a year or two—I've witnessed it firsthand."

"But wouldn't that change them entirely into a new person?" Kaine asked. "You alluded that erasing someone's memory is like starting one's life over again."

Celeste smiled confidently, as if she'd answered the question countless times before. "It's like this: if someone is inherently bitter, erasing their memories won't change that. However, if their bitterness resulted from a specific traumatic event—even one they're unaware of—cleansing their memory frees them from its influence. It offers a second chance for happiness unburdened by past pain."

"I don't believe that," Kaine said. "Perhaps your magic is a solution for some people, but I cannot see how starting over would be good in the long term. Too many years of life's experiences would just disappear."

"Starting over isn't inherently good or bad; it depends on the person's individual circumstances," Celeste said. "What matters is whether my power aligns with their unique situation. After all, it's easier to be told about a horrific experience than to recall and re-experience it repeatedly. Good memories can be rebuilt, while bad ones disappear. Even those who once wanted to die can find happiness again."

Kaine crossed his arms. It was likely that Celeste believed her healing abilities were like Sen's. Her powers functioned as a "cure", and she felt anyone sick deserved to be healed by them. The Lucidian had suggested that one's identity isn't entirely tied to their memories, but Kaine suspected she was wrong. Erasing someone's mind, he thought, was like burning down a ship that only needed minor repairs.

"I appreciate your offer to erase my memories," Kaine said politely, "but I don't think it's worth forgetting everything I've known just to erase a few painful ones."

The princess carefully sealed the final edge of her lantern and set it aside. "My father once told me of warriors who returned from battle, unable to remember who they were or why they fought," she said. "You've used your power as a weapon, not just to help people, haven't you?"

Celeste winced at the revelation. "Yes, it's true. Whenever the Enclave's army captured humans, the Mind Mages handled the interrogations. Afterward, we'd take the prisoners to an open field, blindfold them, erase their memories, and disappear. I deeply regret using my magic for such purposes—that's part of why I left the Enclave's grasp at the first opportunity I got."

Her explanation left Kaine conflicted. Celeste had been forced to use magic against her will, showing not all Lucidians in the war had fought of their own desire. Their magical powers could be used offensively or defensively, and probably many people were compelled into battle. They weren't necessarily all monsters like the stories had portrayed them.

"Wiping the prisoners' minds was more merciful than simply killing them, I guess," Xander said. "As you said, it might have been a cure for what they'd been through."

"The morality of my powers is relative," Celeste admitted. "With full consent, erasing someone's memory can serve as a form of healing. Acting against someone's will, however, might be worse than death, a blessing in disguise, or an indirect path to balance. People are often shaped and burdened by their memories without realizing it. There's no definitive answer on whether erasing someone's mind is right or wrong—it depends entirely on their specific circumstances and needs."

The princess's hands froze midway through folding another paper. Her voice trembling, she asked, "Can you erase your own memory?"

"I can't."

The shack went silent as Celeste opened her mouth to say more but didn't. It was as if she wanted to tell them, "I've already tried, and I failed," but the shame and futility of being unable to use her own magic on herself—an apparent and tragic limitation of her gift—stilled her tongue. She, too, had seen things during the war she preferred to forget.

Kira's troubling question, though likely intended to be lighthearted, ended up being unintentionally hurtful. The princess's lips trembled slightly as she realized she'd ventured into some of Celeste's darker memories—her own shadow. Celeste might have known more than she cared to admit about the memories of others she'd erased, or perhaps some people she'd helped were worse off because of it. Still, Celeste was now uncomfortable.

"It's probably better for her she's unable to accidentally erase her own memories," Kaine commented, aiming to ease the situation. "The hour grows late. Perhaps we should take a break from lantern making for the night. There are many shadows alive tonight."

"You are correct, Kaine Khalia," the Lucidian replied. "I sense a thick fog descending upon us soon. You should return home for tonight; we can reunite after sunrise."

The three of them helped her tidy up the lantern supplies into small, neat boxes, then made their way back outside after bidding each other goodnight. As Xander trailed behind Kaine more than a few paces, Kira wavered directly next to Kaine.

"I hope my question didn't insult her," she lamented.

"I doubt she took it as an attack," Kaine said. "However, we may have reminded Celeste of some things she'd rather forget."

"It's an interesting ability she has," Xander said, quickening his pace to catch up to them. "It might be worth reconsidering her offer, Kaine."

"I don't think so," Kaine replied, shaking his head. "My heart is like an old suit of armor. It's functional and comfortable, despite its dents and scratches. I've grown accustomed to it. Replacing it with a new one seems wasteful when it still serves its purpose. I'm not ready to discard something useful just because it is imperfect."

"You don't believe that writing down everything you want to remember will work?" Xander said.

"It sounds too good to be true," Kira said.

"If I handed you a piece of paper that you could have written, and it told you that you had another sibling you'd never heard of before, would you believe it?" Kaine replied.

"I would!" the prince insisted. But Kaine sensed Xander was only saying so to make himself seem right.

"There's no way that just reading some notes will make everything okay again," Kira countered.

"But if someone's memories are that dark..."

"I appreciate the concern," Kaine declared. "Life isn't always easy, but discarding what I know as good to eliminate the bad isn't worth the cost. I'll keep my mind as it is now. Even if Celeste offered me a shipload of gold to try her magic on me, I don't think anything would make me want to accept it."

30
THANE - THE COST OF ENLIGHTENMENT

The keeper guided them deeper into the forest, where the shadows grew larger with every step. As they neared the valley's heart, its center remained shrouded in uncertainty. A quiet dread taunted Thane's mind as they walked, a sensation he hadn't felt since the last time he entered the Loyalty Circles for the Reminder of Suffering back at home. He struggled to breathe as a familiar but unidentifiable scent overtook his nostrils. He couldn't place it—was it the stench of unwashed bodies or dried blood?

The journey seemed much too quick and yet far too slow. Part of him wanted nothing more than to flee this strange, unnerving forest and forgo learning all the secrets it contained. But a larger part of him urged that they couldn't leave without answers. He and Zeere had come here for a reason, and they owed it to themselves and their causes to see it through.

Dead trees with thicker trunks and a pale hue greeted them as another clearing appeared. The five semi-circularly arranged trees at the far end seemed drained of life, like the rest of the forest. But there was something about them that made Thane's stomach churn with revulsion and pity at the sight before them: they weren't mere trees.

Shrouded figures were tied to each tree's thick trunk like prisoners, their bodies tightly wrapped in dark purple cloaks that absorbed the dim light filtering through the branches above. Ropes woven snug around their torsos forced the Whisperers to press against the rough white bark. Though tied to the trees like corpses, the Whisperers were still alive. Yet the only sound Thane heard was the shuffling of his feet in the dirt, his instincts urging him to flee.

Shadows hid half their faces, but twin glowing red eyes peeked out from above the tattered cloths that covered their noses and extended below their chins. Their bodies were shrouded in robes that hung in strange folds and bulges—limbs seemed to swell where the fabric protruded, while elsewhere, the material clung tightly as if nothing lay inside. Suspended in the center of the tree, the leader of the Whisperers appeared to have no remaining appendages underneath her clothes.

"I AM MYTHREYA NOX," the middle female Whisperer said into their minds, "THE LEADER OF THE ENLIGHTENED, THE WHISPERERS."

Zeere nudged Thane's shoulder and shrugged quietly. "Something's not right. I've heard of Mythreya Nox. She should already be dead, executed by the Enclave."

"Could it be that she somehow survived?" Thane whispered.

The cloaked woman tied to the tree left them no time to ponder further. "WE ARE BEYOND HUMAN AND BEYOND LUCIDIAN. WE KNOW THE SECRETS OF THE WORLD. WE HAVE PAID THE PRICE FOR OUR MAGIC AND MADE THE ULTIMATE SACRIFICE."

Zeere stepped cautiously toward the semicircle of trees, as if they were living gods.

"You speak into our minds, but how?" he asked warily, gazing up at the people suspended high above. "You've mutilated your own bodies for this magic, haven't you? Each of you is missing tongues, arms, legs, and who knows what else. Is this what you've sacrificed to communicate like dragons?"

The very idea made Thane's stomach lurch. Such magic could never be worth it, if it required harming one's own body to that extent. Zeere's conclusion must hold some validity, given the physical states of each of the Whisperers. Yet if destroying one's body could grant magical abilities, how had the Hierophant kept herself together in one piece?

"EVERY CREATURE HAS A MIND, BODY, AND SOUL. WEAKEN ONE TO STRENGTHEN THE OTHERS. DESTROYING ONE, HOWEVER, WILL DESTROY THEM ALL."

Zeere ventured closer to the cloaked strangers. "But how does it work?" he asked. "I almost destroyed my body, yet I gained nothing for it. There must be more to your methods—something beyond words and beliefs."

Somnius had warned Thane not to take part in the Whisperers' rituals, despite their promises of magical powers. He needed to remind Zeere that sacrificing his physical integrity could yield nothing but an empty reward in the end.

"WEAKEN THE BODY TO STRENGTHEN THE MIND. WEAKEN THE MIND TO INCREASE THE ABILITIES OF THE SOUL. THE SOUL REMAINS THE GATEWAY TO WHAT EXISTS BEYOND THAT WHICH PHYSICALLY SURROUNDS US."

"Zeere, be careful," Thane warned. "They have magic, but if what they've done to themselves is the cost of it, then it cannot be worth it."

"You don't seem to understand, young prince," Zeere said curtly. "Magic is the sole means of defeating the Enclave. I must learn their methods and motives to make an informed decision for myself. Don't worry about me."

Zeere's gray history was unraveling before Thane's eyes. As before, it seemed the Lucidian preferred speaking in abbreviated truths rather than full details. Now that they had witnessed the true nature of the Whisperers, it became evident that Zeere was not the only one prepared to make great sacrifices to gain magical abilities.

"When you had the Scarlet Mage burn you, it wasn't just for the sake of hiding from the war, was it?" Thane accused. "You must have imagined more, something about the Whisperers or their ways. You'd hoped to gain magic from having the Scarlet Mage set your body on fire, didn't you?"

Zeere turned back toward him, his face as hidden as ever behind his bandages and wrappings. "The Enclave executed Mythreya Nox because she'd been experimenting with how to give Null Mages and humans magical powers. If she'd only been futilely chasing pointless dreams without merit, then they wouldn't have stopped her. She must have made progress. Isn't that right?"

He looked to those tied to the trees for answers, not Thane. Five pairs of glowing red eyes glimmered from the shadows beneath their purple hoods. The Whisperers pondered, likely deliberating within the hidden conversations of their own minds.

"How can Mythreya Nox even be here if the Enclave executed her?" Thane exclaimed. His suspicions ran high. Something about the forest strongly hinted that everything about the Whisperers was a trap.

"MY ALLIES AND I ESCAPED DEATH, JUST AS THE NULL MAGE BEFORE YOU. THE ENCLAVE BELIEVES ME TO BE DEAD, BUT I STILL LIVE—AND MORE POWERFUL THAN EVER."

Thane couldn't help but wince as the keeper retrieved a ladder, bucket, and satchel of sponges from behind a nearby tree. He proceeded to bathe the leftmost Whisperer while they hung immobile in the tree. From atop his ladder, the keeper reached up into the robes of the Whisperer and cleaned.

"Teach me how you've gained your magic," Zeere said, "and I will use it to fell the Enclave who betrayed you."

"AS I HAVE SAID BEFORE," Mythreya, the leader of the Whisperers, declared. "TO STRENGTHEN THEIR SOUL, ONE MUST WEAKEN THEIR BODY AND MIND. THE SOUL IS WHERE GREATER MAGIC LIVES WITHIN US. THOSE OF US CONNECTED TO THE TREES WAVER NEAR PHYSICAL DEATH AND EQUANIMITY. THIS IS THE COST OF ENLIGHTENMENT."

"So, the rumors were true," Zeere muttered. "Show me where I've gone wrong. I must have my revenge against the Enclave. What they've done to you—I'll pay it back double, I swear it."

"ONLY ONCE THANE ASCHE COMPLETES HIS TASK WILL WE REVEAL OUR GREATEST MEDITATIONS TO YOU. REST ASSURED, NULL MAGE—YOU, TOO, WILL BECOME ENLIGHTENED."

Zeere appeared overly focused on mastering magic, overlooking the broader consequences unfolding around them. Could Mythreya be manipulating Zeere's thoughts, much like the Hierophant had coerced Thane into revealing his name and abandoning his armor? If this were true, then it seemed the Whisperers were attempting to sow division between the two of them. They wanted Thane to translate their scrolls into the Common Tongue, but why? What secrets waited hidden in those texts, and where had they come from?

The way Mythreya spoke of "enlightenment" through physical and mental suffering made Thane uneasy. He feared the Whisperers might be manipulating them for nefarious purposes or that their promises were false. Glancing at Zeere, Thane noticed his friend seemed captivated by the Whisperers' words. It was clear his friend's desires for power were overtaking his ability to reason. Thane wondered if, in the end, Zeere would prioritize promises of magic over his own best interests—or Thane's.

The Hierophant's proven abilities were another factor illustrating that the Whisperers' magic didn't require someone to remove their limbs. How did the owl-masked woman relate to them, if at all? Was the Hierophant a way of proving that Zeere did not need to harm himself to obtain magic?

"Of course, I'll help translate the dragon words," Thane announced. "But first, I have a question about someone we met on our journey. There was a Mind Mage called the Hierophant, who wielded gifts similar to yours. Yet, she had not given up her body to gain her abilities. How was that possible?"

A cackle echoed in his mind as the keeper carried her ladder to tend to the next Whisperer.

"THE HIEROPHANT IS A FAILURE WHO IGNORED OUR TEACHINGS. SHE IS A MIND MAGE ONLY BECAUSE SHE TOOK THE EASIER PATH, THE LESSER PATH. WE ARE NOT MIND MAGES AND THE HIEROPHANT IS NOT ENLIGHTENED."

Mythreya remained as cryptic as ever, but her response confirmed a link between their past encounters and what they were witnessing now. Was the Whisperers' approach to magic genuinely superior to the Lucidian ways, or merely a justification for their brutal practices? Could it be that the people of the trees possessed greater power than the Hierophant?

"So, you would consider her your enemy?" Thane prodded further.

"SHE IS OF THE ENCLAVE." That was all Mythreya said, yet it was all Thane needed to know.

Somnius had sent him here, aware of the challenges he would face. The Whisperers, as influential as they were dangerous, held the key to defeating Zann-Xia-Czul. He might find the required knowledge within the ancient dragon texts. Thane's ability to speak fragments of the dragon language might unlock those secrets and aid their cause. The challenge was whether Thane could find what they needed while preventing Zeere from acting impulsively. Zeere would have to uncover the truth on his own as they unraveled the Whisperers' secrets.

"Then we must ally to defeat them," Thane promised half-heartedly. "Including the Enclave and Zann-Xia-Czul. Our arrangement remains stronger than ever."

"WE HAVE GREAT EXPECTATIONS FOR BOTH OF YOU, THANE ASCHE AND ZEERE MALAAK. OUR POWER AND KNOWLEDGE WILL GUIDE YOU TO GREATNESS."

AFTER THEIR INITIAL MEETING WITH THE WHISPERERS, THANE AND Zeere returned to the keeper's shack and set up camp nearby. Thane, distrusting the keeper, stayed awake for the first half of the night, taking watch. Though it was unlikely the Whisperers could attack them while they slept, the keeper might seize the chance if both were resting. Several times, Thane left their tent to check on the shack and listen. He didn't feel safe enough to sleep until he heard the keeper's snores.

As the days passed, Thane and Zeere established routines within the Whisperers' forest. Each morning, they gathered firewood from fallen trees and harvested vegetables from a small garden. During their afternoons, Thane deciphered ancient dragon texts in the keeper's shack, and Zeere meditated under the Whisperers' guidance in the deeper parts of the forest.

They were not allowed to approach the Whisperers unless the keeper was there to escort them. Thane suspected this rule was intended more to preserve an illusion of sanctity than for any practical reason. It reminded him that only his father had permission to ascend Mount Sephorr and enter Zann-Xia-Czul's cave, while ordinary Son See'ers were forbidden. Thane now understood that the law at home had concealed Zann-Xia-Czul's true identity by design. In contrast, the Whisperers' rule seemed rooted more in pride and a desire to maintain control.

Every day, the keeper and Zeere traveled into the deeper parts of the forest together, leaving Thane to work in solitude. As he spent his days translating the scrolls, disappointment and confusion clouded his thoughts. He had expected the messages to hold secrets of power and knowledge, but they contained only simple and useless words.

"Village, left," one scroll read.

"Nothing south, so seek north," another said.

It was clear that the Throatian and dragon languages stemmed from a common origin. Yet Thane couldn't help but wonder if he was missing something. Were these messages cleverly coded to contain deeper meanings? Among the first scrolls the Whisperers had tested him with, the one about stillborn dragon eggs was especially complex. Perhaps the Whisperers' knowledge of Throatian was too limited to differentiate between simple and advanced sentences.

"I have not seen Axhetharr-Cai-Mir since the full moon," another scroll revealed, hinting at a different dragon's name.

Thane spent hours each day poring over the scrolls, reading and re-reading, deliberately taking his time to try deciphering anything out of the ordinary. Every phrase was simple, but Thane obsessively searched for any hidden code or pattern, finding nothing. It appeared the dragons had used their written language to communicate directions and notes with each other in a straightforward and practical way, but nothing more.

The Whisperers and the keeper had acquired an enormous collection of messages, with crates of scrolls filling the keeper's home. Thane inquired about their acquisition, and Mythreya's fascinating story unfolded. She had borrowed the eyes of a bird, soaring above to observe writings embedded in mountains, fields, and natural surfaces. Dragons, like birds, viewed the world from above, not on the ground. Their words were carved into mountainsides or burned into fields with controlled lines of fire. Mythreya had copied these observations onto scrolls, hoping to uncover the conversations previously known only to dragons.

Despite having many crates of scrolls left to translate—at least two weeks' worth at his current pace—Thane couldn't shake the fear that he was wasting his time or would disappoint the Whisperers. What if the scrolls held no significant knowledge? For now, they appeared to be nothing more than a bunch of trivial messages and poems resembling riddles.

After he finished translating the scrolls, the Whisperers would give him the dragon horn, enabling Zeere to proceed with his magic training. However, Thane remained skeptical of the Whisperers' methods for achieving magical power.

Every day, Zeere and the keeper went to the circle where the Whisperers waited, each bound to their respective trees. He spent his day in deep concentration, chanting or repeating the phrases given to him by Mythreya. The practices resembled those Thane had once performed every morning in the Temple of White, where he revered Zann-Xia-Czul. However, despite years of praying and meditating in the temple, Thane had never left one of his sessions bleeding.

That night, Zeere returned to camp with his bandages stained dark red along his forehead.

"What happened to you?" Thane asked, glancing away from their campfire where a mushroom roasted on a stick. It was an ordinary toadstool, not one of the bioluminescent ones.

It wasn't until the keeper had entered her shack for the night and left them alone that Zeere spoke again.

"I hit my head."

"Clearly, you must have struck it on something," Thane replied. "Are you okay?"

Zeere sat down next to him, curling his knee toward his chest. "I've had better days, but this isn't the worst," he said.

"Be careful of the fallen branches on the ground," Thane offered. "Though the glowing mushrooms light the forest paths well enough, the ground here is uneven in many places."

"I didn't trip."

"You didn't?"

"No."

The crackling of the flames danced against the silent smoky air around them as Thane considered whether Zeere was telling the truth or was simply too proud to admit he'd fallen in the dark.

"Well, either way, may you rest well tonight," Thane said. "Maybe take a day—or two—off from meditation."

Zeere grimaced at him. "What happened to my head was no accident—it was a punishment."

"Mythreya did that to you? But how?" Confined to the tree trunks, none of the Whisperers could have harmed him unless the keeper had been the one to strike Zeere on their behalf.

"I failed to recite one of the longer chants, so Mythreya told me to slam my forehead into the tree," the Null Mage explained. "Further punishment made it harder for me to recall the next part. Resting for a day might help, but I don't want to waste time."

Thane closed his eyes, remembering the times his mother had punished him by making him kneel on piles of seashells. The shells were like glass, each fragment sharp and cruel. They had taught him obedience, but obedience came at a high cost.

"Maybe it's for the best if you don't learn how to speak directly into others' minds," Thane said. "The Whisperers possess magic but look at what they had to give up in order to get it."

"We're talking about this again?" Zeere muttered, folding his arms tightly. "I admit it's strange, what they're asking me to do, but there must be a reason for it all. I should obey. They dismissed the Hierophant as a failure, yet you witnessed her power. Imagine if I could wield a power greater than hers! Surely there was a way for her to harness magic without sacrificing her body. I have to figure out how."

Thane offered him one of the larger brown mushrooms. "I suspect the Hierophant was a Mind Mage from the start, which would have given her an advantage. Just because she has magic doesn't necessarily mean she obtained it from the Whisperers. Perhaps she developed her powers on her own."

"That's true," Zeere said, hesitantly taking the food, "but I doubt the Hierophant is willing to give lessons. The Whisperers are offering to teach me, provided you translate the scrolls. I can always stop if they demand too much of me."

"And how much is too much to sacrifice?" Thane pressed. "A few fingers? Your tongue? An arm? A leg? Your mind? They will ask for it all eventually. None of the Whisperers still have their full body intact. You need to protect yourself against whatever they might ask you to do next."

Zeere took a moment to consider, or rather, admit what he was willing to pay for magic. "I cannot give up my legs, obviously," he admitted, "for I need them to return to the Enclave for my attack. Perhaps I won't have to trade away my limbs—or any part of myself, as it would be unwise. But I must open my mind and learn whatever they can teach me."

"You've given enough already," the Throatian Prince declared, eyeing Zeere's bandages.

Zeere replied, "And yet, I have nothing to show for it," after taking a bite. "If all I need is to sacrifice a little bit more of myself, I'm willing to do that if it means acquiring magic. Without success, all the suffering I've already endured will have been in vain."

"If you sacrifice everything you are for something you believe is right," Thane challenged, "then what will be left of you once it's done? Nothing shall remain—because the very thing you sought to become a part of will have consumed you."

"You have to trust me. I won't do anything stupid. I won't end up hanging from a tree in a cloak, forced to be bathed by the keeper for the rest of my life."

Thane nodded respectfully. "I believe you to an extent, but you shouldn't risk getting killed either. The less harm that comes to you, the better."

"I'll try to avoid it, of course," Zeere said. "Now, can we talk about something else? Frankly, you're starting to annoy me."

"One more thing," Thane insisted solemnly. "Before my parents died, they were desperate for magic. We were fleeing the Darians after the wedding, and they were closing in on our ships. My parents believed that through sacrificial blood magic, they could send a message to Zann-Xia-Czul and secure our rescue. They took hostages—innocents of all ages—and, despite my pleas, they sacrificed them in a ritual to the flames. It was futile, a made-up rite that cost more lives than it could have ever saved. So many men, women, and children died for nothing."

"Horrific," Zeere commented, "but why are you telling me this now? The situations aren't the same."

"My point is that faith, sacrifice, suffering, and power are all related," Thane said. "If the basis of your faith is built on a lie, then everything else that follows will ultimately be meaningless."

Zeere stared into the campfire's flames, his tired eyes resting as he rubbed the spot on his head where his bandages were stained. "You really think we're being misled? But their power must be real, right?"

"Something's wrong with everything," Thane said. "Why would the Whisperers give up their bodies to communicate like dragons? What's the point of gaining such magic if they're confined to the trees forever? And why does the keeper, who can use the same magic, walk freely among them yet say nothing to us? Why are the scrolls she's given me so simple and mundane? They must be hiding something."

"It's because they see you and me as outsiders," the Null Mage insisted. "We can't expect them to share all their secrets. After you finish the translations, perhaps they'll trust us and reveal more. Would seeing the dragon horn you've been searching for strengthen your belief in them?"

"Though I haven't seen the relic myself, I'm certain it's here," Thane replied. Somnius wouldn't have sent him there unless she was sure of its location. "I don't trust the Whisperers. The keeper seems sneaky, like someone who would swindle coins from us in a game."

"I think she's just not used to having other people around," Zeere suggested. "Missing a tongue probably isn't helping her socialize with us either."

Perhaps the Null Mage was right that the keeper's strange mannerisms could be explained by her time in isolation, and nothing was sinister about her. Still, it was of little consequence how the keeper thought or behaved; what mattered was her master, Mythreya. The problem was that Thane could not confirm or test Mythreya's intentions. The leader of the Whisperers always had an answer prepared, and every secondary question came with an even vaguer response.

"What have you learned about their magic so far?" Thane asked, "aside from your punishments?"

"They've made me memorize a bunch of nonsensical words to chant and recite," Zeere said. "The purpose was to help my mind enter a deeper state than I could reach on my own. Once I can successfully reach the depths of my consciousness, my soul should awaken and shape my reality, including projecting thoughts onto others. That's how the voice works."

"It sounds simple in theory, but difficult in practice," Thane commented. "Do you carry any doubts about their methods?"

"The true power lies in the final step, where my mind will fall asleep while my soul awakens. That's where Mythreya's guidance will be most useful," Zeere replied. "Controlling the body, mind, and soul requires an ability most people aren't even aware they possess. It's like a secret muscle within my inner consciousness."

Zeere claimed that commanding his body was the goal, but Mythreya hinted at something far more destructive: the idea that weakening one aspect of a person's being—body, mind, or soul—was necessary to bolster the others. Was there truly any greater power or enlightenment to be gained through self-inflicted harm?

"But you heard what Mythreya said earlier about the three parts of every person," Thane warned. "I think we should confront her directly about it. We need to understand whether harming your body is expected to achieve what she's proposing. There's no hostility in asking her to explain her plan to you in greater detail, is there?"

"No, I suppose there's no trouble in asking questions," Zeere conceded. "Perhaps you can join me tomorrow morning when I go to meditate."

"The sooner we understand this the better," Thane whispered.

"Let's check tonight after the keeper has fallen asleep. Can you lead the way to the others?"

"We're not supposed to go to the Whisperers without her," Zeere said, "but I think we can manage."

"Thank you for trusting me with this," Thane said. "I'll keep my part of the bargain and translate the scrolls. I just want to make sure they keep theirs and that you don't have to lose a limb in the process."

"That's much appreciated," Zeere said. "I too still have many questions about the nature of Mythreya's magic."

31
EISENBERN - THE TRAINING HALL

The tunnel's ceiling lowered as they progressed, forcing Gustav and Ragnar to crawl and everyone else to squat. As they exited the shortest section of the caves, another set of luminescent mushrooms hundreds of feet above glowed white, casting an open, almost sacred light. For the first time since awakening underground, Eisenbern felt small, realizing just how far beneath the ground they had ventured. Thankfully, the tightest part of the journey was brief, having widened out into what Eisenbern could only describe as a massive underground cathedral.

Large bundles of treated leather, shaped together like dragons, hung from the ceiling. The dragons varied in size, some as small as a cow, others as large as several of them. The largest, painted with copper-colored scales, was big enough to swallow at least ten horses. If Zann-Xia-Czul was that massive, he would indeed be a formidable foe.

Beyond the hanging dragons, wooden walkways traced the cave's perimeter, wedged directly into the walls. Eisenbern guessed they were for launching warriors into the open space, though the ladders leading up seemed impractical and time-consuming. Perhaps they were more for emergency landings. He would soon find out.

On the ground level, various crates held spears, bows, and blades. More intriguing were the contraptions Herja had mentioned earlier—leather tunics reinforced with wings, belts, and ropes. Though their inner workings were unclear, they enabled flight, and Eisenbern immediately wanted one.

Near the armor and weaponry stood large, horse-drawn cart-like devices with solid bases and spacious leather cradles. Behind each cradle lay an intricate spring mechanism. When triggered, it would propel the wielder forward, transforming the winged warriors into soaring dragon hunters.

Eisenbern examined the ten sets of wings arranged neatly against the wall. "Do they flap like birds?"

"It's easier to show you," Herja said. "Shall we begin?"

The Dragon Mar approached the nearest set and lifted the thick belt to her waist. The leather wings aligned with her broad shoulder blades as she secured the suit to her body using three ropes. At her sides, two boxes the size of her thighs each contained three harpoon-like hooks.

"This contraption allows me to shoot the harpoons and leverage the cables to change direction or attempt close combat with a dragon," Herja explained. "The cables are detachable to prevent getting pulled along by any dragons."

"Are those hooks sharp enough to pierce dragon skin?" Gustav asked.

"Yes, given how fast we launch them," Herja said. "Then, we can leverage our momentum to close in on the dragon's body."

"The easiest way to kill a dragon is if it's on the ground," Ragnar explained, selecting a winged suit for himself. "Flying is the first phase of combat. I will use a broadsword to chop off the dragon's tail. Without it, they lose balance and can't fly effectively. Once grounded, we gain the upper hand."

The strategy appeared logical, and their equipment seemed designed for the challenge. It had been ages since the last dragon was defeated, and the sheer confidence of Ragnar and Herja was both motivating and slightly disconcerting. Slaying a dragon would be far from simple. These flying creatures were not only powerful but also capable of fire and lightning magic, adding extra layers of threat. Yet Herja and Ragnar had clearly spent their lifetimes training in this hall, preparing to face such a battle. Eisenbern hoped it would be enough.

"Is there anyone here who has fought a dragon and is still alive?" he asked. "Or is it only your ancestors who battled the dragons?"

"Jurek is our oldest tribe member at ninety-three," Herja said. "He's the only reason we learned to use our tools effectively and have so much of our lore recorded."

"Will you introduce us?" Ilya asked. "I'd love to meet someone who's defeated a dragon!"

"Of course," Herja said. "But first, watch this."

She pointed to a mound of dirt nearly a hundred feet away, painted with a red circular target. Herja pulled a lever and a sharp twang echoed as the grappling hook shot forward, arcing across the cavern to pierce the target's center. Reversing the lever, she disengaged the cable, freeing herself from the tether.

"That's how it works," Herja said. "You only have six shots, so you need to use them carefully. Who wants to try first?"

Ilya jumped at the opportunity and hurried over to where the other flight suits waited. As she unhooked the Shadowstone spear from her back, she paused.

"Herja, are you or Somnius considered the leader of the Black Moon Tribe?" she asked meekly.

"It's a sudden question, but a valid one," Herja said. "I am Dragon Mar, making me my tribe's leader. Yet we all serve Somnius now, despite her not being one of us. Why do you ask?"

Ilya removed the weapon from her back and handed it to her with both hands. "This is a Shadowstone spear, our kingdom's most prized item. It's indestructible and will never dull. We brought it with the intention of gifting it to the Black Moon Tribe's leader."

Herja grinned, holding the spear close to her chest and examining its smooth surface. "I've never seen Shadowstone before. Where does it come from?"

"It comes from the mountains near our kingdom," Gustav said. "The material is mined from rocks and weapons forged through a lengthy refinement process."

"Actually, I've been wondering what your armor is made of," Eisenbern added, daring to eye her chest.

"We make the leather from an ocean creature's hide," Herja said, her glare telling him she'd noticed. "This technique has been passed down through generations. The material isn't effective against swords, arrows, or blunt weapons, but it resists the thunderbolts and fires conjured by dragons. Wearing metal armor against a dragon is a wish for instant death."

Though harsh, her warning was one of the reasons they'd made the trip. He never thought about how electricity would affect their armor. If Eisenbern had led the city guard against the Throatians, the battle would have ended when they landed at White Boar's

Landing. Herja had spoken plainly, but she might have indirectly saved several lives.

"It makes sense," Gustav said, "but how well does it withstand lightning and fire? It must lose durability over time, right?"

"Ask questions later, Gustav!" Ilya snapped. "I want to learn how to fly—now!"

Herja helped Ilya remove her Leilan armor and switch into the winged suit. Ilya's body was too slender for the ropes to tighten properly, so Ragnar had to fetch a different set from a nearby supply crate. Once strapped in, Ilya hobbled to where Herja had launched her cable.

"Does it matter which lever I pull first?" she asked.

"Releasing them from back to front makes it easier to track at a glance if you lose your count," Ragnar advised. "In the air, everything seems to move twice as quickly as it does on the ground."

The first cable burst from Ilya's side, sending her faltering backwards from the recoil and nearly toppling her. Though the harpoon spike landed in the dirt pile, she missed the target by a good ten feet. Ilya repositioned herself and fired the subsequent shot, missing once more, and this time by an even greater margin.

"It's harder than it looks," she grunted before firing her third, fourth, and fifth cables. On her sixth shot, she edged nearer to the target, but still not close enough to celebrate.

"Now that she's run out of cables, what's next?" Eisenbern asked.

"In a battle, that's all she'd have," Herja replied. "She'd have to land and hope a supply cart was nearby. Reloading spring boxes takes a long time, making reuse impractical. Replacing the entire set is faster, if possible."

"Reload me," Ilya said. "I'll master this..."

Ragnar retrieved another spring box from a supply crate and helped Ilya remove the spent one from her belt, replacing it with the fresh unit. Ilya took another round of attempts at firing the cables toward the target but still missed each time.

"Again, please," she insisted after her twelfth shot.

"As many times as you want, Leilan Knight Ilya," Herja promised. She glanced in Eisenbern and Gustav's direction. "Who else wants to try? We have plenty of suits and more spring boxes."

"Is it even possible for me to learn this?" Gustav asked. "Given my stature, I imagine I'd simply fall from the sky like a dropped stone. Ragnar, please tell me you've been exaggerating all this time and haven't actually been in the air."

"I felt the same as you during my first training round here at fifteen," Ragnar said. "Weight doesn't matter as long as we can strap you into the suit. Come on, I'll show you how it's done."

He carried a suit to Gustav. As Ragnar secured the ropes, Herja approached Eisenbern with another.

"Come, let me help you change," the Dragon Mar said, locking her brown eyes with his.

He couldn't think of what to say next, so he remained silent as she approached and unlatched his purple chest plate. When her fingers brushed his shoulder, a shiver ran down his neck.

"You know, it's rare to encounter someone who handles armor as well as they handle... cables." He blurted out without thinking. Something about her touch had paralyzed him and jumbled all his words. Though she'd never fought a dragon, Herja was likely the most suited to battle one, and her power left him both inspired and in awe.

"I'd imagine it's rarer to find someone who would be so bold, or better yet, so desperate, to attempt such flattery whilst merely getting unsuited."

She kept her expression as neutral as when she had been under Somnius's potion. He could tell she was holding back—a slight twitch in her upper lip betrayed she was closer to laughing than he was. Without Ragnar's presence, she might have been more relaxed.

Still, Herja was essentially a queen, and he needed to act accordingly. Eisenbern had inadvertently expressed his interest, but at least the matter was resolved now, despite the awkwardness. The two sat in silence as Herja finished equipping him with the Black Moon Tribe's winged suit.

"We can learn how to do this quickly, right?" he let out.

"Perhaps, Eisenbern, perhaps," Herja said, her voice heightened slightly from its usual tone. "Now, aim for the target, and let's see what you can do."

He waddled over to Ilya with the flight suit and bent his knees to prepare for the kickback when he pulled the lever.

"Here it goes," Eisenbern announced, positioning his fingers on the rear lever. He flicked it toward himself, causing his body to be flung backward. A loud thud echoed through the cavern as he landed on his back—the recoil was far more forceful than he had expected!

"Are you okay?" Ilya asked. She approached and offered her hand to him.

Eisenbern pushed himself up. "I'm fine. Thanks—the blowback was stronger than I expected. I'm surprised you didn't tumble over too!"

"The trick is to sort of lean and lunge into it, right as you push the lever," Ilya said. "But look at that!"

She pointed to where a harpoon had pierced the sand hill's target directly in the center. Eisenbern nearly congratulated Ilya on her success, but then his eyes followed the cable along its path to where it was connected to his own spring box.

"Impossible!" Ragnar said. "Nobody gets it on the first try!"

"I'd like to see that again, Sir Eisenbern," Herja said. "If you have such great luck, you might as well go defeat Zann-Xia-Czul on your own."

"I don't believe it either!" Eisenbern exclaimed. Perhaps Herja's touch had somehow blessed him with incredible luck.

He dusted himself off and returned to his original position. On his second shot, he followed Ilya's advice by shifting his weight onto one leg. He absorbed the recoil, but the harpoon missed the target by several feet. He fired three more cables, each landing at varying distances from where he wanted.

"I guess my good fortune has run out," he lamented.

"It will return with practice," Herja said, approaching his side. "Look where you want the cable to go, not where you expect it to come from."

She launched another harpoon, striking the center. "That's how it's done. Let me show you. Position your waist parallel to the target. Even a slightly wrong angle might throw off the direction it goes."

He copied her to the best of his ability, but before he could release his next shot, Herja grabbed his shoulders and tilted him leftward. "Keep your body straight or your eyes will mislead you."

Eisenbern almost blurted out something so embarrassing that he would have regretted it, but caught himself and released his next cable without saying another word. What was it about her that caused him to do this?

When he first met her in the valley between the mountains, her armor drew his attention. However, as he observed her movements, it was the grace of her form that truly captivated him.

"A legendary angel," Eisenbern muttered.

"What?" Herja said.

"It's nothing." He cleared his throat. "To fly with those wings must feel like being an angel."

"It's better to see yourself as a hunter and the dragons as prey," she warned.

"What a fine perspective to hold," Eisenbern let out.

He released his remaining cables, missing them all. After three replacement spring boxes, Eisenbern still couldn't match the success of his first shot. Ilya succeeded in hitting the target on her thirtieth attempt, as Ragnar had predicted. Gustav fired seventy-two shots, nearly untying his suit, before finally piercing the target.

"I can't imagine how much harder it must be to do this while moving and airborne," he commented.

"Mastering the basics can take months," Herja said. "For now, we'll keep practicing."

"Do we have months, though?" Gustav replied, looking at Eisenbern. "I don't want to sound bitter, but we must return to the Leila Kingdom as soon as possible—preferably trained."

Eisenbern gave him a reassuring nod. "The queen didn't give us a set time to turn back, but you're right that getting here wasn't even half the journey. Still, we need to do our best while we're here; otherwise, the journey loses its meaning."

"Does your queen intend to assault the Throatian island alone?" Herja inquired. "What is the size of the Leilan army?"

It tempted Eisenbern to embellish the number, but he knew it was a bad idea. The Leilans had a city guard, not an army. While their numbers were significantly larger than the Black Moon Tribe's forty warriors, without the Darians, they could do little on their own.

"We haven't got nearly enough who can fight," Eisenbern admitted. Herja had already revealed the truth about her numbers, so it was only fair he did the same. "The Darians have far more soldiers than we do, but they don't know about the dragon waiting for them. As their allies, we're here to prepare for this threat and will share this information with them later."

"We'll need as many who can fight as we can," Herja said. "The Throatian way of life is brutal and cruel, but so is Zann-Xia-Czul's method of forging a large army."

"How so?" Gustav asked, then fired another shot at the target, missing terribly.

Herja pulled her hand back from the lever she had nearly grasped. "You are aware of their blood sacrifices, but did you also know about their Breeding Farms?"

"Is it some sort of military training camp?"

"The training camps are called Loyalty Circles," Ragnar said, "but Breeding Farms are far worse. Imagine your only purpose is to grow your country's population, disregarding morality and human dignity. That's what they are."

The implications sank in as Eisenbern's imagination worked its way through the plausible scenarios of how a Breeding Farm might function on a day-to-day basis. His face grew pale as he remembered the terrible events he'd witnessed in the days following the Wedding of the Torn Rose. He'd never forget the horses that were slaughtered or the men, women, and children of Starlight Beach who had been burned alive.

"Even if it turns out the Throatians don't have a dragon, their country deserves the worst we can bring them," Eisenbern vowed. "Their way of life is unacceptable."

"There is a dragon on their island," Herja said. "I'm certain of it."

"It's all because Zann-Xia-Czul poses as their god," Ragnar reminded them. "Everything the Throatians are is because of him."

"Well, it's a good thing we found your city," Ilya said. "When can we learn how to fly?"

"You can practice now if you'd like," Herja said. "However, it will take more training to launch cables while flying. You must first master aiming the harpoon and gliding individually before combining both skills."

Herja led them to one of the ladders Eisenbern had noticed upon entering the training hall, and they began climbing. As they ascended, Eisenbern felt his legs wobble—perhaps because he knew looking down was the worst thing to do at that moment. If any of them slipped or fell, they would surely die; he wondered why Herja and Ragnar hadn't provided safety ropes or tethers. The ascent to the top of the cavern took them nearly five minutes and, as they reached it, Eisenbern realized they had likely made this ascent thousands of times before.

Looking down at the training ground far below made him feel lightheaded, and the disorientation deepened as he remembered he was still deep underground. Though his feet were firmly planted on the wooden platform, he questioned whether he could bring himself to jump off the edge. Were the wings on their backs truly capable of flight?

"When you leap, keep your arms and legs straight," Herja instructed. "Managing your arms is easier than your lower body when starting out. Keep yourself flat to stay balanced until you're more experienced. Redistributing your weight allows you to turn. Whatever you do, don't lean too far forward or you'll enter a free fall, and it's very hard for a beginner to escape that."

"Aim for the sand target," Ragnar added. "It can absorb your crash if you're approaching too fast."

"You both make it sound so easy," Eisenbern chided as his flight suit suddenly grew heavier.

"Watch how I jump off the edge," Ragnar added. "It's important not to hesitate. Your wings will carry you."

"Your wings will carry you," Herja repeated.

Ragnar leapt from the path and entered his glide. Faster than Eisenbern expected, he traced a circular arc around the cave, looping multiple times throughout the training hall as he descended. Upon reaching the ground far below, he transitioned into a brief run, landing near the sand pile.

"Who's coming next?" he bellowed from below.

"Me," Ilya said, stepping forward. Mimicking Ragnar, she leapt and took flight. The moment her foot left the platform's edge, Eisenbern's heart stopped beating, fearing she was about to die.

Instead, she glided across the void space within the cavern, as smoothly as Ragnar before her. The only problem was the dragons hanging from the ceiling.

"Turn!" Herja yelled. "Turn before it's too late!"

Ilya barreled to her right, then evened her course. Eisenbern sought reassurance from Herja, noticing a faint grin on her face.

"Again!" the Dragon Mar commanded. "Return to the largest of them! Don't crash!"

Ilya tilted herself once more, tracing a wide arc to reverse her direction. Moments later, she neared the central dragon, this time aiming straight for its mouth. As she passed, she struck it in the face and giggled maniacally. Ilya only laughed that way when terrified, and Eisenbern couldn't blame her. Despite her fear, she was a natural flyer.

Soon, she landed headfirst in the sand pile. Climbing out, she spat out some debris and waved at everyone above. Ragnar approached and shook her hand.

"Can anyone land better than she does?" he called to the overhead platform.

Eisenbern exchanged a nervous glance with Gustav before patting his back.

"Well, you've seen Ragnar do it," he said. "Your worries about being too large to fly were unfounded."

"Maybe so," Gustav said, "but shouldn't you go first?"

"Should I?"

"I think you should," Gustav whispered, casting a glance toward Herja.

Eisenbern leapt from the platform, exclaiming, "Ha!" without a second thought.

His head and chest pounded as he fell toward the ground before his wings pulled him up again. The cavern's walls blurred as he zoomed near the first dragon, the size of three horses. His fears of flying were for nothing—gliding was exhilarating!

He imagined wielding a sword or spear to slay the dragon as he passed by the dummy dragon. The next time he practiced, he vowed to bring a weapon and strike. After completing the maneuver, Eisenbern shifted leftward, beginning to understand the mechanics of maneuvering in a real fight.

After stabilizing, he veered right, then left again. Lowering his legs slowed him down, though he wasn't sure whether there was a better way of doing it. He would ask Herja later.

Suddenly, something jolted him, and his momentum broke to a standstill. Before he could discern anything else, he plummeted toward the ground.

He thudded as he bounced off another dragon, continuing his free fall. The dragons! That was the key! Eisenbern frantically pulled all his remaining levers, praying to Asura one of the cables would attach to the dummy and suspend him in the air. His harpoons shot from the spring box, but nothing tugged him back. He could hear only Ilya screaming his name as his world went white.

"Wake up, Eisenbern," Ilya whispered into his ear. "Can you hear me?"

He could hear her clearly, but opening his eyes proved difficult. His body felt heavy, pressing into the bed, and he wondered if he was still wearing his flight suit. As he stirred, the room remained a blur, though Ilya's faint outline appeared against the dim green glow of the mushrooms on the wall behind her. As his vision cleared, he strained to make out the details of her face.

"I thought I was dead," he rasped, his mouth dry. "It's good. I needed only a nap."

"Can you move your legs?" Ilya asked urgently.

Eisenbern clenched his toes, feeling an unfamiliar stiffness, but no pain. He flexed his legs, relieved to find them responsive. He breathed laboriously, and each inhale caused a sharp pain in his chest.

"Yeah. It looks like I didn't injure my spine."

Ilya helped him sit up as he took in the room. Mushrooms covered the walls and a large fountain in the center filled the air with soothing humidity. The gentle sound of the water cascading into a small pool had a meditative effect.

"You hit your head on a dragon," Ilya explained. "That's what knocked you out for three days."

"Three days?" Eisenbern's eyes widened. "I feel refreshed, but was it really that long?"

"Given you bounced off two dragons and Herja's cable, we're lucky it took only three days for you to talk to us again."

"What's that about Herja's cable?"

"You grazed a rope holding the training dragons to the ceiling," Ilya said. "When you lost balance, Herja plunged after you—I've never seen anyone tumble so fast. Unable to catch up, she fired a cable beneath you, anchoring it to the cavern wall. She broke your fall, though she also fractured at least one of your ribs."

"Well now, I'll have to thank her for that." Eisenbern said. A dull tenderness ached through his chest as he struggled to chuckle.

"I'm sure she'll be happy to know you're okay," Ilya replied. "And, by the way, you'll be pleased to learn she asked me if you have a wife waiting for you back at home."

"You're joking."

"I'm not, and I saw how you looked at her. Anyway, I told her about Ophelia. Hopefully, you don't mind."

Eisenbern grinned, brushing his fingers along the left side of his torso. "You've done me a favor by spreading that information, and there's nothing to forgive. Thank you. As for Herja, I suppose I can forgive her for breaking my ribs."

He would need at least a month to recover before resuming his flight training, meaning they would spend another month underground. His fall, though unexpected, likely served a purpose. Asura must have had a plan for this, ensuring it would work out somehow. Much remained to be learned from Herja and Ragnar. Gustav had likely already asked if there were any tomes or records for him to study.

"I'll go tell everyone the good news," Ilya said.

"Wait a minute," Eisenbern exclaimed. "I'm not sure how I feel about this situation. It feels as though Ophelia died only a few days ago."

Ilya nodded solemnly. "Based on what you've told me before, she would have wanted you to be happy, rather than hold yourself back for someone you can't have."

Ophelia's words from their final meeting resounded in his mind: "As much as I would treasure it, our destiny will soon become unbound," she had said. "Save yourself for another, Jarret. You deserve a better fate than what I could possibly offer as your wife."

Though Ophelia and Ilya were probably right, pursuing Herja seemed premature. He needed to ponder the idea further as he recovered in bed.

"Not a word about that to anyone else," Eisenbern warned. Ilya just giggled, as though the warning meant nothing to her.

"Don't be silly," she said. "By now, everyone's already noticed."

Eisenbern scoffed, admitting that arguing was pointless. After she disappeared from the room, he savored the peaceful silence that followed. Looking around, his attention fell upon the fountain. It was beautiful, with water cascading into a small pool beneath it. He wondered if the water was safe to drink but didn't want to stand up.

Instead, he let himself drift off again, shutting his eyes for a few moments, and those moments faded into hours.

GUSTAV ENTERED THE GREEN-LIT CHAMBER, AND EISENBERN NOTICED how low the ceiling of his cavern room hung. The tall man had to bend to fit inside, and his towering frame hunched beside the bed. Despite his awkward posture, Gustav appeared relaxed, and his rare playfulness reemerged—a side of him Eisenbern hadn't seen since departing Sky Tower Coast.

"If anyone at home asks," Gustav said with a grin, "tell them you faced a dragon without breaking a sweat. I won't mention the ribs you broke."

"Keep the truth alive, Gustav," Eisenbern wheezed, his lungs still tender. "Crashing a few times is probably a requirement for becoming a dragon slayer."

"Whether you're a dragon slayer or a legendary fallen angel, I'm relieved you're safe."

Eisenbern snorted, remembering how he'd blurted out that impudent title when he'd lacked the words to say anything better to Herja. He imagined she and the others would have spent the rest of the day snickering at him, if not for his fall.

"Thanks for visiting, regardless of if I'm a legendary fallen angel," he said. "That said, I'm ready to leave this bed. Do you know whether the Black Moon Tribe has an apothecary? Has anyone mentioned how long I'll have to stay here?"

"Not officially, but they have the supplies, and Ilya's been taking care of you," Gustav replied. "You're not the first to take a nasty fall —Ragnar's had crashes like this more than once."

"It seems falling is a rite of passage for their tribe," Eisenbern said. "Technically, I'm ahead of you and Ilya in becoming a dragon conqueror. How did your flight go? You're up and moving around, so your run must have fared better, right?"

Gustav gave a nervous smile, his eyes avoiding Eisenbern's. "Actually, sir, I have something to ask."

"What's that?"

"As a knight in the Purple Guard, I formally request to only battle while standing on solid ground."

"Scared of heights, are you?"

"Terribly so, I'm afraid. Climbing the ladder to the platform was hard enough, and after I saw what happened to you, I froze. I couldn't do anything until Herja and the others took care of you. Ragnar had to climb back up and talk me into coming down. It paralyzed me, Eisenbern. I felt naked up there. Heights just aren't for me."

"I can't blame you," Eisenbern said. "If you'll be most effective on land, then that's where you'll be. Humans weren't born to take to the skies, at least not naturally."

"Thank you, sir," Gustav sighed in relief. "If it's any consolation, Ragnar can be the one to slice off Zann-Xia-Czul's tail when the time comes. I won't argue with him for the right."

"He'll appreciate that," Eisenbern said with a smile. "When the time comes, we won't only be fighting a dragon—the Throatians will be there as well. You'll hold your own against them."

"Thank you, sir," Gustav repeated.

"No need for formality. We aren't at Aeon Eve with Queen Blanche."

"Actually, there's one more thing," Gustav said, settling on the foot of the bed. The mattress creaked under his weight, and Eisenbern wondered how many decades old the furniture was.

"What else is there?"

"It's about our training—or everything, really," Gustav said, clearing his throat. "You might recall Herja and Ragnar mentioning that someone in their company has fought a dragon. I had an in-depth conversation with their elder, Jurek, but something doesn't add up. He told me all he knew about dragons: how to track them, how to fight them, and the challenges they posed. The issue is that dragon scales are too thick for ordinary weapons—swords, spears, axes—to pierce. According to his description, even the harpoons from spring boxes shouldn't be able to penetrate them."

While Gustav's concerns seemed valid, Eisenbern suspected a miscommunication or misunderstanding. Jurek had trained many Black Moon Tribe members, including Herja and Ragnar, and their methods had proven effective in the past, as evidenced by the tribe's success in slaying the previous dragons.

"Maybe in his old age, he's exaggerating or misremembering the thickness of the dragon scales," Eisenbern suggested.

"I considered that as well," Gustav said. "But I wanted to bring it to your attention."

Eisenbern intended to inquire of Herja whether the Black Moon Tribe possessed any dragon scales for testing the Shadowstone spear. It was their best chance of breaking through whatever material comprised the dragon's scales.

"The forges at home are making more Shadowstone weapons as fast as they can," Eisenbern said. "We'll arm ourselves with them in case your concerns are valid."

"Not to sound pessimistic, but we'll be lucky if we have even five spears by the time the battle comes," Gustav replied.

"In the end, it will only take one to kill Zann-Xia-Czul."

EISENBERN RESTED FOR SEVERAL MORE HOURS BEFORE RISING FROM HIS bed. On his feet, he realized the crash had left him sore and aching but not immobile. A bittersweet mixture Ragnar prepared for him eased the persistent pain in his lower chest. Despite the discomfort, he felt better than expected—thanks to Herja's quick thinking in breaking his fall with her cable days earlier.

He left his room and followed the narrow hallway back to the central chamber where he had first encountered Herja and Ragnar drinking the potion that had broken Somnius's control over them. Inside, Herja sat at the round table, engrossed in a book. The goblet had vanished, replaced by a pile of tomes now spread across the table.

"I doubt that's a text on how to heal broken ribs quickly," Eisenbern called out. His voice echoed in the empty chamber, suggesting they were alone.

Herja looked up, startled, a faint grin spreading across her face. "It's a record of one of our ancestors' battles," she explained.

Eisenbern envisioned armies of winged knights soaring through the skies, clashing with dragons in aerial battles. They would latch onto the creatures with cables and hack at them with their swords. The Black Moon Tribe's history was rich with heroes who had faced dragons with immeasurable courage. As their leader, Herja descended from such a lineage of heroes. He silently acknowledged the burden of her title and how it didn't yet match her achievements.

Confronting Zann-Xia-Czul was her only chance to prove herself equal to her ancestors. Eisenbern lacked knowledge of their full history, but he suspected Herja was the only Dragon Mar who hadn't faced a dragon and that fact likely bothered her.

He hesitated to ask about her feelings, sensing it was too personal. Instead, he sat beside her. As he sank into the wooden chair, a dull pain shot through his side.

"In the mountains above this chamber, thirteen warriors once defeated three dragons," Herja said, her voice wavering slightly. "I only wish I knew how they did it. My father once said such heroism was commonplace back then, but what my ancestors achieved seems an impossible standard to match."

"A Dragon Mar shouldn't measure herself against those who are no longer with us, despite how it might be your first instinct," Eisenbern admitted. "Perhaps they led ambushes or had more resources. They had greater numbers and different circumstances."

Herja's frustration was evident as she slammed the heavy book onto the table, and a disheartened sigh escaped her lips. "None of our texts explains their tactics. They list only warriors' names, injuries, locations, and occasionally dragon names. It's not what we need."

Eisenbern let his fingers follow along the worn edges of the paper, trapped in thought. "Maybe they were learning as they went along too," he suggested.

"The odds were always against them," Herja said grimly. "Dragons had every advantage in the air. Past leaders sent warriors out on raids, but they only sent handfuls at a time. I don't think any amount of training can guarantee victory—there had to have been more fighters."

"You make a valid point," Eisenbern conceded. "Gustav voiced his doubts about your weaponry being able to pierce dragon scales. I assume he's wrong since such weapons are what your people historically used."

Herja let out a long breath, shutting the book with a resounding thud. She added it to the growing pile of elusive records. With a shaky hand, she pulled the next volume towards her, readying for more disappointment.

"The dragons of hundreds of years ago are dead, and my ancestors slew them," Herja said. "You've seen our weapons, forge, and tools—they are our history. This is what they had and how they did it... somehow."

"I never understood how gliding would prove effective in a true fight," Eisenbern added. "Even though you can fly, couldn't a dragon simply fly higher?"

"I've had my doubts as well, but who am I to challenge the remnants left behind by those before me? I've never even seen a dragon."

"Jurek has enough years past to have fought dragons, though. Did you ask him about any of this?"

Herja's laughter was sharp and bitter. "I've asked him this many times," she said. "Jurek trained Ragnar, me, and others to be as prepared as possible for what we must eventually do. As I matured from a child, who believed every fantasy tale he told me, into a woman who knows reality's harshness, my concerns for the future deepened. Nothing will come easily, even if we've had past successes."

"Your ancestors killed many dragons in their age," Eisenbern replied, "but the one you will help kill might be the most important of all."

Herja stood from her seat. "Come with me. I need to show you something."

They wove their way through a new tunnel route he hadn't ventured down before. Eisenbern walked beside her until the passage narrowed, then fell behind, the damp, chill cave air brushing against his cheeks and neck as they descended deeper.

"Where are you taking me?" he asked.

"You will see," Herja replied, her voice as hard as stone. "But Eisenbern, how many is too many for you?"

"How many what?" he asked, still deciphering the solemnity in her voice.

"How many warriors are you ready to sacrifice in this war?"

He sensed a deep sorrow in her words, as though she carried the responsibility for every Black Moon Tribe member who had ever fallen in their history.

"Ideally, nobody would die," Eisenbern said. "But we know it cannot end that way. Each person should be remembered for who they were, not just a name on a tombstone or a faceless monument. Those who dared to resist the dragons need to be remembered."

"What you say is meaningful and true," Herja replied, "but it doesn't answer my question."

Eisenbern added, "The number of deaths is irrelevant in the face of such a monstrosity. If a thousand must die to defeat the dragons, then let a thousand. If ten thousand, that is the inevitable cost of victory. To lose or surrender to the beasts is to give everyone else over to them in the end anyway. Should dragons reclaim our world once more, every person alive might as well be dead."

Herja's eyes drifted toward the ground as she absorbed his words. Her face glowed with renewed determination and her shoulders tensed.

"I imagine that's what many of my ancestors believed too," Herja said. "And the price came higher than they'd expected. Tell me, Eisenbern, how many wars have you waged?"

"If you include the War of the Torn Rose, only one," he replied. "To be honest, I've only fought in a single battle."

"That's still one more than I've set foot in," Herja said. "Since I was a child, I wondered if my training, studying, and practicing were in vain. The Scourge was believed to be the end of dragons. My people hold a legend that someday the moon will split open once more and release more dragons into our skies. Like the battle records, everything is vague and causes me to overthink."

"You don't have to have fought in a past war to be valuable in a current one," Eisenbern offered. "Your past efforts will pay off."

"That is a belief you and the goddess share," Herja said. "Your battle taught you something important—how to lead men against their fears. But I... I've only led drills. Everything feels contrived."

They entered another small room, similar in size to the one where Eisenbern had rested after his crash. The room was empty except for a single door at the far end of the chamber. It was the first traditional wooden door he'd seen since entering the caves, and it was perplexing how it had been mounted and fitted properly within the stone chamber.

"Where are we?" he asked.

"Somnius isn't ready to see you yet," Herja whispered. "But I think it's time for you to see her."

"Is it wise to sneak up on a sleeping goddess?" Eisenbern asked half-jokingly.

"Every time I mention her name, your face winces as though you think I worship a common swindler," the Dragon Mar said. "By having you see her, maybe you'll begin to understand and believe in her."

"It's not that I don't believe she exists," Eisenbern replied. "I just don't see how you can prove she's a goddess any more than I can prove Asura is real."

"The scars of time build the strongest faith," Herja said. "That's what she told me. I don't fully understand it, but that's what she said."

Herja inserted a thick bronze key into the door and let them inside. They entered a larger chamber with twin rivers flowing on both sides. Between the two rows of water was a plateau of the whitest stone he had ever seen. Overhead, an archway made of similar granite reached to the cave's upper regions. The archway's elegance made Eisenbern wonder how such heavy stones could have been transported and assembled there so far beneath the ground.

Stone roses, painted in dark cherry, wrapped around the entire archway, frozen in time as they protected the white stone behind them. Whoever had crafted it must have spent years flawlessly carving and painting each individual rose. At the center of the archway hung the largest flower, another rose, the most beautifully painted he'd ever seen.

The petals of the largest rose emitted a faint red glow, but patches of darkness outlined each one, setting the overall light in the cavern. The rose wasn't alone; scattered throughout the uppermost portions of the room were stars. For a moment, Eisenbern thought he and Herja had somehow climbed above ground, but it was an illusion. The architecture, the painted sky with its mysterious shades of the darkest purples and infinite stars… only magic could explain it.

As Herja led him under the archway, he finally understood why she and Ragnar insisted on protecting the sleeping goddess and why they'd initially kept her isolated from anyone on the outside.

On the opposite side of the plateau, behind a transparent cloth veil, rested a young woman on a flat granite bed. Somnius's long golden hair, braided into intricate knots, lay at her sides. Her chest rose and fell as she slept, and Eisenbern couldn't help but notice how her white dress wrapped cleanly around her stomach. In the chamber's stillness, the clothing revealed a profound truth.

Most importantly, perhaps the reason for everything else, was the miracle she held tightly between her slender arms.

"She is with child?" he whispered, stepping closer. Before he could say more, Herja extended her palm toward Somnius as though presenting him with a magnificent piece of art comparable to all he'd just admired.

"Now you understand why it is not so simple," the Dragon Mar said. "It's not us alone who will defeat Zann-Xia-Czul, and not even Somnius herself. Our role in this is to support what's coming. Ultima, the child you see growing inside her, is the one destined to save our world. If we cannot protect Somnius and her child, then everything else is lost."

32

BIOS AURAS - THE BREACH OF STORMS

Once Alina had left, Bios slept through the night. As dawn broke, the first light crept through the upper windows of the Golden Mare. He dressed in his crimson armor and helped himself to a stale bread roll. Taking a deep breath, he focused his thoughts on the main hall of the Temple of White. With a brief thought of remembrance, he was there.

The incense's familiar scent mingled with the musty smell of ancient stone walls. The moonlight through the glassless windows revealed that someone had lit the incense recently, as the sticks still had much life left in them.

Voices carried from the nearby room where the Elders were holding their evening meeting. Their words were unclear until he moved closer.

"It may be time for us to open ourselves to the outside world again," Elder Kaelgeth suggested. "Our people have endured enough trials in isolation. If we allow ships to dock once more, White Boar's Landing could flourish."

Elder Valenti protested. "Surely you haven't forgotten about the war? You've told us Darians have gathered near our borders, ready to avenge their princess for our actions. Besides, we still do not know how to awaken Zann-Xia-Czul."

Bios leaned against the cold stone wall near their meeting room, pondering the Elders' words. Their discussion had ignited a flame of curiosity within him. He wondered if they were desperate enough to abandon their dragon's protection.

He entered quietly while scanning the faces of Grimm, Kaelgeth, Valenti, and Cereene, who huddled around a rickety table. Small flickering candles cast shadows on their exchanged glances. He took the last empty chair, joining them.

Grimm's stern expression faltered, and Valenti's eyes darted to where several scrolls were scattered. She instinctively gathered them, arranging them into a neat pile.

"Our food resources are dwindling faster than we can manage," Cereene explained to Bios. Grimm grunted, his mouth frozen shut, his silence confirming the validity of her words. Bios smiled, noting the unease on the Throatian king's face.

"We need to explore other options," Grimm said, pointing at him. "You are our only way to import food from outside our walls. While the raids on Last Hope's silos have yielded short-term gains, they aren't sufficient to meet our long-term needs. Valenti says our population is growing faster than ever. Trading newborns for food could be another option."

"Trade has served us well for generations," Kaelgeth said.

"Even if we opened White Boar's Landing," Valenti added, "there wouldn't be enough large transactions to satisfy our immediate needs."

Bios let his mind wander, studying Cereene's lips, her expression a mystery he longed to unravel. Her eyes, the color of a shiny midnight sky, held an intensity that was both captivating and unnerving. When he brought her to the Silent Deserts to meet Klein, she was a timid Son See'er who had never fought in a Loyalty Circle or even held a knife. After leaving Klein's bedroom, Cereene had taken her first step toward something greater—her first kill—and the experience undoubtedly changed her. She'd also proven herself as one who would follow his commands.

"The next raid on the silo will be our largest yet," Bios offered as he returned his attention to the meeting. "In fact, I plan to ensure we take control of all supplies stored in Last Hope. This would not only meet our needs but also create a famine for them when winter arrives."

Grimm ran his hands through his short, graying hair. "We can't wait much longer for that," he said, his voice concealing a hint of urgency. "In two months, the famine could well be in our lands instead."

Bios nodded solemnly. Maintaining the Throatian food supply had been a secondary goal of his, a means to gain favor with Councilman Ofred and Grimm. Now, it could prove more beneficial to him than ever before.

"Your people will not go hungry," Bios assured him. "I promise you; I won't rest until we have the resources we need." He glanced at Cereene, who sat in her chair without saying a word, her eyes fixated on an empty plate streaked with blood. The sight of Throatians eating raw meat—chickens, rabbits, fish, and whatever else they could scavenge on their island—always left him unsettled.

"Do whatever is in your power to provide for us," Grimm said firmly, despite the stress apparent from his tense neck. "If our people become desperate, we may have to resort to culling our populations again, as before."

Although Bios wasn't one of the Throatian Elders, their secretive meeting to decide the island's future without his input enraged him. Grimm seemed to have forgotten that the Throatians would eventually serve as Bios's army. Why hadn't they simply asked him for more food? Their secrecy felt like a personal insult, undermining his authority and making him question their loyalty. He suspected their secrecy hid a deeper motive, perhaps even an attempt to reduce their dependence on him.

Bios nodded in agreement, though the sour taste in his mouth remained. "I will return with good news. But first, I want to talk to Cereene."

"You do?"

"Follow me."

Leaving the council in their meeting room, he led Cereene back to the main cathedral of the Temple of White, where its polished stone walls reflected the ghastly moonlight.

He looked over the trio of carved obelisks before turning to her. "Is it true what the Elders are saying about a coming famine?"

"It is," Cereene replied. "The food stores are dwindling, and if we don't send the Son See'ers back to the Loyalty Circles soon, there won't be enough grain for everyone. But that's not the issue that demands our focus."

"And why should we not be concerned?"

Cereene hesitated, choosing her words carefully before answering. "It appears the Son See'ers suspect that Zann-Xia-Czul can't read their minds while asleep. Following my sermons, they often ask about their lives. Recently, several have questioned whether he watches over the island during sleep. Do you foresee what problems will arise if their faith in him wavers?"

The Throatian dragon ruled through religion and fear, and his ability to read minds played a major role in retaining his power. For generations, Zann-Xia-Czul could read the thoughts of those around him, making it impossible for anyone to hide their doubts or secrets from him. Anyone who dared to question his authority or dissent had to undergo a test of devotion in the Loyalty Circles. Defiance meant quick punishment, often as lightning strikes from the sky, though the dragon could no longer wield that power while in hibernation. Cereene was right.

"Do the other Elders know of this?" Bios asked. If they did, it would be in their best interest to intervene. Without obedience to Zann-Xia-Czul, they would lose control of the island, leading to its destabilization.

Cereene's eyes wandered toward the meeting room, scanning for eavesdroppers. "Only Kaelgeth knows about it. I've been discussing my concerns with him, and he's been investigating. The rest of the Elders remain oblivious, but I dread the truth will spread soon. If it does, it shall trigger a crisis of faith, causing the people to lose their fear of Zann-Xia-Czul and undermining our control. We must fix this; otherwise, everything's destined to fall apart." Her voice lowered to a whisper. "I've noticed how the Son See'ers glance at each other during my speeches, as if they are wondering whether they're still being watched."

"Perhaps you have some history or lore you can use to convince them that Zann-Xia-Czul is still listening," Bios suggested. "I don't want to resort to using Loyalty Circles yet. We're departing for Yaenia soon to launch our attack against the Darians. Our growing numbers will be essential."

"History and lore won't help," Cereene said. "We both know almost all Throatian history is based on a single lie, so I've already crafted stories to serve that purpose. These tales have swayed some of the more impressionable Son See'ers, but others are growing skeptical of everything. I'm trying my best to keep the country stable, but it's no easy task."

Bios accepted the concession—some islanders would need to die as an example after all. To conquer the world, he needed an army that was completely dedicated, driven blindly by their religion.

"I suggest staying somewhere safe, away from White Boar's Landing," he told her, "and saying nothing to the Elders about what we just spoke of."

"What do you mean? What will happen at White Boar's Landing?"

"Your island is safely guarded from the Darians," Bios said, pausing for effect. "It would be tragic if their soldiers breached the wall of storms."

Cereene nodded meekly in silent contemplation.

"You'll understand what I'm about to do soon enough," he added. "Once you know the truth, tell the other Elders that Zann-Xia-Czul spoke directly to you and warned you of a temporary loss of his powers."

"Is a reminder of what would happen if Zann-Xia-Czul were no longer protecting the island the best course of action?"

"We live in a world where people have too much, where they forget what truly matters," Bios said. "A crisis breaks that delicate, shiny glass. Run now, Cereene, while you still can."

TELEPORTING GRACEFULLY ABOVE THE VAST OCEANS, BIOS AURAS materialized aboard the Darian flagship with a soft thud. His crimson armor gleamed in the moonlight as he landed on the deck, startling the crewmen nearby, who were diligently repairing sails or sharpening their weapons.

"Halt!" one guard shouted, drawing his sword and pointing it at him. "Who goes there? Identify yourself!"

Bios held up both hands in feigned surrender. "I am a Darian messenger from Wargonne," he declared calmly, "sent to deliver vital information to those in command here. I swear I mean no harm."

"How did you get aboard?" a soldier bellowed, his voice like a ghost's scream.

"Though I'm a half-Lucidian and a bastard," Bios lied, "my blood runs loyal to the Darians. My magic allowed me to reach you here from Wargonne."

"Magic?" the soldier's companion exclaimed. "Councilman Conan wouldn't have any half-Lucidians in his ranks!"

"That's not for you to decide, good sir," Bios said. "Now, please take me to whoever is in charge—I have urgent news to say."

"You won't be going with your weapons," the older soldier said.

"Of course," he said. "It's understandable you wouldn't trust me, given my family's background."

"Don't try anything funny. Just come."

Reluctantly, Bios handed his sword to the soldier, who examined it with gloved hands before sheathing it again.

"We'll take you to her immediately," the soldier said, motioning for the other two crewmen to escort Bios below deck.

As they walked, the crewmen whispered about the mysterious stranger and his sudden arrival aboard the flagship. Their whispers mattered little; Bios wasn't trying to convince them of anything. When they reached the bottom of the stairs, they knocked on the door leading to the captain's quarters. Someone admitted one of his escorts into the room, and he returned to the hallway moments later.

"You can come in now," he said. "Captain Ellebar wants to hear about what happened."

Bios proceeded inside, noticing the musty smell and the quaint, cramped space typical of a ship of that size. What surprised him most, however, was the unexpected nature of the captain's belongings. Instead of the expected maps and charts that a captain would likely have, Ellebar's desk was covered with scrolls and papers, each containing drawings of plants and flowers. Each artwork created with ink and charcoal displayed an incredible amount of detail. A finely crafted lute rested against the desk, though a string was missing. The captain, in her forties, sat sketching a delicate rose. Her sun-tanned skin and wrinkles across her face revealed the time she'd spent out at sea.

"Greetings, Captain Ellebar," Bios said. "My, my, you have a remarkable artistic talent."

"The nights at sea drift by slowly here," Captain Ellebar replied. "This is my ship's third trip on this route. The crew and I have little choice but to resort to hobbies to pass the time. Who are you?"

"My name is Alton Dustfield," Bios lied with a new alias he'd not used before, "and I came from Wargonne. I served Councilman Conan."

"Alton Dustfield," Ellebar repeated. "I do not recognize that name. What is your rank?"

"I had no official rank," Bios said, "but I quietly worked directly under Conan. That's where my news comes in."

The captain's green eyes assessed him. "I never would have guessed you were one of the Lucidians—you look as human as anyone else. Why would Conan have taken in a halfbreed and spared you?"

"My mother, a human, was a dear friend of his," Bios lied. "But my lineage is irrelevant. I came to inform you that the Throatians mounted a surprise attack on Wargonne. Councilman Conan is dead."

"What?" she exclaimed as her pen dropped onto her paper, leaving wayward ink on the outer edges of her artwork.

"There was an ambush at Wargonne," Bios explained. "They infiltrated the walls, killing many, including the councilman. None of us could act before it was too late."

"But how?" Ellebar stammered. "We've surrounded their island, and nobody has left their homeland. Just as none of us have managed to enter, the storm wall prevents anyone from leaving."

"I don't know how," Bios said, "but I have my theories."

"And what would you know of the Throatians' wartime strategies, Lucidian?" Ellebar asked, clearly distraught over Conan's death.

Bios touched the edge of her desk, looking over one of her flower drawings. "They must have planned the Wedding of the Torn Rose long in advance," he said, "so that a legion of ships could be stationed near Wargonne beforehand. You agree it's possible, yes?"

Captain Ellebar nodded. "They could have schemed that far ahead, but I still don't believe they broke into Wargonne. The security there, the number of guards, and the watch towers—they would have seen Throatian ships from half a day's out!"

"But there's an important detail Conan and everyone else, including myself, overlooked," Bios said. "The Throatians would know better than to approach Wargonne by sea, as others have attempted before. We must consider the possibility that they used magic."

"What kind of magic? Even with that, they'd still need to get past the sentries and walls."

"Lucidians have many powers," Bios said. "Speaking of walls, you were ordered to breach the island and launch an attack whenever a hole or lapse appears in the storm veil outside, correct?"

"Yes, we've been ready for months."

"What if I were to tell you that bypassing the magical storm wall is no different from bypassing the walls at Wargonne?"

"You're suggesting there is Throatian magic capable of penetrating the storm?" the captain questioned.

Bios nodded. "Not about breaking through but moving past it.

After the attack at Wargonne, I was deeply troubled by what happened to Conan. For days, I was in disbelief. How had the Throatians managed to get inside? It was then I realized their magic must be like my own Lucidian abilities. I discovered I might use my magic against them for my country and for revenge."

Ellebar's eyes narrowed. "I don't need your backstory," she said. "Tell me plainly: what is your magic, and why are you here?"

"I can help you enter White Boar's Landing," Bios said. "My magic can transport anyone—or even an entire army—through a portal similar to the legendary World Veins. Do you understand?"

Ellebar's arms crossed. "Easier said than done. Prove your magic is real."

He let out a light chuckle. "The proof? The proof is that I'm here, and I didn't swim all the way from Wargonne."

"I need to see how it works."

"It's simple," Bios said, opening a portal beneath a single book on her shelf and letting it fall gracefully into his palm. He handed it to her with a gentle smile. "I can move things from one place to another."

"This would allow my knights to begin their attack," Ellebar concluded, pounding her fist on the table. "Why didn't you arrive earlier? We've been waiting out here for days!"

"I never thought to use my magic this way, especially with my other duties to attend to," Bios said with a feigned frown. "Now that I'm certain this is how the Throatians invaded Wargonne, I can help us take revenge for what they did to Conan… and to Princess Lydia. Captain, when might we begin our attack?"

Ellebar scoffed. "To think the breach of the storm would happen this way… through the aid of a Lucidian bastard."

Bios sat quietly in his chair, saying nothing. Though she appeared to be under his control, he detected a faint hesitation in her demeanor. She was exercising caution.

"So, when can we attack White Boar's Landing?" he asked again eagerly. "Now's the time to strike at the heart. Your people surrounding the island are more than enough to outnumber them."

"Not yet," Ellebar said. "I wish to send scouts first. I need to know what we're up against before committing my entire fleet. Can you ensure that all our ships will safely move into their harbors once we're ready?"

Sending scouts alone wouldn't satisfy him; all of Ellebar's underlings needed to play their part in conveying a strong enough message to the Throatians.

"Surveying their territory would be beneficial," Bios began, "but White Boar's Landing has been abandoned since the storm veil came. It would make a sufficient camp for your knights while the scouts venture deeper into the island."

"Have you seen this?"

"I have," the crimson knight insisted, "and I want our attack to be as successful as possible. If we should find ourselves overwhelmed, I can bring our forces back to the other side of the wall."

"I see," Ellebar said as she calculated her next move. She was yielding her trust to him, and it would prove fatal. "In that case, securing White Boar's Landing and forming an outpost would be the best long-term objective. Once reinforcements arrive from Wargonne, we can fortify our position and take the rest of the island."

"A fine strategy," Bios said. "Their island is modest in size. We'll conquer the Throatians in days. However, before we proceed, there's one thing I must ask of you."

"Go ahead," Ellebar replied as she rose from her desk and started putting on her armor. It was painted with hues of red and pink, and Bios wondered whether she had done the work herself.

"Before Councilman Conan's death," Bios said, "he asked me to investigate a group of hermits known as the Whisperers. Do you know anything about them?"

"Tracking them was my previous mission," Ellebar said, fastening her belt and sheath. "My scouts located the edge of their territory but couldn't determine how to proceed further. I was preparing to travel there personally when the War of the Torn Rose erupted, and Conan reassigned me here instead. What do you need to know? What did the councilman send you to accomplish?"

"I'm aware the Whisperers are north of New Ginstown," Bios said coolly. "And now I realize Conan wanted me to find them as well. If I knew their exact location, I could create a portal. Perhaps Conan even intended for me to transport you there one day. Given the distance between Wargonne and New Ginstown, it makes sense. We're meant to work together."

"I can't speak to the specifics of where the Whisperers are hidden," Ellebar replied as she secured her belt. "My scouts suspect they're in a gorge west of the Lowland Graves, but north of the Lucidian Enclave. Look for the path where the trees' leaves are as red as blood—those are your signs. That, or you'll hear voices in your mind."

"Do you believe in their magic?" Bios asked.

"My scouts wouldn't lie to me," Ellebar confirmed, edging toward the door. "Let's discuss this later. We need to coordinate with the other ships for the attack. Defeating the Throatians is more important than pursuing these hermits, who are causing no harm."

The knowledge he'd gained was satisfactory, for it was evidence that Conan had been truthful in his final moments.

"Right away, Captain," Bios replied with a bow and a genuine smile. "Let's take action against those blood-drinking cultists!"

Bios and Ellebar moved above deck, where Bios used his magic to teleport them to each of the other fifteen Darian ships. Ellebar informed her fleet of her plans to strike against the Throatians. After an hour, all the soldiers had gathered on their respective ships, fully armored and armed with blades, spears, and bows. In total, three thousand of them were ready to invade the Throatian island.

"You're sure that you can do this?" Captain Ellebar asked him once they returned to her ship.

In front of them stood the best of her knights and a cache of supplies carried by the other crew. The men and women's faces lit up from their torches' lights, perhaps enthusiastic about finally seeing some action. From Bios's observations, the people had been confined to their ships for weeks or even months. He could identify the veterans, who appeared weary and detached, as if already separated from what waited ahead.

"I'm ready," Bios confirmed.

"Excellent. Move those aboard the ship east of us first, then circle the area until you return," the captain instructed. "This ship's soldiers should arrive at White Boar's Landing in the final round."

"At once, Captain Ellebar," Bios acknowledged with a bow.

"Please call me Lara," she replied with a grateful nod.

Though she had not said so, Bios suspected she was considering asking to replace Councilman Conan upon her return to Yaenia. The decision, of course, would be King Ether's. If Captain Ellebar successfully led the initial attack against the Throatians and established a stronghold, she would likely become the top contender. Bios didn't care whether Ellebar succeeded, but if her ambition drove her decisions, that suited him just fine.

He focused his mind on the first ships and teleported to them. There, an almost identical group of Darian soldiers waited, with a similar spread of enthusiasm and anxiety.

Bios declared, "My fellow Darians, today we launch our first attack against the Throatians! I will lead you through the magical barrier that has long prevented us from reaching their island. Now, march forward in a single line, as if you are about to impale me with your weapons, and do not stop until you've spread out across the beach!"

He chose a spot on the sands near White Boar's Landing, specifically at the bay's edge, and the Teleportation Stone responded to his command. The location was secluded, offering plenty of space for the army to arrive undetected by the Throatian watchtowers. These towers, once used to monitor incoming ships before White Boar's Landing was sealed, were now unmanned. None of the Throatians —not even their Elders—would suspect a Darian army materializing seemingly out of thin air.

The soldiers hesitated as they approached, their eyes burdened with uncertainty. The sight of Bios Auras, dressed in his vibrant red armor, instilled both awe and curiosity within them. No one had ever used a magical portal, and the prospect of following his instructions made them feel uneasy. He understood their trepidation but knew they had no choice. They all wanted to leave their ship, and each of them disappeared through the invisible doorway toward the Throatian island's beach.

After teleporting all the soldiers to the other side of the storm veil, Bios closed the portal and opened another to reach the next Darian vessel. He continued this process until he had successfully transported all three thousand soldiers to the island. Upon completing his task and returning to the main ship of the fleet, Captain Ellebar approached him.

"Your efforts are commendable today, Sir Dustfield," she commented as she moved closer to the portal. "With so many soldiers breaching the storm, we can secure our territory until reinforcements arrive."

"How certain are you of your victory, Lara?" Bios asked, quietly closing the invisible portal behind her.

"We have three thousand at our command," she said. "King Ether and Councilman Conan have prepared for a full assault on the island. We've been preparing for this moment for months. We'll succeed."

Or so she believed. Three thousand soldiers were indeed a sizable army, but the Throatians vastly outnumbered them on the other side of Zann-Xia-Czul's magical wall. Captain Ellebar remained unaware that White Boar's Landing, once a prominent trading port, had become home to the Throatian overflow population. The Darians wouldn't suspect these areas were inhabited at first—it was too dark to see beyond the beach where Bios had positioned them. However, as they moved down the coast from their teleportation point, they would soon uncover the full extent of his deception.

Captain Ellebar stepped forward, her feet carrying her only so far. "Did I wait too long to enter?" she asked, looking over to him.

"Apologies, Lara," Bios said, "but you won't be joining your soldiers in the ambush."

"I beg your pardon?"

"The beach where I sent your soldiers is a suitable location for an outpost," he explained. "It has the ocean on one side and impassable mountains on the other. The only path they can take leads straight to White Boar's Landing. The soldiers will have no problem discovering where to go, but the truth is, they will all die."

Captain Ellebar unsheathed her sword. "I don't appreciate your lack of enthusiasm. Open another portal at once so that they might retreat if you think the odds are so low."

"I have other intentions for them," Bios said firmly with a smile. "The Throatians stationed further down the beach need a reminder of war's consequences. Unless your soldiers have packed enough supplies to sustain themselves indefinitely, they'll eventually be forced into a battle they cannot win."

"OPEN THE PORTAL!" Ellebar snapped, pointing her blade at him.

"I could have allowed you to go through with them," Bios said, "but I chose not to. You should thank me for saving your life. Take your ship home and assume control of the Wargonne for Councilman Conan—that's what you've always wished for, isn't it?"

"YOU TWISTED SCUM!" Lara hissed, shifting her stance to strike. "This is your last chance! Open the portal and bring them back, or I'll end you myself!"

He pictured his room at the Golden Mare, where Alina and

Cassia were likely awake, wondering about his whereabouts. It was unnecessary to revisit the Throatians so soon; the consequences of his actions required more time to unfold.

"Farewell for now," Bios said with a playful wave.

The captain cursed and swung her sword as he extended his arms and fell backward into the portal he'd manifested behind him. Now, he was gone, leaving Ellebar to fend for herself.

He'd let her live because she had been useful to him. Her fate was not yet sealed. It'd be intriguing to see if she'd try replacing Conan. She would sail with her remaining crew back to Wargonne or wherever she wished—he didn't care. Maybe she'd attempt to find Bios again and seek revenge for falling for his manipulations.

But that day was not about Captain Ellebar. Her soldiers would serve their purpose for Bios—three thousand reminders to the Throatians that they still needed him if they hoped to survive the war he'd bring against the Darian's later.

A few days later, Bios returned to the Temple of White. As always, the Son See'ers surrounded the trio of obelisks, their voices blending into a deep, rhythmic chant. He paused behind them for a moment, observing their red robes and white hoods. It wasn't until he paced along the outer perimeter that he noticed the flat golden masks beneath their veils, each engraved with symbols from the obelisks' markings. Their prayers echoed gratitude to Zann-Xia-Czul for protecting them during the recent Darian "attack" on their island.

Grimm stood at the front, nearest the stone pillars. The Throatian King knelt as the others did, his deep voice dominating the chamber. Despite Grimm's apparent devotion, Bios knew they couldn't waste time. He clapped his hands loudly, startling several of the Son See'ers in prayer.

"A timely victory!" he cried. "The Darians perished to your blades faster than the golden sun sets at day's end."

The battle at White Boar's Landing had lasted an hour. When the Darians charged onto the beach, the Throatians defeated them quickly, leaving none alive. Trapped between mountains and the sea, Captain Ellebar's soldiers had been easy targets. Even though the

Throatians won, they were alarmed because they had been caught off guard. The warning was clear: war could begin anytime.

Grimm rose from the ground, his towering figure revealing his annoyance at Bios's intrusion. "The timing of the ambush was too perfect," he said, his tone sharp. "I can't help but wonder if you had a hand in guiding them through the storm veil. If you did, I cannot understand why."

Bios smirked, his mind briefly considering whether Cereene had betrayed his small secret. But it didn't matter; the outcome was the same. The Throatians would conclude that Zann-Xia-Czul's wall protected them from the Darians, but not from himself.

"Your growing army needed a trial," he stated, "and your loyalty to me faltered. It's important for you to consider how your island can survive when the rest of the world comes with their blades. Our arrangement is the key to securing the future."

"I've done no such thing," Grimm growled, gesturing for Bios to follow him into a private chamber where his warriors couldn't overhear. The action confirmed Bios had indeed annoyed him.

They entered the dining hall of the Temple of White, a place where Throatian Elders conducted their daily tasks. Fortunately for Grimm, the room was empty.

"You held meetings with the Elders and made major decisions without my knowledge or opinion," Bios said. "How is that any different from plotting behind my back?"

The Throatian king scowled. "You come and go as you please and we can't communicate with you. The island is suffering from overpopulation, and there are no signs of Zann-Xia-Czul awakening. We had to speculate as we needed."

"You have your commands and my promises of more food," Bios reminded him. "Our largest raid yet will occur within the next moon."

"Why is Zann-Xia-Czul hibernating for so long?" Grimm pressed. "Is he even still alive, or have you betrayed him like you betray everyone else under your thumb?"

"Hold your tongue," Bios warned. "Trusting me is safer than trusting the ancient one. If he had his way, you and everybody on this island would die within the Loyalty Circles."

"The Loyalty Circles have never killed me," Grimm retorted.

"Not yet, but any misstep in a round could lead to disaster. Do not become the next Prince Thane. Remember, Grimm, until I achieve my goals, you and your people will remain under my command. Question nothing, and you will live long and with honor."

Bios had considered having Grimm killed if he strayed beyond his control, but Cereene, though less assertive, was not prepared to assume the role of Throatian queen. At least for the foreseeable future, Grimm would have to suffice.

"Let us lay waste to the Darian Kingdom," Grimm said. "Such a move would resolve most of our problems. Everyone is ready."

It wasn't yet time to bring chaos to the entire country—not until he'd learned what the People's Army and the Whisperers knew about the God Stones. If either group had valuable information, it was best to retrieve it before dismantling their country.

"Soon, the war will enter its next phase," Bios promised, "and we will spill more blood than from every Loyalty Circle combined."

33
KAINE - THE SHADOW'S EMBRACE

"You're wondering whether your mother used the God Stones, aren't you?" Kaine said, looking down at Lily von Stonewall's grave. The God Stones were within reach, but he couldn't reveal their location to Kira without King Ether's blessing.

If anything were to happen to Kira, Kaine would have to take responsibility and would be incapable of forgiving himself. He knew he had to trust the king's judgment that the stones would remain safe and hidden in Gale Village. Deep underground, their magic posed no threat and couldn't be found by anyone. Another day, only after consulting King Ether and Queen Blanche to confirm the prophecy's authenticity, he might return with the princess to retrieve them. For now, Kaine couldn't rid himself of the feeling that everything Orin had told them was accurate.

"No, it's not about whether she used them," Kira said. "Even if she had, it doesn't matter. The truth is... I'm selfish, Kaine."

"I disagree with you on that, my princess," he replied. "You're not selfish at all."

Kira shook her head firmly. "It's true—I don't know what to do!"

He understood the source of Kira's sadness—she longed for her mother's guidance, despite never having truly met her. Lily von Stonewall's death during childbirth left a void in the princess that Kaine couldn't fully grasp. Lydia had tried to fill this void, but now only three von Stonewall family members remained. Besides council members like Iris and Bridgette, whom Kira knew but wasn't close to, there were no other female mentors nearby for her to turn to or relate to.

"You can only do your best," Kaine advised. "And that's enough—don't pressure yourself beyond what is truly possible."

Kira continued staring down at the gravestone. "At the hot springs, everyone talked about the prophecy, about me saving the world. I said yes to please them but hadn't considered its meaning before agreeing. I've been faking my courage the whole time... I want to help, but I'm not sure I can."

Another tremor resonated from the distance, like many others they'd felt recently. Unlike their prior visit to the gravesite, the vibrations didn't startle them this time because they had grown accustomed to the smaller earthquakes.

"You should feel scared, even as you're being courageous," Kaine said, placing a comforting hand on her shoulder. "Courage without fear wouldn't be genuine. No one would expect you to do this without doubting yourself. In fact, Lydia felt the same way."

"She did?"

"After I saved your sister from the monster in the forest, she used the Memories Stone on me. We spoke of our deepest pains, regrets, and fears. It's clear to me now that she didn't have enough time to learn how to use the God Stones to their fullest potential. She knew it too; otherwise, she would have fought the Throatians. She used magical powers but didn't have time to master them."

"I only wish it hadn't cost my sister her life," Kira lamented.

He released her hand and stepped back. "Though our time together was brief, Lydia left a strong and lasting effect on me. I wish she were still here with us."

Lydia had shown him the hollowness within his own heart and its vulnerable state. As she had spoken to him that night in the graveyard, each of her words of truth had hit him like punches to the face, a flurry of reminders of what he'd lost and the choices that had ultimately led him to her. She'd exposed his wounds, forced him to confront every one of them, and then finally offered him solace—and that was how she had healed him.

"She was good at that," the princess said with a touch of admiration. "My sister taught me to be kind to everyone I meet, from the highest nobles to the poorest commoners. She had a remarkable ability to empathize with someone in just a few minutes and fully understand their feelings and values. I wish I could be more like her."

"It's true that Lydia was a great person, but you mustn't forget that you're your own self, too."

"I'm a princess, the younger sister of Xander, and maybe a person with magical blood. Those things describe me, but they aren't me. I'm not sure who I am anymore."

"Perhaps the better solution isn't to discover who you are, but rather, who you wish to become," Kaine said, "and that in itself will take an extraordinary effort. Only you have the right to choose your own identity."

"Only me—or perhaps the prophecy," Kira said. "Maybe I'll become a god-killer or a false goddess, as it foretells."

"Perhaps you will do those things, but what about afterward?"

"Afterward?" Kira asked, gazing at the majestic sight of the orange-crowned volcanoes in the distance. "I don't know the answer right now, but by that time, I'll probably fancy resting on a cozy bed somewhere."

He grinned at her. "If I'm still around after you're done, your highness, I'll buy you a drink. You'll have earned a beer or two, and you'll be old enough."

"I'd rather try some wine, please," Kira said with a faint laugh. "Beer tastes like somebody brewed their tea in an old shoe."

He glared at her. "And since when have you tried beer?" Though King Ether was fond of his darker drinks, his protective nature made it unlikely he'd allow his children to sample any.

"Whoops." Kira grinned, her cheeks burning the wine-red hue of the drink she'd requested. "Xander let me try once. He hoards a stash in his room, ordering the kitchen staff to bring more every few days—and keep quiet."

"Well now, I'll need to talk to him about that once we return to Serenity Keep," Kaine promised, "and also speak with the kitchen staff."

"It's not their fault," Kira said. "He goes around declaring everything he says as royal commands, and so the staff members have no choice but to listen to him."

"It's fair enough on his end, I guess—he is the prince and all. I will address this with him as well. He's been treating this journey as a leisurely rest instead of focusing on his swordsmanship."

"Kaine," the princess said suddenly. "I can't do it. I'm not going to learn how to use magic. Keep teaching me sword fighting."

He sat beside her on the grass; his arms wrapped around his knees. He wondered whether he should press for a reason or offer encouragement. Magic was a realm he knew little of, and his sword-training expertise didn't apply to what she needed to learn how to do.

"I know little of the God Stones," he said, "and I may not be useful to you on your journey. But while I'm with you, I'll protect you and do whatever I can to help you succeed."

Kira brushed her hair back from her eyes. "Father will forbid it. He'll say no to everything. After Lydia died, he had even considered locking Xander and me up in Serenity Keep forever. But Iris persuaded him against it."

Her story was unsurprising. After Lydia's wedding, the king retreated to the throne room, mourning and deciding whether to declare war on the Throatians. Naturally, he wanted Kira and Xander confined to Serenity Keep. No one knew if more Throatians remained among them to cause harm. Letting his children return to any sort of normalcy could be considered progress.

"You made it here. That's proof that he can see reason," Kaine replied.

Still, Kira's worry deepened. "But what if he still insists I shouldn't touch the God Stones—or worse, convinces me to obey him?"

"If the prophecy truly predicts the future," Kaine said, "then there's nothing any of us can do to stop you."

The next morning, they gathered inside Orin's home to discuss the elder's final strategy for approaching King Ether. As Kaine's eyes settled on the weathered armoire, he suspected it might be the last time he'd see it standing there. It felt like ages had passed since he'd last searched through it for a letter from Lily von Stonewall—only to find it was unexpectedly from Princess Zelia. That revelation had opened countless possibilities, but merely hiding the God Stones and leaving without understanding the prophecy would have been far easier. Yet it could also have been catastrophic. Everything must have happened for a reason.

Orin asked, "Shall we wait for the prince to arrive?" as he settled into his chair and offered them a tray of biscuits.

"Xander complained about an upset stomach this morning," Kaine said. "He'll be resting in bed for today. What about Celeste? Is she not coming?"

"There's no need," Orin said. "This meeting will be brief."

"What conclusion did you reach about the best way to approach the king?" Merdel asked.

"As you all know, the situation between Ether and me is delicate, and the proposal we have between Kira and him is equally so," Orin said. "I appreciate your patience this week as I considered everything. The best course of action, in my view, would be to send him a letter first."

"A letter?" Merdel exclaimed. "There aren't any birds here to deliver it. You must mean for us to bring it to him."

"To be delivered by the four of you, exactly," Orin clarified. He reached into his robe and pulled out two scrolls of paper. A plum-colored wax stamp with twin axes sealed one, and the other was unsealed.

Kira's fingers touched the intricate wax circle. "Two letters, Elder? Why?"

"The second one is Zelia's letter," Orin said. "A gesture of good faith. It wasn't easy for me to give this letter up, but I hope it will help ease the situation."

"Thank you, Orin," Kaine said. This would complete their mission to Gale Village, though it had grown into something far beyond what they could have imagined.

"It's intriguing that you've sealed your own letter," Merdel commented. "Would you care to share its contents?"

"After drafting what might have been a hundred letters, I settled on the simplest approach," the Elder said. "I admitted to being an ass over the years and expressed my desire to mend our friendship. I invited him to visit Gale Village to pay our respects at Lily's grave together."

"As honorable as that is," Kaine said, "what about the prophecy? I thought you planned to bring it up with him too."

"That I also intend," Orin said. "With Ether, it will take multiple attempts to get a response. Bombarding him with everything at once will only lead to refusal. The letters you'll deliver are meant to plant the idea that I'm starting to make amends. A few weeks after you leave, I'll go to Serenity Keep and meet him in person. This will show him I'm serious."

Merdel gave him an approving nod. "A well-thought-out strategy, Orin. You know a bit about diplomacy after all."

"Why don't you come with us?" Kira asked. "We're leaving tomorrow. Traveling together will keep you safer. Don't go alone later."

"I considered it, but waiting is the more sensible choice," Orin said. "I don't want Ether to think I've clouded your minds with my ideas and opinions. It's better that I keep my distance until he's open to the idea of Kira learning to use the God Stones."

"You have a valid point," Kaine said. "Still, Kira's concern for your safety is justified. Someone at your age shouldn't travel alone on such a long journey. Even if the path were shorter, the roads are fraught with bandits and wild animals."

"That's why I won't go directly to Last Hope," Orin said. "Instead, I'll head to the Leila Kingdom first. Blanche will provide me with a horse and a few escorts. I suggest you do the same."

"We've reached the same conclusion," Merdel said. "We planned to discuss Blanche's thoughts on the prophecy, so we'll stop by the Leila Kingdom on our way back. Are you sure you won't join us?"

"It's better for you to get home first and take things slowly with the king," Orin said. "Speak nothing of the prophecy to Ether until after I arrive at Serenity Keep. Once I've spoken with him, you can share your thoughts as we work toward our common goal."

Orin's plan was well thought out, and Kaine admired how willingly he took charge. Convincing Ether would require a delicate yet calculated approach. The king clearly understood the importance and danger of the God Stones. Perhaps he also knew that everything about them pointed to something greater and the evidence that Kira was destined to fulfill the prophecy. The question was how much debate and convincing it would take before he conceded to let his daughter learn to use the magic.

"Yesterday, when Kira and I went for a stroll, I told her that if the prophecy foretells the future, then none of us can stop her from fulfilling her destiny," Kaine said.

"Right you are," Merdel said. "I've always believed humans have free will and the responsibility to improve their lives, but recent events have challenged that belief. Perhaps there are other forces in this world beyond our influence."

"How poetic of you, councilman," Orin said. "I hope your

eloquence can convince the king as well—he's always been a bit of a—"

Suddenly, the shack's door burst open. Celeste emerged disheveled, as if she'd just fought off a bear. Her blouse sleeve was ripped, and a massive bruise darkened her forehead. Tears trickled down her chin, and she was shaking uncontrollably.

"He forced me," the Lucidian whimpered.

Kaine drew White Oath as he rose from his chair and glided past her toward the door. He moved beyond Celeste, expecting to confront her attacker, but outside, he found no sign of pursuit. The village appeared undisturbed, with no signs of a siege or wild beast attack. Someone had assaulted her and she'd barely escaped.

"Celeste! What's happened to you?" Orin exclaimed. When he tried to embrace her, she pushed him away, her terrified face still twisted in agony.

"I told him no," she said. "I said I couldn't do it for him. I refused to do it for him. But he..."

"Who, Celeste? Who hurt you? Describe them!" Merdel demanded.

Gasping for breath, she struggled to articulate any more words. Orin guided her to his chair, helping her sit. "One of you, find Sen," he commanded, addressing the crowded room. "Celeste is bleeding from her head!"

Kira ran toward the door, but Merdel held out his arm to block her. "We don't know if it's safe out there," he said. "Kaine should be the one who goes."

"Merdel's right," Kaine agreed, clutching White Oath tightly. "Stay here, everyone. I'll check Celeste's shack and the rest of the village for whoever hurt her."

A choked whisper escaped Celeste's lips, too soft for anyone to decipher. Orin leaned closer as he heard her try again.

"What did you just say?" Orin exclaimed so loudly that his face turned white.

"It's already been done," she cried. Tears streamed uncontrollably from her eyes as she murmured: "The prince."

Celeste's home held the aftermath of the chaotic event—crushed lanterns, strewn papers, and tangled twigs were scattered about the floor. Across the room, the prince lay on Celeste's bed, snoring softly with his arms folded across his chest. His steady breathing reassured Kaine that Xander was alive and only sleeping.

Orin swore in another language, likely Lucidian, then switched to his usual Common Tongue. "This complicates things," he said.

"Complicates things?" Kaine yelled. "Complicates things? Black Sands, Orin! That's all you have to say?"

Kira rushed to the bed, grabbing Xander by the shoulders. Despite his larger size, she shook him hard. "Xander, wake up! What happened?"

He slept on, unmoved by his sister's trembling, as Celeste stepped through the doorway. She stopped behind Orin, surveying the broken room. "I'm so sorry," she said. "He forced me. He made me do it."

Though Kaine already suspected the truth, it wasn't real until she spoke. White Oath trembled as Kaine's next words came.

"He forced you to do what?"

"He said he wanted tea," the Lucidian whimpered. "I let him in. We drank, and then he fell silent. He asked me to use my power. I refused, but he wouldn't take no for an answer. He turned violent… He held a knife to my throat, and I… I couldn't refuse." A sob escaped her lips. "I'm so sorry."

Anger, fear, and betrayal surged within Kaine. It couldn't be true. Xander wouldn't have done this. He was too strong to succumb to such senselessness. Celeste, a Lucidian known for power and magic, had overreacted and invented a story to hide her guilt. She staged the scene, injuring herself to make it look like a struggle. She was the one who'd attacked Xander—he wouldn't have hurt her!

However, the sight of the unconscious prince and the haunted look in Celeste's eyes made him question himself. The truth was… No, it didn't happen like she'd told it. There must have been something else!

"There's no proof," Kaine exclaimed, though his throat strained. "Xander couldn't have done this."

Celeste pointed to a velvet-bound book on the floor. "Look," she said, "he wrote it—on the loose sheet—it's what he wanted me to put in there."

"The prince wrote a letter?" Orin asked.

Kira laid the unconscious Xander onto the pillow and grabbed the piece of paper from where it waited. She read it quietly, but probably only got a quarter of the way down before she burst into more tears.

"Xander," she cried out to her brother. "How could you see us like that?"

Kaine rammed into Orin as he sprinted to catch the fainting princess. Gasping for air, he gently lowered the unconscious Kira to the floor and propped her against the bed. Once he was sure she was stable, he picked up the paper where she'd dropped it and read Xander's final words aloud for the room to hear:

My name is Xander von Stonewall, prince of the Darian Kingdom. My father is Ether von Stonewall, and my mother, Lily, passed away. I have a sister named Kira and an older sister, Lydia, who was killed by the Throatians.

I've wanted revenge for so long, but it's pointless. Nothing can bring anyone back. Kira has magic that might help defeat the Throatians, but I don't. She's better at everything than I am. Kaine will protect her.

They don't need me anymore. I'm tired of being a burden, and they're wasting their time trying to make me into something more than that. I want to start over and live a simpler, quieter life. I don't want to remember who I was or what I gave up. Everyone is precious to me, but this world takes without ever giving back.

I'm supposed to be the next king, and the king gets the final say, doesn't he? If that's the case, then why couldn't I change anything? My only worth is my crown, and I'm unworthy of it. To free everyone from their responsibilities to me, I renounce my claim to the throne and give my birthright to Kira instead.

I want to start over and not be involved with any of this. Please give me a simpler life, one where I can live without bearing the suffering of the world. I don't want to know who I was or what I've given up.

I'm sorry, everyone.

Please go on without me and don't dwell on what I've done.

Defeat the evils of the world without thinking of me or the shadow I've become.

"This is... all my fault," Kaine muttered, his heart pounding so hard he felt it in his head. "I've been such a fool."

He'd been so focused on Kira that he overlooked Xander. Though the prince had always been quiet, there must have been other signs of the pain he'd endured. He failed to see them. Why hadn't he noticed? There must have been hints, mannerisms, or behaviors Kaine could have recognized to stop Xander's suffering.

Why hadn't they seen it?

Why hadn't he seen it?

"The fault rests with no one," Orin offered with a gentle mumble. "It seems Xander wanted this... desperately."

It didn't matter whether the elder was right or wrong. The Xander they knew was gone.

"Why won't he wake up?" Kaine yelled.

Celeste glanced at the prince, her eyes red with sadness and regret. "It's normal to slip into a coma for hours—or even days. His mind is restarting by rebuilding what it can. I mentioned that some things will remain, but..."

The prince would have forgotten everyone and everything important in his life. Even if he eventually woke up, he wouldn't be the same person anymore. Xander was as good as dead, and Kaine had failed him.

Why hadn't he seen it coming?

"We're here," Merdel's voice rang through the shack as they entered. A second later, he realized what had transpired. "Wait, Xander and Kira are... Oh no! Sen, heal them! Hurry!"

The Grace Mage solemnly shook her head, having also deduced what had happened. "It doesn't work that way. I can't heal the mind."

Merdel paused in contemplation. "What's... what's happened here?"

"You have to try healing Xander!" Kaine pleaded to Sen. "Kira's okay—she's just unconscious."

"There's no point in trying," Orin said, glancing at Celeste with a frown. "What's done is done."

"I'll... I'll attempt it anyway," Sen said. She quietly crossed the room and hovered her hand over the prince's face. Her palm glowed purple, just as it had when she'd healed Kaine's arm.

"There must be a way to fix this," Kaine said. "What about the other Lucidians in the village? Can't they do anything? Can't any of you?"

Orin shook his head in disappointment. "There's no such way. Memory erasure is permanent—it can't be undone, not naturally or supernaturally."

"But is Sen's magic working?" Merdel asked. "We can't give up without trying. This could start another war!"

The Grace Mage was still on the bed, holding her glowing hand over the prince. "Unfortunately, there's not. I tried only because I didn't want you to think I don't care."

"Try harder," Kaine begged. "We can't let Xander..." He couldn't even finish his sentence.

"I'm sorry, but there's nothing we can do," Sen affirmed. "This isn't the first time we've faced this situation. What Celeste did cannot be undone."

Sen approached Celeste and healed her head, face, and wrists. Like Kaine's broken arm, her physical injuries would heal completely. However, she would carry a new burden: the aftermath of what Xander had caused. This was likely the first time someone had forced her to use her powers against her will in a situation of life and death. She would be bound by the memories and guilt of what had happened for the rest of her life.

The truth would have been easier to accept if Celeste and Sen had been oppressors, waiting to attack the prince when vulnerable and alone. If only they were soldiers posing as refugees, tricking Kaine and the others into lowering their guard. Having an enemy to blame for what happened to Xander would have made the rest easier to bear.

The problem was there was no villain involved except the darkness within the prince himself. Blaming Celeste for wiping Xander's memory—if self-defense was her only option—was unreasonable, but what pierced Kaine's heart was that Xander had forced her to use her magic. He'd wanted this.

Meanwhile, Merdel picked up the letter from the floor and read it. "Black Sands... Perhaps it wasn't a good idea to bring him to his mother's grave so soon after what happened to Lydia. Maybe we didn't think enough about that. But now... there's no coming back from this, is there?"

"There isn't," Celeste and Orin said in unison.

"But... how can we go forward from here?" Kaine asked. Prince Xander was gone, and King Ether would likely have them all beheaded for failing to protect him.

"Our situation just became a lot more delicate," Merdel concluded. "We should proceed to the Leila Kingdom as planned. We must consult the queen about the situation and the other matters. Meanwhile, Xander can rest until we figure out what to do next."

"I can't help him restore his memory, but I can help him start anew," Celeste said. "I've always counseled those who've used my magic to help them reconnect with—"

"That's not going to work," Kaine interrupted. "Respectfully, Celeste, you're better off hiding somewhere farther from Last Hope than Gale Village. Since you didn't mean for this to happen, I can't blame you, but King Ether won't see it the same way. Lucidians hiding in the Darian Kingdom at the town where his late wife is buried—and they erased his son's mind? He'll send his army against you for this."

King Ether had failed to control himself with the Throatian King Harkbin and killed him despite agreeing to spare his life. What would he do to Celeste, Orin, and everyone else in Gale Village? What would losing another of his children cause him to do next?

"Let's not jump to conclusions," Orin said. "We need to control the situation somehow. For now, perhaps we can make up a small lie."

"We can't cover this up!" Merdel urged.

"A lie isn't going to fix this!" Kaine added, looking down at Kira, who was still unconscious against the bed.

Orin took a deep breath before sharing his idea. "I don't enjoy this any more than you do," he said, "but we must handle this—we must control the situation. While traveling home, a Shadowstone rock fell from above and struck the prince in the head. That accident can explain his loss of memory. Additionally, the letter he wrote should be burned, never to be spoken of again. Ether will have no choice but to believe our story, since there won't be any evidence to contradict it."

When Xander woke up, he wouldn't remember forcing Celeste to erase his memories. He'd be like a sponge, absorbing whatever ideas or stories others told him. Even Xander would have to believe the lie. But it wasn't right. None of it was.

"I can't go along with this," Kaine said. "We'd be lying to the king about what happened to Xander. The king has the right to know what happened to his son."

"Were there any other ways this situation could have gone?" Merdel mused. "Yes, but Celeste used her magic to erase the prince's mind. We can't change that, but we can shape future events. Handing Celeste over to King Ether won't solve our problems, nor will revealing the truth to Ether. To him, her actions would be inexcusable. Though I normally oppose altering the truth, it might be easier for him to cope if he believes it was an accident. Orin is right —Ether shouldn't know what really happened. No good will come of it."

Merdel's conclusion surprised Kaine, and he could sense Merdel's political skills were at play to help preserve the various relationships involved.

"But shouldn't the king know Xander wanted this?" Kaine asked the room.

"It's about empathy," Celeste muttered. "Orin's suggestion is more compassionate. It's less painful to accept that a random tragedy happened to his son than to acknowledge that Xander… that I was forced to do this to him. No father would want to face the truth that their son committed such a sin."

Kaine stared at the letter clutched in Merdel's hand. It was irrefutable proof that the prince had carefully planned everything in advance, absolving Celeste of blame. Destroying the letter would eliminate Celeste's sole protection if Ether ever discovered the truth. Burning Xander's final words would also compel the six present—including Kira—to guard the secret of his actions forever. Yet one question remained: could they trust themselves to remain silent?

Orin, Celeste, and Sen would need to hide their truths to safeguard themselves and the Lucidians of Gale Village. Merdel would stay quiet to avoid a political disaster and simplify their already complex situation. Kira, though—could she bear to conceal the truth behind her brother's fall? Could she hide such a life-changing event from her father? Again, they were placing another burden on her shoulders. When the princess awoke, how would she feel about deceiving her family?

"If Kira agrees with your plan, I will too," Kaine said. "Xander kept his pain hidden so deeply that none of us noticed, despite Celeste's ability to sense trauma. We must ensure that something like this never happens again. Likewise, we must give Xander a chance for a happier life."

34

THANE - THE ONE AND THE SAME

Hours later, in the bleak cold of the night, Thane and Zeere rose from their bedrolls and rekindled a lantern from their campfire's embers. They moved quietly along the forest path, leaving the keeper's shack behind, toward where the Whisperers rested inside their trees.

The trail was unfamiliar to Thane in the dim light, so Zeere led the way through the winding trees. Silence surrounded them, though their boots squished softly against the ground. They paused more than once to listen for movement while Thane held his sword in one hand and his light in the other, alert for threats.

"We're here now, I think," Zeere whispered. "I hope they don't mind our waking them."

Thane raised his lantern, illuminating their success. Before them stood a circle of five trees, each with a Whisperer tied to its trunk, sleeping.

"Good evening," Thane announced into the clearing, expecting a mental rebuke from Mythreya for approaching without the keeper. Instead, there was only silence.

"Maybe they don't hear us because they are in deep meditation instead of sleeping?" Zeere suggested, his voice wavering.

Thane tried once more. "Good evening, Whisperers." His voice was firmer this time yet held calm.

Still, there was no response. The two of them ventured closer to where Mythreya rested and gazed up at her. The night was too dark to see her face clearly, so Thane suggested they retrieve the keeper's ladder for a better view.

Zeere climbed, clutching the lantern in one hand and nudging the side of Mythreya's robe with the other. "This feels very... wrong."

A pair of red eyes opened and peered down at him, and Zeere nearly fell off the ladder in shock.

"We're sorry to wake you," he said, "but we have some questions to ask."

Mythreya's eyes widened, and her shrouded head looked over Zeere and then Thane. Yet she remained silent.

"Um, Thane," Zeere breathed. "You should come up here. There's something you need to see for yourself."

"What is it?" he asked, sensing that whatever Zeere had noticed was likely significant.

"Let me come down, then you can climb up with the lantern."

They swapped places on the ladder. As Thane ascended, his freezing hands gripped the metal handle, causing the light to flicker across Mythreya's purple-hued robes. He saw nothing extraordinary about the leader of the Whisperers—Mythreya remained limbless, jawless, and cloaked in fabric. The leader of the Whisperers was as terrifying, sad, and mysterious as ever.

Her appearance was unsettling, not only because she had traded away her body but for the desperation and desires that had driven her to such extremes. Thane believed Mythreya had partially overcome the barriers in that way—she'd given up most of her physical form to empower her mind.

But as Thane peered into Mythreya's red eyes, everything he knew about the Whisperer came crashing down. Her irises glowed crimson, but behind them lurked a greater darkness—a resignation and acceptance of defeat that Thane recognized from the Loyalty Circles when an opponent was too wounded to fight on and had accepted death was the only way forward.

Zeere had seen the same hopelessness in Mythreya's eyes, a reflection of his own wartime experiences. What could have caused such a rapid change?

"Perhaps it's because Mythreya is sad?" Thane guessed aloud, glancing around to see four more pairs of red eyes watching him from the other trees. None of the other Whisperers responded.

"Something's changed since yesterday," Zeere insisted. "I just don't know what."

Thane had an idea: even though Mythreya couldn't use her magic, there were alternative ways to interact—perhaps more primitive, but still effective.

"Since you can't use your magic, we'll communicate differently," Thane said, addressing the glowing red eyes. "I'll ask you questions —nod if the answer is yes, shake your head if it's no."

Mythreya responded with a silent nod, signaling her understanding, and Thane continued.

"Did something bad happen to you?"

A nod came.

"And it took away your magic?"

The woman hesitated before shaking her head. Thane hadn't expected this response, and now the situation was even more confusing.

"Wait," Zeere called from the base of the tree. "I have a question: was what you were teaching me even magic to begin with?"

Mythreya shook her head, prompting Thane to sigh in relief on Zeere's behalf. Perhaps Mythreya didn't trust Zeere fully yet, or maybe she preferred to wait until Thane completed his translation work before disclosing anything significant. Thankfully, yes-or-no questions minimized the chance of misunderstandings.

However, a new possibility suddenly occurred to Thane, compelling him to pose a straightforward but revealing question.

"Do you actually have magical powers?" Thane demanded, cutting off Zeere before he could speak again.

Mythreya shook her head once more, leaving Thane even more bewildered. If Mythreya hadn't been using magic, then how had she spoken directly into their minds? Was it merely the wind playing tricks, or was someone else manipulating their senses?

"It can't be," Zeere muttered, cursing in Lucidian. "You've been speaking into our minds since we entered the forest! If that wasn't magic, then what was it?"

Mythreya shook her head again, this time more forcefully. Thane sensed that her answer was more than just a simple no.

"Enough with the lies," Zeere yelled up at them. "We had an agreement: you'd explain how you communicate within our minds, and I'd learn to use magic against the Enclave. Put your faith in—"

"That's enough, Zeere," Thane exclaimed. His tone hid a sense of growing empathy for his friend. "You're not going to gain knowledge from them because they possess nothing."

"But they must have it!"

"I'm telling the truth," Thane insisted. "I might have figured out what happened here and why Mythreya no longer speaks to us through our minds."

"And what is it?" Zeere snapped.

If Thane's hunch was correct, their mission had been over even before they arrived. He had warned Zeere that if the premise of faith was based on a lie, everything else following it would be meaningless and futile. Now, it seemed his prediction had come to reality. The Whisperers before them had no magic, rendering their entire journey pointless.

Thane peered into the ghostly red eyes in front of him and asked his final question:

"Are you truly Mythreya Nox? Yes or no?"

The hooded figure in the tree shook her head again, this time, more defiant and insistent than ever.

"But if you're not Mythreya, then which of you is she?" Zeere said.

Thane took his first step down the ladder. "None of these hooded figures in the trees is Mythreya—or even a Whisperer. In a way, they are all the same person. That means there's only one left who could be Mythreya."

"But if that's true," Zeere said, confusion and fear growing in his voice as he realized Thane's conclusion, "then who are these people? Why are they here?"

"We'll have to ask the real Mythreya ourselves."

THE FOREST GREW DARKER AS THEY TRUDGED BACK TOWARD THEIR camp, the air colder now, enveloped in a thin fog that clung to the ground and their waists. Despite the chill, Thane found it easier to breathe, as if the lingering shock of their discovery had relieved pressure from his chest. He couldn't decide if it was more terrifying that the limbless people in the trees were there of their own volition or if the keeper had forced them into that horrific state. The image of those nearly lifeless bodies, tied by their ropes, still haunted him.

"Thane," Zeere muttered, his voice trembling from the same revelations. "I'm sorry about everything."

"There's nothing to apologize for," he replied, his eyes fixed on the ground as they walked. "We both sensed something was wrong with this place, but neither of us could define it. What happened to those people in the trees was horrid."

"My desire for power and revenge blinded me," Zeere admitted with a tone dulled by guilt. "Had I been as careful as you, I would have noticed sooner that the keeper was the one speaking into my mind and that the individuals in the robes were not as they seemed."

Thane recognized how faith's allure and desperation for progress could cause someone to ignore clear signs of deception. The truth was, they had both fallen victim to the lies.

"There has to be more to this than what we've seen so far," he said hopefully. "A meaning for it all. Maybe the people in the trees were there because of their own actions—criminals or individuals who committed terrible sins. That might make it less shocking. We must force the answers out of Mythreya, even though she lacks a tongue."

"Perhaps it's better to do nothing," Zeere said. "We could pretend we saw nothing tonight and wait for her to give you the horn before doing anything else. I suspect confronting Mythreya directly could leave us bound to the trees as well."

Physically, Thane and Zeere could easily overpower the keeper, but it wasn't unreasonable for them to still consider her dangerous. Mythreya, if she had magic, might be more powerful than the Hierophant, if she hadn't already revealed the full extent of her abilities. Whatever had happened to the people in the trees—and whether Mythreya had harmed them and why—was yet to be determined.

"Confronting her doesn't have to involve violence," Thane said, "but it would be naive to think otherwise. Are you prepared if she refuses to cooperate?"

Zeere stopped and turned to face him for the first time since they'd left the circle of trees. "The situation has already moved beyond friendly cooperation. Her deceit and evasiveness make it clear she never intended to negotiate with us; she only wanted to exploit your translation skills. If we're going to capture her, we must catch her off guard. Otherwise, she'll have too many chances to outwit or overpower us. Don't you agree?"

"Are you suggesting we kill her while she sleeps?" Thane asked. "If she dies, then we'll never uncover the answers to what she was doing—or why."

"I'm proposing we hold our blades to her throat," the Null Mage replied. "There's no need to end her—just keep her from attacking us. It depends on her answers what will come next."

"I don't like where this is going," Thane said, "but for the sake of those bound to the trees, we must continue—for them."

A few minutes later, they arrived back at their camp and the keeper's shack. The things they had witnessed had turned what once felt like a safe haven inside the forest into a place poisoned with corruption and uncertainty. Thane and Zeere set down their lanterns, drew their blades, and cautiously approached the keeper's home. Hearing only the woman's labored, congested breathing from within, Thane opened the door and carefully navigated around the scattered wooden crates in the dim glow of two flickering candles on a table.

Thane pointed his sword low, its tip aimed at the floor across the room where the woman—likely the true Mythreya—slept soundly beneath a heap of blankets. Her chest gently rose and fell with each quiet breath.

"Keeper," Thane whispered, trying not to startle her while keeping his sword aimed forward. "We need to talk."

She stirred but didn't wake. Appearing to sense their presence, the keeper sat up slowly, her eyes adjusting to the dim light. She looked momentarily confused before a quiet smile spread across her face.

"You're truly Mythreya Nox, aren't you?" Zeere accused.

Her jaw lowered slightly, reminding them of her missing tongue. "SO, YOU WENT INTO THE FOREST WITHOUT ME. YOU DISOBEYED."

"The people tied to the trees," Thane said, "did you… did you do that to them?"

"YOU BOTH ALREADY KNEW THAT TRUTH BUT DIDN'T WANT TO ADMIT IT. LIKE THE OTHERS BEFORE YOU, YOU DIDN'T RESPECT THE COST OF ENLIGHTENMENT. YOU WERE UNWILLING TO SACRIFICE AND, JUST LIKE THE OTHERS, YOU HAVE FAILED."

Zeere stammered as he pressed the tip of his sword against the edge of the blankets. "Enough with the lies! The Enclave rejected you because of your experiments. Now it's clear—those people were nothing but disposable to you! You used them! You… you used them until they were broken…"

"ONE MUST WEAKEN THEIR BODY AND MIND TO STRENGTHEN THEIR SOUL," Mythreya declared once again.

"THE SOUL IS WHERE GREATER MAGIC LIVES WITHIN US. THOSE CONNECTED TO THE TREES WAVER BETWEEN PHYSICAL DEATH AND MADNESS. THIS IS THE COST OF ENLIGHTENMENT, BUT THEY HAVE GAINED THE STRONGEST OF SOULS. I HAVE LEARNED MUCH FROM THEM. YOU TOO, CAN HAVE POWER WITHOUT SURRENDERING YOUR PHYSICAL FORM."

She was trying to manipulate Zeere's emotions one last time. If Mythreya didn't soon reveal useful information, Thane would have no choice but to end the conversation.

"You sacrificed others to satisfy your own ambitions," Zeere growled. "You're no better than the Enclave. Disgusting!"

The Lucidian suddenly stumbled and gagged at the same time a sharp pain pushed Thane backward from Mythreya's bedroll. The sudden sensation was cold like a knife's edge, yet too thin and focused, more similar to an insect's bite. Thane then realized someone had shot him with what could have been the tiniest arrow.

"Ruik Czharr," the Throatian Prince cursed in his native tongue as he ripped the dart from his chest. "Wavering near madness is an understatement."

Now that Mythreya had attacked them first, Thane plunged his blade forward as Zeere thudded down beside him. Mythreya tried to retreat as she pushed herself across the floor, but she was too slow. Thane's sword entered her chest faster than the cruel woman could react or protest. As he completed his attack, a terrifying ringing pulsated through Thane's ears, and it wasn't clear if it was Mythreya's scream, a side effect of the poison, or both.

The Whisperers and Mythreya were one and the same, and the world was undoubtedly better without her cruelty. Yet, there was no time to reflect on what had just transpired. Thane's vision blurred as the dim interior of the shack dissolved into shifting, indistinct shapes. He couldn't tell if he was dying, but if that was his fate, he hoped Cereene would somehow discover that he had lived a little longer than when they'd last met—and that he had tried to do some good and make up for the atrocities his family had committed against Lydia von Stonewall and her family.

He hoped Cereene would understand that she could build a better life without him. So much remained unsaid between them, but their lives had danced in chaos, which had eliminated any chance for a proper conversation since before he'd sailed to Yaenia. Back then, he'd been different—weak-willed, short-sighted, carrying only faint doubts about their religion. If only she could see him now, forging his own path, making his own decisions. He was free—free from Zann-Xia-Czul's and Bios Auras's control—and he wished that someday, like him, Cereene would be free of them too.

It wasn't the end he had imagined. His body felt numb and clammy, as though he had been submerged in freezing water, but the rough floor beneath him anchored his consciousness. Sunlight streamed through the cracks in the shack's walls, prompting Thane to open his eyes.

Bloodied blankets lay scattered near where he had collapsed, but Zeere and Mythreya were nowhere in sight. Were either of them still alive, and if so, who had survived? Thane's mind was foggy, as if he'd been feverish for days, yet he clearly remembered stabbing Mythreya. Had it even been real, or just a mad dream?

He struggled to rise, but his legs buckled under him and he collapsed to the floor again with a thud. The poison must still be flowing through his veins. Gathering his strength, he pushed himself up, using the wall for support as he staggered toward the entryway.

Outside, Zeere sat beside the campfire, carefully holding a small tree branch over the flames.

"We survived," Thane croaked, his voice raspy from dehydration.

Zeere nodded, his eyes visible through the slits in his bandages. "Indeed. We survived."

Thane took a seat beside him, watching the smoke rise toward the sky. "How long has it been? Where is Mythreya?"

"I've been awake for two days," Zeere said. "The darts were coated with Death's Whisper—a potent sleeping poison. That's likely how she managed to capture and hang the others in the trees. As for Mythreya, well, she's dead. I moved her body far from here. The forest will claim her and punish her for what she's done."

"What she did was unnatural," Thane said. "It's fitting to let nature decide what happens next. Have you checked on the others? They must have been left neglected for a while now."

"I've tended to them," Zeere said, "and it's made me reconsider everything."

He began unwrapping the bandages from around his head. For

the first time, Zeere revealed his face—burned, healed, and scarred, yet bearing the essence of the person he once was. The leathery, pinkish-red skin stood as proof of the suffering he had endured. His physical scars, much like his inner ones, came from years ago, but he still carried them with him.

"This is who I truly am," Zeere said quietly. "Mythreya and I shared a thirst for knowledge and power, and it drove us to do terrible things—her against innocent people, and me against myself. The Scarlet Mage and Grace Mage carried out the act for me, but it was my choice."

"The two of you weren't the same," Thane replied. "Shared interests and goals don't necessarily lead to the same choices or outcomes."

"Still, you were right all along," Zeere continued. "If we sacrifice too much of ourselves, what else remains?"

The thought ate at Thane. What had he given up? Had he sacrificed everything or nothing at all—and why couldn't he tell the difference? He'd journeyed so far from his Throatian homeland, but for what purpose? Was Cereene even still alive? Did the dragon horn Somnius had sent him to retrieve truly exist? Now that Mythreya's deception had been exposed, had any part of their quest held real value? Perhaps Zeere had grown from uncovering the lies, but at best, everything was bittersweet.

"I honestly don't know what this means," Thane said. "Still, thank you for trusting me enough to venture into the forest that night. Who knows how long it would have otherwise taken us to uncover the truth about Mythreya and the people in the trees?"

"About those poor victims," Zeere said. "I went back to speak with them while you slept from the poison. The conversation was limited, but we agreed that setting them free was the best course of action. Now they're buried, and their souls are finally at peace."

Thane recognized a mercy kill when he saw one—many had faced such fates in the Loyalty Circles in his homeland. Zeere's return to aid those trapped by Mythreya was an honorable act. At a minimum, the victims in the trees had chosen their ending.

"They didn't deserve what happened to them," Thane said. "But they didn't deserve to live and suffer that way either. What you did was exactly what they needed."

"The choice was difficult," Zeere replied, "and I wasn't sure if it was right until it was over. You missed a lot of deliberation during the past two days."

"Deliberation can be both a luxury and a curse," Thane concluded. "After everything we've faced—from the guards at Sky Tower Coast, to the Savager Mage, to the Hierophant and her people, and now Mythreya—we're just lucky to be alive."

STILL DETERMINED TO UNCOVER THE DRAGON HORN, THANE returned to Mythreya's shack and resumed his search through investigating the untranslated scrolls. Driven by his obsessive curiosity, he knew he would have to read every scroll to find the key to his quest. With no need to translate them into the Common Tongue, the task would proceed faster, though it would be no less tedious.

Thane opened the crate he'd been working on and pulled out a scroll, spreading it out on Mythreya's wooden table. The Throatian script was as readable as ever, but the content as mundane as the rest. He carefully reviewed each message but came across nothing of value and no mentions of the dragon horn.

As he moved on to the next scroll, his fingers grew stiff from the evening chill now seeping through the thin walls of the shack. He found detailed observations of moon phases, but again, no hint of a dragon horn. Thane's frustration grew as he pushed it aside, knowing persistence was his only hope. With any luck, he would find something—anything—that could lead him closer to his goal.

He worked through every scroll in the crates but achieved nothing. As time went on, he began putting more of his hopes in Zeere, who had spent the past few days searching the surrounding forest and valley for hidden caches or caves where Mythreya might have hidden more items besides in her home.

"There's nothing more out there," Zeere lamented, returning from another hike. "I'm beginning to believe we were deceived on this, just like everything else. Maybe she planned on poisoning us with Death's Whisper the moment you finished translating her cryptic scrolls."

Though his eyes were as red as they were dry, Thane looked at him with doubt. "I can't accept Somnius would send me here to find it if it wasn't real. The dragon horn must be close by."

Zeere sighed as he took a seat and helped himself to some of the bread on the nearby table. "I hope you're right," he replied. "But we've already searched through everything obvious. What more can we do?"

They had checked every surface but hadn't attempted to pry anything open. Given they planned to abandon the shack soon, there was no harm in making their search a bit more destructive. Thane pointed downward. "We need to look inside the walls or under the floorboards—there might be something hidden there."

Zeere nodded. "Alright, let's try it," he said. "If it's not here, maybe she moved it farther away."

Each board was old and water-damaged, with rusted iron nails confirming its age. Thane pried at the sides with one of Mythreya's shovels, trying to loosen a plank. It took several seconds of effort, but he managed to wedge it between the edges and lift the first board free with a resounding crack. He set it aside and continued working on the next.

After what felt like hours of aimless prying, Thane, now covered in sweat, noticed something unusual about one of the boards—the nails were loose and easy to pull out, as if they'd been removed and replaced many times before. With a forceful tug, the board gave way, revealing another layer of wood underneath it.

"I've found something," he exclaimed, wiggling the shovel beneath the next floorboard.

Zeere hurried over and peered down at the new set of boards. "A secret compartment?" he wondered. "This could be it."

Thane removed the first layer of floorboards, revealing a hidden trapdoor beneath. With Zeere's help, he lifted it, uncovering a dark, deep hole that descended into shadow.

"Let's see how far this goes," Thane said, retrieving their lantern from the camp. He lit it and the flickering flame cast light on the natural dirt walls lining the shaft.

Zeere nodded, his eyes narrowing with caution as he examined the opening. "Be careful. It wouldn't surprise me if Mythreya left some traps down there."

Thane attached the lantern to his belt and began his descent, the colder air brushing against his body as he moved down the rickety ladder. Each creaking step made him wonder how Mythreya had managed this descent in recent years—everything seemed on the verge of collapse.

The ladder ended where solid ground met Thane's boots. He stood on squishy, muddy ground at the base of the shaft, his lantern casting shadows over the damp walls around him. The air was noticeably damper, and the low ceilings made it harder to breathe.

Looking up, Thane saw Zeere peering down from fifteen feet above. "It's safe," he called out. "Come on down."

Soon, the Null Mage joined him on the ground after descending cautiously down the ladder. Once they were both settled, they took a moment to survey their surroundings.

The cave was smaller than Thane had expected—only slightly larger than the shack above. Long white rocks lined its walls along the edges, creating an unnatural pattern that was eerie yet mesmerizing. Though the stones glowed faintly in the lantern's light, Thane sensed they were not simply decorative.

"What are these?" Zeere asked, reaching out to touch one of the rocks. His fingers brushed the surface and the stone shimmered faintly under his touch. "It's smooth, almost like glass."

"I've seen nothing like them," Thane replied as he moved closer and his lantern illuminated another section of the wall. "They appear to be crystals. Thin, long ones."

They stepped across the uneven floor, exploring further into the basement. The place was clearly meant to keep something hidden, and Thane hoped the dragon horn waited somewhere inside.

"More lanterns," Zeere announced, approaching the table. He used the flame from Thane's lantern and lit one for himself, illuminating the room better.

More crates were ahead, and Thane chose one at random and opened it. The text inside the first scroll he read was longer, more detailed, and far more shocking than anything he had read from Mythreya before:

Fez-Kor-Czun has fallen, and his body ravaged by human heretics. Axhetharr-Cai-Mir and Zann-Xia-Czul are both missing. I do not know where they have gone or whether they still survive. I will return south at the next moon to search for them.

Thane's voice trembled as he read the text aloud, suddenly realizing the full implications of his translation work. The messages exchanged among the dragons were far more numerous than he had previously understood. Mythreya's real motive for having Thane translate simple scrolls was to use them as a foundation for creating her own translation book.

"All this time, Mythreya never intended to teach us magic or reveal any secrets. She was just using us to speed up her learning of Dragon Tongue."

Zeere's expression shifted from curiosity to shock. "So, all along… she wasn't only a crazed, immoral monster who was obsessed with magic. She was trying to uncover the secrets of the dragons themselves?"

"It might have been both," Thane concluded. "These scrolls, which she kept hidden from us, must have contained something valuable—she suspected as much, at least."

"Wait a minute," Zeere said. "I might know what it is."

The Null Mage carried his lantern further into the room, systematically opening each crate. Inside, he discovered scrolls, random sets of clothing, jewelry, and ingredients for making medicine. Finally, upon opening a crate near the back, he smiled.

"What are you looking for?" Thane asked, wading through scattered crate lids to join him.

"I knew it," Zeere said. "I just knew it."

Thane approached where Zeere had stopped his searching. Inside the box rested a small pile of rocks, transparent and milky white. Each stone was irregularly shaped but looked polished based on how much they seemed to reflect the lantern's light.

"Do you remember the stones you collected from the Savager Mage back in the Lowland Graves?" Zeere asked. "These are the ones Mythreya pulled from the ribs of those she hung from the trees. The people she experimented on were Lucidians—perhaps even the same ones who were supposed to execute her."

Thane shook his head. "That can't be right," he said. "The amethysts you held were reddish, not white like pearls."

"There could be many reasons they'd be a different color," Zeere insisted. "Perhaps their type, age, or quality."

"Maybe so, but consider the stone's color," Thane said, pulling a larger amethyst from the crate and cupping it in his hand. The gem was as dense and heavy as those he'd discovered before. "It is white, not red."

"Do you think white stones are less valuable than red?"

Thane carefully examined the amethyst, confirming his suspicions, then walked over to the nearest wall where the long white crystals ran along the surface. He held the stone up next to one and moved his lantern closer.

"It doesn't matter how much gold they're worth. Do you see it now? The stones from inside the Lucidian's bodies are the same material as what's lodged into the surfaces here!"

"You're right," Zeere muttered, deep in thought. "But if Mythreya took the stones from the basement wall, she was studying them or found them relevant to her research. But about the scrolls you've been translating... Could it be we're not in a cave at all, but—"

"Mythreya built her shack over a dragon's grave," Thane concluded. "This basement is the stomach. The white crystals lining the walls are its bones."

Zeere's eyes circled the cavern, as though seeing it for the first time. "If that's true, that means there's a connection between dragons and Lucidians. I can't believe it. Mythreya has to have a notebook around here somewhere with more hints about what she was working on. I almost wish we hadn't killed her now—she was clearly years into her research. I only wonder how close she was to finding what she wanted."

"Her knowledge came at a price that she didn't pay," Thane said, thinking of the lives Mythreya had stolen along the way.

"Be that as it may," Zeere said, "we should search this place more thoroughly. Everything we need to know about magic and the dragon horn might be in this room—or rather, this dragon's stomach."

They stood in silence for a minute, absorbing the implications of their discovery. The ground beneath their feet was part of an ancient dragon, and Mythreya, as evil as she had been, had been both wise and dedicated in understanding it all.

After a moment of reflection, Thane spoke up. "We should stay here as long as needed to investigate. If anything remains to help us find the horn or understand more about magic or dragons, it will be here."

He returned to the front of the cave and pored over Mythreya's scrolls with reignited determination. Mythreya, driven mad, had given up her morality for this knowledge, yet here Thane stood, sifting through the remnants of the late woman's obsession. They were so close to finding the horn; he needed to find deeper meanings behind the countless scrolls. With no way to distinguish the valuable ones, Thane would have to read them all.

The air in the dragon's stomach smelled musty, as though the ancient creature itself disapproved of their intrusion. Or perhaps it was merely the tension settling into Thane's own gut—a physical manifestation of the unease growing within him. Mythreya's experiments on the people of the trees must have had some greater reason or purpose. What could she have learned that led her down such a dark path? Dragons, magic, and Lucidians were all connected somehow, but what was the commonality?

Whatever the truth was, this creature had rested in undisturbed silence for years—until Mythreya's greed robbed it of its peace. Now, its legacy would carry Thane into a future he could not yet imagine. Would the scrolls and their contents be a blessing or a burden, and where had they come from? Had Somnius known what they would find?

What would come next?

35
KAINE - THE OATH'S MERCY

As the discussion about Xander's actions in Celeste's shack drew to a close, Kira stirred, gradually regaining consciousness. The room fell silent and all eyes turned to her. As delicately as he could, Kaine recounted the events she had missed since fainting; he wished he had some water to drink to soothe his dry throat. The princess remained frozen in place as he spoke, absorbing the news about her brother, and Kaine feared she might pass out again. As he finished, she barely acknowledged anything he said before retreating outside.

"I'm... I need to go for a walk. Alone."

Kaine started to follow but paused at her unexpected refusal of his company. He looked to the others for guidance, but Merdel and Orin shrugged, and Sen gently shook her head. Celeste, lost in thought over Xander, didn't notice his silent question about whether to follow, anyway.

"Maybe we all need some fresh air," Orin finally suggested. "Let's give the princess some space to... process what happened to her brother."

They left Xander under Sen's watchful eye, and each went their separate way into the village, collecting themselves. Instead of wandering like the others, Kaine returned to his shack and examined the bed where Xander had slept the night before. He sat down, the bed frame creaking as if it might collapse under the weight of his thoughts.

For most of the week, Xander had spent his days resting on that mattress, though he was likely also contemplating the meaning and condition of his life. If only they had talked it over, Kaine might have convinced the prince not to go through with his plan.

Faced with his troubles, what made the prince conclude that forgetting his past was the only way to free himself from suffering? Did their talks about the prophecy hold the most weight in Xander's descent into hopelessness? Everyone felt the impact of recent events and Kira's potential involvement, but Kaine hadn't noticed Xander's silent cries or the desperation that led him to make such a drastic decision.

The prince's choice must have been impulsive. They'd only discovered Celeste's ability when the Lucidian offered to erase Kaine's memory. He tried to recall whether Xander had shown any interest in having Celeste perform her magic on him that night. Back then, their conversation seemed minor and insignificant. Kaine attempted to remember what Xander might have said, searching for any clues he might have overlooked.

The conversations he'd had with Xander were blurry—Kaine hadn't paid enough attention at the time, and now he couldn't recall the truth among all the ways his imagination told him their talks might have happened. In the end, Kaine couldn't determine whether it had been his fault for not noticing what Xander intended to do or if Xander had kept his thoughts too close.

Now, however, the prince could be considered dead. The young boy they'd known had been erased, leaving behind only a living shell. Xander's chest slowly rose and fell in a somber rhythm. Nothing else they knew about him remained.

A faint noise from the shack's other end pulled Kaine from his introspection. Muffled footsteps drew close to the door, and as it creaked open, it revealed a figure who had become all too familiar.

Celeste.

She stepped into the room with her mysterious and radiant aura dimmed. Her wrinkled face, though composed, bore the darkness of recently shed tears. She hesitated, approached the table, and chose a chair. As she sat beside Kaine, her demeanor reinforced that erasing Xander's memory had been against her will.

"Again, I'm so sorry," she whispered, her voice breaking from the weight of what they both already knew.

Kaine looked at her, torn between frustration and understanding. Though Celeste had cast the magic, she'd remember what

Xander had done for the rest of her life. After what seemed like an eternity, Kaine nodded subtly, his face releasing tension as it sank.

"You killed my son," Orin's voice echoed from days ago. The truth about what had happened between Kaine and Axel had come to light, and Orin had made peace with the facts, forgiving Kaine despite his direct involvement. Now the roles had reversed, placing Kaine in Orin's position. Harm had befallen Xander this time, and the latest events demanded that Kaine show the same understanding, empathy, and forgiveness Orin had given him.

"It wasn't your fault, Celeste," he finally let out in a mumbled grunt. Though he hadn't spoken entirely clearly, he'd at least spoken the truth.

Celeste's shoulders sagged with relief as her eyes closed briefly, taking in the short but meaningful forgiveness.

"Thank you for believing in me," she replied.

They sat in silence for a moment before Kaine suggested returning to Celeste's home. Upon arrival, they found Merdel, Kira, and Orin already there. The councilman and princess were casually chatting around Xander's bedside.

"Nothing's changed since you left," the leader of Gale Village greeted from Celeste's table, where they'd previously folded papers for lanterns. This time, a map was unraveled across the wooden surface. The parchment was stained, aged, and bore countless notes Orin had made. The map was outdated, likely from before the war—the roads between Last Hope, Gale Village, and the Leila Kingdom were hand-drawn in newer, darker ink, probably by Orin.

"You must return to the Leila Kingdom," he said, "despite everything. The journey will take about a week, but perhaps Blanche can help you with Xander and all the rest."

"Renato might know something useful as well," Merdel added. Noticing Orin's confusion, he explained, "He's one of the Purple Knights, skilled in alchemy."

Kaine had heard rumors that Renato was a wise man and hoped it was true. If there was a way to counter Celeste's magic, a master of natural sciences would know. Anything that might cure Xander was worth the journey.

"Venturing to the Leila Kingdom is a fine idea, as long as we don't encounter King Ether's men," Kaine said, warning of potential danger. "The lie about Xander's injury won't hold up to scrutiny. It seems too strange, especially without a physical wound."

"I'm sorry, Kaine," Kira interrupted, "but Celeste was right earlier. My father can't bear the truth. It's safer for everyone if he believes this was all an accident—I truly think that's what is best. Xander made a mistake, and Celeste and Gale Village shouldn't have to suffer the consequences. We should at least try using the story to protect Gale Village."

Kaine nodded, though he was unsure if she would lie to her father when the time came. "Your decision is brave and honorable, Princess. If this is what you've decided, you have my support."

"This doesn't mean I'm giving up on finding a way to heal him," Kira added. "We'll meet Queen Blanche, learn how to use the God Stones, and help bring him back."

Hope and dread surged equally at her words. The God Stones remained buried with Kira's mother, a resting place meant to prevent misuse by those who would abuse their power. Even if he returned to Lily von Stonewall's grave, dug out the stones, and gave them to Kira that moment, how many years would it take for her to learn whether their magic could accomplish her goal?

What if, in Kira's effort to cure Xander, she instead turned him into a monster, as Lydia had accidentally done to her handmaiden? The possibility of such magic going wrong was frightening.

He met her eyes, seeing desperation mirrored in them. "It's a possibility, Kira, perhaps one day," Kaine said, encouraging her without revealing his apprehension. "But magic, especially from what I've seen, comes with its own risks."

His mind wandered with a torrent of significant thoughts, and a singular truth emerged: if Orin or Merdel believed the God Stones could aid in restoring Xander's memories, they would have already mentioned it. Their silence revealed a secret opinion, clear in its message. Magic, in their experience, had always wrought more harm than good. Now wasn't the time to commit to using the God Stones, even if Kira's sole goal was healing her brother.

"I will always be careful," the princess pledged. But caution alone couldn't ensure everyone's safety—or even her own. They needed a deeper understanding of the God Stones and their use. Blindly wielding them was too risky.

Kaine took a deep breath, grounding himself. "We should focus on reaching Queen Blanche," he declared. "As Merdel said, she might have knowledge or resources for Xander, the God Stones, or the Prophecy of Tears and Sacrifice."

Orin nodded, relief evident in his eyes. "Agreed. The path to the Leila Kingdom is a necessary journey, giving us time to consider all options before involving King Ether. Everything that's happened has shaken me; my thoughts are not the clearest right now."

Merdel nodded courteously. "Very well. If we're found by the Darian Guard along the way, let me do the talking."

"I'm sorry for everything," Celeste said, "but what will you tell Xander when he wakes? I suspect he'll come around within a day."

Kira sighed, her shoulders slumping. "I wish there were an easier way to bring him back without endangering us all… or himself."

Orin's eyes lit up. "I know what to do."

"What's that?" Kaine asked, hoping the Elder had suddenly remembered a cure for Prince Xander's mind after all.

"It's called Death's Whisper," Orin said. "A leaf set on someone's tongue or ground into oil will put them into a slumber for days, depending on dosage."

Kaine already knew what it was. Councilwoman Iris Thorne had explained it to him, as he had once been under its effect. Lydia spiked his drink with it the night before her wedding. He fell unconscious and remained so even when the servants tried to wake him that morning. It wasn't until midday that he finally awoke, assuming he'd slept deeply from too much alcohol. If not for missing the event, Kaine would have considered it a peaceful sleep.

"Why do we need this?" Kira's voice trembled, revealing her apprehension.

"I've had the plant used on me; it's safe," Kaine said, turning back to Orin. "Are you suggesting we let Xander sleep until we know what to do?"

"A slumber will shield him from the world," Orin offered. "Without Celeste or an experienced mentor, Xander's awakening can be confusing and difficult. It's best to have an explanation ready to give him when he wakes, whether it's truth or lie."

He stared at Xander's peaceful face, resting in Celeste's bed. Though empty of his memories, the prince still had more to pay once his eyes opened again. There was too much for him to relearn from what he'd forgotten. Allowing him to remain comatose, oblivious to the group's troubles, seemed both merciful and practical for now.

"There's no danger or side effects, are there?" Merdel asked.

"He'll be as vulnerable as one who sleeps and cannot awaken," Sen explained. "No shaking, yelling, or even physical harm will bring him back until the leaf's oils sweat from his body. Such is how Death's Whisper gets its name."

"If it won't hurt him, let's give him the leaf," Kira said. "Can he stay here with you until we finish at the Leila Kingdom?"

"Pardon me, princess, but he should come with us," Merdel replied. "Renato needs to look at him."

"Transporting him will be difficult," Orin warned. "A cart won't fit through the narrow Shadowstone passages down the mountain."

The elder was correct—they'd already sent their horses home on the journey to Gale Village from Last Hope. Traveling on foot was the only way to reach the Leila Kingdom from where they were now.

"I'll carry him on my back," Kaine said, glancing at Merdel for support, but the councilman's face revealed little. Kira's expression was neutral, and Celeste appeared lost in thought.

"The whole way?" Merdel exclaimed. "It's at least a week-long walk."

"The sooner we get him to the Leila Kingdom, the better," Kaine said firmly.

"Very well," Orin said. "I'll work with Finnegan to craft a cot to strap the young prince onto your back. We used these during the war to carry our wounded. You're strong—you can manage it."

Kaine nodded. "I'll do it. We are now in unknown waters, and every decision carries risk. Our primary duty now is to help Xander." He turned to Merdel. "Until we have a more complete plan, keeping Xander asleep is the best course of action. Do you agree?"

"You have no objections from me," the councilman said. "I wish I could send a letter and summon horses for us. Carrying the prince on your shoulders, Kaine, for what might end up being longer than a week, is something I could never do."

The physical challenge would be tough, but Kaine wouldn't let it stop him. For now, the Leila Kingdom offered the best solution for their current problems. He hadn't been home in years and, deep down, he had been avoiding it. However, even if he didn't need to bring Xander there or consult Queen Blanche, there were other matters still lingering in his mind. Lydia had seen them and called them out the night before she died. Kaine promised himself he would return to settle unfinished business from when he abandoned everything to become a merchant. Ilya was there, and maybe it was time to finally talk to her again.

"Kaine, thank you," Kira said, "for everything you've done for us, and for me."

Kaine looked down at his waist, where White Oath hung from

his belt. He'd promised King Ether to protect Xander and Kira, but his efforts fell short. Kaine knew he had let too many opportunities for deeper conversations with the prince slip by, conversations that could have made a difference in Xander's well-being. He couldn't allow that again—couldn't let Kira lose herself in grief or come to harm. The best way to save Kira from her darkness would be to rescue Xander.

"We leave for the Leila Kingdom tomorrow at dawn," Kaine replied. "We owe it to Xander to help him as soon as we can."

36

EISENBERN - THE STRUGGLE AGAINST DESTINY

Even as Somnius slept on the cold stone platform nested within the cavern, Eisenbern sensed power emanating from her body, its energy causing the fine hairs on his neck to rise. Eisenbern's chest tightened as he doubted the reality of what he was seeing. He refused to accept that she was a goddess yet conceded she possessed powerful magic. Swallowing hard, he knew he could no longer deny that Somnius was special beyond words.

As he approached her bedside, a soothing warmth spread through his body, as if someone had warmed a blanket over a fire and wrapped it around him. His pulse quickened as he wondered if the power was from her or the child inside her.

"When will she awaken?" Eisenbern's voice trembled as he whispered.

"Tomorrow, perhaps," Herja replied, just as quietly, though her tone betrayed her uncertainty. "The remaining Black Moon Tribe members she controls will soon return to Twilight Haven."

Suddenly, Somnius's eyes opened, shining mysteriously and staring up into his wide, shocked brown irises. Eisenbern's heart threatened to burst at the unexpected awakening.

"Our allies can navigate the rest of the way home," Somnius announced, her voice calm yet authoritative. "Thankfully, Bios Auras doesn't know where I'm hidden. We're fortunate he's preoccupied with finding the God Stones, at least for now."

"You're—you're awake!" Eisenbern stammered, his cheeks flushing. "And who is Bios Auras?"

"That's not how to address a goddess," Herja warned, then offered Somnius an apologetic bow.

"Sir Eisenbern did not mean to slight me," Somnius said, bringing herself into a seated position on her bed. "I've been expecting you today."

Eisenbern's fingers twitched. How could she have known they'd arrive at that exact moment? He shot a glare at Herja—had they spoken too loudly? "You knew we were coming?"

"This isn't the first instance where we've conversed," Somnius said, her voice solemn and imbued with a confidence that made him shiver.

"What do you mean by that? We haven't been introduced. I don't understand."

"As I understood, the two of you haven't met before either," Herja added, her eyebrows narrowing in confusion. "I thought this was the first time you've conversed, aside from when you were controlling my body."

"Herja, might we have a moment?" Somnius asked, resting a hand on her stomach. "Please summon the other Purple Guard members and Ragnar. While you gather them, I'll explain our situation to Sir Eisenbern, as he and his allies are integral to everything we need later."

"Yes, Your Grace." Before she walked away, the Dragon Mar eyed Eisenbern warily.

The stars overhead on the cavern's purple ceiling also watched Eisenbern, as if mocking him, as he studied Somnius and the subtle strength in her spirit. Her posture, the slight curve of her lips, the tilt of her chin as she looked over at him, and the approachable presence she exuded told him she held the answers to every question burning within him. His heart ached, wondering if she truly was a goddess. Above all, if she was, could she bring Ophelia back to him?

"I don't understand how we've met before," Eisenbern said, his voice breaking the silence. "I would have remembered you. We came to learn how to kill dragons and seek information about the shield of storms surrounding the Throatian island, yet it seems you already knew we were on our way. Tell me, Somnius, and don't lie to me… are you really a goddess?"

"I am," she whispered, her breath carrying the weight of a thousand years. "But it doesn't matter. You don't have to believe I'm a goddess to understand what I'm about to tell you."

Ragnar once said she could prove herself to Eisenbern, yet doubt lingered within him. Why wasn't her immediate reaction to do so? Was she indifferent to his belief in her, or was this a ruse? Her composure was unwavering; her face was a pale, inscrutable mask hiding her true intentions. Suddenly, he realized: Somnius either knew more than she'd let on or was avoiding proving herself.

"I've lost someone I love," Eisenbern started.

"And I cannot bring back the dead," Somnius replied. "Not even Ophelia. I wish I could help you, but I can no longer break the natural laws. However, you will succeed as both a Holy Knight and a Purple Knight, as was her dying wish."

Eisenbern stammered. For a moment, he thought Somnius had overheard some conversations he and Ilya had in the caves, but he had never spoken of being a Holy Knight or a Purple Knight. It was as if Somnius had witnessed his last talk with Ophelia.

"How do you know all that?"

"You and I have had this conversation before," she explained. "It's complicated to explain, but being a goddess grants a different perspective of time. There is a past, present, and future, but they exist in many versions. In all of them, she loved you the same, and, in all of them, had to leave you as well."

Her words strangled him. Were they meant to play with his emotions by reminding him of what should have been? The phrases she'd used were like strange knives, sharp enough to pierce his armor and enter his heart yet somehow healing it. Peace had come over him, yet Eisenbern wondered what the broader implications of her words meant. She claimed to be a "goddess from another world," but how could she see so much about him while his own god remained absent?

"What about Asura?" he pressed, seeking clarity. "Where is he involved in all this? Shouldn't he be helping to save the world? If you're truly a goddess, then he must be real too."

"A fair question, Jarret. He exists, though not in the manner you might believe," Somnius murmured with a hint of sadness enveloping her candidness. "Unfortunately, we cannot rely on him to help us."

"Is he dead?" Several Asuras—his followers—believed he was, but it couldn't be true.

"Let's say… he is gone," she replied, her mind burdened with unsaid stories. She rose from the bed, her bare feet meeting the floor. Eisenbern noted how her pregnant belly sank lower than he expected.

"Are you okay standing like that?"

"I take it you've never tended to someone with child?"

"The closest I've ever been to a pregnant woman was when I was in my mother's womb," he chuckled nervously, trying to lighten the mood, but then he realized Herja would have scolded him for it.

"We discussed the Wedding of the Torn Rose when you first arrived," Somnius reminded him, either missing the joke or ignoring it entirely. "There's still much you don't know about it, even though you were there."

"You must have been heavily involved in the Darian Kingdom's events," he mused. His curiosity was growing. "There's more to it?"

"Please have a seat, and I'll unravel the tale."

"Where?"

"Behind you."

He twisted around, his eyes widening in disbelief. A long table and six matching chairs, carved from the plateau's stone, stood behind him. How had he missed them? They hadn't been there earlier—he was certain of that. It was as if Somnius's words had summoned the table into existence.

He sat cautiously, his muscles tensed and ready to react, half expecting it to be an illusion or a trap. To his relief, the granite chair held firm, supporting his weight. It was real, but he didn't notice it until now. Surely she hadn't had the time or energy to conjure it all in the past few moments, but somehow, it was there.

Ilya's gasp echoed through the cavern as she, Gustav, Ragnar, and Herja entered. Eyes wide, she looked in awe at the stars spread across the ceiling.

"How did you get stars inside this underground cave?" Ilya breathed. "They're so mesmerizing! Oh! And you're Somnius? You're just as beautiful—and pregnant!"

Everything about the mysterious Somnius was surreal. Whoever she was, she was out of place among the Black Moon Tribe and their caverns. Perhaps she was a goddess after all, but she was not Eisenbern's goddess—he was dedicated to Asura.

"Mind your manners and bow to her," Herja warned, her voice sharper than Eisenbern had ever heard. "She is above all kings and queens of this world, not a friend you chanced upon at a tavern."

Ilya's face drained of color at the stern warning. "Right," she whispered, swallowing hard and kneeling. Gustav's face twitched as he realized his indiscretion and followed suit, as did Ragnar. Eisenbern remained standing but yielded a brief nod.

"I don't understand this," Gustav murmured, "but I suspect everything in this room results from her power."

Despite the tension stirred by the Dragon Mar, a wave of warmth washed over them as Somnius gestured for the others to rise. She turned and said, "Welcome to my temporary sanctuary, Ilya Oleanne and Gustav Reed. Thank you for traveling all this way. Sir Eisenbern and I were just about to discuss the deeper meanings of the Wedding of the Torn Rose. Please join us."

Ilya's eyes widened and glowed with excitement as Somnius waved her hand, conjuring a large glass teapot and cups. She approached the table and took her seat at the head. Drinking tea in an underground cave was the last thing Eisenbern expected to do after waking that morning.

Gustav's hand trembled with fascination as he grasped the cup and sniffed the steam rising from it. "This is no illusion. You've created something real from nothing—a feat beyond any Lucidian's abilities."

"There is always a price," Somnius said as they settled into their seats. "Blood is the currency of magic here—even for me. My powers are more constrained than you might think. A simple tea setting is trivial to create compared to what we'll need in the future."

"Ilya, Gustav—wait, don't drink it!" Eisenbern cautioned, turning to Somnius. "How do we know this isn't one of your potions that will take over our bodies? And how do we know it isn't poisoned?"

A snap blasted through the cavern as the stars in the purple sky above rained down into the rivers like golden arrows. Each light splashed into the water and vanished as fast as it had descended from the cavern's ceiling.

"If you were my enemy, I could have already destroyed you," Somnius said. "But we were always meant to be allies."

"So, the stars weren't for decoration," Eisenbern commented. They had apparently been placed there as a last line of defense to protect the sleeping Somnius.

"You need to stop resisting and trust her," Herja urged. "She's here to help us!"

Eisenbern shook his head. "I'm sorry. There's just too much I don't understand."

"You've come to learn the truth, and I will show you," promised Somnius. "But the scope of what happened before your coming here is too vast to explain in mere words. I must demonstrate, not merely describe, the stakes involved."

She opened her palm and motioned for them to drink their tea.

"You'll show them the same vision you showed us?" Ragnar asked.

"The same vision," she replied, "and it will be enough for them to understand."

Ilya stared down at her cup as her nose wrinkled, trying to sense whether the tea had a strange smell. "This will give me a vision?"

"You have quite an assortment of magic potions from your world," Gustav complimented, raising his cup. "I'll take a leap of faith."

"Me too," Ilya replied. "I want to know what all this means."

She sipped her tea, and Gustav did the same before Eisenbern could object. Ilya asked why the tea wasn't working, and Somnius told her she also needed to drink it before the vision could begin.

"Won't you join them, Eisenbern?" Herja insisted. "If you don't trust Somnius, trust me—drinking it won't harm you."

"It's a vision of the past Somnius recreated," Ragnar added. "You won't feel a thing."

Maybe he was being ridiculous. Somnius could have harmed them or taken control of their bodies had she meant to. Still, taking a magic potion was something else he'd never planned to do that day.

"It won't turn me into a frog or something else, will it?" he asked, his hand wrapping around the cup. If it were a poison that would distort his mind, he hoped it would be painless.

"It is safe, Sir Eisenbern," Somnius reassured him. "The drink is only a means to reveal the truth about why you're here."

"Very well," he replied, raising the cup. "Show me this vision."

NEARBY, THREE STONE OBELISKS PROTRUDED FROM THE FLOOR OF THE Emerald Room. Princess Lydia appeared. Her fair face and sea-foam-colored dress were bloodstained from the conflict, yet she had survived. A massive chandelier, made of a single green crystal, hung from the ceiling, glowing so brightly that no candles were needed to light the room.

"We have to try again," the Darian princess urged as she approached the pair of velvet chairs where Somnius had just sat.

"Return us to the moment just before the incident in Gale Village. We can use a different approach to surprise him."

No, they couldn't take that path again. The disaster in Gale Village—despite Lydia's hard-won acquisition of the Teleportation Stone—had left them with more losses than gains. Holding onto the two most powerful God Stones was meaningless now; the others were gone. To make matters worse, Somnius had recognized a greater threat than ever before.

"We can't try that scenario again," Somnius said. "I've realized how dangerous it was to go there. We must discard the battle in Gale Village timelines and take a different strategy elsewhere."

Somnius wiped sweat from her face and cleansed her body with her magic. For Lydia, who always preferred a direct approach, the goddess conjured a standing basin of water, fresh clothes and linens, and a sunken bath level with the ground.

Lydia scrubbed her face clean and replied, "What did you see that makes you feel that way? We were close to retrieving the other stones. One more try might allow us to succeed."

"All along, the prophecy provided a false sense of safety," Somnius replied. "We've always assumed Bios Auras would be victorious if he acquired all the God Stones. The truth is, he only needs the Time Stone to destroy us, and that's what scares me."

With her back turned to Somnius, Lydia removed her dress and lowered into the steamy cleansing pool. Once submerged, the princess swiveled toward her. "I cannot believe I didn't see it before," Lydia said. "You're right—if he were ever to get the Time Stone in any timeline, it would give him the same power as you. We'd lose our only advantage, and our struggle against destiny would be impossible to survive."

"This is the same problem we've always faced," Somnius replied. "If he gathers all the God Stones within a single timeline, he wins in all of them. With just the Time Stone, he can try again repeatedly, making infinite attempts. Across all possibilities, his success is inevitable. That's why we can't return to Gale Village; in some variation, he could obtain the Time Stone from us. That's why I called the World Vein to retreat."

Lydia soaked and washed the dirt and blood from herself, pondering. Despite being human, she was wise, though sometimes she took longer to reflect.

"Move the stones here if you can," Lydia suggested. "Bios Auras cannot travel to this room."

In most cases, as long as they stayed in the Emerald Room, they were safe.

Somnius shook her head. "He is unable to travel to this room using the Teleportation Stone," she corrected, drawing out more timeline possibilities. "There's still a chance he could sail to this island the lengthy route, which would mean the stones are no longer safe here. There was also an unlikely but possible chance of a World Vein exiting nearby. The Emerald Room is safer than most places, but it's not impossible for him to invade."

While Lydia bathed, Somnius stood and moved to her desk where her notes waited. Grabbing the nearest scroll, an ink bottle, and quill, she drew a large X over the circular symbol representing the timeline variation they had tried. Events in Gale Village and beyond would remain unaffected until she nullified the timeline. Like every failed reality where Bios Auras or Zann-Xia-Czul came too close to success, Somnius would purge it, roll back to an earlier point in history, and start over.

The branches of the various timelines were like those of trees, and it was her responsibility to cut them short if they veered too close to disaster. Through luck and skill, and enough retries, they would defeat Bios Auras and Zann-Xia-Czul, allowing Somnius to establish a golden timeline as the master plane of reality, discarding all other variations.

"If only our enemy weren't corrupted by chaos," Somnius muttered, staring at the paper. Bios Auras was a variable himself, making his actions unpredictable. Even in similar timelines where Somnius had changed nothing, his behavior remained inconsistent. Like her, he seemed completely resistant to fate.

"Perhaps try using the God Stones yourself," Lydia called from the water, "despite the risks."

Somnius shook her head as she let the quill fall back into the ink pot. "Though I am not at my full power, the stones are as corrupt as he is," she said. "They would corrupt me too. That is why you must use them."

"Pardon my forgetfulness," Lydia said, acknowledging what it meant to be human. "I'd forgotten how they become one with the soul."

The princess rose from the bath and let the water drip down her body before wringing her hair and retrieving her towel. After drying, she slid on the clean white dress Somnius prepared for her.

"Considering alternatives isn't wrong," the goddess replied. "It could be the only way to succeed."

"You're sure we must allow Bios Auras to begin with the Teleportation Stone?" Lydia added.

Giving it to him was necessary, even though it gave him an advantage and created unpredictable timelines. Though the God Stones were corrupt, they held honor in their essence—if their wielder took another life, the stones would stop activating for an unspecified amount of time.

Bios consistently adapted to the limitations of the God Stones, avoiding direct murder to ensure their continued activation. However, without these safeguards, he resorted to using his own blade, leading to a higher death toll and an accelerated rise in political power. His invulnerability fueled his greed and ambition, making him crave even more influence. Interestingly, across all timelines, Bios ended up killing significantly fewer people when wielding a God Stone than when he did not possess one.

"If we remove the Teleportation Stone from him too soon, he conquers Yaenia, the Enclave, and the Silent Deserts," Somnius said.

Lydia retreated to the chair where Somnius sat earlier and crossed her legs. "We must find other ways of slowing him down, even if it means temporarily giving him more power… the prophecy is simple, yet we've come too close to failure many times. Something else needs to change. There's got to be a way of defeating him we haven't tried before."

Somnius sighed. "True, there are infinite variations of the timelines, but now it's clear that each risks the Time Stone falling into Bios's control. We should consider the likelihood before attempting further. If he gets it even once, we fail in them all."

"Likewise, we only need to succeed at collecting the God Stones once to seal the remaining timelines and fulfill the Prophecy of Tears and Sacrifice," Lydia said.

"Where did we go wrong?" Somnius pondered. She had robbed Lydia of her humanity by plucking her from the timelines and teaching her to use the God Stones. Every part of the prophecy had been fulfilled except for removing the darkness from their world. That part—the most critical piece—hadn't happened yet in any of the variations, for Lydia could never defeat Bios Auras.

"I wonder if I'm meant to fulfill the prophecy," Lydia said. At some point, the Darian princess might succeed—they just needed to figure out how. Every timeline was within the prophecy's scope, after all.

"All signs hint that you are the chosen one," Somnius replied. "Your sister, whom I trained, could not harness the God Stones as effectively as you. In every timeline where she attempted to use them, she perished."

"It pains me she failed and suffered," Lydia said, "but there's comfort in knowing she's free from these burdens now, and her life will no longer be scarred by the God Stones in any future timeline."

Somnius conjured a pot of tea and a pair of cups, then carried it over to the other side of the room where Lydia sat. After offering the princess her drink, the goddess sat next to her and sipped.

"As always, we must try to save everyone we can," she said.

They were both silent for a moment; the Emerald Room's ambience offered them some solace. Somnius had conjured the room as part of her castle, reminding her of her former home. The grand crystal chandelier in particular reminded her of all she had lost. She couldn't bear losing another world; saving this one by any means necessary was her only way of moving beyond her past failures.

"So, destroy it," Lydia said. "Destroy it all. Make it impossible for Bios Auras to use the Time Stone to create more timelines; then he cannot have a permanent victory."

Somnius scowled at her. "You know the God Stones cannot be destroyed; nor can we move them between timelines."

"I'm not suggesting we destroy the God Stones," Lydia countered, "only the most dangerous ability of one. Make it so that he cannot change anything if he ever uses the Time Stone. Then, in the worst of situations, it cannot happen. You would still have your own power to control time, but he could never have it for himself."

Her words froze Somnius in astonishment. Was it possible to modify a God Stone? A Tear of Asura was supposed to be immutable; at least, that was what she had always assumed. If they could find a way to make Lydia's suggestion a reality, it would prevent Bios Auras from creating new timelines and securing an ultimate victory.

Lydia's plan had one flaw—Somnius herself. If Somnius could manipulate time, Bios Auras could potentially trick or coerce her into using her power for his benefit. The only way to definitively stop Bios Auras from generating more timelines was to prevent them both from doing so.

"If it were possible to weaken the Time Stone's power to a lower level," Somnius said, "I too would need to absolve myself of the ability."

"Therefore, you must erase the other timelines, leaving only a single one remaining," Lydia said. "A final timeline, isolated where none of us can rewrite it. We must ensure it is a timeline that allows us to succeed or at least offers the greatest chance."

Somnius replied, "I need to think about this—whether changing the Time Stone and my own abilities is even possible. Even if we eliminate time manipulation and reduce the universe to a single series of events, Bios Auras could still overcome us in the end. I also fear we've exhausted our major decisions and have made little progress."

Lydia's suggestion to modify the Time Stone was wise. With multiple timelines, Bios Auras would only need to acquire that single stone to secure ultimate victory. However, if they reduced existence to a single timeline, the Time Stone alone ceased to be decisive. The Prophecy of Tears and Sacrifice could no longer be bypassed, meaning Bios Auras would have to collect all the God Stones to achieve his greater powers. The question was whether Somnius dared risk using alternative timelines to try changing more variables. Was there anything else they might do that could set everything in their favor?

She rose from her chair and paced the loop of the Emerald Room. The rows of scrolls neatly stacked on her shelves were her oldest notes, detailing choices made in past attempts and reflections on successes and failures. Could a better answer lie within them?

"There is another variation we could attempt," Lydia said quietly, "something we haven't tried before. Let them defeat me—let them truly defeat me."

Somnius stared at her from across the room. "What could you possibly mean by that?"

"During my wedding, let the Throatians succeed," Lydia said. "I will die, but it would begin a new variation we've not yet attempted. Everything will be different."

The princess too must have realized how dire the situation had become and that they were running out of options. In all timelines so far, Lydia had been a helpful partner to her, even if she had to repeatedly relearn everything she didn't yet know from Somnius by using the Memories Stone. If she died, the goddess would be alone. Would letting Lydia go through with her plan serve the greater good? Somnius suspected that stepping aside and letting Lydia die would cause more chaos than order. In any case, could it be the right action to take?

Somnius nodded, though not fully convinced. "It's true we've prevented the Throatians from succeeding in their plans before, but why would this help us? They would succeed in stealing the God Stones from your father."

"You could let them think they've succeeded," Lydia replied. "Replace the God Stones with false ones, and the Throatians will leave. My father can hide them elsewhere, changing everything else from there."

"I fail to see how that changes anything aside from delaying the inevitable," Somnius said bluntly. "Your death would be meaningless."

"Not if you orchestrate everything else after it," Lydia said. "My wedding was a period of escalation. If I die, Kaine and Thane will live, and their future actions can lead to new outcomes. There's a chance you could come to success without me."

Somnius returned to her desk and began mapping out a potential timeline on a clean scroll. The princess was correct that it would trigger a new sequence of events they hadn't considered. In the previous timelines, Kaine had demonstrated loyalty to the von Stonewall family before dying at Lydia's wedding, and Thane had proven ready to abandon Zann-Xia-Czul. Would letting them live cause more good than harm? Was it worth exploring multiple possibilities, or should they consolidate everything into one timeline?

Regardless, leaving Lydia to be murdered couldn't be the right decision. If she died, who would wield the God Stones against Bios Auras and fulfill the prophecy? So far, despite her knowledge, Somnius hadn't unraveled why Zelia, Lydia, and Kira could use the God Stones' magic. As Kira had proven, activating the God Stones didn't guarantee eventual mastery. If Lydia surrendered to the Throatians and Somnius tried using Kira again, it might lead to another failed attempt to secure the future.

"Even if your deception succeeds, the risk remains of the Time Stone falling into the wrong hands," Somnius warned.

"You said so earlier, and I agree with you," Lydia said. "The more timelines you create, the more chances you have to learn how to overcome our enemies, but we risk defeat if Bios gets the Time Stone. Everything escalated after my wedding. If we diverge from there, there is a chance of new possibilities, and Bios Auras will have only the Teleportation Stone."

The princess went silent as she thought more about the topic. "Every time you brought me from a new timeline, you had me use the Memories Stone to learn from you. I've seen what you've seen, and now I know more than I should—and maybe that's the problem. What if we were wrong about the prophecy? What if putting me into this situation isn't enough? What if my death is the only way to satisfy it and open another path?"

"We cannot deny it is a possibility," Somnius admitted. "However, it's equally likely that letting you die will be the action that leads Bios Auras to achieve his goals. We can't know the future until we create it. Yet, if we create the wrong circumstances, he will prevail. At the very least, we should place Kaine, Thane, Eisenbern, and everyone else on separate paths until we know more of what changes. We must break the old patterns."

"I don't know if it's better to cling to the infinite possibilities or destroy them all and fight for a single true ending," Lydia replied. "But until we resolve the prophecy, for better or worse, we are all forever trapped in the struggle against destiny."

EISENBERN'S EYES REOPENED AS HE LIFTED HIS HEAD FROM HIS ARMS, which crossed the table where he'd fallen asleep. The vision from Somnius's potion came over him like a vivid dream, showing him as a silent observer in the Emerald Room. His cheeks hung low, as if he'd slept for hours. He had no sense of time, but the question was irrelevant given what he'd just seen in his mind.

"That was… quite strange," was all Eisenbern could muster as he watched Ilya and Gustav rise from potion-induced slumber.

Listening to Somnius and Lydia discuss abstract concepts made Eisenbern feel as if he were drowning in confusion. He envisioned timelines as threads, weaving in and out, but each scenario appeared as a fraying rope, with every strand drawing them closer to an inevitable doom.

"The Darian Princess knew she would die," Ilya exclaimed. "She volunteered to do it. I can't believe how—"

"Is this the final timeline?" Gustav interrupted. Eisenbern nodded in response to his question. It was a more important detail.

"Where we are now is final," the goddess confirmed. "I embraced

Lydia's ideas to destroy all methods of time manipulation, and she sacrificed herself to open new possibilities. Now, the Time Stone only allows viewing the past, not changing it. This means permanence for all. I don't know if my actions will lead to success, but everything is different this time, and I have faith we've diverged far enough from what you'd call destiny."

Somnius spoke, her tone as resilient as Shadowstone, yet wavering when recounting defeats. As the vision revealed, she never gave up, and her conviction was genuine. She wasn't lying or misleading them like a swindler or a fanatic. Instead, Somnius seemed weary, as if she'd fought countless desperate battles in mere seconds. Her desperation was the clearest sign of her truth—she was a warrior who'd faced insurmountable odds, perpetually battling yet always falling short.

Herja spoke up. "Somnius and Lydia were forced to retreat and erase the timeline just before Bios Auras would succeed," she said. "Bringing the conflict down to this single order of events limits his chances."

Eisenbern glanced at her and Ragnar sitting across the table and suspected they'd already had similar conversations with the goddess. They had moved from not knowing Somnius to letting her control their bodies using the magical potion. For some reason, they had come to trust her. Was it all because of her child that they'd come to worship her? Suddenly, he realized that the calmness she portrayed, like all her magic, was paid for in silence.

Somnius faced them. "In every prior scenario, Bios Auras would have won. However, in this timeline, we have a chance to change the outcome," she said with conviction. "This is a reality still unfolding, and in a direction never previously taken. Ultima is the greatest new variable."

Eisenbern guessed Somnius was at least halfway through her pregnancy, based on the size of her stomach. Who was the father of her child, if there was one? He couldn't shake the idea of Asura's absence. Somnius never said what had happened to him. Chances were that Asura was Ultima's father, but how was it possible? "A god will fall" was a major part of the Prophecy of Tears and Sacrifice, meaning it must have been Asura who died. Why else would Somnius avoid mentioning his name or acknowledging his existence?

Gustav might have been thinking along the same lines. He rested his elbow on the table and said, "You and Lydia hadn't spoken of your child in the dream, so how did it come to be that Ultima would fulfill the prophecy in Lydia's place?"

Somnius smiled, revealing a faint but mysterious grin. "Eliminating time travel and creating new circumstances would be a gamble at best. Something else was needed. After pondering, I realized my limitations as a goddess from another world, unable to reach my full strength here. Blood is the price to channel what you call magic, and I am not invulnerable. A deity born in this world might be better equipped to achieve what a foreign one like me could not. That's when I realized Ultima was the key to fulfilling the prophecy."

"Before, in the other timelines, you'd tried to fulfill the prophecy, but you could never make it true," Gustav said. "I wonder where the prophecy originated?"

"From the god of your world, of course," Somnius replied. "It was the last gift he could give before passing the responsibility of protecting everything here to me."

Each word she spoke deepened the mystery surrounding her. Eisenbern's mind raced, trying to connect the related points. He noticed the strain in Somnius's expression, making her more human than a goddess in his eyes. The cavern's starlight, once cold and distant, now seemed to accept his presence, drawing closer, as if the stars had shifted nearer to their table.

"Powerful but mortal, Somnius cannot stay here in Twilight Haven forever," Ragnar added. "Bios Auras will discover this is where she's been hiding. We need to help her reclaim her castle and the Emerald Room you saw in her vision. It's much less likely she'll be attacked there."

"What do you mean by reclaiming her castle?" Ilya asked.

"During the previous war, I tried to train someone else capable of using the God Stones," Somnius said. "Though she was talented, she couldn't master them, which spawned the monsters. I understood her destiny, but I let her follow the same path as in other timelines. Her death, along with losing my castle, were prerequisites for the Wedding of the Torn Rose to happen."

"Everything you showed reveals that the fate of our world rests in your hands," Eisenbern said, hoping to guide the conversation back to a more positive direction. "Despite this timeline differing from the others, you seemed to have expected us to visit you here, and you said you needed our help. Did we triumph in defeating these monsters in the other timelines?"

"You ask fine questions," the goddess commended. "The Black Moon Tribe lacks the numbers, but alongside the Leila Kingdom's City Guard and Purple Knights, we will succeed. Once we reclaim the castle, it is going to serve as our stronghold. There, I shall give birth to Ultima and raise him to fulfill the prophecy."

Everything about history was a familiar road to Somnius, and she was aware of when certain events might recur, even under different circumstances.

"You'll have the knights you need from us," Eisenbern promised, eyeing Herja's subtle smile. "However, since this is the final timeline, and this battle might play out differently, recruiting the Darians would be wise."

The Leilan City Guard wasn't an army by any means, but they were skilled enough to handle keeping the kingdom's crime in check. They didn't, however, have any experience in defeating monsters—but who would? Kaine was the only known person who'd fought one and succeeded. King Ether had a larger army stationed in Wargonne—more than necessary to reclaim a single castle. It was better they join the fight.

"The Darian king and I share a complicated history," Somnius replied. "That's why I hid my involvement with Lydia from him. Now, I cannot summon his aid."

Eisenbern wasn't well-acquainted with King Ether but guessed he wouldn't have agreed to sacrificing his daughter to the Throatians. Yet it made sense he'd do anything to save Lydia, even if it meant risking the God Stones. Somnius hadn't sought his approval, for the greater good, and now it was clear everything surrounding the Wedding of the Torn Rose had been a last resort.

"We've cleared the monsters from the castle before, in earlier timelines," Herja said. "The circumstances are different this time, but our warriors and numbers are unchanged."

"By manipulating the World Veins, I will bring us to the Leila Kingdom to rally your forces, and then to my castle," Somnius said. "This will require a great effort on my part, meaning I won't be able to assist with the battle against the monsters. I can, however, guide you to victory."

Quietness settled over the cavern as Eisenbern mulled over what had been shared. If she could prove the existence of World Veins and control them, it would be incredible. He suspected that was how she had convinced Ragnar to believe in her. Somnius had opened their eyes to a greater war happening all around.

Finally, Herja broke the silence. "How about now, Eisenbern? Do you believe Somnius is a goddess?"

He could sense only a genuine persona emanating from her, and she'd revealed her ability to create objects from nothing, making her more special than any legend. The surrounding air shimmered with an ethereal energy, giving truth to her words and promises. Maybe, just maybe, she truly was a goddess after all.

He met Herja's anxious gaze, his eyes reflecting growing hope. "I believe there's more to this world and our destiny than we can ever understand. If aligning ourselves with Somnius ensures a brighter future, then so be it—I'll admit she's a goddess."

"So, you have changed your mind," Ilya commented.

"It's clear Somnius is truly what she claims to be," Gustav added.

"I didn't expect him to change his opinion this fast," Ragnar replied.

"Nor did I, but I am pleased," Herja said.

Eisenbern looked at the group with a newfound and fiery determination in his eyes. Maybe when Ophelia had encouraged him to become a Holy Knight underneath his armor, neither of them had understood the changes that would happen next.

"If Somnius believes in persisting toward this greater future," he announced, "then so do I. We owe it to all those who came before us, and those who'll come after."

"I understand the enormity of what I've revealed, and the challenges you'll face," Somnius said, her voice carrying a calm but undeniable authority. "But believe me when I say this—the past may be unchangeable, but the future is ours to brighten, together."

Eisenbern nodded, clenching his fist. "Very well. Let's gather our allies and prepare for the journey back to the Leila Kingdom. We fight not just for our land, but for the very essence of the world. There's no nobler cause. We have a castle to reclaim, monsters to slay, and a destiny to create!"

37
BIOS AURAS - THE HERETIC AND THE JUDGE

Shade escaped the mountains of Hillside Reach, leaving the sun to sear their skin like an invisible fire. The grass, long ago turned golden, crumbled like dry hay underfoot. With each step of their training, there was a crunch beneath their boots as leaves gave way.

Bios and Alina used their usual swords against Cassia, who Bios discovered could wield a spear. She had borrowed it from the items donated to the People's Army during their rally in the Golden Mare's basement. In their mock duel, Cassia held her own against Bios and Alina until they introduced the new fighting technique they had been practicing.

As he thrust his sword forward, Cassia easily parried the attack. He quietly signaled to Alina, who stepped through the Teleportation Stone's portal and reappeared behind Cassia, ready to strike. Anticipating the move, Cassia tilted sideways, redirecting Bios's blade with the edge of her spear while blocking Alina's advance. Before Alina could make contact, her boots hit the ground, and she froze, her expression revealing both surprise and admiration.

After two weeks in Hillside Reach, the Golden Mare had become a place that felt both like home and a prison. The Magician had insisted they remain until further orders arrived, but the wait was growing tedious for Bios. Every few days, a messenger arrived with letters for others, but none for them. Bios could sense the growing restlessness in Alina and Cassia too, and he shared their frustration.

To combat their increasing unease, he took it upon himself to train them in dynamic portal combat.

Bios was already skilled at combining swordplay and magic, but coordinating with other warriors was an unfamiliar challenge. The Teleportation Stone's invisible portals made it difficult at first, but through repeated practice, they gradually learned to synchronize their movements and harness their teamwork. The women began predicting Bios's portal openings, mastering the patterns until their coordination became instinctive, like a choreographed dance.

"Your reflexes are impeccable," he praised. "Where did you learn to fight? I doubt your former master Klein gave you sword lessons."

Alina exchanged a careful glance with Cassia before answering. "Some slaves are trained for the fighting rings," she said. "The masters like their entertainment. Just... not women for it. Cassia and I had our uses serving drinks at those matches. We watched the men's techniques and steps during the day and practiced on our own in the shadows." She lifted a shoulder in a shrug that didn't quite match her eyes. "Sticks, brooms, and whatever we could use without getting beaten for it."

Cassia pulled her spear back and swung it upward toward Bios's face. He ducked sideways to avoid the attack, then shifted his leg backward for a counterstrike. Cassia spun, blocking the attack just as Alina glided to her from the sky. Alina slammed into the dirt with a metallic thud, her blade clattering nearby.

Bios stepped back, putting some distance between them. "Are you okay?"

"I'm fine," Alina replied, wiping soil from her eyes. "It's hard to attack through a portal without killing someone. If only we had proper training weapons."

Bios helped her up. "We'll get some for next time," he said. "It's easy to forget your mortality."

He redirected his gaze to Cassia, who stood frozen in place. Bios and Alina exchanged confused glances, their expressions reflecting the sudden tension.

"What's wrong?" Alina asked.

"I have to go back," Cassia announced. She glanced around toward the inn before turning to face them.

Bios raised an eyebrow. "Go back where?"

"To the Silent Deserts."

Bios sheathed his sword and rested his hands on his waist. "Why would you want to return there? Surely you have not decided to become a slave again?"

"I must return home," Cassia urged. "I can't linger in the People's Army any longer. I need to check on Sofia."

"Sofia?" Bios asked.

"Cassia's daughter," Alina explained. "We left without saying goodbye."

"I can't believe I allowed myself to abandon her."

Alina's face hardened into an icy stare, an expression Bios had never seen before from her. "Going back now would leave her without our help. We knew the risks when we made our promise. There's no turning back. With Bios Auras at our side, we stand a better chance of repairing our world. We'll return to Sofia one day to make amends for our motherland's sins."

Cassia's eyes were filling with tears. "But I miss her so much."

Bios hesitated. Cassia was useful but less motivated than Alina. Helping her reunite with her daughter might offer her peace and strengthen her loyalty. Alternatively, hinting that she could return home soon may prove sufficient motivation on its own.

Before he could respond, Alina interjected, "Our next mission could arrive at any moment. We need you here when it arrives. Bios's magic will allow us to reach our destination faster. In our spare time, we can visit Sofia."

"I suspect Cassia plans to leave the People's Army," Bios said, hoping to extract the truth.

"She shouldn't have to live without me," Cassia said. "Alina, I believe in you and your cause, but she—"

"How many children in the Black Sands or White Sands grow up without families?" Alina cried, her voice trembling. "How many are ripped from their parents by slavers like Klein? We must fight them, Cassia. Sofia matters to me, but our goals are for everyone, not just her."

He deduced Alina's history from her arguments. She had grown up without her parents, and that came with its own challenges. Alina was once where Sofia was now.

"My daughter is more important than our goals," Cassia declared. "I must see her."

"And then what?" Alina asked, her face flushed as red as Bios's armor. "Once you find her, will you stay by her side, becoming a slave again? Or will you free her, only to watch it hinder your efforts to advance our cause?"

"I don't know yet, but when I see her, I will decide what's best."

"I refuse to settle for vague plans and goals," Alina replied firmly. "We agreed to leave everything behind and return stronger. Why is that so difficult to understand?"

Cassia had sacrificed more than Alina, leaving her daughter behind in pursuit of what they believed was a greater good.

"Very well. I'll take you back to the Silent Deserts," Bios said. "But remember our deal. You both swore yourselves to me. Visiting Sofia won't be an issue if it helps you become a better warrior. However, freeing her and bringing her with us isn't practical and could hinder our long-term goals."

Alina gave him a surprised yet approving nod. "Bios Auras is right," she said. "Bringing Sofia with us isn't practical, and we need you to stay. Let's think this through."

"But you'll take me to see her, won't you?" Cassia asked.

"Yes, of course," he promised. And she would owe him a great debt for it.

AFTER MUCH DELIBERATION, BIOS AND ALINA FINALLY CONVINCED Cassia that they could visit the Silent Deserts once they finished their next assignment for the People's Army. Meanwhile, Cassia could take more time to decide whether to keep her daughter with her or take her to Yaenia, where the child could be under someone's watch as they worked toward their long-term goals.

Armed with their weapons, the three hiked down the hill, heading to the central street of Hillside Reach. Upon entering town, they noticed people passing by—some alone, others in small groups —but none seemed interested in stopping any longer than necessary. Sky Tower Coast, a much larger and more recognized trade port city, stood less than three days' journey to the north. Travelers arriving from Sky Tower Coast likely had no need for supplies so soon. Meanwhile, those journeying from the south, possibly from the Leila Kingdom or Last Hope, encountered Hillside Reach as their first stop after days of travel. Bios suspected the town's founders had created it to profit from these weary travelers, who were near Sky Tower Coast yet far from other settlements. For the

Magician, who owned the bar and inn, this made running his establishment a profitable business venture.

A bell above the doorway rang as they entered the Golden Mare, sending a light chime through the tavern. Most tables were empty, save for the two occupied by a group of seven mercenaries. Bios suspected that they may have been hired without fully understanding their role, although it wasn't clear if they were connected to the People's Army. The Magician set down their round of beers and noticed the trio had arrived.

"Welcome back, my friends," he said merrily. "Today is the day we've been waiting for."

After they seated themselves out of earshot of the others who were drinking, the Magician approached from across the bar. He slid Alina an emerald-green envelope and Bios a second smaller one matching the red reflections of his armor.

"Two separate missions?" Alina whispered, her hands trembling as she picked up the message.

"Not exactly," the Magician replied. "The letter to Hellvar is personal. Yours contains the mission."

Curious, Bios slid his finger under the edge of the envelope. Inside, it held a single sheet, which read:

> *We need to talk after you finish your next task. Meet me where we spoke last among the perished animals. Their staff will summon me.*

Without context, the message was cryptic. Despite lacking a seal or signature, it was unmistakably from Ofred. The councilman likely wanted another bag of bribery gold. Fortunately, Bios already wanted to negotiate a deal on behalf of the Throatians, if only to keep Grimm complacent for another few weeks. They were desperate for food and now more fearful of war than ever. Everyone's dependence on him was its own source of power.

He planned to visit Ofred at the butcher's shop soon. For now, Alina's wrinkled nose caught his curiosity.

"They've ordered us to carry out another assassination," she announced.

Cassia looked around, checking if anyone could hear. "Against whom?"

"A judge named Sigrid Var from Sky Tower Coast," Alina answered. "Do either of you know her?"

He hadn't heard of her, and neither had Cassia. Even the Magician didn't know who she was or why the People's Army wanted her killed. Perhaps she had imprisoned or released someone she shouldn't have. It didn't matter. Their target meant nothing to him.

This next mission would require more time and planning than their previous mission to Wargonne, where Bios had already had sufficient information beforehand to make assassinating Councilman Conan a straightforward task. In contrast, locating Sigrid would demand more effort.

Did she have a regular place where she worked or spent her days? Was she constantly monitored or left unprotected? What purpose would her death serve?

"Does the letter contain only her name?" Bios asked.

"That, and that she's in Sky Tower Coast," Alina said.

"Is that enough information to do what they've requested of us?" Cassia asked after the Magician left them alone to tend to the other patrons in the bar. The nearby drunken travelers were racing each other, finishing their drinks and piling their empty tankards into a growing mountain. One team was losing badly, and their loud yells made it clear they weren't interested in eavesdropping.

"A name and a city are all we need to proceed," Bios assured. "We'll depart for Sky Tower Coast at dawn tomorrow. After completing our mission for the People's Army, I'll take you to the Silent Deserts to find your daughter."

"Bios," Cassia said through teary eyes. "I can't thank you enough."

He didn't want her gratitude; what truly mattered was her loyalty, and he intended to have it.

AS THE SUN ROSE GENTLY THE NEXT MORNING, A QUIET KNOCK RAPPED on his door.

"Come in," Bios said, as he fastened the final buckle on his crimson armor.

Alina and Cassia entered, both dressed and ready to depart. Though they were in their armor, Cassia's eyes revealed she'd had a restless night.

"You're eager to return to your daughter," Bios reminded her. "Don't worry, we will visit her soon."

Cassia sighed, her shoulders slumping. "It's not just that," she said, shaking her head. "The truth is, I'm unsure about what to do with her when we bring her back. The safest option for now is to keep her here at the inn while we figure out our next steps."

Bios nodded, acknowledging her limited options and the difficulty of her situation. "It's worth asking the Magician about that. How old is she, and could she work for him? A young girl working at a bar would be safer than staying in the Black Sands."

"Sofia is ten," Cassia said. "She could work here, that's true. I just don't want her joining the People's Army."

"Is there really no better option?" Alina asked. "I do not trust him yet."

"I'm not sure. The Magician seems kind, but what if you're right and he's not who he appears to be?"

Cassia exchanged a surprised glance with Alina, but Bios spoke first. "Each day, I've noticed the Magician rises early," he said. "Every morning, he heads to his basement, likely to prepare food or check his supplies. Aside from his role in the People's Army, what else could he be hiding? Go to him now and ask if Sofia can stay. Once that's settled, we'll leave for our mission."

Cassia left, her steps slow as she left Bios and Alina alone in the room.

"You're encouraging her, yet you have no reason to care about her daughter's well-being," Alina noted after Cassia had descended the stairs. "Does she really matter so much to you?"

"Sofia is Cassia's weakness," Bios replied with certainty. "If Sofia's fate remains uncertain, her mother's potential will always be limited by fear."

"Fair enough," Alina conceded. "I thought I had convinced her that leaving her daughter behind was better for now. Apparently, I hadn't."

"Maybe at one time, she believed deep down that everything would be okay while she was away," Bios said. "But like any mother, she won't feel at ease until she sees her daughter is safe. We've pledged to support each other in achieving our goals, and this helps us do that—even indirectly."

"I suppose it does," Alina admitted. "Still, bringing Sofia here can't be a wise decision. It carries too many risks, yet I'm unsure there's a better alternative."

"It's more likely to help Cassia than harm her, and Sofia would be free from slavery."

"If the Magician is trustworthy and agrees to the arrangement," Alina replied, her tone revealing skepticism, "then it might work."

"Everyone's got their own risks. But I'd put more faith in the man behind the bar than the one with the whip."

"That, I understand."

With Sofia by her side, Cassia's loyalty to him would be solidified. Now, he turned his attention to securing Alina's unwavering loyalty.

"And what about you?" Bios asked, shifting focus. "Do you have anything you need to handle right now in the Silent Deserts? Once we take Cassia, I expect it won't take long to retrieve her daughter. If you have anything or anyone you'd like to do or see before we leave, speak your mind."

"Killing Klein is always on my mind," Alina said coolly.

"Then you can kill Klein," Bios said with a sly grin.

"You talk as if we're just going to the market to buy fruit and stopping at stalls," Alina remarked with a hint of sarcasm.

"With my power, it makes little difference," Bios said, his grin widening. "With a plan in place, we should discuss the next steps for the mission we've been given."

As Cassia returned, her face bright with relief, she exclaimed, "The Magician will take care of Sofia!" and smiled.

"I'm sure it will be a mutually beneficial arrangement," Bios said. "Now that we've settled that, let's begin our assassination mission. We'll head to the Silent Deserts afterward."

THE MARKET IN SKY TOWER COAST LOOKED LIKE ANY OTHER MARKET Bios had seen, and its generic appearance made it difficult for him to recall the specific details required for the Teleportation Stone to create a portal there. Instead, he decided to teleport to the Sky Tower, a distinctive landmark close to his destination.

He closed his eyes and focused on his prior memories there. The cool sea breeze brushed against his face and the distant cries of seagulls soaring above the waves were a constant sound. Sky Tower

Coast stood out for its towering lighthouse, a marvel built long before the rise of the Darian Kingdom.

The lighthouse was constructed of heavy bricks that had settled into the ground. To prevent collapse during strong winds, its curved walls featured grate-like openings, allowing ocean winds to pass through. However, this design also allowed rain to seep into the inner chambers, necessitating a drainage system carved into the stairwell to channel water back to the ocean. While most lighthouses elsewhere, such as those at Starlight Beach or White Boar's Landing, reached only sixty feet in height, Sky Tower stood nearly six hundred feet tall—ten times their height.

Lost in thought, Bios activated the Teleportation Stone. The portal he'd wished for appeared, and he stepped through with his companions into the sea breeze. He inhaled, enjoying the fresh coastal air after the musty interior of the Golden Mare. Meanwhile, Alina and Cassia looked up at the majestic lighthouse in awe.

"I didn't expect this would be your first time here," Bios said.

"We landed in the southern region when we originally came to Yaenia," Alina replied. "We would have remembered seeing this."

The tower stood nearly half a mile from the shore, so they made their way along the beach. Cassia knelt cautiously, her hand hovering above the ground. A moment later, she slipped her boots off and let her bare feet sink into the sand.

"It amazes me you can do this here," she said. "I'm not burning."

Bios remarked, "I thought only the Black Sands were dangerous to the touch."

"The Black Sands will burn you, yes," Cassia explained, "but the White Sands are like shattered glass—painful and relentless. You won't burn, but you'll bleed, and the fragments are impossible to remove entirely from your skin. Some grains are too small to see, leaving you with an enduring reminder of their presence."

"Yaenians often curse others to die in the Black Sands of Tornaa," Alina added. "But in reality, the White Sands are far crueler. Those who walk among them will suffer a lifetime of torment. The shards penetrate the feet, making the cuts excruciating. Walking becomes impossible."

"What a terrible fate," Bios said, noting it as the perfect spot to dispose of his next victim without having to end their life himself.

They walked along the beach toward the market, soaking up the warm sun and bracing sea air. In the distance, dozens of ships approached the shoreline. Alina's eyes widened as she took in the scene.

"Why are there so many ships? Are they all here for trade?"

"Those who command them are best suited to answer that," he said cryptically. "Still, the likelihood is yes. Sky Tower Coast, the largest port city in Yaenia, welcomes most of the people returning from the Golden Bay Market, bringing back salt and other supplies. The Darian Kingdom now relies more heavily on the Silent Deserts than ever before."

Cassia exclaimed, "How can they continue doing business with such a horrible country?"

Bios fixed his gaze on the horizon. "The Darians have always maintained a complicated relationship with the slavers—one that's delicate yet necessary. Many rely on the slavers for resources they can't or won't produce themselves, and neither side is eager to upset the balance."

As they walked along the beach, the sand beneath their feet felt firm, but Bios soon noticed how easily it shifted and gave way under his boots. The small mounds, shaped by wind and ocean, rose and fell in unpredictable patterns, serving as a reminder of how even the quietest aspects of nature could conceal chaos. The scene made him think of the forces that governed the world—some visible, others hidden—and the efforts of many working to counteract nature's influence.

"There must be another way for the world to get its salt," Cassia insisted. "Is no one concerned about the innocent lives being destroyed by it?"

Bios looked out at the ships, knowing all too well the answer to Cassia's question. Power and profit often triumphed over morality and justice, leaving anyone in the middle at their mercy. Like a Lucidian's magic, everything of value demanded a cost in blood, and so the price was paid. Still, the world survived—and would always survive—in this way.

Rather than revealing his true thoughts, Bios replied, "If the Darians cared about defeating slavery, they would have declared war on the Silent Deserts long before now."

They walked in silence a moment longer before Alina hesitated and asked, "Sir Hellvar—I mean, Bios Auras, could you not put an end to slavery whenever you want?"

Her ideals prevented her from fully grasping the complexity of the situation. Even if all the slavers were eliminated that very day, the Silent Deserts wouldn't magically transform into a paradise. For the time being, it was better not to burden her with this truth. Instead, it was wiser to let her cling to her idealistic beliefs, flawed though they were. He would drag her along for now.

"I'm not sure what would happen to the world once we destroy the masters," he told her. "The Silent Deserts have been the world's primary source of salt for centuries. Without the masters, the slaves would stop working, halting salt production. People being paid fairly for their work makes it unsustainable, you see. Unable to trade for essential supplies, the Silent Deserts would face economic collapse. This would lead to famine in the Silent Deserts and a global salt shortage, leaving everyone to suffer."

"So, you're afraid of unintended consequences," Alina said. "So how will you help us in the future?"

"I'm simply being cautious," Bios said. "Without caution, one might risk creating chaos and darkness instead of order and light as intended."

"If your goal is to eliminate all evil from the world, wouldn't that create even greater harm?" Alina pressed, "The side effects could cause far more imbalance than ending slavery."

Bios turned to face her, his expression thoughtful as if he were pondering her question.

"Before order can arrive, chaos must release its final screams," he replied with a measured, soft-spoken voice, "and the road to order is bloodied with chaos. The challenge lies in choosing the right path—one that leads to the desired outcome. Every step requires sacrifice and compromise."

Cassia grew visibly frustrated as she struggled to make sense of Bios's words. "But what about the innocent lives that suffer in the process? How will you stop that?"

Bios locked eyes with her, delivering the final blow. "They would be the last generation to suffer, ending an endless cycle of suffering."

"I believe I understand what you mean," Alina replied. "A flower does not wither the very moment it stops receiving water."

Bios nodded at Alina, his approval evident, as Cassia fell into a reflective silence. "Come now," he urged, "let's find the judge's home and complete our mission. Our time for our own pursuits will come soon. The Silent Deserts are waiting."

Upon approaching the busy harbor, Bios teleported them to a rooftop, where they were greeted by an unobstructed view of the lively streets below.

Alina scanned the crowd as she asked, "So you've been here before?"

"A few times," he replied. "But I know little about the officials involved in managing it. Should we split up and try gathering more information?"

"Avoid asking people what we seek; it could raise suspicion," Cassia advised. "Instead, observe and listen carefully."

"When should we regroup back here?" Alina asked.

"There are a few hours until sundown," Bios said. "We'll return to this meeting spot at dusk to share our findings."

He teleported all three to an inconspicuous location in the market, and from there they split up. For now, he would let Alina and Cassia handle the investigation, intervening only if they encountered obstacles or failed to make progress.

Wandering through the crowded streets, Bios found a strange sense of inner peace. Despite the thick crowds, he moved unnoticed, observing the lives of ordinary people. Before joining the People's Army and the Throatians, this was how he spent his idle hours—watching traders negotiate deals, guards arresting thieves, bards entertaining onlookers, and drunkards brawling. Each interaction taught him valuable lessons about persuasion, evasion, emotional appeal, and the power of provocation.

"The god is dead!" declared a man, his voice echoing from atop a wooden crate in the center of the road. His black robes were streaked with bold white stripes. "What good can a dead god do for us? Nothing! Asura is dead."

Bios's face turned crimson, matching his armor. He pushed through the crowd, hoping he was merely using shock tactics to attract attention. If the man wasn't about to declare Asura's return...

"The world is doomed!" he continued. "Asura has abandoned us, leaving everyone to rot. We've fallen short of his expectations, and there's no point in having a god if no one heeds his will—that's why he's gone. There's no god among us, no divine presence in human form. If such a god existed, wouldn't they have defeated the evil plaguing our world? Wouldn't they have saved our fruit from rotting before it was too late?"

To believe in the Dead Asura Theory was worse than believing in no god at all; though it meant acknowledging Asura's existence, it also accused him of abandonment.

Long ago, something significant happened to Asura involving Somnius. Yet those who loudly proclaimed their religious views in the squares never spoke of her. Bios didn't have all the answers, and neither did anyone else. However, he understood that Somnius, Asura, and the God Stones were connected somehow. The man he'd encountered in the cold, distant future had confirmed this. Clearly, something had gone terribly wrong. Somnius should have helped Bios gather the God Stones, not opposed him. Why had she betrayed him? If only the stranger in the blizzard had offered more context, Bios might have grasped the universe's true nature. The future would be too bleak if he were to fail in what he'd been tasked to do.

Bios longed for more time with the mysterious man from the future. Learning more about the God Stones and why they were separated could reveal the reason for his mission. For now, he understood he was Asura's chosen warrior, and his duty was to gather the God Stones. Through him, Asura would return.

Bios tightened his fists. Every word the man in front of him spoke was a lie, fueling a growing urge to strike him down. Drawing his sword and ending the deceit would be simple, but losing access to the Teleportation Stone for an indefinite period wasn't worth it—not with his mission still pending. Suppressing his magic felt as grating as enduring the hypocrite's lies.

He spotted Alina's fair face in the crowd. Her green eyes met his across the distance, and she made her way toward him.

"I thought you were looking for our target," she whispered.

"The fool up there stole my attention," Bios replied dryly. "Have you learned anything?"

"I know where she lives," Alina confirmed, "and we can act tonight."

She had approached the nearest city guards, posing as a messenger. Despite Cassia's earlier warning, she had directly asked them where Sigrid lived. It was a clever but risky move, only eased by the plan that Alina, Bios, and Cassia would teleport back to the Golden Mare immediately after completing their mission.

"You've done well." Bios nodded approvingly.

"It will still be some hours before Cassia returns," Alina said.

"Shall we rest somewhere out of sight? I have no interest in listening to this man ramble on either."

"Perhaps, but first, I have another favor to ask," he said with a smile, gesturing toward the crowd's center with his hand low at his chest. "When the blasphemous one runs out of breath, lure him away and take care of him."

Her eyes met his, glowing with reverence that seemed to transcend mere respect.

"Without question," she replied.

He smiled. "So, you believe in Asura now?"

"I'm not sure about that yet," Alina admitted, "but I believe in you."

"I'll find a back door," Alina volunteered as they approached the home belonging to their target.

Judge Sigrid Var's two-story house resembled a box-shaped garden vase, painted in pink plaster with violet trim and artistic emblems of various flowers. Bios's first impression was that the judge had spared no expense on her decorations. He imagined that, once they broke in, they would find many trinkets and useless treasures collected during her years at Sky Tower Coast. Bios estimated the house contained at least six rooms, excluding common areas. Given its size, she probably had servants, and none of them knew their target's appearance. Bios surmised that the most elegantly dressed person would likely be her.

As Alina disappeared into the tall green hedges, Bios and Cassia stayed on the other side of the garden, inspecting the building's exterior. The front door was enormous, large enough to accommodate a cart and two horses. Though imposing, it was of no use to them. Four windows on the top floor remained closed.

Earlier in the day, Alina had revealed her lock-picking skills, and Bios had teleported to a disreputable district in Last Hope to buy her the tools. However, lock picking proved unnecessary. When Alina returned, her face lit up with a confident smile. "There's a balcony overlooking a larger garden on the backside," she said, "and the door is ajar."

She guided them through the hedges to the other side of the

house, revealing her discovery. The balcony would have been inaccessible to a common thief, but with Bios's Teleportation Stone, the open door rendered it as accessible as the ground floor.

Bios teleported to the second level of the judge's home, opened a series of portals so he could bring Alina and Cassia up, and paused to listen, ensuring no one was nearby. He touched the polished wooden door and nudged it open.

To their surprise, neither Sigrid nor her servants were in the bedroom. They examined the empty quarters, noting her strong preference for floral patterns and the color pink. There were fewer rooms than Bios had expected, each unusually large.

As they exited into the hallway, they tiptoed through two other rooms before approaching a massive, out-of-place staircase. Bios raised his arm, alerting them to trouble, as he heard a faint scratching sound from below.

Scratching. Scratching. Scratching. What could it be?

"I hear it too," Cassia whispered, drawing her twin blades. "It's coming from the room on the right."

Bios focused his mind on the floor just outside the doorway and teleported down to avoid making any noise. He peeked through and saw a gray-haired woman sitting at a desk, writing furiously with a large quill. She refilled her ink from a nearly empty ink jar, seemingly unaware if not for her words.

"You're here earlier than I expected," Sigrid Var announced without looking up. "I have final notes to record before you undertake what you've come to do."

Bios held his tongue. Had she truly sensed their presence? Alina and Cassia crept closer behind him as he continued observing.

Sigrid wrote for a moment longer before pushing her chair back and standing. "The Magician and the Hanged Man were displeased," she said, still facing her papers. "That's what they must have told you, but it wasn't my fault."

"You're one of us?" Alina exclaimed. "You're our target?"

He was unsurprised that the People's Army was willing to eliminate one of its own. Sigrid must have done something reckless or serious to warrant assassination, especially considering that a judge was a powerful figure.

"The People's Army thrives because its members don't know who their allies are," she replied. "The lowest ranked blindly obey orders, while the Hierophant, the Cycle of Death, the Magician, the Hanged Man, the Empress, and all the other players pull the strings. It surprises me they sent you to kill me rather than the Fortitude."

"You're a politician, not a warrior," Cassia sneered.

"Yet three of you are here for me," Sigrid countered. "I had guards, but none remain, as you can see. I dismissed them to save their lives. Please allow me to accompany you. I must speak to the Hierophant or the Magician. They never gave me the chance to explain myself before deciding to silence me forever."

Information was power, and Sigrid had more knowledge about the People's Army than they did. She would reveal everything she knew to bargain for her life.

"Our orders are to kill you," Bios said, drawing his blade. "Are you ready to die, Judge Var?"

"Wait! This doesn't have to happen this way!" Sigrid pleaded. "Your mission is to kill me, but the Magician didn't specify when. He never does! The timing is up to you, isn't it? As long as you end my life within a reasonable time, you can take me with you and let me explain."

"Tell us your story, then," Bios said, lowering his weapon. "Why have we come to kill you?"

Sigrid asked, "Haven't you heard about what happened here recently?"

"Go on," Alina said, sensing Bios's hesitation. "Pretend we know nothing—state your version."

"My position holds significant power," Sigrid stated. "I determine who is jailed, who is set free, and who faces execution. I also shape local laws, such as setting taxes. The People's Army relies on me; I funnel some of those funds into their operations. Do you see how this could go wrong?"

"Modifying ledgers is possible if you have access to every copy and enough time," Bios said. "So how did anyone discover you?"

"I didn't change any ledgers," Sigrid replied, brushing her hand over the desk's surface. "Instead, I paid people for generic work that seemed legitimate but was actually nonexistent. The gold went to the People's Army. One of my workers discovered my methods."

It became clear how the People's Army managed to survive—by siphoning taxes from the very people they claimed to represent.

"How much wealth did the People's Army receive from you?" Bios asked curiously.

"Incredible amounts," Sigrid said. "Decades of tax money from market sales, harbor transactions, and even struggling families who could barely afford to contribute. Everyone gives to me, but that part is meaningless. If the People's Army removes my hand from Sky Tower Coast's purses, they'll lose everything. When a worker dared accuse me of theft, I had him and his family eliminated. Everyone assumed they were Throatians. I was nearly exposed, but I wasn't. Anyone who might have known the truth about the taxes is now silenced."

"You executed an entire family for that?" Alina breathed. "No wonder the leaders want you dead."

"Gold is the lifeblood of all religious and political groups," Sigrid declared. "The People's Army represents both. Public executions were necessary—to instill fear in the city and protect the Common People."

"By killing the Common People," Alina added.

"No one suspects me now. I ensured it. Please let me explain it to—"

"There's more to your story," Bios cut in. "And I want to know what else you're not telling me."

Several stray thoughts raced through his mind: Cassia's quest to return to the Silent Deserts in search of her daughter, Alina's mission to abolish slavery there, the Throatians' rapid growth and the need to manage it without losing control, his own investigation into the Whisperers and their possible connection to a God Stone or a dragon, and Somnius's betrayal. However, the judge's response only deepened his frustration. Now was her last chance to share valuable information; if she had nothing more to say, then their mission must be completed.

"That's everything I know," Sigrid replied. "If the Magician, the Hierophant, or the Hanged Man could hear my reasoning—"

"Cassia," Bios commanded.

"No! Please!"

Already prepared with her knives, Cassia charged forward. Sigrid raised her arms in resistance, but Cassia swiftly ended the confrontation, catching the judge and gently lowering her body to the ground.

"I'm sorry it had to end this way," Cassia said, kneeling next to Sigrid, "but you probably deserved it."

"Are you certain she wouldn't have convinced the Magician to spare her?" Alina asked Bios.

"Sending us was already their final answer," Bios replied.

"Besides, there might have been more to Sigrid's story than she revealed."

"That's fair," Alina said, sheathing her sword and striding over to the desk near Sigrid's body. She picked up the paper and skimmed it, her brow furrowing as she processed the information.

"What is it?" Cassia asked, cleaning her blades on Sigrid's clothing. "What did she write?"

"Nothing but poems. What a waste of her last moments."

"Poems?" Bios said as he stepped toward the table. "Or a hidden message?"

Alina handed the sheet over to him. "Lamentation of the end times. Useless words."

He read Sigrid's poem, looking for any symbols or double meanings:

The power of justice, here I stand,
An apocalypse nears, but not by my command,
Lawless reigns, I cannot reprimand,
My power, a mere shadow, now I understand.

"She knew we were coming for her," Bios said, resting the paper on the desk, "and lacks creativity for rhyming words."

The judge understood the relationship between order and chaos, and for a moment, he regretted denying her a longer life. Instead of dwelling on his minor regret, he examined the rest of her belongings, and his eyes fell on her wax seal—a bronze owl encircled by feathers. It served as proof that their mission was complete.

Suddenly, a creak echoed from a nearby doorway. The sound indicated it was the large entryway door they had noticed earlier. It was likely one of Sigrid's servants or friends.

"Someone's coming," Alina whispered.

"Let's get out of here," Cassia replied.

Bios visualized his bedroom at the Golden Mare and activated the Teleportation Stone to create an invisible portal. "Follow me," he said, moving toward the fireplace where the portal had been placed.

As he was about to step through, a familiar voice echoed from the doorway.

"Sir Hellvar, don't worry—put away your weapons. It's me!"

Though he had expected no one, Bios unsheathed his sword again. "Who exactly?" he growled, turning around again.

Alina and Cassia exchanged glances and readied their weapons as well.

"Your friend, of course," the man's voice echoed, "and business partner."

Bios emerged from Sigrid's study into the entryway, where the portly Darian Councilman Ofred stood beside a cloaked man wearing a bronze owl mask. In contrast to figures like the Hierophant, the Hanged Man, and the Cycle of Death, this towering member of the People's Army was both tall and imposing.

He sheathed his sword again. "Your letter specified we should meet inside the butcher's shop. Why are you here if not to confirm that we eliminated the judge?"

"That's exactly why we're here," the councilman said. "I doubted you would succeed so quickly in your missions, but I'm happy to be proven wrong again and again. You've achieved a great deal. Walk with me, Sir Hellvar. We have much to discuss regarding your rewards."

"AND WHAT IS THE NAME OF YOUR COMPANION?" BIOS ASKED AS Ofred led him, Alina, and Cassia outside into Sigrid's garden. The sun had set, but moonlight provided just enough light for them to navigate the hedges as they strolled.

"I am the Fortitude," the man said with a metallic voice. In the darkness, he was nearly invisible except for the faint hue of his owl mask.

His title was as cryptic as the others, but it carried an air of significant political power. Since his arrival, the Fortitude had remained silent, and Bios suspected he was there to observe.

"And who are you?" Cassia asked, walking beside the councilman.

"You don't know?" Ofred exclaimed, clearly offended. "Then again, you are foreigners, so perhaps it's forgivable. I am Ofred."

Curiously, he failed to mention his title. Bios wasn't concerned about the omission; instead, he wondered why Ofred had come all the way from Last Hope to offer their payment. How did they know Sigrid was going to die that night?

"You spoke of a reward," Bios said, hoping to learn about their true intentions. "Have you come with the information I asked for?"

"Soon, you'll have it," Ofred promised. "But first, I have some bad news. Do the women of the Silent Deserts know about our previous arrangement?"

"They weren't aware," Bios replied, "but there's no reason to hide it from them."

"Very well," the councilman conceded. "Our agreement regarding the Darian silos must end immediately. Iris Thorne has grown more suspicious of me. Though the people you steal food for aren't part of the People's Army, she might suspect they are. You understand the consequences if we are suspected of revealing our true identities, even if unintentionally."

"Sigrid turned what could have been quiet executions into a public spectacle," Bios said. "That's why the owl-masked figures ended her life, isn't it?"

He halted and faced the Fortitude. A blank, unblinking stare froze the eyes behind the mask. Their lips remained silent, and Bios realized the full extent of the People's Army's demand for secrecy.

"Our movement thrives through fragmentation," Ofred explained. "Anyone attracting unwanted attention, even if unrelated to our missions, is scrutinized. Sigrid was aware of this yet disregarded it. Therefore, you ought to understand why I must cancel our arrangement."

"I do," Bios said. He would have to assist the Throatians in finding an alternative food source or face the consequences of a famine on their island. Last Hope's silos were not limitless.

As the five of them entered a clearing in Sigrid's garden, statues of giant owls perched on gray stone pedestals greeted them. The judge had clearly stolen tax money, not only for the People's Army but also for her personal gain. The councilman paused to admire the collection.

"I must ask you once more, if I haven't done so already," Ofred continued as he brushed his fingers along one of the stone bases. "Who needed all those supplies? If I knew who needed them and where, perhaps I could help in other ways."

Ofred had obviously come to Sky Tower Coast to gather this information. The person or group requiring such a large quantity of food could pose a threat to the People's Army. While the Throatians were an obvious danger, there was another possibility that could address everyone's concerns.

Alina sat on one of Sigrid's benches, while Cassia stood by Ofred. Meanwhile, Fortitude wandered off to lean against an owl statue.

Bios replied calmly, "Many slaves in the Silent Deserts go hungry. Their masters provide them with barely enough food, and many grow malnourished and are discarded when they can no longer work." He added, "I serve the Common People of both the Silent Deserts and Southern Yaenia."

The response was perfect, satisfying the councilman and further earning the respect of Alina and Cassia.

"What Hellvar says is true," Cassia chimed in. "Lesser masters underfeed their workers. It's a common practice when a master owns more slaves than they can support."

"I've always suspected you were charitable," Ofred replied. "Please excuse me for a moment, Sir Hellvar. I need to step away—I've had too much to drink. Not alcohol, mind you, just water. Wait here, and we'll discuss your reward for completing the mission against Sigrid in a moment."

The councilman bowed and then awkwardly excused himself to relieve himself behind a nearby hedge. Cassia nodded at Bios as they waited.

"You didn't tell us you were sending food to the Silent Deserts," she said. "Thank you for that. You really were an ally all along."

"There's a lot I haven't told anyone," Bios answered with a cryptic smile. However, he shouldn't have smiled. He should have looked up instead.

An overwhelming force, as heavy as the world itself, came crashing down on them. There was no time to think of escape or another place to flee—not even the other side of the garden would have sufficed. The Teleportation Stone was useless without a destination; it couldn't save him. He couldn't react; he could only sense the looming dark object above his head. Bios's fear, however, was short-lived. In a brief yet fatal instant, every bone in his body shattered, and his body burst from inside his crimson armor.

38
KIRA - THE PROPHECY OF TEARS AND SACRIFICE

Her eyes were as swollen as they were red while the day drew to a close. Lanterns with fireflies illuminated the fences along the road, but she couldn't enjoy them like she once did while following Kaine back to Celeste's shack. When they arrived, the door was slightly open, and they entered to find Sen and Celeste tending to her sleeping brother. Xander looked frail, his face pale and distant, as if a fever had consumed him. The sight carved a hollow pain inside Kira's chest. She wondered why he'd chosen this path.

She wanted to slap him with all her might—not only to punish him but also to test whether his memory had truly been erased. The way everyone else reacted suggested Celeste's magic hadn't failed.

Xander had always ruled those around him, commanding them to obey his every whim. Celeste was no exception—just as he had ordered servants at home to deliver alcohol to his room, he had demanded that Celeste erase his mind. But this time, he had overstepped. He should never have asked for his memories to be erased, let alone forced Celeste to use her magic on him. Instead of seeking her help or talking to Kaine about his struggles, he had acted impulsively.

It was too late to change anything now. Xander had left Kira and the others facing an impossible situation—one nobody could find an answer to yet. They needed more time to decide their next move, and Orin's suggestion to keep Xander asleep until they had answers seemed like the best course of action.

"You've brought it?" Sen whispered, her eyes never leaving the prince.

Kaine produced a small cloth pouch, whose contents Finnegan had selected from Sen's stock at the hot springs. "He warned me not to touch the leaf unless I wanted to sleep like Xander," he said.

He handed the pouch to Sen with care, and she carefully untied it without touching the leaves. "It's just like him to over prepare. A single large leaf—or even two small ones—would have sufficed. There was no need for a bushel."

Sen stepped back from Xander's bedside and borrowed one of Celeste's mortar and pestle sets. Kira took her place beside the prince, and time seemed to slow under the flickering candlelight over his face.

"Princess," Sen said after a moment. "This is for you."

She offered her the folded letter, and Kira didn't need to open it to know its contents—it was Xander's.

"Why are you giving this to me?" she asked.

"Will you destroy it?" Her voice carried a desperate weight, revealing her indecisiveness. Meanwhile, Celeste watched them from across the room as if she were on trial for murder.

"The prince's letter is the only proof of both your and Celeste's innocence," Kira muttered. "Destroying it feels wrong."

"You needn't worry about me," Celeste said. "If King Ether discovers the truth and deems me responsible, he has every right to punish me."

"He won't learn the truth," Kaine promised. "We all agreed that keeping it hidden is best for everyone. Kira wouldn't want to see you executed either. I wonder whether we should keep the letter just in case we might need it later. Once we burn it, we can't change our minds. The letter is our only proof—we must be certain it's safe to destroy."

Sen interjected from across the room. "Only pain can come of it, not good. No happiness will ever come from reading the words Xander wrote."

Kira froze again. Sen was right—Xander's letter was too painful to read. What he'd written was so melancholic and dark that Kira barely finished it before becoming overwhelmed and fainting. Even if their father someday learned the truth about Gale Village, she didn't want him to know Xander's final thoughts. It was too much—not just for her, but it would be for him too.

"Perhaps the princess should decide," Kaine suggested as he sat next to the bed. "They are her brother's last words from before it happened."

"I couldn't bear to look over the paper again," Sen commented as she ground the mortar. The paste inside turned a deep orange, and Kira guessed the Death's Whisper was nearly ready. "Orin and Merdel think it's best to get rid of the evidence. But the decision, Kira, is yours. You understood your brother better than any of us."

The letter held Xander's final words and will, along with the darkest secrets of his heart. Would he have wanted these truths revealed? The Xander Kira once knew would never have wished to cause any pain—yet he had already crossed that field. Then she realized the letter didn't just expose painful truths; it was proof of their innocence and confirmation that what happened to Xander was real. But if the truth remained hidden forever, Celeste, Sen, and the rest of Gale Village would stay free from harm, rendering the letter's protection unnecessary. As long as everyone believed that a rock had hit Xander in the head, the existence of the letter could only hurt their credibility.

"Destroying it and keeping what happened a secret is the only way to keep you safe," Kira concluded. "I don't want anyone else to suffer."

Before she could change her mind, she held the letter over the candle flame and set it alight. The paper quickly burned, and she dropped the last bit to the ground, stomping it out to prevent it from burning her fingers. When she picked up the remaining edge, only a small blank corner of the page remained.

"Wait! There's one more thing," Celeste interrupted. "Xander asked me to copy his letter into my velvet book. I granted his wish since it was his last request, but now I wonder if I should burn it too."

She revealed her notebook—a collection of memories, wishes, and facts, echoes of lives reset by her powers. Its pages likely held sad regrets and the deepest dreams of those who had chosen the same path as Xander. Perhaps it was better to let them all be destroyed by the flame as well.

"Why destroy it?" Sen asked. "You've carried the book for decades!"

"It's true they were mementos," Celeste said. "These texts were the last remnants of what people wanted to leave behind. To some, they served as a guide to their next life, filled with hopes and dreams for the future. For others, the writings were a reason to forget everything, believing my magic was the greater option. I've always thought of my notebook this way. Now, all I see is a graveyard of people who've died but kept alive the worst of themselves."

"When you offered to erase my memories, I said it wasn't the right choice for me, though I was open-minded that it might help others," Kaine said, gently gathering the ashes of Xander's letter into his palm. "But now I realize it might never be the right choice. Xander chose wrong—he should have confronted his pain instead."

Kira understood the struggle. Lydia's use of the Memories Stone had forced Kaine to confront similar questions about his memory and identity. But would her sister have supported erasing someone's entire past?

"Facing one's suffering is the harder path, but the right one," Celeste said, gazing at the prince. "I've always believed our lives are too short for bearing so many painful wounds. Erasing memories was my solution for those who couldn't overcome their trauma. I just wanted to help them let go of their pain, but I was incorrect. Perhaps they were meant to bear those weights, after all. Treating suffering as an illusion that can be wiped away is otherwise a selfish errand. One's growth dies along with it."

"There have always been times when using our powers might have been wrong," Sen said as she mixed more water into the paste. "During the war, I healed people, but later those same people committed atrocities. We must do what feels right in the moment and hope destiny balances everything out for the better."

A tear crawled down Celeste's face. "I thought my powers healed those in need and harmed enemies deserving of harm. But I never imagined using them against my will on someone who shouldn't have wielded them. My conclusion is this: erasing trauma is itself traumatic. Kaine, you were right that night—how can someone grow stronger if I erase everything they've faced and survived? My power doesn't erase pain; it weakens people instead."

"I didn't intend to challenge you," Kaine said. "I was speaking hypothetically, specifically about myself."

Sen approached the bedside with the Death's Whisper mixture. "Perhaps Xander will find his own strength in the future, in his own way. If destiny balances all things, then this today may not matter after all."

"There's no way to know," Celeste lamented. "For now, I've robbed him of what could have made him a greater person."

"But look at Kira," Sen said. "Her heart was terribly wounded by what happened to her brother, yet she has grown stronger because of it."

"I have?" Kira replied. The Lucidian was only trying to help her feel better. But she hadn't changed at all—she'd only suffered immeasurable losses.

"You have grown, dear," Celeste said. "Initially, you were hesitant about your role in the Prophecy of Tears and Sacrifice. After your brother's death, you vowed to master the God Stones to save him. I wonder, would you have grown so much in such a short time if I hadn't erased Xander's memories? Who would you be now without losing your mother, sister, and brother? Everything you've faced has hurt you deeply, yet it's also forced you to grow."

"Perhaps we can agree that trauma might either crush us or lead us toward resilience," Kaine said. "The choice is ultimately ours."

"Maybe the shadows of this world only serve to strengthen the strong and weaken the weak," Celeste mused. "If that's all there is to it, then that would explain everything."

"Burn the velvet book, Celeste," Sen urged. "Let go of the past. Your notebook is just a collection of ghosts and bad memories. Vow never to use your magic again, except if you need to save your life, and you'll free yourself from these moral dilemmas."

"The Grace Mage tells the truth," Kaine said. "Defending yourself against Xander was likely the only reason you are both still alive."

Kira didn't want to imagine what might have happened if the conflict between her brother and Celeste had escalated further in another direction.

Celeste gave them a thin smile that barely reached her eyes. "In that case, I plan to destroy it soon after I read through its contents one last time. You're both correct—I need to face it to let it go. All along, this book was my shadow."

"You've made the right decision, my friend," Kaine replied.

Sen, now wearing a leather glove over her hand, dipped her finger into the orange paste and took a small blob. She opened Xander's mouth, inserted her fingers under his tongue, and pressed gently. Sweat dripped down her brow as she massaged the paste into his gums.

"The mixture will absorb into his body faster than a raw leaf," she explained.

"How long will it keep him asleep?" Kira asked, observing the prince's shallow, rhythmic breathing.

"Fourteen days for someone his size," Sen replied. "After twelve days, insert a raw leaf into his mouth. It will take a day to fully absorb through his tongue, extending his slumber by another two weeks. To keep him asleep indefinitely, replace the leaf every twelve days. Carefully plan when you want him to wake up."

"Thank you, Sen," Kaine said. "Is there anything else we should know about using Death's Whisper?"

"Yes," Sen nodded. "Give him a small amount of water daily—just enough to keep him hydrated without risking choking. He can go without food for up to a month. If you should require him to sleep more, you may feed him bone broth directly into his throat. It's delicate work, but if you can get it past his neckline, his body will still digest it."

"I hope it won't come to that," Kaine said. "Hopefully, we won't need him to slumber long once we arrive at the Leila Kingdom."

"I pray so too," Celeste said. "Though I cannot be certain about the chances of his original memories returning, I trust this will ultimately serve Xander for the better."

Kira looked over at the prince again, tears arriving in her eyes uninvited. She blinked them away rapidly and breathed shallowly. "I promise, Xander," she whispered. "We'll find a way to bring you back."

Sen placed a gentle hand on her shoulder, gathering her attention. "You bear a heavy burden," she said, "but remember, Kaine is by your side."

Kira nodded, struggling to regain her voice. "I know, I just… I miss him. Even though he's right here and I've just talked to him, it feels like he's not coming back. What if the God Stones can't restore his memories?"

Sen sighed, her gaze lingering on the prince. "Magic, despite its mysteries and glamour, also hides its shadows. But hope, Kira, is something even magic cannot take away, so long as you choose to keep embracing it. Hope and dedication are more powerful than magic."

"If hope is the one thing magic cannot destroy," Kira said, "then I must learn to never let go of it."

KIRA STILL HAD PARTS OF HERSELF SHE NEEDED TO FREE HERSELF FROM. She returned to the shack alone as Kaine was away meeting with Merdel and Orin. The shack felt lonelier without her brother, yet in that moment, Kira found peace in the solitude.

She commented, "I must hold on to hope, even if it seems stupid," to the empty beds around her. Approaching the one she'd been using for weeks, she pulled Lydia's mirror from her satchel.

The silver frame remained unchanged, and the glass reflected Kira's face with its usual shine. Now, looking into it felt different—less like gazing upon the familiar, imaginary spirit of her sister hidden in the mirror, and more like staring back at herself with no one else beside her. Though Kira knew expecting anything supernatural from the polished surface was foolish since Lydia had died, she couldn't shake the sense of loss the mirror's simple reflection brought now that Xander was gone too.

For the first time since Lydia's passing, Kira found no comfort in the mirror; it simply showed her, and her alone. She still bore a striking resemblance to her late sister—their faces were so alike one could easily mistake them for each other. But Kira's eyes had changed. Though green as always, they no longer held grief for someone who had always overshadowed her. Letting go of the obsession that she was merely another version of her sister wouldn't be enough. Now, Kira understood her strengths and weaknesses didn't depend on comparing herself to Lydia—what mattered more was what she'd learned from her while choosing to create her own fate for the future. Her destiny, whatever it might be, had to become something she could make on her own.

"I love you, my sister," Kira said to the empty room. "And I miss you. But I must go the rest of the way myself. I can't keep looking for you anymore. I have to find Xander now."

She slid Lydia's hand mirror underneath her pillow and took a deep breath. With her final decision made, she pressed her hands down onto the pillow, edging forward with her full body weight. In that brief moment, a crunch sounded from underneath her, and Kira knew the mirror had finally shattered.

THEIR JOURNEY TO THE LEILA KINGDOM THE NEXT MORNING required little packing. Finn had stocked them with enough food for Kira, Kaine, and Merdel, while Xander's unconscious state meant he wouldn't need any meals for nearly a month. Merdel volunteered to carry the heaviest of the supplies, which was their water, since Kaine was already carrying Xander.

Wishing to do her share of the work, Kira insisted on lugging most of their food as they progressed through the narrow mountain rocks. The journey to the Leila Kingdom would be difficult, so she wanted to help the others as much as possible. Everyone else was doing their part to support Xander, and so would she.

The villagers had also built a sturdy cradle overnight, and Kira was amazed. The prince would rest face-up in the cot, secured by four thickly padded straps that wrapped tightly around Kaine's hips and over his shoulders. Kira tested the cradle to ensure it would be comfortable enough for her brother, and for the first time in days, she giggled.

To add to her brightening spirits, the morning's breeze provided a misty calm as they gathered outside Orin's shack to say their goodbyes. Despite recent events, the natural beauty of Gale Village offered a small parting gift. Kira suspected it might be years before they returned, if ever.

Unease filled Kira as she thought about the coming days. She dreaded the possibility of being locked in one of Serenity Keep's towers for her own "protection." As the last viable heir to the von Stonewall royal bloodline, her future was uncertain. Although she wished for happiness regardless of what destiny held, Kira was determined to shape her own path. Only in making her own way could she hope to fix everything that had occurred in Gale Village.

With everyone's help, Xander might recover, even if he would never be the same. In time, he would relearn all he'd forgotten and, hopefully, his original memories as well. Until then, as Sen had reminded her, the best they could do was to hold on to hope.

"Kira?" Merdel's voice interrupted her thoughts. "Are you ready to leave?"

She glanced around at her companions. Celeste and Sen, with their shades of purple-hued skin, were the first—and likely the last—Lucidians Kira would ever meet. Getting to know them and seeing their powers had been a bittersweet experience, leaving her uncertain if their journey had been for the greater good.

Finn, always quiet yet attentive, had gone out of his way to ensure their stay in Gale Village was as comfortable as possible. She couldn't thank him enough for that.

Orin, rough and worn from both past and present, stood nearby, propped up by his cane. "When you reach the Leila Kingdom, Kaine will need a tankard or three. His back will probably hurt worse than mine by the time you get there."

"I'll make sure to rest along the way," Kaine promised. "I owe it all to Sen for healing my arm so well that I can use it properly again. Without her, we might have had to leave Xander in your care."

"Everything happens for a reason," Sen replied, "even when it seems difficult to move a single step forward."

"Beyond our regrets awaits freedom, and we must use that for a brighter future," Celeste added.

"Again, what happened with the prince wasn't your fault," Merdel reassured her.

The elderly Lucidian smiled gently. "I truly appreciate your words. It's been hard to believe it's even possible."

Kira stepped forward and touched her arm. "I didn't want to accept it at first, Celeste, but I've realized the truth. Your magic was misused, not by you, but by my brother. I can't hold you responsible for his actions... So, I promise you, I will not tell my father what happened. I won't let him harm you. Revenge won't help any of this."

"Kira," Orin said with a twinkle, or perhaps a tear, in his eye. "You've grown up."

She smiled warmly for the first time in days, embracing Orin. "There's not enough time for me to be a child anymore. I have to let go of that, just like Lydia did. I'll find a way of bringing Xander to us again—I promise."

"Hard times make stronger princesses," Merdel said.

"Well, what are you waiting for?" Orin said with a playful grin. "Get on with it then!"

Taking a deep, steadying breath, Kaine lifted Xander onto his back and settled him into the cradle. The prince's body was limp, his head rolling slightly as Kaine adjusted him. Though the Death's Whisper still held him, one day it would fade, and they would renew his life toward a greater future.

"To the Leila Kingdom," Kira said, her gentle voice more authoritative than ever before.

"Right away, my princess."

BOOK 4 CHAPTER PREVIEW

Next is a bonus preview chapter from Symphony of Crowns and Gods Book 4: Throne of Deception and Dragons. I hope you will enjoy this glimpse of the next part and what's coming later on in the series. To order Throne of Deception and Dragons, please visit www.theauthorbrian.com or whichever storefront you purchased this book.

Thank you and enjoy!

— Brian A. Mendonça

NOTE ABOUT THE PREVIEW CHAPTER

Please be aware that the following scene preview is from an early or middle part of Throne of Deception and Dragons and has not undergone professional editing yet. Details presented here may undergo changes in the final version. This preview serves to provide a glimpse into the story's early development and is subject to further refinement. Expect minor changes and more writing enhancements in the subsequent drafts as the narrative unfolds...

BOOK 4 PREVIEW CHAPTER

Alina didn't look up. If only she had, she might have seen the giant boulder and warned Cassia and Bios. But it was too late. Instead, her eyes were fixed on the cloaked man with the owl mask, wondering why he'd suddenly raised his arms. She hadn't glanced at her allies, and hadn't seen the massive rock appear in the sky and then crash down on them. The sound of impact—a crunching thud—was what alerted her to the attack.

Cassia and Bios were dead. The Fortitude had killed them with magic. Alina couldn't have warned them. Even when she saw the boulder, it seemed so surreal that her lips froze, her mouth locked open in shock.

She had no time to process it. The owl-masked man might come for her next. If Bios couldn't teleport away in time, there was no chance she could escape. But wait, maybe he had. Maybe he'd created a portal just in time to save them both from the rock. The crunch Alina heard could have only been the ground, not their bodies.

No, it wasn't likely. It wasn't impossible, but it was improbable. There wasn't time to think.

"Don't move," the Fortitude growled. He staggered where he stood, exhausted from casting the magical boulder. Was he a Lucidian?

"Alina Oceansong!" Ofred's voice rang out from behind the hedges. "I'm so sorry you had to witness this. Do not fear; we won't hurt you. We have no reason to bring you harm."

They had no reason to harm Bios or Cassia either, but they did. Meanwhile, Ofred reappeared from where he'd gone a moment ago, his arms relaxed at his sides as if nothing had just happened.

Alina couldn't think of what to say. Was there anything that could change or undo what had just transpired? Everything depended on whether Bios had escaped with Cassia.

"Did it connect?" Ofred asked the Fortitude.

"It did," the man in the owl mask replied, his breath short. Alina guessed they were talking about the massive boulder that had fallen.

"Then it's safe. We'll verify and see that our plan succeeded."

Finally, Alina found her voice. "Your plan?"

"Sir Hellvar was not as he seemed," Ofred said. "You've undoubtedly witnessed his teleportation magic. Your mission to kill Judge Var was genuinely necessary for the greater good of the People's Army, but it was also a test to verify some of our suspicions. It served as a trap to assassinate him if our assumptions were correct. In the end, he needed to be killed. He had his hands in many things they should not have been. I'm sorry that your friend Cassia was taken along with him. You'll be compensated, of course—with gold, a higher rank in the People's Army, or anything else you desire. Our friends with the owl masks can make anything happen to settle with you. That is, if you continue your loyalty to the Common People."

"I-I don't understand," Alina stuttered through her tears. "They did what you asked. We completed our missions as ordered."

"When the three of you killed Councilman Conan and returned to the Magician so quickly," Ofred said, "it piqued our leaders' curiosity. How had you traveled so far and so fast? Magic was the only explanation. The eyewitnesses at Wargonne described a red-armored knight losing an arm, yet Hellvar returned seemingly unscathed. Maybe it had been Ambrose who'd lost his arm and died, but Hellvar was the only one among you wearing crimson armor."

"Hellvar had magic, yes," Alina said carefully, avoiding Bios's real name, "but he was using it to serve you. Why did you kill him?"

But she already knew the answer. Bios had likely been more powerful than others in the People's Army who could use magic. They feared his ability to move throughout the world as he pleased and to recover from any injury. But death was greater than an injury.

"The leaders of the People's Army have their reasons," Ofred replied, "and I promise you his death was necessary. Cassia's demise was not intended, and again, I apologize for that. I know she was your friend."

What would happen to Sofia now? Cassia would never return to her daughter and set her free. No, now wasn't the time to think about that. Ofred and the Fortitude might still kill her if they thought she'd seen too much.

"It's okay, I understand," Alina lied. She had to tell them what they wanted to hear if she wanted to live. "If killing Hellvar was best for the Common People, then it was for the greater good."

Ofred nodded gratefully. "I acknowledge it's often easier to say the words than to believe in them," he admitted. "Please return to the Golden Mare, and the Magician will take care of you and ensure you have everything you need. You'll also have some new recruits joining you soon, and from now on, we'll make you their leader. You've proven yourself capable."

"Thank you, sir," Alina muttered. She had little interest in anything he'd said; the words seemed to pass over her like a nighttime breeze. Cassia and Bios were dead. They'd been betrayed, and it could easily happen to her too.

"Run along now, Lady Oceansong," Ofred continued. "We'll meet again soon."

She turned her back to him and wandered back toward the outer edge of the garden where they'd first come. She kept her eyes up, just in case another boulder appeared above her. Thankfully, it seemed Ofred truly only intended to murder Bios Auras, but even that was too much.

When she reached the gate, she glanced back at the clearing where the boulder had dropped. Alina didn't want to see it, but she had to know if Bios and Cassia were truly gone. From what Ofred had mentioned earlier, they also wished to examine underneath the rock.

Slipping through the hedges, Alina circled back around the outer edge of the garden and crept through the brush. As she neared the clearing where the boulder rested, she spotted a willow tree and climbed its branches. She moved slowly, maintaining her silence despite her shaking body.

Halfway up, she crawled across a branch and hid within a blanket of leaves. From there, she could observe Ofred and the Fortitude and eavesdrop on their conversation.

"We'd be dead already if he had survived," the Fortitude said. "Hellvar is known to be quite vengeful."

"There's no contesting that he's dead, but the Chariot will arrive soon regardless," Ofred replied. "I can't fathom how you create boulders in mid-air but can't lift them again."

"I already told you; it's too large, and I'm feeling faint," the Fortitude said. "More blood is needed. Unless you give me yours, we'll just have to wait for him."

The owl-masked people were Lucidians. Alina didn't understand their magic fully, but blood was their source of power.

"It doesn't matter," Ofred replied. "We were permitted to bring him with us for that very purpose. Still, the Hierophant is taking a greater risk than usual, and for good reason."

"How sure are you of that?"

"Sigrid was long overdue to be gone, and sending the assassins proved the Magician's point that it wasn't a simple World Vein they were using," Ofred explained.

"Even so, you're certain it was fine letting the slave girl walk? She was of no consequence, but witnesses are still witnesses. She might know what Hellvar used or who I am."

Alina's face burned at the insult, but she had bigger concerns.

"She's no fool," Ofred replied. "She knows we could return her to her master at any time. Her loyalty is to us, and any temptation she had to follow Sir Hellvar died with him."

"I see."

"I've arrived," a new voice announced. From the east, a cloaked figure appeared, wearing a cerulean-colored owl mask. At their side was a prisoner, their face covered in a black cloth, guided by a chain.

"Chariot," the Fortitude greeted. "I thought you were already nearby."

"The assassins nearly discovered us when they were searching to enter the judge's home. I had to temporarily retreat."

"Is one donor going to be enough?"

The Chariot looked at the boulder, measuring its size and weight. "It will suffice—we need only break the boulder apart to examine what's underneath. Complete destruction won't be necessary."

"I agree," the Fortitude said. "Shall we begin?"

He moved over to where the Chariot stood with their captive and removed the cloth bag from the prisoner's face. The prisoner, a man in his thirties, was blindfolded and gagged, unable to make more than a whimper.

As the Fortitude wrapped his arms around the prisoner, the

Chariot pulled a trinket from her cloak—a tankard with a thick blade attached at the handle. She grasped the prisoner's shoulder and stabbed him in the neck. The prisoner squirmed but couldn't break free of the Fortitude's grip. Blood pulsed into the tankard-like contraption.

"The pressure is building," the Chariot stated, holding her palm out toward the boulder.

The prisoner continued to struggle. As the tankard nearly filled, the Chariot pulled it free and drank the blood as if she'd found water after days of thirst. Alina nearly vomited each time this happened. The prisoner served as nothing more than a source of energy until he collapsed and the Fortitude released him.

"I'm almost there," the Chariot continued, her arm shaking with effort. "I'll save some drink for you."

Finally, the boulder cracked into pieces, enough for them to examine what lay beneath. Satisfied, the Chariot sat down on the grass to rest while Ofred and the Fortitude approached the rubble. Alina leaned forward, squinting as they began sifting through the debris.

She looked only long enough to confirm the truth. The flattened bodies and their armor were proof. There hadn't been enough time for a portal after all. Neither Bios Auras nor Cassia had survived.

"The Teleportation Stone has to be here somewhere," Ofred said, letting the Fortitude dig through the rubble near where Bios and Cassia lay.

Alina closed her eyes and listened. She couldn't bear to look down again. What she'd seen was already too much, and it wasn't the outcome she'd hoped for. They hadn't escaped.

The Fortitude continued searching among the destruction.

"As far as I can tell, it isn't here," the Fortitude replied. "Maybe that's how we killed him."

"Confirming whether he had the stone is most important," the Chariot said from where she sat. "I'll search more for it while you collect the remains. Use the donor's wrappings as a makeshift bag. The Hierophant will want to study them regardless of how little is left intact. In either case, she will be pleased with our work, with Hellvar out of the way."

The Fortitude scoffed. "She's as obsessive about the inner workings of magic as her mother ever was."

"Blood and magic have always had a dark relationship," the Chariot said, "but you have to give her some respect. She's willing to plunge her hands deeper into those shadows than most, even Mythreya. We can only pray she doesn't follow the same path to madness as her mother did."

Alina took deep, sharp breaths, her eyes squeezed shut against the darkness. The night was tainted with the chirping of crickets, but she forced herself to listen beyond the sounds, afraid of what she might find. Finally, she opened her eyes and looked down.

Ofred, the Fortitude, and the Chariot were gone, having ventured through the pathway leading from Sigrid's home. They left behind only fragments of the boulder they'd used to kill Bios, scattered across the garden like ordinary waste. As Alina tried to climb down the willow tree, her shaking body betrayed her and she tumbled to the ground.

The moist earth was forgiving, cushioning her fall without causing further injury. It jolted her back to reality, and she knew she had to move. She steadied herself and approached the body of the blood donor lying on the ground. Gently, she placed her hand on the side of his neck opposite the stab wound. The skin was faintly warm but lifeless. No information would come from him.

Cassia's and Bios's bodies were gone, taken by the Fortitude, the Chariot, and Ofred. Alina's heart ached with a pain that felt like it would never subside. Cassia had been more than just an ally; they were friends who shared a bond beyond any of their missions and ideals. But now, Cassia was gone without any final words or closure. It wasn't Cassia's fault—Alina should have said what needed to be said: her gratitude, her encouragement, and her farewell. They both knew the risks when they joined the People's Army as assassins, but Alina had never truly accepted that one of them might not return or that they wouldn't somehow die together in their struggle.

She should have been the one crushed by that boulder. Alina had no family; she'd been abandoned as a newborn and raised as nothing more than an object by Klein, her former master. If Alina had died instead, only those who witnessed it would have known. But Sofia depended on Cassia for her freedom. Daughters needed their mothers in ways Alina could never understand. Alina had grown up without parents, leaving an empty hole in her heart and identity.

The crueler truth was that Sofia's grief would be far worse than Alina's loneliness ever had been.

The People's Army bore the blame for this. They had changed Sofia's life irrevocably, all in the name of studying Bios's healing and teleportation abilities. But as Alina stood there, she realized the ultimate fact: the People's Army didn't care about the Common People they claimed to serve. Judge Sigrid was right when she called them both a religion and a political movement. The People's Army was driven only by a desire for power. Their leaders hid behind owl masks, pretending to be wise and moral, but beneath those lies, they were no better than the slavers Alina despised.

Yet perhaps they were more powerful. The Fortitude and Chariot might have been the magical Lucidians she'd only heard about in stories. Their magic was real, and even Bios hadn't suspected it. His abilities were different than theirs, and maybe that's why the People's Army had taken such an interest in him. Did they already know what Bios had told her—that he was the chosen one of Asura?

The cruelty of the evening made Alina wonder if their motivations mattered at all. But the truth about Bios bore more significance. Could a chosen one of a god be killed? Maybe Bios had been delusional, or maybe his magic was just that—magic, not a sign of divine purpose. Was it one of the God Stones that kept him alive and allowed him to regrow his arm?

But he'd spoken of another named Somnius. There was clearly more to the story than she knew. If any of it were true, what did it mean now that he had been crushed under a rock?

Her thoughts circled in an endless loop. She'd seen his body next to Cassia's—crushed beyond recognition. If Bios were something more than human, and if there was evidence of it, could he heal even from death? Had he only been broken, but not dead?

"The People's Army must have had the same questions as me," Alina whispered to the owl statues surrounding her. "I've been such a fool."

There was a truth now—a greater truth than Alina had ever realized: if Bios could heal from his deadly wounds, he would bring an end to evil in the world, and she would stand by him. Whether they faced Lucidians or slavers, the fires they might ignite would consume all who stood in their way. Regardless of what might happen, even if she had to do it alone, she would not let Cassia's memory or the injustice she witnessed go unanswered. Alina, after all, had nothing left to lose.

Bios had once said to her, "I've never died before—I always heal," and Alina clung to those words with desperate hope. If there were any chance of his recovery, she needed to ensure it would happen.

She sprinted in the direction where the others had disappeared into Sigrid's garden.

SYMPHONY OF CROWNS AND GODS BOOK 4: THRONE OF DECEPTION AND DRAGONS

Destiny is challenged—but can it be changed?

The fragile opportunity Lydia created faces annihilation. History cannot be rewritten without new consequences.

Scattered heroes and villains must gather to resist a destiny that may destroy them all. Nobody can survive alone.

As an ancient evil dragon awakens, Eisenbern's knights race to reclaim a monster-conquered castle—but first, the Dragon Mar must confront her father's buried sins and mend her shattered tribe, or their mission will fail before it even begins.

In the Leila Kingdom, Kira and Kaine must find a solution to what happened in Gale Village and overcome the prophecy twisting into something darker and unexpected.

Prince Thane and Zeere have uncovered the secret to dragons' magic that could change everything—just as the Hierophant and her mages are closing in.

Betrayed and broken, Alina embarks on a desperate quest to restore the weakened power of Bios Auras, no matter the chaos she unravels in the process.

Everything hangs in the balance. Together, all must decide: will they sacrifice everything to forge their individual destinies, or let the collective darkness consume them all?

BOOKS BY BRIAN A. MENDONÇA

Symphony of Crowns and Gods Series

Wedding of the Torn Rose (Book 1)

Gravity of Obedience (Book 2)

Prophecy of Tears and Sacrifice (Book 3)

Throne of Deception and Dragons (Book 4) - Coming soon

Available at most major book retailers.

Store links can be found here: theauthorbrian.com

AN IMPORTANT NOTE FROM THE AUTHOR

As the creator of the Symphony of Crowns and Gods series, my primary aim is to transport readers like yourself on an unforgettable journey. I hope that you enjoyed *Prophecy of Tears and Sacrifice* and that it added further depth to what happened in *Wedding of the Torn Rose* and *Gravity of Obedience*. There's still many twists to come in the rest of the series.

I would love to hear your thoughts about it! If this book has captured your interest, would you kindly consider sharing your experience on platforms such as Amazon, Goodreads, BookBub, or any other convenient platform? A few words from you can guide fellow readers and significantly enhance the visibility of the series.

But more than that, your insights serve as my compass in this expansive landscape of storytelling. Your feedback and suggestions fuel my inspiration and aid me in weaving tales that deeply touch your heart.

Thank you in advance for your time and input. You are not just a reader; you are a vital part of my creative journey. And please remember, each review illuminates the path for the next grand adventure someone might embark upon in the Symphony of Crowns and Gods series.

Sincerely,
Brian A. Mendonça

To help, please visit:
https://www.theauthorbrian.com/review-request

Or use this QR code:

SCAN ME

JOIN BRIAN A. MENDONÇA'S EMAIL NEWSLETTER

WHY SIGN UP?

It's simple: fans on this email list get my official updates before anyone else, including any other blogs and social media websites.

Here's what you can expect:

- Upcoming releases and previews of upcoming books
- An open dialog about my author journey
- Deals and sales
- Opportunities for ARCs (Advance Reader Copies)
- Info about fantasy books from other indie authors

Sign up link:

https://theauthorbrian.com/join-brians-newsletter

Or use this QR code:

JOIN BRIAN A. MENDONÇA'S EMAIL NEWSLETTER

SCAN ME

Published by BookPop Media LLC.

Symphony of Crowns and Gods Official Website:

https://www.theauthorbrian.com

www.ingramcontent.com/pod-product-compliance
Lightning Source LLC
Chambersburg PA
CBHW032258020726
47495CB00001B/156